Jáchym Topol was born in Prague on August 4, 1962, son of Josef Topol, a renowned playwright, poet, and Shakespeare translator. Topol's writing began in the late 70s and early 80s with lyrics for the rock band Psí vojáci (Dog Soldiers), led by his younger brother, Filip (the relationship has continued: poems from this novel were set to music and released as the CD *Sestra: Jáchym Topol & Psí Vojáci*).

In 1985 Topol cofounded *Revolver Revue*, a samizdat review specializing in new Czech writing. Topol played an active role in the 1989 Velvet Revolution in Czechoslovakia, writing, editing, and publishing an independent newsletter that became the investigative weekly *Respekt*.

Topol's first collection of poetry, *I Love You Madly* (samizdat, 1988), received the Tom Stoppard Prize for Unofficial Literature. His second volume of poetry, *The War Will Be On Tuesday*, came out in 1993. *City Sister Silver*, Topol's first novel, won the Egon Hostovský Prize as Czech book of the year in 1994. His story "A Trip to the Train Station" was published in a Czech-English edition (the English translation by Alex Zucker) in 1995. Topol has since published a novella and translations of American Indian myths.

Topol lives in Prague with his wife and his daughter.

Alex Zucker has translated *More Than One Life* by Miloslava Holubová (1999), *A Trip to the Train Station* by Jáchym Topol (1995), and a number of stories and poems published in literary magazines and anthologies in the U.S., U.K., and Czech Republic. For several years after the Velvet Revolution, he lived in Prague, translating and copy editing. He now lives in New York City.

Also Translated by Alex Zucker

More Than One Life by Miloslava Holubová

City Sister Silver

by Jáchym Topol

translated from the Czech
by Alex Zucker

Catbird Press
A Garrigue Book

Originally published in Czech as *Sestra* by Atlantis
Czech original edition © 1994 Jáchym Topol
English translation and translator's preface © 2000 Alex Zucker

First English-language edition.

CATBIRD PRESS
16 Windsor Road, North Haven, CT 06473
800-360-2391; catbird@pipeline.com; www.catbirdpress.com
Our books are distributed by
Independent Publishers Group

This translation has been partially subsidized by a grant
from the Ministry of Culture of the Czech Republic.

This translation is dedicated to Mamou and Papou.

Library of Congress Cataloging-in-Publication Data

Topol, Jáchym, 1962-
[Sestra. English]
City, sister, silver / by Jáchym Topol ; translated from the Czech
by Alex Zucker. -- 1st English-language ed.
"Garrigue book."
ISBN 0-945774-45-1 (tradepaper : alk. paper). --
ISBN 0-945774-43-5 (cloth : alk. paper)
I. Zucker, Alex.   II. Title
PG5039.3.O648S4713 2000
891.8'636--dc21   99-16410 CIP

Contents

Czech Pronunciation Guide

b, d, f, m, n, s, t, v, z - like in English

c - like ts in oats

č - like ch in child

ch - one letter; something like ch in loch

ď - soft, like d in duty (see ě below)

g - always hard

h - like h in have, but more open

j - like y in you

l - like l in leave

ň - like n in new (see ě below)

p - like our p, but without aspiration

r - rolled

ř - pronounce r with tip of tongue vibrating against upper teeth, usually approximated
    by English speakers by combining r with s in pleasure

š - like sh in ship

ť - soft, like t in Tuesday (see ě below)

ž - like s in pleasure

a - like u in cup, but more open

á - hold it longer

e - like e in set, but more open

é - hold it longer

ě - after b, m, n, p: usually approximated by English speakers by saying the consonant
    plus yeah; after d and t, soften the consonant by placing tongue at tip of upper
    teeth

i, y - like i in sit, but more closed

í, ý - hold it longer, like ea in seat

o - like o in not, but less open

ó - hold it longer, like aw in lawn

u - like oo in book

ú, ů - hold it longer, like oo in stool

ou, au, and eu are Czech dipthongs

Rule No. 1 - Always place accent on the first syllable of a word.

Rule No. 2 - Pronounce all letters.

Translator's Preface

Set in the first years after "time exploded," *City Sister Silver* is the story of a young man trying to find his way in the messy landscape of post-Communist Czechoslovakia. Beyond that, though, it is the author's exploration of the way language changed in response to the new reality. In an effort to capture the dislocation of this period, Jáchym Topol flaunts the conventions of his native tongue at nearly every step. Indeed his Czech publisher felt it necessary to include a special editor's note alerting readers to "the author's intent to capture language in its unsystematicness and out-of-jointness," pointing out his radical fluctuations in grammar, spelling, syntax, and style between the two poles of written (or literary) and spoken Czech not only from scene to scene, but within a single paragraph or sentence, sometimes even from one word to the next.

Given the history of our own language, in particular the erosion of the border between spoken and literary usage by twentieth-century writers, this may strike English speakers as commonplace. But compared to English, the distinction between written and spoken language in Czech remains far more rigid, and the gap between them far greater. Bridging this gap, moreover, is a vast spectrum of "intermediate" levels for which English has no equivalent. In this novel, Topol works with all of them.

Some features of spoken Czech translate into English more easily than others. Dropped letters, for instance, are common to both languages (e.g., *du* = "I'm goin"). But Czech expresses "spokenness" in a host of other ways — shortening long vowels, for one, or adding a *v* before words that begin in *o* — that cannot be directly reproduced in translation. What makes Topol's writing such a challenge to bring into English, though, is the *way* he combines and alternates forms, and the extremes he goes to in doing so.

Where Topol mixes spoken and written style, I usually dealt with it by dropping letters or using contractions, but inconsistently, to mimic the jumbled effect. In Chapter 8, for instance, Potok asks a downtrodden priest: "Do you know Padre Konrád, father, my good pastor ... kina short and cross-eyed ..." In the original text the sentence reads: "Znáte pátera Konráda od nás, otče, mýho dobrého pastýře ... je takovej malý a šilhá ..." Whereas the rules of written Czech would call for the last eight words to read, "mého dobrého pastýře … je takový malý a šilhá …" a fully spoken rendering would be "mýho dobrýho pastýře … je takovej malej a šilhá …" Here my translation approximates the clash of written and spoken forms by contracting *kind of* to *kina,* a common feature of spoken English, while retaining the *d* on *and,* which I would otherwise drop in the case of "pure" spoken Czech.

Despite the Czech edition's assertion that "valid rules are present in the background of the text," often it was hard to discern a pattern to the constant shifting and mixing, and in my exchanges with the author he repeatedly described his choices as a *pocitová věc* — "a matter of feeling." Inevitably then, my translation too is less about mechanically reproducing the thousands of individual twists on and departures from conventional Czech than about capturing the feeling, the jarring, the dislocation they were meant to convey.

Grammatical and stylistic quirks apart, *City Sister Silver* contains a daunting variety of Czech idioms, dialects, and slang, plus assorted words and phrases from several other languages, and a multilingual tongue spoken by non-Germans in Berlin. Even more challenging — and more fun — for the translator, though, are the words, turns of phrase, and metaphors that Topol invented himself, a private language of sorts.

To choose just one example, from Chapter 17: As Potok and Černá hike through the woods, they nibble on something called "lanceroot." Here I devised a neologism to match the author's own. The Czech word, *kopišník,* to me suggested *kopí,* meaning *spear* or *lance.* Then it was just a question of deciding what sort of nibblable plant it might be, fruit, root, or vegetable; *root,* I thought, sounded more likely than *berry.*

Probably the single most personal invention that I caught in the novel, though, was a metaphor in Chapter 16. (I deliberately say "that I caught," since no doubt there are other references of an equally private nature that I failed to pick up on.) While neither the Czech original nor my translation give any hint as to where it comes from, the story behind this metaphor intrigues me too much not to share it.

In Czech the expression was *mně se to v hlavě mihalo jak v koňský jámě* — literally "it flashed through my head like in a horse pit." In the author's own words: "I still remember this as a little Central European boy: By the river (in Poříčí nad Sázavou) there were these pits, just a deep hole basically, where the horses would go swimming to wash off after work. I remember how suddenly all this sludge and mud and horse shit and rotten branches and grass would start rising up to the surface … when that huge horse body sank in there, into the pit, the depths. Since we didn't know how to swim yet, we were scared to death of the horse pits — that we'd fall in there and drown. So if something flashes through my head like in a horse pit, it means chaos and danger."

Because of the way it falls in the text — "but the old woman intervened again, shooing them off … my head churned like a horse pit, Černá … out there in the woods, she'd better have strong protection …" — it would have been impossible to keep the original construction without sounding awkward (insert it for yourself and you'll see what I mean). Respecting the fact that it wasn't meant to be clear even in the original, my solution preserves the personal content while tailoring it to the context and maintaining the uneasiness the author meant to evoke.

Lastly I'd like to explain how the text was edited and notated. While the first two drafts of my translation followed the first edition, on the final go-round my editor and I decided to incorporate some of the cuts Topol himself made for the novel's second edition, which weighed in at 455 pages versus the original 481. Given that the Czech text was edited with a light hand, we also took the bolder but, I believe, beneficial step of trimming it at points, especially in the case of obvious oversights (e.g., Potok being handed the same piece of paper twice in a single paragraph), phrases or sentences that made no sense (even to the author, in retrospect), and material that would have meant nothing to English speakers without a labored explanation, thereby ruining the effect. I should add that Topol never hesitated to suggest I use my delete button. (Interested readers can find most of the longer cuts on the Catbird Press website, at www.catbirdpress.com/bookpages/sister.htm.)

Naturally the translation still includes a number of words and references that few non-Czechs would recognize. To provide an experience as close as possible to that of a Czech reading the original, these items are marked with an asterisk and briefly identified in a Notes section at the back of this book.

Catching and tracking down these references, along with the various foreign words and phrases found throughout, was a major part of my work on this translation. When possible, I did my research on the Web or in the library, but often I was forced to turn to the source to explain or elaborate. And it is to Jáchym himself that I owe the most thanks, as author and collaborator, but above all as my friend. I know it wasn't always pleasant for him to revisit a work that he considered over and done with, and to respond to the barrage of nit-picking questions I rained down on him.

Beyond my consultations with the author, many others aided me along the way. I cannot name them all here, but there are several individuals I turned to repeatedly, and they deserve to be acknowledged. In Prague, Lucie Váchová and Vladimír Michálek both helped me out by receiving my e-mailed missives to Jáchym, passing them on to him, and sending his replies back to me. Here in New York, Irena Kovářová and Jiří Zavadil fielded questions from me, at all hours, on everything from language to history to geography to pop culture. Karin Beck, who wrote her master's thesis on the novel, aided me in translating the German and Russian portions; apart from that, it was always a treat to discuss the book with someone else who knew it in such detail. Special thanks to Czesław Miłosz for granting permission to use a previously untranslated poem of his, and to Magda Samborska for checking my translation against the Polish original. Czech history wizard Brad Abrams of Columbia University offered valuable input on some of the trickier historical notes. To Peter Kussi, who taught me Czech for two years in graduate school before I lived in Prague, belong my heartfelt thanks for steering me through a tough metaphor or two, but mainly for inspiring me to translate in the first place. I'd also like to thank Robert Wechsler of Catbird Press for taking on the exhausting task of wading through the manuscript, and for bearing with my constant revisions right up to the end. And last but not least Clare Manias, who not only designed the eye-catching cover but supported me throughout with grace, love, and patience.

Alex Zucker
Brooklyn
December 1999

City

1

THE ENGRAVING AND IN THE HOLE.
THE WAY IT WAS WITH SHE-DOG.
WE SEE THEM GO. SHE HELD ME.

We were the People of the Secret. And we were waiting. Then David lost his mind. Maybe the reason his head cracked was because it was the best, sending out the signals that propelled the whole crew, the whole community, forward. That's what we told ourselves, that we were going forward, getting somewhere, but we soon lost all concept which way we were headed.

Some of us might have noticed we had stopped going in a straight line and were turning in a circle. It also struck me several times that time was fading in the pale light, turning more translucent, losing its color and taste again, and I was horrified by that. Probably Sharky was the only one who had a tangible goal: to rid himself of the box and its phantoms. Me, I went like a bear on a treadmill, the whole thing was scary, but it was fun and charged me up. Micka couldn't afford to stop glowing, and he never glowed more than when the metal flowed.

The thing with David happened after the Ministry cleaned out our well. Not only did he constantly sniff at his thumbs. But I also noticed a change in his face, his eyes starting to bulge while his chin seemed to be caving in. His lips hung open loosely, you look like a gourd, I kidded, he didn't respond.

I found him down in the storeroom, sitting under the fabrics like he was in some Bedouin tent, one hand in brocade, it all feels the same, he said, it's exactly the same, it's all the same to me.

What're you talkin about, I asked.

There's no difference. It's all the same. You did the cars, right?

Yeah.

See, he said, you or Novák. You're both the same to me. That's the way it feels to me, physically an mentally. An that's all I'm gonna say.

I gave up and went back upstairs where we sat around and talked the way we always did after work.

So how did it all begin? If I'm going to retrace my footsteps ... back then ... in the Stone Age ... I have to talk about the time me and Bára walked through the square full of Germans, and I will, because that was the place where I began to feel the motion, where time took on taste and color, where the carnival started for me.

We walked through the square full of refugees. Now Prague, the hemmed-in city, the Pearl, a dot on the map behind the wires, had its very own refugees. I'm going to write about how it began, and I have to grab the table with one hand and gouge my fingernail into my thumb, I will, and I have to do the same with the other hand too, and feel the pain so I feel something real. If I want to know how it was. Because the main part of the story, the end, is vanishing into the void where the future and all the dead dwindle into nothing.

It started with the sweeping away of walls and the exchanging of souvenirs, I'll trade you a piece of the wall for a bullet shell from the square, a lump of candle wax, a piece of phone-tap wire, as time went by I lost my collection, it only made sense at first, amid the joy and exhilaration, what use is there in saving splinters, iron scales, an besides: obvious symbols only work for things closed by time. Yet you haven't left that reality. You're still walkin the boards in the same performance, on the same familiar set, your rankled nerves detect the presence of the board of directors, the ones that're runnin the show, and is it? or is it not? part of a plan? is it by design? You still sense the nasty looks on the other side of the curtain, the sneering, the rat, the wicked uncle's grin. The Face.

You still feel the pain in your chewed-up fist, the one you stuff in your mouth to keep from talking, to keep from telling yourself what it really is, what's going on: with you. And you'd just as soon take your share and bury it.

I look into the mirror, a gift from the Chinese, on back is an inscription, letters to the wall. I take a slug of the Fiery, still a long way to the bottom.

Whenever I feel time losing its power, whenever it stops sucking me in and the swirl of chaos and noise in the tunnel falls still, the Fiery always helps. And the next day that rigor mortis is proof that time is dead for me again. Like the way the Chippewas gripped their paddles after they drank the Fiery, seated stiffly in their canoes, heads shattered from inside. They needed it too: rifles and steel knives and smallpox were what smashed time for them. They maybe wanted a circle; I longed for a straight line.

Reaching up to the shelf for the Firewater, I touch a hand groping for it from the other side, a bracelet, fingers chewed like mine, but his hand's dusky, smells of smoke, it's calloused and scraped, mine doesn't have callouses, not anymore. We clutch the bottle, each from one side, but it doesn't want war: this demon wants us both. The bottle splits in two, each of us tugging the cold glass onto our side of the darkness, and on the spot where my hand and the Chippewa's touched, a new bottle stands now, there will always be a new one, as long as we die.

Not anymore, we said. Together. That time with her. I don't know anymore which one of us said it.

As the hangover recedes, everything picks up again, you come to life, feeling that time and motion are back again, you know that it's false but only at the base of your mind, up above the lights are beginning to come back on, falling flatly over the everyday scenery, but you toy with the illusion for a little while longer. You drink because of the hangover, it's an edge, like twilight, not quite day, not quite night. Every instant still sharply fractured. This time still has an end, too far off for me to see, this time can still be reckoned from the moment the first crack in the concrete showed.

The concrete block, stifling anything that tried to move on its own, is gone, you know very well how everything was rotting, gasping for freedom, mutating in the stench, in the bush, in the bushes, the roly-polies under the rock. The bushes: the especially robust runners found chinks in the slowly cracking concrete and squeezed their way out, twisting, creeping, it was doable. That's me too of course, I'm one of the bushes, and for a long time I expected the blow, the command, the deafening whistle, the pounding on the door.

I don't get it, I don't know why it didn't happen to me. Why me, how come you didn't get eight years, an iron bar in the head, a one-way plane ticket out of the country? But it's gone now.

Or is it? And now do we live like this or like that? I saw an old woman and a German shepherd in the morning haze by the train station. Everyone else had just cleared out. A fire blazed in a trash can. The woman was feeding it. Burning old grass, ma'am? I asked. No, these're my files, my *documents*. The dog growled, a beetle crept along the sidewalk, the wind rolled softly over the windowpanes.

Aha, so that's how we're going do it now, people thought to themselves. That before was nothing, that we *had* to do. After all, on the outside you're one thing and at your underlying source you're something else, everybody knows that, it's like ABC. So open up your sources, now, the whole world is theirs. Aha, so what's reality? And what's just scenery? What do we do? And what am I gonna do now? I asked myself in unison with the rest.

Our friendship was the dawning of the firm, the company to be, that was the foundation. I lived with Little White She-Dog back in the days when I knew nothing and had nothing to lose. She made me so in turn I could make someone else, so there would be a tribe. She knew we needed a tribe if we wanted to survive without giving away all our time, and she also knew how to save at least a piece of time for ourselves.

It also works with objects, she taught me. Back then I kept time tucked away in shards of broken glass in the pockets of my shorts. Sitting at home or in class, I'd unwrap a shard from my handkerchief and watch as time began to unwind, gently at first, like a feather floating to the ground (later on she taught me that for gentleness it works best to put time into feathers), and then the time in the shard would accelerate and I'd be inside it with Little White She-Dog, with the grass and the trees, in our hole in the hillside, with her touches, in reality.

She also saw the green eyes of the woman I was to meet in the future, which gifted females can see into. You'll probly end up with some wrestler, she said, examining her bruises in bed one day. I won't toss an turn anymore, I said, yeah you will, she told me back.

Long before I tossed and turned and ground my teeth in my dreams, I was a gimp, in the autumn of my childhood, and my being lame only before her and for her was the beginning of our games, our exploration of human power, it was the origin of the perversion. I would sit motionless while Little White She-Dog set the nerves in my body to tingling, sitting still as long as possible so that she could learn my body, so she could teach my body to feel. My role model was a cripple from an engraving. A medieval engraving peopled with knights and cripples. It was the time of St. George the dragon slayer, and I was a child cripple with a twisted soul and a studiously acquired schizophrenia because what was permitted and required inside was undesirable and dangerous outside. Family pride was a weight around my neck. I was to be the future that would pay back the humiliation, in this I was just like thousands of others.

Just like them, something drove me to bury deceased pigeons and sparrows, making crosses for their little graves and reeling off the words, but She-Dog brought me back to myself, through herself, through her movements and voice and touches, just like a little wife.

Elsewhere I had to pull off the role of the cheerful, inquisitive little boy, bringing home top grades to honor my obligations. The Communists mopped up the floor with families like ours, but that was precisely why fathers and mothers forced their children to study Latin. Fathers waged long-winded debates on whether it was best to teach Latin or English, and always concluded that both were essential. Latin, church, languages; dual geography, dual history, and religion: it was a pretty shabby arsenal for battling the world around us. George at least had a lance. And the dragon wasn't even trying to take away his time, it only wanted to kill him.

With Little White She-Dog I was no one again, a shape born of vapor, wind, moisture. She stroked nerves I didn't know I had, my face took on a new appearance, I started to feel my body. I started to dance. For a cripple, just stretching your hand is a dance. She drew me in, forming me, and that in turn shaped her nature.

As the well-mannered little girl walked to her lesson in classical languages with the former priest, at the time a stock clerk because he hadn't signed out of fear of the Devil, or to the church of the priest who had signed because only the Church is eternal and every regime eventually topples, ending up on the bottom like grains of sand in the infinite ocean of grace … in her mouth she could still taste the seed of the little man of her tribe, because not even the Church is older than the tribe, and we were closer to each other than to those broken-backed families of ours. The present, which our families felt was a world built on falsehood, and the period prior to the invasion, which they clung to, were both the same gobbledygook to us. We weren't afraid of anything. We didn't care about blood and lineage, just like Romeo and Juliet.

With death whizzing by on all sides, we had to duck down and send out feelers, picking up and transmitting the tribal signal. In our hole in the hillside, eyes shut: What do you see? Darkness. Is it far away? No, it's right here. What do you see? You. Other people, small, they've all got the same face. My darkness is red now. Mine too.

Our petting, culminating in orgasm for me and then, much later, for her as well, was more than just the giving and receiving of bliss, it was the ritual of an encircled tribe. Like all my loves, Little White She-Dog was brunette, I called her white because of her skin. I still call her that in my thoughts, even now that everything I'm trying to capture here is gone and I found my sister and Little White She-Dog turned into a ghost, a good she-demon with inscrutable intentions.

He put a wafer on my tongue, the sign of God, she said, and I still had semen in there with your kids, they might not all've been dead yet, I ran the whole way.

Later she wiped off the taste, no longer needing that mosquito net in the jungle, that coating on the tongue we lied with so often, to our families, teachers, priests, to everyone outside the community, and instead she ate an apple, or took a sip of water, using other, more elaborate masks and disguises. Don't move, she'd say, I'm not, I'd lie, reaching for her, the tip of her deceitful tongue vibrating in my ear, still ringing *opidda opiddum, puera pulchrum, ghetto ghettum* as excitement would transform me from a gimp in an engraving where time stood still into a hunk of live flesh gorged with blood, starving and prepared to devour. She was older and liked to toy with me, leaving me inside her, teaching me to sense the powers one eventually prefers to sharpen oneself so as not to burden psychiatrists: the little boy learned when and how to use girl power, the childlike power of the word *no,* and when to be a warrior. As the little boy got older, he didn't just dance the way she wanted. And only then did she really begin to glow, becoming Beautiful She-Dog, with breasts. Until then they had the hole in the ground, curled up in there like embryos, sensing the earth's motion. Afterwards they would go home to their families, living their lives in the wings.

We slept together and played together, actually we lived together, but there was such a flood of filth and futility to fight, the magic stayed somewhere down below, glowing inside her like coals, and in me too, only cooler, kind of like amber, and sometimes when we were alone a long time the magic would show itself, and the day we went to look at the Germans I saw the red darkness again.

Here I am handin out cookies like some pensioner when we oughta be flailin those guys over there, said Sinkule.

The cops were removing a haggard man in a suit from the wall above the embassy entrance, he wanted to take the shortcut, resisted, they pummeled him with their truncheons. He picked himself up off the ground and obediently joined the procession of Germans patiently marking time in front of the embassy. There were thousands of them. The rows wound down the crooked lanes all the way to the square, where traffic had been stopped for days now.

Hey, here they come again, Sinkule slugged my shoulder. A row of white helmets with long truncheons began setting up barricades in the crowd. The Germans who were cut off from the embassy got nervous, tensing up, horrified that this was the end, that after everything had gone so smoothly, like a miracle, like a dream, it was finished, now came the clampdown, the ones who'd gone in could leave, but for the ones they hadn't gotten to yet, it was too late … this was the selection, you in, you out, you yes and you no, the crowd let out a howl and leaned into the cordon, mothers passing children over the cops' helmets to the people on the other side, probly relatives, I figured.

Once the kid's inside, I guess they let the mother in too. That must be why they're doin it. Yeah, but it's not like the kids've got ID. How do the mothers prove they're theirs?

Let's get lost, c'mon.

What if some other lady snatches the kid so she can get out. How do they decide? Like back in the days of King Sollie?

Let's take off, c'mon.

Nah, said Sinkule, it'll calm down again. The cops don't care about the Germans. I been watchin. They'll hassle folks a while an then pull out. They just wanna show us they're here.

I'd rather not stick around. Wouldn't wanna get nailed.

They won't come down this far, take it easy.

Sinkule had been at the embassy every day, he was one of those people the exodus fascinated.

He glanced at me. Anyway, you look German, they won't mess with you. Do you speak it?

Nah, just stuff like *Hände hoch, Los schweine, Achtung minen, Arbeit macht frei*, that crap from the movies. An *Meine liebe kommen ficken,** never used that one though.

Sinkule was right, the cops pulled out, and an eerie silence settled back over the crowd.

How bout me, think I look German?

You? I almost cracked up. Sure, an Goebbels was German too.

I speak it though, my mom was German.

They're back again.

The cops, surrounded by the crowd in the space between the West German and U.S. embassies with the cameras of every TV station on earth humming monotonously, were evidently uncomfortable. These four characters looked like reinforcements from the countryside. Normally the cops didn't take the narrow passageway down from the Rychta beer hall. And if they did, then only in larger groups. The Germans in front moved slowly, working their way up the slope, the rest of them tread in place. Ordinarily a crowd murmurs, the individual utterances intertwining, it's a little like water, you can lap up the words. But these people were silent, as if they'd decided not to talk until they made it through the gate. Suddenly someone in the crowd broke into loud laughter. Then a child burst into tears. Then another. All at once the square was full of weeping children, it struck me that maybe it was like dogs: once one starts, the rest join in. But these kids weren't crying on account of a few silly Czech policemen. Some had been traveling for days now, on overcrowded trains, in Trabants and Wartburgs piled high with junk, on their way out of the cage, on the road to Paradise. Some of them must've been hungry, sleepy, and sensed the anxiety of their parents, wearily lugging them on their shoulders, tugging them by the hand uphill toward the embassy. The laughter didn't let up, it was a high-pitched nervous female laugh, like the wailing of some faraway bird, in an interrupted dream, in the country, in the woods, at night.

Sluggishly the crowd shifted uphill, leaving the lower part of the square empty except for a group of young Germans sitting on the ground drinking tea. Some had spent the cold night on the square and didn't look like they cared much about waiting another hour or two. One or two even looked like they didn't have a care in the world. A pair of cops stopped next to them. The officer lost his patience, knocking the thermos out of the hand of an elderly Czech woman who was pouring tea for the Germans. Where's your permit? he bellowed. A ripple went through the crowd again, and in a blink the old lady was standing alone. I admired her calm heroism in the face of the officer's distasteful outburst.

That's old Vohryzková from our building, said Sinkule. At least now she'll give up that Mother Teresa act, stupid cunt.

Stick it to her, you savage! he roared at the cop, and we bolted.

Thank the Lord they always send those hicks to Prague, we never would've made it through the passageways otherwise.

Just to be safe, though, I crossed myself. We came out gasping for breath by the church with the Christ Child.*

Hey, Sinkule, you notice they're startin to lock up the passageways?

Yeah an that's what did it for me. I've been sneakin through these things like a rat all my life an now those fuckers're lockin em up. You're the only one I'm tellin: I'm goin too. I'm tellin you so you can watch, so I got some backup, so I don't disappear down some hole.

You're goin? With the Germans?

Yeah, so what? I mean it's a farce an you're an actor, right?

You're gonna split with the Germans, huh?

Yeah, Šulc already made it. Went yesterday an he's in there.

Are you guys crazy? I mean this is the end!

Nobody knows that. The Germans're goin over to the Germans, but our guys aren't gonna let go that easy. I donno, but I mean we could all be dead. I mean they got the concentration camps ready. Or they might, an everyone knows it. I mean we're on the list. I mean anyone that does anything's scared these days. Maybe it'll turn out okay an we'll forget it ever happened, but I'm gettin sick an tired. I'm just scared they'll start shootin. You're the one that told me about the tanks.

Hey, I'm gonna stick it out here.

Hey, it could easily go Chinese-style.

C'mon, this is Europe!

Yeah, says who?

So you're goin, huh?

I got it all worked out, me an Majsner're goin together, I mean half of us here're German anyway. Nobody's checkin, an if they do I'll just say they took my papers away at the border, it's such a mess in there at the embassy they're just shovin em on the buses an shippin em out.

So the Bohos've finally got what they wanted, Germans crowdin onto buses an settin out into the great unknown, motherfuckers!

Don't get hysterical. I'll be with Majsner, so if one of us gets into trouble the other one'll clear right out, alles is gut, don't get hysterical, I'll send you back some chocolate an come ridin in on a white tank. Just keep an eye out that we get in.

So the Christ Child was where it began. We walked back to the square and up to the embassy. They waited a long time. I saw them going in.

Glaser got in too, he'd done a year in jail, got caught under the wires in Šumava after lying buried in the sand all day, getting eaten alive by mosquitoes, but he picked the wrong time to crawl out, got hog-tied and left for hours … in a cell full of shit … now he passed through the gate and just for good measure spat on a cop, the Germans picked up on it and started doing it too, after a while the cop looked like he was covered in cum or something, his truncheon hung impotently from his belt, he was scared … Glaser went over to watch … but then I had to stop, he told me later, it was weird all of a sudden, like somethin outta the war, Germans spitting on a Czech, even if he was a Commie mercenary, an I started it … it was weird, my first step in freedom, an instead of breathing it in I spat … there were others who went too, most of them had some German ancestry … but even that idiot Novák got in, got in and then came back out again to go for a beer at U Schnellů, just did it because he liked being able to go back and forth.

And it was then, while that clown was hollering all over the pub, that I realized it had begun … the motion … there was something of a carnival feel to the Germans' exodus that lingers on to this day, from the moment time exploded, bursting out of that locked-up city, time with its own taste and color that you don't know about until you taste it, until you're there inside the color. Exploding time can not only crush you, you can swim in it, or hold it in your hand, like a piece of fabric or a coin. It can be like a gas, or like earth, sometimes you can feel it like wind.

Little White She-Dog and I walked through the streets, sometimes holding hands.

The exodus continued, here and there panic seized the incoming Germans that the Czechs had put a stop to their departure … that there were machine guns on the rooftops … that the Stasi were roaming the streets of Prague along with the StB,* dragging off Germans and Czechs … that the StB was fomenting hatred among the Czech people against the traitors to communism the same way the Gestapo had fomented hatred among the German people against the vermin of the Reich … the Germans, stretching through the streets and across the square, and the Czechs, observing them from windows and balconies, surrounding them down on the sidewalks, silently watching the flight from communism with nowhere to go themselves because this was their only country … all of them well aware that the whole thing could still be stopped, aware of the force that could cut them off from one another, from that silent contact …

when the Germans filled the streets they dragged, slow and sluggish, crews of long-haired boys and girls, holding hands, sometimes, like me and She-Dog, only going somewhere else ... old ladies with purses, parents with little children clutching teddy bears and dolls ... but when the crowd thinned out into smaller groups, alarming reports caught up to them from behind, from all over the city, maybe it was strange vibrations from the Prague train stations, from their homes back there in Dresden, Karl-Marx-Stadt, Gera, Zwickau, from border towns and villages ... where they were hastily packing their last things, jewelry ... food and clothing, and for the last time nervously examining their passports and taking flight, fleeing Big Brother, who seemed to have nodded off for a spell, probably after downing a large bloody nightcap as they picked off another, shot him dead, left him lying there ... by the Wall ... *Die Unbekannten.** But the Monster could awake at any time, refreshed and ready, to dole out punishment ... here and there reports spread that it was over, that they were too late, that they were going in vain, into a trap ... and the clusters of Germans began to move faster, some even sprinting the last hundred, twenty, ten meters, and then it was triumph, a game ... leaving behind in the streets of Malá Strana their heavy bags and suitcases, blankets they'd huddled in at night when the embassy was too full, inflatable pillows, propane-butane tanks, all the things they wouldn't need in the West of their dreams ... forgotten toys lay strewn about the street, a teddy bear with its head twisted off and rubber duckies flung out of the bolshevik pond of the gee-dee-ar onto the cobblestones of Prague, lost in the rush and confusion, no doubt since replaced by that silky-haired slut Barbie ... I saw a skillet and a schoolbag, the square was full of cars, a Trabant with a comforter on the roof lay on its side ...

stride after stride
pots and pans knocking at their side
children with comforters in wagons ride
flaming crosses up in the sky
days with salty anguish undone
and no one here can tell them why
where to go or what will come,
she said.

Well, I dunno if it's all that dramatic.

Hanuš Bonn wrote that, said Little White She-Dog. Only these gee-dee-ar porkers aren't goin into any flaming ovens.

Hey, they're goin into the unknown, they're fugitives, just take a look at those two old women holdin each other up.

Yeah, exactly.

What, like she's some Ilse Koch? An I spose that granddaddy there is Mengele?

I know it's stupid, said She-Dog. But Germans just piss me off. I was helpin em out at the train station this morning, but still they piss me off. German pisses me off. When my grandpa got back, he weighed 40 kilos. Not for long. Plus Hanuš Bonn was a family friend. We've got a copy of *Distant Voice** with a dedication from him. Anyway it's the Communists' fault for fuckin us up with those movies, I've never even talked to a German actually.

Till today.

Yeah. Some cabs bring em here for free, others rip em off like crazy.

Some help em out like you, some break into their cars.

That's the thing about the human tribe, like we used to say when we were little … She-Dog spread her red lips wide, flicking her tongue … when somethin's goin on, that's when people of a tribe find each other. As soon as there's a threat, people divide.

Till then, though, people can be pretty awful.

Yep, anything goes, right up until there's somethin at stake.

So what's at stake now, She-Dog?

I donno, God I guess, or maybe everything.

The thing is, people bring on bad stuff by actin crazy.

You never know, there's various paths an everyone's gotta choose for themselves.

That's our contract.

The contract's valid.

Sinkule thinks they're gonna lock everyone up.

The contract's valid, even if we're not scared anymore.

Of what, machine guns on the rooftops? Good luck puttin a halt to that.

Halt. It's wild how many German words we use. I could go for a lager right now, how bout it?

Let's duck into a building first.

Yeah yeah, said She-Dog, nudging open the door of a place with a lion on a shield, how bout here?

Here it smelled of wood, another place it was a septic tank, we searched out cellars because we longed for that hole in the ground where she had taught me, where for the first time the world had been real, where our bodies had grown up together, where we had come to know every centimeter of each other's body and our own as they grew larger and coarser … there was also time preserved in those cellars, intact and compacted, in corners and under vaults, in every nook and cranny, even in the spiderwebs that served as the delicate dress for our wedding, our intercourse. Often it was damp with groundwater, sometimes old as time itself, time had a heavy fragrance, it slaked our thirst. I would hold Little White She-Dog on top of me, or she would sit down in an alcove, spreading apart her legs, and in that clench of male and female, in the motion, the screwing, slowly the rhythm would come and in it the red darkness, and in the darkness images. We set the time around us in motion, it swirled and spoke to me. Sometimes She-Dog would whisper into my ear, today she spoke of fear, and as she ran her nails down my sides, shredding my skin, it was like lightning flashing down through the red darkness under my eyelids. I couldn't hear her voice, it was like the sounds were forming letters, but it was only the idea of them, just her speech echoing in my brain, now it was the speech of fear, fear of losing power, losing it as the city set against it the power of all the others' fear, the fear of the crowd, it's sour, I heard She-Dog's mind echo. We knew that time also flowed up above, but we didn't have the strength to reach up there anymore … up above the rooftops, where there might be machine guns … and might not … it wasn't so much them, though, as the nests full of mutant pigeons born with the plague, chemical freaks, plunging to the pavement on their first try at flying, without any soft palm between them and the world, nests full of little birds peeping in terror, and it wasn't a bird's cry but the wheeze of a new sort of creature, nobody heard them except maybe Starry Bog, they were born into nothing but terror and hopelessness, and they didn't know it, but I did, and that was why I couldn't go that high.

We were also losing power because the reign of cruelty glowed in colors as bright as the sky when the twilight is aflame and filled with the demons that descend on the city at the first stroke of nightfall.

We aged in those twilights, by now every cell in our shared body was a combat veteran … and She-Dog's power was turning against her because she wasn't living just for herself anymore, she wanted to go farther … and take me with her. But I was afraid … to be in the world the way she wanted me to, to give it to her, to be inside someone else ... I was losing my power by acting, feeling out the world in assorted costumes and characters because I was fearful of direct contact.

We screwed in cellars whenever we could, whenever we got the urge, we became absolute virtuosos at finding places where it was warm and dark and the old time murmured like a living thing. It would've meant death if either of us had pushed the other away, or let go. When lions mate, the male grips the nape of the female's neck so tight with his teeth her neck would snap if she moved, that was the way we held on to each other, with every single pore. I opened my eyes and the red darkness was still there, She-Dog watched me, smiling, she knew that the red darkness came from inside us but also existed out in the world, a part of it, like an animal, say, or a desert, or the shit of the tenants in the flats above our heads. Firmly fastened down to the darkness around the edges, that cloud protected us, sometimes an electric light swang past when they came down for coal ... but no one gifted with power had ever seen us, I thought ... no one else came here for time.

We were moving in bliss, and then She-Dog's brain sent me to an old woman shoveling coal into pails, suddenly I heard the clink of shovel on pail, clear as a bell, and then she sent me on a journey through the old woman. As my eyes sank into She-Dog's, I saw myself as a little bead, then as a micro-scopic Gulliver, traveling through every fold of skin on the old woman's shriveled face, feeling every wrinkle, feeling the chill of time in the tunnel of death, where it lay in wait.

In my eyes, fixed on the smiling eyes of She-Dog, I saw my horror as I traveled along the skin of the old woman's belly, and then she sent me farther, now through time as well, I felt the moist cells of an embryo, and it wasn't my body anymore, I had become one of the embryo's tissues, I was inside it, time suddenly turned the other direction, and I was with them as they matured in the woman's belly and went out into the world in blood and tears, I felt time come to a stop as the pain came, shaping reality, and then She-Dog sent me off again, into the old woman's innards, and as they opened up I made my way out, and then I was in She-Dog, feeling the pressure build inside my cock. I spurted, hoping to get to the bottom and out, but She-Dog held me firmly ... now I could feel the time of life, the old time we searched out in the cellars, beginning to carry us off, sweeping us out of the alcove, we went soaring through the air, She-Dog's body growing heavy in my embrace, I saw her face sag, her hair turning gray. She had rough skin, I touched her belly, scarred from giving birth, but I won't show you you! was the sentence she gave me.

Think it started already? said She-Dog. We stepped out of the building, back onto the set. There was a rumbling from the square, as if those permanently parked Trabants were all starting up at once. Could be personnel carriers, I thought. Maybe they sent in a few tanks after all. She-Dog adjusted her skirt.

Look, I'm not gonna wear em, I mean c'mon, they always get wet.

You shoulda left em back there.

Are you nuts, some pervert sorcerer finds em an we're goners.

She was referring to the fact that I made her wear panties. There was a time when she hadn't worn them out on our strolls, but then I discovered I preferred to fuck around them, running up the inside of her thigh and wedging my cock beneath the elastic, the feel of the fabric, the resistance, turned me on. Besides, She-Dog really was little, so the distance it added between me and her sex was negligible. Maybe also my member needed to feel something besides her, anything, in those days when I was losing it. Maybe her grip was getting weaker. Or, then again, maybe it was just that I wasn't so young anymore and my cock demanded rougher treatment.

It was buses. Dozens of buses lined up in rows, full of Germans. The people inside them were different from the herd in front of the embassy. I could make out individual faces, each with its own expression, not just faces in a crowd anymore. They were somewhere else now, they were in their own time, and it wasn't sour, I lost interest in them.

Hey, said She-Dog, I spotted Šulc, so he made it!

You knew?

Yeah, he came over to my place all freaked out askin me to teach him how to say "They took my papers" in Deutsch. Then he had a faint planned.

So how do you say it?

I donno. I thought he was kiddin, musta had him repeat *Ich bin der auslander** like a hundred times.

As the buses drove off, one after the next, bystanders moved into the square. From adjacent streets, out of shops and pubs, filling the empty space left behind. Emerging from their homes to join the silent demonstration, abandoning the archways where they had stood, as if hidden, for hours now. Watching the Germans' departure. The ones in the last buses no longer looked like fugitives, foreigners trapped in a foreign city, they were smiling, some even seemed to enjoy it, waving to the crowd. A hand reached out one of the bus windows holding a can of Coke, a German no longer squatting on the cold cobblestones, handing down from on high the shiny greeting of capitalism. All of a sudden three boys were hopping up and down on the spot, jostling for position, the biggest one snagged the can, stuck it under his jacket, and bolted. The two who came away empty-handed wandered along the buses until some-one tossed them a pack of gum, then stood there divvying it up until the driver of one of the buses honked, wrenching them out of their trance. In the quiet of that historical moment it sounded out of place, like a fart during Mass. The Germans in the last bus smiled happily and wearily, some flashing the V-sign, now they looked like sightseers. And the Czechs in the streets, the ones block-ing the route, the ones who took a few steps after the last departing bus, fur-tively filling in the space from which you could clear the iron hurdle with a turn of the key in the ignition, not that you'd want to, maybe not … but the possibility was there … to disappear, suddenly the border was just a few steps over the cobblestones, nothing out of the ordinary from an everyday pedestrian point of view … maybe they felt the wings of time, maybe now time was like an angel, or a dragon, here and there its feathers grazing a person or two in the crowd, knocking someone's hat off maybe, shattering a window somewhere.

Down through the streets from the Castle, the cops closed in again.

This time they weren't marching with the routine stride of extras in some movie about the Crusades; they were sprinting. I couldn't make out their faces behind the plexiglas, but from the way they were moving it was obvious they were eager. Wild pigs get a whiff of the watering hole, a jungle scene came to me and I danced it out with my feet, grabbing hold of Little White She-Dog, but she was already crouching down, her sense of smell too was better than her sight. The first row of cops had their truncheons out. No more foreigners now, no more cameras to sully the dictatorship's reputation. We don't go throwin our dirty laundry around for everyone to see, an that includes your soiled shorts, you son of a bitch, an your stinky socks, it's time to clean house, whenever the Monster's in the mood.

Let's go, I said, more forcefully than usual.

Slowly at first, then faster and faster, the crowd began to disperse, nobody bothered waiting for a head-on collision, where a threatening mass had stood before suddenly there were clusters, and then just individuals, and all at once everything was the same as before, here and there a pensioner passing by, a college student, a worker in his blue jumpsuit, a lady with a baby carriage, people in their old roles, pub doors creaking familiarly like at the beginning of the world. Once again trams rattled to a stop on the square. Suddenly Jícha materialized.

Ciao, Bára, ciao, Potok! You guys saw it! Pinch me if I'm dreamin!

It was a perfect time loop, said She-Dog. My love's an expert when it comes to that stuff.

What a protest! That was great! Those cops were scared stiff, Jícha said gleefully.

Oh definitely, beside themselves with fear, said She-Dog.

Did you guys know Sinkule booked? An Glaser too, course he did time. I'm surprised bout the rest of em, though.

What're you up to tonight? I asked out of curiosity.

Nothin, he said.

Come see the show, we can get you in, I said condescendingly.

What? You guys're performing?

Uh-huh.

You know Jirmut's back in jail, an so's Pečorka. An they locked up those Slovaks. When they cracked down on Solidarity, every theater in Poland went on strike! An here?

Huh, never thought a that, said Bára.

I mean somebody's gotta start here too, said Jícha.

That got my attention … start … that was a time thing. Half-assed activists like this guy, though …

But … I said.

Maybe you guys could be the ones, said Jícha.

But … I said.

We're just a little troupe, said Bára.

We just wanna bring joy to the people, I said.

Jícha stood tight-lipped. He's gonna remember this, I thought.

We're just a little troupe of perverts, She-Dog came to the rescue.

No thanks, I got somethin tonight, aright ciao, said Jícha.

Aright ciao, we said.

Let's go for a coffee, Bára, I'm feelin kina battered an beat.

Not me. You're gettin old.

We're gettin old as monkeys. Maybe when the Communists bite the dust, we'll get capitalism.

Could be, maybe, said Bára, they're both just words.

Everything'll be private, belong to somebody, I mused, even the trams, even that cup of coffee that I'm gonna have by myself.

An the owners'll lock up their buildings.

Oh yeah, I said, hate to have that happen.

Forget it, when things get normal here, we're gonna make so much cash we won't even care.

You think?

I donno. I'm goin.

How bout that drink?

I'd better be goin.

You're goin? Yeah? Aright then, later.

Aright, later.

But I set out after her, watching the street, and when we passed the place with the sign, it seemed suited, I spoke again. We were there. And you, She-Dog, on your way, made a move, arched your back, turned the corner, that's how I'll put it: she turned the corner and I guess kept going, I guess, or maybe she did soar off into time, maybe she used that trick with power she taught me once at some boring party: you stick your fingers in a socket, reversing the current with your power, an go with it, seeing the streaks in your brain, the colorful streaks of electricity as they travel through the building, an you go, through every outlet, every wall, and when you stop the current with your fingers the streaks come circling back, weaving together, an you go, racing in the closed circuit as long as your breath does not give out. As long as you don't want it to. It's a colorful game. I'm going to say it, let it be so: you grabbed me in the cellar and held on tight … and maybe you were playing now too, with a socket, say, with air, a stone, some male, somebody's you met, because we put on the show without you that night and I didn't see you for years, if I'm to refer to time in conventional terms.

I missed her during the performance because it was my piece, a piece I'd written for her, or for someone else from the community. I played the part of a human rose, budding, blossoming, flowering, withering, and wilting, all in an hour. The best part of the show was a string of short scenes, witty skits, got the audience rolling in the aisles usually, I went on acting off to the side …

slowly croaking … here and there we mixed in some porno as our part in the struggle against the regime, having the gardener tickle the elves, for instance … a child walking across the stage now and then to make it obvious the emperor was naked … I played the rose and tried to get into its time, into its life … seeing as I had to kill it in the end … Little White She-Dog played a swarm of flies, voracious aphids, we had some pretty good scuffles up on stage, her biting me full of holes, I was the rose, not too manly a role, I admit, and by the time I shed my petals, there wasn't much light left on me. And since She-Dog wasn't there that night, Cepková, a blonde, had to fill in for her, and as she was sawing off my thorns I saw She-Dog's face beneath her makeup, sending me a message, I heard her brain from inside the rose's red darkness and I knew she wanted to free me of fear, but I didn't want to be free of it because without fear I couldn't act … without fear I could do anything except create … because the only way I can make up human characters and play around with them is if I know the wicked old horror of life and the horror of its ending … I chose fear … so She-Dog cast me out of the community, cut me off from herself … she promised to send me a sister, though … to fulfill my future … and two green spots like magnets flared in Cepková's face, like a blaze of heat … but then the fire died out and the female features beneath the makeup settled back into clown face as called for in the script, and She-Dog was gone … my tears flowed onto the rose … the people in the front row saw it and thought, Potok the dancer, stoned again … but I didn't give a shit … after all, even that old sadist Nero needed a sizable cast of extras for his poem about the fire … and my colleague pranced around me, acting out scissors and a greedy hand and a cloudburst with falling branches, all things with a negative sign in the life of a rose, and then she brought my drooping time to a stop, playing water and a sunbeam … the audience went wild … and She-Dog wasn't there … so after consulting with the stage manager, I acted out the watering of the rose, inserting a tube in my mouth and coiling it around my body and into a demijohn of red wine, I drank liters of it that night as I thought about my girlfriend, because it was obvious to me if she hadn't come it had to be serious, and then it was dark, Firewater-dark, with shards in my head. And in the morning I looked at my colleague Cepková, a blonde in my bed, that's pretty sick, I said to myself, and tried to wake her so she'd take off. I thought maybe She-Dog had kept her promise and sent me my sister, so soon? But when I touched those blonde tresses, it turned my stomach.

Lemme sleep!

Cepková, get up, listen …

Leave me alone … what time is it?

Hey, there's other worlds!

Aw baloney, there's just this one.

Really? Yeah, for real?

Same difference.

Yeah, I guess so.

2

WHAT MADE MY HEART. CHARGED OBJECTS.
BACK IN THE SEWER. THE CONSPIRACY.

And then one murky post-bolshevik day I stood in the street and I was alone and nothing can sear that day out of my memory. At the Tchibo coffee shop I had a memorable appointment with Micka where we laid the cornerstone of the Organization.

Nor can anything sear out the era of the Sewer, because that was what made my heart. You could zigzag through the streets and test the weight of the buildings on your back, and you can ask your mirror on the wall: Tell me, who's the fairest of them all? and the mirror takes a while to answer and it's scary, and you draw on that while for the tension in your motion, and then the mirror is just an object again and:

the shattered mirror is cut-up snapshots, I look around and it would be nice to write myself into third person, but no, says Potok: I lived in various flats and packs, and when one smiley streetwalking day they let me out of the wicked old city insane asylum, they gave me a social service key and a hole to crawl into. There wasn't any family around I could stay with. I didn't want to put up with any anger or affection for a while. So I lay my head down on Gasworks Street and filled my wardrobe with disguises. She-Dog was still in my dreams.

There were boyfriends and girlfriends and conspiracies, you could grin and say yep and nope, hah, and give a wink … there was Bohler and Micka and Čáp and Cepková and Elsa the Lion and others, each traveling in his or her own circles, which sometimes intersected under the pressure we all felt … and there were objects surviving with spirit stored inside them, objects generated in the war against death, shit, and fear, and these are often the material in which images, sounds, and speech originate, including written speech, so ferocious, so meek. And just by the way and like it was no big deal, there were people walking the streets who knew how to make these charged objects. Some of them were survival artists, even if self-destruction was the price they paid to survive. Some of them lived in the Pearl. I wanted to learn. I was hungry. Most of the other inhabitants were too slow for me, dangerous even, sour time's grayness had gotten them, but I full-throatedly wished good luck to all, contempt is best left for oneself.

No charged object of mine ever stopped water cannons or tanks, brought my dearest girlfriend back, or staved off a single wicked wrinkle. All they did was lap up time; sometimes that's enough. I ate em up like bread, putting them into my tongue.

Coincidentally the tongue I use is one of Czechs, of Slavs, of slaves, of onetime slaves to Germans and Russians, and it's a dog's tongue. A clever dog knows how to survive and what price to pay for survival. He knows when to crouch and when to dodge and when to bite, it's in his tongue. It's a tongue that was to have been destroyed, and its time has yet to come; now it never will. Invented by versifiers, spoken by coachmen and maids, and that's in it too, it evolved its own loops and holes and the wildness of a serpent's young. It's a tongue that often had to be spoken only in whispers. It's tender and cruel, and has some good old words of love, I think, it's a swift and agile tongue, and it's always happening. Not even the Avars* could get this tongue of mine, not tanks or burning borders or the most repulsive human species of all: cowardly teachers. What will eventually get it is cash in a shrinking world. But I still have time, as Totilla the barbarian said back in that wicked time of his, before his battle began. Before they got him.

As soon as we'd served out our childhood, the theologian Bohler and I started wheeling and dealing with the Poles. There were times in my youth when I wanted to be Polish. Watching from under a rock. There wasn't much time, I watched primitively. On account of the avalanches. What I liked best were the simple things; the trick was to make my mind up fast. The Indians were dead already. Poles clobbered cops. Prayed. Drank vodka. Romantics always and in everything, but standing up. Our hatred of the Monster was so great and our feeling of humiliation so strong, we sometimes dreamed about our own murder.

Another of the overlapping shards of glass, a snapshot: Čáp, white with rage, reads a statement from our fathers and grandfathers calling on us to abandon our protest because it might lead to shooting.

Look, this is crazy, says Čáp, they all left town for their cottages! Yeah, so, if they stayed they'd just get locked up, I said knowingly. Yeah but that's the point! It's all right for people to be dancin around the truncheons if they know those guys're in the slammer. But out at their cottages!

So Čáp took up the responsibility that was lying out in the street and put together his own band of juveniles. I was first in line to sign his declaration, because his vision was the wackiest one around. Hey ... nothin works, but a guy's gotta try ... our Polish brothers've got the Church, all ours're destroyed ... hey! Oh yeah, sure, I nodded, yeah right ... it's like Blake said, either create your own system or be enslaved to someone else's. Bohler reappears in the shards of mirror: Take that watch from Tokštajn, we'll hawk it to the Poles, toss in some ideological diversionism. The bazaar of course was illegal ... stupid Czechs, they really piss me off, Bohler would say, smiling at the Polish bandits, the Bohos just don't get it, I mean at least these guys're men, if they didn't trade their families could starve to death, what else're they sposta do, they don't go for the disgusting sin of whimpering ... they steal ... the Poles're always bleedin an fightin, Bohler said dreamily, the Polish nation is the Christ of crazy Eastern Europe, he blasphemed ... as the Polish bandits unloaded their cars full of smuggled Kazaks, one strode into the setting sun with a rug thrown over his shoulders, hence the vision ... and who could that gentleman hanging there be ... the one with his arms spread wide like an airplane?

The older and wiser ones who said, don't go, they might shoot, were forfeiting us, and if things hadn't gone so fast they would've also lost Čáp's juveniles ... he was getting skinnier every day, curly hair flapping, eyes shining ... we'll hand it out, but not till after the prayer! I told him inside the church ... out of the question! Čáp protested, so what if we interrupt, dammit! ... half of em can't make out the words anyway ... he had a point, we passed out our flyers with the picture of the Czech lion tugging at his chains, the Christians snatched them up and gaped in terror, stuffing them under their coats, into their bags and purses ... one fellow told me "thank you" and in his eyes he had a smile, a smile of joy, he knew there was a time for war and a time for prayer and that the two of them merge together ... a single sister shook my hand ... she smiled too ... let's hit Ignatius, said Čáp, and off we flew, through passageways and carriageways, swift and agile, glancing left and right, with eyes in the back of our heads, fast and silent, with that good old Katholik joie de vivre ... Čáp's teachings were more and more appealing every day, because he knew the war against communism must lead also to the liberation of ants and every other living creature, that no one must harm the helpless and the young, and that whosoever does must accept the punishment ... only his kingdom was a kingdom not of this world. And Čáp's juveniles amazed me too ... the most jaded bunch I ever had the honor to meet … hardcore cynics, extraordinarily reckless at times … at the age when we'd been struggling through school, they skipped out, didn't give a damn … at the age when we'd torn down a flag here and there and on the sly, they learned to dance under the truncheons … some of them were really young … practically kids … we took our experience from insane asylums and prison cells, first from the ones ten years older than us and then our own … and passed it on to them, only they were tougher … at the age when we'd collected stamps, they collected tear gas cartridges off the cobblestones and had a blast doing it … the Poles were their model too … and their tongue accelerated with their motion along the cobblestones … our eyes sometimes glowed with fire … the machines of the enemy rumbled through the air and underground, but we had a vision.

I mean everyone knows … back in today's central woman, Europe, there's nothing but dogs, they wiped out the wolves, on this reservation the only thing left to do was devote yourself to illegal shamanship and just here and there and occasionally, for a fleeting moment, dance and possess the strength of a warrior, a mortal prepared to die.

There was beating in the streets, ready and waiting, but the people with vision went back for it again and again because it was the realest thing they had left.

Čáp hurling cobblestones at a personnel carrier on Železná Street, giving his juveniles a thrill … because the kingdom won't happen all by itself, that's just common sense. It was motion, it was new. It didn't matter how many people accepted the motion, all it takes is one rotten tooth in a loyal healthy smile to give the Monster a headache …

And none of our citizens, whose stupid heads contained a shrewdly manipulated image of Poles as the hungry, wretched enemy, had a clue … and no one over in Poland had a clue about those rowdy Czechs … no one had a clue how crazy we were … no one eavesdropping from a satellite or dangling in an airshaft listening in on the scarred speech of our cooperatives, that accelerated city-speak … sitting in their cottages or squatting in the slammer, no one had a clue what the conspiracy was really about … all those scattered gangs of the city underground preparing for the important assignment, hastening toward a final solution for the soul's design … auguring from their own dread-filled intestines, tensely watching the quivering skies … secretly going for the future's throat in a conspiracy to nothing less than murder … namely, the brutal and conclusive assassination of Josef Vissarionovich Švejk.*

3

DAVID LEARNS. THE BYZNYS PATH. THE LAOTIANS.
WHAT WAS WORN. THE WELL.

And then I stood in the street, it was freedom, half past six, weather roughly March. Clouds above, asphalt below, people with shopping bags walking the street, children and dogs in tow, it was freedom and time out of joint was going mad. I let it drag me in, it was a different dance than with She-Dog, different than the dance of the rose, different than with the truncheons, there was no end to it, it seemed endless. Human time had accelerated, I was disguised as a young man with a tiger-stripe tie, files under my arm, walking to an appointment with my associates. Walking at just the right pace to be there on time, fifteen minutes early, that was part of the social contract, our own little entente. I could've afforded a car if I'd wanted one, I was just afraid to drive. Micka had changed too. Tiger stripes suited him. He wanted to make cash spin the way my She-Dog spun on electricity, but he didn't know how to send out the signals. Micka handled the paperwork, forgetting all his past hospital treatments he'd finished school and become a lawyer, it was freedom and he began smoking cigars. For the signals there was David, strategist and head of our little entente, the only one of us from the countryside, he'd climbed trees till the age of eighteen, which also made him the only one of us in sound health. All he needed to learn was the basics.

Hey, last time we went to see Mošna, he looked at his watch three times, Micka tutored him. What about it, David said studiously. Next time Mošna peeks at his watch, we get up an go, said Micka, it's an unmistakable sign. How's that? our boss wanted to know. Every textbook for future psychiatrists strictly forbids lookin at your watch, it gives sensitive patients the feelin they're takin up too much time, an rightfully so, said Micka. End of doctor's story, I added.

Micka was the first to enlighten David about the Secret. But it wasn't totally necessary, because David was born a man of the contract, all he lacked was the terminology. Together then we taught him how to eat with silverware, have eyes in the back of his head, talk with women, hand out bribes, be in three places at once, ride the subway without holding on, smear invoices and puff on them, creep through the fax, and use the phone. Which is better to eat with in a Vietnamese restaurant, David, chopsticks or silverware? Chopsticks I guess, right? With chopsticks you've got one hand free, with silverware you're at least holdin a blade, think about it now, think hard. David nodded and Micka gave me a look of pride. I tried too: Okay, David, what's heavier, a kilo of feathers or a kilo of garnets? Dummy. C'mon now, what's lighter, a liter from the head or a wheel? He hesitated, but he knew.

We knew that Slovaks were fast Moravians, Moravians were a few bricks shy of a load, Czechs thought around the corner, Praguers were stuck-up pigs, and all of us were on the same map. Micka and I had been born with asphalt between our fingers, Bohler didn't know who he was but had a degree in theology, and David was a hick but caught on at the speed of light and didn't have any hang-ups since we were there to hold his hand. Even in his innocent phase, when he was still getting up to speed, not one Prague pig ever said a thing about the ludicrous way he moved or his overall appearance, not to mention the threads and the accent. Many a hanger-on was tempted no doubt, but we never gave them the chance.

If I didn't know him, though, or didn't get that vibe right away, I might like to slug him one myself, Micka admitted one night during a dance party at the Dóm. We watched the horrified look on the face of one of our girlfriends as David attempted to move with her. Bohler just gave a perverted laugh. I felt a passionate longing for She-Dog run through me, something between a toothache and the thought of a sharp knife, careful, what's the connection with David? Is it a sign? I asked myself, or maybe my power. It didn't reply.

Micka organized the papers, tampering with rubber stamps, tuning in the contacts, pressing the lever to the ground, it was just about to begin, we were letting the genie out of the bottle, and I for one was hoping it would go in a straight line, I stretched and twisted my body, rehearsing my speech for the play.

Bohler stood by, the helper, also waiting for motion, eyes fixed upward. We were ready.

David meanwhile ridiculously rolled his eyes and cocked his head, paying no attention to how he moved his knees and elbows, sometimes even walking without moving his arms at all, as if he were herding cows. Whenever we went to the Galactic Bar, Černá's, or the Dóm, he would sprawl out and stare around at the carpetbaggers and local rabble, guzzle down the Water and not pay attention at all to his left, where the angel of death most often lurks. He didn't see why he should spit whenever he saw a black cat, ain't packin no chew, fellers, he puzzled. He didn't see why we always kept handy a toothpick, clothespin, or length of stick when we ate at snackbar counters, not realizing how many times knocking on wood had warded off serious screw-ups. He climbed into cabs headfirst as a rule instead of with his feet. He wasn't afraid of fog or gloom. He didn't know to weep at the right moment, when your world is complete and like a cup that's overflowing, to relax the motion of your sweet red heart, but that was one thing we couldn't teach him. He didn't know it was crucial to puke after drinking cheap wine or liquor to avoid breaking out in goose blotches. We weren't drinking the cheap stuff for long, though. We also banned him from wearing necklaces ... then you're sweaty an unflexible, Micka lectured him. That made David sad, he was used to wearing necklaces of teeth and claws from bears he'd killed back home, up in the mountains. Rings're all that's allowed, an earring at the extreme, bracelets're up to the individual, silver's good if that's your thing. Silver's always good, I tried to comfort him. Micka went into the details: short hair, long hair, normal ponytail, okay, but never one a those thin little braids, you're a man, not a rat.

David studied hard and we were amazed how much we knew. Micka taught him the fundamentals of hand-to-hand combat, I taught him how to run for it, and Bohler taught him the Our Father and gave him his first rosary. It was moving to see the way he gaped at that holy rope. Bohler's Laotian lady was the first person to truly touch David, and it was such a beautiful experience for him that he spent weeks tagging around after her like a puppy, not realizing it wasn't some special trait of hers but that all our female friends were more or less capable of the same.

From the moment Micka found David at the train station, spotting his hidden strategic capabilities with that old practitioner's instinct of his ... man, I saw him standin there starin ... right into the chrome parts, through all the guards an everything ... he was hungry ... an I could feel it in the air, he was runnin through combinations, it was intense ... it was obvious he was broke, an then he disappeared, an three minutes later he had it ... I could tell he had no idea where he was, but without even stoppin to think he took off in the right direction, under the bridge, hand raised, keepin the edge of his left pinky between him an the river, I don't think he even knew he was doin it ... there was just somethin in him *sensed* what to do, I mean he walked right through the Ghoul's shadow an didn't even get scared … an I could see that the kid knew how to get what he wanted, sniffin it out, wanderin through the usual spots, steerin clear of the useless stuff an gettin through the essentials without a scratch … an it was obvious to me that he saw, that he knew what was goin on … so Micka brought him in, and by a tacit but irrevocable decision the young David instantly became a member of the pack, which took care of him from then on.

David constituted a solid clause in the contract, we protected him as long as necessary, and later on he protected us too.

We were a community, and while a strong shock could've caused it to crumble, one of the reasons we had it was in order to withstand the shocks. And besides, we actually liked each other. Despite all the jokes, the gags, the booze … the daytime paranoia, when the street turns gray and the buildings at either end suddenly start tilting toward each other … and the nights when you feel the pounding of your heart, like the sound of some distant hammer, the forge … dark love tearing you up, because it's a serious thing when you couple with some stray bitch amid the chaos and you don't really know … who's who … despite all the low blows and fast moves, despite all the spirals of speech, when you hurl the fury of your hangover into your partner's face, suddenly a bare hand is offered, palm unarmed, your droog's bare back, exposed for the biting, it seems, but you know that in reality it's there for you to defend … and that person with his eyes turned the other direction is going to defend you too … because you both want to survive, waiting as long as possible … at first we went everywhere with David and only took him to our establishments. He had to change the way he talked. Look, better yet, don't even say another word to that girl … cooch … don't call her that, aright? … just tell her the air pressure's weird today, Micka lectured the boss, slicing into shapely morsels the animal flesh on his plate, David was still growing, and he scarfed it down like crazy. Yeah these pink earphones're pretty cool, I told the boss, no seriously, they go with your scarf, aw shit, they just fell in the ditch, don't worry, I'll buy you some new ones. No, David, really, Micka lectured our boss, you can't have Kyusu, I'm serious, the only ones you can use are Toshu, nothin I can do, that's just the way it is.

David was very quick to grasp what is, what isn't, and what could be, and which truly mattered at any given moment. He started to think around the corner. Suddenly he was popping up in underpasses and vanishing down hallways, waving to us from the ramparts while we were still dashing toward the moat. He got into the slang so quickly and used the right words so perfectly, it hit me that Czech had exploded along with time.

Then he began to pull away from us, sending out signals on his own and keeping in motion the octopus whose tentacles wound their way into government offices and out among byznysmen and goon squads, whom we also had need of now and then … he began to steer us, which suited us just fine … since all us savvy Praguers with the heroic past of the Sewer were actually a little squeamish of the warts on the tentacles … and then Sharky came in as foreign minister and we expanded.

I saw She-Dog again and David violated our little entente, tripped up on the water mill, lost all fear of anything, it all merged, and he lost his mind.

At the outset, though, good spirits prevailed. We were the Knights of the Secret and we were waiting. We and our assistants worked like robots. It even struck me once that if there was anything human about this transformation, it was something out of *Frankenstein*.

Sometime at the dawning, in freedom, we decided to make money, to engage somehow in the changed world around us. What I liked most were the coins, the eyes of a wide-ranging organism, their gaze as cool as the distant stars, the cold wind blows over them too … we soon realized money wasn't the metal we used to buy our beer or red wine and the Northerners their rum, but that money was debts, stamped and unstamped papers, money grows from money, multiplying by division like cells … money is words, friendships, low blows, promises, money reacts magically when the right doorknobs are polished, stacking up with each smile in the right place at the right time … currency is attracted through courtesy to this bank and hostility to that one, and the one with the most money on his hump isn't the mad dog, or the exotic tattooed dragon from the murderer's dream, but the clever eel.

Micka wanted cash, I was killing off the rest of my power and feeling the motion and searching for my sister, and David was taking shape, starting to live, he'd been born into freedom. We were cranking up the machine, and though we suspected it might destroy us, death during those tense moments of conveying the treasure out of the cave was just another sparkling secret you could set your own rhythm to. In that single everlasting instant of frenzied time, death is there as your invisible girlfriend; and we also relied on instinct.

If the Monster, with all its tanks and troops and police, hadn't cut us down back in prehistoric times, what did we have to fear now? Prison … if anything leaked out, if all those cleverly scattered connections were unable to cover it up … would be like a leper colony for kids, once you'd seen the spooks' ugly mugs *from below* … prison now: yeah right. Either the laws didn't exist, or they did but no one was paying enough attention to catch us in a loophole, those paragraphs didn't apply … I'm still talking about years 1, 2, 3, etc. after the explosion of time … didn't apply to us because we were fast.

So instead we concluded a little entente among ourselves, because we feared for our souls.

We said no, David told Bohler, no rackets, no Ukrainians, no Yugos, no Russians. Eyetals maybe, Greeks maybe, no Albanians, no Poles, nobody from Prague, no tough gangs, fuck em. You're racists, Bohler mumbled upward, imploringly, in the direction of his Bog, he's been bought off, I thought to myself. You're racists, Bohler the helper pleaded one more time. No we aren't, but you're a moron, said David. From time to time Bohler tried to cut his shady business friends in on our ride, but David, now the boss, kept a firm grip on him. Whenever we began to give Bohler a hard time about his great compassion for dubious types, he countered by dropping a few words to the effect that our buildings, a dependable source of revenue, had in fact been obtained through his prayers. After some consideration, I had to admit there was something to this.

The member of parliament who along with his little clique forced through the legislative exemption on the termination of leases owned five buildings himself. Never even got a chance to throw the poor tenants out. His tough luck Micka used to work in a boiler room with his archenemy, now a police officer. And I knew the MP's stepdaughter, she used to sleep with one of my droogs from the active era. That did the trick. We drank a toast the day she brought us the photocopies of the MP's real estate contracts with the dates retouched, but we had no clue David would work so fast that three of the buildings fell right in our laps. I stood up for Bohler, so he got the rentals. I still felt like I owed him a lot. As helper, he could only dream of sharing. But he didn't give a damn, he was interested in more important things.

It was also his idea to gobble up the space in front of the buildings. By now David knew how to stand politely if Mošna the civil servant glanced at his watch, but he didn't. It didn't even occur to him. He just looked at the piece of paper David held up to his face. It was a copy of a collective death sentence dated 1952, and the name of the judge was legible. For Mošna it served as sort of an orthographic mirror. The Devil knows whether those unavenged old convicts still dangled in his dreams … in his other hand David held another sheet of paper, and he could've said something like: Now sign this, cunt … but he was a polite boy and all he felt for cunts was a mix of grateful respect and tenderness … but I couldn't think of any other word, he said. So he only said the first part. And Mošna the civil servant signed.

Ludvig the civil servant was sent down to us from heaven itself. Boys, you've got it made, you don't know what it's like passin the buck all day long, you boys're livin! Got a little drum kit back home myself, haven't picked up the sticks in years, though. In his mind we lived wild, exciting lives, for him the adolescent demi-vierges slouching around the basement clubs, the jaded huntresses lining the bars in the places we took him, were all bohemian sexpots. He was our man in the government. When Bohler handed him the aspirin that Micka passed off as LSD, I wanted to rub off the name at least, but David wouldn't allow it. Sometimes I'd get furious about how easy it was, I'd go totally berserk, but I knew we were just trying to see how far we could push it, testing the spring, we wanted to fly.

Ludvig held the ceiling up with his eyes, panting loudly. Trying not to lose contact with real life. As the conversation rewound from art back to byznys, he miraculously revived. I'll get you eighty of our best architects to build that palace, terrific boys, every one, Artists that aren't in it just for the cash! Those architects of yours'll rob you blind, man! Micka had him spellbound. But we were all "terrific boys." He never actually did take home any of our female friends, so maybe he was gay. Either it was enough for us to see how desirable he was, groping one of them off in the corner, or he genuinely wasn't interested.

Pisses me off, said Micka, I'd like to hear what kina setup he's got at home. Maybe he's scared to go to a hotel an at home he's got a wife, I said. More likely he can't get it up, the theologian said. Micka gave the nod and another terrific boy joined us at our table. Give this architect a break, Ludvig, or I'll rip your ass to shreds faster than you can say Frank Gehry! Micka yammered. Ludvig pulled out a break and tossed it across the table, for once in his life he had plenty of them for everyone, and amid the general drunkenness it even seemed normal for the artist to be dragging around his diploma, it had gold lettering, we all saw it. Micka was getting better every day, and our man in the government melted, the contract was in the bag, all that was left was to seal it shut.

Then it was up to me to sneak through the window of opportunity with my rich assortment of disguises. David sent out the signals designating where to drop off the envelopes, where to speak plainly and where to be slightly shy, when to stand awkwardly in the doorway with a radiant boyish smile, which decision makers would appreciate a bottle of Water ... which officials enjoyed reminiscing about the Sewer days and were eager to pop some wheelies ... the sparkling party favors of real life, with girls or without ... who said art with a capital A and longed to hobnob with the Names ... and since a lot of atelier types were our friends and most of them were poor ... they'd get a blazer and a signal on when to be where, now and then someone would speak intriguingly of suicide ... and I knew where to stick out my chin, and my shiny teeth and shoes, and where to be just a regular Czech, a little sharp, a little naive ... when two hands join, the cause prospers, but if you're not interested, fuck off an don't hassle me ... who clung to the good old dissident ways, now battling corruption, so I could assure them as a former brother-in-arms that this dynamic group of young men ... and the new government building began to be mapped out right on our land ... and we weren't surprised when the price climbed dizzyingly high ... we cashed in on the cobblestones ... and the funny thing was, we could see the construction site out Bohler's windows ... and coincidentally the firm that won the contract was favorably disposed toward us ... they knew why, they weren't stupid ... and when the deliveries got held up, the envelopes would start to rustle, and they were always fatter coming in than they were going out ... it tied my guts in knots, how could we get away with it? ... the fools, but I wanted it, all the way down to the bottom of the filth and the fun that I got out of it ... Micka came up with the gadgets and the threads were my idea, the fabric came from India by way of various tracks through Mongolia, it was unbelievably cheap ... we bought up tons of the stuff, and then, with the help of a little baksheesh for various fifth- and sixth-division Ludvigs, coincidentally the rest was slapped with outrageous duties and we became the Indian fabric magnates of our crumbling republic ... and while I expended the fleeting remains of my power on hypnotism, sailing through bedrooms and offices and, in one or two delicate cases, fifth-division Ludvigs' cottages ... to get them to bang the stamp ... Micka bought some warehouses on the outskirts of Prague for a song … they were full of unsalable dry goods, cheap T-shirts and undies: two million for family, six m. for suckers … and with the help of Bohler's Laotian lady, they flew to her homeland, where they dropped out of sight for a while, together with the plane, before resurfacing in the form of lotions, ointments, incense, hats suitable for the stony fields of reeducation camps, multicolored ribbons, bamboo boofalo spears, everlasting candles, miniature Buddhas, noisemakers for scaring off birds … we nearly gave Bohler the boot, a pink slip for four m. would've meant at least a fall down the stairs, I was there to protect him, but David was tough and Micka always did have a cruel streak … just in the nick of time, though, six cousins of the Laotian kitty flew into town, and they paid in dollars, because those T-shirts and undies had earned them millions in that zany currency of theirs, which they put toward the purchase of crude rubber and got a racket of their own going with Hong Kong. When the communist soil of their homeland got too hot for comfort, they took a quick trip around the world to see their cousin … and no wonder, she was a gem, from her smile right down to the roots of her short hairs, I could sense them whenever I activated the remains of my power … I didn't even want to think about her belly or her behind, and if my power hadn't been dying I would've taken her away from Bohler … also they wanted to meet the amazing wheeler-dealers we were by then, and get a little or big something going in Eastern Europe, B-o-g willing.

Put em in the buildings, David told Bohler.

C'mon, that's crazy, everything's taken, they'd hafta live with me!

One policy we adopted immediately so as not to please the Devil too much was no throwing out tenants. There was one thing, however … our sole infringement upon the domain of tenant rights … that we persuaded them to do … which was to take all their disgusting wall-size screens and various heathen TVs and lug them out to the lawn in back … where Bohler took an ax and chopped them up, one by one, because there's no reasoning with Evil. Then we knocked their satellites off the roof, and of course we paid them back for it all, down to the last haler … it's just that all sortsa Tides an Mr. Hydes come crawlin outta that satanic tube, the old ideological stupidifier, an they're hungry for human heads …. especially children's … an hell if we're gonna share our home with a bunch a ghouls, Bohler argued, the rest of us nodded approvingly.

Only now he had a bunch of agnostics crashing right in his own flat. Aw c'mon, that bag on the third floor's gonna kick the bucket any day now, Micka consoled the theologian, just stick it out, c'mon, you got the biggest place.

Bohler and his Laotian blossom had five rooms to themselves; true, in one he'd built a small altar, but it was our assessment he surely still had room to fit in a few Buddhas.

Hey, try to get along with em, Micka continued, they're great, really, I'm tellin ya, an once we get asylum for em, he gave me a meaningful look, they're gonna come in damn handy, David nodded. The yellow race is gonna dominate for the next century, minimum, plain as day, even says so in the Bible, doesn't it, David? Yep, David said. Hah, hah, said Bohler.

If worst comes to worst we can make the Laotians passports, no big deal, I thought to myself, standing on the second floor of the imposing skyscraper of the Department of Foreigners, it seemed hostile from the second I walked in … but then in the hallway I ran into Lexa, hey there, nice a you to drop by, he said, c'mon into my office. I didn't know I had a friend from the active era sitting in such an important seat. Guess I oughta update my lists, I made a mental note.

Once upon a time the two of us had packed books together in the same warehouse, actually brochures, mounds of brochures, Marx and Lenin and Krupskaya and Engelmord, it goaded us so much we started planning to build a balloon to fly us over the wires, I expressed concern about the firepower in the guard towers, but Lexa had a solution: We'll just metal-plate the thing. That was the last of that. Maybe this time, though, he'd come up with something better.

Listen, Jituš, said Lexa, switch A over to C for me an keep it down, will ya, I got an old buddy in here. Miluš, get a move on with that two-o-five, the Boss'll be comin in any minute! Irča, he called, and as the beauty walked in he said: Irča honey, I want you to meet Potok, he's an artist, an actor. Wow! What were you in? Well, there was *My Sweet Wittle Willage** … Wow! Who'd you play? Actually, I, uh … just Šafránová in that one. She walked out. Lexa didn't laugh. Sorry, I snapped, I said … Nah, forget it, I just wanted to show the girls that I'm … you know, now that I'm a pencil pusher an all. Hey, how bout you guys, how bout you, how's life? Still actin? Oh yeah, and how, I almost burst out laughing. Then I thought of something, hey Lexa, you know a Major Mrkvica, works in passports? Yeah, good guy, just got promoted. He's that piece a shit that wouldn't let my first wife see me, I said. I'd like to spit in his face, that's the scumbag that advised me to emigrate … in the interests of the state, he told me, that Major Fuckface …

Hey, Lexa stood up. I know this stuff as well as you do, darn it. But he's a pro, we need these people. I come up against it each an every day. But Christ, you're out boozin it up, playin around in some theater, someone's gotta do this stuff.

Father Bohler prays for you, I said, for alla you that've taken on the responsibility. If it helps any.

Prayers always help.

Hey Lexa, ever get the feelin that all you guys that went into politics feel guilty about not havin a normal life?

Hey Potok, ever think maybe you guys that aren't involved in politics feel guilty about leavin it to somebody else?

Well now, that's a serious argument.

So let's drop it. What do you need? The only time old friends ever come around here is when they need a favor.

I need asylum for six Laotians.

Got any IDs?

I laid the six exotic passports featuring a picture of an elephant, hammer and sickle circling above its tall forehead, on his desk, near the paperweight.

Come by tomorrow. An wanna know when we'll stop feelin guilty?

When?

When we all get used to it. Some to the fact that they got power, an some to the fact that they don't.

But I mean it must take a heavy toll on you, it must be a problem, I mean power over people, that's heavy stuff.

Power's only a problem for those that don't have it.

Aha.

Yep.

Aright, ciao, an thanks.

Bye now.

Hey Lexa, I turned around in the doorway.

Yeah?

She's a real beauty.

Don't I know it.

I went around babbling and acting, David sat in his leather armchair, pondering and combining and sending out signals and directing the tentacles, and Micka was everywhere, handling the paperwork.

We were the Organization, and Micka worked magic with so many papers at once that we were all things in all shapes, and if a black wind blew our way we could roll right up and cease to exist.

The occasional explanations he gave us went in one ear and out the other, so eventually he gave up. This was in years 1, 2, 3, etc., when he started to speak in the bewitching tongue of economics ... and sometimes he would talk to himself: So you'll sail through the new tax, we're a cooperative, only bound by the old contract, which is registered with Rycký, but he's okay, he's one of ours ... look, s.r.o.'s Czech for gMBh, but it's the same as politics, right is left an left is wrong ... take cartels, we're talkin 19th century, man ... as for the gadgets, anybody that's not with us we persuade, an anybody we can't persuade we flatten ... What's this? They got us hangin on the hangars still, so we deduct the rent, that gives us ... movable debts at Commercial an Early Bird, hah hah ... an invoice here, an invoice there, just keep it comin's all I care ... hey, Micka, I told him, I don't like this, Community Organization, Manufacturing Cooperative, sounds like shit, how bout a Syndicate? Can the romance, you hack, wait'll after the elections. If those half-assed eggheads from SOP pick up a decent percentage in the fourth an the sixth an good old Břevnov, we'll get it goin there, that'll be Švejcar an Špála ... hey how bout this Rybka guy, do we know him? ... He was in the slammer with Křenek in '79, David mumbled as if hypnotized. An Bohler knows Křenek from the Expressway, they worked on the chain gang there in '82, he fished from his memory bank.

David carried the whole matrix around in his magical head, into which in regular sessions we deposited every thread: former classmates, pseudodroogs from the Sewer, coworkers from boiler rooms and warehouses, ugly mugs from loony bins, tennis courts, and prisons, two-bit artists from cellars, attics, and the Academy, ess-tee-bee agents, Charter 77* signatories, journalists and train engineers, officials, friends, enemies, men and mice, gals, guys, and dogs, civil servants and their secretaries, Poles, Ruthenians, Jews, and Kanaks, every face we ever glimpsed through the windows of our fast-moving vehicle, model 1, 2, 3, etc. ... after the explosion ... but also from long before ... contacts, connections, situations ... who did time with who, who slept with who, who hated who, all the gossip, facts, and information, when dusted off and combined by David, formed the silver net that was to snag the golden fish with platinum eyes and scales of precious stone, the financier's dream, the Al Capone Cooperative's nightmare.

No shit? They did? Micka said gleefully. Go an find me that priest, Potok!

Most of Bohler's friends in those days were heathens. He'd kept his old racket from the era prior to the Organization, before we had David. He would drive around the countryside in a big black beat-up delivery truck, then head back to the city with hundreds of liters of stupefying red wine. He called his truck Maria. He li'e tha' truck li'e coffin an' wi'e li'e bloo', like blood, I corrected Lady Laos on the subway home from an office where she'd played the role of Madame Hoi-Tsu, a big-shot Japaneez industrialist.

I was the interpreter and they swallowed it, hook, line, and sinker. We didn't actually want to buy anything; we just wanted to keep the firm in question out of the hands of another outfit that we needed to squelch. Before the officials could think to call the embassy and check on us, we were gone at the speed of the setting sun.

Bohler's wine shops turned a pretty good profit, though he didn't need the cash now that he'd become helper. He taught the Laosters to love the red stuff. It was a pleasure to see that crew coming home in the evening from one of their trips. Bohler enthroned at the wheel, all in black, with that happy, perverted smile of his. In the back, six sloshed Laotians, sitting or reclining in various states of bliss, eyes shining joyfully. Through the glass of the old funeral wagon they looked like life-size statues of Buddha ... except for the belly ... they were agile, nimble fellows ... sometimes, when drunk, they sang songs ... dark, wild songs, about their dark, wild women, I guess ... or the water boofalos ... no longer waiting ... out in the jungle, there were times it sounded like two bamboo stalks scraping against each other, and the only one who could stand it then was Bohler, with the divine patience he'd learned in seminary ... but occasionally it got on his nerves too, so he taught them a few Czech tunes ... the one they liked best was "Re' ke'chief, re' ke'chief, roun' an' roun' you whi'l, my swee'hear' is angry, I don' un'erstan' the gir'."

The Laotians managed to sell off all the junk that came in on the lost-and-found-again airplane, we gave it back to them in return for a percentage. Through the Organization they hooked up with Hadraba, a Northerner with a company called Fab Rocker a.s., and soon those bizarre caps and hats and fans and pipes and stimulants were all the rage at the clubs, which Hadraba had his dirty paws all over. Teenage boys flocked to his stores, buying heavy leather jackets and T-shirts with skulls, some even went for the boofalo spears. And girls began carrying fans around, to refresh themselves and their pet lab rats.

Sacred Buddhist incense burned on every dance floor, it was hip and the metal flowed and Bohler just grinned pervertedly. It dawned on me that the reason why he was unleashing those heavy fragrances into the face of his Katholik Bog was in order to spite Him, he had a beef with Him, he'd betrayed Him, or been betrayed by Him, when as a boy in the slammer he'd been raped and kicked, or the other way round, and now Bohler had hardened, waging war on Bog from the doomed position of the lone warrior, like all of us in fact.

And when the Laosters opened the last few boxes, which we'd overlooked, there were masks inside ... magnificent, terrifying masks ... and Czechs were stunned when they saw those ghastly masks from Laos, yellow and green and red and wooden, boarding the trams in years 1, 2, and 3 ... after the explosion of time. They were slaving masks, Bohler's Laotian lady told me. Not too long ago in her country, she said, warlike tribes had come down from the mountains, slaughtering the French and hunting for slaves, and the cruel demons of the mountains and forests must've been laughing now ... to know that people in the Pearl were wearing the masks of mountain jungle killers. Even the skillful Javanese who ran the tattoo parlors in Hadraba's clubs got a little unnerved, and there was nothing for them to do except burn the new, mystical tattoos off the masks and prick them into the skin of people's arms and thighs and backs ... our Laotians rode and sold and piled up the metal, which came to life in their nimble hands, changing into other metal, more metal.

Hadraba tried to take them away from us, and despite their having already put their thumbprints on a contract with him, we persuaded them to stay with us and spun them off a percentage, and when the lady from the third floor finally passed on ... we persuaded the ground-floor tenants from another of our buildings that they would be better off in the smaller space upstairs, and we did it in such a way that they were quite willing and happy to squeeze themselves in. The Laotians opened a shop downstairs, we gave them the cash for another plane, this time with Micka and David keeping a sharp eye on the percentage, and the commerce in Asian junk started up anew.

To tell the truth, the tenancy of our buildings did drop off a little, Bohler gave a bit of a dressing-down to the ones that occasionally complained about the noise from his flat … and there were other problems too, for instance when he told them they were forbidden to walk across our lawn … that lawn is sacred, people, the theologian said, and he who does not hold good housing in high regard deserves tough treatment that he may discover and open up the sources of humility within himself … another few relatives and pals of our Laotians arrived unexpectedly on the next plane … and on the next plane … and the next … securing passports for the stowaways took up a lot of my time, Lexa started to bridle, and violated the law of the community, so Micka and I dug up a few minor allegations, some staler, some fresher, and shot him down, because to aid fugitives is an especially righteous deed, particularly when they turn out to be so good at taking care of themselves … and at bringing in proceeds … and the Laosters just kept selling and selling, and some of them lived in our buildings too … and our slightly disgustingly racist tenants claimed they were scared of them when they went to fetch water from the well … it's true that around that time a few of our tenants' children went missing, but we just assumed they'd taken up with the scamp packs … Bohler shuttled back and forth settling disputes between the tenants and the Laotians, a few of whom he'd already persuaded to be baptized. Things came to a head when the Laosters converted the drying room into a pub and the baby carriage room into a Buddhist temple, which Bohler oddly enough permitted … he was getting a little worried though, and one day at our briefing he said the well had begun to lose water again and there was something weird about it. None of us cared, since we preferred the Fiery stuff anyway, but we gave Bohler approval to make Vasil the superintendent. Vasil was a young Ukrainian he'd brought in from South Station to our greasy pots and cruel freedom.

In those rare moments between business and pleasure, we would lounge around our private domains, take naps in Bohler's flat, play backgammon with the Laosters in their dive … and the new time, in the years 1, 2, 3 … etc., kept us warm and cozy, and a few times, spinning around abruptly, I glimpsed it, even touched it … and several of the Laotian women gave birth … we threw enormous parties, which as a precaution against openly racist sentiments we required all our tenants to attend and bring lavish gifts for the happy mothers … and as time went by, it was sweet to see some of the children growing beautiful flaxen hair, genuine manes … some of the men congratulated me … I just smiled … maybe I forgot to mention that my buddies … well, most of them were Balkan-Ugro-Finnish-backwoods Romany types, Bohler had a few traits that were positively negroid ... Micka was missing a few teeth from birth, and the dark-skinned David, like most mountain men, had some difficulty walking on floors ... all of us were a little damaged from various acid storms and accidents, but I think I had a few genes that were actually European ... as the M.D. eventually confirmed ... from the olden days of the Lučan Wars,* the genes of my foreforemother, who stuck by foreforefather Čech* when he chose to settle down here ... I've got fair hair, totally typically Slavic ... and it came as no surprise when my friends Cepková and Elsa the Lion said they had a hunch a few of the Laotian men would happily return the favor, I wasn't at all opposed, but I left it up to the girls, after all it was freedom ...

We held frequent byznys meetings and sociable briefings, sitting around telling stories and fables and mythical parables ... mixing narrative techniques and shaking our heads in amazement, spitting tobacco ... jingling our silver ornaments ... trading experiences ... various silver things were worn in those days ... talismans, charms, each crew had its stars and crosses and menorahs and labyrinths ... animals ... dogs, snakes, and dragons are good ... my dragon was green, but I hid him in my skin, I'd had him tattooed on ... by putting him on my chest I thought he'd help me find my sister ... various tribes, most of them actually pseudotribes, but they had protective colors too ... the Vonts' color was yellow ... that struck me as unsafe ... clans, groups, defensive alliances ... the Cellar People, spider worshipers, they put on plays ... BKS, also believers ... the Ginga Disciples, they took their power from trees ... the Machines ... the Window People, devotees of cyberspace ... the Northerners ... the People of the Tower and the People of the Castle ... various clubs, gangs, and bands ... it wasn't too wise, back in those days of today, to be on your own ... the other reason for wearing silver was that in those fast times it was best to know right away who you were dealing with and who belonged to who, there were multitudes of muddled sects from all over the place ... I myself wore one important silver thing that helped me out a lot later on at the Dump ... my mom hung it around my neck one day as I was going out ... said something like: Hope to see you soon. Dear son! And it hasn't happened yet, and due to certain circumstances, whether favorable or unfavorable I hesitate to judge, now it never will ... my most powerful piece of silver was a medallion of the Black Madonna, the Blessed Virgin of Czestochowa, the one with the spear slash on her cheek, the one that weeps eternal ... it was a real old thing, some great-great-great of mine'd hiked all the way to Czestochowa from his home in Lithuania for her, made a pilgrimage … I was real fond of that Black Madonna, she had great power, I wore her under my byznys suits and all of my disguises, even slept with her on … some people cleaned and polished their silver, but I let mine live its own life, and that ancient artifact, that piece of jewelry, turned black …

Various stuff was worn … Bohler for instance had an eagle, eagles see a lot … yep, he's a seer, said Bohler … tends to be seen up high, an besides he's fast, an admit it! he looks good too … he's medieval Indian an isn't afraid, an besides, there's not many eagles left, are there? Yeah, cool, Cassock, your eagle's cool, seriously, way, we all jingled our silver … and maybe that was also the reason we got along with the Laosters so well, they had all kinds of wild pig tusks and shark teeth … they were also believers … being accustomed to the relatively homogeneous population of Bohemia, we confused them with each other at first, this is Tino, said Bohler, well that's not his real name, but we wouldn't know how to pronounce it, it's too tough for us, an that one with the shark tooth's a great hunter, Lady Laos told me …

It didn't take long for the Laosters to spread all over the city, all over the country in fact, because the planes just kept on flying … Micka began to forge plans for a small private airport, a definite potential was shaping up to dump Asian junk on a few other countries that had shed the yoke of communism and were in dire need of fresh goods for their nonfunctional markets … our ground floors and cellars turned into a Laotian initiation camp … and bastard Bohemia's hardened arteries got hit with a fresh dose of Asia.

With their immaculately forged papers, the Laotians were just getting going, the only ones that still lived with us were the original six-member crew, plus a few wives and kids now as well. And then Vasil showed his stuff, teaching the Laosters how to make samurai swords … he'd picked it up in Kiev from the Vietnamese … with the help of various tricks in the metal shop, tricks with the temperature of air and metal, soaking them in water and burying them in sand at the right point in an appropriate place, soon Vasil and the Laotians were making antique samurai swords. Production soared as Japanese, American, German, and other tourists began bringing home not only imitation Czech glass, rubbery Czech dumplings, and shooting-gallery-prize Czech Švejks but gleaming Ukrainian-Vietnamese-Laotian-Czech samurai swords … Bohler authorized the construction of a forge in one of the courtyards, and Micka went shopping for a few thousand dull rusty surplus bolshevik officers' sabers to use as raw material. Vasil's value climbed, and if not for his howling Chernobyl nightmares we probably could've arranged for him to move in normally instead of sleeping on a shaggy cloth down in the cellar.

It was a bit surprising when, at one of our parties, Vasil began to speak Czech ... a twisted Czech traveling a roundabout route through the roughly two centuries since his family had left for the land with the dark rich soil called *chernozem* ... entirely without warning and out of nowhere and in a blink it seized him, right under the picture of the Mother of God: kottige, kow, feeldz, gorse, plou, fyer, sojers, he spewed out what was evidently his family history in a nutshell, and collapsed in an ecstatic fit ... Bohler daubed his temples with acid and Vasil came to and began to tell his story, and he has yet to finish to this day, because the Great Mother's people got him when she decided that bad good old Prague was a good place for her and the People of the Faith ... I'm getting ahead of myself. But it was chiefly his good fortune that the Miraculous Doctor Hradil and his family stumbled into our path. Because he gave Vasil a blood transfusion that cured his epilepsy, for the short remainder of his life, anyway.

It was like this: one day our little group was playing and singing in Micka's mobile on our way back home from the Rock when we saw the Doctor's family pack. A dappled old nag towed the caravan, and walking at its side, into our life, was a slightly battered example of our generation, a scarf with a red cross wrapped around his neck. Various children, big and little, peered out the caravan windows. It was the Miraculous Doctor Hradil with his sons, daughters, and wife. Just to be safe, we pulled over and jumped out. Seeing this, the Doctor got nervous and reached for a small silver scalpel hanging around his neck. But then he noticed Bohler's cassock, our crosses and amulets and altogether friendly armaments and accoutrements, and gave us a slight nod. We stood leaning into the hill a little, waiting to see what power he had, and he spoke: All right, all right, okay, if anyone should ever need an examination ... a minor operation or two ... or even something more ... all it takes is a few dumb moves at some inappropriate moment.

It was obvious right from the start that this was our man in medicine. One word led to another, and around the fire that night we learned that thanks to restitution, in those magical, adventurous Klondike yesteryears of today, the Doctor had been able to reclaim his predecessors' good old autopsy lab, located, coincidentally, right in the capital's center. The Miraculous Doctor Hradil worked mainly with blood, and after dinner, once the littlest children had gone to sleep, he showed us some of his cupping glasses, and he was also the proud inventor of a new medicinal trick: the laying on of people to leeches and vice versa. It works, fellas, like a charm, he wound up his lecture, rubbing out with a metal-tipped boot the graphs he'd drawn in the sand. We learned that the U.S., especially the army, had shown interest in his discovery, and that the Miraculous Doctor Hradil had lived some time in Canada, illegally, on their tab. He and some of his sons had spent a few years as hostages of the Mohawks, and in fact it was the old medicine men there that had given him the basic ingredients for Doctor Hradil's Miracle Elixir. He was from the old school. Taught the Mohawk shamans Latin. Understood aeronautics even. I see I can trust you fellas, but do you trust me, Priest? said the Doctor, clutching a flask in his calloused palm. Yeah sure, said Bohler politely, and the Doctor stabbed him in the face with his scalpel, slicing open his cheek. Then, quieting our crazed war whoops with a reassuring nod, he splashed Bohler's face with a jellyfishish liquid. The priest gasped for breath, sorta tingles, right? the Doctor said proudly. Yeah. The wound was practically gone. All you'll have left is a minor manly scar, actually I concocted it for those little rascals a mine, they're always pretendin to be Mohawks an slashin each other up cause they think scars're cool. A couple of his growing sons smirked. What else can it do? Micka asked. I could sense his financial timepiece ticking into action. David nodded approvingly: it was obvious. You name it, said Hradil, M.D. The Elixir can fix anything, but there's still a few kinks in it. Sometimes it acts organically, sometimes inorganically, sometimes as an acid, sometimes as a base. Depends on the patient. Bohler blanched. We soon realized one important thing: Doctor Hradil was indisputably an excellent physician, but human life was of absolutely no interest to him. He preferred gutting corpses. The autopsy lab was his now and he was looking forward to hanging up health care. Micka took the Doctor over behind the trailer, and they sat down with a calculator on the grass. Occasionally we overheard: School in winter: 19 pairs of shoes. Or: per week: 7 kilos of flour and 6 pots of boiled beef. Or: we're Katholiks, no big deal, the Lord'll provide, man … Micka's astutely persuasive voice. And then: Breakfast: 8 kilos of molasses, large melons, jelly doughnuts … it went on like that almost all night. Meanwhile we traded experiences with the Doctor's growing sons, ever so slightly, properly, and over our shoulders sneaking peeks at his growing daughters. Doctor Hradil's wife was the first normal human the Medicine Man had tested the Elixir on, and she was so kind and beautiful, and moved with such fawnish grace, we kept confusing her with her sixteen-year-old daughters. But we had Jesu in our hearts, and we hoped the Miraculous Doctor Hradil didn't confuse them too. The next morning we learned that Doctor Hradil had been persuaded.

In return for a single monthly payment he would treat our mental problems, work up case histories, take urine samples, X-ray our livers, and photograph our blood. He kept us fit on the crazy merry-go-round of byznys, and soon he was raking in a decent percentage on the Elixir.

We're takin the nationalist tack, men, Micka announced at our daily briefing. Alla that foreign crap — Taizé, Finnish drops, Wajza vodka — it's all shit. Czechs can always cure Czechs best. Czechs know best what ails other Czechs. All through the Hitleriad an the bolshevik era, every Czech ate the same crap. Czechs're all the same. Czechs're buddies. Even that dead old Romany Gypsy poet Mácha* said so: "Who's better than a Czech?" With ads like that running in every political weekly and cultural quarterly favorably inclined toward us, we soon broke through. The ancient Chinese selling technique also helped tremendously: Doctor Hradil's Miracle Elixir was far and away the cheapest health care product in the then crumbling republic. Nobody but total derelicts and lonely old crones bought the stuff, so when the wrong kind of patient took the Elixir there were never any dangerous what-have-we-heres and the coroners banged the stamp for the casket without a fuss. And that bestial Mohawk the Miraculous Doctor Hradil had himself another vagabond to strap onto his autopsy table. It was a perfect circle. Besides, by cleverly specializing in the stratum between the urban poor and the urban underclass, he usually gutted only the wrong kind of patients. And the sign on the door of his old downtown lab — MEDICINAL WORK FREE OF CHARGE — did its bit too … pulled the poor folks in like a magnet.

Medical care was one thing our hard-earning little crew truly needed. Besides, all those tablets, capsules, and draughts went great with Firewater. At 7 a.m. each morning, we were up and dressed in our fine white byznys shirts and immaculate pinstriped suits, Bohler in a fresh cassock, prepared for the daily briefing, but every now and then all at once those dog-hard years under the bolshevik knout would show. Especially the years in the loony bins. We didn't get goose blotches anymore, now that we drank expensive booze, but the new improved kapitalist vodkas gave us turkey blotches instead. Doctor Hradil's treatment for that was to bathe us in a laser beam. It helped a little.

With David combining and Micka steering, we managed to nab the strangely popular Gamma Knife. That's just like today's folks, Bohler railed, pitchin in all that cash for some space-age knife, then stick some innocent little boy under it, see what it does. Before we put the Gamma Knife back in the warehouse, we all exchanged bone marrow. Bohler groused a bit, but we persuaded him. Afterwards we felt better. But I have to admit I felt sad … a little … from time to time … seeing the fantastic, chivalrous, gallant way Doctor Hradil's sons treated their sisters … it wrung my heart … watching the little ones play their good wholesome Katholik games … pirates … doctor … the Clan of the Woolly Mammoth … their nerve-racking Mohawk battle cries echoing through the buildings … Doctor Hradil's sons kicking around the neighborhood … they were good boys … and whenever only the right kind of patients had been buying the Elixir a while, and Doctor Hradil was getting bored, the boys would go dig up some stiffs from the scrap heaps, or the Dump … troll the toxic Moldau … engaging in heavy battle with the scamp gangs along the way … but they showed em a Mohawk trick or two, especially the ones for man-to-man forest combat … and soon the city brats would break into tears and flee at the sight of them … and when Hradil's boys eventually came up against the real goons, and I'll say something about them later on … they weren't afraid to take a little swig of Elixir in the right place at the right time … they took after their dad … and knew how to take risks.

My heavy sorrow and my insane longing for She-Dog were giving me bad circles, worse and worse every day … so I pestered the Miraculous Doctor Hradil, visiting him for checkups: Uh-huh, mm-hmm, mm-hmm, discombobulated joints, run-down cartilage, beat-up ribs, fucked-up skull, quick shoulders, slowish knees, cracked Adam's apple, buzzing calves, demented heels, profession? Dancer. Aha, ah-hah, well, what else've we got: sunken eye sockets, hungry glances, coarse fast hair, clogged pores, old hump, dark malice, yearning, eagerness, mysticism, harsh booze, avarice, gloves, fill in the blank: Actor. Uh-huh, uh-huh, hold on now, we're almost done, how many times've you been committed, hoochmeister? Six, boss, Doctor sir, but that was under the communards. Just the opposite, old rat, those count double, and moving right along, this is going to hurt: Aha and oh my: yellow Slavic blotches, Celtic somnambulist, Germanic dummkopf, Jewish ganef, transitional AIDS, you stud, incipient raw graphomania, insane heavy perpetual adolescence, and good old schizophrenia. Capable of living defect-free. Good luck. Next!

Doctor Hradil's family pack was a welcome addition, a fabulous diversification. But one day, two of the M.D.'s sixteen-year-old daughters disappeared. They were last seen high on weed, carrying pails down to the cellar to fetch water from the well, laughing that distinctive pealing girlish laugh of theirs. Some of the Laotians saw their torches and heard the girls cranking the winch. Laughing the whole time. Then silence. Desperate, the Doctor's wife rounded up the Laosters, and armed with boofalo spears, just in case, they combed the entire cellar, but the girls' footprints were Čapekesque* … they went as far as the well and then vanished.

Even Jesu in all his greatness left no footprints on the lake. He walked across and put his imprint in the suddenly holy sand on the other side. Not the girls. One Laotian, the former shark hunter, dove into the well and scoured the cracked and muddy bottom, ten meters down, but the girls weren't there. It was odd. It was dark. Bohler paced gloomily around the courtyard while the Doctor's family pack prayed woefully and sadly and insistently by the fire. The tenants were tucked away in their rooms. Vasil sat under the picture of the Mother of God, where he felt safe, and sobbed.

As the evening shadows thickened, sinking into the courtyard, the Laotians went into their temple and performed a ceremony. The men lit incense, and the women separated the smoke from the fragrance and sent it out to search. Around midnight Bohler's Laotian lady came to me and touched my forehead. She had ashes on her finger, and something else besides. I didn't let on how flattered I was that she'd chosen me to pass the message along from tribe to tribe. The smoke had told her something, I could see it in her eyes. Where're the girls? I asked. Wa'er too' them. Where? Into we'. I went to tell my tribesmen.

Some of Doctor Hradil's younger kids began to sob. Micka assured them that everything would turn out all right, plain as day. They bawled even louder. The M.D. showed up and began to pack without a word. There wasn't much, the children gathered up their winter caps and a scalpel or two here and there, and the Doctor's family pack abandoned the suddenly strange and inhospitable environment of our buildings for the autopsy lab. Finally a little elbow room, I tried to joke. He's used to makin em, not losin em, Micka chimed in. David just sat glumly. Hey guys, I don't mean to bleat, but've you noticed anything weird about our street lately? Not a whole lotta cats or dogs, bird or two's about it, said Bohler. An I'd say we been losin tenants too, not that their petty gelt matters. They're probly a little freaked out by your buddy Vasil an those screamin meemies of his, Micka retorted. No, it isn't that … I putter around a lot, talkin with everyone … an there's somethin strange in that well, or strange about it. I been thinkin. An my guess is it's somethin that doesn't work on goons like Vasil. An not on the Laosters either, they've seen it all before, in that yellow bolshevism of theirs. Hold on now, David said, are you tryin to tell us there's somethin here that works on tenants' little kids an cats an dogs an the old M.D.'s pure virgin daughters … but not on us? I finished for him, and only then did I realize what it was. Aright, okay, said Micka, but we can't deal with it right now. He was right, but we were too caught up in the whirling merry-go-round of byznys to get around to it later on. As a result, we nearly lost all of our rackets, and all of our worries too.

4

GOLDIE AND HIS PROPOSITIONS. IN CAME SHARKY.
THE CONTRACT. BOHLER SHOWS ME THE TOYS.
I DO THE CARS. HE BRINGS HER IN, FINGERS THE STRING.

And one smiley day when the sun shone down on the cool city neon as sweet and heavy as grapes from the vineyard of the Lord, Micka brought in Shark Stein. He'd been hinting for some time now that we needed to expand ... hey Potok, all of a sudden there's like thirty thousand Americans here in our hometown, go an find out if they're all just a buncha half an quarter henry millers, or if any of em also know how to make the metal flow ... and I brought in Golden Joe.

Joe dressed in gold from head to toe, had to sling up his fingers because they'd gone limp from all the rings ... tied his ponytail back with a golden band, instead of bookshelves, cupboards, and a fireplace at home he had showcases full of gold ... and most of the gold in the little shops that spread like mold after the explosion of time belonged to him as well.

Goldie was American, a Hungarian with an excellent passport, each month he flew to Bangkok to expand his hunting ground of connections in the Hungarian colony that had sprung up there in the wake of that bloody year when the Hungarians attempted to set off the time bomb ... the Monster sent in the tanks, which, as everyone knows, don't bother persuading, they just roll on through ... the Hungarian colonists in golden Thailand, where the oldest whores're thirteen forever and some of them never die, worked for Golden Joe ... some, I soon realized, out of sheer joie de vivre and love of motion, and others because Goldie's men persuaded them it was better to cough up a few gold chips than to risk tangling with their countrymen, especially when the nearest dark and silent jungle lay right at the end of the local bus line.

Joe'd been drawn to Prague right from year 1, having sensed the motion, and as one word led to another suddenly there were whole sentences of Inglish with the unfamiliar accent of the Sewer of Buda and Pest, I listened with great interest, leaving the content to Micka and David ... and in came the Firewater, and since Goldie was interested in our gadgets, we agreed to make a deal ... it got a little hairy when David had to advise him of our little entente … Goldie didn't live by the contract and didn't know about the Secret, he had intercourse with those thirteen-year-olds whenever he went to Bangkok, but seeing as he could tell that our interest in metal was real, he tossed out an idea he said he'd been toying with for some time now in the hope of giving gold a rest and enjoying life a little in his golden years, of which so far there were nearly thirty … maybe get a few massage parlors goin, staff em with sweet young things, I'm talkin *real* young, an white! Praga could be a minor branch of Bangkok, no problem, fly in a few tea roses to brighten things up a little, but mainly to give some classes, cause your girls here … well … they're a little on the comfy side … maybe I'll fly Amber an Coral over … but we'll recruit the rest from the finest old Prague Katholik families … inasmuch as possible … an bam, we're swimmin in metal, with the legislation the way it is here we'll be pullin in the sickest pigs from every desirable state, suckin the metal outta their pockets before they can get a grunt in, an afterwards too … but first David had to advise him of our little entente, which we had mutually bound ourselves to so as not to please the Devil too much … porno okay, but never with fleas … an fleas means kids … said David … that's cool, said Golden Boy, but when he made his next proposition David had to raise his voice again … we don't transport, distribute, or offer drugs to anyone that isn't already hooked … that we don't think is already hooked … then Goldie, by now openly amused at what odd tradesters we were, whipped out another proposition, this one slightly soggy with Water and wheelies of truth, which I'd slipped into his Jack Daniels with my usual agility … I'd used them in negotiations with guys like him before, whenever Micka screwed up his nose in that special way and said the password: Aunt Madla may be dumb as a pumpkin, chief, but your proposition is quite attractive … I'd insidiously trot out the wheelies of truth … got em from a KGB major I knew … usually the chiefs would get tangled up in their words, and now and then they'd own up to their innermost, generally dark intentions, which was important, since maybe we wanted to be their contacts and maybe we didn't, but we definitely didn't intend to wind up as somebody's sacrifice, like the son of humble Abraham that almost got his throat slit up there on the mountain … that's what I call a close shave, and back in the days of today's fast times that I'm talking about here, the eardrums we'd gotten from Starry Bog were pretty ground down to start with, so there was no guarantee we'd hear the command from the heavens that stopped old Abraham's blade …

and this time Goldie started off with a detour through liberated Czechoslovakia's foreign policy, before coming back to Thailand and then up to the border ... with Burma, and then he crossed over and stopped his speech there, casually tossing in a word or two about this tribe called the Karens, a pretty powerful nation, and a minor conflict with the Burmese government, inserting a mention or two about a few tens of thousands dead ... and slightly and heavily wounded ... villages burned, men executed, women raped, children kidnapped ... in other words, the usual ... adding how fascinating it was to track the constant improvement in armaments and accoutrements on both sides of the conflict ... see, the Karen rebels began to suffer heavy losses when the government boosted its arsenal with wicked old lethal long-range AK-3s, which as every little kid knows come from Czech factories ... now that was a racket, boys ... Goldie smacked his lips ... and that wasn't all, because the clever Karen chiefs took all the gold they had stashed away in those bamboo stems of theirs and bought the very same perverted Czech weapons, and they had so much gold saved up in those thieving households of theirs that the Bohos also outfitted their rifles with infrared telescopic sights, and at night the government ranks wore seriously thin in spots ... so the government had no choice but to pick up the phone and call the death factories about installing chemical warheads, and when the orders were filled ... Goldie smacked his lips and took a slug of Firewater spiked with wheelies ... the Karen shamans, in those old caves full of moonlight and eerie drawings in human blood, opted for the final solution and telepathically roused the death factory managers, and each invoice for special rocket hookups to fit the AK-3s ... meant a huge profit for the intelligent byznysman ... said Goldie ... an it's still goin on ... just a stone's throw from Bangkok ... Igen! said Goldie, reverting to his native tongue just before he fainted, which tended to happened to other crews' chiefs after sampling my cocktails ... allowing us to confer in peace ... without any foreign hick's bat ears around ... and David didn't have to cite him any more clauses from our little entente, which was a good thing, since he probably wouldn't't've been able to take knowing what a pack of angels we really were ... the main point of our contract was the Secret, because the one thing we prayed for more than anything else back in those days of today, after the explosion of time, was for the Messiach ... to come ... even though we enjoyed ourselves most of the dwindling time, death lurked around every corner, as always ... and sometimes life was so insane ... as always ... and a knight isn't allowed to do himself in

... not even if he's taken hostage ... not even if they torture him ... he's gotta suffer through it all ... every one of Starry Bog's traps ... and we all contained so much cancer and human misery and fear and hunger that sometimes it leaked out our eye sockets and Bohler had to step in with his cross.

To be brief ... sometimes we were like spiders in cloisters, and the feeling of eternity and frustration, the fear of life and the fear of death, of cold and heat, were unbearable ... sometimes you could drop acid and glimpse life pulsing in everything around you, and the trees were friendly creatures, just like you, and then it snapped and the trees were just another scary life form trying to take you out so they could suck the sun's warmth without interference ... and both were real, and you have to know and cope with both, and you have to know when not to fear and when to be full of dread ... only he who doesn't dread his fear can cope with both in the now and here ... and live in time on the move ... so we crossed paths in the perpetual war of the creatures to get a spot at the watering hole ... and every battle was so tough that sometimes even when we switched off, hopped into Micka's mobile, and drove out to the Rock in the countryside, it didn't help.

The Secret concerns small creatures ... the unfinished ones that can't defend themselves ... and also children and small dogs ... we were waiting for the Messiach, so we weren't gonna lay a hand on any little kids, that was obvious ... look at the first Jesu, rolling around the manger in his diapers ... he had the good animals standing guard, and no doubt old chief Joseph gave a proper going-over to everyone who came bearing gifts or "gifts," confiscating the juveniles' knives and turning the adults' fiendish devices right back into their guts ... and sixteen-year-old Mary with long black hair was a mighty sister with a soft, hard gaze, she kept an eye out too ... checking Jesu's lollipops to keep some fool who didn't know about the contract from handing him a sucker laced with smack ... the first Jesu had a good bunch around ... customs agents, sturdy carpenters and masons, whores, actors, and Peter the skillful swordsman ... and in the end they got him anyway, but that's just how he was, that was the way he used his power, and as he died his ears and eyes filled with the soft, golden light of God, which in fact according to Bohler and other authorities he was ... but having a hotline straight to Starry Bog might not be enough for the Child of today ... who knows what cold urban hole our little Messiach is shivering in now ... who knows if his plastered dad's not wavin a carving knife at him as we speak ... the Devil knows if his strung-out mom isn't smotherin him under the sideboard ... me and the guys would sometimes wonder, spitting tobacco and nodding our heads ... jingling our silver, Bohler fingering his eagle, me patting my Black Madonna ... we gotta be careful, Micka summed up every time ... no weapons or drugs, no porno with fleas, David spoke the living parts of the contract aloud and Bohler raised his eyes to the heavens ... Sure, sure, I'd add at some point when I wasn't adjusting my mask.

An maybe right this minute those Burmese hunters, with their golden velvet Czech AKs, are sneakin up on some forest hideout where the little Dalai Lama is playin around with the first signs of his power ... Bohler said ... an they're soft as tigers, not a claw click on stone ... an the little Dalai Lama doesn't suspect a thing ... an he doesn't have any protection cause his disgusting father's off in the nearest village gettin tanked on the local Fiery ... an his dirty old mom's out makin bacon ... an the hunters're after his little scalp ... Bohler had us hypnotized, standing over the unconscious Goldie, then he whipped out a garrote from under his cassock, ready to terminate the poor guy ... we had to step in and subdue the priest.

We went by the contract, and though we decided to use Goldie for the byznys with the gadgets we kept our ears and hearts locked tight against his black chicanery.

Our other American, Shark Stein, was a man of the contract. His dad had been born in Terezín,* and for the first year of his life his world had been confined to the inside of a shoe box, good old Batas,* Sharky said. He survived to have Sharky only thanks to the fact that in every one of those foul camps, where his childish soul had its eyes opened to all the worlds and where those worlds began to merge into reality, he always bumped into people of the contract. He hung around the mass graves, collecting the knowledge that he would later pass on to Sharky. After Shark Stein became a member of the pack, he taught us a few things. Probably the best was the one with the box: the trick is to watch the world from inside, especially when it's a world of metal-tipped boots and you're on the smallish, fragile side, and then, when the right moment comes, you climb out and put your power into play.

Taking after his dad, Sharky was a survival artist specializing in the many discomforts of mass graves. You could sense it in every light and heavy move he made. Sharky had a face as sharp as mommy's morning razor. We all admired him, and Micka glowed, because he was the one who'd brought him in, just like he did David. Only this time we didn't have to bother with teaching. Sharky already spoke the Organization's language, along with slang and argot, plus a host of other tongues the usual way. Every language you know makes you another person, Micka lectured us one morning. Every language you know means you can lick my bunghole, I said like a proper actor. Bohler caught on: Hey guys, know this one? This lady goes to the doctor an says, hey doc … I got this like itch in my throat an … I'm all sweaty an dizzy … an I'm sittin there stark naked, Bohler got confused … I broke out in mad laughter, David turned red, Micka opened the door, and in walked Shark Stein, sprightly, swift, and silent, in a pair of black leather shoes.

Sharky knew about the Secret, he knew that you have to treat every unfinished small human creature like a vessel full of light because you never know which one might be the Child, the Messiach. And here in the hostile territory of the spinning wheel, he's got a mission. Namely, to gather the salvation that's always going on, gather it into the ultimate noose, and kill the pain. Once he's had a little stroll through the vale of tears and taken a look around … that Child's got a real big job waiting for him, namely to *persuade* the Old Bloodhound, Starry Bog, that Dogass Fuck, in other words his plastered dad, to turn a blind eye to all the filth and murder. And that's quite a job. So why not make it a little easier on him, huh? On that we all agreed.

Luckily our new buddy wasn't as overzealous as Bohler, who'd already been to court a few times for snatching sons and daughters away from their plastered degenerate mothers, who in his opinion were treating them cruelly.

Roaming the city parks, Bohler handed out chewing gum and holy pictures to wild boy thieves with keys around their necks and snot running from their noses. Bible in hand, he prowled the city scrap heaps, blessing the runaway brats who went there to lick out cans. A few times they chased him off with bolts cast from their homemade slingshots with fiendish accuracy. Loitering around supermarkets, he kept watch over the little shoplifters whose tricks he'd come to know well. And they came to know him too.

Hey, y'old Cassock, they'd sneer at him. Hey, y'old vampire, Terminator, Alien, Golem, Nosferatu, Medoosa! hurling video lore in his face. Rabble, I bring you God's word, Bohler would begin when he managed to get hold of a few. Shuddup n fork over the moola, the grins, the jingle, the duckets, ya wormy old Dracula! He gave them the cash every time. But instead of buying soup with it, they'd get smokes or toyfils* or toluene.* I force charitable acts of baptism on em, said Bohler, like with the Apaches. Once he got shot with a police special, and a few times the little do-badders stabbed him. But Bohler would always just sew himself up, rinse himself off, and head back out on his crusade.

When I imagine our little Messiach joltin along on some train right now, Bohler said wistfully, his good, hardworkin carpenter dad an his kind, virtuous mom lookin out for some Egypt-type place to escape the Balkan or Angolan or Kurdish or maybe Cambodian ... Herodiad ... an the Messiach's got just one sweater an only one pair of socks ... an there isn't a single country that'll take the saintly family in, since they're obviously economic refugees ... Bohler let out a savage howl and rushed off to the train station to reward the next trainload of Gypsies from Romania.

But there was one other thing about the scamps that disturbed me, and that was their toys. Those abominable toyfil spiders from space ... time flew by so fast in years 1, 2, and 3 ... that all of a sudden there were totally different toys ... I shook my head in disbelief, and when me and the guys talked it over we reminisced about our own childhood worlds.

I think those dolls and teddy bears littering the ground outside the German Embassy were the last normal make-believe beings before the Atomic Galactic Skeletons burst onto the scene ... the Pearl's toy store windows looked like ads for a Vampire Ball ... hideous bloodsoaked grapplers everywhere ... Nuclear Asexual Homonucleoids ... all kinds of extragalactic wicked witches instead of that good old hag Ježibaba, alias Baba Yaga, the one the Grimms' Hans and Gretel, or their Czech siblings, Jeník and Mařenka, polished off at the end, giving children's souls a chance to recover from the horror ... me and the guys reminisced about our childhood castles and teepees.

Back in the time before I had sperm or She-Dog, who relieved me of it with childlike innocence, I too played at the world, fighting countless battles with miniature knights and Indians, learning the ways of war to avoid getting lost in the Jungle, or at least not right away ... just as my grandpas waged endless battles across the floors, golden soldiers in the castle, pinecones in the village below, tin soldiers everywhere imaginable ... and in that world of childhood games, the Cheyennes and the Arapahos won, tearing across the prairie and stealing horses while the villains yowled at the martyr's stake, and not the other way round, and the white knight struck the black knight down, and not the other way round, and Captain Cormorant and his bro the tiger saved the day instead of rotting up in the rigging, that's the way it was and not the other way round, and maybe Brutus had a dagger but still he gave old Julius a chance, don't try to tell me he didn't … and maybe the real, cruel world turned out to be different, but at least that sweet little kid was clued in to a few of the basic rules … at the age when we'd towed around wooden ducks and dug through coal trucks, playing miner, the scamps were inventing worlds full of all sorts of fascistoid bolshevist Freaks and kapitalist Phantasms … Alien Space Invaders … toyfils and toyfilkins … the un-Christian Japaneez of course produced most of the merchandise … all sorts of small-scale dragons, spitting images of that blind old serpent in his underground lair … Gamera vs. Gaos, Monster X from Outer Space … in the end old outer space was just too scary and there was no use trying to be happy and quiet and wary, like a dolphin gliding through the sea. I mean if you don't believe you've got a chance even in outer space … then what? … a dumb ending with no beginning … just one trapdoor after another … Spiders … *El Beso de la Mujer Araña* … Thinking Machines and Unthinking Furies … all those toyfils and not a single positively charged hero in the bunch, an accursed band of demented postmodern pests … apart from cute little critters of every race and species, all of our creatures were people at least, in most cases knights and men, whether cowboys, Indians, old carpenters, soldiers, scuba divers, or maybe, at worst, cosmonauts … little girls had princesses or Ribannas* or babies or elegant ladies with changeable wardrobes … all that's left of that now is that stupid Barbie, the robot clone, may AIDS drag her into its pestilent grave! I cursed as Bohler and I drove out to Toy Central in his hearse.

He turned off the headlights, and then we went a pretty long way on foot, which irked me a little since I'd just put a nice good high on with some weed. He dragged me over to one of the windows and switched on a flashlight. It was hair-raising. Toyfils filled the shelves, and those freaks were alive! They busily communicated among themselves, the Thinking Machines whirling about spewing flames at frightening speed, Draculas jockeying Spiders, Gargoyles of Zador bearing down on the valiant Batman, the Mutant King and the Purple People-Eater chatting away in the corner, and Barbie … yeah, doin the nasty with a team of grapplers … good God! … talk about a wild ride … The most awful part, though, was what the nine-handed Blinking Martians were doing to a few Cheyennes I must've somehow overlooked back in my tough childhood … they had them bound and gagged, and in each hand they had a … nah, forget it.

When the freaks spotted us, there was a big commotion. Squirming like worms in a hunk of old cheese, they were back on the shelves in the blink of an eye, safely wrapped in boxes and cellophane.

Now you get it, said Bohler.

Yeah, you mean …

That's right, he plants em here, the Dark Prince, he's after the kids, it's obvious.

An those stupid dads …

They buy em like robots …

I guess the problem is the human tribe's fallen apart, said Bohler, yep, families aren't what they used to be. I'd even go so far as to say the reason why moms an pops buy toyfils is cause they hate their offspring, deep down in their souls they're happy to bring the dark stuff home, only …

the stuff's power turns against em, I finished Bohler's thought …

yep, they're scared a their own offspring, wanna destroy the kids before they grow up … but a lot of kids survive their dark upbringing, an then they go out an start stranglin old codgers …

which explains all the family murders these days, I tossed out …

Raskolnikov, before he killed, had to train his power pretty hard in old Nietzsche's superman theory … Bohler filled in my knowledge of literature and philosophy …

an nowadays scamps bump their weary old dads off just for a fistful a coins …

yeah, but Raskolnikov at least had that painted slut Sonia, said Bohler, she helped him out …

what? he had a sister? that caught my interest …

nah, said Bohler, just some whore … but she did bring him a Bible … later on … in the slammer … an before, he had that crybaby Marmeladov … an his mom an sis came all the way to mangy Moscow to see him, an he had buddies too …

wait, Bohler, what about that sis?

… yeah, I guess the problem is scamps're so lonely these days, TV's all they got, so they fill the hole with toyfils …

wait, Bohler, did Raskolnikov have a sis or not?

… the human community's fallen apart, just a bunch a tribes fightin in the dark, Bohler mused … allied or opposed based on commercial considerations

… an the scamps're so all alone, he said, choked with emotion … an they take to the warpath, them against the world, but they donno the rules, they don't have any contract, they're either on their own or they belong to bad tribes, pseudotribes, an since they donno about the contract they smother everyone else, an then they turn around an have more forsaken scamps … an they do it all over again … it's just one great big circle …

wait, Bohler, was Raskolnikov sleepin with Sonia or was he sleepin with that other sis?!

… like atoms in some fucked-up model, wandering aimlessly through space, I bet some of em don't even know they're alive, Bohler concluded his discourse.

I wanted to ask him whether Raskolnikov had a sister and slyly ferret out somehow what kind of power she had, but our work was cut out for us. We broke into Toy Central and combed through the storerooms. We didn't find any more Cheyennes, but we took the ones from the window at least, and it goes without saying we also roughed up a toyfil or two along the way. Then Bohler rigged up something around the edges of the rooms, and by the time he lit the fuse we were moving pretty fast. We hopped into the car and put a good couple hundred meters behind us before we heard the soul-soothing blast, a splendid red glow laced with green and yellow flashes lit our way as the sources of the toyfils' evil power crackled in the blaze, or so, dear Lord, I firmly hope. As soon as we got home, we took the Cheyennes out to the lawn in back and set them free.

But to return to our commercial enterprises: Sharky, like us, was expecting the Messiach, so it was no big deal, he just signed a few papers for Micka, and the razor-faced Shark Stein became a full-fledged member of the pack. Micka glowed and glowed, because with all the years he'd spent in Tokyo our new pseudodroog was an exceptionally valuable acquisition.

Your attention, gentlemen, Micka announced at one of our briefings. Düsseldorf, that means Bank of Japan, they got their hounds at the border right this second, waitin to see how the breakup goes. As long as we're not swimmin in blood, the hounds'll come runnin. An a little bird tells me Suzuki's makin a deal with Volkswagen to buy Škoda, I.G. Farben, an bloody old Krupp! Cash on the barrel! They'll have computer samurais here on every corner before we know it.

And David combined and Micka negotiated, and they plugged in the well-traveled Sharky, who we made our foreign minister … we're still in years 1, 2,

3, etc. … and Micka pulled the levers calibrated for cross-border transfers … mainly at the ministry, but also in various companies and outfits, and David did his combining, and they sent me out to play my part … this time it was pretty enjoyable, since I was riding with Bohler's Laotian lady, alias Madame Hoi-Tsu … the gadgets, complete with cheap spare parts from Thailand, compliments of Golden Joe, were taking several of the slower countries by storm all at once, and the Laosters peeled us off a percentage, and every so often we would quietly and without needless ado unload a few less important buildings on the outskirts of town … that actually didn't exist … since the treacherous MP we'd shot down was working for us now … we'd persuaded him of the benefits of some fast work in the silent company of a few certain land registers stored in a particular office … and the Miraculous Doctor Hradil's Elixir was taking by storm one East European market after another, because the farther east it went, the more poor souls there were who either wasted away into lifeless vagabonds or adjusted into entirely healthy individuals … here and there we also received reports that in certain mutated regions the Elixir worked as an aphrodisiac … out toward the Urals, Doctor Hradil's Miracle Elixir was winning more and more enthusiastic devotees every day … both right and wrong patients, in exact accordance with Darwin's theory … and with the good old Russian roulette principle … and the label designed by our art director, picturing the deviously smiling M.D. Hradil with a rented white lab coat and a borrowed stethoscope, fending off the Grim Reaper, was the hit of the new, post-bolshevik world, and the days when Vasil sat in the cellar licking labels and pasting them on were long gone … now the Elixir was produced out of a few old factories in the new Bohemia's capital … and we were still the Mongolian Indian fabric magnates, and the construction of the government palace on our government plot of land was going at such a snailish pace that it actually didn't exist, which meant it didn't block our view … and another scheme or scam … would pop up every now and then … and there was no shortage of them … because this was and still is the Klondike … of the Wild East.

And we went like whipped dogs hitched to a sled that we just had to get there, because the second you stop, your time is gone and you end up freezing to death in hostile territory.

We cracked the whip on each other just as hard as we did on ourselves, that's the way it is in the human byznys tribe. And whenever we felt our bodies pining, like an unexpectedly cold morning breeze, the M.D. would find us a remedy ... his sons were wholly absorbed in the search for their sisters, and no one understood that better than me ... but time was flying like a demon from its lair ... out of that crack in the concrete ... as if time were hungry, as if time were feeding on the flesh of the people who lived in it ... its enemies, it struck me ... I told Doctor Hradil about it one day, but he said: only paranoids have enemies ... and the metal flowed ... and Prague was changing ... and the ones that couldn't find their way had to crawl ... slower and slower, till they perished in time ... and the ones that had harnessed time broke the others' backs, shot them down, as long as there was something in it for them, but if it didn't seem worth their trouble they knocked around the cheap eateries in the town below the Castle, keeping to themselves, till they perished too ... and that's the way it's been from the very beginning ... there's something baroque about it ... and the way the people who live in the Castle perish isn't a whole lot more elegant ... and the M.D. just cracked a little smile over his autopsy table and, eyes glittering, plunged into his research ... the avid anthropologist ... and then one of his sons got killed for carelessly erasing an evil swastika down in that accursed subway ... the hitlers were starting to swarm.

At first our little group wasn't too concerned, just the wrong rumble in the wrong place at the wrong time, but soon we were to hear more about them.

The Laotians, who'd taken a liking to the Doctor's pack, even teaching the littlest ones some of their words, gathered under the lab windows the night of the young boy's final journey. It may've seemed a little strange to them to see the deceased rolling off the old conveyor belt onto the bier in sacks. The M.D. had dissected him in order to be certain ... of the strength of the blows ... the direction of the wrath ... so he'd be better able to protect his other children.

The Laotians also got their butts kicked every now and then, and every now and then they kicked ass right back, but until they saw those sacks filled with the little white boy who'd spoken their language, it didn't really hit them ... they'd stared down death's bony sneer for a pretty long time in that cutthroat land of theirs.

But now, for the very first time, they got a nice sharp look at their new free land, and except for the ones Bohler had persuaded to be baptized and rewarded with rosaries they all began to howl ... and the ones that had been baptized knelt down with clasped hands and began twisting their necks and tossing their heads ... damn, what's with them? I hissed to Bohler ... well, he said tentatively, I donno for sure, but if y'ask me I'd say they're turnin the other cheek, guess I went overboard, they musta misconstrued it.

Just then Bohler's Laotian lady came up to us with a terrified look on her face: Horry, horry! What's up? I inquired. Lao'ians ou' to ki'. So what do you want me to do? I said. Call the cops? No, no, she said, they ki' cop too! Bohler and I traded looks, then took in the scene with panicked eyes. The Laotian pack was calmly howling away below the lab windows, but the ones who'd been baptized started popping up out of the crowd here and there … samurai swords glittering in their hands, boofalo spears hoisted high … one guy right in front of us, the one that used to hunt sharks, tore off his clothes, snatched a boofalo spear away from one of his softly howling neighbors, and dumped his clothes on his head … uh-oh, said Bohler, I was tellin em just today, "If you have two coats, trade one for a blade an go fight, if your strength tells you to," I mighta been a little off on that one … another Laotian, armed with a sword, dragged an old woman out of the howling, wailing crowd, slammed her into the wall, then slapped an elderly man in the face … the rest of the armed anabaptists clustered around the shark hunter … what else did you say in your sermon today? I asked the blanching Bohler, maliciously, I admit. "Cast off your father an mother an rid yourself of your family when you take to the warpath against obvious iniquity," shit, they didn't get that those're just quick metaphors, Bohler added. But then we heard the wail of sirens and Micka's raspy voice. A dark line was forming in the street, again I saw the plexiglas. The shark hunter let out a savage roar, quickly joined by his blood relatives. Luckily Micka and David got in on the act, recognizing the footsoldiers' leader. It was Micka's pseudodroog from the Sewer days, owed the Organization for all sorts of things, I'd performed the corruption on him myself. Arms raised to the heavens, Bohler reined in the Laosters with a frightening string of international swear words as David handed flowers to the cops in the first few rows and the Doctor shouted down at them from the window of his lab: He was my son, not yours, you sickening pigs! His teenage daughters draped themselves over the boofalo spears while the little ones ran back and forth translating. I noticed the Doctor's sons had knocked out a few windows with their slingshots; that probably explained why the tenants had called the cops. The scene quickly settled down. Bohler led his Christians away. We held a procession for the son.

And next morning at our briefing we were back in our byznys suits. Riding the tentacles and cranking up the mill and whispering and roaring with laughter and phoning and faxing and shooting up and forging plots and raking it in and winning and losing. Drinking Firewater. Sleeping with pseudo-drooginas. Chasing cars. And paying off cops and gangsters, who every now and then we needed, and who we didn't have anything to give but cash.

Sometimes it took a house, a hotel, a rubber stamp or two, a smile. One signature cost twenty, another the right sentence at the right time. Some places on the eternal wheel of the world there were death, solitude, and insanity together with love and compassion and the solidarity of the human tribe. Here it was dark and there it was light, and we lived mostly in between. I trained my eyes to see the dividing line. I stabbed myself in the heart and it healed itself up, ripped off my fingers and next morning they were back. Cut the nerve and they wiggled. Wanted to die, but just made money. And that night, as we sat under the light, laughing and stroking each other, death gave me a light prick of his sickle, grazing my eyelid with the tip, just a touch to say: Hey, you fuck, I know you're out there. Sometimes it seemed like nothing really existed, other times it was full. I couldn't get to sleep that night.

The Galactic Bar was for ungluing our heads, the Dóm for eroticism, and Černá's for both and more. We dealt in trade. And we flew into fits and shook with spasms, because it was unbelievable what we could do. Then Sharky came up with towing BMWs, my job was to sell the things, and even when I had the addresses in my pocket and knew just how to get there, it took some wild dancing ... joints cracking and heart charging up as I obtained information ... dealing with guys who'd spent their whole lives polishing their one Oktavia or Zhigula, and who, via commercial enterprise or inheritance or magic or sleazy rackets or divine grace or murder in the Congo or hard honest family work or sheer chance, had struck it a little rich, what do I know about all the ways there were in the years when time broke into a run ... and I listened to their astonished speech, old and new ... interweaving ... because, astonished at all the gold to be had in that suddenly sprinting time, these guys walked straight from their grubby factory workbenches and concrete engineer's feed troughs into the newly reestablished millionaires' clubs ... instead of the old standby, soccer, now they broke up their lives with golf ... took things at a slower pace ... and adopted the new terminology of social mobility ... instead of bats and biddies it was madam or mrs. or my dear lady ... instead of hobbyhorses, maracas, fuck bunnies, wham-bam, or poontang they vied for cuties, cupcakes, receptionists, assistants, and secretaries ... and their wives began to exercise a little here and there, because suddenly it occurred to them they actually had something to live for still … sunbathing in the Canaries, say … lovers, for instance … and as their husbands got rich, there was plastic surgery all over the place … and brand-new handsome vitamin people … and the men settled into their new old legally acquired smuggled BMWs, happy, as if suddenly … I'm afraid to write it … never blaspheme unnecessarily, Bohler had admonished us … they'd spotted their sister in the rearview mirror outlined in the flames from their eyes … they dressed in suits and hired photographers and cruised around in tax-free duty-free cars … and being used to their smelly old bolshevik jalopies, occasionally they'd lose control and knock off some old or young beggar's head … because there's always somebody standing in the rain by a milepost and somebody driving by … and it's fairly rare to run into a saint who'll whip a gleaming sword from his briefcase and hew his jalopy in two as a gift … and that's the way it was, is, and always will be … and I cruelly fleeced my parvenu clients and donated the leftovers to Bohler for the scamps and goons and refugees so I wouldn't please the Devil too much … so I could get through the eye of the needle before that camel.

Perhaps I've neglected to convey sufficiently and exhaustively in both common parlance and my golden mother tongue Czech what a truly big-hearted fellow Bohler was. Now that he had cash and a flat, even if it did belong to the pack, he was constantly sucking up to his Katholik, church-and-pew Bog by caring for stray sheep, usually shaggy with wool the color of coke from the filthiest bolshevik boiler room around. He sprinkled his little altar with tears while we cranked out the cash, a portion of which he squandered not only on the scamps but on all the other characters he dragged in from South Station whenever the urge seized him. Delousing stray Romanians, returned to the way station of Bohemia from every corner of fucking white man's Europe, rubbing Dalmatian ointments into Albanian hookers' legs, swollen from pounding the pavement, and running baths filled with Fiora perfumes for underage Gypsy girls from the worst urban holes of the Wild East … he sobbed his eyes out to David about how whenever there was some odd job, arranging fabrics in the warehouse, say, or packing gadgets into crates, or the painless removal of spiderwebs from the hallways of our buildings, the kinda dumbfuck peasant work we usually paid some lush from the nearest dive to do … he could go down to the station and pick through the rejects from all the countries … where the delicate flesh of baked pigeons gently and readily … passes through the razor-thin lips of emaciated faces … and continues down in the shape of mouthfuls … those desirable states whose officials were absolutely right to decide that no way're they givin asylum to that shady-lookin greaseball … because either they've got demogracy at home or they goddamn well avec deus ex machina better fight for it, by nonviolent means of course.

Bohler had an infallible nose for the biggest badasses … we had to throw the craziest fucks out on a regular basis … a destitute Romanian concentration camp escapee turned out to be a Portuguese pickpocket … a Bulgarian divinity student that Bohler nabbed in the station dive turned out to be an Indian witch and violated his altar … torture-scarred Armenians, after eating, taking a bath, changing clothes, and buying tickets to the nearest town in Germany (all on the pack's tab), turned without warning from members of the first Christian nation on earth into savage Azeris tired of murdering in the woods … but then again not too tired … Croatians fleeing the most awful horrors imaginable, after a fit of Bohler's generosity, underwent a bizarre transformation into Serbs … Serb dissidents turned into Bosnian Muslims … asking the way to the Black Stone of Mecca and salaaming endlessly … apage Satanas, Bohler shrieked in his sleep, and Lady Laos kept a sawed-off shotgun under the bed … I do' know if i's fo' him, me, o' them, she said with an apologetic smile … all of Bohler's good deeds were followed by swift and just punishment … and one day he brought in a gorgeous Slovak … as it happened Sharky was out in eastern Slovakia looking into an intriguing plan Košice had to become a Hanseatic city of free byznys … we'd just sat down with the Water after some difficult negotiations in which we'd managed to extend the patent on Doctor Hradil's Miracle Elixir to include its sale as a guaranteed anti-hair-loss product … also caused weaker links to lose their skin, unfortunately … with a little fast work, we nailed down a monopoly in Bohemia … and that in turn meant more moola and chuckles and loot, Micka was the only one even keeping track anymore … as the theologist nudged the beautiful girl into the room, Lady Laos turned visibly pale, which for a tea rose is pretty unusual … this is Helenka from the University of Trnava, Bohler blushed, she's applied for Czech citizenship … says she wants to study anthropology, human evolution … Bohler said into the silence. Hey, hi, I majored in anthro too, course they gave me the boot, cause I was the best, I said amiably. Yeah, cool, when they shut down the border she'll be crossin the Iron Curtain, back an forth, back an forth … Micka daydreamed, already drunk. She was beautiful. She was mysterious

... she was brought in. I fell for her right away. She was quick to grasp what it was all about and wanted in on the action, tearing right into Praguese. I listened to her tongue, and when she and Lady Laos went at it I got it in full stereo. Even Micka had to smile.

But I couldn't stop longing ... for She-Dog ... my childhood sister, Little White She-Dog. I wondered about her promise ... of a sister, what sign would she give me and when ... and if so, then it all has meaning ... while our women argued in the kitchen, we sat and dreamed ... bottles of Firewater on the desks, weapons close at hand ... outside our windows the battle raged ... we were brutes and terrific boys, thieves and entrepreneurs, drunks and junkies, artistes and wheeler-dealers ... low-down and dependable ... and above all we were a community, don't forget, there was a war raging outside our windows ... and this was before we knew what would happen ... and we were ferocious and meek and ferocious and meek and ferocious and meek ... and we were fetishists and sexists and superstitious, the power of water and fire were in the air ... and there was a time for prayer and a time for song ... a time to get your ass kicked and a time to kick butt ... and from time to time we'd just sit back and dream, in the community but by ourselves ... Bohler told us we were *miles Christi* ... but we were actually more like Dog Soldiers* ... it was the time after the explosion and we lived in the ruins ... robots thundered through the air ... and time went by ... because time is always running.

Slovak meanwhile got Bohler completely. *Olovrant,* yeah, how bout that, he said, stroking his rosary with the massive lead beads touched by the Papa himself after Bohler went on his knees all the way to Roma the great ... founded by those two Gypsies that sucked at their she-hound, that She-Dog of theirs ... but no one was interested in that except me.

Maybe the reason Bohler went was because of what happened to him in the slammer ... because of what that gang did to him ... Hey, how bout that, said Bohler, fingering the string, this is an *olovrant* too. It was a peaceful evening, one of the few when we weren't either in the city or out at the Rock.

5

THE VOICE. AT THE ROCK AND AROUND THE COUNTRYSIDE. I'M RUN-DOWN. THE THINGS OF THE BOX.

You see … back in the Stone Age of the Organization we would drive out to the Rock to celebrate every m. earned, rustled up, or extorted, but not anymore … we would've celebrated ourselves to death … now we went out there to switch off. Prague was the place of byznys … this was before the thing with the mill, before what happened to David … the Rock was our mystical sanctuary, our castle. It was a house that belonged to Micka, the property we'd used as collateral for our first loan from Early Bird Megabank … back in the '70s Micka had lived there with a bunch of hippies who attempted to stave off the miserable world around them by erecting a fortress out of their time, to bring it to a standstill. The cops dragged them out one by one, like rabbits from a hutch, and most of the boys and girls wound up emigrating. The first time we went, we had to empty the closets of old hippie bells and ponchos and sugar wafers and poems and headbands and records and flutes and lutes, moldy weed and moldy shrooms, and Micka grinned happily as he burned the things of the old time … the past, but suddenly Bohler leapt into the flames and plucked out a Yanis Yoplin album, and that was the first time he said: Thou shalt not blaspheme … unnecessarily … she knew Fiery Jack an all sortsa human tricks … till the dog from hell got her … she had a strong *voice.*

And as Bohler spoke, I heard a woman's voice, a throaty song, like a green flash of light … coming to me from the distant mountains, and in spite of its power and energy it was twisted … and full of longing … maybe trying to show me the way, I thought. What is it? Who is it?

And then, oddly, my heart brimmed with She-Dog's now quite old but not entirely forgotten words. They were soft and peaceful and filled my body's nerves with tenderness. She said to wait. She said to be ready. And again she let me hear the voice.

Lemme see you! I cried, unfortunately aloud, and everyone looked at me funny, amid the general and joyful destruction of the dead packs' cult relics I suppose I appeared somewhat sentimental … and the power I had felt from

She-Dog's hidden presence drained out of me so fast and, it seemed, irrevocably that I tried to chew my way down into the dirt and stay there.

Switching off out at the Rock meant … shrooms and weed and LSD and Firewater and liters of red wine and not talking much and trying to just *be* … now and then we'd bring along various pseudodrooginas, various close female friends … no conceited rant-and-ravers, no dumb yapping cunts … it was nice to be able to dream a while … that one of them was my sister … I took Cepková once … hoping, I guess, to see in her face a flicker of She-Dog's … just one more time … but it didn't come, not even when I stopped talking and concentrated hard … she was just another blonde … but at least she was from our old troupe, so we played around a little … put on a little makeup and put on a little show … around the barn, past the gate, and back again … in the wind … and at first we'd be a little uneasy without any bad new ads crowding our ears and eyes … instead of Barbie, just wicked old Slavic Polednice* occasionally appearing on the sunstruck hillside across the way … no toyfils flying around, just an occasional wicked old werewolf roaming the nearby forests, but they knew to stay away from the house or we'd've busted those bloody chops a theirs … just a good old Goblin or two calling out in the woods now and then, no copters circling overhead, like during the ancient gothic Orwelliad … Bohler brought the Gobs food … but I'm sure the old werewolves ate it all anyway … and when from time to time we got an uncontrollable craving for those disgusting rubber city burgers, we'd drown it out with red wine and Firewater and go to the pantry for more shrooms, and then it was enough to sit at the edge of the frozen lake throwing stones onto the ice … and in the crack of the ice you could hear life's blows, like slow music … with the certainty that come summer the stones would make circles and that every plop they made would send a greeting to your power.

Micka got the idea for us to exercise now and again, on some of those freezing mornings. Sharky wanted to see if he could stay on his feet in the air, David was almost in favor, and it was all the same to Bohler, I was the only one that refused … mornings I'm usually useless after a long hard night of dancing, I get plenty of motion as is, so I watched from indoors, basking in the cheery morning glow of my half-naked pseudodrooginas, including Lady Laos, while those madmen, my pals and partners, hopped around, doing push-ups and sit-ups and sparring with each other …

That's what makes the un-Christian computer samurai so cool, Micka lectured us, they go by a contract too, Bushido's what they call it, they travel in clans an teach their scamps to fight at an early age, the coolest way's with bamboo swords, alias kendo, Micka the lawyer explained. Damn straight: healthy body, healthy mind.

Yeah, Micka, I said, only they're in it for the long haul. I mean we're just testin it out here an there, seein how far it'll go, right?

Hm, oh yeah, right, maybe, I guess, said Micka, and David turned a little red. What's up? I said.

Well, now that we got the treadmill goin, said Micka, it'd be kina hard for you to get off.

It was only afterwards I realized that maybe that word *mill* was the unlucky charm that eventually played into the mill in Sudan.

Yeah, and? I said.

Look, David said a little too slowly. Look, Potok, this is all I know how to do anyway.

Are you crazy, man, I said, you can do anything in the world. What's up, Priest, tell me what's goin on, right here, right now, an you too, Sharky, am I dancin the wrong way, is my timin off or somethin?

No, you're dancin just right, said Micka. Only you seem a tad pissed off lately. Maybe you ran outta gas towin all those BMWs, maybe it's all your language research, maybe you're pregnant, or it's time for your more or less regular monthly circles, but we'd like to see you back to your cheerful dancin self again.

Forget it, pals, I said, nobody's gonna squelch me with that cheerful crap. This isn't some bolshevik summer camp here. You just have to accept that I've got my monthly circles an they're draggin on slightly longer than usual.

We accept it, dear pal an knight, we know you take holy communion on a by an large regular basis, Bohler frowned a pinch at that. We just want you to know that we're your essentially devoted personal friends, an if ever a dark cloud comes your way … you can count on us … you know that as well as the rest of us.

Thanks, chief strategist, thanks, chief lawyer, thanks, chief priest, thanks, chief minister, thanks an likewise an same to you too.

Only … we knew each other well, we could measure each other's breathing by the clearing of our own throats, so it didn't escape the pseudodroogs of my tribe and war community that from time to time I was a little run-down. My longing for She-Dog was driving me crazy, and all my speculating about the sister she had promised me as my future, my power, was eating me up ... cause, as I've shyly noted a few times already, my power was dying, and I couldn't picture myself powerless in the cruel and insane world around me ... this was years 1, 2, 3 ... etc., and I knew the community was a gift direct from Starry Bog and that lots of other human beings were living on their own or in the wrong tribes, bad tribes, tribes without contracts ... but I longed for Little White She-Dog and her complicated displays of love, if I'm to use an old term.

But I didn't want to tell my buddies about her or her disappearance. I had a secret, which meant I wasn't totally and entirely just a Knight of the Secret, unlike my pseudodroogs, as far as I knew. In a moment of wholly unnecessary blasphemy it even crossed my mind that compared to Little White She-Dog some little Messiach didn't mean ... but I put a stop to it and, just to be safe, had a nice long talk with my good old rosary ... even through the whizzing of the lead beads over my fingers, though, I could hear the sound of She-Dog breathing as we made love ... and the beads started to burn me, an unmistakable sign. I wasn't doing too well in the love department.

But I nodded off my pseudodroogs' worries, and seeing as we were out at the Rock we sent a few of our dear female pals and occasional partners out to the pantries and iceboxes to fetch the shiny bottles, and Bohler made his delicious mushroom turnovers, and another amazing evening flew by, like so many times before, in pleasant conversation about the magical world of byznys.

Every now and then, though, we still got slightly bored, especially toward the end of our stay ... bodies tingling, fingers twitching, itching to start taking again ... no one blasphemed unnecessarily by speaking his thoughts aloud, thoughts of faxes and phone calls and appointments and conferences and lists and consultations and contacts ... but I think all of us were eager to be back cranking the mill, creeping along the tentacles, feeding the Organization ... since we still had three days left, or however many Doctor Hradil prescribed, it was obvious we had to squeeze out another drop of enjoyment to keep our work in Prague from giving us all a nervous breakdown.

At moments like these, the thing to do was climb or hop into Micka's mobile and take a trip round the Czech countryside. While Micka revved the engine, warming it up, we roared: Hey, coyote mama, let er rip an let it ride! ... step on it, old dog, so what if we kill ourselves! ... put the pedal to the metal, lawyer, so what if we kill somebody! ... give it the gun, old skinflint, so what if we kill a cop! and Micka peeled out, and then it was time for pranks on the driver ... which Bohler's Laotian lady excelled in ... maybe because she could count the number of times she'd been in a car, the only thing she'd ever ridden in her native Laos was boofalos ... covering Micka's eyes on the curves, dropping a sack over his head ... strangling him savagely all of a sudden as he took a hairpin turn ... firing a gun off next to his head ... imitating police sirens ... but Micka just laughed and glowed, he knew how to handle it ... from the days of his rickety old motorcycle ... and being fast and alert for him was part of the code of Bushido ... and Lady Laos got wilder and crazier ... shrieking into his ear ... popping champagne out of nowhere ... and as we bore down on some poor old dog she took a broken lollipop stick and rammed it into Micka's ears, piercing both his eardrums, the lawyer started screaming as blood gushed down his neck, but he couldn't hear himself so he started screaming louder, and even if unlike us he didn't hear the crunch of that kind old stray dog's spine, he saw him ... what was left of him.

Micka stopped the mobile, and while we searched through the tangle of bodies, rags, bottles, and other junk for bandages and Doctor Hradil's Miracle Elixir, Bohler took Lady Laos into the shadows behind the car and smacked her up a little. Seeing the grim look on the now bandaged and recovering Micka's face, he spluttered something about the unique Asian sense of humor ... an if anyone tries to make a little fun an games into some kina racial issue ... he said ... set off any pogroms ... or stir up ethnik conflicts ... I'm here on the side a Good, said Bohler, an anyone that does'd best prepare to get his ass kicked ... but Micka couldn't hear him. And the storm blew over, and the sun poured down on the scenic mountainside of fragrant evergreens, and we drove in peace the rest of the way.

The mobile hummed and sang, weaving through the narrow lanes of Řepákovs and Vidlákovs ... braking for ducks ... picking its way through chicken droppings ... singing its old engine tunes to its amazed and miraculously silent passengers ... taking in the small towns and villages ... I enjoyed the motion ... watching the way they'd changed since time had exploded.

Everywhere people were constructing local byznysses, pubs buzzed with fast talk full of loopholes and taxes on declared and undeclared income, licenses and contracts flew left and right ... and we had to smile, cause that old familiar tingling was running through our fingers, and now and then, just for the pleasure of it, I'd sit down with the old buggers dabbling in real estate, and I had to roll my eyes cause it was all the same game ... gangs crushing lone warriors ... people working magic with rubber stamps ... friends of friends of friends of someone else who fit the bill for your paracousin's son-in-law's new little racket ... we all come from the same chimpanzee after all ... and the guys that had voted DOA wouldn't vote COD anymore, even though they were all good family men too, carpenters ... they lived only in and for their own tribe ... and only bigwigs changed tribes at will, feeding the papers some bull about "chemistry" or "necessity" ... and they dug up the old aqueducts, hidden from the bolsheviks ... and dusted off the monstrances full of Christ in all his glory, and paraded them through the villages, blessing the new old irrigation system ... while hired goons were poisoning the carp pond behind the neighbor's barn, or blowing up his cow, or planting the red rooster on his roof ... and the mischievous Maryša* was dumping dead ashes in Vávra's beer again, and the silos were filling with golden Czech grain, and the cost of animal flesh rose and fell and rose, cause now instead of some shitty old bolshevik fiddling around with prices, there was some new Community ... indexing them ... and the old flimflams flew through the air, embracing the new tricks or in conflict with them ... and some saw it and some didn't, and there were those who took advantage and those who were afraid ... and the first shy touches and fleeting kisses and smoked cigarettes ... in a haystack behind old Bárta's barn, not in some city tunnel full of rats ... and *Mrs.* Schoolteacher smiled ... skirt fluttering in the cool breeze, embroidered blouse swelling with virgin breasts ... and *Mr.* Pharmacist shyly smiled back as meanwhile he mixed his poisons ... and the only place you saw the word *comrade* anymore was on a few tombstones and a monument or two ... beloved freedom was everywhere ... waiting for its Lada to immortalize it in pictures* ... a crock of milk ... and a fattened pig ... and the wall where that bloody old drunkard Švejch once hung was bare now except for maybe a damp stain, till the innkeeper scrapes up the moola, the lint, the bobs, the lootage, and whips his new old establishment into shape ... nothing at all hung on the wall, and the mystery of it made me feel good, the empty space charged with expectation ... the motion ... even the most deserted ghost towns were coming alive, sprayed with time's explosive colors ... and proud old ladies stole through the backstreets peeking into garbage cans in case of any bread ... and crazy drunken dope-smokers begged right out in public ... and the local *villon* robbed to pay for his booze, and then in the clink the old bailiff illegally bashed his face in … just like under the lamebrain bolshevik, only this wasn't some shitty bolshevik summer work camp anymore … it was nobody's business but yours … you might spin m.'s, you might spin zeros … you might have an ace up your velvet sleeve, or just your own lousy tattooed pickpocket's arm in a dingy T-shirt … cause God knows why, cause some just yep and some just nope, and you okay and you uh-uh, and some've got what it takes and some don't, and why that's the way it is back in the days of today's world of ours, well, that's a mystery too.

I was cruel and I was tender, and I liked it. But I was run-down. I even caught myself thinking that maybe instead of taking a trip I should spend some time at home on Gasworks, and I had to ask Bohler to kindly clout me a few times with his rosary, see if that'd clear my mind. He was more than happy to oblige, but added, listen, Potok, dear friend, that sparkling nugget over there in the creek, the one deaf Micka's drivin by in his singin mobile at this very moment, informed me that my pseudodroog, the gallant actor Potok, would prefer to hole up in his place an fear life with great dread.

My dearest buddy Bohler, despite all your time behind bars, I said, turning a wee bit red and uncertain, I swear, you speak the absolute truth, an I can see you've got the great gift of seein into the human soul.

Bohler nodded. I understand, pal, sometimes I too lock myself in a momentarily free room, never the one with the altar, an emphatically ask my Lady Laos for peace an quiet, an sit by myself, an indulge my thoughts an emotions.

You're right, my clever theologian, our pals're in byznys an they're doin a brilliant job of keepin the treadmill runnin, but maybe the two of us're a little cracked … you're a scholar of Scripture, an in the course of your daily an nightly wanderings you've gotten a glimpse into the endlessness of human suffering … through the open gate into the place where souls howl in various degrees of terror an confusion … an me, I'm just an outstanding actor who also knows how to act an dance off the boards of the cruel old crazy real world, I can move inside people an with people, an create an act out characters to the point of total exhaustion an eclipse … in other words, we know it, an all this byznys stuff is just another form of motion.

Yeh, yeh, you put that pretty elegant, brother … said Bohler … for an actor.

And then we pulled into another town, picturing the new private dives and touring a few attractive developing or foundering private byznysses, and even squeezing in a few bolshevik monuments, and then we picked a hotel and began having fun. And it happened to me, later on, in my room.

I was with our pseudodroogina Táňa, coincidentally a blonde, known as Elsa the Lion to a close circle of friends, and she was very kind and beautiful, and relatively gentle as well.

Except then it happened, and I demolished the room a little, cause all of a sudden I realized that the floor of the room was sloped and we were slipping down it, and instead of the pretty face of Elsa the Lion I was looking into the repulsive snout of a hound with jaundiced fangs, and a voice ripped into my brain: Caution: Slippery slope! and on one side the floor actually started to rise and on the other side was a trapdoor. I got a glimpse inside, and I think I saw flickering flames and heard a suspicious metallic grinding, like spits rotating around. The hideous dog started growling at me and rolling around on the bed in a puddle of its own vomit, and I realized my Little White She-Dog, wherever she was out there, probably wasn't doing too great. I attempted to calm the fiendish cur, but letting out a menacing growl he tried to slash my belly open, and then he began to grow, bigger and bigger, crowding me toward the trapdoor, and then I heard: Caution: Slippery slope! and I couldn't back up anymore, and as I groped for the blade in my pocket the dog fixed me with burning eyes, trying to pierce right through me, going for my heart. Desperate, I tried to do a dance and summon up my power and She-Dog's words from out there where she was suffering, something evil was happening to her … I could sense it … but the beast took up so much of the room I couldn't do even an ankle dance, couldn't even move my heels … and as I finally got hold of the blade I heard it a third time: Caution: Slippery slope! and something clamped down on me.

We caught you just in time, man, you woulda slashed her up. Luckily you were screamin so loud we heard you, even Micka, my boss and buddy David explained after approximately twenty hours of piercing darkness.

You probly oughta see Doctor Hradil about a vacation. Ah bullshit, there's too much work right now, I objected. There's always too much, said David. We'll see, but I got a feelin it'd be a good combination. We won't talk about any major or minor operations yet, dear Potok, said the boss. Nothing to object to there of course. An anyway what really got Táňa mad was you kept callin her a dog, said Micka. I mean every little kid knows that she's a lion, added the brilliantly acclimatized Sharky. My mistake, I was thinkin of She-Dog, I corrected myself nonsensically.

Táňa, dear Táňa, lemme make it up to you, I pleaded with my somewhat battered and slightly slashed pseudodroogina. At least lemme set you up an account so you won't hafta punch the clock for a while. Well, all right … but still … even if you aren't the absolutely totally worst dancer, you probly oughta find some other pseudodroogina to take along on your next trip … outta the question, I said, tonight I wanna be with you, that was just an evil spell, we gotta test if it's back to normal now. That was my argument, and Bohler solemnly nodded in agreement.

The next night, then, we made ceremonious preparations for our copulation. Just to be safe, we persuaded the other guests that they'd be better off finding someplace else, and rented out the whole hotel. The boys agreed to stand guard in case it happened again, but a minor tussle ensued over my knife. Micka didn't want to take any chances, but David pointed out that without an instrument my anger's power might not show itself, and besides, I wasn't *that* fast. That irked me a little bit, and there might've been a minor spat if Bohler hadn't intervened in time, passing out relics and amulets, setting up the aspen stakes and demon nets, and meaningfully clearing his throat.

Táňa and I got down to it then, this time not quickly, in our usual old city style, but gently, kind of country-style like, with blue skies and trees and apples, with foreplay and nibbling and touching all over … we were probably showing off a little for the pseudodrooginas gathered around our bed in case the situation called for litanies. I must humbly note, at least some of them peeked … shall we say … with interest. All of them except for Bohler's Laotian lady, who, I assume, got a laugh out of our relatively clumsy euro-missionary moves. But she kept herself in check, apart from baring her teeth a few times as she suppressed a catty smile; she checked herself because it was serious. And it worked and it was okay and nothing out of the ordinary happened.

We nearly forgot about the well. Hradil's boys took turns standing watch down in the cellar, a suitable distance away from the water's surface, which frightened them. One of the boys, who went by the Mohawk name of Montague, regularly came by to report that the sisters were still missing.

And once upon a smiley city day, finding ourselves with a little free time after our daily briefing, we decided to try Sharky's trick with the box … spotting Montague, who was trudging back to the cellar to take over from one of his bros ... Sharky said, it's a good thing for a little boy ... and told Montague to give it a shot. Given the relatively old age of the box in Sharky's mind, the price tag was the first thing that intrigued the young Hradil, he was a practical boy. Then he gave the nod and got inside the box. Sharky sent it back to the foul concentration camp, and it took all the strength little Montague had to dodge the furious metal-tipped boots, the whips that could tear right through the box, shredding its fragile contents, not to mention the foul sounds he had to withstand ... because Sharky carried around inside him the shuffling of forty-year-old old men, death rattles, shrill commands, soft weeping ... more than enough to kill a small creature ... but Montague, inside the box, was surprisingly calm and cautious, and then he began to grow with his power, and damn fast too ... Sharky turned pale, we were all surprised ... none of us had handled it as well as little Montague ... screams of insanity and pleas for mercy ... he didn't let anything inside his box ... our eyes were popping out of their sockets ... he even steered clear of the SS riding boots ... Sharky's showstopper ... but all at once Bohler broke out laughing, Micka joined in, and then I saw it too ... and Sharky, sweaty and pale, switched off. Hey, Micka explained, the kid pulled a scalpel outta his sleeve an cut a hole in the box, he *saw* the whole time, he gave eyes to his power, man ... then David added an appreciative comment about Montague's strategic capabilities, and the boy, now out of the box, flushed with embarrassment. It was great the way you stayed in there with that scalpel an didn't cut yourself, or cut yourself down, an turned your eyes' power outward, Micka praised Montague. An just the fact that he saw all that stuff an it made him stronger ... testifies in and of itself ... to a certain quickness an agility, said a slightly emotional Sharky. Hey, uncle boss, Montague said to Sharky. Yes, my boy? Know anyplace that still sells those cool Batas? We froze a little stiff. If all he cares about's the shoes, if he cares about getting anything else out of that trick besides his own life, he's damned anyway, no matter how fast he is, flashed through my mind ... the others, with sadness in their hearts, were probably thinking the same ... the boy went on though ... if we could scrounge up somma those boxes an rig em up for small sizes ... for dogs an cats an squirrels. What for, boy? Bohler wondered. Cause all those city critters that used to come an drink outta the well're startin to disappear. Why didn't you say so, boy?! we asked. I figured my sisters were all that mattered to you guys. Besides cash an booze, you don't seem to care much what goes on around here. My mom told me so, said Montague. From the mouth of an innocent babe the bloody truth has spoken! roared Bohler. All right, boy, go run along an play or whatever, Bohler continued in a more subdued tone, that box belongs to your old uncle Sharky, an givin it to squirrels would be like givin away his identity, like losin part of his head … an next thing you know he'd be lying belly up in the nearest cruel city hole. Montague brooded a moment or two, then kissed the ring on Bohler's hand and ran off to the cellar.

6

"I HAD A DREAM."

We sat there in our club chairs and luxurious leather armchairs ... the truth had spoken from the mouth of an innocent babe ... David sat all crumpled up, positively reeking of intense city sorrow ... I had an urge to uncork the Fiery and take myself a little vacation ... Micka wrung his hands, gnashing what few teeth he had left, Bohler leafed through his dog-eared copy of *The Married Priest* ... then he slammed the book down and said firmly: Self-criticism! He was right, we all sensed it. It was time for suicidal self-criticism, the byznys day was down the drain.

It was only extremely exceptionally that we engaged in self-criticism, only in those heavy-duty cases when we'd seriously crushed someone, not that we ever broke the rules of our little entente, oh no, but every now and then the dictates of the market economy obliged us to pull a dirty trick or two. Our victims we didn't care about; if someone gets under the wheel, doesn't know how to use his power, that's his business. We performed self-criticism in order to be purer ... more ardently prepared for the coming of the Messiach.

Supposedly self-criticism was an old bolshevik class invention developed to perfection by that bloody Mao, a teacher. We dusted it off so we could use it, not abuse it, in freedom. Bohler always went first.

I had a dream, he said. I was walkin around that old city of ours, slacks an a sport jacket on, decked out in my civvies, makin the rounds of the bars an the usual spots, keepin my eyes peeled for sinners, some infected whores I might persuade to leave behind their disgusting ways, a scamp or two to reel in, you know how it is, guys. An I admit my bosom was warmed with satisfaction an heinous pride, because the day before I'd snagged three little goons, herded em into an old garage, trampled their toyfils, an baptized em. After some deliberation I let em keep their weapons, they wouldn't get far without em, an they seemed to be genuinely contrite, so I went ahead an sanctified their little guns an knives. An the day before that I set a few hookers straight an also succeeded in heavily stigmatizin this one disgusting sinner I caught abusin his kids ... so now Bog'll easily recognize the fiend ... an O my pals, that selfsame day, I overcame stiff resistance from a band of revoltingly bloody butchers to save two blind old forsaken horses from slaughter an set em free on our lawn … I admit, as I strode along, I felt nothin but good feelings. Well … as we all know, our first free president's lovely new vision, namely clean quiet streets an cozy little pubs an delightful little shops sellin all kindsa grub, is becoming a reality all over the place, lots of folks're enjoyin vitamins in the comfort of their homes an plenty of folks're movin outta the village up to the castle, but we also know that the cellars're full. So I'm walkin around, an I see the human misery an the vice an the falsehood, an the sinners an their victims, people whose hearts're red with rancor an people whose hearts're broken in two, an as I'm strollin toward the landing in the stench of the toxic Moldau, I'm warmed with pride that I'm on the right side … doin what I can to aid His coming … an then I see this derelict standin outside a taproom … a disgusting old guy in lousy rags … face totally ravaged with goose blotches, the skin drippin off … an his filthy body was shakin all over from booze, or the lack of it … an people were stoppin to laugh at him, subjectin him to ridicule an scorn, this guy was absolutely under the wheel, an I mean deep … just these baggy things smeared with shit for pants … whimperin for change in this shaky voice … an little scamps were chuckin mud an dirt clods, one of em hit him smack in the face an he didn't even feel it … so I stop next to the freak an start fishin around in my pocket … I admit I too felt scorn an contempt … the bozo … starin down at the ground the way old panhandlers do … but just then he lifts his watery eyes … an I see it's my father, my dad … an he recognized me too, an he's so out of it he says: Michal, Michálek, get me outta here … which was what he always said when my mom sent me to bring him home from whatever dive he'd blown all his cash in that night, an he'd be just sittin there blitzed in the corner, an the guys'd all laugh an say … your angel's come for you, Bohler, get up … an I'd take him home, an he'd always find enough strength left to take a few swipes at me … coulda killed him, that piece a shit … then I split … left my mother to deal with him, since she was the cow who'd married him … an it didn't take him long to drive her into the grave either … an now here he was, standin right in front of me, the creep, an his eyes livened up a little … but he was just too out of it, an he goes: Help a poor soul, mister … didn't know who I was anymore … but I knew … an I knew he could sense I was there … caught that greedy flash in his eyes, an suddenly I didn't give a damn about all the people around, an I go: Do you know who I am? Do you recognize me? Pop! An that ugly mug opens its eyes an says: Yeah, you're my son Michal, course I know you … I'm tellin you, guys an buddies a mine, I felt like deckin him on the spot for all the things he'd done, for what he'd done to himself … but then came pity an I realized he was in there somewhere … there musta been somethin we'd never talked about, some evil spirit that cut him down … somethin I didn't understand … now he was really bad off, worse than a battered animal … an I was scared to death that we would never get to talk about it … scared it was too late … an it was, he didn't know me anymore … an, O my friends, I asked a couple lamebrains in the crowd to wait there with him while I raced off to find a doctor, or whoever it is you go for in those kinds of situations … but I couldn't find anyone, an by the time I got back that old lush, my pop, was gone of course … an when I burst into the taproom they probly thought I was nuts, nobody knew him, nobody'd seen him. An that's that. I figure by now he's gotta be dead. An I never did give him that change he was askin for …

Bohler concluded to the pack's guardedly approving grumbling. We took hold of our partner's shoulders, where the sources of pity are, and whacked them a little here and there, and in the course of our efforts to provide effective aid our partner also got a slap or two, and then his shoulders straightened up again and he was basically all right.

Next in line was Micka. I had a dream, he said. I was maybe ten, give or take, an I was playin around the garden of our kultchured family's old Prague home. An it was a weird day, the kina day when the air is new an a little guy gets in a weird mood, the kina mood where he feels like tryin out worlds an testin his power to see what it can do. A little annoyed an a little antsy, I poked around the old sheds an the raspberry bushes a while, but they didn't hold any more mystery for me. I kept lookin, waitin for somethin to happen, there was definitely some kina force pullin me. I scratched around in the dirt a while an tried to lift this great big rock, but nope, it was no go. I kicked around the cracked old swimming pool, built in the pre-bolshevik era, actually it wasn't ours anymore, actually neither was the house, but anyway the tenants used it to store their coal, so I got in there an started tunnelin around. But somehow that wasn't any fun either. I wanted to break through the surface, an get to somethin new. I moped around back an forth, then tried to lift the rock again. Still no go, I fell down an banged my head. An I think right then the Devil possessed me. I picked myself up, a little dazed, an spotted a bird's nest up in the tree. It was full of all these bald little crows, cheepin an stickin their long bald necks up towards the mama, who was feedin em a worm. I'd never seen anything like it except in pictures at school. It was new, it was interesting. I snuck over to the tree so I wouldn't frighten the mama, but she spotted me of course, an started flappin around the nest an beatin her wings. I donno why but I guess it freaked me out a little, so I grabbed this rake off a pile of leaves. The little chicks were really startin to squawk, an I wanted to get a better look, so I took the rake an like tipped the nest up a little. They started cheepin even louder, an I could see em wigglin their heads all weirdlike, snappin their beaks open an closed. I got goose bumps, it was a funny feeling, all of a sudden I was their master. I could decide what would happen to them. They were so cute I got this totally burning desire to cup them in my hand an pet them an cuddle them. But at the same time I got excited at the thought of suddenly clenchin that friendly hand into a fist an squashin em to pieces. I felt both at once. I still could've stopped it all, but instead I lifted the rake up, bit by bit, till the nest began to wobble. I needed to know so bad what it would do, what would happen. I guess I needed to know how my new power worked on living creatures. I didn't see it that way at the time, but I guess I needed to find out how death works. An that there really is such a thing. The first baby fell onto the ground. I went over to get a look up close, an when I touched it I could feel its frenzied little heart poundin away under the down. An somehow that frenzy got inside me, or I got scared the mama crow was gonna punish me. She started dive-bombin me, disappearin into the branches an then swoopin down, closer an closer to my face each time, her wings even touched me a couple a times. I guess I got scared she was gonna call in the other crows, or my parents, or I donno what … but I realized whatever I wanted to do I had to do it right away, an what it was to this day I've yet to figure out. I took the rake an started bashin the nest an the little birds started fallin down, an then the nest tore open. I think I was screamin. When the nest came down, the babies started cheepin an squirmin around on the ground … an all at once they were disgusting, like some kina worms or somethin, an I jumped on the nest an stomped it to bits. I stomped those baby crows to a pulp, an then I took the rake an knocked down the mama an she started to wail … don't anyone tell me birds don't cry, I heard it, anyone says different … I'm warnin you … an I started hackin her up with the rake, over and over, till she was all mangled an just crawlin over her children … an then, O my brothers, I pissed on them …

I was so fired up, I just had to keep goin. So I urinated all over em, an I knew what I was doin was evil, but it was also beautiful, it was strange … an it wasn't over yet, cause there I was peein all over those birds an pokin em with my shoe, when all of a sudden I hear: Lukáš! Lukáš, what're you doing out there, what're you playing around with? It was my mom an she was standin right there an all at once she saw everything … an there we were, face to face, me with my fly undone … an the birds … an if I'd broken down, maybe, or at least started crying, I might've been able to snap out of it … but instead I let out this awful scream, I was scared I was gonna get punished an I hated my mom for catchin me. I punched her in the mouth an shouted every swear word I could think of. She got all frazzled an turned to get away, but that only got me more riled up, so I took the rake an whacked her one, an then another … an she went down, bleedin from her nose, an suddenly it hit me. I threw myself down on the ground next to her an said: Mommy! It's okay, it's okay … but she just pushed me away an staggered off. I went an locked myself up in the shed an stayed there, I donno how long, but I guess pretty long, cause when I came out again it was nighttime an the birds were all cleaned up. I noticed right away cause the moon was shining. Somehow I snuck back into the house, an the next day I stayed in bed with a fever. I wished so bad it'd been just a dream. But it wasn't. My parents never even talked to me about it, just sent me to see some fuckhead psychiatrist, who I told to take his cuntlick questions an shove em up his ass. An my mom never spoke to me again, except for the usual: Do you want milk, or tea? Finish your food, bring me this, show me that, an all that stuff, never asked how I was or … gave me a friendly pat or anything, wouldn't touch me at all, that was when she cut me loose for good.

Micka concluded to the pack's guardedly approving grumbling. We touched him a little here and there, patting him on the stomach, around the stomach, and on the scruff of the neck, where the sources of malice are. But since the sources of perversion are as yet unknown to medicine, we also gave the rest of his body a good going-over as well. I admit it didn't come off without a couple kicks in the nuts either. And then Micka sat down, a little whipped but basically all right, and it was my turn.

I, however, by general consensus ceded my spot to David. Because even though Bohler handed out some pretty tough penances after our self-criticism sessions — 600 Our Fathers, or 1,000 push-ups, or Climb out on the roof an stay there! or Go hustle a Kalashnikov off the Castle Guard! — when it came to our mountaineer, ordinarily Bohler just waved it off, or let it go at two or three Our Fathers. And after all the depravities we'd heard, we were hoping that he wouldn't let us down this time either.

I had a dream, said David. I was back home in the mountains, with my family tribe the Losíns, and a mighty blizzard raged outside our cabin windows, and the trails were all snowed under so we couldn't go out hunting. My paw was chopping up a tree trunk, hacking out a roofbeam, but every now and then he'd stop, stretch till his joints cracked, and say: Coupa poods a frish rawh meat shir'd hit thi spot raht nah, agh, agh igh, oyvay Maria! And set to swinging his broadax again. My younger bros huddled on top of the stove while old Gramma told them the local legends. But the boys didn't pay much heed to the mythical feats of old Choroš, chatting away among themselves: A-yuh, sum a that bludsy grizzle, oo Lord! shir cud suk ohn that, haw bowt yew, Medor? Aw, don go tillin me thim tayls, lahk t'eat m'own hand, replied Method, another brother of mine. My youngest bro, Benjamin, sat propped on my oldest bro Abraham's knee, the two of them drooling on about the last bear we'd had before the storm. As the cruel tempest gathered fury, my maw broke out the Candlemas candle.* I peeked over at my kind, virtuous maw, and she says: Bet choo'd lahk ti sink yir teeth inna sum bludsy cartlidge too, yew rascul yew, hoy! Cud do with a baht masilf, ma little Davidko, hoo! You see, buddies, wilderness was just a regular thing for us, normally not a day went by without one of old Losín's boys bagging a bear. We just weren't built for that kind of hardship! Not that we were in danger of starving … out in the pantry we had pork and veal flitches, new and old ham, all sorts of bolshevik meatballs, heaps of eggs and taters, cauliflower, a hidden buckwheat pit or two, sacks of oats, bushels of wheat, cornstalks tall as a man, blindworms, rice with oil and sunflower seeds, dried fruit, millet, kabobs … we were just short on vitamins. The storm wasn't letting up and Maw was running low on candles. Old Gramma said she couldn't remember a winter this bad, not even in the legends. It looked like the Losín clan wasn't going to make it! And, friends and knights, I couldn't stand it anymore! So one night, when everyone else was asleep, I quietly donned my little fur coat, slapped my foxfur cap on my head, gathered up a few arrows and Paw's old crossbow, and out of my bro Abraham's boot I took the bowie knife that he had for jamborees. Then I pulled the sled out of the lean-to, loaded up the broadax, and untied Paw's old bear-dog, Azorek, whose eyes lit right up when I told him where we were going. Azorek was a cross between a city cocker spaniel and a werewolf, and some of the younger bears died of fright at the mere sight of him. So I hitched him to the sled, threw in the crossbow, and off we rode. Into the tempest. That was some Siberia out there, believe you me, guys and buddies. Just a few meters away from the cabin, luckily, we came across our first bear nest. While Azorek furiously set to digging, I tried to draw the crossbow, but soon discovered that it was beyond my boyish strength. Then I got a salvational idea! Taking some heavy rope out of the sled, I tied the bow to old Azorek's legs, then jumped in the sled and sped downhill. I don't think I need to stress how tight I held onto that bowstring! Azorek, meanwhile, dug and dug and dug, until suddenly he let out a triumphant roar and an old she-bear sleepily tottered out onto the snow ... I let go the bowstring, and the arrow went whizzing through the slightly surprised Azorek's legs and hit that old she-bear right in the heart! As I clawed my way back uphill, sled and broadax prepared for portioning, I noticed that Azorek, crazed as he was ... licking his chops and flicking his forked red tongue in and out ... still held back, because he knew the meat was for all the Losíns! And I took pity on that good loyal beast. Ull raht, Azerek, naw we kin have irsilves a litta bitty tayst a that fahn blud n fayt, nummy num num! Overwhelmed with excitement, David fell into his old tongue and burst into tears.

We just sat there, frozen like statues, because self-criticism is sacred and it's forbidden to interrupt ... An as you probably realize by now, buddies an pals, we went an ... David beat his breast ... wolfed down that old honeysucker, every last bite ... an I forgot all about my Maw an Paw ... the happiness in their eyes as they nibble on the snout an the paws, slurpin out the marrow ... an my bros, too ... I ate that bear! An as long as old Azorek lived, we never said a word about it to each other, not a holler, we were too alienated an ashamed! David wiped his eyes between sobs. An I stuffed myself so full my bros had to come out to the old shed at dawn an lift me off Azorek's back ... an I lost the sled an Aberham's bowie, an just like in my colleague Micka's woeful tale, I stretched myself out on the stove an lay there with a fever ... an even though next day happily the sun came out hey! hoy! an everyone was elated ... an crazed ... an my bros dashed out into the woods an hunted up dozens of bears, an Abraham wasn't mad at all about his bowie, he had lots more ... David blubbered, gushing tears ... an that night my bros dragged home the dead bears, an we gorged an gorged ... an gorged ... an the Losín tribe was saved an happy again, I was never happy again after that, couldn't look my family in the eye, so I left my tribe … an got lost in the stars an had to slay all kindsa innocent wolves … an jaybirds … for food, an I wandered across nine mountain ranges, trippin over roots, an then I came down from the mountains … an got lost again, an somehow ended up in this city … n yew Knahts a thi Seekrit fahnd me heer, n Ah fahnd yew n … and the bear hunter broke down sobbing again.

David concluded to the pack's guardedly approving grumbling, here and there interrupted by a friendly cheer or two, and here and there and right here and over there we gave him a few gentle pats on the head, because it was obvious to us what it was all about, because we were twisted crooked swindlers of the Pearl, old champions of sin and repentance, so we exchanged happy grins and yodeled manfully and congratulated each other that our little Davey hadn't wound up frozen to death … the boy showed courage, huh? An at his age too, just think, guys, damnation, damnation … nodding our heads and spitting tobacco … glad that David could blubber over that kinda crap and didn't have to wail bloody tears from his heart when he caught a glimpse of the horrible wheel of the world … he doesn't see, we whispered to each other … it's a miracle that mangy old Azor didn't take a chomp outta him, none of us would've come within five steps of that wicked old dog without a club, or better yet a good old AK-3, well anyway it turned out all right, we congratulated ourselves once again, and Sharky whispered kindheartedly to Bohler, two's enough, don't you think? meaning Our Fathers, and Bohler patronizingly nodded, as if to say, it's understood, pal … and David sat there flushed red, but after a while he was basically all right, and then at last it was my turn.

I had a dream, I said. It was a long dream, O brothers and blood brothers, so please be patient. And don't forget that I'm only a humble messenger, the bearer of the dream.

There was a little buzz among my friends, because in the history of the community those opening words had only been spoken two or three times, and never by me, and they indicated the person in question had something urgent in his heart that concerned not only him but the entire community, and though it came from him he believed that it had been sent down to him to pass along to the others.

I'd been stifling the dream inside me for a long time now, it had been given to me by my spirit, my power, and I was glad at last to be able to share it, but also despondent because the dream was dark and I had only a vague idea what it meant. A community dream has its rules, though, so I still had to field the opening questions to fill my associates in on the picture.

Bohler: Take any stuff?

Me: Shrooms, weed, wheelies, but just a few, really. An red wine, lots of it. Also jumbo shrooms, Green Power, I think, I specified.

Sharky: When an where?

Me: Three, maybe five weeks back, in the time we're in now. An for a long time goin in I didn't take anything at all, to make sure it wouldn't throw me. My place on Gasworks.

Micka: Anyone else around?

Me: Nope. I was solo.

Bohler: How long'd it last?

Me: Two days, I think. I spent all morning drinkin an druggin myself up, an then it started sometime after noon.

Micka: D'you eat?

Me: I tried some chevabchichi or somethin, but then I spit it out. The only thing I could keep down was spinach. An lotsa Water. When the wine ran out.

David: Did ja lie down the whole time?

The boys grinned knowingly.

Me: No, David, mostly I walked around, shakin an dancin a little.

Seeing David blush, though, I quickly added: Yeah, an I did lie down a little, towards the end.

What kina carpet? Bohler was curious.

Me: None. I tried beer, but it was still a rough landing. Got a headache an I was scared. I wanted to be alone an think it over, but I was afraid to stay there. But I did.

Micka: Right, now I remember! You sent me that fax from your place that you were takin four days off. You shoulda said you were havin a dream! I wouldna taken it outta your bonus.

Me: Whatever, I forgot.

Sharky: So go ahead an mark it down for him, why doncha.

Micka: Yeah, in a sec. C'mon, spill it, Potok. Any more questions, anyone? No.

I'm sorry, O brothers and buddies, but right at the start I oughta mention … I recited the formula … a few basic blasphemic doubts. Don't forget, I'm just the bearer of the dream, so this doesn't necessarily represent any of my own worthless opinions: namely, is our Teaching, the teaching of the Knights of the Secret, truly correct? Because this dream, O buddies an knights, led me into dark lands, an I donno if they're only mine. It's got two traps, as far as I can tell. The first one right at the start, the second one at the end, an they're both traps of the old time.

As I spoke, it occurred to me that the whole dream was one big trap ... but when it comes to important dreams, interpretation and commentary are forbidden, we're no eurojournalists, as Sharky once quipped. I was about to say it anyway, but then I felt the voice entering me, speaking through me, so instead I just said the words:

In my dream we were high in the air, on a flying carpet like. David sat in front, watching out for clouds, Micka stood at the helm, Bohler was meditating, Sharky was trying to hook up to some telegraphic waves so he could figure out where we were, an I was stompin around, testin the strength of the wind. We didn't have any Water, but we were havin fun. There was kind of a casual feelin about it, like we knew that we were safe, driftin along in the stream of time, like we'd saddled it or somethin. An then all at once, hey: some sign with a blinkin arrow. So we go blastin over there an the sign says: OS 5 km. What could that be doin here, way up high above the earth in the middle of flowin time? we wondered. Aha! I've got it, the clever Sharky shouted, it's the old abbreviation for OSADA, settlement! So we paddled on over in that direction, lookin forward to seein our pals the Black Crows an the whole Apache band, old Ludvík Crow Feather an the blood brothers Kopcem an Veverčák,* those guys all hunt together nowadays! Yeah, we'll build a big fire, an if it turns out to be some hobo camp, that's aright too, we'll give em some of our songs, yeah, do a little drinkin. So we went on driftin along in time, feelin safe an comfortable. An after a while, another sign! What a cool machine, friends, it's a heavenly timemobile! Micka hollered, an then we came to the sign, an this one said OSVĚ 2, an it was a bit on the dingy side, probly from all the campfire smoke, so we whooped for joy, because it was obvious it was OSVĚŽOVNA, a refreshment stand, as the ingenious Bohler realized, an so we flew on in that friendly time, enjoyin our heavenly journey, an then in the distance we spotted another sign, so we made a beeline for it, an when we got there, O my brothers an chiefs, we saw that it said: OSVĚTIM, Auschwitz, an it was too late for us to turn back, no matter how badly we wanted to, an our heavenly mobile all of a sudden started to plunge, O my brothers, because we'd come to the place where all the time from every world in human heaven collides ... suddenly there was a vertical wall with time suckin us down into a black hole like a whirlpool, a huge maelstrom straight outta that paranoid Poe. An then we landed.

An we landed softly, brothers, the ground there was so soft we even bounced back up a little. An when we dropped down from that bounce, dear buddies, some of us found ourselves in ashes up to our waists, others just to their ankles, depending on how we fell. It was the ashes of cremated people, my brothers, the ashes of cremated Jews. Any last hope we had that maybe there'd been a mixup, an that at least we were in some slightly cosmopolitan wicked old gulag, was lost. An the ashes stirred up by our landing stuck to our shoes an clothes, an made it hard for us to walk. An where there weren't ashes, brothers, there were bones, human bones, an endless ghastly sea of bones. Then we saw towers in the distance an so we started walkin ... usin one of the taller towers as our point of orientation ... an we were afraid cause the skulls were watchin us, lookin at us, an we asked ourselves: Why are we here? Why us? Why did it happen to me? An some of the skulls seemed to answer: Why not? Some of them lay there softly, jaws set in a knowing smile, but more, far more, just peered out blankly at us, what was left of the jaws twisted into a grimace of pain, cause these'd got it the hard way, brothers, an heavy-duty, alive. There was a sea of them, an ocean. An this comparison occurred to us when we couldn't walk anymore because we kept plunging into the bones an so we tried to swim our way through, we tried to move an crawl an shove our way through with our arms. But it was too gruesome. An the worst thing about our fear, O sea wolves an blood brothers, was it kept growing. Our horror, my brothers, spread, expanding inside our brains to truly vast dimensions. An as our horror grew, it was obvious its borders were shifting an we could only look forward to more.

Crawling didn't work either, because the bones kept caving in an we were afraid that we would suffocate under the weight of all that death. So then we started to jump. An because we were a tribe, we tried to boost each other's courage. Who ever said Jews stink? This place doesn't smell like anything, let alone the appetizin aroma of garlic, shit! Yeah, shit, at least if it smelled like that! said one of us. Hey, what if we're tanked? Why don't we just pretend that we all drank some kina snake oil, one of us suggested. But David said: Nah, there's no way to get this wasted. This is reality, an a pretty dumb one if you ask me. An at that moment, knights an gentlemen, we heavily an seriously detested David. An one of us biffed him with a shinbone an said harshly: Shut up! An we inched along toward the towers, trying not to catch the skulls' empty glances so we wouldn't go insane.

There were children's skulls, my brothers, an there were piles of skulls smashed to bits, an there were skulls shot full of holes, an skulls that looked like they'd been crushed in a press, an skulls with small holes mended shut with barbwire, an one of us, O knights an skippers, cracked another joke: Guess that's what you'd call his-and-hers skulls, ho! ho!, but then started to vomit. An the one creeping in front of him didn't hear him because he was weeping, an the one crawling behind him didn't hear him because he was praying out loud. An, friends an brothers of mine, it wasn't hell we were going through but whatever it is that comes after it. An we realized that our horror, now independent of our brains, outside of us, exterior, like some kina demon, was toying with us. We realized we'd never know if we were just terrified or actually insane, an it began not to matter. Every now an then one of us would fall down an flail around, dancing with the skeletons, till he caught hold of some bone he could use to pull himself back up on. Some of the bones were rotten an crumbling, but most of them looked as though they could've been put there yesterday. It was yesterday, I thought to myself. Wherever there weren't whole skeletons, or at least heaps of bones, we carefully picked our way along broad pelvic bones, flat-footing cautiously across fragile rib cages, an then we figured out that the thick calf an thigh bones, the ones that came from men, were also pretty safe, an the shoulderblades were okay too, an eventually, O my brothers, we just about learned how to move. But the second we started to think so, one of us went plunging down into a chasm of skeletons, one of us, O bosses an sling shooters, an we looked at each other with eyes full of horror an left our brother behind an crawled on, hearing him scream an beg … an though tears began oozing into our hearts, where the water of the warpath flows, like worms … we crawled on … but then one of us went back … an tore off his threads an made a rope an tossed it down to our pseudodroog, an the rest of us stopped, improvising nests out of bones an waiting there inside them, or laboriously building skeleton bridges an making their way back … an the only music we had on that planet was the splinter an crack of bones in tune with our slow motion, an now an then a racket as a pile of skeletons caved in, an otherwise nothing but silence.

Finally we came to what we'd thought was a town, but then we saw it was the ovens that they'd used to burn the Jews. There were bones an skeletons surrounding them too, we made sure we were extra careful when it came to children's bones, cause they just snapped, an we would've broken through, since there was nothing else beneath us. Here at least we could grab hold of the ovens' sturdy grating, an the walls were solid too, the bricks seemed almost new even, not a single crack. It probably would've been easy enough to trigger the mechanism, fire it up, but except for us there was nothing to feed it. We all sat down, sprawling out around the nearest oven, because this was the end. But then, feeling pain, we started to move around again, though only slowly and with great effort. An the source of our pain, my brothers, was the bones underneath us, cracking beneath the weight of our bodies, scratching an stabbing us. Mainly our thighs an elbows, but one or two of us even got a scratch on the face here an there ... an the worst thing, brothers an gentlemen, was when one of us accidentally trampled ... somebody's fragile or rotten chest, an crushed the sternum an broke through, an the sharp thin ribs clamped shut on his foot like a trap ... an the ashes of the dead got into our wounds ... so we tried to wash them out with saliva, an then Bohler tore up his cassock an Shark Stein his byznys shirt, an we tried to bandage ourselves a little ... an then we just sat there.

After a moment or two of oppressive silence, O brothers an buddies of mine, I decided I would try to pump up the conversation: From far away that chimney looks kina like a TV tower! Weird, huh? An one of you, O pseudo-droogs an brothers, replied: Hm. An another one said politely: Yeah?

An then Bohler started shrieking an quick made the sign of the cross, an then we all saw it: there stood Death. The Grim Reaper. At first, I admit, I was slightly in awe: You mean *that's* what he looks like? An I think the rest of you also recovered a little. At least now it was obvious why that crazy flying carpet had flown us all the way out here: to die. An Bohler got up an walked across the bones to Death an let loose, Iesous Christos Theu Ios Soter, an made the sign of the carp with a shinbone, I thought he'd finally flipped. Death didn't say a word, just stood there looking at us through empty eye sockets. All that scythe stuff was bullshit, Micka whispered to me. With those claws who needs one, he added. I shuddered. Bohler came gloomily walking back an sank down on a bone next to me. What was that all about? I asked. That was the first Christian greeting from the days of the evil Roman catacombs, I was informed.

He'd used it as a test, figuring Death's old, he oughta at least know that. Next Bohler gave Latin a shot: *Ora pro nobis* … we all joined in, except Sharky, I noticed. But Death didn't say a word. Just stood there. Then Shark Stein got up an said: Enough aready with the Christian cockamamie, this here's my turf. My people were the ones killed here. Alla that old-time bastardized Greek an Latin doesn't mean a thing here. An Sharky walks up to Death an goes: Shalom aleichem! an starts chanting, Shma Yizrael … an rocking back an forth … an jiggling all over his body … who'da guessed, I leaned over to Bohler. C'mon, he's an old kibbutzer, Bohler whispered back … baptized. Sharky sang … whined, more like it … an Death just stood there. Disgraced an unhappy, Shark Stein walked back over to us an then turned around an told Death: Mazeltov! an he didn't mean it sarcastically. But Death didn't say a word. What do we do? whispered Micka. Nothin, said Bohler, leaning back against the grating. Wait. Like always.

But then Death took a step towards us, slow an hesitant like, an then another … an I felt like shouting: Move it aready, you blasted old swine! But I didn't, an we began crossing ourselves, an David yelled out: Not to fear, boys, we lived by the contract! An when Death heard that, he pulled up short.

We heard a sort of hesitant cough. An then a voice, soft an raspy: Beg pardon, yer worships, but I was advised some young gents from the Czech Lands were here. So in case ya'd fancy a little tour … at cher service, Josef Novák's ma name, sightseein's ma game, heh.

I thought I was hallucinating, an when I looked around at the rest of you, O friends an chiefs, it was plain you were meeting with the same feelings as me.

Hey, said Sharky, when that skeleton talks, it opens its … mouth.

Course that's only natural, said the skeleton.

So you're dead? David went to the heart of the matter.

Yep, said the skeleton.

An you're really Josef Novák?* Bohler said, giving Sharky a wink.

Am now, gentlemen, said the skeleton, course who I am … I am … as the sayin goes out our way in the wild blue yonder.

An you were baptized with the name …

Sure, said the skeleton, at that little church in Žižkov.* But if ya might fancy a little tour? See it's gettin late, yer worships, though course out our way … wull, things're a little diffrent.

Excuse me, Bohler said, but would you mind tellin me … you see … here … with a name like yours …

Oh that ole story, said Josef Novák the skeleton. That ole mixup. Yep, like that all of um were Jewz, yup? Most all of um. An a couple a Gypsies, briefly. Alla the gentlemen from the Czech Lands ask that one right off. Wull back under the Protectorate* I was workin this honky-tonk Mincík's down on Wencie Square, an there was this dishslinger there name a Roubíček, an we had a little thing goin wid invoices, nowadays course I'm above it all, wull an the thing was some signatures for schnapps, up at the till an oud in the storeroom, I'd jus useda fill in for im when there was a need, ole Rouba he was in on it big time, I'd jus play the dummy when there was a need, so as ta get me a spot at the water hole, right, wull nowadays I'm above it all, the bag of bones rattled on, an one day I'm pullin the ole snotrag oudda my copacetic zoot suit an Kasal, that was this walleyed kid, posthumous child from our little Adinka, heart a gold on er, wull an this kid Kasal useda cover for us durin handoffs, I mean I'm tellin ya! An I didn't notice cause a my snotrag but he's goin nuts makin all these secret signs how we're busted an the raid's on the way, an was it ever, bingo! Wham bam thank ya ma'am that same day the Gestapo comes bustin in lookin for Roubíček, which that day was me, an I was expectin somethin, I mean it's like I told ja before, contacts, deliveries, handoffs, crates an bottles an whatnot, wull nowadays I'm above it all, laugh right at it now, as Adinka* useda say, right, an they're: Where's Roubíček? An I'm: You're lookin at im, pardners, there some kina problem? An them, course they're Czechs, nowadays I'm above it all, they go: Yeah, you! An they gamee a bit of a brutalizin, never got a chance da say, hey I'm a good Czech too, straighten the whole mixup out wid em somehow, you scratch my back, right, that's the fix, eh? Nowadays, wull, I laugh right at it. Wull an down at Gestapo HQ when they found out I wasn't the wanted Semite Roubíček but some Josef Novák from Žižkov, temporarily employed as a blond barboy, which is ta say a dancer, an a highly sought-after escort to boot, wull nowadays I'm above it all, they were floored: Here we are huntin Jews an there's Czechs goin around impersonatin um! Wull an off I went wid the first transport. Yep, otherwise it was nothin but Jewz here, all of um, yes siree.

And we just sat there, chiefs and brothers, quiet as mice, no longer feeling the pain from our wounds.

Wull then, yer worships, ring-a-ding-ding, let the tour begin! Ordinarily I'm advised ta awways start the gents off wit the ramp, but today, gentlemen, I … today, hm, anyway … things're diffrent for us … it's just that I got somethin ta do later on, so if ya don't mind I'll just give ya a little peek, right, yeh? Wull, silence gives consent, as ole Brychta useda say when he was coppin coins oudda farmers' dampers on Coal Market Square, kapisch, pardners?

Over there then, the skeleton pointed to the sea of bones, that was the ramp an that's where Mengele useda separate the wheat from the chaff's how he put it. Over there, when the cattle car I was on pulled in, wull it's all behind us now, there's an incident from my first day goes wid that, when those Jew boyz see us fallin oudda the wagons, suffocatin ta death an dyin a thirst, they come flyin in there wid the whips, chop-chop everyone out, ess-ess're standin behind um, wull an we go down the ramp an there's Mengele an all the rest of um wearin these white lab coats, an he sees me an says: Now there's a showpiece! an the whole hullabaloo stops on the spot an I strip down to my birthday suit an he takes this pointer an points an all the resta the docktors an ess-ess're lookin an some brass band's playin along in the background. An he says, course now I know what he said an I laugh right at it: Note here the typical degeneration of the cheekbones … an he like jabs me wid the pointer … the typical Jewish nose … the flattened palate … here we have Beelzebub's hump … notice the striking size of the sex organ … proof of pervertedness … depravity … Wull hell, it tickled. An I donno hardly any German, jus the stuff the guards're screamin, an what wid all those folks in the cattle car sobbin an moanin I figure they're givin me some special welcome, like I'm some upper crust or somethin, which … now all that's behind me, things're diffrent out our way … I figured since all he's tellin the rest of um is Rechts! an Links! an flippin his pointer back an forth. An so I raise my right hand an go: Heil Hitler, meine offizieren und docktoren an scholars. Ich bin eine kleine tschechische schweine, geboren aus Žižkov,* howdy do, Novák from Prague here. Greetins, everyone, an long live the Führer an the Thousand-Year Reich! Hip hip hooray! An Mengele hears an turns all white an swishes his pointer, an the guards kick me inda the line for the gas, yep nowadays I'm above it all, but what wid the hubbub stoppin an restartin, the lines got all tangled up, an they start tearin dames' kids away … confusion sets in … an the Jew boyz fly back in wid the whips, chop-chop dividin it up like … like, pardners, kapisch? … but they jus made an even bigger mess, an I'm down there floppin aroun in the mud an they're at me wid the whips, wull I'm above it all now, an then this one kid kicks me back inda line, wull an that was the wheat line, nowadays, wull, I laugh right at it.

And suddenly I realized, brothers and skippers, I was walking behind Josef Novák the skeleton, and so were you, we were walking across the bones, but it was safe, just a little bit hard on the feet, like concrete. And the skeleton stopped and turned to us. Wull, pardners, that's like how it was ... and then he picked a bone up off the ground, a man's shin, I think, and said: Fall in!

And all of us, brothers and buddies, obediently fell in line like it was some fuckin army drill.

Wull, pardners, Josef Novák the skeleton walked up to Micka: Let's see yer teeth, swine! Heh heh, scared ja there, scoutie, he laughed, waving the bone. Rechts! Yer a strong fella, you'da gone on road detail. But watch it! That was ess-ess Bauch's kommando, an he'da only been happy if you misbehaved, only real pleasure for him was breakin strong fellas. Nice an slow. There there, scoutie, what's a matter? the skeleton stopped at Bohler and ran the bone over his rags. Cassock? That's too bad, an yer a strong one too, but preacher men only got three days da live aroun here, kapisch? An then it was nach oven an I'm talkin ein zwei drei! Then Josef Novák the skeleton comes up to me and goes: Hey, scout, whatcha shakin for, ya sure yer not a touch meshuga? But then, noticing my slightly frazzled elbows and the minor permanent sprain in my left shoulder ... he bent down and listened to the rhythm of my heels ... and Josef Novák the skeleton tossed away the shinbone, threw his arms around me, and said: Colleagues, heh? And I went, yes ... Mr. Novák. Wull, ya mighta been able da hop aroun the camp fancy house a while fore ya hopped cher way inda the oven. And then the skeleton passed Sharky and just snickered and let out a hoot: Wull that's an obvious one, and then he stopped at David. You're a pretty young good-lookin boy, I'd give ya the road, but if Oberst Prochaska gets a gander a ya, that's yer tough luck. Wull, boys, alla ya'd, cept for this gent here, he said pointing to Sharky, end up, long as ya got cher paypers all shipshape down at the rathaus! the skeleton admonishingly lifted a bony finger, in an Aryan camp. Wull but it's twelve a one an half a dozen a the other, as ole Vaněček said durin that blackjack game down at Kalenda's when he lost the last thou he'd got for those horses he sold to Kropáček from Byteč an hadda dig the coins oudda his pockets, heh! Wull never mind, move it along, pardners. So over there ya got cher tattoos, pricky pricky, heh heh, wull nowadays

I'm above it all, an how bout a little shortcut, we'll jus swing over this hill, keep that spinnin top spinnin, keep those wheels from standin still! Wull then right here ya had jer gallows, yep, got used whenever someone misbehaved, or whenever they were empty … and, brothers and buddies, I took a few steps back because Bohler was kneeling there vomiting, and when he had nothing left to vomit then he began to choke, so I gave him a few manly kicks in the back …

Yep an when I got ta my digs those Jew boyz that plucked me oudda the gas let loose on me wit that gibberish a theirs … wull, pardners, you had me mixed up too, carryin on wid all that talk a yers at first, I was advised some young gentlemen from Prague were here, an I mean it's like I told ja! How bout that sweet little mother of a hundred spires of ours … don't cha go poopin yer you-know-whats now … how bout ole Fensterer, still got that butcher shop a his up on Klamovka, pardners? Just got it back, Micka reported dejectedly. Wull an those Jew boyz let loose on me, an when they found out I was no showcase Jew, or even an ordinary one, when they found out I was a mixup, I mean I told ja, goddammit! they kicked me oudda the barracks, wull nowadays I'm above it all. An the tour moves on, shake a leg, make it snappy, gotta keep the wifey happy, hey! Wull, pardners, this right here's a good one, in spring of forty-three me an Broněk jumped this one ole Izzy an scarfed down his potatoes, wadn't that a treat, yep, yep. An this right here's where yer Jewish soap was made, as in out of um, yup, an so me an Broněk snatched some an plugged it to the Polaks, word was it kept the lice off, yep, yep, it's all behind us now, swingin the lingo yet, pardners? Ya know you fellas talk funny, like some kina goody-goodies, ya sure yer from the little mother? Hey an right over here's where they killed Bonn, Hanuš, yep, right over here by these stakes, told me bout it when we went fishin, yep, yep. Right here then ya had jer store-houses, boyz, right here ya had yer ess-ess canteen, yer fancy house, heh heh, an right here ya had jer offices, here's where I'd useda see Poláček,* awways makin like he was in a rush fillin out forms for the transports, cross out one, put down another, yeah he was good, that ole Hebe, all it cost was a little margarine, yep … Enough! roared Bohler. We turned around and saw him standing behind us with Sharky, and Sharky started in again, shimmying all over the place and wailing in that voice that didn't go with him at all, some-thing like asmoel … yizgebal … oooeee … chayil … ay-ay-ee … shoah … ey-ey-eee … an Bohler stood next to him with a cross resourcefully fashioned out of two bones tied together with a strip of his cassock, roaring: Stand back, infernal power … diabolical delusion … unclean force … and as the two of them came walking down a path of bones toward us, I could almost feel the power of the warpath … but Novák the skeleton just laughed and said: Oh yeah, folderol, shenanigans, yep, gentlemen carry on all sortsa ways here, rollin aroun the ground, oh yeah, it's got all kindsa diffrent effects, yep, yep, I'm aware a that … but … and the skeleton scratched his skull with the shinbone.

Look, Mr. … sir, said Micka. Whoever you are, whatever you want with us, where we come from every little kid knows that Poláček died in Terezín an he definitely never put anyone … any Jews, uhh, any people down for the transports, just the opposite, he saved em … for Chrissake, Micka, cheeks flushing, turned to Bohler, he was a writer! An Hanuš Bonn never left Terezín either! Sharky chimed in, tears rolling down his cheeks like peas. Yeah, I said, that's where he wrote: Flamin crosses up in the sky an days undone with salty anguish … I suddenly remembered the song that She-Dog had told me. And Josef Novák the skeleton, seeming a little embarrassed, shuffled the bones of his feet in the sea of other bones, and said: Oh yeah, boyz, plenty a gentlemen lose their tempers durin the tours cause things're a little diffrent out our way … than what ya got in those arkives an paypers an facts a yers, yep … An besides, there were no transports from here, this was a Death Camp! Sharky said furiously through his tears. Suddenly Novák the skeleton was next to him, patting him on the shoulder with that bone. I saw Sharky shudder, but he kept right on bawling and, O my brothers and chiefs, I was shaken because I'd never seen the tough, cruel Sharky sob with grief … like some helpless little kid … I was afraid we'd lost him … he wept and wept, and that normally razor-sharp face turned blurry … and the horror began to creep into my heart, I was scared … Novák the skeleton soothingly patted him on the shoulder, and said: Oh yeah, it's a lot ta take for the Israelite gentlemen … but look at it this way, pardner, that in spite a what they had planned for alla ya, you grew up ta be a strong, good-lookin Jewish fella … an there's lotsa you … an gorgeous Jewish girls … all over … An they failed … an you can kick their asses! Micka roared at Sharky … an we'll help! he added, menacingly waving a bone … Amen! Bohler said in a resounding lion's voice, and Sure, whatever it takes, I said somewhat unconvincingly. All right, scouts, we get these kina cases an outbursts all the time here, yes sir, now movin along … apropos, gents, this lager here wadn't all that big … transports ran oudda here roun the clock … now yer genuwin lagers … yer death factories, those were unnerground … an don't think there wasn't lotsa heftlinks happy da be here, I mean I'm tellin ya! Right here in Auschwitz! But yer genuwin lagers the ess-ess kept hidden unnerground … in Russia … an those kindsa places … no one knows a hoot about them yet … all those paypers an rekerds an facts a yers! … Pff … Auschwitz wadn't diddly! Baloney, roared the freshly outraged Sharky, why else would Jehovah have sent us here? What Jehovah, Bohler cried, tearing up what was left of his cassock, what Jehovah I ask! … it was Starry Bog … Whoever it was, pardners, guess he just felt like it … said Novák the skeleton, I dunno, I'm a little man, all this sendin stuff … yer here, yer here … and he added to himself: These edjumucated gentlemen, graddyates … awways pickin arguments … never stop stickin their two cents in …

Then it was Micka's turn to vomit, and Bohler wept, and David knelt down and crossed himself, and Sharky had his tough razor face back on, and I didn't want to but I heard Novák the skeleton … wull an here's where we tossed um inda the ovens, even if they screamed an fought back, Broněk knew how da handle um, he was this boxer, a sorta Jewish Goliath, wull an I hauled in the ole Jews, an they didn't fight back cause right up till the last minute they'd be hopin an prayin the Messiyah might turn up … somethin wrong, pardners? said Novák the skeleton as we all screamed in horror … an put out the fire. Those ole Jews believed it, sure as can be! Wull, he never made it. Me an Broněk worked together on the sondercommando, an it was ess-ess Wagner came up wid burnin um alive, got bored one day … we'll get ridda those lice for um, boys … an he'd awways arrange for the canteen da bring us over some bread an a couple cups a melta, an salami too! Yep, dee-licious, wull nowadays I'm above it all, right.

I'll kill him! cried Sharky, leaping at the skeleton … but he froze in mid-leap and dropped on his back in the field of bones, whimpering … it doesn't work! Wull there ya go, the bag of bones rattled on, doesn't work, I mean I'm already dead, wull, I mean I told ja! Boys! An whadda alla you do by the way, you damnatious boys … shtudents? on hollydays … yeh?

Bohler fell to his knees and clasped his hands: Sir … Mr. Novák, whoever you are, an especially if you're … if you used to be Czech, I beg you … tell us what all this means, why we're here, what happened … why us … what Starry Bog intends for us … standing on one leg bone, Novák the skeleton stuck an index-finger bone into his skull where the ear used to be, and wiggled it fiercely … we fell to our knees and Micka groveled in the ashes, jabbering … c'mon, we're just byznysmen ... why us, for Chrissake, whadda you want from us ... and I chipped in: We don't get it ... we wanna live decently, within limits ... an anyway, how're we sposta understand when you just keep rattlin on nonstop ... Sharky stubbornly held his tongue. This is insane here, said David, people, what's become of you ... Mr. Novák ... you went through all that hellishness ... so what the fuck for? said David, spitting out the ash that was stuck to his tongue just like ours.

Wull there ya go, boyz, said Novák the skeleton, stirring the ashes around with the bone, finally the right question, yeh-yeh, alla those back there were wrong questions, why're you here an all, question is, what about us, the ole heftlinks, an how come we got so brutally slaughtered an how come this whole camp thing happened, wull, least that's what I was advised, never mind me, I'm jus a little man, an I told ja before! I'm jus a little Czech, course nowadays I laugh right at it, nowadays things're diffrent ... nowadays, hm, anyway ... things're diffrent here ...

Mr. Novák sir! Bohler howled ... don't digress, tell us: Why?

Wull, pardners, said Novák the skeleton, see I was advised ... like special for ya ... seein as how ya troubled yerselves da come all the way out here, young gentlemen from the little mother ... I was advised back at the gate ta tell ya, yes siree ... how come there was Auschwitz ... an alla that hellishness ... but a big apology, pardners, beggin yer pardon, I jus plain forgot. Wull you curious little scouts'll hafta figger that out for yerselfs. Guesser guesser guess away guess, with all the strength that you possess!

And the skeleton headed off again, flapping his jaws nonstop ... So right over here, boyos ... Micka tugged at what was left of my sleeve, hey man, I thought a somethin ... What? ... What if he's God ... y'know, Bog ... Who? ... Him, the skeleton. What if he's Bog an he's playin a joke on us. And suddenly, O brothers and skippers, I was terrified. You think? I said to Micka ... well, could be. We decided we'd rather not think about it, and hurried off to catch up with the others, because if you lingered too long in that sea of bones, and got left alone, pardners and Indian chiefs, it brought on some mighty unpleasant feelings.

Josef Novák the skeleton walked on in front of us, rattling away and pointing to the sea of bones, and I admit, O my brothers and free wolf cubs, from that point on all I did was try not to see or hear. And I think the rest of you felt the same. Still, now and then I'd prick up my ears and try real hard ...

to listen, because we hadn't ended up where we were for nothing, there had to be a clue, some hidden meaning … but Novák the skeleton just babbled on, and what he said didn't make any sense.

Heh, boyz, get a gander here! the skeleton's raspy voice interrupted my thoughts. Right over here ya had jer bunkers an this is where Oberst Prochaska had his kommando an I tell ya that fella was one s-o-b. When he gave those Jew boyz a shapin up, you could hear um holler all over the lager! Took um down in the bunker an locked imself up wid um! Had it all figgered out … he was Czech! Yes sir … from Jičín. Time they kicked me in there … wull I'd done some misbehavin too … stole a carrot … the jitters I had! All kindsa talk went round about im … yeh yeh, pardners … but us Czechs awways manage da straighten things out wid each other, I like said da myself, not out loud, I mean that goes without sayin! … So there we are alone … in the bunker … jus this funny little bulb flickerin … wull I'm above it all now … an he's all over me wid that German gibberish … an I'm still kein deutsch, yah? So I tell im … I dunno German! An he kina like screws up his eyes, had this look … yes sir … a regular devil! None a that goody-goody stuff! One look at him an it was obvious he was evil! Not just goin through the paces like some a those young German boyz! Those fellas, when they came in an saw what was goin on here at Auschwitz, they lost their lunch! Almost felt sorry for um! But this Prochaska fella … he was a downright animal! An I'm lookin da see if he's got the hammer … Broněk tipped me off … whole lager was eatin offa that one! That was obvious, yeh! Soon as the oberst goes for his hammer, that means he's hot to trot an bingo! It'll be a long long time till yer comin oudda that bunker … till he fells ya … wull that's somethin you damnatious boyz don't get in those scout sayins a yers … this fellin … it's not like cuttin um down, yeh? … it's like he'd cut away at cha piece by piece, an I'm talkin itsy-bitsy teeny-weeny pieces … yeh? Ess-ess sometimes'd make bets … how long the oberst could drag it on wid this or that heftlink … picked out the real strong types for im … fattened um up even, some a those numbers … an made bets … cause Prochaska was the champ when it came da that, yes sir, knocked those ess-ess flat on their cans … too sharp for um! Golden Czech hands* that butcher had … that cutthroat … a pro! … tops in his field … greetins an please, right this way, valued customers, an pull up a seat, heh heh … an those Jew boyz'd be prayin for their turn not to come, for im not to pick up that hammer … or whip, or whatever … prayin for the pistol … that woulda suited um … bang!

an that's it … an this butcher he figgered it out! oh yeah, snitches pricked up their ears … an Prochaska, when word got back to im, he switched techniques … an just when some Jew boy'd be blessin his Lord cause the oberst had a gun … or a plank … he'd just smile an put it down on the chair … an reach for the hammer … or the other way round! nobody ever knew wid him … so I'm scared he's gonna fell me … an he says … Eh, a Praque Chew zat dussn't spik Cherman, vot iss diss, vot iss goink on? That's the way he talked, boyos, like some kina pig … an I trot out the whole mixup thing an connect up all the dots an da wrap it all up I yap: Commander sir, I'm a big anti-Semite … picked that one up from Broněk, he awways useda say that bout imself … An while I'm standin there sayin this, Prochaska he sits down … stretches out his legs … an says: Interresstink, ant vot in yorr opinyon duss it mean, zis anti-Semite? An I say: Means I can't stand negroz! An he starts laughin an says: Mann, you musst be a total idiot! An gets up an walks out, found out afterwards sent a yardbird down da the gate for my file, yeah over where Poláček was, I mean I told ja! Wull an when he found out it was all true bout me an the mixup, he kept me in the bunker as a kapo, heh! An that was a jumbo jackpot, my golden boyz, cause what was in there? Wull, golden soup, heh-heh! An when I was down there in the cellar cleanin out those battered wrecks that the oberst called by their first name, did I tell ya that, my boyz, how he'd start out callin the heftlinks mister an then bingo! he'd switch on um? … soon as he knew he'd felled um … those were some cases down there … some of um I'd hafda examine afterwards … an feed … an he'd act nice to um … let um go walk aroun in the sun, I'd take um out … an talk um oudda their sinful thoughts a suicide, an when they'd start bawlin for their mommies I'd tell um: there there … an the oberst'd talk all nice to um, like how they'd been reformed an they were goin home … an some of um he'd tell the war was over … an they were goin back to Amsterdam, or Pest, or Košice, or whatever place it was … an then it'd start all over again … the torture an the screamin … till he'd felled em … had a few favorite characters … felled em lotsa times … an the ess-ess'd be grinnin ear da ear … yeh that was some number, that Prochaska, yes siree! What's a matter, boyz? Not pukin again on me, are ya, big boy? What cha all blubberin for, blubberheads! Nothin's happnin ta you! Us ole heftlinks is the ones it happened ta … we're the ones got brutally slaugh-tered … an ja never saw us blubberin about it … couldn't! Wasn't anythin left ta blubber, ya whiners! They don't give two shits about that bleatin a yers, the ole heftlinks, all them're in heaven, case ya wanned da know … hey you there, shakin like a gorilla … whadda they call you? Potok, Mr. Novák sir. Well hullo there an how's it hangin, aren't you related da some Chaim Potok from Odessa that croaked out on the wires here? Croaked an croaked till he was all croaked out, heh, that's right, idn it, sokol?* … We don't have any relatives by that name, I donno … Wull a course ya don't now, how could ja … an don't gimme none a yer lip, scoutie, all of um're related! Wull an I mean I gotta tell ya, heh heh, scouties, I got my spot at the water hole, yes siree! See cause sometimes the oberst got sad how all the boyz here in the camp went an croaked on im so soon … turned weak on im, all of um … no kiddin … they didn't have that golden soup … and right then, O my brothers and skippers, I could've sworn the skeleton went: glug glug … course I earned it, too, but chou wanna hear bout that fix now, don't cha, boyz, heh? Wull sometimes Oberst Prochaska he'd come round the train, the transports like, an he had this handshake with Mengele that he could haul off some a the healthy ones … yer suspect ones though, careful now, boyz! Yer healthy ones went straight da work, yes sir! Wull but Mengele he was innarested in what Prochaska did wid em … kept tables on alla those exercises an innerviews … like what an how much each type could take, yeah? So they made a deal! … an I got a whip, an when the oberst made his pick I'd herd that Jew boy oudda line an lock im up … some of um were gals too, my boyz, wull we'll get to that, all in good time, as Aladdin useda say …

NO! we roared in unison, and we turned to make a run for it, why didn't we think of that sooner, I wondered in those first moments of elation as we pulled away from that raspy needling voice, just run off an hide somewhere, that's what I thought, pardners and chiefs, but as you surely realize by now, that was naive of us … because the only place to hide in that sea of skeletons … was underneath them … and we weren't about to do that … and the second we got out of range of that voice we started breaking through an getting speared again … an I was crawlin along next to Bohler an he turned his sooty face to me an the ashes looked like mud … with trickles runnin through it … from tears … an maybe vomit … but my face looked the same, I guess, an Bohler said to me: Brother, I fear that that skeleton is none other than the Devil himself. An I too felt great fear, O skippers an slingsmen, but I just started cacklin away like some scary old witch, cause, as I told Bohler … anything's possible an possibly we're already damned. An so we kept crawlin an fallin through an lookin for wedged-in bones … an we ended up crawlin right back to Josef Novák the skeleton.

He spread his jaws wide in a smile an started rattling on again, an at last we could get back on our feet like human beings.

Wull then, my spooked little laddies, I'll leave the gals for another time, seein as yer such nosewipes, touchy types, heh, just start snifflin again, wouldn't cha? Wull then about that fix, pardners, see the pieces I herded in straight from the station, those fellas … an gals, now easy there, creampuffs, an kids too, see the oberst started fellin them too later on, yeh? Kapisch? An those kids can take a lot, you gents'd be surprised … an they got diffrent responses, yeh? Oberst Prochaska an Dochtor Mengele were fascinated, yes siree … an the oberst was a bit of a perv, like, yeh? Kina sweet on the red stuff, if ya know what I mean … heh? Pardners? No time for alla the happenstances, let's jus say the oberst duhveloped a taste … sometimes he'd treat um like they did somethin wrong, like reeeal reeeal nasty, an sometimes he'd treat um reeeal reeeal nice, heh. Like rewards an punishments, yeh? An when an who, he knew that, but never the tots, yeh? Kina like a big Parent, kapisch? See, down there in that cellar, gentlemen, down there in that bunker, he thought he was God! Yep, that was the thing … that was it, that's what he loved. Lived for it! An whenever I'd bring some fresh nipper in for his first innerview, Prochaska's peepers'd be like saucers … he'd be tremblin! Wull an the nippers were tremblin too! An Prochaska says: Vot are you starink at, you idiot! Couldn't stand it when anyone else was aroun. An I'd clear out da go sweep the roll call square or whatever, I mean I was a kapo! An that, boyos, right there, direkly in fronna ya, the skeleton waved toward the sea of bones … now those're storees, boyz, heh. Stiffs galore! Wull an these pieces here that didn't make it through the gate, ess-ess called em Prochaska's kindergarten, heh, an they weren't even tattooed, yeh? Kapisch? An if they weren't tattooed, they weren't what? On the list, yeh? An if they weren't on the list, they didn't exist, gentlemen. Meanin they didn't get marked down till they were dead! Heh? An so what'd this lil noggin right here come up with? The skeleton tapped his skull with what once had been a finger.

Wull, even if they aren't marked down, they still got what … teeth, right! An some of um're gold! Get it, pardners? An those aren't marked down in the paypers either! Kapisch? Wull an then it was paradise. An sometimes, sokols, it boggled me alla the gold teeth those nippers had! The oberst he picked out the healthiest ones, goes without sayin! An most a them were what? From the finest rollin-in-dough famblies, right? I tell ya, pardners, it jus boggled my mind, bustin my buns for ole Rouba at my age … playing escort ta nasty ole biddies … workin like a dog … for a couple a peanuts! An here were these nippers wid gold teeth! An Broněk … he hadda box like hell … an when they ran oudda fellas for im da knock down … he hadda work in the slaughterhouse … bust his balls! An these nippers here … they had it all … till they got to Prochaska, that's right. Whimperin … bleatin … alla those Moisheles an Itziksheles an Paisheles an Basheles … an I'd take their teeth … heh! … but before they went to the innerview wid the oberst! He'da noticed, yes sir! He knew bedder n anyone what he did to em! I covered my butt! But when he'd see a piece for the first time an he'd notice the nipper was missin a chomper, wull, it was a milk tooth, kapisch? Or an accident on the ramp, yeh? The shovin, the pushin, the hubbub, got it, pardners? Smart thinkin, right? An the teeth'd go da Broněk an he'd plug um to the Polaks … an we got … pardners … one day we got meat! Honest-to-goodness dog meat! An it was dee-licious, I mean I'm tellin ya! How da ya think you'd measure up, pardners, you edjumucated scouties, heh?

I didn't know, O brothers and skippers, because I'd been trying to lose consciousness, but unfortunately, O bosses and entrepreneurs, it was working just like the horror, all at once it was like independent … like there was something just forcing my consciousness to be … and take it all in. That skeleton's voice and that sea of skeletons and those skulls watching us … maybe they were just lying there, but my consciousness told me: Nope, they're lookin at you.

Mr. Novák sir, David spoke up, excuse me, but how come you're in heaven now if …

Ya mean like, what I did da those nippers, yeh? Wull I got tortured too, so what. It was … pardners, this life a mine, even wid that golden soup it was … it was hard, don't go thinkin it wasn't! Hell, boyz! When they brought Broněk inda the oberst … an he was still a strong fella … a boxer, I mean I told ja, fellas, goddammit! Wull Broněk didn't know what he was in for yet! No sir! I knew … an those dead folks that went inda the oven … they knew, elsewise though nobody else in the lager … an Prochaska, that goes without sayin! An I'm takin Broněk oudda his first innerview … he's on all fours, boyz! He's crawlin! So I get im back ta the cell an I'm goin lockity lockity lock! an he says: Kill me, Josef! Kill me … I beg you! … but I knew he still wasn't brutalized enough … ta die … an Prochaska could tell! I mean he was an expert … in pain … yes sir, I mean it's like I told ja, boyz! An I says: Broněk, pardner, stick it out another round or two … an then I'll kill ya … an he starts sobbin an says: It's no good, Josef … I can't take it … it's too awful … do it now or I'll turn you in. Wull an what was I sposda do, pardners? Figgered if I strangled im maybe the oberst wouldn't be able da tell, but he was a real strong fella … I mean he couldn't stand up … but he was thrashin all over … an I was a boy! An I don't ever wanna be a boy again! I mean I'm tellin ya straight! So I stuck im … an I'm thinkin I'll talk my way oudda it … like he put up a fight or somethin … an I go da Prochaska an there's these two other ess-ess in there besides, Wagner … an Bauch … jus my luck! I mean my nerves were totally jimjammed … I was up shit creek, gents! An instead a askin me bout the little mother like the oberst awways did … he was fond a her … an he'd smile an say … vot about Praque! Zat stepmuzza hass some clawss! An … finish op zis shtroodle, I kent stant zat hunkry look uf yours, you idiot … awways treated me good, yes sir! I gotta tell ya! An I told ja! An he'd speak Czech wid me, that way a his, he'd say: Uf course vee are Cheks, Herr Novák, bot nobotty hass to know! Herr, that's how the krauts say Mister, Oberst Prochaska called me Mister! an he didn't hafda, I mean I was a heftlink … an there were milliyons a them, I don't hafda tell ya! Wull an when I see he's got company … a meetin … I back on oudda there, but Bauch gets a load a me … an next thing I know he's got ahold a me … an slap! slap! Boyz, an me wid my nerves in a tizzy … from back there wid Broněk … my pocket rips open an sparklin in there … two gold teeth! An when my oberst sees it, my Oberst Prochaska, who I betrayed, don't think I don't know it, pardners! Wull he stood up … an then it started … the whimperin an the bleatin … the tortures … an the ess-ess makin bets … wull nowadays I'm above it all, my sokolites.

And, O skippers and sokols, if you think now came a break so we could concentrate and mull it all over, you're mistaken. Because Josef Novák the skeleton started right back up again, and by now we knew we had to follow, to stay within reach of that raspy voice, or we'd start breaking through the bones. So we straggled after the skeleton like on some stupid field trip from bolshevik days.

Yep an movin right along, let it fly, let it ride, like three grannies down the slide! Hola hey hola ho, watch my tour an off we go! Wull but I'm in the wild blue yonder now, boys …

So you're seriously in heaven, Mr. Novák, for real? asked David.

Wull yeah I'm in heaven, I mean what've I been tellin ya, hell!

So why're you there? said David. And the rest of us, dear lords and standard-bearers, kept our mouths shut, but I think we all considered it the right question at the right time.

Wull now, boy … that I dunno! Hooty hooty, woods an booty, Novák the skeleton started up again, guesser guesser guess away guess, with all the strength that you possess, he hollered back at us over his collar and shoulder bones, and we had to pick up the pace again.

Wull all right, boyz … the wild blue yonder, I rode in there on a copacetic shinkansen, knocked me flat on my can! That was somethin new! Peek at my turnip an there she is, pullin up to the ramp, right on the money!

Oh boy, said Bohler.

Uh-huh, said Micka.

Really, Mr. Novák? said David.

There he goes again … it's never gonna stop … said I.

I'm goin outta my mind … said Sharky, gnashing his teeth.

But first I hadda go through this tunnel wid alla these other stiffs an there was plenny a other heftlinks an some was heavily brutalized an I mean I wasn't exackly a knockout either! No siree! Wull what wid the oberst an all! I mean you know, boyz! … so we're goin along an I see this Angel standin there so I say: Greetins, yer worship! I'm Josef Novák aus Žižkov … but my legs gave me away, yes sir, boyz, yes siree … an the Angel he tosses his hair an says: I know, Novák, but things're diffrent out our way. An since we also happen ta know, ole pardner, that you can swing the techneek, which is ta say yer one seriously slick operator wit golden Czech hands an callouses all over those sticky little fingers, we got a copacetic shinkansen here for ya. Course the Ole Man'll hafta take a peek at cha first, but between you an me, pardner … it's just a formality, got cher paypers all shipshape an where yer goin now ya won't get no cheap shots, no one's gonna try an stifle ya or poison ya or any hanky-panky ever again, ya warped ole chiseler, I swear on my momma's death, umtata umtata boom! An the Angel spat good an hard. An me, boys, I broke down right then an there! Every one a those tears I'd held back, I bawled um all out, cause I didn't snuffle once in four years in that lager! Not one little bitty teardrop, jus so we're clear! I couldn't! Not there, I mean I'm tellin ya! An ya know what I was bawlin for? Cause somebody'd talked normal da me! Cause that Angel

swung the lingo my style! … that Angel, he was a personage, an authority …
my new boss, the commandant, for cripe's sake! An I'd awways had some kina
pop … ole Rouba … the guards! … the oberst … but I couldn't ever sling it
my style wid those fellas, call a spade a spade … awways twistin my tongue in
knots for the bosses … an it was the end a all that now, I could feel it … an
maybe that Angel had long hair like some kina perv, but this was his home turf
an he came down da my level … that Angel was the boss, an he definitely had
a piece a the action on everythin beautiful an clean an new! An who was I, a
blond barboy an … a brutally slaughtered heftlink, I mean you know! A nobody! Boyz! Wull an when we pull up da the ramp there's this ole gentleman
sittin there, up in this like armchair sorta, real ole gent wid long white hair an
whiskers, an he's smilin all kind like an noddin to us …

Jesus an Mary! cried Bohler.

I bet, said Micka.

That's beautiful! Just like my mom told me! said David.

Yeah, cool, said I.

Heh heh heh, said Sharky …

… an there's lines comin in from every which way, cause not all of um rode
in on shinkansens! Don't kid cherselfs now, boyos, cause that'd be brutally
miscalculatin! That'd be a mixup, ha! Cause some hadda slog through the mud
… on foot, some of um in coaches … an that kind ole gentleman, that was
Mr. God, my boys, an as the lines went past he'd jus smile an go Rechts! und
Links! wid this like white cane, an in the line I was in, the Angels took care a
us an treated our wounds an consoled us an sang an all … but the debbils tore
inda that other line wid pitchforks an whips, an talk about cher hubbub! Talk
about cher uproar! Chunks a flesh flyin! An there was more an more a them
debbils every minute! I noticed that like right off! An these debbils … they
weren't like those Jew boyz … an me … back there in Auschwitz … here
akshally … wull nowadays it's diffrent … but debbils're worse, don't chou
think! An this one boy, he's worked over all nasty an done in like me, but
suddenly he starts hollerin an hoppin for joy, an he says, in German, only now
I know how da swing it, right: Hey, it's that swine ess-ess Kupner, ha ha, hey
everybody from Dachau, look what they're doin da him! ha ha ha, an a couple
a heftlinks take a look, an they start in, ha ha ha, an the debbils when they
heard that, wull I guess they wanned da show off for us, an for Mr. God a
course, so they take their pitchforks an fire an start hazin an brutalizin that ess-

ess Kupner, makin sorta like a showpiece oudda him. An all of a sudden I hear Mr. God talkin da us ole heftlinks: Really? Is this what cha really want? An a couple a brutalized pieces hollered: Yeah, mister, give that swine what he's got comin! Or somethin like that, an the Lord says it again, he says: Really? An do ya wanna know what they're doin to him? An a couple a us said, yeah, an some jus nodded, like yers truly … an all at once, my boyz, we were in the picture … all at once we knew what they were doin da him … an it was awful, boyz … an if we hadn't awready been dead we'da dropped right there on the spot … not that anythin was happenin da us, boyz … no sir! But we knew what was goin on wid that Kupner … an it was goin on in eternidy … he was sufferin … an every teeny little second a pain was an eternidy … wull you dunno that one, boyz … those scoutin storees a yers don't tell ya diddly bout that … wull even the most done in an brutalized heftlinks stopped yellin at that ess-ess fella an jus kep goin … an I turned aroun … an saw his face … an he wasn't holler-in … it was past hollerin now … he was sufferin an he had an eternidy in fronna him still … on an on … nothin but sufferin … all sortsa pain … us, though, we were in heaven.

Look! Sharky shouted.

The ovens were in front of us again.

Wull, boyz, seein as ya need it, go ahead an squat yerself down a little, way we been runnin aroun the lager, yes sir, kep me a while there, boyz, damnation! Curious little buggers! said Josef Novák the skeleton. Wull an every so often I go down there da peek in on the oberst … down there, boyz, by those spits there's tubs a water an whirlpools an all sorts a contraptions … an whoever wants to … but only if ya know um! Wull an I remembered that strudel an alla those soups … so I awways stop down there time da time an give the oberst a drink … that swine oberst a mine … an he goes: Sank you, Mr. Novak … misterin me again, heh! … the oberst's on his own down there … there's lots of um burnin an sizzlin all by their lonesomes! Ya got some strange cases, sokolites … an some a those spits got crowds round um too … families … husbands or wives, frinstance … other wimmen too, dependin on yer setup … go down there an fan um … can't help too much though, boyz, now whoa there … not wid alla those giant knives … an fire all over, yep! An the debbil pitches in wid his pitchfork … loves it! Course that's what they live for, that's why they're there, I mean I'm tellin ya … there's all sortsa cases … people from heaven they … people, hm! Pff! Someone's got a thing for some sinner they can go down there, easy as pie! No checkpoints at all, yer in ein zwei drei, I tell ya! … yep, came through here after Auschwitz, sokols, yes sir, oof, said Josef Novák, bones cracking as he dropped into a squat … think I'll pop round the clinic, see if Mengele's in, he'll put me all shipshape, yep, nothin that can't be fixed … things're diffrent out our way, sokols, us ole grandaddies we like da chew the fat wid the dochtor time da time … shuffle on in, get a shot or two … even Hanuš, wull not like we need it, but cha know … things're diffrent out our way …

Bohler sank to his knees and for what must've been the hundredth time now, O sling shooters and free lancers, broke into loud moans. Micka spat, this time David didn't say a word, and Sharky walked slowly up to the skeleton, until his face was about 2 cm away from his … face … and spat through his crooked teeth: Are you tryin to tell us, whoever the hell you are, you Novák, that the man who murdered the Jewish nation, that devil Mengele, is in heaven?!

Whoa there, boyo, now slow down wid that devil stuff, cause see lotsa people … people, hm, anyway … in the wild blue yonder wondered bout that, an lots of um Mengele sent there personally … see, news gets aroun up there, oh yeah … whole place is like one big latrine … rumors an agitations … wull but things're diffrent out our way … an I was wondrin too, but then one day Hanuš tells me, cause see he's inda negroz an he translated … propriated … all sortsa negro storees, an he tells me how Mengele's down in Argenteena, boyoz, yeah? an those modern Izraeli boyz're huntin im, so he hops a plane an drops in on one a those negro rain forests an some a them negro boyz find im there, Bororoz or somethin, Hanuš tells me, ain't talkin through my hat, boyoz, no sir, jus sell it like I bought it … Hanuš like surmized it all, yeh? Jus so we're clear, ha! An these Bororoz, wull, they're out huntin Vaiz, these other negroz … been fightin for years out there in those forests, cuttin each other's heads off, like trophies, yep, inhyooman negroz! Like champeenship cups, boyoz, yeh? Swingin it yet, are ya? Wull an so they bag Mengele an take one look an leave im alone … an so there he is, what's he gonna do … an he's sittin there in fronna his hut, happy as can be cause those new Jew boyz, those modern ones, won't be comin afder im there … no sir, boyz, all there is there's anacondaz an lizardz an parrots an spiderz big as a cottage, all sortsa kina critters, Hanuš tells me … no smart Jew boyz're goin in there! Not even for Mengele! I tell ya, no mixup there, nope, ha! Wull an one day Mengele sees this negro walkin through the village an he hollers an foams at the mouth an drops an he's a goner. An Mengele goes da the negro king an says, what's with that pardner there made im holler like that? An the king says, yeah we dunno, hey Mengele, yer a dochtor, go give it a gander … an Mengele goes an aha! Cancer! The ole familiar, yep! No mixup there! An Mengele goes inda his hut an surmizes an reckons an mutters an snorts … three days he's in there! That's the way it was! Cross my heart an hope ta die, pardnerz! Wull an so he reckons it all up … draws some formyalas in the sand … an he tells this negress: Go an get me this stuff … an then tells another one: Go an get me that stuff … an this other one he tells: Go an get me this other stuff … an he nods ta the formyala, wull an that's how it goes, an the negro king gives Mengele some palm wine an cigars, an Mengele shuts imself up in his hut an dumps the stuff in a satchel an stirs … an stirs … an three days later, bingo! pardnerz, he's got it! But careful, it's not over yet: cause afder he went an cured the Bororoz, this delegation a Vaiz comes an says somethin bout some ole feuds … an buryin the pipe … an they got alla these gifts for him an the king … carvings … an heaps a gold … precious gems … so Mengele goes an cures alla those negroz … an peace breaks out all up an down the Ammazon … an alla those negro heftlinks, all of um prosperin an diggin gold … no more cruel diseases or fires or killin or nothin! It was paradise. Yep an him there, boyz! Lived there like that fordy years! An made a deal wid the tribes so they wouldn't go an stab im. An they went an stabbed im anyways! Yep, go trust a negro.

You're a racist, Sharky said disgustedly.

Nobody's found a cure for cancer yet, David said boldly.

Did Mengele do penance? Tell me! Bohler roared.

C'mon, the guy's fulla shit, Micka barked.

I kept my mouth shut, my buddies had said it all.

What's it now, boyz, awways mumblin! What's alla this racist talk … I worked the bar, never played in no orkestra, I told ja loud an clear! Wull an how're they sposda find the cure when the fella got stabbed! I mean I tell ya! An how bout chou, preacher? Penance, yeah, did he do it, did he not, like how'd he get ta heaven afder what he did ta alla those boyz … an dames an kids … yep, I dunno, preacher, I'm a little man an anyways, guesser guesser guess away guess, wull ya know the rest by now, sokolites … sit cherselfs down! C'mon, yer tired!

He was right. With great relief, friends and flag-bearers, we flopped down next to the nearest oven and leaned our backs against the grate.

Wull now, my weary sokols ... rub-a-dub-dub, five ducks in a tub, till one sank down an blub blub blub ... Heh heh, boyz! Spose I'd better be ...

So long! said Micka.

Thank you very much! Bohler said for the rest of us.

That is ... wull jus one more, know this one, boyz? Hitler's meetin wid Chamberlain an Stalin, an Hácha* walks in an says: Hey, fellas ...

Yeah, Mr. Novák, we know it, only with a different cast, Micka said.

On a different set, I clarified.

Wull all right, boyz, yeh! An hey, pardners, heh heh, I mean we're all men here ... how bout this one? This lady goes ta the dochtor an says: Hey, boss ...

Yeah, yeah, Mr. Novák, we know it, we assured the skeleton in unison.

An how bout chou, boyz, know any? Somethin I might pass along ta Poláček ... that ole Hebe ...

Well, maybe, if ... I cleared my throat ... and said: Hey, Mr. Novák, ya know the one about the nun?

Heh heh, the skeleton shuffled eagerly, heh heh, guess not, try me, young fella, give it a go, my silvery sokol, speak an tell!

Well there's this nun walkin down the street, an she's goin past this doorway, an this guy jumps out with this metal rod an biffs her in the head. She goes down, an the guy biffs the nun again, an she's gone, she's history. An the guy spits an goes: Huh, I thought you could take more than that ... BATMAN!!!

Micka and Bohler collapsed in a laughing fit, I just wheezed, David howled, and Sharky went into hysterics, falling flat on his back on the skeletons.

Wull now, boyoz, boyoz, Josef Novák the skeleton shook his skull ... I sorta didn't ... whatchamacallit ... what's wid all the hee-haws ... I mean that nun musta ... pardners?

Guesser guesser guess away guess, with all the strength that you possess!!! Bohler shrieked and, O my brothers, maybe it was strange, out there with that sea of skulls and the ovens and ... Josef Novák! ... but we couldn't stop laughing.

Wull, pardners, if I could like, yeh? Cause I got a riddle too, boyoz, so like what cha gonna do now then, heh?

We stopped dead.

Wull then, pardners, yep, this here ... all the best, sokolites ... guess I'd better be, I mean I was advised ... an maybe I'll be seein ya ... up there ... wull it all depends on you ... arrivaderchee!

And next thing we knew, the skeleton fell to pieces, bone by bone, the skull first, then the arms and legs, and a few seconds later Josef Novák the skeleton was just another one in the sea of millions.

And it was quiet again.

An I was chosen, brothers, an I realized after a while why I'm the bearer of the dream ... in all modesty, blood brothers an industrialists ... maybe the reason the Face singled me out was cause I'm a dancer an an actor an therefore an artist, an as such've already got within me the proper dose of insanity, an maybe that's why I was able to take what I saw an now I can share it with you. It started inconspicuously.

See, I sat down on a bad skeleton an it slipped out from under me an without even thinkin, just on instinct, I did a dance, a little elbow here an a hand or two there, an suddenly I was flying, soaring, an from way up high I saw you down there, relaxing or dying, an I was down there too, an I saw the skeletons in the ovens, from the last ones killed I guess, they were shattered an cracked from the heat, an then all I could see was ashes, an lying there among them in one of the ovens, brothers, was a little piece of melted metal, it was there under the grate that we'd been leaning on the whole time. An all of a sudden, O my brothers, the Face was there in front of me, an it was kind ... an up there in the air I did a little skip for joy, cause I was convinced this had to be Bog, but I didn't know what to do ... so all I said was: Hello.

Hey there, fella, the Face rumbled back.

An I was totally devastated, cause when I realized it could be Bog himself I had hoped to hear his speech, thinking his words would be old an beautiful, splendid objects, like rare wood ... but for him to talk like some arrogant city hooligan ... that I hadn't expected.

You get what you deserve, said the Face. Watch closely now!

An that metal lump in the oven was a key ... I saw it via the same technology a satellite up in space I guess uses to size up a sneaker ... an ordinary key, an all at once I knew it was the same key you see around the necks of the scamps that live in those ratty tenements where their moms an pops don't trust the neighbors ... an with good reason, they're all the same beasts ... an they can't hide the key in the hallway cause everyone knows all the tricks already, every hallway's the same ... so they put the key around their scamp's neck so he can get in when they aren't home cause they're too busy chasin cash an vitamins … boozin it up … writin poems … gettin laid … keepin appointments … always on the go an they don't have time, an city perverts, all sortsa Chikatilos,* have known it for a century at least … so they single out the brats with the keys around their necks, an when the right time comes along they say: Can I help you, son? Little girl? Your folks aren't home anyway, an what grade're you in, princess? C'mon now, you can tell me, I'm consumed with curiosity, an here's some candy … an next thing you know they got their foot in the door … an the brats're defenseless … cause some muffled scream, neighbors don't give a fuck … all neighbors're idiots.

An then, O my brothers an free lancers, I realized, or more like the Face put the thought in my brain, that that Jewish boy or girl … that used to lug that key around on his or her neck back in his or her time, that Moishele or that Bashele, wasn't gonna come … the Child's not gonna make it cause they burned him in that oven. An that was the Messiach. An all that awaits us till the day we die is the hopeless, meaningless life of a worm.

An as I hung there powerless, O my brothers, I started to wring my hands, which as an actor of some standing I've always considered bad form … but then an there I realized that even that can be appropriate at the right time in the right place.

An I screamed at and into the Face: How come? An what're we sposta do … it's not our fault!

An the Face didn't answer, but suddenly I felt somethin push on my neck an I started fallin down … an I was back at the ovens with you.

An we started running, O my brothers, over that field of bones, an though we weren't breaking through anymore, every skull we stepped on screamed in pain, an we'd jump aside in horror but we'd always just land on another an then its jaws too would open wide an let out a scream, an there was no way to stop because wherever we stepped or tried to stand still the skeletons would pitch an scream, an wherever we tripped or stumbled an fell there were cracking sounds an moans of pain … an some of the skulls' empty eye sockets had tears rolling out of them, an some of the skulls in front of us kind of like tried to get out of the way but just sort of twitched an we had to jump onto them, an whenever we slowed down, in the blink of an eye we saw flesh an blood … an so we kept running, hoping to find a spot where we wouldn't wound anyone an the horrible moaning would stop, but there were skeletons an skulls all over the place, an all of a sudden I heard what it was that all those skulls were screaming, an it was like thunder, slow, rhythmic, an rolling: Our blood on you and your children! And again: Our blood on you and your children! An then I went flying back up, an the Face was there before me.

Know who they're screamin at? said the Face. Your grandpas.

An I go: But … they couldn't do anything!

Oh yeah, right. I guess not. Said the Face.

An I gathered up my courage, because just hanging there like that I coulda been tossed anywhere at any time, an it occurred to me that actually I didn't care anymore, an I go: Like that our grandpas didn't slaughter those guys before they slaughtered the Jews, yeah? An what if they had … somehow … what if the Messiach had been one a those other guys that got slaughtered!

But he wasn't. Said the Face. And it sneered.

An it occurred to me up there that it didn't matter anymore whether our grandpas had been slaughtered or kept quiet or took part in the killing, it didn't matter anymore for what reasons or by what coincidence, but the Messiach wasn't coming. He'd been here an they'd burned him. That's what flashed through my mind while I was hanging there, O my brothers.

Exactly, said the Face. I don't like the way you keep killin em. An if I give it another try, said the Face, it won't be till … well … we'll see.

So why'd you let it happen? I shouted, no longer afraid.

But the Face didn't answer me. An suddenly I was holding that key … an ordinary house key … made by the thousands all over the place … but then the key started burning my hand … turned white-hot, an I let go an watched it drop back into the human ashes.

It dropped down in there an the ashes swallowed it up. So that's it, brothers an chiefs, that's what I saw. But one more thing: I was hanging there in space over that land of ashes an skeletons. An the space wasn't moving because time'd died with the Messiach in Auschwitz, an I grasped my enormous mistake. No time bomb exploded, brothers, an some of the acting an dancing I'd done was the dance of the dead, of a man without time, an that was a mistake, an arrogant mistake. Time died in the land of ashes, it hit me. Because one tribe had tried to kill off another an it almost worked an the wheel of the world of human tribes had been broken. An if I hadn't heard that cry of pain, I donno if I would've come down from up there … ever, brothers, but then I heard a scream … an I saw it in the sky, like the sound of a sharp knife ripping through canvas … a scream out of a nightmare, an I got scared that whatever it is that comes after hell had come back to life again down there below me … but then I recognized the voice, it was our helper and superintendent: Vasil.

An in the dead timeless sky I saw a dark star glowing … time had shifted … an that star was Wormwood, brothers. The Face showed me Wormwood, an it was scarlet, an there in the sky stood a man-at-arms with animal horns on his helmet … an he was draped in a scarlet cloak, he wore the color of rage with pride … it was the Dark One in all his power, the Prince … an the Face gave me power too, an I shouted: Hey hey! An in my heart there was joy because suddenly it overflowed with the cruel water of the warpath, an once again I was happy, my sinful hopelessness was gone … an maybe it was the joy of a worm with a meaningless life who now knows it'll never have meaning, but I was joyful … because the Face was here an I was here an you were here, O blood brothers, an the Devil was over there … I was joyful … I was back in the wheel of war, I was alive … an I knew many traps're hidden to man but there's still somebody to fight against … an then I was back by the ovens with you.

Looks like we're gonna be stuck here a while, said Bohler.

We leaned our backs against the grating and the sun shone overhead but it didn't give off any heat. Still, we weren't cold. An as for me, O skippers an pseudodroogs, I forgot all about my flight the second I sat back down on a bone an leaned against the oven.

We were five* an there were millions all around an we had no clue what was to become of us.

But Josef Novák the skeleton had shown us so much horror … we had no more tears or vomit left, an even though we were still afraid, I saw a couple of my buddies with smiles on their faces … but they weren't ordinary smiles … Micka bared his teeth grotesquely … Sharky squatted down, pouring ashes on his head an wailing again, but then he gave up an came over to us an curled his lips back too … it was a wicked wolfish smile … because we didn't know what to do anymore, the springs we had inside us had bounced back against the horror … so, fine, if some power wants it, we'll die right here an maybe we'll go to hell an shove it up your ass! I had the same smile too, I think, wicked … a wolfish grin.

Bohler stretched an stood up.

I know what you're thinkin, said Shark Stein, but none a that, there'll be no collective baptisms of the dead in this place!

An why not? asked Bohler, readying his vessel.

An no consecrating either, I'm tellin ya!

Now now, son, find your humility …

These are my tribe's people, damn it, an it was Christians that did this to em, for cryin out loud …

Go on, cutiepie, whadda ya mean your tribe? My little Praguish bastard blend.

Where're you from, Cassock? Micka spoke up.

Since when've you got somethin against the little mother, priestie, I took the stronger side at random.

What, are you crazy, Bohler, askin Stein about his tribe?! C'mon, we're a tribe! said David.

Yeah yeah, Micka cracked a grin, I'd say the gentleman comes from the mighty nation of Crybabies!

We're on the site where millions died a large an weighty death, brothers … Bohler stepped back in.

Yeah exactly, said Shark Stein.

Yeah exactly, an that's why it's all the same, said Micka.

Unfortunately I hafta agree, I said.

No, said David. Look at us, we're not dead.

We had to think about that one a little.

David walked over an gave me a slap. Ho ho, who'da thought the sissy had it in im … I hunched up slightly, cocking my hands at the proper height, a little above my thighs …

See, you macaque, you gotta be alive if that hurt, said David.

I readjusted my hands to their original position.

Vida, vida, the old ploy still works, Bohler snickered with delight.

We strolled around, back an forth, walking across the skeletons, all of a sudden it worked again. It didn't affect us anymore.

How bout that, said one of us, now it works again. An maybe it won't in a while, another one of us added.

If we had the Fiery here, this stuff'd be like dry leaves, said one of us, poking some bones with his shoe; one of us, an incorrigible human being.

An then, O my brothers, knights, an skippers, we each settled into the dream our own way. We got used to that timeless place, brothers, to that Auschwitzian grave. After all, we were well aware that at the end of each life is death, as Comrade Stalin used to say.

Bohler walked around, anointing whatever skulls Shark Stein would permit, the more crumbled ones that Sharky conceded might be ... partially ... of Aryan origin ... maybe. Sharky didn't take his eyes off him, an meanwhile tried to get his bearings. Once upon a time the wind blew here, he said, and once upon a time it shuddered at the sight. An you can definitely tell your compass points, it's always good to know where you're at. Which way's left an which way's right.

I just hung around watching the others until it occurred to me that if I found a few strong thigh an calf bones, an maybe a pelvis or two, I could set up a little podium. I spotted Sharky behind the ovens ... testing out the box trick on location. But I gotta come clean, chiefs an bosses, I got a pretty good laugh out of it: never mind Batas, he was curled up inside a box barely big enough for the Keds of two tin soldiers!

An Micka, Micka the helmsman, said: Well, might as well! An started looking around for gold teeth. At first he was only kidding: Ho ho ho an Heh heh heh, but then he got obsessed an started poking through the gratings, an believe it or not, dear chiefs, in the old clogged unraked gratings on the ovens' outer wall, where the heat I guess wasn't as fierce, he found a little lump of gold! Right away him an Sharky started arguing how much it could fetch. Sharky played hard an heavy, quoting figures off commodity exchanges an fuming at the ridiculous sums, but Micka glowed, because he'd found his time, Das Kapital.

And shortly after we'd gotten acclimatized, so to speak, to that place left over from hell, a terrifying gale kicked up, whipping bones around, picking them up in bunches and flinging them in our faces, and all those protective playful structures we'd built in anticipation of death were lost.

The first one to go was my small, perhaps I could say impromptu, outdoor stage, right after I had finally gotten it stabilized and somewhat tentatively rehearsed the short but justifiedly popular monologue of a dramatic figure from olden times, the young aristocrat holding a skull. His question, put as much to the skull's empty eye sockets as to the bulging, bloodshot eyes of homo sapiens' arbitrary representative, was also a question for me: the right query in a suitable place.

Good old English rang in my ears with unusual urgency. And especially of course that important question mark; the reply to the dead Dane's question, coincidentally negative, could only be made with great discomfort ... and only thus do words become deeds … but the thought of running my heart through with some old bone grossed me out … and I didn't have my dear old knife with me, but from historical writings I know of a certain widespread practice employed by the Aztec princes at that fatal turning point when Cortéz and his pack of metal-plated rednecks shattered their time: biting off your own tongue and swallowing it, resulting in strangulation … I found my tongue with my teeth, clamped it in the gate, and held it there a second, but it hurt too much … I simply lack the upbringing to be a son of the Sun … so I went on polishing my monologue while searching for reinforcements for my stage, but then another unruly thought got me started laughing again … about the skull the brilliant playwright inserted in the young man's hand for his immortal monologue … with the kind of props I had handy, the playwright known as the Swan of Avon would most likely have given up composing his titillating pieces for the enjoyment of strapping journeyman butchers and gone out screaming wildly in the nearest local loony bin.

And then the aforementioned gale interrupted my speculations … grasping hold of us, lofting us upward, circling over the ovens, which we bid, with what we hoped was our last glance, finally farewell, and then we were flying … like a squad of celestial aquabelles, we were five, and suddenly the sun was warm, and then, O brothers and blood brothers, I sighted the Face once again, but the happiness I felt at that instant, stunning me from my capillaries right up into my medulla, suddenly turned to fright as something happened to the Face … and then I don't know … I was flying in front, until suddenly Sharky went flying past, shoes first … And that's the end.

And the voice left me. I dug my nails into my palm and looked around the room. Shifted my head and saw the sun. Setting. The lawn behind our buildings glittered in the last rays. Then it was dark. The grass is black now, I thought to myself. Went to the window and looked out. I was expecting the ritual of friendly muttering, but instead someone smacked me in the head, somebody else gave me a kick, I didn't fight back. It would've been only normal if I'd gotten a bit of an ass-kicking. But nobody was up for it. Best bring in the Fiery, I told the shadow leaning over me. My dream had been so dark and long, it had swallowed up the whole byznys day. We didn't get to Sharky. Or to the well and its mysteries either.

7

THE METAL FLOWED. ON THE SUBWAY WITH L.
BOHLER THE GREAT. I LEAP AND HEAR SHE-DOG.

And the next day we turned up for our regular briefing in byznys suits unpunctured by any dream bones. And began spinning metal. I had the delicate task of pitting a second-division Ludvig against two fifth-division Ludvigs. Usually it was no problem, given that most superiors squelch their inferiors just to prove their manhood. Power instead of balls, drugs, and a smile. That's the way it was, is, and always will be … we, however, were only out to squelch certain inferiors, and only at the right time.

One of the lesser Ludvigs' wives was sleeping with the second-division Ludvig. They were fond enough of each other but too pressed chasing cash and the social limelight to plan a common path. The superior Ludvig sank a claw into the two officials, failing to realize the inferior Ludvig knew about his sweet secret. Jarmilka herself wanted her lesser husband to know that she knew that he knew. It was never spoken aloud, so as to preserve some sort of dignity. This way they all got something out of it: the greater Ludvig in bed, the lesser Ludvig in the office, and Jarmilka got both. The claw was sunk in over a few skillfully chosen sentences during lunch with the avant-garde actor Potok … following a small sample of a certain irregularity in the two officials' files, and in one of them in particular … Potok, as if by a miracle, and it's no longer any secret … above all through persistent nosiness, and last but not least with the luster of metal, had obtained the file from the other crushed official and, being an upstanding citizen, saw to its rectification.

These, to put it gentlemanly, irregularities could've meant surefire easy cash … all you had to do was bend forward, casually … with a smile … as meanwhile a breeze wafts, schoolgirls sing, the day grows sweet. It was purely by accident that the starving artist Potok happened on the 24-carat irregularities, and he has no intention of making a fuss, writing the newspapers, raking the muck … of course not! … he's merely a poor bohemian, kind of a fool in fact … BUT. Let her leave me! I'll walk out! confided the earnest fifth-division Ludvig over their next lunch, and the slippery Potok knew that the official tucking into the delicate strips of gleaming meat in je-ne-sais-quoi sauce à la Mouchon on the other side of the table … the shrewd Potok was treating … could just as easily walk right into the slammer. My Jarmilka's got a thing for him … but he's harassing me! You got a cousin, right? asked the patient Potok, that sly psychopath … Yeah, what's that got to do with it? A lot, pal, a lot, Potok the good guy in a pinch leaned across the table … Shortly after that, the suffering fifth-division Ludvig decided to leave his Jarmilka to bang the second-division Ludvig, and went to see his cousin the MP, who in turn arrived for his appropriately high-level meeting with the troublesome superior Ludvig equipped with documentation of a scandal worthy of a first-class tabloid … the teeth-gnashing second-string ministerial official felt his glands wilt … upset, and with his high-ranking seat suddenly irretrievably slipping out from under him, he unconsciously and ever so casually and furtively dropped his left hand under the table and touched his quick-as-a-wink miniature member … no, not that, smiled the genial MP … and a few seconds shy of a heart attack the high official learned that he could keep his high seat, along with his bedmate and devoted coworker, and that the irregularities in the files … the date of a certain ruthless audit probing for those same 24-carat irregularities was conveyed with a whisper … and the old ticker kicked back in at the usual gallop … BUT.

And not long after, a danced-to-death Potok, trembling with emotion, was accepting congratulations from his elated pseudodroogs, and Jarmilka turned up for her percentage flushed with happiness and full of sex, which was her ABC … in addition to chuckles, the Organization gave her a bouquet and of course a couple slugs of the Fiery, and then she got acquainted with our buildings, putting in a word or two with lowered eyes about the things we could do together … I mean business-wise though, boys. And the metal flowed.

Just for thoroughness' sake … Potok was sick to his stomach, but well, might as well, he said to himself … and the next day set out in a spotless byznys suit with Bohler's beautiful Laotian lady, alias Madame Hoi-Tsu, a Japanese industrialist with a fragrant jasmine blossom tucked behind her dainty ear … and sporting the perfect ensemble, a subtle gray discreetly fading into dark green … my friend Cepková, the actress, had been teaching her how to walk in it. Ha, check me ou'! No bi' deal! You look like a duck! Toes out! Cepková commanded. Don't swing your ass, twist it. Give it a little toss. She doesn't know what *twist* is! No, you nanny goa'! An' since whe' you know how Japane'e lady walk! You don' know bean. We had to give her that. And from then on Bohler's Laotian lady could move however she wanted. It was better like that anyway.

I've already referred to the misfortune that met one of the doctor's sons, put to death at the hands of bandits. It was back in that old familiar ferment of the new unexplored era that the troubles with the hitlers began. And I saw Bohler the Great swing his *olovrant*.

The hitlers and stalingos came along right after time exploded, the blast having unplugged even the crummiest pipes of the Sewers, however worm-eaten they were and wherever the hell they went to, whatever disgusting Devil's butt they went up ... and the hitlers started slithering out ... into the light straight from the eggs of the poisonous old serpent ... they'd never heard of persuasion, the only thing they respected was violence ... they were whores to power, the kind that makes problems for everyone else except the one who wields it ... the stalingos crushed only those weaker and smaller than themselves, which there was no shortage of ... they lived on the opposite side of the coin, the only power they had was dark ... even Bohler miscalculated when he claimed it was under control, that their days were already numbered ... because until that holy time comes, they and they alone will be counting the wounds and knocked-out teeth and shattered skulls of the others ... those stalingos and gotwaalds* ... and it takes the Lord an eternity to do the arithmetic ... so defend yourself, Starry Bog tells you again and again ... in all sorts of ways, by various means and methods ... and all our pals that had any dealings with the hitlerite stalingos said it was worse than back in the Sewer ... since after all you knew the spooks and they knew you and everyone knew the old time was spent ... and some of our battered pals from friendly outfits sadly nodded their heads and spat tobacco ... but now and then in the morning, since they were getting up early anyway ... they'd polish up their bayonets ... the good old warpath leads into the new time too ... and there were new hitlers born every day, and they were acclimatized to the new time, to time in motion ... and some weren't even human ... I myself caught one and kept him out in the yard ... he'd never read a single sentence by Foglor or Landon or Kcharal ben May,* never heard of the human tribe or compassion, didn't know how a person should treat the weak, especially widows and orphans, never heard of deference toward each and every woman ... all potential sisters, or of great respect for them, stronger than any flamethrower, his dark heart was filled with nothing but complexes ... which in order to survive he had to get out of his system ... and he was eager to, all right ... I ended up feeling so sorry for him I wanted to let him go, but David and Micka said no.

The attack came early, unexpectedly, and on several fronts at once.

Lady Laos and I were riding the subway back from an office where we'd pulled the old Japaneez bluff ... we always arrived in a car with a driver, and he was Bohler's man, a former parishioner of his, but I kept his palm greased so I could drag Lady Laos off, at least for a little while, to a hotel or my place on Gasworks ... she wasn't opposed to the idea of an occasional escape from the altar, the endless rackets with Buddhas, the blood-red wine ... we'd always cuddle a little, but mainly we would talk, because I was fascinated by her tongue, now that I knew that Czech had exploded together with time, her tongue actually fascinated me more than all the rest of her beautiful golden-brown body.

Lady Laos sensed the dark wave first. I sat absorbed in daydreams. The train was just passing under the Vltava where an iron gate straddles its path, so if anything went wrong, the tunnels between the stations closed, and the metal plate chopped the car in two, hopefully we'd both be on the same side of the guillotine, together till the water washed over us ... I thought to myself, it's always good to be prepared for every possibility ... meanwhile Lady Laos crept off to a seat in back, in the corner, and huddled up, even managing to shrink a little, cats have a knack for that ... I look up and see a pair of skinhead stooges garbed in black, obvious hitlers ... know why those jerks're bald? I flashed back to a recent conversation with Micka, cause they're not men ... he'd said ... remember the advice Chief Joseph gave General Champollion: Tell your young men to let their hair grow long so it'll be an honor to kill them ... so said the chief of the Nez Percé tribe, that old murderer ... till they killed him of course ... they're pussies, they're scared a losin their scalps ... Micka concluded, but unfortunately he wasn't here right now ... he'd've seen that these two weren't scared, they were champin at the bit ... from the next car over two more shuffled in ... one stalingo was in the car with us already, I'd been too busy daydreaming to notice ... he stood up ... so five supremacists total, an that's plenty ... they stood there leering at me ... one made a grab for Lady Laos's hair, she knocked his hand away ... an here it comes, the whole folklore. I narrowed my eyes, preparing to take all my power and dance my way into the real world, summon up my darkest demon, the one with eyes set in dark slits, gashes of wrath, and howl and twirl in the air like a beast, and bite, and always land on all fours … the hitlers were so much in love with their dark power that only pure insanity could stop them … sometimes … but I can wait, I thought, I've got my rosary … and Lady Laos's moist palm slipped in between my cold clenched fingers. Meanwhile two of the boys in leather jackets casually passed a bottle of Myslivec* back and forth, spluttering with laughter, the third flashed his skull-and-swastika T-shirt, the fourth the chains around his hand and a spare around his waist. The fifth calmly surveyed the alarmed faces on the rest of the passengers, I'd forgotten all about them. How long till the next stop, three, five minutes? Can we make the door? An then what? I ran through tactics like a field marshal. But the graves in the distance looked dark and damp, as victims' graves tend to be. Fine, I put on my tough-guy face, I got a blade in my pocket too, dickheads. Yeeellooow whooore, the chain guy warbled, the chief, I figured, rocking up and down in his boots. He was still just playing around though, the frenzy hadn't caught him yet. The people around us stared into their newspapers, at the ceiling, at each other's shoes. A little girl next to me dropped a tasteless pink-and-yellow webbed toyfil on the floor, looked at it, opened her mouth. "By underground rail, through all Prague we sail, on steps another elderly mother," a tune buzzed in my head … slaaant-eyed scuuumbaaag, warbled the guy with the chains … "the cat's aboard too, purring loudly for you," I lay Lady Laos's arm around my shoulders so it'd be obvious to everyone, "riding the metro, the underground track, Vanya with his bass and kitty in back," I hummed the tune to her. Hey, the chain guy leaned toward me, Potok, you old brook,* I could make you bubble so bad you'd pee your pants, dumbshit. Zat so? I replied bravely. Fok yu, the Martian said to my face, even thumb contracts don't get broken, an if you wanna know more be at Černá's tonight … Černá's, I realized he'd said. And I was pretty relieved, for a second I thought they'd found out that I'd stopped tossing scraps to their bro in the yard. The train pulled into the station. Die, human pieces a shit, the Martian bid the other passengers farewell and got off. So did his boys.

Trash, said the man with the little girl next to me, are you from Japan, he asked Lady Laos, r yu jappaneez, ma'am? Yes, I said, she's looking into buying the City Brewery. I was pretty prompt in my role as interpreter. Good for her, another passenger joined in, we can't afford it anyway. Can't afford it, you wanna sell it all to the furriners? someone else chimed in loudly. A wave of satisfaction rippled through the debaters. So we end up slaves, yeah, mister, you can stick it up your you-know-what! Look everyone … if the Castle sells out to the Jews, we're screwed! What are you, some kina intellectual? … Stupi' hiyenaz, bluddy fucksy itty-its, said Lady Laos, full of fury, her beautiful Czech tongue so brutal it tugged at my heartstrings. I comfortably stretched out my legs. Lady Laos too. It was behind us.

But not entirely. As we pulled up to our buildings, back in the car with the chauffeur again, I saw Bohler the Great swing the *olovrant.*

It was almost high noon. We'd spent some time in a certain hotel … and now it looked like we were too late, me and Madame Hoi-Tsu, now slightly raspy from speaking … it didn't look pretty, the sun, the roar … in shock, our driver slammed on the brakes, then immediately shot right off again … the car jumped, I swear, like a living thing … straight at one of the runts, and we saw the Laotians' shop gasping its last in the flames … their fans, made with love and fear and inspired by the butterfly's ineffable charm, fluttered amid the random occlusion of glassy fangs, the remnants of shattered windows, crackling in wreaths of sparks … not to mention the joss sticks and incense, whose fragrances had long since lapsed into the old walls, their perpetual moistness now being licked by an at first glance clearly obscene tongue … and as their red and yellow scorching breath reached up to the second story, there wasn't a soul around … not one of our dear tenants … the street was empty … and two Laotians held firmly in check by a clamoring pack of hitlers were parrying with boofalo spears, what else, and one of the chrome-domes dropped to the ground with blood coming out his neck … skinhead scum, I almost wet my pants right then, and my legs began to dance on me, but this wasn't the time for flight … *now* was a good time to die … this was the fast time of Chief Joseph … and the chauffeur lurched forward, screaming the car to a halt just two centimeters away from one scared-to-death skinhead's mug … close enough to accommodate those gorilla mitts of his, I was glad the driver had em … and Lady Laos dropped into a crouch, ready to pounce, claws artfully trimmed and subtly adorned with henna … always prepared for loving scratches, I'd naively thought till then … and she let out a shriek, a shriek of power with hatred in it … because one Laotian lay on the ground, samurai sword snapped in two, and Bohler, now Bohler the Great, stood by the wall of the building as it blistered in the heat, and spotting us grinned through the blood on his face, flashing his teeth in that perverted old smile … and as a hitler with a crowbar came at him, he swung that *olovrant* of his and swatted him across the eyes so hard I hope the last thing that fuck ever saw was the bared teeth of the Lord's dog … Bohler the Great … I approached the Laosters, and before they recognized me I sustained a minor stab wound over my left collarbone … to this day I wear the scar as a tattoo of that moment … but then I laughed and they knew who I was … I laughed because I knew it all, this was the old time back again, the time of the corpse, the time of the Monster, and I knew that I could handle it … my power was coming back, and good settled in where it always had been, face-to-face with evil again … and there were just two colors, black and white … like back in the body of the Monster, the intoxicating red darkness glowed inside my head, but not like before, when it had come while making love, because the time for that word too had come, only now in a brawl … I danced the attackers a first-rank dance, they were in the first rank and Potok was in top form … and had good shoes on … and in and through my dance, as the first bone snapped, I begged She-Dog to come back to me like my old power had so suddenly now … and because I still loved her, I danced as well as I had back then and only then and once upon a time in the dance of the rose … but instead of dancing the death of a rose, I whipped out my knife and cut a tiny étude of a rose's life into the pavement, softly … carving out a few dance figures … till the boys were fairly dripping … and then She-Dog swore that she'd come back … that I'd see her … again she put words in my brain … not in some dark cellar this time … but on the blood-soaked pavement, in sunlight … in the fire's warmth … in freedom, and then I saw the Martian … and his eyes showed neither anger nor fear … like the eyes of the ones the Laosters and I forced back step by step to the sound of their pained screams … he was eager … no bat … no crowbar … no chain, none of those fashionable items, just a long Solingen in his hand, gleaming, solid and grooved, wonder what for? I managed to ask one of the louts before finishing off his face … plainly the Martian didn't give a damn about any showy bouncer stunts … and then the Laotians started howling, a furious throaty howl, and I felt the rhythmic frenzy of war drums pounding in my brain … I guess their forest spirits answering back … howling, with an instinct inherited from the slave hunters, they could sense the end was near, one way or another, and in fraternal harmony the two of them wanted a chance to kill their own Frenchman, before it was all over, whichever way it turned out … and the parishioner lay on the pavement with two lying underneath him but one standing over him … and Bohler swang his *olovrant* … but one of the boys snagged the string with his crowbar, and while they were playing tug-of-war a few more came at Bohler from behind, with a certain cautiousness, but still pretty fast … and the Martian left behind the dopes in the front row … and waited … and then I danced a hoof chop and one of the animals dropped and I felt like I'd knocked down a riser, clearing the stage for the Great Director's latest dramatical tour de force … the Martian stepped through a gap in the bodies, parting in waves to make way for his fury, and She-Dog cried out: Darling! … for a little tenderness I gotta go to the threshold of death? you bitch! … I sent my words back into the darkness to her, and the knife blade sparkled at my chest … and out of the thus far incomprehensibly silent sky came a RRRRAAWWWR, a hole opened up in the ground at the Martian's feet, chunks of cobblestone flying, and again: ROAAWEE!, this time different as Lady Laos sprinted out of the building holding the shotgun at her hip … I felt pretty proud that she'd saved my life first, I'm a little conceited, I admit … just between us actors … RRROWEEE, this time blasting into the air … and the wounded went quickly limping off after the ones that were still whole … and due to the intoxicating feeling of victory, our wounds didn't even hurt that much, luckily that's how it tends to be, they say, in those kindsa battles. Only then we went into the building.

Sister

Shards, they have the time of those days in them too, it was she, my dark star, who took me by the hand and stood me in this room. In outer space. There's a mirror. She turns me toward it, I'm in it alone, just my face. That woman left me in it. At the bottom of solitude. At the bottom of a solitude more deep and awful than I ever imagined. Until I felt the chill that blows from the stars, I knew nothing about life. Perhaps the noose of my path had at last drawn tight and this was the despair of the trap. No, her hand turned over the mirror, and written on the back was: "Only dogs have a destiny." I read on:

8

THE NORTH. ČERNÁ'S. I FIND OUT WHAT THE WELL IS. THE SHADOWS. I FIND OUT WHY THEY DON'T RING. HADRABA'S OFFER.

I went in, slightly dazed an proudly blood-spattered, first. I still harbored some hope that as the first one in I'd grab the morning mail an then, brushing aside Micka's invoice reports an sundry promotions an ads for poisons, bury myself, at least a short while, in *The Fool World, Clokwork Pomegranate, The Anchor and the Cross* an find out the details, a new classic work came in the mail almost every day.

But then through the open door, where the fire was meekly breathing its last, I saw the two Laosters' dead bodies, an David, streaming blood, came downstairs, having chewed through his ropes. That was hard-core, Bohler said, standing nearby. He looked awful, lips gushing, but that was from Lady Laos's biting kiss, the first one after the victory, back on life's track, which any old iron bar can easily knock you off of.

I'll call Hradil, said David, an I noticed he had blood on his hands. The tips of his thumbs had been sliced away, or chopped off. He went back an forth between nervously twirling the little bones an holding them stiffly up in the air, I guess waiting for them to dry. As Bohler stood over the Laosters' dead bodies, into the room walked the shark hunter. One of those I'd fought alongside. He clutched my shoulder, spun me around, an touched my wound. Then went to the dead ones lying on the floor, I noticed they weren't even that bloody, except for the gaping wounds of ruptured flesh around their stomachs. They weren't beaten to death. Bohler stood at their dead feet praying, the shark hunter kneeled down an spread his arms. Knelt there like some hesitant bird. Helena! cried

David, an rushed back upstairs. I dragged along after him. I was astounded to fall twice along the way. Get up! I told myself, an probably thanks to my whipped-up emotions assumed the feet-down position each time, in stride, precisely as prescribed by Stanislavsky. Lady Slovak lay by the smashed altar. They were gonna give her a ride, David turned to me, but then they dragged me off … there were too many of em … They found out I wasn't … Czech, so they didn't … Helena's face was cruelly aged with two bloody slashes an sprinkled all over with some kind of powder. I hope it's powder, I thought.

I went downstairs. An then fell again. I woke up to some stalingo stabbing my rear with a boofalo spear. But no, it was the M.D. with a needed injection. David's thumb tips were sewn back on now, he sniffed at them. Don't worry, the M.D. told him, the guy was clean. Lady Laos an the bandaged Helena were soaking rags in dirty water … you wan' pay someone e'se clean up you' own bloo'! she raged. Fo'get! She decided for us. She was right, who knew what some hired phony might conjure up with the blood. Are you guys nuts! Screamed Micka, who'd just driven back from some trade negotiations. They're not nuts, helmsman, they're bleedin, the M.D. explained, momentarily interrupting the melody of the air whistling in between the sewing an the washing, full of bad post-battle feebleness. No elixir, Micka ordered, quickly finding his bearings. What, do I look like a murderer, the Doctor mumbled. The Laotians withdrew to the cellar with their dead … bodies in the building an an empty street, said Sharky. Where were you? whispered David, eyes glued to Helena, who squatted, back to us, scrubbing the bloody stairs … In the box, said Sharky, turning red. An then this string got knotted up … I got stuck in a shoe actually … I shrank … explained Sharky, embarrassed … Bring in the Water! the freshly stitched Bohler thundered, an Sharky, for once obediently an without any back talk, went for the booze. The thumbs, it's obvious, I shouted, an told the story of our encounter in the subway. He said even thumb contracts don't get broken … that was that time with the Laosters, when Fab Rocker a.s. tried to swallow em up. I told the story of our encounter, perhaps slightly exaggerating my role … Lady Laos nodded fervently … the lone witness, apart from the random and apathetic passengers … to my heroism. Once I had colorfully described how the Martian and his armed horde took flight, she went back to her rag, furiously scrubbing bloodstains that were already washed away … maybe my exaggeration set off her fury, those graceful staccato movements as she rinsed out the rag, dribbling water, I watched the lady carefully … an decided to cut off my story. You're sposta be at Černá's tonight, yeah? asked one of my blood brothers. There's no way though, Hadraba's an old pseudodroog from the Sewer, there's just no way he'd hire stalingos! On us, Bohler cried. Times may be changin, added Micka, but that's too hard-core. Not to mention commercially futile an totally perverted. He's a Northerner, don't forget! But … this isn't his style, I admitted. An if it is, Micka said, I see Ústí an Teplice an fuckin Chomutov* in flames, an they're outta the little mother, those hicks, back to their Sudeten graves.

Northerners: Many slender threads and cables connected us with our cohorts born in the north of Bohemia, in nooks and crannies whose shapes on the map remind the more susceptible of nothing so much as a demon's head. The North was full of evil spirits, in the air, on the ground, and especially underneath it. In the days of the Sewer, while we, the Prague city slickers, were constructing the complex clauses and short punchy sentences of petitions demanding the immediate release of now long since forgotten political prisoners … the northern longhairs were taking it hard in the teeth, because their interrogators knew the most effective thing was a beating … In the days of the Sewer, when reports of beatings of Prague burghers carried over the global airwaves … and photographs of city dwellers with scruffy hairdos filled the free world's glossy weeklies … the beating and torture of northern longhairs was usually done to nothing but the more or less approving howls of the smog-choked wolves in the nearest deep forest, where the coppers pulled over their Zhigulik with the victim inside … When in view of my frequent involvement in the drama demimonde my interrogators were changed, in place of the dwarf sadist Duchač and a pair of backwater thrashers appearing under the almost chauvinistically Czech names Dvořák and Svoboda, suddenly into the gloomy room leapt a handsome man with an evidently artificially high forehead, brimming with a knowledge of French poetry … That idiot, that slimy bolshevik pig, that mutant so totally blatantly in the service of the Devil, took the liberty of placing his hand on my thigh: Just sign it, Mr. Potok, Charlz Bowdlair was also insane an dwelled on thoughts of death, "Carrion"! know that one, don't cha? he said as if it were a joke … well you're gonna be dwellin on those thoughts here, too … In the days when I graduated from interrogators concerned with hooligans to interrogators concerned with artists, the northern cops had long since realized that the two concepts often merge, and treated the artsy Northerners accordingly. In the days when we were being thrown out of schools and kulchur, the northern longhairs were killing off their hangovers in the nastiest toxic factories, where the only way to get thrown out was over the cemetery wall. It's a cursed land those wretched hicks live in, Bohler assessed their situation one gloomy bolshevik day in the preliminary holding cell where by the grace of God we met. That's what they get for their granddads' gold digging,* he went on cruelly. They kicked out the Germans, battered em in concentration camps, an now they got what they asked for.

The fact that the Northerners were more stifled than us wasn't the only difference. There were also insurmountable cultural chasms. While we favored leather boots, the orthodox Northerner never took off his sneakers. He didn't share our fondness for jackets and sportcoats, being too much in love with his shabby olive-drab field jacket. And even on the steamiest summer day, he never took off that abominable sweater, often frayed at the elbows. Prague was predominantly Catholic, among the Northerners there were many Protestants. Given our hatred for the Communists, the only thing that still bound us to the territory of Bohemia was the lion we so happily and incomprehensibly bear in our emblem; the Northerners were obstinate Lambs. The memory of German bones haunted them in their genes. Where one of us had a glass of wine, the Northerner drank a bottle; where the smug Praguer slowly sipped his beer and discussed global issues cagily, to avoid getting right to the heart of the matter, the Northerner guzzled rum and hollered. So it was impossible to ever agree on anything. In those lamentable little smoggy northern towns, each patrolman soon knew the defiant Northerner and kicked his ass whenever he could. Northerners came to Prague to relax and gain experience, but whenever the cops here picked them up they generally would thrash them just for being where they were from. It was a fiendish circle. Broke the weak, steeled the strong, like life itself, only much faster.

Hadraba. And now I have to go and clash with him, my head buzzed.

Even though none of us could stomach the idea that Hadraba was capable of hiring stalingos, I didn't much feel like going. Černá's was Hadraba's main tent, and whatever he wanted, the Martian wouldn't have invited me there without his knowledge. The hitlers were a new, foreign element, and allying with them for the sake of commerce … the contract the Laotians had put their thumbprints on … would've put Hadraba out of the loop. He'd be turning time, which once clenched him so cruelly, against himself. There's no way, we concluded, and we were right.

Only I didn't know that yet. I tried to think of some of the tricks Daniel used in the lion's den, but except for that one, nothing came to me. I just relied on Bog and myself and went.

Maybe Černá* will be there at least, I thought. But then it struck me I could easily be subjected to general ridicule and scorn and outnumbered by my assailants, so instead I hoped she had the day off.

Thinking of Černá I went on foot, in order to loosen up my slightly achy and danced-out muscles. Bohler was right, our street, the last one within city limits, was conspicuously quiet. Just our three buildings, plus the usual sheds and garbage dumps, and some stuff that used to be gardens, in antediluvian times. Jutting up from the dirt were the foundations of the government palace that would never exist. Rust-stained scaffolding. A pipe here and there. A pool clouded with chemicals, unrippled by worms. Ordinarily there were city dogs and cats chasing around, a grinning squirrel or rat or two, but now there was nothing. I noticed the grass in back of our buildings had been all trampled down, and that made me wonder. What with the battle and the fire, we had expected most of our dear tenants to finally take off. But how fast they did was surprising.

As I made my way into the city, an illegal light flickered here and there in the demolition sites and buildings, entries locked and boarded up. There's probly a hole here too, I worried, better tell the others so we can do somethin about it. Wouldn't want it to spread out to us.

Then I decided to take the tram. On the outskirts I was alone, no one else got on till later. Candles flickered in the cemetery by the chapel of the Virgin Mary. As the tram rode along its shiny route through the gray urban canyons, from time to time an ad would flicker for Happy Family or Pepsi Cola. Few glowed steadily. Both flickerings were about hope: one here, one there. People began to get on. I didn't like their looks, and if they even noticed me they probably didn't like mine either. I thought about Černá instead … recalling this song she did at the club, never mind the words, she's obscene enough herself … but always at the right time in the right place … at the club called Černá's … "I'm aware of what you're begging for, lemme wrap my legs around you" … the old-time "aware" struck a dissonant chord with "lemme," and that created tension … the childlike "begging" gave it spice and brought the serenaded guy to his knees … the way Černá sang it, all the others hated him, after all she was offering … lemme wrap my legs around you … what's more, she had black hair and cloaked her relatively petite though no doubt dance-firm body primarily in white, black, and red, the colors of light in the most important knowable worlds. Up on her miniature stage, behind the sorry piano, she observed the stir in the club with a sharp, no-nonsense look, and a few times it struck me … in my battles with the Fiery … or with my colleagues, but also with Cepková and Elsa the Lion … in the olden days of instructing David … it would beautify any chair to have Černá planted on it. She also had a voice, I remembered how Bohler, after rescuing that record from the flames, had added voice to the list of recognized virtues … in fact one night, after some especially difficult negotiations, Černá's voice got me so confused I dipped my hand under the table next to me, it sounded close, I guess it was the way she twisted the words, maybe she wanted to be close … and when I raised my head I caught her eye … I tried again … and again, clear across that big, ugly room, she looked at me, slightly offended … if she'd actually been sitting nearby, she might've said: Keep your paws to yourself! … a third time … yet again she shifted her head toward me, incredible, it works, I told Elsa the Lion … yeah, but you don't work anymore, said my pseudodroogina, and she was right, I didn't work on her … not for a while. And then I froze in the tram, recalling that voice out at the Rock and the last words She-Dog had given me … promising I'd meet a sister … and I couldn't remember whether or not Černá's eyes were green … suddenly I didn't want to go … too many things were happening at once and I wasn't prepared … but you can't very well drag your private affairs into a byznys outing, that's one of the ABC's.

I remained seated as the tram came to a stop, the doors opened, and the city spread its welcoming arms right at the site of a new, extremely suspect frankfurter shack by an old statue of a forgotten patriot. I got off at Hangman Street, formerly Marshal Time-Vulture Avenue. Bad old Prague no. 5 chilled my aching feet. Feeling light and warlike, I sprinted the length of an empty lane called Swingshift, formerly In the Tentacles (later it bore the name of some favorite horse of Budenny's*), and swept through the Galactic at a trot. There were a few familiar faces, but I just gave a wave or two, ran out to the courtyard, and continued on over the wall. Crouching down on the other side, I stayed there for a while, hearing nothing but my own soft, wary breathing. Not a soul around. Then, hooligan slow, legs firmly planted and my hands above my thighs, the edge of my left pinky cocked against demonic whispers, I went down a few ordinary streets to Liberation Avenue. That name hadn't changed, it fits every time the old rats jump ship.

Since I was going to negotiate, and into the lion's den at that, my blade stayed at home. I moved better in the spot around my hip where more often than not my friend weighed me down, but it wasn't totally me, like I'd suddenly gotten younger. Wouldn't do me any good anyway. In case of anything. Hope Černá's not there today, better not be, I sang to myself, wandering along that filthy street that smelled of childhood lindens.

I came to a portal, but the Church of the Martyred Sisters was closed. I didn't wear a watch, but it was still light. I wanted to pass through saints and angels into a place of Bog. I turned into Station Street toward St. Bruno's. The bar wasn't far and I still had plenty of time, so I hung around and observed life a while. You get that hunnerd back to Padevět first thing tomorrow night! a woman in curlers nagged a sulky fellow dumping out the garbage. He made a face up at the second floor and issued a heartfelt threat. The lady vanished. I sympathized, not everyone had to know he owed the guy such disgracefully petty loot. Townspeople walked home from work, stopping off at dives, ladies lugging shopping bags, here and there I even spotted a baby carriage with someone new inside, from time to time a dog passed by. An old lady, basically a crone, clutched her heart, set down her bag, I looked for the nearest phone booth, there weren't any there, before I could peek around the corner she'd snatched up her bag and chipperly set off again, moving the meat and the bag another piece of life forward. I just let myself drift, happy to pay attention to something besides myself for a while. Hey dylyna,* hey you ... three older Gypsies suddenly were standing around me, the meanest-looking one gripped me by the collar, everyone else in hearing range expertly sidestepped. Nah, that's not him, Fána, uh-uh. Said one, disappointed. Seriously? said Fána, my new enemy. Nah, this one's got hair, dylyna. It's not me, really, I rasped. Looked like a slap or two would've done Fána some good, guess he didn't get enough boxing in at the Warehouse today. In the end a sense of justice prevailed in the rot of his scarred soul, Fána let me go, and they trudged off again to see to their affairs, revenge, vanishing from my time. I noticed they had two or three Romany scamps romping ahead of them as feelers. Smart thinkin, I muttered to myself, only it's not in line with the little entente, it isn't kosher ...

The Church of St. Bruno was closed too, what's goin on? But there was no one trustworthy around for me to ask.

A college student, I guess, walked by, comely shoulder stooped as she squeezed a tome to her side, I deflected her cool unquestioning gaze and looked:

not the Book, but *The History of Art* beat her hip in time to her stride, she walked like a calm sea, moving up and down, kina like little pedals if you were ridin real, real slow … I stood in front of Černá's, now in twilight, as the day went out again and the lion's golden head, the ball of sun, sank unstoppably behind Petřín Hill.

A kid lay flat on his back on the ground, I bent down to the victim … his green mohawk soaked in a puddle, the cheap dye turning it green, like a promo for some movie about the Wild East, maybe Hadraba stuck him out here to attract thrill-seeking tourists. I was careful not to get my hands near his pockets, we know that one, the old police ploy, hah, wallet up the sleeve and on the sleeves go the cuffs, just tryin to help my neighbor, heh, the cop is tickled pink as a prawn, the villain quakes on the ground, and from the heavens sounds the good news of the glorious promotion without any work or prayer. The kid lay there. I quite gently caught hold of his left eyelid and tugged it up to expose the pupil, an oyster without a pearl, like some book about the underworld, youth gone bitter. But unless I was having hallucinations, he was breathing.

It was time to go inside and get my bearings before I came face to face with Hadraba. Halfheartedly I told myself we might be underestimating the danger, and our basic assumption … even if that dumbass was ridin totally without a contract, not even a northern one … why would he make rabid dogs outta us, with all our friends an connections, the guy's not nuts, he's a man of business … hitlers musta got revved up an acted on their own … sure, Hadraba's like the bolsheviks, just wanted to perestroikicize us a little but couldn't keep the dummies in line, forgot that in their version of freedom, namely dictatorship for everything else that moves, they slip out of control, the way our newly free citizens did when they kicked to pieces the bolshevik's carefully laid plan, that time in November … when we all filled the squares and loved one another … doubt vibrated lightly through every bone and vein of fear in my wrists … then I remembered the Laosters' massacred bodies and Helena's cuts and David's blood … and last but not least my own, and I made up my mind that if Hadraba really had planned it that way, I'd kill him. Didn't matter how, I'd find somethin there to dispatch him with. And gripping the door handle, I ever so slightly, and at first a little guilefully, the way you should, summoned up anger … the Laotians and their ruptured stomachs helped, they were my brothers too, this is going to earn me a star in Starry Bog's thick black book … and anger arrived: head intoxicatingly clear, water rising in the heart, shoulders heavy with frenzied strength, and you feel like having a little dance … running someone over … so I cut it off, trying on the questioning and slightly sharp-edged smile of the brief time between friendship and what comes after, then settled for the mildly tough and somewhat disgustedly bored look with which one enters such establishments, opened the door and was in.

The first room you had to go through was a dank chamber with a single glazed window, a ceiling that dripped, and reeky old rags all over the floor. Behind the bar stood a hulking Northie, I knew him by sight from my frequent visits. This repulsive room, with a couple of broken chairs that looked like the dead had just risen from them, was Hadraba's flimflam … for deterring normal citizens looking to spend a pleasant night out on the town, bosses proposing to secretaries, mafiosi seeking a quiet box, tuckered-out farm workers crumpling their caps, and similar unwanted guests. He had it all figured out, the signs saying, DITCHDIGGERS KEEP OUT, GO FIND A DIVE, were more or less routine.

Yuck, what a cave, an I wanted dinner, my mom said you do a mean boar here … I gave it a shot. Mirek, like, the boss, like, yeah, said the Northie, was expectin you later, but I'm sposta tell you you're his special guest an whatever you want's … the hulk thought hard, scratching his typically thick, long, and greasy northern hair … like, you can drink on the house. Yeah, an like I'm sposta tell you that like Mirek knows all about it an he's like takin action to make sure everything's cool. I collapsed, but more out of relief than anything else … if he's lettin me drink on the house, I guess it means he wants a truce, since he's a tightwad an he knows I can put it away … Hey, you heard me, so like go on in an we don't got any food. Huh, I said, startled by the sudden detour. Yeah, you said somethin bout some meat you ate here with your mom. He looked pretty puzzled. I was talkin shit, some stoner's lyin outside. Yeah, I know, I booted him, guy was fightin. But he's lyin out there … Hey, what do we care, the hulk said in a Hadraba-like tone of voice, lifting his hands to the sky. Not in the club … not our worry. You goin in? Yeah. How many are there an where're they waitin? I fired off the bazooka. Hey, like I told ja, Míra's not in an like you got those drinks … he obviously couldn't get over the fact that I could get plowed for free … much less that I wasn't doing it … but my old Iroquois trap didn't work, and I could only hope that he was really as dumb as he seemed.

He drew back the curtain, I bounded down the hallway, and then calmly, like an elderly gentleman out philandering, maybe like Goethe, stepped inside. The scene was the same as always. Tables and chairs and on and around em people. First I scanned the stage, just some half-naked lout staggerin around up there, no Černá rollin her eyes behind the mike, makin like she's eating it, that was a brilliant stunt … I didn't see her red sweater anywhere, black pants tight on her thighs … could be a shame, if I end up triumphant … the room in front of me, haze at my back, I struck out toward the bar to talk to the guy with the earring shaped like a spider bobbing above his shoulder. The crowd here was irrational and international: off to one side a crew of Chinese gorging on some disgusting old fish, alternative youth all over, I remembered the first time Bohler heard that word, he just snorted, hmf, what alternative, no such thing, it's obvious. I agreed with him: just life and death, death and life, both. I was pleased to note the smell of incense, trade was moving, fragrant weed was everywhere, that trade was moving too.

Out by the trash there's a young boy lyin, I told the bartender some words from a song. Lonesome an sick an maybe cryin, I added from my own head.

Least he ain't dyin, the bartender said, and I gave up.

What'll it be? he asked, tossing a sheet of paper in front of me. New menu today.

I ride free, I informed him.

No prob.

I checked it out, two sections. Nothin familiar. I'll take a beer! I blurted.

Ran out.

Don't tell me Stalinism's back?

Came an went, he corrected me.

Then a bottle of red.

Locked up.

You're kiddin.

Míra said the drinks might suit you. Warned us you were his special guest tonight. I aim to accommodate.

I studied the names.

I-n-c B-b. Zat some crossword puzzle?

That's the Incest Bomb. Little sister tequila an big brother mescal.

Make it a double.

The other drink was called Secret Urge. I asked what was in it.

It's a secret.

I slammed my alms voucher down on the bar. Tell me! I got a permit.

But then it wouldn't be secret.

I drank the Incest Bomb, tasted good. I knew there was no way for Hadraba to know what She-Dog had said, but still the coincidence struck me as suspicious.

Since when'd you get this stuff? An since when do you guys use hitlers as bouncers?

The drinks since today. The second question I'm deleting, doesn't compute. You work for the Ministry of Fear?

I'm in the pay of the Ministry of Love. So there's no hitlers here?

Just the ones we throw out.

When I tried the Secret Urge, everything turned brighter.

What's this?

Whatever you want.

It's kina weird …

Just your secret urge, man, who knows what strange desires you got inside … passions …

Now don't go analyzin me like some Moravian* …

Yup, Freud, Freud, we're all paranoid, the bartender sang, his spider jiggling.

I noticed some pale kid with glasses on waving to me from one of the tables … I'm used to being relatively famous from the days of my acting career … nodded back … he went on waving an pointing to the chair next to him … all right, all right, I started over, glasses in hand … passed Padre Booze sitting at a table in a dirty frock, famous character, priest … had to hide out a long time in Romania, or Albania … got mixed up in some killing in Mexico … bad priest, Bohler said. He was a skinny little man, teens made fun of him, giving him their confessions, he took it seriously …

 Hi there! I told the kid, I'm Potok … yes I know, he nodded eagerly, the way they always do … but I didn't want to look stuck-up, so instead of asking his name right away I jabbered something, sat down, and said: Oh I know, we … you … we met … you're … it never failed. Benito! he blurted. Oh right, hi there, Benito, cheers. He sat hunched over the table, jotting something down in a smudged notebook … What's the time? looked at his watch and answered himself. Then looked up. Oh no, I'm not Benito, he just walked in, Colombian's thewordrountheministry … coke, he gibbered, but that's secret. And turn the page. Romul* sends his greetings.

Now I knew which way the wind was blowing. Romul was a pseudodroog from the Sewer. A warrior who knew how to be in several places at once. Fought for rule of law. Drank vodka. Our ways had parted when he took on the responsibility of being a bigwig at the Ministry. The Organization had never exploited it though. He was probably the only one we knew wouldn't climb on a tentacle, would've chopped it off. There were more than plenty of others at the Ministry to bend.

How the heck is he? I inquired politely.

Great, amazing! the kid shouted.

I'm an Agent, he offered me his hand under the table.

You new there?

Yeah, he said blissfully.

He was obviously one of Romul's discoveries. Romul had this thing for dragging unknown gravediggers out of their villages, musty geeks out of libraries, country bumpkins that looked like they couldn't count to five away from their beers and plows, and making top-notch agents out of them. The young ones especially admired him. Apart from fighting for justice, Romul was fond of two things: booze and high-speed driving. Since he didn't have much time, he had to combine the two. The young agents who worshiped him grew beards like Romul, dressed like Romul, screamed at people like Romul, taught themselves to draw a Colt like Romul, and learned to guzzle booze like Romul, mowing down hens in out-of-the-way districts. "Romuling" even became an expression around the Pearl. The mortality rate at the Ministry soared. They sloughed it off on the KGB. Leaked factoids about Mosada and MC5. The devotion of Romul's youngbloods reminded me of Micka and his beloved samurais.

The main reason I'm here is that scuffle of yours with the juveniles.

You mean the stalingos?

Could be the Leftist Front, Pioneers for a Red Future, Defenders of Flora and Fauna, them probly not, Black Horsemen, Terror Brigade, hah, it's all over the board nowadays, comin in from the Balkans an Ukraine, well, that's secret, an there's gonna be reactors, uranium, stuff's movin's thewordrountheministry ...

Huh?

We have to go by process of elimination. Logically. They were hitlers.

We know that. But how do you know?

We've known a while now ... we saw it ... in a crystal ball, how do I ... our prognosticators ... fortune-tellers an poets an psychotrons ...

I nodded understandingly: the Ministry was known for its tendency to mysticism.

Let's just say our clairvoyants saw the whole thing a long time ago. No doubt the question of intervention occurs to you, yes. But you have to understand, the Ministry is rebuilding, we lack vehicles and personnel, we're looking for able recruits, and the main thing is, what's done can't be undone! In other words, once our clairvoyants focused in they saw it, and if they saw it, then it already happened!

But why focus in on us? We're lily-white. We've got a contract!

That may be.

But?

There's a few things here …

Past, present, or future?

Always.

So what, we deal in trade. Bohemia's a landscape an a lion an late childhood … the shadow of suspicion being cast upset me, I explained … the Organization doesn't give a damn about the state, that's all we know. At least we're not responsible for those warheads blessed by the Kiev Metropolitan. Or those rifles you send to Central Serbia!

So what, the same shipments go to the Bosnian Jamahiriya! We're maintaining the balance. Plus it's just defensive an preventative weapons. A colleague of mine, you donno him …

We know that Hunkie warrior alright.

I know, said the Agent. But what're we supposed to do? The United States of Europe won't let us in. An MATO won't take us either, we don't even have standardized ammunition! So what're we supposed to do, we have to look out for ourselves.

An those contracts with the Kavkhaz Emirates …

If we don't sell arms, someone else will. When those assassins got our first free president, it was written in his will. That's the word round the Ministry! It may be somewhat apparently absurd … but even Mauretania and Oceania don't want us. We have to act sensibly.

Hunt for the mote in your own eyes. We don't give a damn about your laws. Those judges a yours, sendin people to the penalty box. We're a tribe, we got a contract. Fuck if I'm fetchin coffee for some monster that used to interrogate me in whatever piece-a-shit office he parks his ass in now.

But you do business with em!

So what, that's my free choice. No one's forcin me. My business. An besides, it's perverted.

But we've got constitutions!

Made by the same guys as the old ones. Doctors with degrees from bolshevik instytutes. Lawyers from hell, Agent. Constitutions're scraps a paper. Sworn on by the same guys that went by the old ones, an now they're laughin. Never been happier. Used to be they squelched whoever they were ordered to, to get a spot at the watering hole. Now they squelch for whoever pays. What we've got here's bad old early England. The outbreak of industry. The pirates've got the cash, an they hire moppets to keep the wheel spinnin. There's no law, just old Darwin. I know. I'm in on it too. I say that sincerely, as an animal. Apologies for getting upset!

You guys're mafia, Potok.

Aw, come on, we're just a buncha pals helpin each other out.

That was my pat response and I enjoyed using it.

This isn't about your rackets anyway.

So what is it about?

Fine then, straight up: that well a yours is a Zone.

Huh? My eyes popped. I couldn't believe what he'd said. There were two or three Zones in town already, and they were bad, real bad.

Are you serious?

Yep. But stay put, it won't do your buddies any harm an they're the only ones there. I'll check it out.

He toppled back in his chair, this time it was him whose eyes were popping. I kept waiting for him to whip out a transmitter, but I guess it was in his neck. I turned to where he was staring. Behind us was a table of girls. Is that what threw him? Hey, I said. Still pop-eyed, he'd begun to sweat.

Uaagh! he wrenched out. It's okay. We were worried about the Slovak girl, but it's all right for her there too. I saw that in you just now, I'm also a little ...

The enigma of extrasensory perception, I said so he could see.

Well, I'm still learnin, he added. But at least now you know the Ministry is fighting ...

Quickly I repeated to myself: Zones are evil, Zones suck in the pure, Zones are tunnels. That's all we know. I realized I was talking out loud.

The Agent nodded his head, pleased. He didn't seem so young anymore.

Correct, he said. An a few more things.

A Zone's not just any old hole, where you basically survive if you're fast an agile enough, I said. It's Evil.

It's a path to it. That's what the hitlers went there for, said the Agent. The Laotians just got in their way. An Hadraba, poor guy, gave em an excuse.

That bastard!

Well, said the Agent, he's still pretty new to the little mother, he grinned and apologetically threw up his hands.

I silently congratulated Romul on his discovery.

Did you like the drink, an how bout the name?

Heh, wha …

Yeah, I thought it might remind you of Závorová … Barbara.

Shut up or …

Or nothin. That old theater troupe a yours left a nice little file behind at the Ministry. We know Závorová escaped to Germany.

You know where she is now?

Weelll, the Agent shrugged and rolled his eyes.

She didn't escape anywhere, she soared into the air, flew off in time … She-Dog! I spoke her name out loud in front of another person, a cop … I finished my drink and stood up.

Well, maybe we know, an maybe we don't …

I sat back down.

It all depends …

On what.

He leaned across the table and delivered that beautiful spook line:

It all depends on you.

Okay. I'm all for it. But …

But what?

I've got a contract.

Oh of course. You're such a moralist bunch, Bohler, that Bog-lover …

Save it, I snapped back.

First we'll take the second an then we'll come back to the first, he said Prague-style. I think we found a way to clean up the Zones, or at least to stop em from spreadin. An force em to give back whatever went into them. Except for the hitlers of course. It's a process based on telluric magma, internal incandescence … but you wouldn't understand anyway.

Nope. What's in it for you?

Ahead a you there's the Spessart Society, they're a buncha beggars, then the Abdulimah, we'll let them bite the dust, next some Yezidis, an then you. You come last by law, but you mentioned old Darwin yourself. So, one m. for the medium, another m. to the Ministry account, one to another account, one more for me, an we'll take a look at that little well a yours first.

Now he really didn't look like some pale young kid. Potok the actor trounced by another hack. How many masks does this guy have, I thought with a touch of professional envy.

As many as I need, said the Agent.

Know the rest? I asked, and said in my mind: The pumpkin eats the carrot, rods and wands slice.

The beetle hops, let's roll the dice, he said hesitantly.

Hah-hah. Okay, I'll take the first thing, but when'm I gonna see her, where is she? Závorová … as you put it.

I can't see that far either, the Agent said honestly. But be ready.

That's what she tells me.

Be ready. You'll hear from Jícha.

Huh, he's with you guys?

Never let anything surprise you. My name's Rudolf, an at least now you realize that the Ministry …

Hello, Rudolf!

How bout the second thing, change your mind yet? The medium can come by tonight.

You didn't see it in the ball yet?

I saw it, nodded Rudolf.

So what was there?

That you'll take it. Without even consulting the others.

Aright then. We'll take it.

Hey, Potok, at least now you realize who the Ministry is up against …

Hm?

… the Devil, he whispered, and rose.

I stayed at the empty table. The hubbub was picking up, so luckily I couldn't concentrate. A Zone, that's bad. We might have to move out. 5 m.'s a good chunk, I'll see what Micka an David say. I shot the bartender a questioning look and tapped the spot on my hand where people wear watches. He shook his head and made the sign for time, lots of it. Fine, I'll manage. But I couldn't stop thinking about the doctor's two daughters … and all those cats, dogs, and squirrels, I couldn't take it, so I relocated to the bar. Along the way I stopped off at the girls' table. Some seventeen-year-old had just arrived, shaved bald and, as was apparent thanks to her modest attire, heavily tattooed. Hi girrrls, didja hear the Blue Negroes're playin tonight! she shrieked … yeah, just don't freak, chapel girl, said another seventeen-year-old with long black hair and a Madonna-like face, the old one, I mean. Scuse me, do you know if Černá'll be here tonight, I asked politely. Naw, she's in the maternity clinic, said Madonna. Huh? You mean she's … got a bun in the oven? Tee-hee, the girl sputtered, are you outta your mind … she's in for scurvy, foot-n-mouth, some booze thing, hey, how bout buyin the sisters some refreshments, don't just stand there, entertain us! No, you're not my sisters, an I gotta fight for justice, maybe I'll stop by later. Maybe there won't be a later, Madonna said in a voice so heavy with booze I could barely crawl out from under it.

I went to get a drink, trying to tune out everything except the racket and the snippets of conversation … at least then you can't dwell on darker matters … I guess that's why everyone was here … I took up a post at the bar. Onstage the half-naked singer was working himself into a state of ecstasy, prancing around as he whipped his back bloody, his ponytail was tied with barbwire, I noticed … "you turn around once or twice, then you're pushin up daisies, oo-wah-ee," couldn't disagree with that, "like slaughtered cattle, man, it's crazy, oo-wah-ee," that was too harsh, I relocated again, to the corner. And even before I heard the soft voices, my skin broke out in goose bumps.

Human women eat flesh, take a good look.

And that one there …

She has an embryo in her belly. The flesh grows within their flesh. Sometimes they kill them.

To eat?

No. To burn. And that one there too, only she doesn't know it yet.

They give birth to live young?

Usually. Now they do. But even the dead ones are bound to them by a cord of flesh. They used to bite through it. Now it gets cut.

I think the one in front of us can hear us. Should I kill him?

I didn't shudder. I tried to listen to the singer again and smoothly, casually, rise from my seat. But I couldn't budge.

Wait. Let me test whether he hears.

And then: Honey! It ran me through like a white needle of pain. And then her laughter, soft and friendly: It's me, little brother, here I am. Turn around so I can give you a hug! I knew it wasn't ... couldn't be She-Dog ... this was the old tongue: Turn around and look at me! I want to see you. Turn around and we'll be together forever, I promise. Come to me ... my love.

If I turn around, Death'll be there, I knew it. But it was starting not to matter anymore. I was sweating like in an oven.

Hey ... nother Bomb? the bartender yelled.

Yeah, I mumbled, and took a step and then another ... and turned around, but no one was there. No one was there anymore.

What's up? said the bartender as I leaned on the bar, exhausted.

Aw shit, shit, c'mon, man, he added, spotting a manly tear or two running through my stubble. Hey, maybe it's the new booze ...

gimme an Incest ...

... it's funny, people see important stuff sometimes ...

fork over the Incest an can it ...

... this ain't some counselin center here ...

The Bomb!

Quit sobbin then. It's only nine.

I left him and sat down in the first free chair. Teeth perched on the edge of my glass, I gave a little hiccup, because I found myself looking straight into the hungry eyes of Padre Booze.

Good evening, son.

Good evening, father, I said.

He looked pleased. He wasn't used to that form of address. They usually called him Pachanga.

Your tall boots, my son, may conceal the knife of a warrior, or mere filth, your uncut and unwashed hair may be a lion's mane, or a golden fleece awaiting the first strong hand, your silver ornaments, dear son, may signify the confidence of a man, or the vanity of a fop, your tattoos may contain the hidden truth, but they may also be a snakeskin hiding a wicked heart, your scar may be testimony to the fight for justice, or a blow bestowed upon you ... he started choking.

But he had me read. That was quite a feat.

What are you drinking, father? You'll have to go and get it though.

Thank you, he said proudly, scraped up the money, and made for the bar.

I stretched my legs, finally some space … alone by the wall. In one leap I was at his side; startled, he clutched the money in his fist. No, not that, I reassured him, I'm just afraid to be alone, if you don't mind … He gave me a look of surprise, nodded. The bartender slid him the menu, I grabbed it away.

Brandy, said Padre Booze. Brandy please.

You know Padre Bohler? I resumed the conversation back at the table.

O, the apostate, living with a sect of Bog-lovers, communing with a heathen … you know him, son? he stopped short.

Yes, I said. From hearsay. People in our congregation say he's a good man … it had been a long time since I'd spoken the old tongue, but when it came to a priest, even if he was a mop, I made the effort … an that group, that they support each other, that they're all right, father.

They are unfortunates who distort the Church's teachings, they are mutants, beware them, son. And which congregation do you attend?

Uh, here, boss father, Praga five.

Then surely you know the reverend Father Dobiáš. Sort of tall, red hair?

I knew those tricks. No, father, I don't anyone by that name.

Good, said Padre Booze happily, he doesn't exist. Sorry for that little trap, son. It's just that you don't look …

Do you know Padre Konrád, father, my good pastor … kina short and cross-eyed …

Certainly, my son, he is the Lord's faithful servant. We know each other somewhat.

Father, may I ask something …

Whatever you want, son. Whatever you want.

Why is Starry Bog such a bloody pig? Why is He always devouring us? Sometimes I get scared that I'll go insane.

He just tipped his head.

And sometimes I fear that I already have, he said. It does not surprise me that you are also one of them … there are no rules anymore, that is why we have fear. He finished his drink.

Your church knows all the rules, but it doesn't know a single human heart, I read that somewhere.

Let each man search his own heart, that is his freedom. In any event he shall only come to know it by following the rules, said Padre Booze.

Bo … that is, a friend a mine says some're damned even before they die … in eternity, I mean, like, for it.

If one single … Padre Booze scanned the club, then returned his gaze to my face … if one single sinner in this room is damned, then I want to be damned with him. I suppose that's blasphemy.

So you really believe in God?

If not, I would shed these … this vesture and go unload freight cars, maybe work in some office, or beg, it would make no difference, but I am a limb of the Church, and the Church watches over the rules, it bears witness …

C'mon, they wrote you off! You're a lush!

I may be a miserable priest, but that is beyond my control, I cannot revoke it. I might also … kill myself, or kill you, son, and it would make no difference, nothing would exist anymore.

I guess that's what Starry Bog wants, I smirked.

Shut up! Padre Booze tore into me. Shut up! Shut up! Write it on your floor, tattoo it onto your filthy skin, look at it whenever you get up in that hole of yours you call home!

What's up? The bartender stood over us. Should I toss him?

No, I said. Bring us a brandy. You'll have another, father, won't you?

He nodded almost imperceptibly.

I trust you, came out of me. Come with me, you can live with us. It struck me suddenly … I had a feeling I wouldn't be so scared with Padre Booze around, I don't know why, after all he was worse off than me.

No, I can't.

Bohler is all right, he's a … good person. I mean, c'mon, he's just a helper, I sputtered.

It's not him, you misunderstand me. How can I go with you … when there are still so many people who have never heard the Message, who know nothing. You at least live in a community.

Guess he means the News, I thought, maybe it's the same thing. Where do you live?

I sleep here, or … around.

Do you live at the Dump?

There too, and the station.

You can't keep that up long.

Sometimes I pray that it won't last long. Which is of course a sin as well. You have a refuge, that's a good thing, value it. Those tribes of yours, that's been here before, and surely all shall begin anew. Therein lies hope.

There was something doglike about him. But I trusted him anyway … that he really meant it all.

I'm the only priest who takes confessions … from drunkards. He said it as if he were bragging.

An junkies?

Them too … sometimes.

That's not allowed, is it?

No, but … he put that dog look on again … that rule I modified, otherwise these people would never … and perhaps, once I break one rule, the entire structure collapses? he added, eyes shining.

He's drunk, I realized. I'm off, I said. I got up and went to the bar. Making sure I kept people around me all the way. The bartender eagerly rushed over when he saw me, I told him to bring the Padre a bottle.

Hadraba said you free, not the rest.

He's not the rest, I'll take a drink.

Then I thought of something and went back over to Booze.

Father, there's these two churches I go by from time to time, an today they were closed an there was no one around I could ask. It's some new thing.

So you don't know, you poor devil.

What?

The Pope declared an interdiction. The bells haven't rung for a week now.

Yeah, I don't read the papers. But why would the Papa … ?

It wasn't in the papers. I do not dare to presume why … the Zones, the sects, us, what do I know. Of course in my position, he chuckled, in my position I am not reluctant to say it is cruel.

Yeah, it's harsh.

Even the last sheep now have nowhere to go.

So let em change inta wolves, heh heh, the bartender unexpectedly inserted with a grin. One fine bottle a brandy for my dear pansies. Enjoy your meal, fellas, Spidey said.

Padre Booze quickly poured himself a glass, as if worried someone was going to take the bottle away.

Interdiction. Now everyone is like me. Almost, he said.

Guy's a crazy old coot an soon he'll be six feet under, the bartender whispered to me.

Shut your mouth! I said pretty loud. Shut it!

What the hell? Hey …

That wasn't to you.

Seating myself at a free table, I told myself I might turn around if I heard the Shadows again. That *might* was a thin plank I left myself to leap across. As I slowly tightened my calves, right heel dug in, left swinging into the air, Spidey tapped me on the shoulder.

Boss is waitin. He gestured upstairs with his thumb.

I laughed.

You mean Bog?

Donno bout that, I mean the Boss.

It took him a while.

You won't be disappointed though.

I'll see about that. Thanks.

I went down a hallway and up a winding set of stairs. Even before I got to the top I saw the lights were on in the office and heard voices. Two, but that didn't necessarily mean anything. I shook out my neck and shoulders to kill off the last little bit of fear, and skipped up the last few steps to ease my breathing. Opened the door. Hadraba and Jícha sat at a table. So soon? I flashed a grin at Jícha the spook. Hadraba had his feet up on some sack, looked like it was coated with tar. He motioned to a vacant chair. I sat opposite them.

All actors're fags, Hadraba began.

But I'm a woman. I was curious how he'd take it.

Where's your tits then?

Tits aren't everything. Besides, all musicians're washed-up dope fiends fulla junk, I unfurled the banner.

Not me, I'm fulla God's light.

More like rat light.

Maybe that rat's Jesus.

Your gramma's Jesus.

Yeah yeah, said Jícha.

We smiled amiably at each other, I knew now it hadn't been Hadraba's plan.

Next time watch who you go siccin the kids on, huh?

There won't be a next time, said Hadraba. Promise, cross my heart an everything. You guys want compensation for fear incurred?

We don't fear people, I said. We want 5 m.

I don't have it an're you guys out to ruin me?

The well's not his fault, I realized.

I got somethin else to offer you, said Hadraba. He leaned down and peeled a piece of tar off the sack. I saw the Martian's face. What was left of it.

Is he alive? I asked.

For now, yeah, that's up to you guys, said Hadraba. Wanna give him to the Laotians? It was him killed those two. Knifed em when they answered the door. An smashed your altar too, scumbag, said Hadraba, and spat on the face. The Martian's eyelids fluttered once and opened wide. He was looking right at me.

Greetings from the old brook, I told him. He stared at me and my stomach was in knots. Not that I felt sorry for him. No, he still frightened me. That's your sick messenger, the Martian, I said.

I don't care where he's from, he stopped livin when he handled it his way. He was my messenger, but I've done my penance, said Hadraba. We could just leave im be, it's not like he could hurt anyone now. Or we could, Hadraba made the sign for the end.

I didn't have to think long. Okay, I said, giving the right sign.

So we're cool now, yeah?

Yeah. I gotta tell you though, for a second we thought you forgot what you were doin an didn't have a contract.

I'm not the suicidal type, said Hadraba, covering up the Martian's face.

It's not your death, it's what comes after, Jícha wisecracked.

Free press runnin all right? I asked him.

On paper.

Jícha was another one from the Sewer. Complicated personality, young poet. I'd heard some talk about him recently. Now here we were, opposite each other again. I traveled down the darkening path of my memory to the pre-days, every face, gesture, and scrap from then I keep saved away in my foggy filing system.

For close to a decade now, Jícha had featured as the country's top young poet, but since he'd drowned his debut works in samizdat, hardly anyone knew what he wrote. His fame came from his underground past. His one collection, *I Love You Under the Horologe of Insanity,** had been bought up by silly high-school girls and their depraved female teachers. Having exhausted the romanticism of the erstwhile underground, Jícha dropped poetry in favor of something really bloody. I vaguely recalled some articles by him about attacks on *gastarbeiter* dormitories. They were the stepping stones to his career as a postrevolutionary journalist. He infiltrated the Vietnamese, of which in those memorable bygone years 1, 2, and 3 … after the explosion of time in Bohemia, there were tens of thousands …

I settled in comfortably, reminiscing about the Sewer: people, and I can only speak for Prague, were so pissed off sometimes that the only way they could deal with it was by doing the sickest things imaginable. The need for human sacrifice always hangs in the air. And who worries about fulfilling the deep-rooted human need to hate? It's one of the basic human rights. The sacrifices in my time weren't performed on some block of concrete, oh no, they were done down in cellars, down where the sickness fermented, where there was so much criminal energy. So much unused energy. Frustration and powerlessness. Pinning the hatred on a couple men dangling at the end of a rope, as in years past, didn't work anymore. The picture of the enemy, whether the old USA or the new Charter 77 signatories, was faded and unusable right from the beginning, even for the ones that painted in the colors.

My soothsayer explained that it was essential to find an enemy, some anonymous mass, to assure the domestic population they didn't have it so bad under communism in the heart of Europe. That anonymous mass was communism in Asia. But the slogans of brotherhood came heavily loaded: the shrimpy Asian men and odd Asian women in their quilted jackets and work boots two sizes too big showed Central Europeans a different model human. Beneath their two red lids the communicating vessels exchanged a few bubbles. The organized migration of nations for labor's sake reestablished the validity of the law of conservation of energy. It couldn't be flushed away down the factory floors. Because, thank God, one unforeseen side effect of the *gastarbeiter* transfers was a change in the ethnic face of Bohemia, often remarkable blossoms of interpersonal relations sprang up from the treaties and figures and graphs. It's quite likely I'm lying again, but that's exactly how the ancient soothsayer put it.

They came by the hundreds of thousands. Feeding the factories and bolstering the native workers' self-confidence, not just with their small builds and the ludicrous slop they ate instead of sausages and beer, the only legal and proper meal, but also stories of war, starvation, and killing in their own country, where it was still yesterday. Crossing these two human species was forbidden, and if it went on in spite of that, because love is insanity, then only when the authorities closed their eyes. Because the system for controlling people was highly perfected, I remember it. Only neurotics slipped through the cracks … just a few heroes fought their way out independently, tearing a flag down here and there, typing out copies of K…a, for instance, hijacking a plane, trashing a bulletin board of the Revolutionary Trade Union Movement, learning languages, fighting for justice, praying, stealing melons, ecstatically assaulting a cop … even the slightest attempt to erect your own watchtower in that wired-in land possessed the drastic elements of Babylonian ruin, it's in my memory. The frenzy of scattering through the world, whichever way the wind blows, stayed on the inside. There was only the frenzy of circling in a cage, frenzy turned against itself. I'll kill myself, you, or somebody else, is the final slogan of frenzy, the last stop. And the victim of course is to blame.

The heroes (of which the versifying Jícha was one) occasionally found themselves coming to in a shattered store window at the point between plastered and hungover, right at that point where there's no turning back, waking up to the pain of a body cut by broken glass, stirred to life by police sirens. One even managed to cut his ears off in his cell.

But these heroes, destroying their bodies by jumping through windows with frenzy's proud feeling of self-satisfaction, were complicated personalities. Neurotics. Artists. Criminals. Masochists. With serious Promethean liver problems. And no eagle around to soar up from the horizon, ready to rend. No one gave a damn about them. They accepted the responsibility and paid their own way. I'd rather pay than say thank you, as Timpo put it. He went Buddhist. Shaved his head and got new teeth. Munches grains with em. Lives somewhere.

Yeah yeah, me and my colleagues would sit around at those gloomy conferences of ours. We guys had it somewhat easier, at least we had to show off for the girls … of our tribe … which made their lives less rich, since any woman with half a brain is naturally kind, gentle, and beautiful, they don't have to try that hard. Yeah, if we look back at our history, said Čáp one day in conference … it's no disgrace … to survive, is it? All that massacring … it never stops … the Picardians, the Waldensians, Hus, White Mountain, exterminations, imprisonments, a few executions here an there … censorship an exile … German camps, Soviet camps, Czechoslovak camps, some folks even managed all three … Kulakistan … light bombin, heavy bombin … buzz bombs every which way … nothin but wires all over … an German shepherds … the best people slaughtered, driven out, locked up nonstop … always someone gettin their ass kicked … an you wonder why folks on the street look so bad! There's no spark, no flair … it's a flop … Yeah yeah, we nodded our heads, spitting tobacco … an wait'll the bolshevik goes down an they open up the archives an we get a look at how many spooks there really were … they won't open em, don't worry … they'll just draw up a new social contract an everyone'll button their lip, better to just forget, close your eyes an move on … Where to? … No way! I can't forget anymore, I'm not lettin anyone rob me of myself, or my time, ever again … one of us shouted hysterically … come off it, the bolshevik's not goin down in our lifetime, don't worry … we won't go, this is no Tobruk, or even Warsaw, we'll just keep gettin beaten down over an over an over … here in the Sewer … history? What about the Hussites? Ick, pitooey! Those pigs killed priests. All right … the Battle of Britain!* Cool … but with a foreign army! Milan, King Vladislav!* Cool, cool, that's ancient stuff … People might remember somethin or somebody … if they hadn't all gone stupid … Absolutely, there was that one courageous old teacher that that actor played in that movie, one of those high-powered gothic bloodbaths they were always takin us to … Russians killing Germans and everyone else … and each other … me and my classmates sinking down into the darkness while some bestial red bolshevik blabfest or necrofilm unfolded up on screen, the only trick was taking out Bajza, outwitting Hála, and not tipping Glaser off … as I deftly and discreetly occupied the seat next to Věruška … often it worked and then I'd regret there weren't two of me … to protect her from the other side … and as the body count grew … at first some kids got sick to their stomachs … girls puked … but then we got used to the bazookas and shredded bodies and crumbling buildings and flamethrowers … in retrospect I'd say it had the emotional charge of fireworks … they didn't take the older kids, since it only provoked ridicule … and ridicule in the relative safety of a dark theater full of screams, giggles, and shouted advice: Kill im! Rat-tat-tat-tat! Fire, Russian scum! Shoot im, stupid! and so on and so forth, and our cowardly teachers, the ones that stopped being *Mrs.* and turned into *Comrade*, couldn't handle us, and then bottles started passing around … we felt up the girls, just the ones that wanted us to, and kissed them too … Bajza handed out pills one time … he'd been on drugs since he was thirteen, picked it up from his bros … and the screening was heavily disrupted by visions, at least for me, Věruška squirmed and tossed uneasily … I didn't move … but there was also a Moral principle to the whole whacked-out spectacle, and that was the fictitious courageous teacher played by the old actor … A higher moral principle, he told his assembled students after a few of their classmates had been coincidentally killed by Germans: Dear children, to murder a tyrant is not a crime! It was a movie about the Heydrich-iad,* which some streets still dream about to this day, a few people killed a tyrant before themselves being killed for treason … in a church! … and we had good reason to wink, cough, and shuffle our feet guardedly, and blow our noses conspiratorially, because that was a good slogan … and the movie ended there, but we went on shuffling our feet and grinning, because we knew very well how it continues in reality, after the movie ends … that teacher said it in front of the whole class, no doubt afterwards someone told on him and they killed him too, it was obvious … but it didn't matter, that's the way it goes, and there were approximately as many brats in the class in the movie as there were of us … and I kept waiting for one of my teachers to stand up and say … something … but they all just said the invasion was great, a happy event all in all, and the Russians're our Big Brothers … yep, that's how it was back then … we nodded our heads and spat tobacco … someone here and there battled injustice … got high … and Hála learned Chinese and Glaser did time.

Feeling jilted was a lot of it, both boys and girls got a slap in the face from the world too soon, and too soon they saw that the map was blacked out … and only the stupidest humor worked anymore … it was part of their development and they lived in bugged flats … and our conferences were gloomy till Čáp came up with his teaching on ants, but I already said that … and the sun came up in the morning, pretty much every day, and from time to time history gave somebody an idea or a seizure. And out came the Fiery and the day survived on its own.

Good old tribalism … only … I mentioned circling in the cage, frenzy and victims. Anyone who leaps through windows pays for himself, for his demons. It's easier, though, to catch yourself a cat, a stray dog, a baby swallow, someone quiet and mute, a slave without any rights. Someone who it hurts and who isn't gonna talk.

Every little kid knows all this, steal his scooter so he gets his bearings early on, so it's obvious right away; it's a war of good versus evil, went the word among us.

The *gastarbeiters* came like manna from heaven in the last years of the old time.

Even the simplest citizens found something to relish in their massive influx.

Hatred threw open its discharge valves and went far into the new time. And Jícha had a job and remained on the scene along with the hatred.

And I tell myself: Everything's obvious and always has been. I get it all, understand it all, listen with sympathy. Look at myself. I'd do some kicking too. It's best to get the devil down on the ground and finish him off with your boots.

Jícha also had a knack for recounting his dubious experiences and occasional wheelings and dealings in a pretty entertaining way. Even squeezed some cash out of it now and then. But the old horrors paled with time, the new stories lacked strength and listeners, and his stock plunged irreversibly. Most of the *gastarbeiters* either left Bohemia or fled to desirable states. What's more, killing was an everyday thing in the new time and people got tired of Jícha's reports. He grew glummer and glummer. Just when he realized he could finally write whatever he wanted but nobody cared, the paper dumped him. He got bored with traveling, so he'd put a bomb in the office to give himself something to write about. It went downhill from there. I'd heard he even began writing poems again. But meanwhile the high-school girls had turned old and gruff and lived their own poetry now. The new high-school girls didn't even read. And Jícha wasn't interested in teachers. Now and then and more out of habit than anything else, some pal of his in the press still put in a word of praise for him. After all Jícha could get pretty hostile, and the Pearl's a small place. And the culture section addresses are listed in the front of every dream book. So at least the scrawnier critics were careful. Through some error Jícha even scooped up a few literary prizes. No one knew what for, least of all him. He hung around editorial offices, living off crumbs. Invented dead poets for radio shows. Word got out, and had he been at the zenith of his underground glory they would've let it go, but as it was they booted him down the stairs. I'd heard he vanished from the Pearl for a time. Didn't matter to me, I didn't exactly miss having him around.

Great to have you back, Hadraba said in Jícha's direction.

Yeah, haven't seen you in ages … where you been? I inquired politely.

Faugh! went Spider, I hadn't noticed him come in.

Guy had a grant! he added with envy.

Yep, Jícha nodded. Went out into the world a literat. And returned a literat and a globetrotter, he proclaimed in a deep voice.

Spider shuffled his feet.

Yep, my friends, dear pack, I returned because it dawned hard on me, Jícha continued. But that's not what my story's about.

Hadraba comfortably stretched his legs. Spider clambered over the sack with the corpse and nestled into a chair. Jícha stretched out his back, shut his eyes, and started swaying in place from side to side. I knew what was coming.

Every group in those days used a different storytelling technique to solidify the community. I guess due to my congenital diffidence, I failed to sufficiently highlight the fact that as the Grainy began to cast its flickering glances from the bowels of all sortsa dead eyes on a variety of talking heads, we, the believers and the epicures, were returning to three-dimensional storytellers and actors.

We preferred to let conversation take shape directly before our eyes and purely by means of the pertinent organs, totally like the old times, when life was lived in mud huts and lean-tos. That living speech made for less chill in our rooms. The chill on the inside remained, and if you weren't satisfied you could deck the three-dimensional being in front of you. Shyness made one stingy with praise.

Jícha, perhaps due to his soul's violent twistedness, employed the forest method of Kaa the Snake, who all of us knew from the Mowgli movies: Kaa swaying back and forth, his slick, powerful body looping through the sand, then sinking his poisonous fangs into the leaders of the Bandar-log, the Monkey People. But everyone knows that.

Personally, I prefer the rising-voice method.

Yep, yep, O my buddies, I struck out on a journey, said Jícha, eyes shut … swaying ever so slightly left and swaying to the right … set out into the world an I'm gonna tell you about it, friends, Jícha's body tipped to the left, then to the other side and back … might be good as a brief introduction, boys … hm yeah … listen closely … you can hear me, right, buddies … this'll be a little tale just for you, for your ears, for your soul … he said, and I noticed Hadraba's eyelids drooping, Spider I couldn't see, but he didn't breathe a word … as for me, my sight went fuzzy … and Jícha let loose … and I wouldn't be at all surprised if he'd had it planned in advance … the faker …

9

JÍCHA: "I GOT TANGLED UP. THE TRAP.
CARNIVAL. LIVING TONGUE. HEAVY SNOW.
SPRING OF NATIONS. DANGEROUS BUS."

You all know that in the days of my bolshevik youth I occasionally suffered from existence, O my brothers, and I wasn't ashamed to put it in my tongue, filling sheets of paper with it and drawing attention to myself. Some of you did it too. You scrawled on paper, brothers and pirates, don't tell me you didn't, and whatever words they were, they always said the same thing: Here I am. Do you like me? You all know, O wolves and sling shooters, that's a trap for yawning readers, they don't know beans. And just like you I walked the city, my turf, searching for objets d'art, objets d'esprit, those antigenocide tablets. You all know, you logrollers and dung beetles, how charged objects originate: through the art of surviving by self-destruction. They don't win a single thing, but they're here and you know it, O porters and carters. And as I so crassly and desperately drew attention to myself, O my brothers, little by little I got tangled up in my tongue. Because as I kneaded it for my own use, trampling, stroking, and twisting it, my tongue fought back. And that created tension. And then I got trapped. But before all that, I saw that woman, and here's a tiny question for you, O archers and sharpshooters.

There's various possibilities … many … but you're walkin along … you just got up an you're walkin along … the landscape's hostile … on the horizon even a fire or two … walkin along, cold, you need to shit, an you're hungry … an over in the bushes, lo and behold! a dead body … an you're walkin along … feelin pretty bad … an not only that, you're a woman! … but a bit of a floozy, I'd say … an not pretty, not young … pregnant … by someone … probly some soldier … there's various possibilities, various stuff … you walk through a wisp of filthy air … nothin but scraped-out tin cans lyin all over … it's somewhat of a junkyard … you hesitate … there's possibilities … what lies beyond the horizon? doubts begin to sneak in … another horizon … an beyond it … you walk, hesitate, but when you turn around, O soldier's delight and sutler, when you turn around and look back, dear sister … there's Egypt! Slavery! And ahead of you and around you … freedom.

I'll take it!

We nodded fervently, exchanging smiles and whispering, heh-heh, Jícha won't fool us with that one … nope, uh-uh.

I took it too, O sculptors and stone cutters, but I still wasn't rid of my passion for tinkering, for the simultaneous cultivation and degeneration of text, I longed for the workshop, O my brothers, and so I set out for Europe. With the Druzhba. Surely you remember years 1, 2, 3, etc., when we came crawlin outta the Sewer, slowly and cautiously, so the air wouldn't get us right away. But, O my brothers, before I struck out on my path I got tangled up in Kulchur … and maybe I ceased to be a slave, but instead I became a servant … to Kulchur sections … I had to deal with young authors and old texts, and go begging to ministers and banks and tomato importers, nothing against them! and wait in the wings and talk and be quiet and go psst! and toot! toot! in my mad dash to get … somewhere, but it made me lose my savagery, and if slavery kills and servitude tames, what's heavier? A kilo of fish? Or a kilo of flesh? And I saw what the others in Kulchur did, and it was appalling! Utterly useless! And that's what I was racing towards. Boredom of boredoms! Boredom of speech! A pond where the fish don't even fight anymore cause there's nothin left to fight over! They thought I was deranged … many didn't even know the basic rules of Schiller's robbers: Between you and your readership the only possibility is war … dear reader! Blitzkrieg is best. It's the only way. They messed with my articles so they'd be readable. The stupidity! These were the people who got the robber and put him on the wheel. I knew I had to get out before it turned nasty. Be careful! Watch your tongue. And that was all I had in those days. My editors greeted me thumbs down, I didn't have it easy there. Whispers and searches and speeches and slanders. First a meeting, then a meeting, and after that a conference. And paranoia. Kulchur sections, when I see you I keep my finger on the trigger! It's pulp and grit, and the Kulchur section servant's a flunky to the dwarf called Advertising. I'd get these visions: You know what you're gonna be when you die? Not yet, Boss … an earthworm? … a shoe rack? … or maybe … a Czech studies major, a queer? Nope, you're gonna be an aesthetics professor! Beggin your pardon, but that's harsh. An if you don't watch it, you know what you'll be even longer? No, Boss, what? A reporter in the Kulchur section of a mass-market weekly! Ai-yi-yi, oy vey. Jesus Christ! A health food bar and an ambulance. On the double! That was about the size of it. You know how it is, you canons and Capuchins, there was nothin anyone in Kulchur could tell me that I didn't already know … an you either, O collectors of charged objects, you know no chicken farm's gettin me. I longed to get away, turn my back on the carnival, I lurked by the side of the stagecoach routes … waiting for an opportunity. And then, O my brothers, I found out, the usual way, through the grapevine, about the Druzhba Homes for Artists. I'd been making my living as a young author, collecting heaps of prizes and hundreds of titles and a dochtorate or two in morality … totally pissed off everyone else … I knew I hadda get lost for a while … outside town they were building me an Arch of Triumph … I was eatin bay leaves … shootin gingerbread* … flyin on Pegasus, hangin from his tail … upside down … went all the way to Brno once to be on TV* an nod my head … other young authors an writers were hangin themselves, it gave me alleys … I was livin the life of a young author, livin like an animal … an my mangy drivel was published in Pekingese an Malaysian cantons, an in Paraguay too, cause I had lotsa pals, maintained various friendships … intertribal blood brotherhoods, bribery an flattery … an as my TV an radio plays started airin in Kitai, Slovač, Moravanian, Mordvinian, an Comedian, in tongues beyond an tongues apart, certain ink-spillers' jealousy membranes were so agitated that all sorts of anony-mous an homonymous threats an fiendish contraptions came pouring in, my wife hadda open em up in the kitchen, I threatened to take her computer away … yep, so just to be safe I split, took off to the Druzhba Homes for Artists … an when we arrived, all of us from the bad lands, in that nameless desirable country, my brothers, we were amazed … the Druzhba Cottages … an the stores! The stores in that rather isolated town, isolated so we could create in comfort without getting in the way, were filled with delight, with incredible packages … we feasted on vitamins … it was wonderful and beautiful … Bene! … the Romanians said internationally … Very bene! I replied happily … there in France … and in our cottages we were free to write poems and chisel titanic busts and sing arias … the Hungarian men and the Bulgarian women swapping hot peppers for sweet peppers … the Polish poets briskly bustling about … the Ossies measuring out gardens … the Kanaks tearing up floorboards and grilling boofalo … the Lithuanians, Estonians, and Latvians circling the Russian, eyeing his vodka … the old Chinese man practicing calligraphy … I looked out the window and laughed at the Slovaks, I was the smartest of all, the Czech! Yes, friends, I was there on behalf of the Czechs, somehow it had fallen to me … I wrote nothing but nonsense there … often it was so egregious I had to air out my room … and that desirable Belgian land told us: You're free an you have time … it was a gift from an organization of theirs called Kulchur, yes, just like home. And when I didn't feel like writing I would climb on my horse and ride, barking at German shepherds and cawing at ravens and vice versa, and then by the woods I saw wolves! I called out in greeting, but they were munching grass, and said: *Was?* There in that desirable country they hadn't killed off their wolves, they'd tamed them, O my brothers! I rode home an had feverish dreams an my tongue got tangled an mean. The next morning I called the caretaker, but he wouldn't talk to me … so I took a plane to the mountains, O my brothers, and climbed, you know where to, bosses and chiefs, to find a place of my own … an the first anthill was fenced in with wire mesh over it … to protect them, I laughed wickedly … and kept on climbing, and then I saw him! He circled overhead and came gliding down … but! The sun glinted off his talons, he had a ring on, O my brothers … and around his neck … a collar! He didn't speak … git, I shooed him off … and kept climbing and there was a wolf, and I cried, Brother, here's where you live! An he rolled over an begged … I fled down the mountain an went back to my cottage an subjected it to a thorough inspection … the floor was cracked … I didn't go down to the cellar … that was a little too scary … and I took a look around for the others … not as many as before … the nearest town was a long way … some couldn't stand to drink solitude, sang out their arias and went back home, or ran off to explore their possibilities in other parts of that desirable state … I stayed, my tongue a little wounded … and the days went by … the Ossies scattered throughout the country … their tongue was in the neighborhood … some of the others got lost among the supermarket shelves … the Russian's liver was in sick bay … the Balts went off to fight … the Bosnians were being drafted too … the Chinese man disappeared into Chinatown … the Kanaks hunted skinheads in the subway … the Vietnamese disappeared into Viettown … the only man left was the Hungarian, because no one understood him … the Bulgarians went on singing in those cracked voices of theirs, they were afraid to go into town … it was their first time outside their borders and they had no idea where they were … and then something happened … winter set in, and my cottage had no heat … and I, the young bard and writer, was reduced to warming myself with hard liquor … I drank a lot … truly considerably, you know me, you burglars and blackmailers … and I got scared to go to the supermarkets, because the pesky sales clerks kept forcing unfamiliar items on me, and how could I refuse as a guest and an author … and I forgot to wash and it showed on my tongue … which I began to neglect, I didn't know how long I'd been there anymore … and it started to snow … I ran out into the yard and screamed: Get back in your hole, I'm cold! But it didn't give a damn, it fell anyway. I felt myself getting stiff, and I knew a kilo of snow was heavier than a kilo of iron … one of the Bulgarian women comes up and says: Akva? Yest u tiebya sum akva? Akva minerala? Vasser, you mean? I ask stupidly. Nein, akva normal dlya drink ent … evrisink. For two days there'd been no water, O pardners and blood brothers … and I couldn't understand her too well, I think her voice had frozen over, ice fell from her mouth when she spoke. I crawled back to my cottage and into bed, under my comforters, and wrote, O bossmen and day laborers, using that ice. The windows wouldn't shut, I didn't get it … I drank liquor, O my brothers, and my liver grew heavy … I knew that erstwhile eagle wouldn't help me … bad! and when I tried to write at the desk, my kidneys got heavy too … there was a draft, now it was gettin nasty … the young author and writer there in that desirable country took ill … forced to warm body and soul by the flames of booze, because winter's an element too … it's everywhere … there's no escaping it, it gets everyone in the end … there was water at the Hungarian's … and the Chinese man had left behind a sack of rice … the Vietnamese their chopsticks … we stole it all … and at the Ossies' we found a stove! But it didn't even heat the Bulgarian's cottage … we'd drawn straws, she got the trick faster than us … that little stove wasn't for beans … the hot plate! shouted the Hungarian … we glanced at each other, amazed … that's right, O my brothers, we'd begun to communicate via extrasensory perception. What chou writin bout? said the Hungarian … oh, this an that, dynamite an pigs an bones, tongue stuff, you know, language … tumbled out of me … yeah, sure, that's my thing too, said the Hungarian, a young author and writer … the Bulgarian stretched out between the stove and the hot plate and rasped out a song: Hey hey dynamite, hoola hoola pig, hey hey boney-woney … we gave her some help with the chorus, we were authors after all … how bout we poke our noses inta the other cottages, see what they got, said the Bulgarian … we found all kinds of poems and translations and plagiarizations … the Poles had fat tragi-comic novels, the Romanians shepherd's pipes, the Ossies documentation, the Russians icons, we chopped up a couple pianos too and built a fire in the yard, I pulled what Wojaczek* had out of the flames and put it into my tongue … the Kanaks had lard, we fixed it up with liquor … I mixed it in with my tongue …

the next day we strapped on snowshoes and headed into town … but it was Carnival! An that means shops an cathedrals're closed! The people in that nameless, desirable country lived in a sort of coexistence with the state, so there were always a few days of reckless, intoxicated merrymaking … all over Sweden! … merry allegorical floats in the streets, bottle rockets and firecrackers, I got a nervous seizure … my eyes started tearing, but I wasn't crying, it was from writing, from sitting in bed in the cold for so long, staring straight ahead … we were puffy-eyed from lack of sleep, and dirty … but the people in masks walking past … I guess thought we were in costume too … disguised as some East bloc dogs … the vitamin people laughed at us … made a circle around us and started to dance … the Hungarian roared at them in Hungarian … they thought it was some folklore gag … the Bulgarian woman cursed … furiously … her face covered with scrapes from falling down drunk in her cottage … she looked the worst of us … some duded-up fellas an ladies walked up an started to talk in the local tongue … we didn't understand a whit … but then we realized they wanted the Bulgarian to be Carnival Queen, our masks were the best, they said … *authentisch* and *pintlich* and *super* … cowboys and draculas and sailors and devils swarmed around us in store-bought masks … we turned and fled … back to the cold … the Hungarian was thinking the same thing as me … we kicked in the door of the last villa … the singer stood lookout … we found an electric stove in the kitchen … grabbed all the food … the singer made sure we didn't wolf it down right away … the trip through the woods was awful, that stove weighed a ton … leave me here, the singer said, I don't live, so what, big fuckin deal … there's eight million of us … we carried the stove and then went back for her … chafing with chilblains … panting like dogs … at least we got some food in our stomachs … we dragged that stove home, step by step … not even talkin anymore … an there's no outlet! … just these weird, suspicious thingamajigs … so we crawled off into our cottages to create again … leaving that one little stove for the Bulgarian … she was a woman after all … some elementary chivalry remained within us … why didn't we all just climb into one bed? They were short and narrow … plus the one time we tried it, the bed collapsed … at least the wreckage was good for a fire.

I wrote and drank and the dreams came and went, my wife's anxiety weighed on me from afar, and that made my tongue … somewhere out there, my wife was playing computer games all night long … I was in bed too … but I was freezing. I worried about getting sick, but I was so sick already I didn't even know it. My head blew up like a balloon.

The three of us would meet by the phone and try to get through to the caretaker, but he'd either say something incomprehensible or just hang up. We thought about phoning home … I'll call up the hordes, said the Hungarian … don't do it, Attila, the singer said … you know how that turned out … we didn't want to tell the folks back home … what it was like here … we were ashamed we'd fallen into a trap, they all thought we were livin it up in some castle, they envied us … an it was obvious to us now what was goin on … the old Kulchur flimflam: Need to launder some cash? Just get yourself some artist type, give a little to him, a little somewhere else, it's all in the interest of the common good, an the wheel keeps spinnin an the tanker sails through the taxes, flag hoisted high … Kulchur figured we'd scoop up the cash, which we got the first day, an bolt … like everyone else there did … that's why the floors, that's why the windows, that's why the heating. An that carnival of ghouls in town. It was obvious why the artists from the desirable states used the cottages only in summer. We were idiots. Idiots. East bloc idiots. Toss in a bone! the singer croaked. An a pig an some dynamite, the young authors said. We went our separate ways to create.

And the days went by. And several days, O brothers and chiefs, I was touched by death. I knew I couldn't look over my left shoulder. It was there and it had time. I fought for my time and had visions. I lay in bed, only getting up to go to the bathroom, and sometimes not even then. The days rolled over me, sometimes fast, others extremely slow, and I forgot myself. But often I wrote. There were times it didn't work. My tongue slithered up from the pages and coiled around my neck. I was losing strength and that's what I wrote about. But death was out to get me. I would've put on my paint, leapt on my horse, and gone to meet death like a man, but I didn't have the strength. And besides, there was no horse, I made that up, or we would've devoured it ages ago. And after one distraught message from my wife, it struck me she was no doubt out there somewhere this very moment full of tenderness savagely fucking … striding along, hopeful of dark and dirty intercourse, of several in succession, or maybe coldbloodedly coupling. I had no charged objects there, nothing to help. My nerves were inflamed and my eyes kept tearing. All I could do was write, so that as the letters added up I'd know I was alive. My wife sent me anxious inquiries, and stayed home alone, playing computer games all night long. At least I knew she always prayed afterwards. I wrote:

My wife plays computer games all night long
she's alone
and I want to die
then she prays

and nothing else came to me, but I didn't put a period. I opened another bottle and wrote something different. And what I wrote, O hunters and chieftains, was a book, I wrote it in nothing but my own words, I was in a trap so I didn't give a damn if that book was hygienic … what came out of me, sisters and girlfriends, was blather, babel, and babylon, what it was, dear good she-demons and cuddly soothsayers, was a sort of lesser pornography with a humanist spin, and Prago-centric to boot, what it was, kind potential she-reader and nosy Nelly, was cheap trade, on the trashy side, but in my own slave tongue … so I'd no longer be a slave … but it was so powerful I coulda not even been … I hacked my tongue, and stroked it, and it gave it right back, my tongue was alive! And it's a secret and open tongue. And the days went by, and there were tough days and tougher days, and they mixed with the night, which could now set in at any time, because it was the night of my mind. And I began to seek out those black holes, something happened … I didn't want to write anymore … I was scared … but there was no stopping it, the book began to live its own life, feeding on me, and as it grew it squeezed me out of my room into the freezing cold, where even my breath couldn't warm me up. And I couldn't destroy the book either, because by then its tongue had devoured so much of me it was stronger, someone else would have to destroy it. But there wasn't anyone there.

I dragged myself outside one day to find no sign of my pseudodroog or -droo-gina. I was the last one. I said: Why me? And the answer came back: Why not? I was on the threshold, I was on my way … and the snow fell like it was nothing. Why wouldn't it? I thought, and went on writing my tongue, no longer a gift but a curse. Sometimes I told myself, as long as I'm here … just then Jícha raised his head from the typewriter and cried: But I'm still here! Jesus an Mary! And feeling a prick of dread he burrowed into his comforters and quick began writing again … so if anyone back in the little mother says anything about a castle … I'll kick their ass on the spot! And things began to happen … letters assaulted me, sentences wept … and all of a sudden I hear peep! peep! One of the letters was peeping at me. No big deal, a pretty trivial matter, the kind of thing that belongs in the Gwinness Book of Records. But then the letter sputtered and spat. It wouldn't stop acting up. I told it, knock it off an get back in line, move it! Took a look up close, eyes still watering … it was the ř! The little hook slightly quivering … an I was happy again for a while because I realized it was my treasure, I mean nobody else has that letter but Czechs, it's our national property, a rare an sacred gem! Anyone who doesn't work with ř is a furriner an a chauvinist! An their writing is nonsense … Then I heard footsteps, it was the Hungarian and the Bulgarian, they'd just gone off to try and rustle up a little something but were forced to turn back by the snowdrifts. Out in the woods they'd found one of the Romanians almost frozen solid, rattling on about highrise hotels … giant Ducks … Pepsi light and Pepsi heavy … gargantuan billboard people … he'd been living at some train station till all at once it hit him and he started trying to find his way back to the colony … he was a musician, but he never did find those pipes of his, the Hungarian and I gave him a few words of advice: dynamite, bone, sow … Langwidge! said the Bulgarian, and before he started writing we all sat down together and munched a few beechnuts he'd stolen from some tame wild pigs in the woods … he'd been surprised they didn't put up a fight. And the rest of the artists began coming back too … the Poles with sacks full of goods … the other Hungarians with goulash … the Vietnamese with old fish … the Russian, now cured, with caviar … and I sat and wrote. And then it came to me and I typed:

My wife plays computer games all night long
she's alone
I want to die
then she prays
and I'm still living.

I pecked the period and out came the sun. My eyes stopped watering. It was obvious. Unmistakable. I opened the window and shouted to the others. The Bulgarian was tanning herself, singing some mountain cantilena. The Kanaks were waving scalps in the air, wasn't much hair on em. The Hungarians and the Slovaks had occupied the sandbox and were building a dam. The Lithuanians were playing chess and checkers with the Russians, the Serbs were hugging the Croats, the Chinese were playing water polo with the Vietnamese, the Armenian was doing a handstand and the Azeri a cartwheel, that's what it looked like, a regular spring of nations. I stood proudly in the window, hair aflutter, I had a book! I screamed something at the Slovak, because I was the best, it was obvious, in a word … Czech! An I told that band of nationalist chauvinists, too. Which was funny, since you helmsmen and smugglers know very well what a loyal Czech I am, hah. Well, eventually it broke down into various scuffles an frictions. Skirmishes. A Russian and a Ukrainian locked themselves in the barn. But the pitchfork'd been stolen by some Bosnian ages ago. The Slovak swiped my clothespins, so I took an axe to bed with me. The Kazakhs brashly complained to the management about the food. Wanted more of those fuzzy dirty dumplings of theirs, bosnians, they call em.

Then the caretaker took us on a walk into town at last. It was so gracious, I nearly bled to death with joy. The town hall for example was gigantic. And we only crossed on green. Red means: Stop and wait! At least then we could gawk at the cars: Talk about hot rods, cruisers, an calibers! We were droolin … The tour moved on. But we couldn't get away with any hokeypokey or messin around. Look! The Bulgarian cried. The supermarket doors opened all by themselves! You just went up … one more step … an they opened! An step back … an they close! Incredeebeelay. I tried it out a few times myself. Everyone gathered around. The caretaker looked on indulgently. I was afraid somebody was going to get mad they didn't have doors like that back home and break them before I got a chance. I gave the English levers a shove, but shrewdly, so it'd look like the Chechen's fault. I broke it! Alarmed, we huddled around the miraculous doors, jabbering one over the other. But the caretaker didn't even get mad. And no one came racing out of the place with a cane. Strange. We went on. I was about to take the Bulgarian's hand, or grab her ass, I donno anymore, when someone tripped me up from behind. Lightning fast I spun an slugged the Pole behind me in the belly. But it wasn't him! It was the Albanian behind him. I recognized my mistake from his grin, but it was too late to back out. You dog! the Pole roared. Dog's blood! I roared back. Smallpox! the Pole roared. Cholera! I roared back. *Di do prdele!** the Pole roared. *Chłop zasrany!** I roared back. The others were quick to join in. I saw an Afghan kick a Russian in the head, a Bosnian put a Serb in a nelson … and off it went … the Chinese, Vietnamese, Cambodian, and Laotian women ran around, terrified, wobbling on their crooked legs … the Gypsies got a big laugh out of it, dipping into an open pocket or two. Here come the officers! On horseback! I quick made like nothing was up. The others also reined it in and began scanning the area for someplace to hide before the armored cars rolled in. But too late, surrounded! Nowhere to run. It looked like we could kiss our human rights goodbye. The Poles, the Afghans, and the Vietnamese started tearing up cobblestones and building barricades, a fancy car or two caught fire, loud prayers, weeping, and teeth gnashing all around. Anyone ready to tattle and at your service got off with a slap on the wrist. It still worked! The Kanaks charged the police ... I, admittedly, was a little hesitant, but I took advantage of my hesitation at least by stompin the Slovak's foot ... reinforcements arrived ... white overcoats ... some religious-type crosses ... and no beating or shooting ... some tricky new technology! They kept their distance, politely negotiating with us through megaphones ... put on some boring mellow music ... offered us gift baskets ... ham, potatoes, shrimp, everything ... old I.Q. Pavlov set to work ... we put our heads together ... they had us surrounded, we started crossing one another, nothing but: Forgive me, brother! Kind neighbor! Dear friend! May Mother Earth be my witness! Visegrad ... Sarajevo ... Gabčíkovo ... Hanoi ... Saigon ... Bucharest and Buchara, as long as I live ... an never again ... and then those desirable people at a distance offered us ... jeans and jeeps and cars and chateaus and chewing gum ... if we'd be good!

We gave ourselves up and boarded a bus. Then we drove down a stunning high-frequency highway, lotsa intersections, all kindsa lights, overpasses, underbends, concrete, no people ... an then Gejza notices the bus doesn't have any windows! There's glass but it won't open! We know this one, the Romanies roared, whipping out their razors. Never again! Same old tricks! *Churi des churi hudes!** Betrayed! Now comes the gas! Gas. *Plynyata,* the Croatians translated for their Serbian cousins, *plonovyeshcha,* the Russians translated for the Ukrainians, drinking vodka and kissing each other, *plynovodstvo! plynka! plynoubitiye! plynuii! plyndura! plygur! plona!* the Slavs lamented, the Asians still didn't know what it was, *bezpelészrzvéketil!* the Hungarian screamed. The Bulgarian singer kept pushing me off, I didn't get it, I mean we're gonna croak anyway, so why not gimme some? But she wanted to cross herself and curse the Bulgar-killers a few more times still. The Popes whipped out icons, the Navajos kachina dolls. Where're the jeans? the Albanians screamed, they're takin us to a concentration camp, the Ruthenians cried excitedly, wonder what it'll be like? And the shaman from Yakutsk whipped out his drum and horseshoes, and the bus came to a stop. We were at some gigantic town hall again, out in front were mayors, scientists, and doctors with medals. It was Timbuktu for all we knew. Someone started a rumor that the buses aired out automatically. A miracle! It's a miracle, declared the Galician Hasidim, tugging at their beards ... from the time of Abraham the Angel and the holy rabbis of Belz ... great, great wisdom and progress. Pff, bullshit, I said, showing off for the Bulgarian and a couple of Gypsies … they can take their acclimatization … an shove it! There's holes in the bottom! Hey, the guy's right, said one of the swarthy men. And then they led us inside for the reception. We ate like pigs. The Kanaks put jeans on their arms. After the cake fight, they washed us up and we read a few of our beautiful, sad, and bitter poems. We traded em around at random, an anyone that didn't know how to write got somethin written up for em in some tongue or other, no sweat. The artists unlingually reached into their warm-ups and sacks and whipped out their artefacts, pictures, cult figurines, and gallows. The mayors applauded that too. Success! We were a hit. Then they gave us the medals, an I got one of the biggest, cause I'm Czech! An that's somethin! That means somethin in this world, dammit!

Jícha raised his hands an went to wash em. Also rinsed out his mouth an gargled at length. Which meant we could speak without being called on: Good job, Jícha! You really got it goin over there! That was way Czech … progressive an deep, like the Stag Moat.* At least there was somethin goin on! Just no intelligentsia or small works,* there's various ways, various possibilities, there's many things out there! We know, we know, O beloved Jícha. We applauded our representative. An how bout the pseudodroogina? What's with the Balkan, huh? She still around? You guys write? Is she Varana or Ljubita, does she float like a butterfly or sting like a bee? Or both?

The whole thing's a little intricate, said Jícha, settling back down.

Hey, Jícha, but anyways. So how bout that book a yours, what'd ja write back there? Spider inquired.

Lost it soon as I finished, buried it somewhere, thing's unreadable, never mind talkin about it. I don't have it exactly. But the main thing is I'm back, no? East, west, home's the worst, eh? An also the best, isn't it? Why search for happiness abroad when you can find it at home with the family, huh? Yep, things're great here, an they're only gonna get better, right? But somethin's gotta be done. To wash out the filth. From this land. Our country. Yep, that's what I'm tryin to get at. This has been a little tale to welcome dear Potok into our midst.

10

**WHAT THEY WANT FROM ME. I GO OUT AN I'M NOT ALONE.
A GREEN LIGHT AND A WORD FROM SHE-DOG. AND THE MILL.
AND OUR DEAR TENANTS. HUNTER.**

Good to have you here, said Jícha. We're countin on you, Potok. Your tribe …
yeah, fine, but there's other outfits here. We're employin you! He yelped in my
face.

An we're a war outfit, he added in a deep voice.

Tribes, hmh, Hadraba stretched. It's a different era, man!

After a rapid-fire exchange of glances, Spider got up and said his goodbyes.

Jícha dumped some photos out of an envelope onto the table.

Look here, you got Olda, this here's Svoboda, then Nutcracker, Side Pocket,
Duchač, an who have we here? Jícha was plainly on cozy terms with the
collection.

So they're spooks, ess-tee-bee, what's the big whoop? The poet astounded me.
I wanted to know more.

Doesn't it strike you as interesting where our old enemies're turnin up now?
I arrange the private settling of scores. These pricks here just go right on playin
detective, pokin around the embassies, an even, get this, our friend Side Pocket
happens to be an occasional guest at a certain Asian embassy you're no doubt
familiar with.

I'm not interested in embassies, what's your point?

You guys're the ones that started this, you an that Organization a yours, an
you don't even know who you got in your own backyard.

You're crazy, what do our Laotians gotta do with the ess-tee-bee?

Well first of all, said Jícha, they aren't Laotians, at least not some of em.
They're Hmongs, he said triumphantly.

I don't get any a this, but if Hadraba here thinks he can take over their shops,
well I'd say it's gone far enough already …

No, that's not it, it's the spooks I'm after, said Hadraba. Side Pocket an this
bunch here. They're the ones interested in those Lotions a yours.

You tailin these guys or somethin? I asked.

We tail em, Jícha said proudly. Dostoyevsky, our private persecution agency.

Why Dostoyevsky?

Crime and Punishment, never heard of it? Powerful prose …

You're through with lyricism, I see.

Won't fill my belly. If you don't want the spooks interested in you, get interested in them, Jícha recited. I can't let you keep the photos, but take a good look at em. Remember these guys' handles. Some of em you know. I don't like tellin you this, but there's certain … indications … that they're in on a few things with the Laotians, that is the Hmongs.

So what's this really about, Jícha? I don't trust you.

Could be anything, ideology's down the crapper, that leaves cash, he livened up. Christ, I mean we did amazing trade with these countries, an the KGB an our idiots were in on it. Look, Semtex, weapons, drugs … we're talkin billions … in dollars, an you think those scumbags're gonna give it up? Debts, liabilities, secret couriers, under-the-table expenses, established channels, Jícha was delirious.

Get a good look at these mugs, an if any of em start buzzin around, get word to me or Rudy. Or drop by here. Those Hmongs a yours draw em in like bugs to a lamp. We'll let the mosquitoes get a little suck, an then bam! the hero thumped his fist on the table.

A little suck, an whose blood, Jícha?

I don't remember now what his answer was, but whatever he said it came true. In a different way, in a different place, and by then he wasn't around anymore.

Hey, I don't wanna see those ugly mugs anymore … ever again.

That's the whole thing, Jícha slammed his fist down. Christ, no one wants to, but I mean we gotta put these guys to the wall!

Hadraba nodded solemnly. Member the Šistecký case? he asked.

Yeah.

Recently, briefly and over breakfast, the Šistecký case had been a nationwide source of amusement. The papers were full of it. Unidentified perpetrators had given a certain sadistic ess-tee-bee scumbag from the fifties the classic forty-eight treatment from the eighties. Kidnapped him, locked him up in a cellar for two days, and then let him go. It was a just demonstration and provocation. The Communist Party declared him a victim of terrorism, which he was. The martyr's hair turned gray, he didn't know how long they'd leave him there. Rightfully he'd expected to have a few of his own interrogations performed for him on a new stage with a revised cast. No one beat him up though, no one even spoke to him.

Yep, that was us, said Hadraba. An that's just the beginning. You read about Major Razseda?

That'd been in Poland. They'd killed him. And his wife.

Yep, jailer bitch, just like the rest. An Honecker! We don't give a damn what deals the new governments made with the old ones. This is about concrete individuals ... these guys ruined ... lotsa lives ... they gotta pay. The folks that were in the camps're old, lots of em're dead, it's up to us. Sooner or later. I mean a lot of us've got active experience. You too, Potok.

Aright, aright, I said. But I got my own life.

You're a racketeer! Jícha sputtered.

My business, I said. I'm not goin in with you guys.

If you're not with us ... Hadraba said with a laugh.

I've heard that one somewhere before.

Yeah an you'll hear it again, it's the leitmotif of every community, said Jícha. What about Čáp?

He's a nut, said the poet. Ravin on about earthworms.

An you about people!

Worms don't have souls!

You donno beans, porter!

Degenerate sectarian!

Don't argue! Hadraba barked, and we stopped.

You still got a chance to play ball with us. Know this guy? Jícha tossed another photo on the table. It was the Shark Hunter. Only he had glasses and a European suit on, and no tattoos on his face.

No. I refuse to testify.

Závorová.

That got me, now he was talking about the light of my life, my one miserable hope, and he was smiling.

I'll keep an eye out, ask around, I said. Laotians, Mongs, Kanaks, what do I care.

Lemme explain, that repulsive person said, drumming his fingers on the tabletop.

The Hmongs live on the border between Vietnam and Laos. The ess-tee-bee's interested in this guy. Someone hired em, maybe the KGB. The factories here were fulla Vietnamese, an their agents. Some worked for the Sovs. But this guy, Jícha tapped the photo, he must be somethin special, he just came now.

Seems kinda wild to me. I find it hard to believe.

Never let anything surprise you.

I've heard that one too.

Well here's somethin you haven't heard: this guy speaks Czech.

Aw baloney, now I started laughing.

See, you do know him! shouted Jícha. That's proof!

Learned that one in the spookhouse, huh.

I picked up a few things.

Bowdlair, "Carrion," know it? I asked.

Sure, how could I not? You had that moron too? The one with the forehead? We don't have a handle on him yet.

No doubt you'll track him down, I said sarcastically.

Spare the sarcasm. It might come in handy later.

We went on sparring like that till we'd had enough. Said some sort of goodbyes to each other.

Though it was still pretty early, I didn't feel like sticking around the bar, Padre Booze had already left. Maybe I'll look him up sometime an talk him outta livin at the Dump, persuade him to move in with us, no doubt that'd be a worthy deed. The street was empty, dark. I felt a twinge of anxiety, I didn't like what Jícha had pulled on me back there. Why go diggin around in old stuff when time's flyin like a mad horse ... but there was somethin strange about Hunter, that photo with the glasses, it was definitely him ... gone were the days when we mixed up the Laotians ... he stood out as the only one with a powerful build, plus he was the chief, had authority ... gotta peek at a map, see where it was he hunted those sharks, I made a note to myself, striding along a street lighted only by windows, the streetlamps were broken ... my city, me, I talk with this city. An I got nowhere to run to. So I look.

I picked up the pace through Prague 5, with its dilapidated old gardens, the bushes' slender arms reached out for me, beckoning me inside the bars, into the heavy stench of soil and rotten leaves ... yeah right, I thought, I also felt bad I couldn't tell my buddies ... this was my business, but what if Hunter ... then we'll get rid of him somehow, I'll see.

The pavement was broken in spots, but I like to jump ... by the time I got to Liberation Avenue I was feeling pretty weary ... but not enough to drown out the anxiety … my temples throbbed, today was too much, as usual … the run-in with the hitlers had been short but tough, the talks at Černá's had culminated quite unpleasantly, plus if they knew about her … it might also be bad for She-Dog … an me! The day should've been at an end by now, I just wanted to be with my tribe … an fast … a person or two walked the avenue … APOTHEKE, a big pharmacy on the corner blinked in green neon, the light was strange and sharp, and I sensed somethin still in the air … Don't take it easy! I howled to myself, following the example of my Hungarian great-grandmother, mother to a smuggler, an skidded to a halt … A car had been followin me for two blocks, here the streetlamps were on, so I used the old shop window trick an caught its reflection in the glass. Just before the pharmacy I noticed a bookstore, an I'd love to have She-Dog here now! maybe she could shrink me down an slip me into the pages of some, if possible, noble-minded book, cause old actor Potok is more or less all danced out for the day.

I came to a stop beneath one of the lamps, and to make damn sure they could see it was me, I lit up a smoke right in front of my face.

Engine cut, the car quietly glided toward me through the night air, big an black, the way they like em … I leaned in the window to find Side Pocket staring right back at me. Hadraba'd named him that after the spook kicked him in the balls. Those eyes hadn't changed. Once upon a time I'd had the chance to see them cloud over with rage, the black dots of his pupils rising out of the mist of his psychopathic gaze like two pinheads, the shafts buried in his brain. Once upon a time I'd been afraid of him, once upon a time I'd dreamed of killing him, but that's a whole different story. He laughed.

Surprised?

Yep. Government fall or what?

Not yet, citizen, said the other one, Jícha had shown me his photo too, Viška was his handle, and seeing him now in the flesh I had a hunch I knew him too …

What're you doin here? Why're you followin me?

An what's it to you, sir? He didn't mean the *sir* seriously.

I'm callin the cops, you got no right to hassle me … just be glad you're not in the slammer. I stepped away.

Side Pocket practically moaned with pleasure: Just a second, just a sec, hey, look here. I turned around to find a badge in my face: Enigma Private Detective Agency. He smiled blithely. We're still cops! An good ones!

I can't believe it. You guys even got pistols?

Peashooters too, he squawked with glee, we're clean not mean, ha-hah. Pay attention now, though. You an your buddies might've gotten yourselves in a bad situation, an we can help. Get in back, let's go for a ride.

No thanks, I've got a physical aversion.

You'll be sorry, said Viška, you've got no idea what kind of mess you're in. We're just … regular employees now.

Just doin our job, added Side Pocket, cockily honking the horn.

Climb in, said Viška.

Just a little ride, said Side Pocket.

No, I said.

Don't think we donno who you were talkin with just now, said Side Pocket.

An maybe the guy you were talkin with wants you to know that we know, said Viška.

An maybe not, said Side Pocket, giving another honk.

I couldn't care less, I said, stepping back from the car in case they got any dumb ideas, and also to get a better look at Viška … those shoulders …

Mr. Viška, I said.

Ah, Mr. Potok has seen the snapshots. Yep, those were the days, those were the days, so many names, you know.

There was a moment of silence. Me standing, them sitting. I knew that one.

So, see you again, Mr. Potok, yes?

I don't think you'll be going to heaven.

Hah-hah, good one, said Viška, waving goodbye. Side Pocket put the car in gear and finally they took off.

I realized I was sweating. Will we ever get rid of those spooks? No. Or just one way. If by a sheer twist of fate, instead of a velvet takeover there were a lesser civil war, and if good triumphed over evil, at least for a while, those two'd probly hang. Enigma Agency, laughable. Damnable.

I walked on, considering and speculating, till I came to the pharmacy on the corner and there stood Černá, under the neon, leaning against the grille with one hand, looking at me through green eyes, and my heart stopped.

It's closed, fuckin slaves, she said.

What do you need?

Nothin you got.

She seemed a little … wobbly, clearly she wasn't doin too hot. She looked … ready to travel … she never looks the same way twice. Dark jacket, dark pants, tall boots. Hood. Around her neck a thin thing, gold maybe. No silver stuff, no jewelry either. Small scar on her chin, never noticed that, I realized. I'd never seen her up close like this before. She came across as the fairly guarded type, momentarily in distress. Hair raven-black. Shorter than I remembered. She was looking at me. Bathed in the neon's glow, my palms, when I glanced down, were tinted green … we stood there in that tent of light, the streets and their darkness all around, my mouth was dry. Černá cocked her head sideways, studying me, must've known me by sight … she's drunk, it struck me. Somewhere overhead a lightbulb burst and a gentle rain of shattered glass floated down to our feet.

I guess it's her, I said to myself.

Yes, said She-Dog.

Before I could notice whether Černá had moved her lips, she slumped sideways, still holding onto the grille but leaning on me now, I felt her cheekbones against my face, her hot breath on my neck, wrapped my arms around her, she would've fallen.

I need a man … now … a guy I can lean on, she said drunkenly, but … she hiccuped … I shoved him, he fell. You … flag me a cab. I wanna go home.

Very cautiously and very gently I pushed her back, peeled her hand off the bars, gripped her by the shoulders, and propped her up against the grille.

I took off her hood. She drifted off into relieved microslumber, but there was a dream, her eyelids were quivering. Her hair color swept off the wings of a black bird. Couple silver ones … face pale an fragile, a sharp wrinkle or two at the corners of her mouth, hair curled around her ears. She-Dog never told me when I met her she might need to lean on me, it took me by surprise, maybe what was left of my power was there to protect someone …

What're you doin? Quit screwin around, I told you you can come over. She stood there, legs spread, eyes open, looking off over my shoulder … I gave her a shake.

I'm tellin you, it won't work. It hurts! Flag a cab. Please, she whimpered.

So I did. Holding her up with one arm and waving with the other.

Take off my jacket, she said after a while. I think I'm wasted.

What for … it's not warm.

But she insisted.

One guy stopped, but then got a look at us in that tent of green light and drove off again. Not the next one. I took her cold hand in mine and led her to the cab, spread-legged and teetering, it probably looked hilarious, but there was a strong emotion in my heart. Tilting drunkenly, she tossed her jacket on the back seat, sat down on it, and slammed the door. Just then I noticed drops of blood on the sidewalk, leading from the spot where she'd been standing, it had soaked right through her pants.

If you don't mind, boss, I'll take the cash in advance, said the cabbie.

Wait. The address, Černá, the address!

She said it. The man rolled down his window. I gave him something.

Then I walked through the city to the home of the tribe, through the labyrinth of my world, where I live, and in my heart was peace. Because now I knew I'd found her, I gave She-Dog thanks and my power grew, I think. Just a few matters to settle an I can forget the spooks … tell my tribe see ya, the byznys path has been great an all, friends, but my motion diverts me … an on my frequent visits I'll watch as Micka glows an Sharky gnashes his teeth an Bohler meditates an David … we were five … hope David's thumbs're healin up … it didn't even cross my mind that Černá might not want me.

I walked down our street past the burned-out Laotian temple, it was already boarded up, the boys hadn't been idle. Now that I knew I was so close to a Zone … and that it didn't work on me … there was plenty of time to get used to it. I walked into the building and into Bohler's place and there they all sat. Bohler's head was wrapped in bandages. My pseudodroogs were very abnormally quiet and downcast, I sensed it right away. Both the flat and the building had been cleaned up since the battle, but whatever it was I'd sensed in the air on Liberation Avenue was back again.

What's up?

Take a seat, Potok, said Bohler. We know bout your thing, that guy Rudolf was here. An we know we're in a Zone, that'll be dealt with later. An we also know bout the Martian.

What's up?

Better take a seat, pal, he nodded, I've already explained to those present that the end of the Organization's gonna bother you least of all anyway.

Heh, so, what's up? I pointed my chin at David. He lay there, head propped on the table, bandaged thumbs dangling down at the end of his arms. Bohler walked over to him and put them up on the table. His arms seemed unnaturally long for his frame, but it was probably just the gauze. He didn't move.

He's in bad shape, said Sharky. It took a lot out of him.

Sharky was on the pale side too, gnawing his nails in the chink of his razor-sharp face.

Micka! Buddy, pseudodroog, you look awful!

The helmsman had aged. His glow was gone. He smiled wearily.

I'll run through it one more time for Potok's sake, least it'll gimme a chance to get used to it.

First of all, the hitlers destroyed all our papers, apart from what we've got in the safe-deposit box at Early Bird Megabank … but they made off with all the cash, that means operations, salaries, bonuses, miscellaneous … a couple m., fine, that's my fault …

Aw baloney, said Sharky.

Nonsense, said Bohler.

I shook my head.

All right, it's not … but Early Bird was a front for Salman Brothers, an those guys went under, our rating from the computer samurai was quite unparalleled, you see. The bank flopped worldwide. Bad luck, maybe I should've looked into em more …

Did what cha could, pseudodroog, no one doubts it, said Sharky, the foreign minister.

Bog giveth, Bog taketh away, I accept it in peace, said Bohler.

Yes, I said. What's up with David, has Hradil seen him?

Just wait, we'll get to that, said Micka.

Where're the girls? I asked.

They left for the Laosters', they can wait till the Zone's cleaned out, but …

The Laosters're all gone?

No, Hunter's around, that's on the agenda, but wait … basically, Potok, we're wiped out! Micka roared.

I didn't realize, you know? An today I met … my sister …

You've got a sis? someone asked.

Yeah! Yeah, but apologies.

There's money scattered around various banks, except that as you know most of it's in receivables, the big invoices can wait, you know how it is, but we're swimmin in little ones, yep, of course then there's bonds an principals …

I didn't understand a word, and Bohler was nodding but I could tell his mind was elsewhere. Sharky was probably the only one who had a clue.

… so it'll take all the gold we have to keep the fabrics in motion, an not for long. So that 5 m.'s actually all there is, an that's goin to the Zone, an Rudolf knows it, so we can take our pick. Bust, or jail, or both, or bust.

What jail? I perked up a little.

Goldie tricked us. Micka said gloomily. It was real simple. Bought off customs an probly also had a deal with Rudolf, I'm just guessin on that. Those gadgets weren't clean.

Yeah, they never were, I said.

Micka raised his eyes to the sky. He doesn't get it. You're out of it. Nothin we did was totally clean, but the way that Goldie breached the contract it put us in breach too, there's nothin we can do. That's the way it is. The stuff didn't come here in the gadgets from Thailand, we were watchin for that, it went from here over there!

The era is overtaking us, Bohler said thoughtfully.

That's intense! I had to say something.

That Goldie's a real scumbag, said Sharky.

In other words warpath, I said, but I felt fatigue.

No. First of all, he's gone, Micka continued, disappeared as soon as he got us, an second, it already happened. We're defenseless against him.

I was surprised but relieved.

But now comes the main thing, Micka said. We dissolved the contract.

No way, my throat constricted.

Micka went on: Me an Sharky made a move with that water mill you were working as the interpreter on with Lady Laos …

But I always said it was a power plant!

Same difference, said Micka, it's an outstanding government liability … it sat in the Sudan for years, they had a war there, as I'm sure you know, an the new government refused to pay the debt … it was available for two … Micka got up. Go on, Sharky, I can't, I don't wanna.

Where's the Fiery? I asked.

Right in front of you, someone answered.

We put everything we had into it, almost everything, said Sharky … funny thing was, the government backed out … there was no way to negotiate directly with the Sudan, it went through various middlemen, Mozambique, Argentina, the cash is laid away, that's all right, it was IOUs, careful now, we didn't lose a thing, only, Sharky sped up, it was an old bolshevik front an now the rockets're in Libya.

Rockets? I didn't get it.

Yeah, plus equipment. They were Russian, actually ours an the Soviets', belonged to the Warsaw Pact but they were Czechoslovak, Czech after the split, I guess … no one knows.

So how'd they get there? Libya's a long way.

Well, they just shipped it in off the books with the Organization's velvet reputation as the guarantee, I mean not entirely, again it all went through somebody else, but we were the ones that cleared it an everyone else was hands off … almost everyone, couple a Swiss are in on it … An the Poles an the French … but that's not for sure, added Micka. Tell him the rest, Sharky.

Some stayed in Libya an some's … Sharky lowered his voice an said almost too softly to hear … in Iraq. An the Palestinians got some an, gentlemen and brothers, I'm going home. We've gone bust an it's been nice, up to now, but I gotta be on my way.

It's too fast for me, I said.

Everything's fast, Bohler noted.

Where'll you go, Cassock, I asked.

Out to the Gobs', I guess. To the Rock.

I still don't get it, I'm sorry, but you know that transnational byznys stuff never was my … we sold rockets to Libya … an some other places … an they can pin it on us?

Can now, said Micka. If they wanna.

How could we screw up like that?

It happens, said Sharky, these fronts stay underwater for years sometimes. There's just one consolation for me in all this: that we got caught on an old anchor.

An the Zone, don't forget, said Bohler.

Get it now? someone asked me.

Yeah. But I was lying. I might've got that we were broke, that we were wiped out byznys-wise, and that … we'd violated the contract and were a bad tribe, and I knew what we had to do now, and what I ought to do too, I shook my silver ornaments an stroked my hair … but what I didn't get was we were splittin up, that Sharky was takin off, so was Bohler, an probly everyone else too … I still didn't get that the tribe had fallen apart, that we'd be without protection … I looked around at the others, they were thinking the same. What's up with David?

I went over to him and lifted his head, it was … a mask of a face, it frightened me, that gourd look, it was spooky …

Well, said Bohler, Hradil thinks that David … that he's gone insane.

What? I recalled our recent encounter in the warehouse, the weird way David had rattled on, confusing me with Novák.

Today he's just … I donno, said Micka, scratching his head, not talkin at all … Helena was with him the whole time, an she wanted to take him away, but we figured since there was a briefing …

… the custom oughta be preserved to the end, Bohler added.

Maybe he'll get over it, I said, maybe he caught some pain in the neck or whatever from the hitlers …

Hradil … look, there's just too much today, said Micka.

Hradil said to leave him alone, that it's shock, temporary paralysis …

Damn it, tell him the truth, Sharky snapped, I mean we all know it.

Hradil said he'll probly … that it's probly for good.

No, I said, and I could tell that even though the others knew it was true, it was still too much for them to digest.

Maybe Hradil made a mistake!

He doesn't make mistakes, you know that.

We were all tired, but we couldn't scatter through the building and leave David there by himself … it didn't occur to us to call up one of our pseudo-drooginas … maybe it'll ease up when Helena gets back. Those two spent a lot of time together.

There's one more thing, Bohler said, clearing his throat. It's about Hunter. I was waiting for Potok.

I froze stiff.

It's about that attack today … those two Laotians that got killed … an that's not all … I guess you noticed the lawn out back is trampled, totally ruined …

Yeah, I nodded, the others too.

There's this thing Lady Laos told me … when the hitlers came bustin in, slashin an bashin, I was out in the street, as you know, Bohler ran a hand over his bandaged head with a bit of a smile, a proud one I think, the thing is, when it started, what tenants we had left came tearin outta the buildings, but then they saw the hitlers were only goin after the Laotians … an yours truly … so they turned around an went out back an stood there clappin an eggin em on, they stomped down all the grass back there an showed em how to get into the shop, not only did our tenants not call the cops or the firemen … they applauded … the Laotian women took their kids an hid in the cellars, an when they smelled the smoke an saw the flames they figured the stalingos had set the place on fire … so they start passin the kids out the bars to the neighbors, those brutes had all the exits blocked so they couldn't escape … the neighbors didn't give a damn though, an Kučera from number three, he was crocked as usual … an he goes up to the window … an just stands there lookin while the women're stretchin their arms through the bars to pass the kids out to him … an he whips out his dick an pisses through the bars all over those kids in the cellar … an Lady Laos told me the Laotians' opinion is that won't do, an Hunter's here waiting.

I don't know which of us screamed, but it was a mighty scream.

Well, maybe Kučera's not so dumb he didn't split, someone said.

Unfortunately the idiot's still here, said Bohler. Vasil's guarding him in case the Laotians … in case of anything rash. But they said it's up to us.

We didn't have to nod our heads and jingle our silver for long.

It's obvious, said Micka.

Sharky just gave the sign.

Aright, I said, what else can we do.

I'll take responsibility too, said Bohler.

But Hunter wants you to go with him, Potok.

I remembered the photo of Hunter looking like a computer samurai or a perfect agent, which can be confused … and the way he used to walk around the buildings in that rag of his, with his tattooed face and that shark-tooth necklace … I didn't relish the idea … and it showed.

Lady Laos told me Hunter was extremely depressed an embarrassed that he stabbed you, an it's a great honor that he wants to take you along, she said any one of his people would be thrilled to be chosen … when honor's at stake.

Yeah, aright, I'm honored.

Hunter smiled when he saw me walk into the courtyard, bonjour, he said. I looked around, we were alone.

You needn't bother, I know you know my language.

Excusez-moi?

Aright then: Je sais que vous parlez tchèque.

Non, excusez-moi, je parle français, pas beaucoup.

Have it your way, I'm tellin you though, the ess-tee-bee's after you, I mean the cops … no wait, not cops … underground cops … komunisten banditen, vous connaissez?

Non.

Fine, fine. On y va.

And we went.

Vasil stood outside the door. Bot iz dere hiz voomin, he said. I come heer, I bek him, I say him, run fest! He no unnerstant notink, durak!

His business. Get outta here, Vasil … but don't go to the cellar, go to the priest, harasho?

Da.

I'd barely knocked when the door swung open. There was his voomin, they made a cute couple. Both were big drinkers and he had a slightly criminal past, none of that bothered us. My memory of Kučera, a shard: typical Czech guy, in his fifties, the type you see hangin around the trash cans on your street from time to time. Carrying out the garbage in his undershirt. Sweating. Likes soccer, TV, meat, porno, his money, his memories, his car, doesn't love anything. Coexists with his wife. Beats her every now and then, or she beats him, their business. They had a son. He took off. Wouldn't surprise me if he'd taken up with the scamps. Wouldn't've hesitated if I were him.

When we first took over the buildings, it was an extreme shock for some of our tenants. Instead of their people from the old national committees, suddenly they were required to consult our amulets and hardware. Kučera had a problem with it, but Bohler persuaded him. And they all discovered there were certain benefits to having us as bosses. We didn't always bother to collect rent, for instance. We'd just forget, plus I think Bohler, whose job it was … felt sorry for many of our lodgers.

Please, ma'am, I think it would be better if …

I'm not goin anywhere, mister.

Listen, there's been an incident …

The place smelled like somethin was burning … an cabbage … her face was red, eyes puffy from booze, or maybe tears, or both … tousled hair … she held on to the door.

I stuck my foot in. Hunter stood quietly behind me. She saw him.

I'm not goin anywhere, if he dies, I ... it'd be the music of paradise for me ... go ahead, mister, squash the louse, you donno the life I've had ... you donno shit! she flung open the door ... Hunter slipped inside.

Don't be silly, ma'am ... go on, leave ...

Don't you try to run me out ... mister ... she followed Hunter in, I couldn't stop her. Kučera stood at the window, on the table a bottle of beer and a newspaper, staring at us in disbelief. Hunter stepped in front of him and turned to me.

Il connais rien. Vous parlez pourquoi ...

Oui. Yes, I'll tell him.

Hey, get cher ass outta my flat an take that gook wit cha. Mařena, call the cops ...

You brought it on yourself, Pepa.

Mr. Kučera, not only did you not help, but ...

I looked at Hunter, he didn't have anything on him, but then I looked at his hands and it was obvious he didn't need anything else.

Goddammit, you can't do this, we got laws ya know, get cher ass outta here!

Unfortunately, Mr. Kučera, you've just violated every law there is. And I told him how.

Mařena, no, you can't ... you wouldn't.

But she did. I turned to Hunter: Il connais, maintenant, je pense, and I followed her out.

Before making my way back to the pack, I wandered the halls a while, just to unwind. It was obvious the other tenants had left. But not all of them, somewhere downstairs I heard a radio, a fork clinking against a plate. But the sounds were lacking their usual dimension. No fights, no weeping, no new humans' laughter, no opening and closing of doors, or clatter of high heels, no old granny shuffling up the stairs ... to gossip, no fella in a blue jumpsuit stepping out from around the corner. No one luggin a baby carriage, alone, till someone comes along to help. Just the building's old, heavy smells. Sad. And downstairs the Zone.

I quickened my gait.

11

All right, Number Five is here, Bohler welcomed me.

They called me that sometimes because I was The One Who's Usually On The Way, and generally they had to wait a little before I came bounding in … but it didn't bother them, I was working for the common cause.

I think it's time, said Bohler, beginning to unravel the silver from his hair. Guess we'd better go to the forge, huh?

Guess so, said Micka. On the table lay a pair of scissors and a razor.

No, said Shark Stein. I had a dream.

We all froze. Night had finally come at the end of a long day. We hadn't expected this.

What's the use of self-criticism? said Micka. The tribe's dissolved.

I don't want self-criticism, said Sharky. I had a dream.

We took our seats. For the time being we left our silver alone. And our hair. We just let it hang down.

You know, O skippers and brothers, that I'm merely the bearer of the dream an I don't mean to insult the community with some kina worthless opinion. But it was a very long, hard dream, an I'm not sure I understand it, but I think it wasn't meant just for me, I got it so I could share it. It picks up where Number Five's dream left off, an now I know why in his dream I was flyin in front of him. In my dream, O brothers and bluebloods, there are many snares an puzzles, an it's not for everyone. It's a dream about dreams an charged objects, the tribe, the end of tribes, the individual, an Possibility. In case you've got questions, here's my answer: I had the dream today, when I couldn't get outta the box, while you guys were fightin the stalingos.

As I sensed the voice enter Shark Stein, I took a look around at my neighbors. Cassock had his eyes shut, Helmsman sat resigned, knowin the next thing to come wasn't a byznys day but the exorcism of the Zone. David just lay on the table, an there was anguish for him in our hearts. Sharky spoke:

My dream's also about what the earth is. An you have to hold out till the end,

O fibbers and squealers, because then I'm going to give you a Possibility.

Go for it, cruel Sharky! Bring it on! We're ready! we cheered on the Scheherazade, settling in more comfortably.

My dream starts where Potok's left off. We were flyin over the field of bones an then we came to the Face, an it was kind an glowing, an the same thing happened to me as to Potok: I was flyin in the lead, you know that, O pimps and shoplifters, but all at once the Face turned hard an rough … evil … an all the kindness drained from my arteries an veins, an they grew heavy with blood, an I was scared, a great fear came, you murderers and marauders, an as the dread circled inside my skull my vision dimmed … an the Face constricted into the grimace of the Evil One, a hardwood mask. An then suddenly, you perjurers and falsifiers, I was lyin in the grass an I saw you, highwaymen and brigands, in the grass beside me. We must accept these lives too, I thought, and when I looked again I saw you, Micka, as Brawler, in a tattered fur with blood dripping from a gash in your hand, you, Bohler, as Sad Man, sword in one hand, hammer in the other, and you, Potok, as The One Who Leaps, leaning on your spear, and you, Kral, you were unarmed. And I was The One Who Is In Many Places, and I had a bow and quiver but few arrows. And our eyes, dear conquistadors and infant slayers, were all turned in the same direction, toward the wooden idol of our god, the one farther back in time's memory than even the city's Starry Bog. We were gazing into the face of Svantovít, lord of lightning, supreme god of the Elbe dwellers, The One Who Drinks Blood From The Heart Of Darkness And Renders His Children's Enemies Lame And Fearful, and despite our wounds and hunger and fear of our pursuers, we were happy.

We were the people of a tribe that had gotten under the wheel, or into the scissors, as I believe, dear huntresses and she-judges, is the term in fashion round the Pentagon these days. But in our tongue of the time we said: under the hammer. And this Svantovít … he was no lightweight flower-and-sheep lover, as our revolting Marxist teachers claimed … he was an idol of rage for the old people of Bohemia, which of course in those days was called something different … the wood of this statue had been drenched countless times in the blood of sacrifice. The more sacrifices there were, the stronger our idol and the more strength it gave us to hunt fresh victims. It's only logical. But our teachers didn't tell us that, it was forbidden. They had to say the new, modern-day man was different, more amazing, better. Extremely gifted, they told us, you recall, you psychopaths and paranoiacs. They didn't tell us anything. So we had to find out for ourselves. We served Svantovít and he protected us. Only … we were a small tribe, and even though we had many young warriors … one by one they fell in battle … and as a result there were more women and girls in the tribe than men … priestesses, sisters, girlfriends, and brides, very many indeed … we couldn't keep them satisfied … we were too worn out from brawling … so they decided we had to move on, butcher a nearby village or two and bag them some guys and boofalos … why should I be givin birth all the time, said one, it's a pain, let's just steal someone else's kids, what's the diff … so we obeyed the mighty Eva, O my brothers, you idol worshipers and fanatics, and sallied forth … leaving the statue of Svantovít behind … we were proud and thought we had strength enough … we wiped out a few settlements of soft people and bagged some guys for the women so they could find satisfaction in the arms of slaves … so they'd shut their mouths and stop complaining … we preferred hunting and hacking … only then we got under the hammer.

We had the Pšovans pressing us from the north, the Axe People closing in from the south, the Zličans' sturdy stockades before us, and suddenly the Curly Heads charged from the rear. A classic hammer and pincers. At first we fought back … but they kept pressing and pressing us … we fell into booby traps … the women started grumbling again … we even considered a truce … temporarily … that's how much of a mess we were … dunces, Eva scolded us, why'd you leave Svantovít there? Fools, see if I sleep with you again … but she was the one who'd decided not to drag it along! It was unjust! As things got worse and worse, our only strength was fear … it was kill or be killed … no more killing out of exuberance and joie de vivre … now the tables were turned and we were the hounded ones … we had to leave our old people behind in the woods, there was no one to carry our charges … we'd already lost all we owned anyway … fleeing. And then we came to the deep forest, the hunting ground of the Lemuz tribe, an especially hateful and brutal horde of subhumans who'd formed an alliance with their age-old enemies the Doudlebs in order to crush us. After we managed to fend off their attack, our female comrades put all the little children to death … we knew what awaited them otherwise … surrounded on all sides by inconceivably loathsome tribes … we began to resign ourselves to the thought that the human race would soon be extinct … the women also took up arms … in battle they were even more savage than us … it was out of the question that they would end up with some other inconceivably loathsome guys that didn't know how to do things right … they knew we wouldn't be bringing them any more slave boys to put through the paces … like us, the only thing they could do was appeal to Morana, goddess of death and winter … they touched our ribs and led us into battle … all we had to eat was roots … and apples.

We got pulverized in that last awful battle, only thirty of us turned up at the agreed spot afterwards, the tribe was devastated. There were just three women left … where's Eva? we wondered, she was powerful, gave us strength … she was wounded … and one of us had to kill her and bring the rest her hair, so it wouldn't fall into enemy hands, we divided it up … we have to get back to Svantovít, we've got no choice … but the prospects were poor … of us making it all the way through those savage inhuman tribes … we were ambushed by runts in the swamps, we'd never seen such inhumans. They carried wicker shields with a turtle painted on them and their bodies were coated in mud. They attacked screaming Ninja! Ninja! and killed two of our comrades. Then we encountered the Croots, with whom we had once maintained a shaky alliance, since they were as pitiless as us, it made sense to join forces and hunt down those who were weaker … but the Croots turned us over to the Chebeks, whom we'd tyrannized since time out of mind, in return for boofalo and slaves … only a few of us escaped … the women had all fallen, and without their presence, their other fragrance and other agile moves, we were done for … we needed to steal some women … but out of eight men to start with, just five were left, and one of them was Kral … who didn't even carry a weapon, the nut, he'd only survived by a miracle … for days on end he'd just doodle in the sand … whatcha doin there, Kral … we teased him … hey doodler, come have a dance an jump somebody … the only reason he'd lasted in the tribe was his powerful sister Eva, she protected him … leave him alone … he makes letterz, we're gonna need them so we don't forget anything, so we can be with our fallen ones … c'mon, Eva, we remember every bone, every bit of flesh, we've got every slain tribesman in our hearts … you do, yeah, but not your children … oh yeah, right, we scratched our greasy manes, and whenever we didn't happen to be out murdering and ambushing, or being murdered and ambushed, which tended to merge, we pestered Eva and Kral, whadda you wanna remember all that nonsense for anyway … none a your business, said Eva, go hunt me up a couple slaves, I'm gettin kina restless … finally the five of us, Brawler, Sad Man, The One Who Is In Many Places, and The One Who Leaps … and Kral, made it to the statue of Svantovít. And the four of us, you bandits and cattle rustlers, just you recall, the four of us stood there and pleaded with him, and Kral, the poor wretch, broke off a twig and scribbled in the sand while the four of us waited, and Svantovít spoke ... remember, you defilers of virgins and slayers of children, you know what he told us ... and we went and stood around Kral, remember, you scalpers and censors, we stood around him on all four sides and Brawler struck first and Sad Man tore off his fur and The One Who Is In Many Places spat in Kral's face and The One Who Leaps speared him ... and then we beat him to death.

We obeyed Svantovít, you generals and dispatchers, and when Kral was dead we cut out his heart, chopped it into four parts, and ate them ... we sacrificed our brother, you judges and undertakers, so we could survive ... and his heart was sweet and pulsing, and our strength began to come back to us ... and Brawler looked at his healed arm and screamed and The One Who Is In Many Places stomped the ground and Sad Man laughed ... The One Who Leaps dashed uphill, holding his nose ... he smelled smoke, and pointed his spear in the direction it came from ... and we raced off, no longer feeling hunger or fear, but intoxicated with savage joy, we were eager ... Kral's heart lived in us, we felt it like armor in every artery, every hair on our body ... and we ran downhill, four brothers united by sacrifice ... at the bottom was a fence of posts ... we probably should've waited for nightfall ... but Brawler whined impatiently, Sad Man nodded, The One Who Leaps licked his lips, and The One Who Is In Many Places rose ... and off we went, creeping through the grass like snakes ... The One Who Is In Many Places suddenly stopped and spun around, eyes flitting, arrow at the ready ... a dog came running out and Sad Man hammered in its skull ... The One Who Leaps scaled the palisade and opened up the gate ... and Brawler charged in first and cut down two men ... they didn't expect an attack in broad daylight ... and the rest of us charged in after him ... swift and silent ... darting in and out of cabins, killing left and right ... our enemies were too stunned to react, they'd never seen a horde or heard the cries of foreign warriors ... we slaughtered a lot of them before they rose to the defense ... and that only made us more eager, we let them feel our skillfulness and new strength, and then they didn't feel a thing. Lying glassy-eyed on the ground, chin up, in their beards an arrow, a bloody sword wound, a bite mark ... some of the slaves welcomed us and rebelled against their masters ... but we slaughtered them too, our strength was great and it grew with the blood ... the women put up more resistance ... scratching and biting us, some ran themselves through ... and we only spared the ones who resisted, beating them till they lay still ... any women who begged for mercy we kicked aside and chopped in two and smashed their childrens' heads open against the cabin walls ... then everyone was dead and we went to the few women we'd spared ... and raped them and gave them our seed, because we knew our time had come.

And we were never naked and miserable again. We made the women we'd spared dig a pit and burn all the corpses. We watched them closely, taking note of anyone who wept over the body of her man or child. A few of them fled ... we let them go. But three stayed. They realized who we were. They didn't weep. We wanted sons only from them. We forayed through the surrounding area, massacring settlements of soft people. And then we came across a new tribe. They had yellow skin and slanted eyes and rode beasts we'd never seen before. At first we thought it was a single creature with two heads and six legs. Then we slayed a few and realized what they were. They didn't have any special power, they bled like all the rest. And they too left behind only flesh. They were unsuited as slaves, didn't like to work. We took their horses and our strength grew. After that the yellow people too avoided our lands.

We were four: the dark princes of Morana, protecting one another from four sides. Our land was desolate, anyone we hadn't slaughtered or enslaved had fled, so we ordered our slaves to build a tower. It had to be tall so we could see far. We wanted to see like eagles. We wanted the tower to touch the clouds.

Our first women all had died, but not before giving us children. Our sons slept on dung out in the cold. We humiliated and beat them to make them hard. Those who survived did not love us but they feared us. Our daughters could fight as well as our sons. But they also knew how to do other things. They would gather roots, and from them and pebbles and the claws of beasts of prey they could divine our direction. They could heal their brothers' wounds by applying spider webs and saliva and birch compresses. One of them was powerful. Her name was Soaring and her strength was great. She governed the slaves and directed the building of the tower. Even her brothers obeyed her.

One day she divined a direction for us and we rode a long way, to a great river. We came upon a beaten path and stopped the caravan. Spears came raining down on us. One of our sons laughed and rode forth into the forest of spears, screaming at the foreign warriors in our tongue. They answered him in gibberish. He returned with foam and blood spurting from the flanks of his horse. What to do with such rabble, fathers, our son the wolf called out, they do not even know how to speak, they are *němci,* they are mutes, and that was how the Germans got their name in Czech. In one of the mute people's carts was an old woman and a little boy who spoke like us. Maybe that's why we spared them. The boy had an odd thing. A transparent stone, bright red in color, and when we held it up to the sun it turned gold. There was a fly inside, but it didn't move. We shook the stone, trying to make it fly. Maybe it was dead. But it looked like it was in flight. Its wings weren't bent and they still had their colors. Cautiously we examined the stone. It was magic. The stone had stopped life but without crushing it, it had the life inside it. How did that happen ... we wondered. And what are you called, boy, one of us asked ... respectfully, in case he was a sorcerer. Samo,* said the boy. One of us gave him a dagger and a sword, another draped him in his crimson cloak. We also loaded his bow and arrows onto the cart. To ward off his wrath. After all, we had killed his servants.

The magic unsettled us. We possessed the strength of Morana, we'd seen our enemies scream and die in convulsions, begging for mercy. Seen them flee. Knew all about the movements of the slave girls when we lay down with them. Some realized what awaited them, and squirmed beneath our weight, sensing that this was already death. But the boy's stone was death of a different kind. We spent our time running and fighting, in the stone there was no time. Maybe we should've killed the boy and destroyed the stone.

We put our new slaves to work on the tower. It grew, but slowly. Ever since we'd seen the stone, we knew that new things were happening. We feared for our time. And we were more frenzied and cruel than ever. We were at war with all peoples, hunting and hounding them. They were wretched. Morana loved us alone, Death herself was our sister. The four of us were bound by the pact of the torn-out heart. Only we had had the strength to sacrifice our brother, King David, and eat his heart.

Soldiers from other nations began to come into our forests. Before, we had always driven them out. This time we waited though. The tower was growing, but didn't yet touch the clouds. How far is it to the sky, we wondered. The top wasn't even as high as the mountains on the horizon. We hunted down more slaves, but many warriors preferred to die rather than obey our commands and the lash of the whip. As time went by, though, we reared a new breed. A slave breed. Our sons tested their swords on the old and the weak. The slaves were afraid to grow old.

Then it happened. Soaring ran away. With one of the slaves. Our sons, humiliated, begged us to take them along. But we felt this was our business. We rode off. Brawler and Sad Man, The One Who Is In Many Places and The One

Who Leaps, riding in silence. We urged our horses on. We didn't know why Soaring had done it. She could have had any man she desired. Her brothers would've done anything for her. All she had to do to end her solitude was give us a direction. But instead she had abandoned us. With a slave. From some cowardly clan, not even a warrior. We urged our horses on, we knew we'd catch them.

Soaring sat on a hillside, a dog rolled in the grass a few steps away. We climbed off our horses. We looked at our daughter and none of us wanted to do it. She'd had enough time to do it too. And yet there she sat, head bent. Waiting for us. My fathers, she said ... you know who Soaring is ... she lifted her head and looked up at us. She was very powerful. You do not want to do it because you know who I am, she went on, and because you want to know ... why I left. So I will tell you ... something happened ... I directed the building of the tower ... and I was driving the slaves, but then something happened ... this man's heart spoke to me and its speech was very beautiful ... I wanted to listen, my fathers, I blushed and turned away ... but he spoke so beautifully, his speech sang inside me ... and I knew, my fathers, that if that slave wanted me to, I would kill every one of you ... you know who I am ... and I would torture my brothers and set fire to the stockade and the tower ... if that slave wanted me to ... but he wanted only to leave ... he is no sorcerer, my fathers ... he is but a man ... and a dog. She stood and went to the slave, who was rolling around in the grass whimpering, afraid ... she spat on him, then gave him a hug and wiped him dry with her hair. She walked up the slope, stopped, back to us, then swung her arms and fell to the ground. One of us killed the slave, and then we stood over our daughter, knowing it still hadn't been enough after what Soaring had done, we needed to renew our strength, make it greater. And one of us rolled Soaring over with his foot, and another opened her with the tip of his sword, and the next one cut out her liver, and the fourth one divided it among us. And we went on ruling the land and feeding Morana. And waiting.

Then a new tribe came out of the forest. Driving the multitudes before it. The fleeing tribes mixed with one another. Our sons told us these new men were Boii,* People of Battle, and wore helmets with bull's horns. In battle they chewed the edges of their shields and sometimes tore up trees, roots and all, hurling them forward as they attacked. Nothing could stop them except death. We erected new palisades and dug the moat deeper. When the fugitives pounded on our gates, we drove them off with arrows and stones. We whipped our slaves, hoping they would finish the tower so we would have a chance to climb it. The People of Battle stormed us in broad daylight. The men howled like wolves, suddenly they were behind every tree, charging out of the woods in droves, leaping rocks, dodging arrows. Some of our sons dashed out the gate, seeking to test the new warriors. They greeted one another with howls and laughter. But we saw that our sons' swords cracked and split under the blows of the Boii. Their swords and axes were different than ours. We slayed a great many with arrows and stones, but not one of our sons returned.

We knew our time was finished, and went to the slaves. Unless we killed them, they might attack our rear. They knew what awaited them and tried to chew through their ropes. The Boii will defeat you! one of them cried. They are gods, forest gods, and your land will be theirs. Then we heard the howling again and ran out on the ramparts. One of us went back and set fire to the tower. We appealed to Morana for the last time and felt an icy touch on our ribs.

We were blinded by sparks from the flaming tower. And as they ran the first of us through, we began to lose our strength. The new people tore our bodies to shreds. The tower fell and the slaves burned with it. That's the way it was.

Ugh, Sharky … Bohler pleaded, c'mon, enough aready … Yeah, I said, I mean we all know the wheel turns … Hey, an did I really get two guys at once the very first day? said Micka. We looked over to where David had been sitting. He wasn't there. Cripes, it's just a fairy tale, Sharky cried. I only dreamed it! It's just a dream!

We went racing out of the flat. David wasn't in the hall. We ran downstairs. Look! one of us cried. On the light switch by the front door was a bloody thumbprint. Oh yeah, it's been bleedin, I noticed that, said Bohler. He went out, Micka said despairingly, but how far can he get like that, I mean the guy's like some kina zombie. Maybe we can find him, I said. Sharky was off and running. He went out in back of the buildings. I'll check the sheds an the yards, you guys run out to the tram, barked Bohler. Micka and I took off. I gotta say, that pseudodroog's one strong fella, but he can't take me in a sprint. Maybe he's on that one, I pointed. The tram pulled away, heading into the city, its curving route illuminated by sparks of electricity. The lights in the distance sat ready to swallow it up, to merge with its hazy yellow glow. Outta luck, Micka kicked a stone, sending it skidding across the tracks. Maybe he's feelin better, maybe he changed his mind. C'mon, Potok, you know the tribe's bust. Yeah, but where can he go?

We've got to believe, said Sharky, that he's all right. Yeah, nothin else we can do, said someone. We can check out the usual spots, ask around, I suggested. Yeah, we will, all in good time … Right now there's the Zone, that's the first thing. After all, he left on his own. After all, guys, his business. He can look out for himself … he'll hafta. But we knew our pseudodroog was very, very weak. An unless he'd made some kina arrangement with Helena, the Scarred One … he didn't know anyone in town except for other crews' bosses and byznys officials … can't rely on them … all those guys care about is getting a spot at the watering hole … we'd taught him how to get around all right, but not when things change, we reflected.

Settle in now, O vultures and scavengers, cause things've gotta come to an end an I haven't even begun, Sharky warned us. My dream continues, an it's about another pack. It's fast and slow, and you'll find out what the earth is under your feet. So don't shake your heads an quit tryin to solve the unsolvable a while, believe me, there's various paths, various possibilities, various things … an one of the paths was the path of the people of Dull Knife when their pack's G-night began.

The fleeing tribes mixed together. And then what was left of them was herded into corrals. And enemy tribes were herded into the same corrals so they'd kill each other off … the tribes' time was shattered, and the new people, who wanted to give the land their own name, couldn't stand them … they put collars on Dull Knife's people, forcing them to eat the same ridiculous things and move the same ridiculous way … at least that's how it seemed to the people in the corrals … and they called their slavemasters Wasichu, white spirits, on account of their ridiculous skin color, and didn't consider them human, because only they were Déné, people. And coincidentally, the people who locked them in the corrals considered them to be the subhumans.

The Déné were dying because the grass there stank and the water was undrinkable … there weren't any moving animals to shoot at or chase, and no eagles either, there was nothing there but vultures … the Déné didn't like them … and soon there were no more enemies either, the Déné wiped them out, all except the Wasichu, of course.

And … for the Déné this was the worst part … the corrals didn't have any trees in them. The Déné, you see, laid their dead to rest in the treetops. They knew what the Earth was, they knew the Earth was a mass human grave. It was totally obvious to them that only fools and slaves to Evil buried or burned their dead. They knew the heaps of dead and ashes were overloading the Earth. They had dreams about the next tribe or nation thrown into the pits sending the Earth veering off its path. Forfeit its place, lose its mysterious way, and go shooting off somewhere, up the ass of the old Invader, or more likely the Devil.

That was the Déné's teaching. That was why they gave their dead to the trees, the air, the wind, and the eagles and their ravenous cousins … some of them they didn't like, but what could they do, that's the way it was … and since the corrals didn't have any trees, they buried and burned their dead Wasichu-style, but they knew what it did to the Earth. They got bored and died, and in between they drank the Fiery, of which oddly enough there was plenty … in spite of its being strictly forbidden, since, as stated in numerous studies and dissertations, the Déné after consuming it in large doses turned into "psychopathic murderers." However, there were several kulchural foundations that for tax purposes supported basket makers, poetasters, and daubers, and so the Fiery went to the reservations by the wagonload … and some dailies even ran humanist articles about the subhumans' art. When the juries laid eyes on the hungover works, they said all kinds of crap, to keep the metal flowing and earn their living, the critics tuned up their ballpoints, and the guilt-tripped idiots expounded their views with impunity ad infinitum … and, dear listeners and anchorwomen, it got to the point where all the boredom and pointless death drove Grinning Man to kill his wife … he was under the influence of the Fiery, so no one blamed him for it, but it was no good … and when he came to again, Grinning Man bitterly regretted his deed and slashed his wrists and spoke to his wife, begging her to forgive him … and maybe she did and maybe she didn't, no one knows since she never revived … and then Necklace cut off his little sister's nose, laughing as he did it … also under the influence, so he didn't know what he was doing … and everyone realized he did it because of the collar, no one said a word, but they knew that what was going on wasn't any good. And it has been objectively established that Natanis's collar made him climb a tree, tie his legs to a branch, and drop headfirst into an anthill, and as numerous prominent studies and several dissertations have noted, the Déné said to cut it out … but he told them to cut it out an watch, and they shared his fate like brothers, because he suffered his collar in silence, until at last he was so ashamed he decided … to have it out with death … overnight he sobered up, but he didn't change his mind … and along came Pte-San-Waste-Win, and she said: Firewater is worse than Thunderstick! Smash the bottles and slaughter the Wasichu who sell you this filth in exchange for your women. You immoral drunkards. You've forgotten everything. Are you still people? The men were all drunk at the time, and it seemed like a good idea, so they went ahead and did it. Pte-San-Waste-Win was powerful and they usually did what she said. When nobody was watching, she put an end to Natanis's suffering too. The Déné slaughtered all the Wasichu, including the corral overseer, who had the most titles and sat on many boards of directors. Whenever they had complained to him that there was nothing to eat, he had told them to eat grass. So they killed him and stuffed his mouth with grass, and he's still eating it now. They had their fun, but they knew it was time to disappear.

They put together rifles and pistols, which they weren't supposed to have. Some time ago, though, they had taken apart a bunch of them and braided the barrels and triggers and hammers into their hair, along with their clasps and feathers. The Wasichu laughed at them, rattling on about stupid barbaric ornaments and childish superstitions. But there were no more Wasichu around now. And when the people of Dull Knife's G-night began, a great many more Wasichu stopped laughing at those ornaments. They stopped smiling, they stopped being.

The men on horseback led the way, followed by the women and children on foot, they didn't have too many horses yet. Not far from the corrals, they knew, were a few squadrons of cavalrymen. It is said that Grinning Man and Necklace led the charge. They had sinned greatly and nothing mattered to them anymore. The cavalrymen weren't expecting it, and that day plenty of them stopped laughing. Grinning Man fell and found out whether his wife had forgiven him. He wasn't the only one to fall. But they got lots of rifles and horses and their strength began to return to them. In a nearby woods the riders dismounted, and Dull Knife took on the responsibility that was tumbling across the prairie. All right, all right, brother, said the others ... Chief Joseph, Little Bear, Ollokot, Sleeping Rabbit, Abenak, Bloody Knife, and the rest ... okay, but you know ... they didn't have to say it, but they began to live by the rules again ... and Dull Knife nodded because he knew ... what would happen if he didn't steer his people through the pitfalls and they fell in the traps and snares, if he didn't make the right moves, if his heart turned sour with fear. They headed north, back to their home.

They had their own language and clung to it, foolishly, dully, fatuously ... just as they clung to their motion, and with every step toward G-night, away from the corrals, their strength returned to them … they were from various tribes … Chief Joseph and his son, Necklace, were Nez Percé; Wovoka, who taught them to dance the forbidden dance, was Paiute; the rest were mostly Cheyenne … but it made no difference now, they were a new defensive community, and they traded words because they needed to understand one another in order not to perish, or at least not right away … they were the Dull Knife pack.

And Dull Knife's heart did not turn sour, just the opposite, now it was sweeter and redder than ever before, and the pulse of Dull Knife's heart helped his people move through the pitfalls … steering clear of the traps and turning the snares inside out.

But the cavalry encircled them. Charging out of places where before there had been nothing. Dull Knife's people soon discovered that even though the earth was still just as big, it had shrunk. Wired and wireless links guided the cavalry unerringly. But Dull Knife's people had links to other worlds and began using their powers. The forces of Nature were favorably inclined to them. When there was fog, they used it. When the rain fell, it helped them. When the sun beat down and the soldiers' palms were breaking out in blisters from their rifles' cocks and barrels, Dull Knife's warriors would emerge from the glare, hammers and hatchets cool in their hands. Sometimes it was good to walk through the water, sinking happily into its soft, shiny world, to throw off the dogs of the citizens' search parties. Little Bear fell. Abenak, the young men's leader, was slain. Even Wovoka danced his last.

For every man of the pack that went down, a new throng of pursuers sprang up on the side of the Wasichu. It is said it was obvious to Sleeping Rabbit, and he saw fit to tell the others, that it was like a man's corpse and a thousand maggots. It is said the others nodded. When Sleeping Rabbit fell, they didn't mourn much, remembering what he'd said about man and his maggots, and their lips curled back in a smile. They bared their teeth to the leaves of the forest and the sand of the pits and the rocks among which they hid. And they say the things of the trees and the soil adopted the wolfish smile as their own and helped the people of the pack.

Chief Joseph and Necklace brought up the rear. Circling. The others rode on the flanks and in front, protecting the women and children, who obeyed the words of Pte-San-Waste-Win, Buffalo Calf Sister, Many Baskets, and Yellow Woman. Most of the women were from different tribes, but they abridged their vocabularies and mixed their alphabets in order to understand one another. Supposedly they were upset that they couldn't use many adjectives, given that they lived in such a wild and colorful time. But they had to give things names on the run. Sometimes a couple of nouns were enough to name the things you had to dodge. Often the most urgent sentence was nothing but a muffled cry. A whisper and a gesture. Dull Knife's people knew that as long as one warrior and at least one of the Protected Ones survived, the seed of the pack would not perish. But Ollokot, Bear Head, and Heap of Meat had fallen. Crooked Lightning and Carrying Pumpkin had passed on. The people with those ridiculous and incomprehensible names in a tongue that almost no longer existed, even as it was being created, were dying one after the next. By now they had lots of weapons, so the old women, or anyone else who didn't want to live anymore, rode on the flanks and at the head, putting enemies to death. Some cavalrymen boasted to their companions of the distinguished decorations they'd won in their war with the tribes. They carved out women's private parts and slung them on their saddlehorns. The decorations quickly dried in the air and never turned moist again, except in the rain.

On receiving this old information, the man of the time of reading, swallower of a full spectrum of data flows and deaths, the cripple of today's age when there are no rules and all is permitted, should conceal any potentially unwarranted and pseudohumanistic indignation. And not just because of the fires all around us. Because when the women of the pack got to the hostages, they tested their manly strength with instruments. In the scholarly volumes and history books it is written that it lasted a long time and that it hurt. No one knows who started it.

It was the cavalry versus Dull Knife's people, bullet to bullet and knife to knife. That it was a hundred knives to one, and then a thousand, is a different matter, but there were rules. Then something happened. Chief Joseph told Necklace: Ahem, ahem. Respectable citizens joined the hunt from every village, every town, every farm where cows or chickens were raised in slavery. Sheriffs, bosses, chefs, bankers, psychoanalysts, jailers, teachers, politicians, voters, brakemen, and eurojournalists all flipped through the channels and, finding no reruns of *Dallas* or *Denver*, grabbed their rifles, said goodbye to their wives and little ones, and walked out the door. Chief Joseph caught a lot of them. But then he fell too. The citizens ran the pack out of their backyards, then went home and told stories and wrote screenplays and drew up assessments, convening peace conferences and printing moving accounts. Some even produced resolutions calling for an end to the hunting of subhumans. They made lots of resolutions, right up to the end.

The land of animals and people was transformed into an unbroken tract of cottages, one great big never-ending chicken farm, and wherever there wasn't a building someone had a backyard. Nothing lay fallow or untamed anymore. And new citizens were constantly coming along who hadn't learned their lesson yet. The ones who had could no longer speak. Their experience was incommunicable. Some only wanted to get a snapshot of the savages, but their incomparably dull subjects couldn't tell the difference and took their scalps along with their cameras.

Winter set in. The pack found itself in its usual situation: encircled. But this time there were settlers gathered in droves behind the string of cavalrymen. Holding carnivals, raffles, and peace conferences. Having fun. Bloody Knife thought they were out of their minds. Let's slaughter them, he said. But then others will come, said Wolf Cub. Too late. Bloody Knife had ridden off. The grandstands fell silent, his singing the only sound until he came into shooting range. The pack charged. Some fell under the hail of bullets. They say Bloody Knife caught the bullets in flight and deflected them into his chest, many shots were fired. Thunderbolt, who prided himself on his singing, couldn't take it and decided to outdo Bloody Knife. Their voices crossed in the night, catching bullets. They couldn't afford to waste time killing settlers. Their pride was too great to make meat out of them, they measured their strength by their songs. But many shots were fired. Afterward, at the agreed spot, Dull Knife counted his people. Only thirty of them remained, they say, a few braves, plus old people and children. Just three women were left now: Pte-San-Waste-Win, Armadillo Sister, and Yellow Woman.

It was winter. They dug a ditch and hid inside it. Fortunately the people of the pack still had the old free animals' hides; those snowflakes weighed a lot. That night they were heavier than bullets. Many old people froze. Some of them threw their furs over the ones who were asleep and crept out of the ditch to go look for their time, thinking it had disappeared. Next morning the ones who were left had to kill the horses and eat their flesh. The horses' blood was the warmest thing they had. The spirits surrounded them, but this time they broke the rules: they didn't kill; they waited. A couple of journalists with Camerama, Inc. snuck across the line to Dull Knife's people and began shooting footage; they're still shooting there to this day. Then shrapnel began to fall on the trench.

I shall not surrender another one of my men to the scalping knives of the inhumans, declared General Sherman. It is said that some of his men vomited on seeing the shredded bodies fly from the trenches. They no longer felt like warriors. They say some refused that method of warfare and were punished. When the head of Pte-San-Waste-Win rolled across the snow, it cried out Natanis's name; she had taken away her brother's freedom and now feared to meet him. Dull Knife's remaining people climbed on their horses and charged the cannons. It is said the clouds carried them, releasing an avalanche. Few were the horses not shredded by grenades. The next day the survivors found out how strong the frost was. They cut open the horses' bellies and put the little children inside to hide them from the cold. They knew they were going to die but still hoped the spirits might spare at least the littlest ones. They wanted the new tribe to live on in their songs. But soon there was no one left to sing them.

But it is said ... Yellow Woman tethered Wolf Cub to her horse and broke through the encirclement. They couldn't tell which way they were going, the snowstorm blinded them. But they reached the mountains and spent the winter there. Yellow Woman tied branches to Wolf Cub's broken arms and the bones grew back together. They hunted. Somehow they survived. Wolf Cub saw that Yellow Woman's belly was growing. She wanted to go on though, high into the mountains. The Earth is full of graves, she told him ... the Earth is a grave, c'mon, you know ... we have to go as high as we can.

The Earth swallowed up Dull Knife's people and turned into a pit. No one knows where Dull Knife lies. All they know is he threw off his collar.

Yellow Woman took Wolf Cub higher and higher. She avoided the gullies and gorges where there might be bones. When they came to a place where there was nothing but rock, she suggested it might be appropriate to build a cottage there. Then she and the child rode on. They were trying to get to Kanaka, where there were still people who lived the old way, and lots of trees.

It is said that two braves, Wanatabe and Ishtu, spied their silhouettes on the horizon and rode off to face them without telling anyone in their pack. Great joy, brother, Ishtu said ... I'm sick to death of hunting those stupid Wasichu ... they don't know the rules, they get frightened ... they smell disgusting ... they don't know how to speak. And Wanatabe was joyful too, because now he was hunting people again, which required skill and strength. Because even a small child of the Lakota tribe could tell that the two beings riding toward them on the horizon were also people. No Wasichu knew how to move like that.

As soon as Wolf Cub saw the horsemen, he knew what they had in mind. He reached for his club. But Wanatabe and Ishtu left their arrows in their quivers. Are you people? Wanatabe asked formally. Ishtu made the sign for *tribe.* Yellow Woman replied that they were from the pack of Dull Knife. We heard … Ishtu signed … that you had done away with tribes and that all of you were slaughtered. Wanatabe left his fingers in his horse's mane … this is a great … a great and sacred moment … dear brother and brave sister … welcome among the people of Sitting Bull. The child opened his eyes and reached out for the braves' shiny ornaments … he remembered them from previous lives, but his father and mother had lost theirs … the four Déné knew the Lakotas had more than enough ornaments … so they dug their heels into their animals' flanks, riding fast.

One other member of Dull Knife's pack, Necklace, the Nez Percé, also made it out of the encirclement … but he didn't remember how, later he claimed to have been carried off by an eagle … he wandered the region on foot until he stumbled across some chicken reeducation farms, trounced the subhumans, and helped himself to their armaments and accoutrements … the militiamen dogged him, tightening the noose, but he sliced through the knot … and made his way to the forests, where there were neither people nor Wasichu … he nursed his wounds there, feeling at peace … I'm a person, he said to himself, but after a time he set out again, he didn't want to be alone … they hunted him and killed his horse with a machine … but he crawled on … and after many days he came to a forest where the Crows still hunted and the nonpeople hadn't been yet … he saw some girls gathering wood … there were many trees … the girls screamed in fright at the beast creeping toward them on all fours … but one of them, She-Raven, recognized him … she knew who he was and wasn't afraid. Welcome, she said … this is a good moment, for coincidentally … she said, unbraiding black strips of skin from her hair … by truly rare and remarkable coincidence, today ends the time of mourning for Little Shield … he was a good husband … and I'm cooking a doggie in the kettle as we speak … the meat must be quite tender by now, and I venture to presume, O warrior, you would not spurn a morsel … provided, that is, you have the time and the inclination … be my guest. Ugh, Necklace said, and he collapsed. She-Raven assumed that this was his way of expressing consent.

And so, dear friends and enemies, said Sharky, of the last thirty people they say three managed to escape, thereby thwarting genocide once again. And a certain crackpot, that is to say mystic, infers from these numbers the identity of the man who at a certain age chose to take on the responsibility that was lying out in the desert … spread his arms … and tried to do away with tribes … but seeing as you're practical types and the cream of scholarly society, boys, I'm sure you know the name of this nearly extinct people. Bohler! The Irkuts, Mr. President! Outstanding … Micka! The Ingush,* boss minister! Marvelous … Potok! The Ikvas, fuckbrain hippie! Brilliant … our spiritual caretaker will answer on behalf of our missing colleague … the Inuits, potatohead! Very good. You're well prepared. There's various things, paths, snares, an pitfalls … various possibilities, you know what I'm sayin … an as your reward, tattoo the name of this people a thousand times on your sweet little hearts. Got it?

Bohler banged the window shut, it was getting cold outside. Sharky went on smiling and talking to us. We were almost the only ones left in the building. Beneath us was the Zone. We knew our pseudodroog was relating his dreams so persistently because he was parting with us … going home, as he put it. I had no idea which place on earth he called home. His business.

An now I'm gonna tell the lot of you, said Sharky, another made-up story from my dream about reality, but not about the pack, it's about the Individual. Once upon a time lived a man named Rimbow, who wrote: I die of thirst beside the fountain, blazing hot with chattering teeth … or maybe it was someone else … probly a woman, same diff … but shortly after Rimbow ditched his old *maman,* he got tangled up in kulchur sections an went through some horrid stuff with phone idiots, an that's what I'm gonna tell you about.

Rimbow put colors together with vowels an consonants, changin his tongue … inventin an alphabet … pavin the way for those that came after … but there was always someone phonin him up, cause there's lots of idiots that donno what it is to drink solitude … an they wanna talk about their thoroughly boring lives an discuss the problems of tribes an crews … Rimbow mixed his solitude with Firewater an stuck it in his alphabet, which he was makin for people without a tribe, cause he was a seer an knew what traps were yet to come … it was obvious … but the idiots kept phonin him up an schedulin appointments an gabbin away at conferences, expressin their views on the things of the knowable world … there were frictions and squabbles, and voting too, mostly about chuckles and slavery, as usual … he needed the chuckles, after all he was human … he'd tried making a meal of air, rock, coal, steel, but it didn't work … so he had to go to the conferences and listen to the views and speeches ... it was awful ... and since he didn't pick up the phone, the lobbyists would come over with plans on how to get rid of the other lobbies, which is in every special-interest group's job description, and since he happened to live on the ground floor, when his friends passed by and saw the lights on, they'd knock on his door ... so he lived in the dark ... drew his eyelids down like blinds and flapped his ears back like a dog ... girlfriends and secretaries made him appointments with psychiatrists ... saying: Don't be crazy! He was, but as he wrote once from the woods ... it's all the same how it ends, it's my power, my path, that's what's important ... and when his friends broke down the door, he had a fake beard on, and said: I'm someone else! And just to confuse em he added: But that's not me either! He was trying to stop the wheel of the world, at least for himself, if no one else. And every time he hit his stride and the mysterious symbols of his alphabet were beginning to take shape ... his friends would steal into his place, plug the phone into the wall, and call an ambulance ... he'd wake up in a straitjacket and his friends would come and sign him out and say: There, you see, it's gonna be fine now ... and he pretended not to see the wheel in motion, and with all the shots and pills he really didn't anymore ... he tried his best to give the impression he was satisfied again, and his employers in Scabieville, smiling benevolently, withdrew the black mark ... and he began going to conferences and presenting his views on the visible and listening to other views and excitedly debating them, and the whole thing started all over again.

And Rimbow turned his back on the carnival and left, because the Earth hurt his feet. No, he told his mom, no, he told the kulchur sections, no, he told the city, an when Satyr called from the slammer: May I kiss you again before I kick the bucket? Rimbow said no an killed the phone.

Sharp bones jutted out all over the Earth, lacerating him. So he decided to split. My heart dribbles tobacco off the stern, he said, and hired himself out. Deserting to Ceylon, he made his way through the rain forests and up into the mountains so he could get firm rock underfoot instead of a mass grave.

He knew the important dreams were the ones that hit hard on hard earth, not on soft, which is ... you know what by now. Being a seer was all that saved him from the gorilla raids and macaque attacks. He was *maestus et errabundus,* and knew it didn't make any difference whether he survived the climb to the summit. He was a seer and knew that up there, especially in Ceylon, there were freedom-loving ants, and it was enough for him to meet one that could pass the news on to his partners ... so the things he wrote would remain puzzles and snares for those that came after him ... one single proud, freedom-loving ant was all it would take, because all lives're interconnected, that was obvious to him. He was a VOYANT, a seer, he was a clear-sighted eagle, and in his important dream he saw Mussolini offer him his daughter and half the republic if he would bow down to him, but he also saw the Abyssinians and their ruler, King Menelik, counting out flints for spears.

He felt the gusts of icy wind as the wheel turned round, and looking ahead he could sense what awaited the Abyssinians, the pit opening to swallow them up ...

So he blew off his stupid poems, left them in Ceylon, and rushed off to Abyssinia ... took to the byznys path, buying Kalashnikovs from Ukraine and lifting them in to the Abyssinians ... didn't get much cash out of it, he never was good with numbers, but he knew what his reasons were ... he needed something concrete to keep from going totally insane ... and thanks to Rimbow the Abyssinians were able to hold off the stalingos' tanks for a while ... and thanks to the fact that they slaughtered a lot of them, the Abyssinians were preserved and their name has not been forgotten. And the circle of tribes remained intact, and apart from the letter G there's still the whole alphabet and the Abyssinians' tongue, and G is just one of a number of letters.

Then they cut off his leg and he died.

Yep, colleagues, Sharky smiled at us, that's how it was with the Individual that didn't have any tribe ... I simplified it a little ... an it might seem hard to believe, but even without a tribe there's things you can do ... an that's why I sprang this character on you ... without a tribe, I say, cause that's what awaits you, you Subeuropeans, you Czechs an other carpetbaggers ... it's gonna be tough because, my apologies, free horsemen and masons, but you didn't have any good, free animals around your more or less smelly cradles back in those cold ratty tenements, the donkeys and cows had gone to pasture for reeducation, not to mention Chief Joseph was long gone by then, just remember, you rejects and sinful vessels, who stood at your cradles, none other than Adolf himself an Uncle Joe, come on, you remember ... Mowgli roared at the wolves ... an they sank their claws into your craven little hearts, so cover yourselves with protective tattoos, you're the last of the old time an you're gonna need em ... and remember! Remember how it began here, remember who it was that unified the tribes ... Sámo, a Frank, a traitor to his own people, it began with betrayal ...

he got so messed up from those tall tales his old Czech nanny Sláva told him that he turned against his own tribe, your grandfather, the father of miscegenation … remember the days when the Christians rendered unto Caesar not just a lousy penny or two but took their children outta the rec rooms an school-sponsored factories an gave him them too, an that was you … an I'll tell you right now, straight up an full force: entirely unintentionally it led to the creation of a subeuropean bastard megarace, rising up like Venus from the foam, or like Baba Yaga from the muck, whatever you feel, I'm not givin any orders here, heh. An those two that stood at your cradles were regime installation artists, they knew what an efficient killer the state is, they knew how to let the G-arrow fly … you dear listeners, future possible defensive snipers an potential humanist ethnic cleansers … Sharky lectured us … you know that part of my bastard Prague constitution derives from the People of the Book … an that they tiptoed out of G-night through the holes between the hinges was nothing short of a miracle … but these People of the Book have an old and amazing alphabet, an they wrote down, wrote out, an compiled what happened, an that's why it exists today, that's why it's real an isn't forgotten.

But there's yet another people here, trained in the art of survival, an this one doesn't write, its only chronicles are scars, occasionally on other peoples' skins … an no one knows the names of its dead, it's like they never existed … they're not written on the walls of any bloodstained house of prayer either, cause on G-nights this people's blood gushed without anywhere to pray … this people lives in rough coexistence with the state, an for them the state's always been a killer, they're the People of the Pack, who tend to the family an don't mind a bit that it's crawling with lice from time to time … an no one from this tribe was ever so fatuous as to invent a mobile wheel so no one could escape from anyone anymore … or electric-powered torches so people could scrape away at the lie of progress absolutely nonstop … or the unnatural telephone, which shortens life as well as distances … on the contrary, this people cleverly tears down ads to use for occasional fires … an wages its miniature war with pockets an shivs, an what is that next to genocide … a very unusual people they are, never marched into the field or destroyed another tribe, cause they've got no talent for organization … never dug a pit for another tribe, cause shovels an picks don't interest em much … quicklime only gives em the hiccups an makes em fling up their arms … this people knows very well how important it is to daydream and slack off, that it's true art when a dream and a color fill in the spots where once the menacing lions of the subconscious roared … and Goliath said: Who is not with us is against us and will be killed or reeducated … and David said: Live and let live … gimme a break aready, why doncha! And let his slingshot fly. You know, you illustrious rec room dwellers … let live … and keep a close watch on the colorful boisterous throngs of criminal Romanies … because their tribe keeps the pack and the family alive, and will be the last that knows what a pack is … and that there's more than just the rules of the state with its markets and its ads' duper-super cookie-cutter freaks of the near-distant homogenized future … and Rs don't look like ads, not even from far away … and even the newfangled dragon pseudopit of the Meediya won't swallow the Rs but just spits them up … they're drunk and noisy too much of the time, and don't look good on the Grainy … put the beast behind bars with the rest of the beasts … but the earth must never again be a pit for another tribe … it wouldn't be able to take it, you know what comes next … and that it's starting again, literally every day, like everything else … every G-day was yesterday and goes on smoldering … but there's various things here, various possibilities, all sorts of paths, dear brothers' sisters and dear sisters' brothers, and it's not a pretty sight. The earth is entirely overburdened, it seems, but there's still one more possibility, said the mytho-maniac Sharky … and then Dolphin the *brujo* storyteller darted off into the dark and heavy tide, plowing through the surf and surfacing near the sandy beach, he fixed us with his sparkling emerald eyes and said … you know … there's possibilities here, and one of them is hope.

How magnificent! cried the first of us.

How banal! cried the next of us.

Both! cried the last of us.

And then we gave Dolphin a round of applause, he was totally hoarse.

12

HELENA'S NEW CONDITION. THE WELL AND
WHAT'S NOT IN IT. BOHLER'S NUMBERS. "LATER."

We went down to the forge and tossed our silver ornaments into the fire, our tribe was finished. I'm keepin my eagle, Bohler said, he's all anyone would take from me ... nothing else is worth it. I kept my Black Madonna. Everyone kept their one strong thing, the rest ended up in the furnace. Whoever felt the need trimmed his mane. Our hair twisted in the flames, probably crackled, we couldn't hear it. I seized the opportunity to cut my nails. When we came out of the forge, Helena was in the courtyard.

Where's David?

That's what we were about to ask you.

She gasped.

You let him leave ...

We explained what happened.

I gotta go after him, she said. Maybe he went home. To them. The Losíns.

That hadn't occurred to us.

Tell me the address.

It also never occurred to us, though, to ask what village, what mountains, our brother was from.

It's urgent ... said Helena.

Well, maybe come summer ... some mountains, Bohler said hesitantly.

By summer he'll be born already. David and I are having a child, said Helena.

Neither proud nor alarmed, she was just informing us.

So he doesn't know? I asked.

That guy doesn't know anything right now, said Micka.

Bohler stepped on his foot. You oughta find him, he told Helena, but maybe later ... an don't just stand there, go tell Lady Laos goodbye, we're wrappin things up here ... aren't you goin home?

Home. Hah. Said Helena. With this thing, she touched her cheek. The Elixir, oddly enough, hadn't helped or hurt, either way.

Helena honey … Bohler went on … get some plastic whatcha-macallit, go away … we've got a Zone waitin for us, you can't be here if you're expecting, you know that. You gotta go right now. The baby might get hurt.

There was nothing we could do to help. We had to stay and wait for Rudolf, finish things up with the Zone. We watched our pseudodroogina leave, alone and empty-handed, the same way she had come to us. Carrying the new life inside her away, far from the Zone, I hoped. Wait up, Bohler ran after her, need any cash, you're goin to the Laosters', right? You are, aren't cha?

I don't need anything, she shoved him out of her way.

Helena, hey, so later! I shouted.

Later, said Micka.

Yeah, take care. Later.

She knew that word of parting, she knew what it was about.

She walked out of the building and went away.

We stood around the courtyard, smoking and waiting for Rudolf. Talk about a comedown, huh? Sharky said hoarsely. You can say that again, Micka replied. Got your ticket yet? Yep. Said Sharky. Hey, Potok, where're you goin?

I figure I'll stay here a while. There's a girl I need to find.

You were sayin you found a sister, Sharky walked over to me. What's she look like?

Hey, that's my sis you're talkin about.

What's she look like, for Chrissake? What's up? I'm goin away an I wanna know about you guys, Sharky said.

I described her. Knowingly I spoke of her relatively slight yet firm figure. In plain terms I referred to her hips in stride. And I said all sorts of things about her gorgeous face with its squarely prominent cheekbones. About her paleness, indicating a soul in struggle. I made a comment or two also about her fluttering lashes, nor did I leave out the occasional flashes of green. I spoke of her tender breasts, neither frighteningly huge nor uselessly tiny, and also of her back, I could almost feel my fingertips, one by one, brushing over the tender skin … I talked about the vertigo of the moment when my sister touches my rib and it hardens back into ice … I babbled on like a soldier, bubbling over with warmth … my buddies clustered around … that stuff alone's gotta help fight the Zones, said Bohler, touched. I … said Sharky, I think I might know her … a good friend of mine on the Masaryk kibbutz … a sabra … Cruel Micka's eyes were shut. I strutted around the yard like a peacock. She's graceful! Once in a while, probably … cruel as a cat, but not at heart. She's mine! No, hers, no, whoever she wants to be!

And then we heard the signal. It was Rudolf. We opened the gate and a car drove into the yard. It stopped by the stairs leading down to the cellar. Rudolf climbed out, collected his checks, and said: Now watch yourselves, an don't let anything surprise you. An don't talk if you can help it. Just the four a you here?

Yep.

Good. They know you. Nobody else's got any business bein here. A pair of men in black stepped out of the car and walked around to the trunk. What cha draggin along the black sheriffs for, Rudolf? I teased. He just laughed. Standing there, scrawny and four-eyed, he looked like a little boy, but I knew he was far from it.

I told you not to be surprised. Those aren't sheriffs. They come with the skirvolya.

The who?

The medium.

The pair opened the trunk and lifted out a buggy with a canvas over the top. It was about the size of a baby carriage. They pushed it past us to the cellar entrance. I took a look at them and felt queasy. I noticed Bohler was sweating. Both of these guys looked exactly the same. They must've been twins. They even moved the same way. Their skin, or whatever it was, was a rubbery grayish-yellow. Their eyes gauged us carefully, unblinkingly. Each gripped the handle with his left hand, in unison. It occurred to me maybe they were machines. The carriage squeaked as it rolled by, something was moving inside it.

I glanced over at Bohler. We didn't like the looks of it.

Trust me, said Rudolf. If anyone or anything … he chuckled … can lick the Zone, it's the skirvolya.

The two robots, or whatever they were, lifted the carriage gently down the stairs. We walked behind them. Holding candles. There's gonna be more than enough light in a minute, Rudolf grinned. We stepped into the darkness. The carriage gave off a glow. Like the color running out of an impaled sun, sprang to my mind. The two men pushed the carriage up to the well's edge, which in the peculiar light looked like the mouth of a crater, and stepped back.

I fixed my eyes on the winch. That old wooden structure, iron-plated and grooved with age, seemed like something familiar. Something from the human world. I heard the murmur of churning water. The water's surface sparkled darkly, like a wrapping over the depths, rippling with waves. I hadn't seen that before. The water was expecting them. The murmuring seemed to fill the cellar as far as I could see. Even the vault above our heads. I'm hearin the Zone breathe, I thought with a shudder. The water was still rippling. As we stood behind the carriage, someone, I guess Bohler, began softly praying, but Rudolf shouted him down. Be quiet, everyone, nothin's gonna happen to you.

It was like the water was moving inside itself, and then in the depths I saw light spilling out and making its way up, climbing to the surface. The two men pulled the canvas off the carriage and I saw the Head. It was freakishly large … the circus, I thought … big and bald, with ears like funnels sticking out. The Head was black and sat upright atop its slender neck. I only saw the creature from behind. That was enough. Some eyes it's better not to look into. So that's a skirvolya … I thought … the ancient Slavic forest creature … they still exist then … standing a few meters in back of the Head, I saw two hands rise from the carriage, the long, powerful hands of a fully grown person. They were bare and ended in claws, thick claws, that sparkled in the greenish light exploding noise-lessly up through the water, illuminating us in its glow, the water began to boil, but there was a chill coming off of it, maybe ground streams churning up from below … I looked at my pseudodroogs' faces, I'd say like me they were trying not to have too many feelings or opinions about what was going on.

We wanted to believe the Head's power was on our side … Rudolf was smiling haughtily, that reassured me, he was human, so if there was any threat of danger … so what, I said to myself, maybe this power's too strong for me to escape anyway … the long bare arms went back into the carriage, and then the hands were holding an object, pouring something into the well, a liquid … there was a hissing in the well and the light was right beneath the surface, ready to punch through the lid, break out … then the long arms' hands were holding an idol, might've been made of wood, and flinging it into the well with all their might, I caught a glance of the figurine, it resembled the pair standing by the carriage, motionless, as if switched off.

I just shifted my weight back and forth, wiggling my toes, a habit of mine. Then the clawed hands were holding a book, they opened it up and shred it to pieces, the bits of paper falling into the water.

The water was like the plasma of a thousand bodies lumped together, grasp-ing at the shreds, waves spraying and splashing around, snatching the paper in flight. As the book's shreds hit the surface, the water closed over them, sucking them in like a huge mouth. The light in the well was energy, I guess, the surface sealed it in like a crust, but the light forced its way up from the depths, trying to break through the wrapper … just beneath the surface it condensed, first pale, then the color of runny silver, it probably would've blinded us but for the darkness of the water.

Then the Head poked up again and the creature began to sing … we looked at each other, amazed … the voice was so strong and beautiful, for a moment I doubted whether it really came from the Head, but it did.

The song went straight into the well, you could see it, or sense it, penetrating the surface and disappearing … the water was boiling and now the air was hot, the song bounced off the walls and the vault and tumbled down around our heads. The water in the well squirmed as one body.

I memorized the words to the song:

> Holy pools contain mere water.
> I know, I have bathed in them.
>
> Gods carved from wood and ivory give no reply.
> I know, I have sorely begged them.
>
> Holy books contain naught but words.
> I know, I have looked in them.
>
> Kabir speaks only of what he has lived.
> What you have not lived is not truth.

The water boiled over and spilled across the edge of the well. I leaped out of the way, but suddenly it turned to mist, and rising out of the seething water I saw … a serpent's spine, a monster's veiny tentacle, and up from the depths in a silvery foam climbed two lights glowing like bloody targets, the serpent's head. In the blink of an eye it shot out of the well and the giant body was wriggling high above our heads, like it had gone right through the vault, like the vault had never been there at all, its spotted hide glistening with scars and sprinkled with warts the size of mushrooms, some of its scales were shiny, others like deep festering wounds, and the sound of hissing filled our ears … lifting my head I saw the serpent's maw, its eyes no longer glowing but blind, covered with skin, flaps of skin … water sprayed everywhere, but not a drop landed on any of us, maybe we were still in the power of the song, and then the serpent disappeared.

I don't remember whether back into the well or if I just stopped seeing it. Nor did I hear the murmuring water, the breathing of the Zone, anymore.

And suddenly a cat was perched on the rim of the well, stretching and meowing, it hopped down, followed by a dog, then a squirrel darted past, and other animals too came trodding across the surface, one little doggie leaped up on the railing, scratching furiously behind his ear … the lost dogs were back, along with their fleas, and then all at once a girl came striding across the water, and another one after her, holding her hand …

Don't move yet, fools! Rudolf screamed. The Head had dropped out of sight and the two men were fastening the canvas over the carriage.

Doctor Hradil's daughters clambered over the railing: Hi there, Uncle … said one of them, are Mom an Dad around? I took her hand as she hopped down, it was cold, she leaned on me a little … Hi there, she said again … her eyes were chilly as icicles and shone with a silver light, she touched me … What was it like? I asked. Different, the sixteen-year-old replied. Then I heard … shuffling across the water toward us … it's Granny Maceškavá, Bohler shouted, hastening to her aid. Yes indeed, sonnies, it's me, I'm back. An I brought this little fellow here. Anyone else in there? said Micka. No, not anymore, said one of the sisters. It was just us, the other one added.

We stood there without saying a word, cats and dogs racing out of the cellar. I was glad they were back, but I felt extremely tired. The little boy's eyes shone silver too. Are Mom an Dad around? he asked. I'll be damned, Micka whispered to me, it's Kučera's kid.

Hradil's daughters seemed to know. About the little guy's parents. You can come with us, Jožka, you're our little brother now. We've got lotsa little bros you can play with. The boy giggled happily and took one of them by the hand. I'm goin home, sonnyboys, said Granny Maceškavá. We were too surprised by the whole thing to ask any questions. The water had taken these people away and given them back again. We knew the Zone was done for.

Bohler and Lady Laos were headed for the Rock. Micka wanted to poke around town and try some other byznys, Sharky had a plane ticket in his pocket. I couldn't wait to go after my sister … and David … David had disappeared.

We weren't up to asking any of them what had happened. That was their business. And besides, we were kind of embarrassed that a Zone had popped up on our territory. The main thing was, it was behind us now. It didn't matter that we'd lost all our cash. Looking back I realize it was all the same to us. We were of the opinion that only fools and bad people don't clean up after themselves.

Rudolf was waiting out in the yard. The two beings sat in the car.

Hey, Rudolf, said Micka. We wanna thank that … skirvolya. An you too.

Forget it, said Rudolf. The ducats'll do the thankin for you.

It's great, I said, that skirvolyas're still around.

Hah-hah, laughed Rudolf, still around … that's a good one. You guys just dreamed the whole thing.

Oh sure! I said.

Yeah, suckers, said Rudolf, I had you guys under heavy hypnosis.

Do you mean to say, said Bohler, that those checks're real?

Rudolf stuck his hand in his pocket. Yep, they're real.

Enough fun an games, said Micka. Thanks anyway. To the Ministry as well.

I'm not there anymore, said Rudolf. Now I'm in the private sector. An, Potok, I'll be seein you tomorrow night at Galactic. Got some news for ya. You're stayin in town, right?

Yeah.

I know. All right, boys, take it easy. An if I was you I'd let those people go. Nobody knows what the Zones do to em. Those girls're beauties an all, but still.

Thanks for the advice, we can handle it from here, said Sharky. Take it easy.

Who wrote those words the skirvolya cleared it out with? Bohler inquired.

Miłosz, Rudolf instructed us.

Is that someone from the Ministry? I asked.

Nope, said Rudolf. Or actually, I donno. Some Polish guy.

Aha, I said. Cool words. An that snake! Man, you coulda gone sleddin on those scales!

No, you couldn't've, Rudolf said. Well, you guys work it out somehow …

Aright, later! He climbed back into the car. I tried to get a glimpse of the carriage, but all I could see was the necks of those two men in black. Sitting there like they were carved out of wood.

The girls had gone off to find their folks, they knew about the autopsy lab. We didn't ask how. They took the boy with em, Micka informed us. Vasil said Macešková went back to her flat. An he wants to know if he can stay when we leave. I told him no problem, cool?

Yeah, said somebody.

So … friends, said Bohler … I reckon Lady Laos is packed by now … we're drivin out to the Rock in the morning, an anytime you want … the door's open an the Water's poured … my little lady's gonna miss you guys too …

That was obvious to me. Ahem, I said. I'll be happy to make a trip out sometime, Bohler buddy, check in on you an the Gobs. But I'm gonna stick around here a while still. Or catch me over at my place on Gasworks. An how bout you two, I turned to my pseudodroogs.

I'm takin off *nach* Israel, you knew that, said Sharky. Joinin the army.

I got a little somethin in the works, said Micka. An I think it's gonna start takin off. An if any a you should happen to get the urge for some byznys … I'll be leavin my info at the usual spots. I'm sorry bout David.

You guys know, said Bohler, I don't bother much with quotes. But we've gotten to be a pretty disgusting an coldhearted buncha wrecks, including yours truly, an we've got all kindsa stuff under our nails. Least of all the Sewer. So I think it'd only be right to say a prayer for David. Things aren't lookin so good, but there's always hope. When you were tellin us your dreams, Sharky, specially that one about the tenth lost tribe of Israelites, I thought of a quote from old Isaiah. The numbers're 40 an 31, in case anyone's interested. I wouldn't want to blaspheme unnecessarily, especially after what we've been through together … well, I'll take my chances … listen up:

> But they that wait upon the Lord shall renew their strength;
> they shall mount up with wings as eagles;
> they shall run, and not be weary;
> they shall walk, and not faint.

Cool, huh? said Bohler. We nodded our heads, clutching out of habit at the spots where until recently we'd worn our silver. Thanks, thanks, O House of Prayer, that's good stuff, we'll keep it in mind, sure thing, Cassock … our voices rang out here and there and maybe for the last time in unison … in the courtyard's thickening half-light. Then Bohler said: So right … I'm goin … an you two guys're takin the tram too, right?

Why don't we all hop in the mobile, Micka suggested. I got my coats in there, byznys threads an whatnot. I'm holdin on to that stuff.

Hey, take it easy, I said into the car window.

Bye, Potok, one of them said.

An make sure you shut the gate.

Aright, bye now. Later.

Later.

I watched the mobile getting smaller and smaller, till it came to the first street and turned the corner. I shut the gate. My steps sounded strangely alone in the courtyard.

I was glad that Vasil and old lady Maceškova were still in the building. I went off to lie down in the former pack's old flat. Summoning all my brainpower I tried to conjure up an intoxicating image of my sister. I wasn't feelin too great. I even felt lonely.

And then the doorbell rang. Hard.

I jumped up and quietly went to the door. Then went back. For my blade. The ringing didn't let up. Who is it? I said. Why it's just me, sonnyboy! Maceškova. I was pretty relieved.

She stood in the dark hallway. Why don't you turn on the light, Mrs. Maceškova? Oh, I can see fine, young man. She tittered. I switched on the light. Her face was even more sunken and pale than it had been before the well. As far as I remembered. What do you need? Oh nothing ... I was just curious where you boys go nighty-night. Who's around still an who isn't, she giggled again. Nosy old hag. But ... maybe she was just surprised to see the building nearly empty. I tried to explain. But she didn't seem to be listening. Stared at me. Licked her old lips. Looked like she was out of it. There was something wrong with her. But hey, after all, she'd been in the Zone a pretty long time.

I made an effort to be polite, but all of a sudden she just turned around and shuffled off ... no neighbors to gossip with, poor thing. Good night then, I called after her ... and don't be afraid! She didn't answer. No sooner had I shut the door than Vasil started pounding on it.

Come on in, malchik. An sleep here if you want. Plenty a room.

Jou know dis babushka, he asked.

Yes, she's been living here a long time.

Vhat she like?

A hag. A regular old witch.

Vasil's eyes popped.

Naw, c'mon, it's just an expression. How bout a nip of the Fiery? Vodka?

Da! Jes.

We drank till we fell asleep. Vasil kept asking if it was really okay for him to be in the flat. That dope had no idea how glad I was to have him there. He drank so much I think he didn't even scream in his sleep.

The next day I discharged the most pressing morning functions, put on some fresh clothes, and took off. I tried to clear my head of everything past. Černá was all I longed for now. The tram was too slow for me.

I also tried to be practical, and when Vasil wandered off somewhere I'd counted up my funds. Back in the Stone Age of the byznys path, the only serious money I'd spent was on byznys suits and ties and shoes, and the Organization reimbursed me for it. Usually we'd eaten and drunk together, Bohler handled that. We ran tabs at the usual spots, I knew Micka took care of those. In that whole time all I'd acquired were a few cool street jackets and a couple pairs of running shoes. I don't like when every nail I jog over hurts. No need to make your heels cry. The rent for my hole on Gasworks still corresponded to its appearance and location. I didn't spend anything, actually. Not counting the occasional depraved hamburger. I still had a good few months of take-home pay stuck between the sheets. Even got by the hitlers. When I dumped out the pillowcase, I was pretty amazed at the total. On the other hand though, I had no idea how expensive stuff was now. Some went in my pockets, some in my shoes, and the rest I put back in the sheets. I realized I'd never seen Černá in anything except handsome but rather bedraggled tops. And I seriously doubted she washed those pants I'd seen her suffering in. Guess those songs of hers didn't bring in much. Maybe I'd start with a gift ... out of courtesy and friendship ... I had oodles of cash.

I got off the tram and trudged along the street, a nobody without a tribe. It was still early morning, an unusual time for me, no doubt my little sister was still asleep ... there were people swarming all over ... charmless receptacles full of nothing but their own destinies ... flashing by in trams, hopping on, reading newspapers ... some talking to themselves ... honking cars stormed the streets ... everything flashing by, changing constantly ... there were moments it looked ridiculous, the sidewalks were full, everyone on their way to scrape by, scrape through, scrape along, I got in line.

Without a tribe I didn't belong anymore. Who'm I now, I wondered. An what'll I do when I find her ... Then I remembered ... I'd met a Queen once, back when I was abroad ... maybe it was Jícha's story from that relatively recent period, which now seemed tucked away in the corridors whistling with time ... he'd talked about his trip to Europe ... I recalled my own trip there. That time in Berlun. With Jakob Kopic, my accomplice. Jakob gave me a good sentence there, that time in the subway. I remembered it, it was liberating.

We had a fast little group back there in Berlun. And there was no way we could pay for the subway, or any of the other transportation we had to take so we could see, hear, touch, and smell everything. Our finances weren't in any great shape. We were stowaways.

13

THAT TIME IN BERLUN. THE KINGDOM OF THE KANAKS.
THE DARK LADY. I FIND A QUEEN. AN LOSE HER.

Berlun, I reminisced ... we're ridin along neath one a the strasses, checkin out the advertorials, happily sittin, happily purrin, an they got us! Ticket check! The whole train starts buzzin. Black, yellow, white, spotted, everyone splits. We get nabbed. Kopic fakes a heart attack, I'm sobbin. We whip out our cards from the camp. They wave em off. An again, later ... we're sittin. An here comes security. Headin straight for us. Hey, says Kopic, isn't it weird how they always head straight for us? By then we'd gotten normal haircuts, brushed our teeth, shined our shoes, and our *odyezhda* — it was super. We went by the ads: impeccable black-and-white checked sportcoats, trijeans, nightingale kneesocks, Kopic had a fab cap with a Pi Beta Kappa insignia, I was jealous. It was all ... found clothing. But we looked just like the natives. I mean we had our own tongue, that's obvious, but nobody talks on the subway. Hey, Kopic looks at me ... now I get it, it's your mug! Huh, I yelled, what? I donno ... but it's in your mug, it's different! I look at him ... look around at the other whites on the train ... aha! Guess what, dear Kopic, you've got it too.

And then it happened. Jakob Kopic gave me that sentence. We're ridin the subway again, goin to check out a few department stores an a Nazi monument or two, there's colorful groups all around makin noise, an ticket check! An again straight for us! Kopic can't take it, pulls the brake, I kick out a window, Jakob throws down the ladder, an we go flyin into the tunnel. Police flashlights flicker, they're not gettin us! We race, breathless, around a corner, an again another corner, the cops right behind us, an all of a sudden some hands shoot out an snatch us into an alcove. We don't resist, outnumbered. The cops go whizzin by, Kopic sprinkled pepper to fool the dogs. We knew that one. Very well. I look who nabbed us, Kopic goes on reconnaissance. Before me stands a little man, black as a boot, with a tusk through his nose that shines in the dark. Ungara, Bulgara, Polisha, Rumana ... he probes. Nearly guessed. It's in my mug. Ich bin Chekoslovakiya! I beat my breast. Ich weiss, kommunisten, nix gut! says the little man, his teeth're shinin too. Ja, ja, I chime in, grosse scheisse, nix gut, führers!

Blah-blah-blah … sure, guy. Und you? I ask, Angolak, Congan, Ugand … eh? Nein! Nein! Ich Kanak! he pounds his tiny chest with his fists. Gut? I say. Nix gut! Kommunisten? I try. Nix, he says. Banditen. Nix essen, kein vitaminen, grosse problem. Aha! I get it. Dokument? he asks. Nix. Nix identifikatsionpapir, legalité keine! You? Keine! he says. Arbeit, mark, gut gelta? Keine, I reply. Ja! he says, thinks a second. Ich arbeit heer. Tunnla! Huh? I don't follow. Tunnla! Tullers! Ch! Ch! He makes like he's diggin. Nein, not me! I say. The Kanak tugs at my elbow. We go into the back. My eyes bug. There's some mine or somethin back there, lotsa nimble little black guys. Diggin up dirt an cartin it off in wheelbarrows.

Kopic comes runnin up, gaspin for breath, air's clean, he reports, his eyes bug too. My Kanak friend explains: Tullers, ch, pa! Essen heer grosse, grosse, bik! Kanakland keine! He curls his fingers and scoops his hand toward him in the international gesture for stealing. We chime in. Tunnelers! Nach Kanakland! Aha, Kopic understands. They're diggin home. Globe, I say. Globe, thru? Ja, nach globe, the Kanak says gleefully. Essen konzerv und joos supermarket Doychland nach Kanakland fur kindern und fraulen Kanak und nix problem! Grosse und grosse gut. Frishten sie? Ya, says Kopic, nach Kanakland thru globe wieviele kilometrs? Kimtr? the Kanak is stumped. Kopic, an old hand when it comes to language, shows him how long ein metr is. Wieviele metr nach Kanak-land? Ja, our rescuer catches his drift. He draws a number in the sand. Hey, I say to Kopic, if you look from this side it's 60, an the other way it's 90, that's doable. The Kanak rubs the numbers out. Keine problem! Kimter nix problem. My guess is they donno how far it is, says Kopic, an they don't give a hoot. Ja! says the Kanak as if he understood. Arbeit?! He points to the shovels and wheelbarrows. We shudder. But … could be nice in Kanakland … palm wine, beaches … Are you kiddin, says Kopic, we don't have time. Maybe they'd make us overseers, I say, I mean hey, we're white … We don't have time, says Kopic. He's right. Auf wiedersehen … an lotsa luck, we wish the Kanaks. Farewell. A second later we're on the surface. Stridin along. Yep, says Kopic. Kanaks … hey, we're Kanaks too! Oh yeah! I realize. In a blink. That was the important identity sentence. The holy ghost musta come over you, Kopic, or're you from the clan of Elijah the prophet? Could be, Kopic said solemnly. He was right. We were all Kanaks. The megarace of the tunnel. That whole crew in Berlun on the way back to Europe.

Deringer's a Kanak, we also called him the Commander, cause when he got drunk he'd turn to stone. Šiška's a Kanak, worked for British intelligence, kept a close eye on us, gun at the ready. Borowiak, Polak, also a Kanak, then Šimuna, a.k.a. Šmelina, guy had all kindsa passports ... Shimako an Chiharu, both Kanaks, always holdin hands, strokin each other, nibblin at each other's lips an clackin their teeth like lovebirds, they lived together, rapturously intertwined, always lugged around various balls an rods, they'd laid it on too thick with the feminism in Tokaido, got socially under the hammer an psychologically bottomed out an ... hit the road an ended up with the rest of us in Berlun, or was it the beginning? Vasiš, he's a Kanak, slept around the clock, scared of lethal traffic, perforated sleeper, brother of the needle ... Petrák, Czech as a log, always drawin maps, knows everything, never goes anywhere, he's a psycho too ... but Kopic, your woman an lawful wife is Doych, she can be our language bridge ... till she took my splendid name, Kopic smirked, she useta be Yablunkovskaya ... that's old Ukrainian. Heh, Kanak to the core! Kopic's kids're Kanaks, we're all Kanak. Maybe even the good Lord is ... basically ... ? Slews of Kanaks. Rosie Simonides, she's a Kanak too, we pitched our tent at her place, that was our lair. There were thirty cats livin there, we put special crawl-through doors in for em, they would gobble hash, an as it came rollin outta their bowels I realized why they called it shit. We were a Kanak kingdom, boys solid as birches, girls sweet as virgins, eurotrash for the most part. Mark was a Brit, at home he'd been hit, ended up in Berlun. A Kanak. Then there was a Dutch foursome straight outta Breughel: professional Kanaks. We introduced our own currency, the kanaka. Slept in rocking kanaks. Picked through the heaps at Aldi, ruthlessly and Kanak-style. Once or twice I even got a case of the kanaks: A nun came riding out from around the corner on horseback, but in the blink of an eye she turned into a guy on a bike, an old Kanak. And slowly the most important thing of all came into being, the secret and open tongue of the Kanak kingdom.

We didn't have much time. A lot of it had already been devoured by that freak of freaks, the scavenger Colonel Time-Vulture. How I loved the demonstrations! Free, truly, in every sense ... Au! sland! er! raus!* The first word like a pterodactyl, the second like the creak of the spit. Drums, whistles, bagpipes, panpipes, waving flags, I loved it. Didn't miss a single rally. *Auu*, I roared, *sland*, that sounded almost Celtic, then a very solid: *er!* and the glittering finale: *raus!* like the rip of a scythe. The ice queen rattled her frozen train. I marched. No one could tell. I'm very handsome, everyone thinks so. I've got fair hair an blue eyes an clear skin with pockmarks. An I was in the right spot on the globe at an opportune moment. You're so smart, Kopic said enviously. Tell me, he begged in the lair afterwards, what was the protest like? First gimme some cash! He clammed up. Are you kiddin! He couldn't go to the rallies. He would've got his head bashed in. Those boar fangs, brown almond eyes, kinky hair, an that beak a his! Not him! He was obvious! When anyone at the demonstrations addressed me in a friendly way: *Kamerad* … I'd flash a grin an point my thumb to my ears an lips … a deaf-mute *Kamerad* … even they're with us, the Nazi lovers would say to each other, even though they know what awaits em the next time we win, won't be long, isn't that touching … my roars were drowned out by the thundering voices … so I lied my way through an finally I could protest freely, an one day I notice … these guys walkin around at the back, shaved heads, uniforms, but they're luggin burdens, beams an stakes, prospectors? I glom on to em an I can't believe my ears: If I'm lucky, Mirek, maybe herr oberst'll lend me his bullwhip … someday … maybe they'll notice us, Jarka, if we try real hard … yes, Jindra, we're an inferior race, but they're so amazing … Czechs, and they were blind … I was seized with rage … but then pity, they don't need any help croakin, poor bastards, ugh! They're just carryin the load.

We didn't have time. An it was all so fabulous! Foreigners out, oh definitely. We were like pigs in clover. Meals practically free, drinks too. All kindsa interesting stuff. Sometimes we'd test it out, bump into some cop on the street, stumble, like accidentally, drunk, an the cop'd go: entschuldigen sie bitte, toss a dirty look, an that's it … I'd clean the looks up, toss on a stamp, an send em home to my mom as postcards.

We were a kingdom of Kanaks. I didn't work, never had an hour free. Kopic did, he was restless and had a family to support. Took odd jobs, sweeping and cleaning. That brought in plenty for everyone. At work he stole rags and nice plastic ashtrays.

We also went to the huge bazaars where folks from our neck of the woods learned to market economize. Kopic demonstrated his genius. Got on first-name terms with a roulette wheel. Found it on a dimly lit side street. It was a Kanak wheel and he spoke its language. Greeks, Eyetals, and Assyrians spun there. Gypsies, in short. Just don't gimme that small works spiel, said Kopic: it's better to live large. If there's any surplus, we can always destroy it or donate it to the needy. He was right. I sat and gawked, watching the ashtrays, while Kopic hunted among the market people. We hustled to the Moroccans, who hustled to the Poles, who hustled to the Turks, and then we'd buy the ashtrays back and send em on down the line. Often we'd net as much as 600 percent. We also stole bikes. As a favor to the natives, so they'd know what to expect.

On my wanderings along the way to Europe, I met lots of outcasts. The penitentiaries were interesting. That was nothin for alla those craggy Siberians, heavy-duty mobsters from Katowice an Gdansk, Ceauçescu's children, or any Albanian! Hah! The Crimea! With rest homes like that, the mayors and city councils might as well've put up a sign: Interhotel Paradajs. The Russian gangster said: I won't talk. And he didn't. You see, dear children, torture was forbidden in the desirable states. Not that they didn't … occasionally strike someone down … some nigger, Ayrab, yellow bandit, slow Polak … oh sure, but it didn't compare to the hellishness these people had in their cells. Hungry vacationing Kurdish peshmerga, Turkish gray wolves, Ukrainian rabid dogs, Volga ship pullers, Romany crooks from every which where, galley-scarred Chechens, Bucharest mafiosi, all kinds of Angolans, mercenaries … some had spent years in the mines, in slammers where the groundwater flows onto the night concrete straight from … we know where … and just when the guy is such a wreck that even Satan feels sorry for him and sucks the water out … the jailer takes the hose … just in case the fucker was thinkin he might actually survive, and a lot of them did … and they were amazed … You're serious, all I gotta do is say I'll never do it again? And this is soap? A whole bar, for me? Well … I feel like ataman Ralfo Valentino Belmondovich himself, finally! But they didn't wash anyway, they stole it to sell at market, or to give to their Lenochka or Stazichka, their Agla, Vanda, Latka, Varga, or Monka. And what's this … three blankets, three blankets for one night, Mother of God! And this? Those are pajamas, said the kindhearted old sergeant. And which meal will you be having, mister convict sir? Corned beef, sirloin steak, or tofu? All of em. Splendid, splendid, we apologize, but we have only five kinds of tobacco today … an the ones that'd already been in the desirable countries' slammers before knew what to answer … Oh yeah? Then get cher ass in gear, you old reformatory, how bout my human rights! And next thing you know there was a minor insurgency … and the only ones happy were the local eurojournalists, because their light-fingered packs're joined with humanity's outcasts like a communicating vessel. Finally they had something to do. If it bleeds, it leads, we know the old slogans.

I'm just talkin about the underworld now. The most amazing thing was the papers. After all those entry forms an exit forms an hassles an archivalia, finally you could run around the desirable states on your own. Pleading in the slammer, yes I'm goin home, right away, to my family. Only … I can't afford a ticket, never mind a kennkarte. I don't suppose there'd be any cash? Yes? Most grateful. Just a ticket? Great. And will the Railway Armed Forces be accompanying me? Are you nuts, you're a grown man. Yes, sir, pardon me, boss boss, of course, herr commander. Hawk the ticket in the station restaurant and you had yourself a party. The next desirable state was across the border, true, but only wackos bothered with customs. To this day I could make it through with my eyes closed. I walked around like that sometimes anyway, just to see where I'd be the next time I rolled up my eyelids.

Refugees! City councillors met with economists and physicians and Ph.D.'s. Phones at army headquarters rang off the hook. Those riffraff, said the councillor, they're buyin up all the cat an dog chow an feedin the stuff to their kids, what about my poor little Dagmar. An there's more of em on the way. And the city councillors said to themselves, Stalin, Pol Pot, Hoxha, Hussein … maybe those guys were onto somethin. But they couldn't send in the machine guns or they would've shattered their time. They were on the spot where two worlds crossed, two different times. All those flawless Swiss-Japanese timepieces of theirs were useless. Come winter they're gonna tear down all our colorful ads an stuff their shoes an shirts with em. Let's just give em cash. And they got a couple affirmative actions rolling. But the eastern outcasts only went and bought more canned food and juice and a better gun or two and higher-quality smack, none of it went for self-education.

And then one of the councillors trapped by time said, Leave it be, just string up the wires, leave it be, it'll rot away … in time. Maybe he's right, for now, but … especially around the penitentiaries, here and there a jailer or two lightly fingers the gun on his hip, a breeze ruffling his locks as he tilts his ear to the outcasts' uproar … they've just refused the spinach an they want an extra blanket … an then he touches the one in his underarm, an when he sees some free protest goin by, doesn't seem that bad to him … an when an absurd Kurdish nest or two, an irrational Angolan dormitory, goes up in flames … the telegraph's not workin, the dispatches don't get through, the wheels grind to a halt … an the dead bodies roast in the blaze … let's wait, we'll see, the councillor said. Yes, wait and see what happens.

As I knocked around, tryin to see an hear as much as possible for myself, I managed: Berlun: disturbing the peace and riding the subway without holding on; Dormut: hooliganism and provoking an officer (it was the first time in my life I'd ever eaten an artichoke, which I only knew from books before, an I got carried away); Milan: I donno; Paree: I don't remember; Gibraltar: I'm not tellin; Munchen: sleeping in a private doghouse, an that was the only one that pissed me off, cause the dog couldn't've cared less; we had four guys snoozin in there at the time.

After my successful sightseeing tour filled with Kanak studies, I came back to the lair and gave all my soap and blankets to Kopic. I kept one fragrant box for myself, just in case … and off to market we went.

And as I stood around, picking up all sorts of words and expressions as the tribes mixed together in byznys to survive … stealin cash an words from each other … experiences an words … it struck me maybe somethin was happenin here, maybe the mixing was givin rise to a new tongue … a Kanak one … an maybe it was a tongue of peace, a pre-Babylonian one … I mean they're poor, they gotta communicate … till everything's tremendous again an we all look like the billboards an pitch in to rebuild … they need each other … only most of the folks at the markets looked pretty bad, shabby, emaciated or bloated, all kinds of deprivation peering out of their eyes, and hunger … for safety and things … they would've had to mix with the handsome natives too … to put an end to tribes … but they're not wanted, that's obvious … the rags the Romanian Gypsy ladies bundled their lousy young in … weren't fit for a dog, I know, I saw em. I was there. Maybe unfortunately what it'll take, I thought … truly unfortunately, is another couple Auschwitzes, a Wall or two, a Gulag … an even longer path … till it dawns on everyone.

Beat it! Beat it! Quit gawkin, move! Kopic oftentimes interrupted my daydreams and meditations as the noose drew tight yet again, a raid … we grabbed the ashtrays and hopped on our steeds, if ours'd been stolen we stole someone else's … and the prairie stretched out endlessly under our ponies' hoofs as we rode, deftly hunched down in our saddles, zigzagging to safety from the Haida and Mandan bullets.

We didn't steal much … just here and there … like sparrows, I guess, we were fed up with organizing and didn't have the time for heavy-duty crookery. We weren't in the mood either. There were huge quantities of colorful stuff to see. Look at that yellow, zaps me in the eyes, I donno that one, said Kopic. I get it, I said. We swung off our saddles, hitched up our bikes, walked into the department store, and came back out with beautiful sunglasses on our noses. At the next ad, I panicked. I donno that beige, my old WWI wounds're gettin itchy an openin up inside, it's definitely gonna rain. We stopped and went in a department store, came out with raincoats and umbrellas. Kopic had a radio, too. Switched it on. Oy, some unfamiliar, ponderous, industrial, fanatic music! Kopic blanched. But it played. We'd made a good purchase. Now and then we'd get off the bikes and dawdle around on the sidewalk. Then off we'd ride again, each with a packhorse tied to our saddle. How's Iltschi? Kopic called out. On her last legs, I replied honestly. Hatatitla's* barely swingin his hoofs too, grumbled Kopic. We switched to fresh bikes to confuse our pursuers. Sometimes we had to save ourselves … by sacrificing one of the bikes and riding the rest of the way on the better one, each of us standing on one side, holding on to the seat, pedaling in turn … they never did get us. Ah, Berlun, a true sanatorium!

Then I got a job in a brothel. Washin spitoons, takin out trash, sweepin up, I was the spitboy. It's perfect, the spitboy sees everything, goes everywhere, an he's lower than the sawdust on the floor of a pub, no one's gonna usurp him. His rag an bucket make him invisible.

I soon made friends with the whores. There were dumb ones of course, blabbers an screamers an whiners, but some of the girls were great. Fistfuls of Czechs, wagonloads of Romanians, armies of Ukrainians, pastures of Poles, heaps of Hungarians, one gorgeous Jewess, and others. I noticed the movement of nations began in the brothels. One of the great human urges it's got on its mute conscience: the desire for fresh meat. The Italians an Greeks an Turks bemoaned the loss of their position. They organized an underground. No petitions, just vitriol. It got intense at times. Whores're a tribe, I guess, like toy makers or gladiators, clans're a byznys thing. My heart burned for a sister of my tribe. Howdy, whores, I'd say. Howdy, wage slave, they'd reply. Peace and quiet prevailed. I often eavesdropped on their fabled phlegmaticism: You don't watch out, there it is, turn to the left, there it is, lean to the right, there it is still. Cocks, knives, toyfils, crabs, whatever, it's all the same.

I taught them the saying: Singelosh, bangelosh, split right through, quality work's what we aim to do. It had a good rhythm, the girls said it helped em deal with alla those sickening pigs. From time to time they'd express their gratitude, but for real, briskly, in the prenoon hours, before the wheel spun up to full speed. So they weren't totally wiped out yet. They told me about things I didn't know. Permutations, combinations, variations, uriny, greasy, moist, an bloody. Some of the girls, the foolish ones, began to get nostalgic here, dreamin about the petroleum ponds and tractor-filled fields of home. They'd come in search of treasure, but it didn't take em long to rack up a debt the very same size as that chest of sparkling ducats. Housing, heat, meals, makeup, clothes. Protection! The door out of the cage to the golden West slammed shut in their faces. They were under the wheel now. Pieces of meat, not much to look at. Others were smart an strong an didn't let any drool near their bodies, even if that body was as broken and plowed over as Mother Earth herself. They knew their way around. They knew how to get the cash outta the wild pigs, an what to do with it afterwards … they were the ones the students an the killers fell for. One yep, another nope, you in, you out … same old story. I raced around with a mop, tampons, a broom … set up a little hairpin-and-condom byznys, plus lipstick, least they didn't have to cross the street. For some of em that street was the only thing they saw on their way to Europe.

Litka was Slovak, or Slovenian, I donno anymore, I took her to the fair. They're lookin at us, she said in the pastry shop. When it came to sweets, she was like a little girl. No, they're not, I lied. You could tell. What she was. It was as plain as Mars on fire. Wow, she lit up, look at the swings. She gave em a whirl. The bumper cars too. Another coffee. And then it hit her: we gotta go back. C'mon. Let's get outta here. Los! Bitte! Wait, I wanna go to the shooting gallery, squeeze off a shot or two first. I'll shoot your heart out! The way she looked at me, it dawns on me in retrospect, she must've been Slovenian. We stood in the amusement park arguing, in Kanak of course. People all around. Bumping into us. They came to have fun. And we were in their way. It was embarrassing. She wheeled around on a high heel and ran off, she thought toward the exit. Ran all the way to the back of the park, I almost couldn't keep up. Ran right into the fence, stupid whore. Collapsed and began to sob. Her purse spilled out on the ground, she tossed all her doohickeys back in with the mud. C'mon now … Litka! Get up! Finally I got her into a cab. Some date, I thought glumly, all that cash! I looked out of the car at all the people, buildings, machines, phantoms. What else was I sposta do. Didn't wanna look at her. We rode in silence the whole way back to the brothel, the place where she lived. The place she couldn't get away from.

But next day she greeted me as merrily as the earlybird. Howdy, wage slave! Howdy, whore! I appropriated that word, I think, in every post-Babylonian tongue. And I was gettin fed up too. It was better flyin around on bikes with Kopic. All the combinations and permutations and multiplications and alphabets were startin to make me sick. Light and heavy private odors. Too many moist things. Sheets, shits. Too many stains. Pubes and hairs. Every dirty line of work's got its sad or brutal consequences. Their business. But most of those whores were slaves. And a lot of em weren't there voluntarily, that's bullshit, and anyone who says so deserves to get his face bashed. Some were obvious victims that would've gotten under the wheel anytime anywhere. Some liked it. Some were chasing the golden dream and refused to give it up. They went right on dreaming, eyes shut, taking wheelies for the nightmares. And many were forced into it by slaps, poverty, fear. They'd run away from wars, scary streets, factories. Idiotic dads and dangerous lovers. A couple girls there couldn't've been a day over fourteen. They got old fast. Coke and booze and bed. They didn't know anything else. And what else's a slave? The pimps' mugs were as bad as the spooks', if not worse. The girls got beatings. Whenever they acted up, and sometimes just for the hell of it. So they'd know where they were and what they were worth. The romantic, picturesque life of the whore was probably dreamed up by some delirious writer as a reward for an unreal amount of pumping, licking, pinching, blowing, and stroking … his nerves must've been trembling pretty good … by the time he got it up. Maybe there's other brothels. But if this is one …

There was one strange thing there that no one ever talked about. And that's what did me in. I couldn't even pry anything outta Litka, who'd worked her way up to the bar, and that's up there in the hierarchy.

This woman dressed all in black, down to the veil over her face. She also had a hat, a very elegant one if I may say so. I was somewhere off in a corner, stationed behind my sword, a.k.a. my broom, dipping a rag into my shield, when she came clattering up the stairs past me like I didn't even exist. She always went by at the same time. Slicing through the air as she moved, or more like outside of it. I know what a dance is, and this woman danced with every move she made, yet with extreme dignity. In her cold and mechanical movements she was … free. That's how she wanted it. Any marshal, any statesman that nods to the crowd from a red carpet, could learn a lesson in dignity. To see this … lady walking up the brothel stairs. She had her own room, just to herself. I wasn't allowed to clean in there. But one day, swayed by curiosity, I knocked on her door. I knew she didn't have anyone in there. Her door had a peephole, she slid it open. I saw her face, actually just part of it, without the veil, that was enough. She was wearing a black mask, so I couldn't see even a wedge of skin, only her eyes. Those eyes were naked, like there was nothing behind them anymore. Domineering, icy, very evil. I dropped the rag and stammered something. The peephole slid shut.

I knew what Domination was, what it meant here in this brothel. Whipping, just another one of the numbers in the matrix. Only this was something different. I ran downstairs to the bar and told Litka: Make it a double. An if you got any feelings at all for the wage slave standin in front of you, tell me who that woman is. Ich verstehen nichevo. C'mon, Litka, don't do this to me. She could see I was a total wreck. And what she told me stuck in my head, my brain translated it from Kanak. You saw her, huh? Yep … the mask, the eyes. Hey, how much does she go for? One trick? Girl behind the bar oughta know these things. She's not for you … she said a sum that took my breath away. You could get a Rolls Royce for that! Maybe two, said Litka. She started wiping glasses, all at once she had her hands full. You know they always come in the back way for her, through that hallway where we're not allowed. They built it just for her. Sure I know, I faked. But she takes the stairs. Walks around here like she owns the place, I said. Yeah, she even stops at the bar sometimes. I got a feelin she … likes it here. She gives people these looks sometimes, the girls. They're afraid of her. She never talks to anyone. An you know what else … the girls say she's dead. What? No way! The girls say she's dead … but I think maybe she's a famous actress, some star or somethin … an guests like havin her here for the atmosphere. Well, Litka, you're no dummy, kein durak. That's gotta be it. What those girls said, there's no way. Then again, you know what the Russians say: vsyo mozhno, anything's possible … myezhdu nyebom i zemli, between heaven and earth, I added, flipping my thumb up and down. Und under zemliyo, the whore added in Kanak. We laughed. Have another shot on me, Litka. I got a new job. Difrent verk. Luchshi rabota. Grosse marka. Geld. You're leaving? Varum? It hit her hard, I could tell. There'd been more than one of those shots. She said to definitely stop by sometime … just to say hi. But I didn't. I knew she was halfway hoping I'd get her out of there. I just wasn't up for it.

And it was back to riding with Kopic, making merry and whizzing around. I put the brothel out of my mind. Shimako and Chiharu began teaching me words. Omako, they'd whisper, leering. Omako, omaku, omaken, rite nau, Chiharu san, et aussi, Shimako san, heh? Koishii avec moi, yoo super ober lesbien sistrs, ja? Nein, nein, nix omako avec moi, nix omako avec nous! Rien! they giggled, holding each other's hand. We went for walks through Berlun, alerting each other to landmarks and miracles. One window had an effigy strung up in it. Its face was bloody. Ketchup dripped from it onto the pavement. Nagel für präsident! Any president that'd let this stuff go on's got some strange ideas about runnin a country, I politicized. Guess they're just different, Jakob concluded. I went into a bakery to get some rolls. There was a little lake with swans swimming in it. Plus there were like 60 kinds of rolls and not one of em looked normal. I fled. The Japanese Kanaks cracked up laughing and went off to shop on their own. I waited outside, chain-smoking and observing life. When they came out, I carried their bag. They enjoyed it so much, I think sometimes they went shopping just so they could have a guy behind em carrying their bags. It was new for them. They'd look back and giggle. Wave to me every so often. Those two had wads of yen. They were in movies.

I liked their moola, it had holes drilled in it. Reminded me of the shells some of the black Kanaks wore around their necks. Maybe money started somethin like that. People from crustaceans an people's money from crustaceans' protective armor. Anything is possible. I pitched yen with Kopic's kids. They kept winning. Yeah … yeah, I thought to myself, you don't hafta win every time … looking into the pools of their almond eyes, sparkling as they cleaned me out … just make sure you never lose for keeps, Hansel, an you too, Gretel, be wary on your path in the woods, steer clear of the traps, an torch that monster when it tries to gobble you up.

Chiharu and Shimako were constantly soaking and scrubbing each other. Berlun seemed filthy to them. What snow-white pastures do you hail from, O copper-skinned maidens, golden ones? But they'd escaped them. They knew their way around shopping, the rest of us other things. I was very astonished to hear they thought the salespeople were rude. I always got embarrassed in stores. Exotic-smelling beauties wrapping my pair of potatoes or kilo of milk in silk, tying it up in a bright-colored ribbon, and smiling at me like a newlywed bride. Too many smiles, nothing but considerateness, excessive kindness. But then Shimako san explained that it was just another tribal contract. Dis woman, she pointed a long painted nail at the salesgirl, in Tokyo owt of jop. Imposseeblay to tuch yor noze. Vhen tok to kunden. Before the poor newly unemployed girl could finish blowing her nose, I got it. A smile lit up my face too, though not so my cavity-ridden fangs showed. Oll rite, na ja, panyahtno, honto, tribal contract. And what's fermenting down there, beneath the surface … I'm quite familiar with that.

I got almost no sleep. But I fell in love with the Carpet Bar. Everywhere else, I'd suffer like an animal. Think strange contradictory thoughts. Get carried away by strong emotions. Just generally be bizarre. But not at Teppich Bar. I'd follow the carpets' strings and threads as they intertwined in ornamental patterns and then went on to vanish into the inscrutable underside. The top, which was what I could see, was covered with beasts and birds and flowers and people. All gathered together in dazzling colors, and nothing disturbed their peaceful presence. Riders on horseback, falcons on their outstretched arms. An eagle on high. Waiting. Musicians holding their breath, not sending it into their barbaric instruments of twisted wood, a princess in midstride, prepared to dance, prepared to please her beloved, standing full of love, not even stirring. I saw it, it was in the carpet.

But then I started to suffer again. I saw that woman. It was love at first sight. Her pale fragile face framed in thick black hair. And every bone in that face! She touched her companion's elbow gently: Now you may lead me where you will, but only as long as I grant you permission, I may take wing at any moment …

I knew I loved her strides, and the way they made the air swish along the edge of her dress … the way she would fix her little finger, for an imperceptible instant, at some point in space, space which until she entered it merely existed … uncharged … empty and desolate … I could've loved that space alone, preserving it in a silver-trimmed ivory case till the end of my time … naturally, though, I'd've rather had her. They settled in a few steps away. The native snapped his fingers, and terrifying the waiter with his crude, vulgar voice, forced him to take their ridiculous order. I cleared my throat … she looked at me … I had to lean on the table. I felt extreme psychophysical desire. I glanced in her direction. She was still sitting there. All of a sudden I felt sick. My genes were going crazy. Those tiny little beasts that everyone's got inside them were regrouping their ranks. My biorhythm began a new chapter of living. I'm a sensitive guy.

But then … I tried to be reasonable. I studied her escort. In times of turmoil it's best to hone in on the adversary, render him an object of hatred. But he was … I had to admit, a likable guy … tall … after all, my woman wouldn't spend the evening with just any old bum, that's obvious, I set my mind at ease … he was dressed normal, didn't overdo it, shoes, pants, somethin underneath, somethin on top … yeah, he's alright … an me? All kindsa stuff under my nails, in my hair, yeah right, whores an spittoons … I was a spitboy, a Kanak … but if she could've seen through my rumpled warmup jacket into my wild red heart, she would've seen herself in there, reflected as if in venetian glass … she didn't know about my tender, hungry, crooked arms … yet … I scoped the room and ducked under the table, the carpets blurred into a motley jumble … calm quiet colors melting into chaos … I struck out under the tables … cautiously, like a long-tailed monkey … eluding prying eyes … I got in there and listened … back home, on Charles Bridge … she's some kina hat seller, one of us, I rejoiced, and then suddenly I froze: Sir! She called him sir! Since when does any Kanak woman, daughter of a free people, have a master, I just about lost it … and then I heard: cir, cus … oh I get it! Circus! She's tellin him bout the Kludskys, from the good old First Republic, they must be pitchin their tent in the Pearl again … great … and then he let loose, speaking Kanak, but in reverse, he was learning her tongue! He loves her, it's obvious, there's no other possible reason, I let out a howl, they jumped … but then went on … he was feedin her all this talk about huge tours, unreal concert halls, rabid fans, schedules and stripteases … then I overheard … translatsion, reductsion … and so forth … I gotta remind her what happened to Švanda the Bagpiper,* I realized … sůstaň tady, ztay here, the man told her, you wir mate for sis citty … sis citty iss at yor fit … every city's gonna be at her feet, but with me, dammit, I mumbled to myself under the table, I'll arrange it somehow … or maybe just that one city, hers, the city of her mother tongue, that wicked stepmother … just hope she doesn't have a screw loose, I mean it'd be curtains here for a girl like her … I gotta rescue her somehow, by force if necessary … but not like this, some creepy Kanak under the table, what I gotta do's I gotta … disguise myself, yeah, an take her by storm … I knew I shouldn't cause a rift right off the bat, but I couldn't resist … licked her knee, she slapped him in the face. It worked! I scurried off. That knee tasted good.

I hopped on my bike. Not a minute to lose! Instead of cooling me off, the night air drove me into a frenzy. I'll kidnap her. An marry her on the spot so she can't run away. Kopic can fill in for the priest. I flew through Berlun like King Kong himself.

On your feet, Kanaks! I burst into the lair. Quick, everyone, gimme all you got! I gotta get duded up for a rendezvous, amour is here, big coucher avec ma femme, ma princesse, sheez grozz beeyutifull! I dragged some threads out of boxes and the Kanaks out of bed. Berlun's the capital of bohemianism and hit parades. Subkulchur. It's gotta work! I went for the alternative look. Kopic had a tie. That's for the market, he protested. We tugged back and forth till the choker tore in half. I'll fix it up somehow, where's the sewing kit. There! You owe me 60 DM, Kopic pouted. I took his blazer, it was the only one we had, he swept in it. Lend me your Pi Beta Kappa hat, I pleaded. But he was pissed off. I took his kids' ice skating cap, it was a good color. Wait, no, Chiharu, vayk op, help an merci, hilfe! Where's that chic headgear a hers … she was in the shower … Shimako was eating snakes … they didn't wanna be disturbed … they were always takin showers or eatin snakes or flyin kites. Chirina! Chirina! In Kanak that means: Hurry! Hurry! But it's understandable in other tongues too … lend me your mikado … be a sweetie, sweetie, be muta, mutasana san, honto? Daivak! Iamb, dact. Hai? Hai! In the end I wore them down. They laughed pretty hard. But I didn't care. I took Agent Šiška's handgun … just to be safe … and he had the perfect suspenders! I put em on right away, my leggings were sagging. Jumped on my bike … shit, no socks or shoes … but off I rode … pedestrians stopped an stared … I called attention to my indigence … picked up a couple cigars an some change, that'll get me off to a good start … snatched a robe off a clothesline an put it on … took the clothesline too, in case she put up a fight … people gawked … so what, assholes … gawkin at my multiculti garb … the hell with em … I rode like the wind, like a tempest, pedals squeaking … here comes the prince of the Kanaks! Burst into Teppich Bar, there she was! But … everyone was lookin at me … uh-oh, total silence … jaws dropped … an oh boy … maybe … I was bright red … mikado red … an my loved one … my loved one smiled as the others roared with laughter … just smiled … my heart ached … waiters came over, chefs … Have you any maté, mate? I got tangled up in Kanak … I was sweating, dripping, ran outside, the bike was gone. I had to walk, it was awful.

But no, I didn't give up. I acquainted Kopic with my plan. I've discovered the Queen of the Kanaks, I told him. I described her. Told him what she was like! He believed me, why not. We'll wrap her up in a carpet an drag her back to the lair. I can handle that man a hers, hah. We'll attack from the roof. Chiharu an Shimako'll disguise themselves as flower girls an cover for us. Šiška'll iron things out up top if the plan falls through. We'll take the Dutchmen along for backup in case there's any screwups. An Deringer'll be the commander … he'll scare the wits out of em! Rosie Simonides'll push a fake baby carriage … Petrák'll draw up a map, plot out the directions an distances, to head off any mistakes … Everyone was in favor. Except for Chiharu and Shimako … they'd gotten used to our intimate community … didn't want to get off track … I had to promise them the Queen of the Kanaks would be their slave, that they could put her in their movies ... then they gave the nod ... promises are sworn, fools are born ... we set out ... that night, in raincoats, with ladders ... but she wasn't there! Just the carpets ... she'd vanished ... my love ... and I never saw her again, I don't think.

Enough already, I told myself. Quit thinkin back on your youth, there's other things, Potok. But ... it struck me, if a guy like Jícha can write a book, why not me. Only I'd write mine in Kanak. On the body of a changed world, in the ruins of the former time, I'd open the first glorious chapter of Kanak literature! I'll write the book in raw post-Babylonian, the way I heard it on my wanderings through the past, present, an future.

Sure ... it's all been written before ... but a guy's gotta try, as my fellow warrior, the worm lover, put it ... it's all been done, it's all worn out, I'll have to go round an round ... over an over, but that doesn't matter, no one listens anyway ... an the crates full of my book, no, make that stacks of crates, will read: Fragile! Very fragile! Seulement pour Kanaks!

I had visions of moola, piles of loot, from publishing groups, sages an literati, subscribers. I mean everyone speaks it now ... I mean we're all ... Kanaks. That was the idea my reminiscing gave me. Silly idea.

14

I SEARCH AN SEARCH, ALL I COME UP WITH IS KNIVES.
SPIDER'S RIDDLE. OTHER CLUES. VASIL. JÍCHA .
THE WELL AGAIN. LOVED ONE IN WATER.

I looked up and realized I'd reached the part of town where my little sister
supposedly lived. I made my way down a few Gypsy streets, the last one with a
straw mattress burning on the sidewalk and a group of dusky children hurling
mud at one another. I carefully bypassed them. Then came factories. And sparse
grass, dust, old fields. More blocks of flats, in rows. Chebků 33 was the address.
Once I find the building, I'll track her down easy enough. It'll be a pleasure. My
hands were cold but not clammy. There was a pounding in my throat. The
ground floor of no. 33 was all glass. Office space. A sign announced:
RUTHENIAN UNION, CZECHOSLOVAKIA. The last word had a line through it.
CZECH, someone had shortened it to. That was also crossed out and scrawled
over with: Czech never! And another citizen left the message: Russkies go home!
The office was empty. I rang the buzzer. Immediately a woman opened the door.
What can I do for you? I described my sister. What's her name, asked the …
office worker. I don't know. You don't know your own sister's name? We've
been apart a long time. Separated. That might've moved her a little. I lived a
long time … ajiz … owverseez, I said with a Western accent. Ah. She fell for it.
I'm tryin to find my sittle lis … little sister. I'll tell you what, I don't know
anyone here in the building, she said … but Miss Mariaková matches your
description almost perfectly … she helps out here at the Union … You mean
she's your cleaning woman? I asked sympathetically. She wrinkled her eye-
brows. Excuse me, she said, but Miss Mariaková has a degree in computer
programming, she set up our database … guess it's not her, I said ruefully. Does
she have a little scar on her chin, the Russian lady went on, from falling off her
bike? Yes, I blurted. That's definitely Miss Mariaková then, my informer declared. But she won't be back for another two weeks. Tat's teddible, I said. I have
to go to Brussels on business. Why don't you stop over and see Mr. Meždek
then? He's … Mr. Meždek is an architect, he's the young lady's gentleman friend
… What?! Well, your little sister's not so little anymore … Mr. Mariak, why

she's all grown up now! So Ruthenians're Russians, right? I displayed interest. No, she said, bristling slightly. We're primarily from Subcarpathian Ruthenia. Yep, they're Russians, I said to myself … the Carpathians, Romanians, Dracula, Ceauçescu, yep … I thought silently. She handed me a piece of paper with an address on the other side of town. All right, thank you very much. We parted the same way we'd met: coolly.

I took the subway and walked through the tubes. Trying to ignore the swarms. Černá a computer programmer, ridiculous, maybe I should've taken a pass through the building. I can always go back. Sooolingens! Step right up an get cher Solingens! someone on the platform hollered. They slice, they dice, they chop up chives, Solingen, the sharpest knives! Some old bag was harassing the commuters, a cutting board strapped to her belly, with sliced tomatoes, a few scraps of meat, and something green. A set of blades glinted in her hands. I went over to check if the green stuff was kiwi, still hadn't seen one of those yet. Turned out it was just a pepper. But the old bag wouldn't let me go. It's a miracle, look at that, she flourished a knife before my eyes. For a mere two thou, incredible, wow, tell me what does your sweetheart cut with now? She got me. Go ahead and wrap me up one, mother. Comin up, professor, comin right up! Stuck me with a full set. And keep the change, mother, I told her kindly. A hundred thousand thanks, God bless you, professor! As I stepped on the train, I heard her say: I'm not your mother, you lousy creep! My face flushed a little as the train pulled away. The other passengers smirked. I put on a menacing air. It helped.

Meždek. Photo studio. Whole place reminded me of some dictator's hospital. Too clean, too white. Death and pain discreetly tucked away, under a pall, off in the corner. Every doormat the same, right down to the last fiber. In the lobby they had a rent-a-cop with a gun. Who're you here for? Mr. Meždek, I said. Ah, photos, yes? Testing me, like it wasn't written on the mailbox. How'd you guess, I said saucily, and went in. In front of each door were slippers or shoes, depending who's home and who isn't, it hit me. They're scared of thieves, that's how come the gorilla downstairs. Somehow I didn't picture Černá's fella living in a place like this. I had a feeling she was more the type for places where folks weren't scared. Assuming I was on the right track. I stood at the door a pretty long time before I heard footsteps. I prefer to play it safe. Something snapped shut, sounded like a fridge. I knocked. It's amazing how this works. People're so used to the buzzer that when you knock they usually open up even if they don't want to be bothered. Just curious what the change is all about. The footsteps inside fell silent. I knocked again, softly but insistently. Confidentially. The door slowly swung open. I couldn't believe my eyes. Granddad outta some fairy tale. Pink robe, slippers with pompoms. Peering at me, terrified. Deep blue eyes and … pink lips, the guy had on lipstick! His smile drooped when he got a load of me. Some folks don't like my looks at first. He tried to shut the door, but I strong-armed him and stepped inside. Guy was victimhood incarnate. Every bone in his body begged for mercy. Didn't start yelling or swearing. Looked more like he knew he might get what he had coming. I chose my tactics accordingly. Where is she, I rasped. Not a word. There was a plea in his silence. Where is she, I said, where's my sister! Here, I said dramatically, touching my chin, she's got a scar here. Ah, you mean Maruška, he shed a little tension. His voice was what I'd expected, high and reedy. Tremblin. But Mařenka isn't here, she only sits for me once in a while. Where do you do it, I roared. Guy got on my nerves. For God's sake, what … what do you mean … sir … backin away from me, his voice wasn't the only thing tremblin now. I followed him, still walkin backwards, into the next room … there was a rocking horse in the middle covered with ribbons and bows … pink curtains on the windows, couches around the walls with some stuffed animals, all kindsa dolls, one huge one … a beach ball, I spotted a jump rope … Maruška never told me she had such a big brother, we could have worked something out … she just came here to relax, do her homework, why I never … I'm an old man now … she's a good little girl … I wouldn't've laid a hand on the old fart, but if he was talkin about Černá, if she was so bad off she hadda come over to this freak's place to relax …

Don't lie to me! The police'll be interested in this studio a yours! I beg you, Mařenka can do whatever she … but I just have to see my little girl, look what I have for her … he ran, actually more like danced, over to the closet … opened it up, look what good care I take of her, I only want the best for her … pulled out a dress, white with red polka dots, luxury stuff, gold stitching … this one is her favorite … a white summer frock with a bolero, he said … I plopped down on the couch with the stuffed animals … this chick couldn't be Černá … bolero! … looked like the photographer was in his element … we never, don't think it for a minute, Mr. Brother sir, that's not my sort of thing, all she did for me was … dance … he dropped his ass down on that heap a glad rags … frocks … I want the pictures, I said … I don't have any!

I got up and walked towards him. No, really … wait a minute, there's just this one from Paris … Laurent put it out … he ran across the room, robe fluttering, dug through the papers on his desk, pulled out some fashion mag, flipped through it till he came to the spread, and offered it to me. I yanked the sacred pages out of his hand and went over to the window … two photos of a very young girl … that's one thing Černá's not anymore … still there was somethin … maybe the nape of her neck, the face floated in half-light, her legs were bare, I didn't know what Černá's ankles looked like yet … one of the pictures showed the girl from the side, and there was somethin about the way she had her arm raised … for an eternity, the way her hand was bent at the wrist … she's beautiful, so very beautiful, Meždek said standing next to me … it is a mystery, they are the mystery of life, the gateway … Yeah right, we all come outta cunts, I felt like bein mean … and of death … their mystery is on the inside, like their sex, it is invisible … not like ours … I'll take this, I yanked out the photos and tossed the rest on the floor … ach, he said … I despised him … even if that Mařenka girl wasn't Černá … takin their pictures, robbin em, babblin on, what's he wanna go showin em to everybody for, the world the way it is … what if someone decides to kill that girl for bein so beautiful, it can happen … he stood lookin at me, you want to destroy her just like you destroyed that magazine, you aren't her brother, you just want her for yourself … just then the doorbell rang.

Is it her? I croaked. No, he said hesitantly … I don't know which of us got to the door first, but I opened it.

A woman stood there as if carved out of stone, holding the hand of a little girl that looked like an angel from one a those paintings of the Holy Virgin. Maybe it was on purpose. Golden hair down to her shoulders. Tiny lips slightly garnished. Standing somewhat defiantly. I guess the way little girls look when you promise them the biggest cake in the world and a pony named Pony to get them to go to the dentist. I've had it, the stone woman said. Leaving us out here like that where all the neighbors can peek at us. She swept past me, dragging the girl after her. Meždek shut the door behind me.

Back out on the street, I stuffed the pictures into my jacket next to the Solingens, a cloud covered over the sun. I'd hafta go back and see Hadraba, that was obvious, I'd run outta leads. Maybe that was just some random street name she'd blabbered out to the cabbie. I wasn't in the mood for Hadraba or Jícha. But those guys hadda know somethin.

Ach, She-Dog, your pupil and your chief, Potok the patient, Potok the wage slave, convict and merchant, the old actor has forgotten his part. Lost in the wings, plot forgotten … she made no reply, only I knew why. O my She-Dog, give me strength, together we were like Beauty and the Beast, it's just that now and then we forgot who was who … till then it happened, and it happened to both of us, not just to me, you went and flew off into the air, cause that's the way it was, I've gotta believe it … you went and flew off to a better world … hope you're doin all right, wherever you are.

I waited for an answer from her, but heard only silence, the street full of sounds a city person can't perceive.

Salutations, I uttered, nodding to Spidey. May your camels be as grains of desert sand, may your wives be forever pregnant, may your sons humble the tribes under their yoke …

Ah, ciao actor, you talkin Macbeth? inquired the simpleton. Care for a shot?

Absolutely not. I'm on the prowl. Beer.

The bar was empty. This time of day it was closed actually. Pleasantly dim, so the chance wayfarer could concentrate. And also to make it easier to relieve em of their dinero. Spidey was solvin a crossword puzzle. Can't stand those things.

I need a four-letter word for *alebezener*.

Nura.

Huh? How'd you know?

I donno. Intuition.

This is nonsense. The riddle's not comin out.

I know whatcha mean. Černá singin here tonight?

Nope. Seven-letter word for *metal* … starts with U. That's easy.

How bout tomorrow?

Černá's through singin here. Six-letter word for *sty* … shit …

Huh? Wha jou say?

Sty, huh … *corral?*

What?

I donno. I just donno.

Wha was zat about Černá?

Her? Black Maria's through giggin here, finito. What's wrong?

I stood up.

Hey, Potok … with you there's always somethin. C'mon. Have a beer. Relax. It's early.

I need to find her. I want her address. Why isn't she here?

I was articulating like an automaton. I had a terrible urge to slug Spidey. I don't know why. He hadn't done anything. Besides, he looked stronger than me.

Look, ask Hadraba. He's the one gave her the heave-ho. His byz. I'm the bartender, get what I'm sayin? An what's up? You got some kina deal goin with her? She owe you some cash? Cause tough luck, pal, she owes the club too. That's all she was doin here was workin off debts.

I don't got anythin goin with her. I just like her.

Well, she is good-lookin … if you go for that type. Want that beer or not?

Yeah.

But she's a weird one.

Yeah?

Place like this, people gotta stick together. You know the hordes we get comin in here. She's too into herself. Acts like the boss when she's not.

But she is, Spider.

Not here. She's her own boss, period.

Exactly, one of the few.

Few, heh, that's a good one.

You havin anythin? One a those drinks a yours? Or'd you pull em off the program?

Nah. Not for me. Beer.

Hadraba comin in?

Any minute. I'll buzz him you're here. You're one of us, right.

Absolutely. How bout Jícha?

Aw nothin. Cool. Carved a nursery rhyme here. Spidey leaned over the bar and read: I die of thirst beside the fountain … heh-heh, he looked up, good one for a bar, right? … blazing hot with chattering teeth, in my own country I'm in a distant land … nice, huh? said Spidey.

Yep, those're real pretty words, I said. So old Jícha's writin again?

Guess so. But, you know, we got work.

Crime an punishment?

Shut your mouth … an speakin a Černá … she's always like no big deal, but that chick's got eyes an ears everywhere, she's a slippery one … she knew.

You're nuts! She's not like that. Not her … you're outta your mind.

Hey, I ain't sayin nothin. Ask Hadraba. He's the boss. I'll give him a ring.

If you'd be so kind.

I sat and sipped my beer. Tasted awful. Anything would've tasted awful. Spidey forgot about his crossword. Just stood and looked. Lotsa people earn a living that way.

Hey, Potok …

What's up?

That Ukrainian a yours … they been askin around about him. Bout you guys.

Who? The spooks? Which ones?

Nah, some Russkies. Talked funny. I told em I donno nothin. Like always.

Who could it've been?

I donno. Some wackos. Weird getups. An ya know what they said? They said his mom was lookin for him! Good one, huh?

Weird.

Mm-hm.

I noticed they had a new bulletin board. Shifted over towards it. You guys show movies? Since when is Hadraba a cinema buff?

Brings people in, said Spidey. Stuff theaters don't show anymore.

I studied the schedule. All cult stuff: *Blue Velvet, Winnetou, Land of Dreamers, Tame at Heart, Blade Runner, Mrazík** … I'll come by sometime, as a reward, I promised myself.

In walked Hadraba. Spidey beat it over to the glasses, pretending he had a heavy workload. Yep, that's what it looks like when the byznys path comes between former fellow warriors, which I'm assumin those two were back in that hicksville of theirs. Hadraba took me into the back, out of hearing range.

So how bout that Laotian? Where'd he go, he asked breathlessly.

Threw me for a loop with that.

I'll be hearin from him, I'm sure. Hadraba, listen, we're finished. The Organization's done for.

Rudolf mentioned somethin bout that. You goin in with us then?

They stopped me on the street, Side Pocket an one other guy from those photos a yours.

Víška, Hadraba chuckled. Ex-jailbird. Diaper diddler. We got em shook up. Now the thing is to get hold a that gook an find out what he wants. Ess-tee-bee're crawlin outta the woodwork for this guy. Find him. An … Rudolf tells me you're lookin for a girl. Your colleague, Závorová? We got the nets in the water. If she's out there, we'll find her.

I strongly doubt it, I sneered. There's somethin I need, Hadraba.

Hm?

Spider was talkin some shit about Černá … or whatever her name is …

Yeah, Černá. Hey, I know it's stupid, all these suspicions, but she's … weird.

Got any evidence?

No such thing when it comes to that. But hey, better to make a mistake ten times than screw up once!

There's no way.

Hey, tween you an me … it was Jícha's decision for me to give her the heave-ho. He was interrogatin her an she just laughed in his face.

It's obvious! That idiot! He was just hot for her an she wouldn't give him any! Jackass! That poet. You're all dummies, the spooks're turnin your brains to mush. It worked. They finally got you, Hadraba!

It's still far from over. An don't get upset. Hey, she won't get lost.

Already is, far as I'm concerned. You got her address?

No.

I thought my head was gonna explode. But I just laid it on the table. Hadraba was surprised.

You got a thing with her?

No, but I wanna. Bad.

You're nuts, Potok. She's a headcase.

But she's beautiful. She's amazing.

She's a drunk!

Who isn't.

Yeah, I kina get whatcha mean. I got bit by the bug once too … Hadraba scratched at his beard … it wasn't even the slammer that got to me so much as not bein with her, it's funny, Hadraba chuckled, but I was so wrapped up in it I wasn't even embarrassed, like you right now … makes you feel like a little kid … but it's nice.

It's awful, I said.

That too.

There's somethin weird with her though. I can't tell you how many times I've seen her gettin a guy all hot an bothered just for kicks. Chick likes it best when she's got six wolfhounds sittin around her droolin an goin at each other's throats. Understand, even that doesn't get her off. She's just messin around.

Her business.

Yeah, an the guy that gets dumped on's.

I can handle it.

That's what they all say.

She with anyone?

Always towin someone around. She doesn't give a shit. Chick's got cocks comin out her eyeballs … an what's she got? Nothin! I mean she ain't exactly a work of art, c'mon, she's all skin an bones … got her voice an her pussy an that's about it.

Drop it.

She always liked draggin some kid in here, get him all steamed up, totally fuck with his head, just till things got goin, an then leave him, drunk. Way most a those poor bastards ended up! Stewbums were happy to take a whack at em. Fresh meat. She'd watch. An on top a that she'd pump em for cash. It got so I couldn't stand watchin her games anymore. Yeah an finally these sailors got in a fight over her. She got em goin. You know how she sings an what she does durin her act. You know she sometimes dressed up like a little girl? I mean you know how she is. This shit was sick though. We hadda give the guys the heave-ho. One stayed. Think he lost some teeth. He was so tanked he didn't feel it. Face all busted up. An Černá just sits there. Watchin. Chick was into it. This guy got the worst of it, but basically won, if you catch my drift. He was after her. She provoked em. I could see in her eyes how happy she was. Purrin like a kitten. An the guy walks up to her an goes: Would you care for a shot, miss? An she goes, Fuck off, faggot. Who's been fuckin you, you stink like shit. Yep. Every-body shuts up. She's sittin there in this little red sweater, skirt down to her knees. You know she wears little kid outfits sometimes? Guy was totally floored. Shoulda popped her one. I woulda let him, Spider too, heh, I'm tellin you we'd all had it up to here. But the sailor backed down. Chick was givin off some weird kina vibe. He went back an sat down, she got him. First they beat the shit outta him for trashin their buddies … all over that dumb bitch lousy whore.

Drop it.

Calm down. I liked her. But she started to overdo it. Not the ordinary crap like every chick. Every dude. She was testin how far she could push it. That's what got her off. Everybody saw that thing with the guy. Hey, people started gettin pissed off at bein made into spectators for Černá's passions. It was enough to make you puke. Anyway, brawler splits. An she steps up to the mike an says: Any a you urban poor wanna song … slaves? Or'd you rather have somethin else?

Then she walks back to the bar an starts suckin it down. Secret Urge, that's all she ever drank. An that's not a drink for everyone. You know what I mean. What right's she got insultin guests? What's she so nasty for? She gets paid, she oughta toe the line! That's how Spidey put it. She spit her drink in his face. Spider made like it was no big deal. Put on some hard rock. Things got goin again. But this sailor didn't know when to call it quits. Had a drink, got up his courage, an went over to her. Guess he wanted to prove how tough he was. So he goes up an grabs her ass. I woulda stopped him … that's the one thing Černá can't stand, an I don't blame her … all the weirdos we get in here … but at first she's like nothin, just turns around nice an slow, says: Oh it's you, honey … she kisses him, man, shoves her tongue like halfway down his throat, they're standin there … I relax like, whew, she's wasted … only then she takes a step back an nails him with her knee, the guy doubles up, just moanin … she grabs a bottle an smashes it over his head … he goes down, she jumps on him … that was enough … Spider went after her, it took three of us to drag her off … bitch.

Three Northies, not bad for a skinny little girl!

You moron. She fractured his skull. Serves him right, scumbag, she says when she found out. I figure she's hidin now. Probly didn't hear he survived, stupid cow. That chick loved it when guys fought over her. I've heard stories about her freakouts. Nonstop recently. I'm glad she's gone.

Gotta admit though, she brought em in. With those dirges a hers.

Yeah, that's true. Helped a lot at first. No doubt. But lately … a little guitar an some mood music, that's the way to go. That stuff she's been singin lately … human flesh … flowers made outta skin … I donno who's been writin her words, probly some perv … or maybe she writes em herself … Jícha was furious … she's got a good voice, I know. But I'd rather show movies. Let folks sit an keep their mouths shut. Peace an quiet. Černá just caused trouble. It's the only way she knows to have fun.

Listen: If I don't find her, the first thing I'm gonna do is go see the Laotian an tell him everything. An the next thing I'm gonna do is I'm gonna get in touch with Romul an tell him everything I know about you guys. You're terrorists. If you weren't blackmailin me, I'd be gone in a second. An Jícha's a moron.

Yeah right, Potok. I was expectin somethin like this. I think you're not normal. The address is 7 Balkon Street. That's all I know. We need you cause you know the gook. Nothin personal. But seriously, I wouldn't advise any leaks. You're not just dealin with people who know you anymore.

Hadraba, buddy, I know you too. Thanks for the address. Nothin personal to you either. I'm glad you offed the Martian an all. But I got my own stuff. I'm outta here. If she turns up, tell her I'm lookin for her.

Yeah yeah.

What district is it?

13.

Thanks. Ciao.

Ciao.

It was a typical ratty building. Too many of em on the map in my head. Outdoor walkways linin the courtyards, ruinin all hopes of solitude at the end of a long day of drudgery. Another site where neighborhood life is played out. Another place where you're exposed to bullshit. Where they peek in your windows. Good Lord, so this is it: Černý, it said on the door. I'm gonna see her father, I can't believe it. Platinum balls. A dazzling, illustrious man. Kill him slowly for all her suffering. And the cellar downstairs. Here comes a little kid goin there now, luggin a coal bucket down from the walkway, and there's times he feels like he just wants to die but he doesn't know how to describe it yet. A woman opened the door. Tall, thin. Curlers in her hair, suds on her arms. Cigarette hangin off her lip, face worn haggard from runnin around and: I can't make it! Interrupted in the middle of endless errands, futile prayers, only the devil or nobody knows. Old gray she-wolf. This could be her. Same housedress on as every woman in these places at this time of day. Kitchen to living room and back again. They've all got the same one. That or sweats. I used to imagine the Midday Witch in that kina getup when I was real little. Good afternoon, I say. I came to give your daughter her check. I'm from Barrandov, the movie studio. That gets every mother's attention, I think. It didn't cross my mind for a second that Černá might actually be livin here still. Or even that she might be hidin here. There was nowhere. C'mon in, young fella, a voice thundered. Guy in his undershirt, newspaper and beer on the table. So how much is it … I heard Mařena was on TV with that singer, Korn,* he said from inside. One peek and I decided to stay out in the hallway with the lady of the house. "God grant this home happiness," said an embroidery. Not likely. Where's my little girl? the lady said, mouth hanging open. Can I offer you something to drink … Mr. Producer sir … I'll sign that thing for ya, the guy boomed. You're not her father, the lady shrieked. And oh boy, another tragedy, right in the eye of the hurricane, I thought. How much is it, said the guy. Come in the kitchen, she said, taking me by the elbow, he's got nothing to say about it. I'm supposed to get her signature, but we can work something out, I whispered to the lady before the guy came barrelin in … and saw me … you, from Barrandov? he crowed, fat chance. Get out, boy. I went. Whatever's supposed to happen is already goin on. I waited in a passageway. Then relocated to the dairy next door. Stepped in line so I wouldn't stick out. It was a long one.

Finally she showed up. She stood outside lookin around. With the scarf on her head she looked older. Do you know where she is? she said. Do you know? No, ma'am, I'm trying to find her, I'm a friend of hers. So then you don't have any money for her. I do, I do, and I'll give it to you. But can you tell me where I might find her? Are you with the police? No, ma'am, I swear. I believe you. Martička … I think that lady was truly fond of her daughter … she was living in a flat with some friends at one point … I begged her to come back … but she had a mind of her own. That was when she was working down at St. Francis, the night shift …

She's a … doctor?

No, oh no, just a nurse's aide, she wanted to go to school, but …

Where's that flat she was staying in?

Růžová 3. South City. Who are you?

Who does the flat belong to?

I couldn't say. These days, you know …

Who's written on the door?

Mr. Hozner. From the TV station. He used to give Martička a ride home sometimes …

Any girl friends?

Martička? No. None. I donno. Who are you?

I gave her some cash. Looked right at her, tryin to drink in her face, since if this was my sister's mother … but no, it didn't work.

So. Černá used to be a nurse's aide, huh? I woulda thought she'd've made it at least to nurse … sister of mercy, yeah right. I picked up the pace.

I'd been through this underpass once before. Somebody'd thrown a cobble-stone at me. Missed. When I caught the bastard and asked him why, he said he didn't know. Today it was empty. Guess he grew up.

I found the box I wanted, got on the elevator, and rode up, alone. Everything the same, anonymous. Nobody knows anybody. No questions. I kina liked it. Here comes justice, Mr. Hozner, you're through givin lifts to Martička … I buzzed, nothin. Just a second ago, though, I'd heard footsteps and coughing. I waited half an hour, then tried my luck with a different Open Sesame. Three buzzes in a row, fast and urgent. Pause, then again. There isn't anybody that hasn't used this simple signal at least once. In their childhood, say. Pound on the door and it'll open. You just gotta know how.

This character was real skinny. Eyes swimmin, doubt he could even see me. Hair down to his waist. T-shirt on, perforated arms hangin off him like twigs. Turned and walked back into the flat, totally ignored me. I followed him in cautiously so the needles wouldn't scuff my speedy leather. Another two sat in the kitchen. In chairs at the table. That's all there was practically. Except for the smell. Is it Morti? Did Morti come? No, that's not my name, I said. So whadda you want, asked one of the junkies. I told them. The kitchen table was covered with baggies of powder. Mounds of wheelies, medicine bottles. Alchemy kit on top of the stove like out of an old Ed Kelly catalog.* The one that let me in was totally wrecked. Went off to huddle up somewhere. The other two beamed. They were in a witty mood.

We donno your vahine. She's not here, can'tcha see? Hey, he can't see! He can't see us, we're not here! I think he wants ta crawl unner the table, said one. I think he wants ta shoot up, said the other. Found it so funny he pitched onto the floor. Černá, you kiddin, we got colors galore ... wait, he means Bardot, no, Dietrich ... no, dude, Diamanda!

I left the door open, I pointed out, and there could be more coming after me. Huh? The one in the knit cap got up. Look, guys, I said amiably ... she's the one we're lookin for, the girl with the scar, we don't give a damn about you ... but ... it all depends on you ... the boys could be here any minute, and if they start takin turns on you down at the station ... You lie, junkie, said the one with the cap ... I underestimated him ... he slugged me hard ... but the other one jumped on him ... take it easy, Francek, he soothed him, be reasonable ... That's right! I said in a forceful tone, like some kinda Colombian judge. You can enjoy your shit or not, it's up to you ... hey Francek, he means Evie Blue Eyes, the one with the scar ...

That's her! I shouted. But they aren't blue though ... the third one got up again: Ask me if I care. Oh yeah? Yeah! Which one a you's Hozner? I demanded. None, said Knit Cap. So where is he? He ain't here. He ain't anywhere no more, hah, said Knit Cap. His witty mood was coming back.

Look, the reasonable one told me, we don't got nothin to do with her, she's someplace else now ... Where? She's been stoppin by old Dernet's place ... downstairs, second floor. Aright, but if you're bullshittin me I'll be back, I promised him. I was serious. And I said it so he could tell. Real passionate like.

I dropped back down the shaft in a crate hooked to a cable. This whole thing was gettin to be a drag.

I was so absorbed in my drug squad role I didn't lift my finger off the buzzer till the door opened. First thing that caught my eye was the bump on his head. Second: his hushed voice. Come in, my lost child, he said. Which of the brothers sends you?

Sister.

You mean Sister Asmorgas?

I mean my sister, I said.

We are all brothers and sisters.

You're no bro a mine, parasite, I thought to myself. Yes, I said.

How much does she send to the poor? How much did she collect?

Place didn't look at all like the others. For one thing it was almost totally dark. Rugs on the walls. Tapestries? What's the difference? One you don't walk on. I figured Dernet for bout as old as that photographer guy. But he was all in black. Almost like me.

You too seek solace, young man ... you are lost, fumbling your way in the dark ...

You can say that again, I admitted.

Search no further!

Mr. Dernet, I'm tryin to find Černá, Evie they call her. Tell me where she is.

Sinner, yelped the oldster, kneel down!

Only place I kneel's in church, I said, perhaps with unnecessary harshness, an they're locked up. I patted the Madonna on my chest.

Dernet looked at me. And well you should, for Piyus, that Prick, that hydra, is leading the throngs into the flames! Kneel, dog.

Mr. Dernet, please, I'm just lookin for my sister, my girlfriend!

Sister Asmorgas is dead, boy ... and you can only pray ... that is why she sent you here ... we are all her murderers ... he had some statuettes around the room, the window was shut.

I started to sweat a little. Excuse me, Mr. Dernet, I don't think you can help. Kneel, he screamed, and opened the closet door, actually it mighta been a wardrobe ... Asmorgas seeks young men such as you, drink her light and you shall find peace ... an altar came shootin outta the closet, some kinda mechanical setup, artificial light flooded the room, Dernet kneeled down on the floor ... it was a regular Mary statue, musta cost a good couple grand for that motor though ... I had a buddy over at the Tatra factory, I knew this stuff ... gave Mary a pat on the forehead, just a light flick, they produce it for export to Latin America ... the thing rolled back in again, stopped glowin ... Dernet picked himself up, eyes poppin outta his skull ... You know the sign? I drop and bow down to you. Command me and I shall be your servant.

Jesus, I gotta get outta here, I thought. The madman grabbed my pantleg, on his knees.

Tell me, Dernet, I gave it a try, where can I find the girl with the scar on her chin who sought out your presence?

Walk straight down the street and you will find her, he yelled. That wasn't good enough. He kept pawin at me.

People are diseased and unhappy, said Dernet ... perhaps you will find her, but living in terrible sin.

He was startin to piss me off, I shoved him away, pretty gently though ... those tapestries were covered with crucifixions, but not of Christ, they were women. Women's bodies. Just lookin at em made me sick.

I took the elevator up by mistake, but at least it gave me a chance to calm down. There's gotta be *some* normal people, I thought, look at Černá, she's not ... depraved. Or maybe I'm just chasin a phantom, but c'mon, I can't be that dumb.

I checked out the buildings one by one. I knew I couldn't keep it up long, but I didn't wanna throw in the towel just yet. Guess I'll hafta go back to Balkon. With a bonus check.

Here I was trampin around South City like Little Boy Know-Nothing,* it was no good. I'd lost the trail. I hate when that happens. My only option now was Rudolf. They want me, I'll make em a deal. Though I didn't much like the idea a them knowin what ... who ... mattered to me. That's no good. That's nobody's business but mine. Once they know that, they got you in the palm a their hand.

Yep, eatin in stand-up snackbars, and yep, ridin the tram ... same scenery, same faces, life as usual.

I lay on a bed in the former flat of the ex-pack, tryin not to think … about nobodyhood … where's Micka now, I wonder, who's he forgin plans with these days … Bohler and his beauty must be settlin in by now … so Sharky really went and signed up, yep, said he'd been in the army before … said everybody over there has. And David. Poor guy.

I got up and grabbed a rag. That bloody thumbprint of his was still on the light switch downstairs.

When I got back, I noticed the place was different. I stood in the doorway … and sniffed. Something had changed. I listened. Someone was in the bathroom. Only so was my jacket with the knives. And the photos … I yanked the door open and hopped outta the way. It was just a soapy Vasil, he gave a shriek of horror. I stood there snickerin till finally it hit him … but he kept screechin and fumblin around … blinded by the soap … snagged hold a somethin, my jacket. Asshole! I said, yankin it away, you're gonna get it all wet, tossed him a towel and then I froze.

First I thought they were just ornaments, but then I realized he had fingernails growin outta his chest … like armor … like some creatures inside him were pokin their thumbs out, like pieces a mica or somethin. The nails were in his skin.

Sorry, Vasil, I stuttered, I'll be next door … I shut the door and went to lie down again. It'll never be over. It'll never be over for me, I told my pillow.

I think he woulda split if I hadn't been lyin there. Woulda walked out the door and gone somewhere else. Most likely back to the train station. That's how ashamed Vasil was. He tried to rush past me, red all over.

Don't be stupid, hell, I said, your business what genes you got. There's people missin legs, ears, so what?

I mutant.

Baloney! So'm I!

You know nothink.

Well, you're right about that, I thought. I know.

Eto z Chernobyla.

Oh yeah, here come the horror stories. He'd told them before. About how when it blew they all went outside to look at the beautiful glow. About how the murderers fed them all kinds of crap about everything bein all right. About how various bandits and wretches snuck into the evacuated villages and lived there. And mutated. And died.

Wheeler-dealers took a fancy to the thatching on the roofs of the former Czech villages and cheerily sold them off. And not only thatching. Zones're big byznys. Radiation, who knew what that was? It won't kill you now, Vanya, so what's all the fuss about? Can't see it. Doesn't exist. There were other things you could see. Later on.

Vasil told stories about children who thought a two-headed calf was normal. Wondered why their dads buried the sweet little thing on the spot. Three-eyed birdies. A zoo's about the only thing that would've amazed the children of Chernobyl. A botanical garden probably would've bored them to tears.

Vasil was a champion of monstrosity, a connoisseur of curios. He told us how when he was fleeing the area, people on trains got up and changed seats when he told them where he was from. One time he hung his coat on the rack in some pub and they tossed it into the fire. Cause it'd touched the other coats.

The people they evacuated from the Zone, and we're talking entire villages, were cursed wherever they went. No one was allowed to write about Wormwood,* and people believed that radiation was contagious like the flu. Some evacuees couldn't stand it and went back. Ran the army barricades and returned to their land. Illegally. Vasil was afraid they might spot him from the helicopters. So he dug a pit in the cellar and spent the winter there. Come summer he couldn't believe his eyes. The grass wasn't green. The trees weren't trees. He didn't see a single living thing. Then a pigeon. He couldn't eat it though, it had something wrong with its eyes. It had something instead of eyes. Vasil thought it was the end of the world. That God had gone mad and he, Vasil, was the last human left. It never occurred to him for one second that he might be the one who'd gone insane. That intrigued me. I made him tell me that part more than once. He reached the barricades, but the soldiers saw him and chased him away. Said he needed a pass. He got through somewhere else. But he couldn't stand to be around people. Nobody believed him when he said what was going on in the Zone. The radio didn't report anything out of the ordinary.

He went back. And there were others. He met a girl that was also alone. All her relatives had died. Couldn't get a foothold anywhere else so she went back on her own. They ate the animals. When it got really bad they lived on eggs. He said, you don't know … what's in those eggs. They traded with people on the other side of the barricades, farm tools for food. Hid from soldiers. Vasil always enjoyed describing that period … it seemed like he was happy then.

No chairmen, no meetings, no statues of leaders jutting up absurdly, nakedly, from the empty village squares … he didn't have to bow down to anyone, he wasn't a dog anymore … he had a woman.

But then he started growing the nails. I don't know if there was anything wrong with the girl, Vasil never said. Once he told us about the thing the girl gave birth to. She snapped. He buried her and fled. Felt like a monster. And he had no idea what would happen next. To his body. He expected to die soon. That explained why he was so shy and preferred to sleep down in the cellar. He saw himself as stigmatized.

Seriously, Vasil, I don't give a damn. If you got a trunk growin outta you. Your business, hell. Everyone's different. It's all the same.

Da?

You Chernobyl Czech you …

Bot I no haf legitimatsya.

You want some ID? What for?

Legalizovatsya.

We'll fix that! I still know people! Got any proof though?

He brought me some tattered papers. We did a little lookin into em. Yep, issued in a city that didn't exist, in a region that'd changed names, in a country that'd split up … signed by dead people … somebody else's picture … classic.

It'll work somehow, don't worry.

But it didn't. Vasil got taken in by the People of the Faith, servants of the Great Mother. Or whatever.

The People of the Faith were the only ones that took him under their wing during his destitute trek across the Union. Probably would've ended up in the clink otherwise. Didn't have any proof for the two years of his life he'd spent in the Zone. Made up some story about workin on an oil rig. But he was scared. Even back then he knew it was dangerous, he knew too much about the Zone.

Then he found his way to some journalists … from the desirable countries. Met with em in somebody's flat. That was the first and last time he let anyone look at his nails. They rolled the cameras and he told his whole story. Gave a fake name though, he didn't want to take any chances. A week later the story came out in one of the desirable world's leading weeklies, duly dressed up with quotes from the poor fugitive railing against the Soviet government. Splashed across the cover was a photo of the man with the nails. With his real name of course. All the other prominent glossies ran the story too. He had to make himself scarce, in a hurry. Go to meet Anyushka. That was what his new colleagues from the cheap seats called death, he explained. That intrigued me too. Anyushka. Really? Such a tender name? Da. Vasil didn't expand on what kind of enterprise he and his new colleagues were involved in. But in Moscow he'd also met People of the Faith.

At that point you could say all kinds of things out loud. The Great Mother, who got money from her followers, said them over the radio. From what I gathered from Vasil, she promised to change people ... the same old song ... give me all that's yours and I will strike you like a bolt of lightning, tear you up by the roots, change you ... I think Vasil ... and he never said this ... I think he wanted to get rid of his nails, sure, he could trim em, but I think he wanted to be free of all the horrible things he'd been through ... and the Great Mother found a lot of people like him.

Skolko, Vasil? How many?

Miliony. In Ukraine. Many in Bulgaria. Balt!

When he saw how interested I was, he brought me a picture. A photo actually. Of the Great Mother.

Is icun.

Icon?

No, is new. So: Icun.

On the back was a strange picture, a drawing. In color. A face, a woman's, with a cross in one eye, a star in the other. The eyes followed you wherever you moved, like those photos of the deceased they put on tombstones. Same technology. What was even worse, the face had a ... nail through its forehead. Or a screw. I didn't like the look of it.

Behind the face was a railroad car. But the Great Mother's face was kind. She looked to be about forty. Dark-skinned. Like some woman from India, I guess. Where's she from ... this lady?

Is born in Chernobyl.

Right there, yeah?

I no know. Nobotty know. Ana ... change? ... She change people to her rebyonky, her children ... ana yeh zashchichayeh.

She protects them?

Da. Protekts.

When Vasil finally got the chance to make his plea to the Great Mother ... she told him no. She told him he was on the right path ... nails or no nails, and that he had to stay with her. That he, more than anyone else, was her child. And then Vasil told me, and this was one thing he didn't share with the others … maybe Bohler, I donno … that the Great Mother had chosen him, along with several others, to send to Prague, just as she sent people to Sofia, Bucharest, Bratislava … Poland, all over … to herald her coming and gain new adherents who wanted to change themselves … and give her all their money and land, because the final great change was approaching, and only those who changed in time would survive …

I think I yawned a little.

Guess it hurt Vasil's feelings … he said the prophet's rebyonky weren't all just dumb and destitute like him, there were also scientists. Atomic scientists.

Yeah yeah, I said.

Patok! Vasil shouted. I'd never been able to teach him not to do that. Plus when it came to the Great Mother, he tended to get emotional.

Eto seriozno. Ana tozhe rabotala v etoy industrii … The way he told it, she was one of the engineers that survived Chernobyl, and she was there the whole time. She knew what people could take so the radiation wouldn't harm them. But they had to change. He said she spoke every tongue on earth and she was there for the whole world.

Every tongue? Ochen intyeresno, Vasil. So why'd you run away?

He gave me a look.

Aha, I said to myself. And casual-like, randomly … moved off the bed. So maybe he didn't. What's he pullin on me. Probly been workin for the sect this whole time. Nailhead. All this stuff that's been goin on … Vasil!

Ty hochesh s nye gavarit? She in Prague. She … want see you.

Me? Why me?

And Vasil told the story … claimed he really had run away from them, that he'd wanted to make his way in the new world, the West, on his own, but they'd found him … by his saliva, from the labels he'd stuck on the bottles of Doctor Hradil's Miracle Elixir.

Said he was back in contact with the People of the Faith and the Great Mother wanted him. And he … thought he had no choice. He said the Great Mother wanted me because of the Elixir. I patted my Madonna. Vasil watched. Smiled. He knew something.

The Elixir's gone!

Vasil gave a shrug.

She know vhat is Elixir … superadidas!

Great, Vasil, we'll see. Tonight though I got an appointment. Rabota. I'd be thrilled to meet the lady later on, panimayesh? Zaftra!

Vasil smiled kindly again and nodded his head. I pulled on my shoes and went to get my jacket. Emptied out my safe, that pillowcase was getting pretty deflated. Vasil stared. And didn't blush and didn't avert his gaze. Then I stood lookin around the flat, a relatively long time … gave Vasil a friendly pat on the back, see ya later!

Da. See me.

I took the stairs slower than usual, knowing it was the last time. Goin to Gasworks. I jumped for joy a couple of times, it's solved where I'm gonna be then. Until I find my love … Great Mother, gimme a break. Drop dead, fanatics.

Galactic was almost empty. I sipped gingerly at the special house tea … I noticed: ever since I'd been lookin for Sister I'd cut back on the Fiery. Gotta be prepared.

Galactic didn't have a stage. There were other things here. But I wasn't interested. It wasn't in Prague 5, like Černá's, wasn't so out of the way. I appreciated the view of the street. Entertaining sometimes.

Every now and then there were demonstrations out there. Today as well, but I wasn't too wound up. I was almost lookin forward to seein Rudolf. Touched the tiny scar on my left shoulder. I don't care if he's a sextuple agent, I'll take that Laotian over the Great Mother any day. Why is it the Russkies're always so tragic. That cattle car on the icun … aha, that must be it … long as no one's packin the Russkies in em, they go and pack someone else on. Most of the time there's room for both … that's how vast a land it is. Little nations like us … we've got an advantage. There's not so many of us to wipe out, even though on the other hand … I got tangled up in the philosophy.

So instead I flipped through my mind, goin over my morning visits. Those musta been false leads. But if Černá thinks she seriously injured … too bad I wasn't there! … that sailor that harassed her, she might've left the country. What would she do … out there … with her tunes.

That time at the pharmacy … she hadn't looked too healthy. The pharmacy. The green neon. I'm an idiot! That's where I hafta start. She must live around there. After all, it's not like she'd go to the other end of the planet in the middle of the night. If I don't find her at the pharmacy, I'll go back to the first address.

Mariaková, that Ruthenian musta made a mistake. There's tons a girls with scars …

I was about to take off, but then calmed my agitated muscles and nerves, ordered my heart to be still. First I gotta clear things up with Rudy. After all … I'm gonna need some work. I'd been checkin out prices in town, the streets were friendly enough, oh sure, but the cost of living had soared.

All that tea picked me up a little. Still I wasn't gettin any bright ideas … didn't feel much like makin up jokes. But I wasn't in the mood for anything serious either. My clothes didn't seem as clean as they'd been that morning. But I was lookin forward to Gasworks. To my new life in general. Finally Rudolf showed up. He took a seat and blurted out without any intro:

So the girl's name is Eva Slámová and she was born in Ponořany. Her father did time. Heavy stuff. Now he probably works for them. You oughta have a word with Vohřecký.

What girl? He means She-Dog, knucklehead, doesn't know shit … or is he talkin about Černá …

Who's that I'm sposta talk to?

Vohřecký, Side Pocket. He's ess-tee-bee, but he works for us too now. Rudolf explained.

And that means he works for who? I fired back.

Don't bother rackin your brains, said Rudolf. Adding: Listen, Jícha's dead.

What?

They found him in a building on Eastern Ave. I was waiting over at his place, and when they gave me the news I went through his desk. Found a piece of paper with your name on top. Want to know what it said?

I wanna know who killed him. And I can't help it, but my legs're shakin, how bout a shot? You think someone was tryin to rob him?

Nope, Rudolf shook his head. We got infiltrated. They had someone on the inside. You know who, Potok. Sámová. He leaned forward and looked at the paper. Or Slámová, it's a little bit smudged.

I donno who you're talkin about, and I don't care. That's for you and that agency a yours, Dostoyevsky, you amateurs. The spooks killed him, it's obvious!

Not at all, said Rudolf, not quite. You're going to meet with Vohřecký. He wants to talk to you.

Why would I meet with a spook? Whadda you want from me? What're you guys up to?

Not many people know about Dostoyevsky. You're one of the few.

Well, pardon me, but I hope you're not tryin to pin this on me.

No, you and your pals were just tellin each other goodbye when it happened. You put transmitters in there?

No one ever took them out.

I tried not to look at him. He left me alone. He knew I needed time. I sat with my head hung down … drowning my spoon in the green tea … the world, the whole map, every horizon suddenly reduced to a few sharp lines with me bogged down at the spot where they intersected. One thing no one could take from me though was that pressure … the desire to be with her, to taste her skin. Slámová, maybe that really is her name. Big deal. Maybe she even … does work for them. That's awful. That's ridiculous. And even if she did.

I peered out the window. An armored personnel carrier cruised down the street, slowly and majestically. Tore up a few cobblestones and rumbled off. The sun high outside gleamed like a trinket, cool and metallic. Over on the square, a demonstration had begun. It was on the bar TV too. With the sound turned off. The speaker waved his fists, opening and closing his mouth. If somebody had picked him off, I wouldn't't've heard a thing. The figure on the screen would've collapsed, incomprehensibly, a stain appearing on his shirt out of nowhere, without warning. Maybe I'd think it was just some stupid movie. Maybe I'd expect the hero of today's episode, Tidy White, to appear, and the shirt in the ad to wash and press itself. Doesn't matter who's in it. Just as long as it's clean. I don't even care who it's for. I want Sister.

You know who the Laotian is? Rudolf continued. Here's what we got from Vohřecký. He pulled out a sheet of paper and read: "Nguyen Dai Vang, general … chief of special forces … South Vietnam. After forced unification of the country in 1975, active in the opposition movement. Served ten years before escaping to Hong Kong. Headed the foreign resistance against the Communists in Vietnam until 1985, when he vanished into the jungle. Commander in chief, Thai partisan camps."

Zat a fact? For real? You're not shittin me?

Vohřecký claims this guy's recruiting gastarbeiters to go back and fight the Communists. Thousands of them've already taken off to the West, don't like it here in the factories, that's obvious. But sposedly this Vang's only after a couple ex-officers. When the Commies took Saigon, these guys just dumped their IDs, got new identities, some of em even new faces no doubt, and melted into the crowd.

Rudolf informed me.

Well, I donno politics, but if the communards were pourin in there, it's no wonder.

Ever hear of the Vietnam War?

Sure, hippies an stuff. Forman did that movie about it.

Sheesh, said Rudolf. Well I won't burden you with the details ... but when the Americans, despite all the promises, finally pulled out of South Vietnam, the Communists started up there ... know what reeducation camps are?

Concentration camps? I was just guessing.

Yep. That's where most of the ones that Vang's after went. But as the situation changed, some of them resurfaced and got sent to work in Eastern Europe. A few of em ended up here.

C'mon, Rudolf, that's a pretty long time ago now.

Yeah, but this time is like vacuum-packed, get it? It's still the same over there. It's suffocating, it keeps on going.

I perked up. Believe it or not, I get it all right ...

He nodded. The general needs these, shall we say, specialists for his partisan camps in Thailand. Where else is he going to find men like them? Seasoned cutthroats, Rambos in the sheep's clothing of diligent factory workers, you might say. They're the reason Vang's here. You've got to realize ... there's a hidden battle raging! Neither side makes any noise about it ... Vang and his men're kidnapping Communists, Vietnamese secret police, embassy staff. They dope em up, interrogate em, and then they kill em.

You're not shittin me? I mean, it's possible, but ... I said.

Don't let anything surprise you! said Rudolf.

Uh-huh. Reminds me a some kinda wildcat Wiesenthal.

I know you've heard about that, Rudolf leered. But there's one other thing. He leaned toward me and said: According to Vohřecký, Vang's also got people in Ukraine. And they're interested in a certain seven-letter metal, beginning with U.

Cut it out, I told him. You remind me of Spider.

What spider?

Where'd this Vang learn to speak Czech?

Huh? I donno. What makes you say that?

But you told me … or was it Jícha.

Uh-huh, said Rudolf.

I still can't believe it.

I know.

What does Vang need me for? I asked.

He knows you. Maybe he trusts you. You helped them out. Plus you know your way around here.

A rock crashed through the window, showering us with glass, Rudolf quick dipped under the table. I followed him. The cops wrestled a pair of uncouth protesters in black hoods into a paddy wagon. We changed seats. Up at the bar they switched off the TV and turned on some music to drown out the demonstration.

We're counting on you to help Vang find those men. That crew of yours was their only contact here. And you're the only one left. If Vohřecký's information is right, Vang's ready to roll. He's gonna need a Czech to take him around the dormitories. You're the only one. We bet on it.

Sorry, but dorms aren't my style. That was Jícha's thing.

Yep. Exactly.

Huh?

I donno. But he knew it wouldn't be easy for a Vietnamese. Even the ministry doesn't know which gook's where. There's no way to keep track. And the dorm managers, the factory people, they're not gonna talk to some zipperhead. Even if he does speak Czech.

Why was Jícha killed?

You want that girl?

What's with Side Pocket an that other guy?

Vohřecký's a complicated figure, he was in Angola. He'll find you somehow.

You drive me nuts, Rudolf, seriously. Since when was there anything complicated about a spook.

You can't see things so black-and-white, he assured me. It's a different era.

So I'm a mercenary now?

Soon as you say the word.

How much?

Let's say five.

Been gettin expensive, I noticed.

Ten.

Deal.

I sat by myself. Jícha. Yeah, I wasn't wild about him. But the least they could do is publish his books now. Who though? I tried to remember that thing Spider recited to me at the bar. Bout the fountain. I'd forgotten, but … maybe I could put out somethin a his. With the cash from Rudolf. That'd be classy. What's it matter to Jícha now anyway though. What's it matter to anyone, I mused. I'll grab my girl and we'll bolt. Somewhere far outta reach of any long fingers with nails so filthy no constitution can touch em.

A couple kids in hoods dashed into the bar, cops on their tails. They swept em out in a second. Without any reporters' flashbulbs in sight, the kids didn't even resist. It was like the moment never happened. Then some beggar walked in wearin blindman's glasses, but it was just an act, they'd never swallow that étude at DAMU.* The waiter gave him the heave-ho. Had a pretty good view from behind the bar. Probably got a show like that every day. My homeland's in convulsions and the rats're rompin along the surface.

Almost forgot about that stuff from Jícha Rudolf'd brought me. I tore open the envelope. At the beginning was a note: "Do as a novella and also try as a play. See what Potok says, it could work for them. They're still performing." Behold! A message from the dead … from the old days. I took a look.

> Initiation ceremony, font of the story, hero must pass through a tunnel whose slimy walls crawl with repulsive spiders, taunting him with their long furry limbs, the cold wet slap of a monstrous worm beats beneath the sound of his footfalls, in whose echo we hear the stealthy tread of his doppelgänger, as the whoosh of scaly wings pierces the silence. At each and every step the threat of a sudden fall, brutal murder. Pain. And a mocking cackle. An endless train rumbles somewhere overhead.
>
> A story of life as initiation, the final passage into maturity while staring death in the face, a maturity separated from the grave by nothing but a thin wall, three bricks thick, and from the neighbors' you hear the sound of muffled conversation and coughing as a harbinger of mysteries to come, some plot, you don't know what. Those few moments in the protagonist's life extending from the winter of the first encounter in a shadowy bar to the golden sparkle of mountains in summer (to be described later), when he lay stretched on the rack of passion, writhing near death at the mere illusion of his little harlot's mouth, be it in his cell or in that sunny home where their limbs so feverishly intermingled, or

in a solitude filled with gnawed fingernails, poorly digested booze, and indigestible paranoia.

In this time of trial he most resembled the dancers of the ancient people, treating the slender threads of his perception as recklessly as an old rag, an unwanted painting received in the course of a drinking spree. His perception was frayed with the same effort with which our fathers and grandfathers once drove wooden spikes beneath the skin of adolescents' backs and thighs, and dragged them into the wilderness, where they were left to alternate between waking and dreaming, and the weaker ones died of exhaustion. But he who lived through the sacred delirium of the dream dance acquired strength and saw his protector in animal form. He returned to the circle of the tribe, and was solemnly invited to take part in normal life, as if nothing had happened, and then went on, obedient to his power, in the dance of love and death, drinking solitude, which did not kill him, maturing, nearing the end.

For our protagonist, however, there is no barbaric brother, no tribe, awaiting him at the end of the journey, no one but he himself. The forest, a nest of thorns, the harlot, and her honey. Good.

Well, to tell the truth, dear Jícha, I said to myself. But I decided not to say the rest … a little one-act maybe, some kina emotive-type thing, sort of like in remembrance … but.

I walked across town to the pharmacy. The neon. A diamond in my memory now. A fixed point swathed within the purplish, oozing flesh of my brain. The place where I first saw her.

I combed through all the buildings. Nothin. Feeling hungry, I walked into a greengrocer's shop and rejoiced at the sight of unfamiliar fruits. They had the vitamins goin on decent here! Ate a couple bananas, that did the trick.

Cleared out. And it was night. A very frustrating one. Didn't have the strength left to ride out to Chebků. I stretched my strides toward Gasworks, back to my hole. It can wait'll tomorrow, I gotta sleep.

Walking up the stairs to my den, slowly I switched off again, absorbing the old building's sounds. I was back in my refuge, this was where I'd come from. I knew the damp map of every wall here, traveled them many times. I kept my back to the windows as I went along the walkway. Learned that early on, couldn't've lived here otherwise. I opened the door … and froze stiff. There was somebody in the chair at the table. The room was dim. No, it's not her … a man stirred and switched on the lamp, it was Vohřecký. Side Pocket.

Come on in an close the door.

I did, it was a relief actually. I've always been a fan of fast cuts, but this Rudolf … the guy was a little too fast.

Makin yourself at home, huh?

That's right, said Vohřecký.

Where's your partner? You don't look whole on your own.

You'll get over the wisecracks soon enough, sit down.

I didn't like his bossy tone, but I knew I'd get used to it.

So tomorra you go inda action, said Vohřecký. Vang's got almost his full team a gooks together, just a couple missin he can't find still. Tomorra you go see um, pay a visit to your old pals the Laosters. That's what you guys call um, right, the Vietnamese? The ones that slope chick a your pal Bogler useda rub shoulders with. One of um works for us. Vang'll be there too. You're gonna offer im your services.

Fuck alla you.

That's your business. By the way, bein the diligent guy that I am, I combed through all the leads on that girl a yours … Závorová … the one that emigrated. Or did she? Huh, Mr. Human Rights Activist? Or maybe she did somethin else? Somethin ugly an hadda pull a fast vanishing act? Didn't even give her snookums a smooch?

Boring!

You punks, toss around a few flyers, thinkin it's who knows what … human rights!

Baloney, cop … you'd never understand … that was real life, what're we even talkin for.

You really think so, Vohřecký rocked forward in his chair. My chair. Lemme tell you somethin about real life … I was in Angola! You punks back here writin your petitions … we knew alla that … alla that was covered an I … you didn't even vote, you chump, an you thought you had a life. Only fightin you ever did was with your weepy-eyed mama! Bitch was climbin the walls when we took you in.

It occurred to me maybe Vohřecký was liquored up. Why else would he be tellin me this? But actually … maybe I can pry somethin outta him.

Would you like a drink? I've got some Fernet.

Yeah. But listen da me, that whole time you were needlin me, you little punks … an those jackass philosophers, yappin away bout human rights …

literati, they were just burned up they weren't on TV! Only reason they worked in those boiler rooms was so somebody'd take their picture an send it to the West. They knew how da sell themselves. But you punks. You know I felt sorry for you? That guy Čáp, hadda bash him up good da get him da understand. That pal a yours, Hadraba … hah-hah, my pal now too, least he's a man. You know he clocked me once? Human rights! So I laid offa him. Rights my ass. This Cuban down in Angola, Jesu Morales … walkin death, that guy, even the freedom fighters were scared a him … I'm down there, little buddy, drivin in my jeep, an I see this broad … I pull over an bang she hits the deck an spreads her legs, my first day, those Cubies had um trained all right. Morales dressed all in black, had a machine gun on the hood of his jeep … Baby Jesus, they called im … couldn't stand priests, shot up a weddin one time cuz of it … people'd run for their lives when he came da their village: Okata, okata Chesito nagada! It's Baby Jesus, everybody run! … first few nights it kept ringin in my ears, then I got used to it … he'd tear down the road, just honkin at people da get oudda his way … didn't give a flyin fuck … he knew the freedom fighters wanted his ass like nobody else's … you punks didn't know jack about real life, as you put it … real! Real was when they caught im an we found his head afterwards … in the kitchen … strung his legs up on the gate so we'd find pieces all the way in … never knew who was who down there, what with some a the Cubies bein niggers an all … there were uniforms lyin all over the place, from all kindsa armies … didn't strip um off the dead down there … an me an the rest were Czecho-slovakia, wasn't a lot of us, just specialists, special forces … the hell you starin at? Yeah people keep quiet bout it these days. But without our doctors those Cubies woulda been dancin on air! An who da you think built the bridges? I was proud to be Czech … real was when we were crossin the water an Franta Mázlů got picked off, hadda leave im there in the mud … that stuff a yours, that was just a game! An we let you play! An guess what we learned down there off the darkies … guess. Lectric current, that's right, little buddy … those darkies can take it … Cubies droppin like flies an those darkies'd crawl right off through the mud an find those mines no problem, yep, always found just that one … one black girl … got stuck with a bayonet in the belly, our Doctor Rak sews her back up an next thing he knows her bed's empty … found her over in the women's barracks, eatin an apple! What were you punks doin then, writin petitions … Vohřecký started laughin his head off.

Y'know I got a doctorate, he said ... in psychology, you know that? You all think we're just a bunch a gunslingers ... an know what socialism brought Angola? Sposedly women's liberation. That's what the feminists from the West wrote! Sontrag, you wouldna heard a her. Real cow. Down there women were slaves, an every man had five or ten of um tillin the fields ... that all got ripped to shreds, those families were hidin freedom fighters anyway, then famine hit, men couldn't handle it on their own, but an important step'd been taken, little buddy ... there's plenty a things I could tell ya ...

You guys were on the Devil's side though ...

Oh gimme a break, how da you know? You peabrain fanatic. Alla you an that tego svego Polish Bog crap a yours, you idiots. We got the goods on alla you. Too bad you lost your boogeyman ... Nobody can say what side we were on, you'd hafta be clairvoyant. Enough fun an games though. You got your instructions. You'll stick with Vang as long as you can an then let us know where his team's holed up. Our man can't find out. We gotta shut these guys down before they head east. An don't get any ideas, one of um'll be watchin you! Rest assured!

Guy can't handle it by himself, huh?

You donno beans! He'll be with um right up till the end. You no, there's no point. Well, he picked himself up. Quick and steady. Guy wasn't drunk, he was just actin. I donno why. Hasta la vista, baby, he waved from the door. Then shut it behind him.

Another door that I thought I was the only one with a key to. I gave it a little kick. Kicked around the chair too. Slammed the table a couple times. Hard, from over my head, with both hands. Didn't help much. I noticed he'd taken the bottle with him. Some slender bug was crawlin along the wall, killed him, left him there. Lay down on the bed. Then got up and opened the wardrobe. From bed to wardrobe, that was my path, about four steps. Behind the wardrobe the sink. And then the door, my den ends there. Then the world. It was a long trip to the toilet, all the way to the subway. Sometimes I'd dream about vitamin factories finally comin up with a food that didn't make you shit. Mornings here my poetic states tended to be consistent: head empty, bowels full.

My wardrobe was full of disguises, threads. A box of calling cards. Interchangeable names and professions. Anyone who thinks they already know what they are suffers from a lack of imagination. And all the way in the back, several dresses and a jacket ... women's things, what remained of She-Dog. Some poetry books she was fond of. And a couple kerchiefs and barrettes … that was all I had left of her. That and my dreams.

It was beautiful when I'd find a hair of hers lying around every now and again. In a corner. In the dust on a shelf. All of a sudden on the ground when I got up in the morning. Blown there by some good wind. Hairs don't rot. One of her kerchiefs I put on my pillow to carry me away. And fell asleep.

The buzzer woke me. I leaped out of bed, musta been night already. But I didn't want to open the door, not anymore! I said to myself. I can't … but the buzzing was steady, it wasn't a signal, whoever it was was ringin nonstop. In my dreamy daze it occurred to me that if I opened the door, it'd be me standing there.

But you can't think about these things or they happen. I tugged the handle and there stood Vasil with two reinforcements. Vasil was smiling.

Let's go! Mother is waiting for you.

Vasil drove, the other two on either side of me in back, I guess to keep me from jumping out. An unpleasant arrangement. I looked to see where we were goin, crosstown, in total silence. Nighttime, not a soul. A couple bars with lights, but not a single *Nachtigall* flappin around.

Vasil knew the way, handling the machine with confidence, and then I realized we'd taken a turn out of town and were heading toward the pack's old buildings. My new companions … Russians, I figured, both stocky, smiling. But there was something about them … somehow they were too neat. Suits, ties. Proud crewcuts. One even had a handkerchief in his breast pocket, they were clean, freshly shaven. Like they'd just stepped out of the bath. I smelled cologne. Peeked at their shoes: shiny, not a smudge. But the make was nothin much … bout twenty years behind, maybe more, I got an eye for this stuff. Unlikely gangsters. More like good-natured farmers … country bumpkins. Volga ship pullers died and gone to heaven. No river or ropes for them ever again. Muzhiks from Tuzex, I thought with a smile.

They smiled back at me, looking pleased. Smooth skin stretched taut over their cheeks, they were probably about forty but … not a single wrinkle. Weird people. Vasil stopped the car. We walked into the building. I was expecting to go to the pack's flat … but Vasil veered off into the cellar. Vasil, no! I shouted, wheeling around. Behind me stood those two, politely smiling. No! I tried to shove past, but it was like they were made of granite. Vasil grabbed me by the shoulder, come! he said. Eto nado!

They dragged me down the stairs, and I walked the rest of the way on my own. Then I saw her. Sitting in a chair, back propped against the well railing. I walked toward her, something pulled me. Her eyes glowed out at me in the half-light, but I wasn't afraid. It was the Great Mother.

I noticed another few ... yokels around ... Her face was broad and kind, a little swarthy, like in the photo. No extra color though. Neither old nor young. Her eyes glowed with ... peaceful joy. She looked pleased to see me. All at once ... I thought I saw ... Micka, Bohler ... it couldn't be ... I blinked, no. It was those peasants ...

Where are your buddies, where are your friends? the Great Mother spoke to me. I knew what she was saying was just for me. I felt something like blissfulness, a caress, the voice was caressing me ... like I was floating in a warm sea, bobbing in waves ... where are the girls whom you were so fond of? Where is everyone, where have they gone? Vanished, scattered. Where are the little ones with whom you once played? Someone must be here still, you can't be all on your own ... did the water take them away, are they bound in wire, were they carried off on a train? There must be someone somewhere still. And your loved one ... you wish to honor only her ... you love only her ... you would give your life for her ... where is she ... in distress? Alone? Frightened? In a house ... on the street ... lost in the forest? Perhaps she is all alone ... in the dark ... perhaps she cannot hear you ... and perhaps she is you ... where is everyone ... why did it have to happen ... and why is it always going on ... the ball has gone flat, the sand castle has crumbled ... the dragon has swallowed all of you up ... you set loose the paper dragon, and for a while it laughed, for a while it fluttered on the string, and then it soared off into the distance, out of sight ... and now it is returning from the heights ... and it is a Monster and wants to devour ... but I also have happy fairy tales ... for Hansels and Gretels ... that cottage, that was their mommy's heart and they ate it ... the heart of their mother ... but mommy forgives them and takes them back ... into her, into the earth ... I am the Great Mother ... and I will warm and soothe you all ... you will be inside me and feel neither hunger nor fear ... nor cold ... I am the Great Mother ... in me there is warmth, in me alone the sun shines ... in me you will change, you forlorn little children ... I am the Great Mother ... and you, the children of change, Mother will gladden you and you will be children ... safe and sound ...

I think I didn't hear or see anything else but the Great Mother's voice and face. Her face, so beautiful ... warm and splendorous ... I walked slowly toward her, very slowly, so I could hear her as long as possible … and I knew all I had to do was nod and say: Okay! And everything would change and I could live in this feeling of bliss forevermore.

But … I looked into her face as I drew near … and saw her eyes and their splendor and felt myself wanting to sink into it, and then I saw her hair … her black hair, and jerked away.

It was the hair. It reminded me of my longing and brought me back.

I stood face to face with the Great Mother, about twenty centimeters away … and now … the face was toothless … ancient … the face of an old Gypsy soothsayer, she curled her lips and shot me a furious glance, and then turned her attention away from me.

She stood up and went over to Vasil. He was lying on the ground. The others … followed her. She grabbed him by the hair, speaking in Russian, rapidly, but I understood.

Liar, she snapped at him, fool, you thought you could run away from mommy, now I must punish you … she said more or less, it was a farce … and it was disgusting. Vasil lay there on the ground. You should know, the woman told him, there is nowhere for you to run … I went over to Vasil … she stepped back, everyone watching.

Vasil, Vasil, get up, don't be stupid, it's just an old hag … an a couple a geezers … the two of us might've been able to take em … but he just lay there, the Nailhead. Vasil, c'mon, up an at em! Even that didn't help. I gave him a little kick. No, he said.

I tried hoisting him onto my shoulders. But he was too heavy. He didn't want to. And that hag was smiling! As soon as I moved toward her though, the geezers moved too. I knew the well was there. Ten meters to the bottom. And down there … I didn't give Vasil another look, inching back towards the door, a moment later I was out in the hallway, escaping … and all of a sudden, like the corner of a rag … some bird or bat or I don't know what whipped me across the eyes with its wing … brought me to a halt, heart pounding from running and also with fright … I walked to the door, slowly, curbing my fear … and then I heard footsteps, quiet and shuffling, but how could … Granny Macešková came shuffling out from around the bend in the hallway.

Whew, granny, you scared the daylights outta me. I leaned against the wall.

Good gracious, what is it, sonny, your heart? Acting up? said the little old lady.

Did you know we have visitors, Mrs. Mašešková?

You mean those geologist gentlemen? What fine young men, they brought me up some coal. Helped me take down the curtains … she mumbled something to herself.

Mrs. Mašešková, I asked, I don't suppose you have any … relatives, friends … somewhere to go if you couldn't stay here anymore?

Good gracious, what do you mean, sonny, why on earth would I want to move?

She peered at me, those eyes … full of silver, like when she came out of the well … Uh-huh, guess she'll have to stay here, I thought.

Why don't you come up to my place for a nice cup of tea … a growing boy like you needs healthy things.

Thank you very much, Mrs. Mašešková, but I've gotta be … I heard footsteps on the cellar stairs and cleared out fast. It was the reasonable thing to do, I think.

I ran down the street, no tram. I set out for town along the tracks. They seemed to stretch into infinity. I don't gotta do everything I can, occurred to me nonsensically. When I came to the streets, other things occurred to me. Day was breaking. I watched. Poked around in the spring mud a while, there's always stuff lyin in there, that's what archeologists do. You can tell from the sediment what's goin on. Even if the whole plain's bustling with mobiles threatening you with their fumes, give the stuff a little blood from your eye … investigate. I studied the shop signs. There were names on the shingles now. Usually people's. Some made sense. I touched the plaster here and there. Some signs I had to laugh at, others were upsetting. None conveyed humility. Then I lifted my head and saw: RUTHENIAN UNION, CZECH REPUBLIC. I felt a prick. Here I am, I marveled. But then I spotted him and ducked around the corner.

Must've been comin off the night shift, he was draggin, he'd had enough. Actually I don't know why I followed him. Something told me to. I think I was trembling a little. I trailed him tensely, ready to jump … he tottered a little, just a little, didn't look back even once … then finally he entered a building … I broke into a sprint … followed him all the way up to the attic, treading lightly one flight below, and when he opened the door I jumped inside, shoving Spider ahead of me. He just groaned.

She was lying on the bed. I turned on the light, her eyes didn't open. Black hair on the pillow, flat on her back. I threw up the shades and opened the window. The room reeked. At the head of the bed … of my loved one … bottles … empty, half full, a whole battery … I bent over her puffy face, a thin blanket covered her body. And underneath … I yanked it off … straps around her hands, across her chest too, only her legs were free … and all she had on was a ripped T-shirt, drenched in sweat … I roared, knelt down, and whipped out my knife … Spider cold-cocked me from the side … dropped on me … only … rage … then I was pounding him, on and on, I could've gone on pounding forever, I didn't even know I was hitting him, there was a fog in my head, it was red … and then I heard … What're you doing? she said loud and clear.

She was looking at me. I don't feel good! she said. I cut her loose, held her in my arms. Drinky … drinky winky? her swollen face pleaded grotesquely. She shut her eyes, head slumping onto her chest. I felt her forehead, touched her cheeks … must've had a fever, she was limp in my hands, I laid her blazing-hot body back down.

Ahem, said Spidey. He stood behind me, holding my knife. I didn't totally trust him till I had the blade back in my hand, edge toward him. He raised his arms. He was a little scratched up, but these Northies …

Hey, he said …

What's with her, you freak. Tied up?

Hey, that was Jícha's call. She … an booze was the only way I could keep her here.

How come she's got nothin on. Where's her clothes. I'll kill you.

No, he swallowed. No. I took em so she wouldn't split, trust me. I … that's not my thing.

An Jícha? Talk to me.

He's dead, you know that.

I don't care, did he … did he interrogate her here?

Yeah, said Spider.

No, I said. That's too much. An who else? Hadraba?

Nobody, I swear. I was just comin to let her go. Hadraba's call. She was for you. We didn't wanna, it was Jícha, believe me. He knew she'd been meetin, know who with? Viška, he said. She musta squealed, no shit.

That's what Jícha said.

Yeah.

Got a bathroom here?

He lifted his chin.

We carried her over and set her down in the tub. Get lost, I told him. I ran the water, dumpin in all the salts and shampoos that eight-legged playboy had in there. I didn't really want to see her naked without her knowing. It was hard work keepin her head above water and washin her up a little. Skinny. Shame slapped me, but I couldn't not notice … her firm breasts and rear end. Gorgeous! Unbelievably small nipples. No tattoos. Maybe something … on her inner thigh. But I resisted.

Am I home? she said, opening her eyes. You're with me, I assured her. She shut them again. Started bobbing her head around a little and whipping the foam with her hands … suddenly a smile spilled across her face … It's cold! she said. I added hot water. And then: Are we in the yard? Guess she thought she was in some washtub, she sat up and I scrubbed her back a little … then she wilted again. But kept on smiling into the foam. I soaped her up and rinsed out her hair. It stank of booze. She held on.

Ahem, ahem, Spidey said from behind me, gaze discreetly averted, and handed me a glass. Alka-Seltzer, he mumbled. New thing. I put in four. She obediently drank it down. Bulged out her eyes, then began slapping the foam and humming to herself, she still didn't know where she was. Me and Spider sat on the edge of the tub, backs to her … we'd hear the glug-glug if she went under … had a smoke.

Hey … I said after a while, you guys shouldna done this.

You know how it is … he said … an I just …

You fed her the booze. I mean it coulda killed her!

Sister snorted and slapped the water. Splashed us.

Not that chick. All she needed was one hand free, heh.

Followin orders! I've heard that before. You too!

Damn, yeah, that's what it came to.

Anyway, screw it.

Right but … now what'm I gonna do.

Yeah, well. Sorry for poundin you like that, hey, I didn't know …

Forget it, an don't get upset, laughed Spidey, but that was nothin, I coulda flattened you if I'd wanted.

Zat right?

Yep. You know it.

Aright then, bring in her stuff, huh. Do as you're told.

Just as long as you clear out ASAP. I'll call a car.

He walked out.

I know your address! I hollered.

You, my dear little Potok, pokin his head back in the door with her clothes, you I'm not worried about.

I yanked her things outta his hands and pressed them to my face, they were clean … and I felt strength in those important colors, Hunter, the Laoster, sprang to mind … and all at once I knew I'd track him down, no matter what Rudolf and Vohřecký were settin me up for, cause if there was one word of truth in that story about the mysterious general, I wanted to know … about him and his people, who cares if they used the Organization and lied to us, there was probly a reason, I wanna know … and I'm not the only one.

You might be surprised, Spider.

Let's drop it, huh, he said. Maybe another time.

Fair enough. Shoes?

I stood her up on the towel. She sat right back down. Somehow I managed to dry her off. It took both of us to get her dressed, she was still loaded and put up a struggle. At least she wasn't so bloated now. Her face was starting to come back to life. Even kept her eyes open a second or two, but her gaze was totally glassy. When it came to the shoes, I waved Spidey off. Tall boots like these call for delicacy. He had to hold her a minute as we dragged her across the room, though, while I performed a full-steam flying kick into the bottles, busted up a few. Stomped em to pieces. Spidey stared, exasperated. But kept his mouth shut. We put her in a cab. Careful with the knees.

Bye now, said Spider, take care.

Ciao.

We took off. I didn't tell the driver the real address till after a couple blocks. My little sister was snoring a bit. It was tremendously cute. I made the vehicle stop its wheels and climbed in back. She slept, holding my hand. I didn't even move. I didn't want to wake her yet. That would've been nuts.

And it began. I could see she was a little scraped, so I rubbed her with ointment before she woke up. I was glad Jícha was dead now. Once upon a time this strong female ointment had belonged to She-Dog. Like everything else here. But it still smelled good, so I risked it. There were a few other tiny scars scattered around Černá's body. It was weird … they were all almost exactly the same as the one on her chin. Sown at random, not in rows.

She threw up yellow foam. I was afraid it might be brain poisoning. But her breathing was regular. Then I noticed her hands were clenched in fists, and tried to pry apart the fingers, I could see the nails gouging into her skin. Guess it was her dreams.

I slept on the floor. Next morning she wasn't on the bed, I never knew I could jump two meters high. From on my back. But then I heard water, she was standing behind the wardrobe. At the sink. She must've been amazed how clean she was. Černá, I said so she wouldn't get frightened, and took the two steps. I guess thanks to the booze, she wasn't fast, the pan just swiped my shoulder, and then I caught hold of her wrists and looked in her eyes and saw fury, the blanket wrapped around her body dropped, leaving her naked, I shut my eyes and let go, because this was it … you fuckin bastards, she hissed through her lips … they must've been swollen still … leave me alone aready, you beasts … Černá, I screamed, you got it all wrong! You can … I'm just askin you to stay, no one's … keepin you prisoner, go if you want, but …

Who're you?

My name's Potok, you know me.

She tossed the pan on the floor, it made a clanging sound, we let it die out. I stepped away from the door so the way was clear … if she wanted, but I didn't want to move in her direction unless I had to … and in that small space it was difficult. She stood by the bed, blanket on again, rubbing her wrists, I could see her body's outline. She was more petite than I'd thought.

Got a cigarette?

It'll make you sick.

I know. I'm … they call me Černá.

Like I didn't know. Get dressed.

The blanket's fine.

Over coffee we agreed that we did know each other. That we had absolutely definitely and totally positively been eyeing each other for a pretty long time.

You sang that time, that Tuesday night, or was it … Wednesday?

Yeah, you were sittin with some redhead. You were smokin!

Yeah, that's it. But with … Táňa … she's blonde!

Get out … I coulda sworn …

Well … hm … yeah, an you left with Pikna!

No, impossible … actually, wait, but he was just escorting me!

That's it. An then at the coat check, you lost your jacket …

Riiight … so you were the one that had my ticket!

Ticket? … I donno bout that.

Ah, never mind. Anyway … I always liked you. How you'd look.

Really?

Why'd you close your eyes … back there by the sink?

I couldn't take it.

I saw some a your plays. Way back when.

Yeah an … what do you think?!

Mm-hm … good. My head hurts.

I really love your songs. Want some pills?

Sure. What kind?

Are you hungry? What do you eat?

Our words … as we talked, merged. I didn't know this voice of hers. We assured each other we understood. She wasn't in the mood to go out. She told me Hadraba promised he'd hide her. Didn't say why, guess she figured I knew, or that it was none a my business. And then … her face twisted in disgust. I didn't tell her Jícha was dead. Didn't bring up the sailor either. It was a little bit low-down of me, I know.

Being in a confined space didn't bother us at all. We got to know each other. Breath is crucial for that. She didn't know what was going on yet. I was filling the time till it hit her and she realized … She laughed and laughed. Still looked tired though. I clowned around … crawled the walls. She gave answers. Put my Chinese cap on and made silly faces, tried on some corset left from the whores … her body might've fooled me, but her eyes gave her away … I quickly realized she was a grown woman putting on an act.

I pulled out my photos, because the words were running out and the monumental silence after our initial mutual attraction was tearing up my insides … it was just like holy Sunday in the cultured Prague families of olden times … minus the Sacher tortes … she flipped through my collection of butterfly and mouse pictures, occasionally brushing a finger over the face of a common acquaintance. We debated back and forth what they might be doing in the new era … and from our confrontations, blathering, and disputations we came up with our best guesstimates … and not a single gesture of weariness in the flowing veil of her beauty escaped me.

Then I pointed out my assortment of caged hedgehogs and the various household enigmas of keys, hot plates, and so forth. I knew I didn't need to show off with some kinda hotshot outlook on life, none a that manliness, masochism, or machismo stuff, not to mention political convictions. It wasn't the next night I was angling for, but every night. And every day. She accepted me easily, like an open gate. We didn't talk about it, I knew she was holding back. I was actually glad she was so wiped out from the booze … even her face. I could sense she was the one that I'd had under my eyelids ever since a woman's face had first gone flashing past. I knew that She-Dog … was cleverly guiding my steps. From out there, wherever she was. If Černá had been standin here in all her nighttime beauty … I don't think I could've controlled myself. This way we began the day slowly, her emerging from her hangover the way she had from the foam the day before. Then she said she wanted to lie down.

Černá, I, I gotta go out.

Can I be here? She was already closing her eyes.

I'll be back tonight. An sorry, I know it's dumb, but the plastic bags're here, just in case … the trash can's out on the walkway.

Yeah, I saw. After, we can go to my place. Be back soon.

And she fell asleep.

15

I swung round the essential spots, flyin. Gave the tram a try, but it was a total bore. I wondered if she'd still be there when I got back. It was her. Sister. As I thoughtlessly plodded the pavement toward where Bohler's Laotian lady's pals lived, images came to mind: my encampment, where for years I'd been subjected to tiny fly attacks and buzzing helicopters, that ridiculous den of mine with a fax and a phone, all for the sake of the pack ... but I guess I was expectin a different kind of message ... in my mind the den became a massive edifice, a palace of Hermaphroditus, a shelter and survival home. And it grew to the clouds, far from the fields of ravens, up toward their migrating brothers.

I cut off the street talk, Sister's talk was inside me now. My heart was sweet and red. And in there where love had never flowed but baked into a hardened lump, fending off the waves of hatred so I wouldn't kill or go crazy or I donno what ... two bare hands now bathed in the ripples ... hands of a body of love ... caressing the water ... or something like that ... to exaggerate a little.

I opened my eyes as I bashed into a lamppost and noticed a tree blossoming in the midst of the filth, probly some mutant apple tree. In the gutter. Boards around it. Put there by people who wanted it. Proud ants crept across my heart in overalls that said Freedom or Death, the second component was crossed out, not with enemy blood but some trivial scrawl.

I couldn't stop smiling. But I knew they wouldn't take it wrong, the smile's their tribe's basic facial expression. Actually I think they were glad to see me. Even if I did bust in without knockin.

All the Laosters wore store-bought threads now. Even glimpsed an occasional tattoo, on the men. They'd managed to create all sortsa outfits and new combinations with those ridiculous foreign fabrics. Some a them cracked me up. So my laughter was merry, a thing of pure joy. They could always sense that anyway. We still spoke in French-Czech-Laotian-Russian-Indochinese, but mainly in gestures, back slaps, and toasts. I'd arrived just in time for dinner, it was some kina holiday for them. Right off I realized it was a holiday for me too. There were about twenty of em there, some I still remembered. Somebody told a truly fabulous joke. Or so I thought. From the heightened merriness. Somebody gave me a wink. Somebody nudged me off my chair. Probly just tryin to rile me up. Tino, that's what we called him. Dragged a girl with a little kid out to the middle of the room. She was shy. I started to clap. I donno why. Guess I got taken somehow by that long blue-black hair a hers, like all the Laotian girls have … those guys a theirs donno how good they got it, they're into the Czech mares, I'd observed. Giantesses. Fascinates em. I on the other hand lived for the movements of those petite, fragile creatures. It's always opposite aspects, parts of a body … that attract. I just kept drinkin and noddin my head. It took me back to the merry … old days of the Organization. I clapped my hands and danced around, curious what kina fun Tino had in store. But the only joke was that the child was blond. I probably overdid it, but everyone laughed and joined in the applause, except for Tino, face frozen in a smile. I wrapped my arms around a bottle of liquor. I had my sister's two eyes inside me, and that was all that mattered.

There was no end to questions about my buddies. And: Luna, said one. Yep, Mácha,* that guy hadda invent a totally secret tongue for his stuff, otherwise they woulda killed him. Had his own alphabet, him and his sister watched what they were doin, they knew what it was all about! I edified some old man sittin next to me. Je ne compris tchèque. Moi aussi! I hollered so he could hear. Luna, he said. Luna! another one tried to explain, excitedly drawing circles in the air, oh, lůno, womb! I rapped my forehead. Oui! my friend cried, guess he had female bodies on his mind … shyly I looked around at the ladies, bringin out dish after dish heaped with crab eyes and slugs, and smilin the whole time … I guess over in Asia they know that fucking is the love and blood of a living body, as long as it works … when you get right down to it, God is love too, theirs and mine, I thought, guzzlin rice wine, here I was thinkin those gestures were their lascivious way of inquiring about their cousin, Bohler's Laotian lady, but it was just some Moon Day or somethin, some Lunar Festival, they lit the lamps, the incense fumed, I'm a somnambulist too … I tore into the slugs, hungry as a wolf, all that rompin around was startin to wear me out … sitting across from me was a fellow I didn't know, tie and everything … color-coordinated, real smoothy.

People kept tappin me on the shoulder and askin: Où est monsieur Bohlira? Il est okay avec femme à la campagne, he's … I clasped my hands to show he was prayin … et monsieur Miska? Oui, Miska okay, byznys, et monsieur Sharqui par avion, Israël, la guerre, vzzzzz! I went … il est rat-tat-tat-tat-tat, which is Kanak for Kalashnikov, or Uzi, same difference. Tu es bien, somebody shouted, ploppin another mound of somethin onto one a my plates. I thought about bringin some back for Sister, she probly didn't know this stuff. I threw out the lobster claws.

I totally forgot what I'd actually come for, I was feelin all right. And in the leftover moments not taken up with fast and friendly conversation, in between jokes and drinking, my heart only seized up from time to time … would she be there, or would she take off … if she did, nothing would matter anymore … all at once someone doused the lights, the Laosters began jabbering, and a clipped voice rang out … probly Tino's … What's up? I yelled, grabbin a plate … not to worry, somebody in front of me said, he'll be turning the lights back on in a minute, I was startled, this Laotian spoke perfect Czech … What's goin on? Nothing out of the ordinary, a minor inconvenience perhaps, everything will be just fine. Oh yeah? Zat right? I stood up. Sit back down, and whatever you do, don't go outside.

My companion lit a candle. It was the smoothy, everyone else'd vanished, apart from a few girls clearin away the dishes, pullin off the tablecloths.

Then I heard it. A scream of pain, and another, murmuring voices and stamping feet and another scream again, and that one I knew, that one I'll remember from the fiery day forever. I was startin to get a hunch what was goin on out there … and somebody hit the ground … probly chin-first on the pavement, bad sound. Nearby. Then the voices began to get farther away. Stamping. Feet goin after someone. And then they went away.

What was that? I asked Smoothy, pointlessly.

Oh nothing, they come out here occasionally, he said.

Who?

Now now, Mr. Potok, you're here for another reason. You have, so to speak, a mission. And I personally am pleased that there are still people here willing to aid the struggle for a great cause, even now that your splendid homeland has cast off the yoke of communism.

I sobered up. Yes, thank you, think there might be another drop a that rice wine around somewhere?

But of course, of course. He wouldn't even allow me to pour it myself.

We talked about an hour. He explained what they wanted from me.

Then the others began to come back. It wasn't so merry anymore.

Monsieur Tino, I followed him into the kitchen and asked, okay?

Mais oui, okay. Okay.

And it began. Moving through the plowed land, the factories. I was amazed at what still went on in that disgusting, lovely, and absolutely childishly brutal Bohemia of mine. It was just like Rudolf said: Nobody would talk to em.

Every now and then I'd have to lash into some manager in a pretty raised voice — so he'd pick himself up from his chair and drag out the list of workers. Sometimes, just for kicks, I'd pass myself off as some bigwig government type. All you had to do was say: Our reason for being here today has nothing to do with Precious Gems or Cellulose, but Mr. Jindřich, I repeat, Mr. Jindřich ... *from the district office!* has an eminent interest in foreign workers ... we're setting up a new department ... you mean you've never heard of Comrade, eh-hem, pardon me, *Mrs.* Maturková from the Ministry ... No? Well, I'm sure the director will clear that up, where is your phone?

At that time in this country, see, nobody knew who called the shots. Most of those who had spent their whole lives following bosses' orders couldn't keep up with the accelerated movement after everything had done nothing but rot for so long. And nearly all of them had notched up points for loafing, stealing, informing, whatever. And the only thing that worked on them was fear for their dumbass job.

In short: there wasn't ever anyone anywhere who knew who was who.

I dragged my outfits outta my wardrobe again. Jackets through gates, jump-suits over wires, I rarely made a mistake. Occasionally we'd latch onto a feeler at the bazaars where the Chinese or Vietnamese or Laotians or whoever hawked their goods, but Smoothy didn't have a chance, they didn't know him. I at least could pass myself off as a wheeler-dealer that owed some cash to Pu or Minh or Lan. And when I whipped out the bills, sometimes it helped. But usually they gave me the runaround. Those guys didn't trust anyone. And I didn't even try to talk to the girls, they'd just vanish and then suddenly, in a wink, instead of their charming bodies I'd be starin at some golem ready to bump heads or make a run for it. Or both, always with a smile.

To get into the factories and dorms, I used various press IDs. At first it helped, but I soon discovered people were used to scumbag reporters turnin up once in a while ... and bein called names in the press didn't get anyone bent outta shape anymore. We drove from dorm to dorm. Lookin for "relatives," as Smoothy put it.

I only saw Hunter once. In a flat on the outskirts. We got in somewhere near the Angel subway station, this time Smoothy drove. He darted in and out of the buildings, jabbering away in earnest as darkness descended all around, and it was obvious he was driving in circles to wipe out the map I had in my head. Then one of the guys in back blindfolded me, thanks, Godfather, I joked. He didn't reply.

We drank tea, spared words. It was all too obvious. I didn't know if Smoothy … who else he was working for, but I couldn't imagine Hunter not knowing. He wasn't a bit surprised to see me turn to stone as he walked into the room in a suit. I remembered the way he'd drifted into Kučera's flat that time … and I shuddered. He knew I knew. I was hoping he hadn't forgotten that souvenir on the shoulder he'd given me. The tattoo'd been erased from his face. He laid some cash on the table, plenty. I jabbed my index finger into my T-shirt, he nodded. Contract, byznys, payoff, nothing personal. I wrapped it up. Smoothy smirked in the background.

But I folded. Afterwards … in the car, when Smoothy got all chatty and started tellin those horror stories … the fella we were bringin back from Slovakia, bout fifty I'd say, laughed raspily as Smoothy prattled on in that way a theirs they got. In the pub where we ate, he showed it to me. It covered his whole chest, plus his arms. Even the back of his neck. Some came from the camp, some from the sharks that almost got him when he climbed in a dinghy and pushed off from the shore of his cruel homeland.

This gentleman here ate his children before he'd crossed the ocean, Smoothy informed me with a sugary smile. A piece of the ocean, that is. And not having any fingernails hampered him at first in his work in the chemical industry.

They didn't try to make me finish my fried cheese. What he'd eaten in order to cross the ocean … had been for the sake of his mission, there was no need for Smoothy to stress that. I figured Smoothy … was a sicko, but probly the reason he kept feedin me his people's sagas of suffering was because they ate at his brain.

I get paid to drive an talk, leave the rest out of it.

History spins in circles, Mr. Potok, note that the gentleman whom we are going to see, and whom we hope to find today, was an officer. A very able para-trooper, we have his dossier. Our superior, whom we may refer to as General Vang, truly values him. Just imagine, this man executed an entire village of trai-tors with his own two hands … in the Mekong Delta … and truly, he took his lumps as well … when they captured him, you see, they took bamboo chips …

Enough! I roared at Smoothy, pulling the car over. He was laughing. Aright then, I started the wheels back up.

My working hours were unlimited. And something happened to my time. I might've been out racin around with Smoothy all day, but when I got back ... Černá was there.

The first night I came home from the Laotians' and collapsed next to her sleeping body. I awoke to something touching my face ... her fingers ... and the way they touched me, every second my skin lived a life of its own ...

Sorry, you're snorin like crazy ...

What, like a dog?

Like a pig.

I was a little insulted. But ... she'd come back. All those touches brought me back to me, so I could fly out into normal life and come back to her at the end of the day.

We didn't bother with whether our touches were sensual, sensuous, or total nonsense those first few nights, because that was the only time we had to see each other, I didn't even know if she stayed in the flat the rest of the time ... and I didn't ask ... I discovered that being with her in reality was actually all there was.

Černá, hey ... this is gettin ... freaky.

But it wasn't, not with her, with her it just ... was, I swept my head clean of all the rags, splinters, and bandages a person wraps around his brain over the years, out of self-defense ... to better survive in a world full of mystery.

But even though I was nearing bliss ... even though I was with her, I still had dreams. Sometimes they just come out of your head. I used to have to dance because of them, wear myself out in the day so I wouldn't live at night, but now: even despite my work with Smoothy and his horror stories, despite all the every-day, chaotic, waking stuff, only she was in my dreams. Daytime, nighttime, she was my love, my buttress against the world, she herself became my world, but in my dreams ... many times I saw her face and reached out, body straining, but the face would turn into a grimace, a sneer ... that time in the cellar, She-Dog had turned into an old lady ... Černá, on the other hand, turned into something ... monstrous, I wanted to scream but couldn't make a sound, then woke up, relieved, her above me again, naked, smiling, I laid my hands on her chest and the face began to fade into a grimace, an unfeminine mask, the shining paths of fangs traveling up through her skin, I screamed and woke again, Černá, I blurted ... What is it? You want more? I snuggled up to her ... and her smile rippled and the lips disappeared, exposing the flesh and the empty darkness beyond it ... I would travel like that from dream to dream, and sometimes, sometimes I couldn't take it and would ricochet out of the dream, plunging down and down, until at the last second, using all my brainpower, I would stop myself and reascend ... rebounding off the bottom ... and there was my love and it wasn't a dream, I could feel her touch, her lips ... and she opened her eyes, leaning over me, speaking soothingly ... her hair on my shoulders, and I opened my eyes and the Monster was back again.

That was how I lived at night, it lived in me, through me. Rising up out of the dark pit to find my loved one gone and a pendulum swishing through the air.

But I also knew if I stayed down there in the depths, fleeing the sneer of the one that I loved, I would never return.

Well that sucks, she said. Should I leave?

No.

My mate, my unearthly star, the one who gathers up the ashes of my heart, my sparkling jewel, made breakfast. A couple of times we even went out. To look at the Czech kings' graves, for instance. She'd never seen them before. She quickly picked up my habits, tapping her ashes into the coffee grounds too. Sometimes she washed the dishes. I guess it was like being married. I let her go through my wardrobe and look at She-Dog's clothes. She didn't think much of them.

This one's too modern. An this one ... too postmodern. This is cool, she triumphantly whipped out a white, polka-dotted dress ... the one She-Dog wore to her confirmation.

That evening I'd come home after some especially unproductive talks with the board of an aluminum factory ... had to convince em we were shooting a film about the Vietnamese. Talk about stupid, who'd be interested. I buttered them up though. What a drag. Better to go with the envelope strategy, like I did with the Organization. But I oughta explain, this was real fast work ... I had no idea when Vohřecký would turn up again, and whenever I asked Smoothy where he was shipping his foundlings to, he'd just laugh and launch into his horror stories ... I didn't have time to figure out who to give the envelope to, the boss or the janitor ... so I could find out.

One day I walked through a gate ... it was near the Austrian border, and despite the barbwire fence all around the dorm, the wheeling and dealing proceeded unchecked … I walked up with an armful of stockings, guard stretched out his hand, gave him a pair of kneesocks or two … lively place, I tripped on a bone and rammed into a baby carriage, the tot started bawlin, I was intrigued … rocked the little shaver and sang him a tune, a teeny-weeny half-breed … damn, what'll he speak … the hallway was plastered with busty singers, giant white women, and yep: Bruce Lee with nunchuks, he was all over the place … three guys came up and I suddenly forgot the name of the fella we were after … left the stockings there. Smoothy wrote it down on a piece of paper, I went back. Get lost, said the guard, this time empty-handed. Crime unit, I told him with delight and an exclamation point, flashing my ID. He didn't look sure … I shoved the paper at one of the three … waiting faithfully by the stockings, studying the Latin characters … Whe'e Mis'er Viet who wri'e dis? Out in the car. You ou' frien', ti? Huh? Ti, li'e drink? All right, thanks, just for a minute.

In the room the television mesmerized. Couple guys loungin in sweats on the beds, sound turned off on the TV, I looked at the pictures, my new hosts … weren't like the Laosters, who'd come illegally, true, but it wasn't the same … some, caught up in the folklore, merrily flung themselves onto the path … the sweats, the TV, I sucked in the air … weariness, flat beer, and nasty questions, all boiling down to a very unsettling one underlying it all: What're we doing here? What next? Where else? And why?

Couple a them got up and slipped out, I noticed, a machete lay under the bed, dust balls all around, but not a speck on it … right, in this place, surrounded by wire … and this here was slavery and the tea was nice and hot.

Peered out the window and all at once the gate opened and a cop car pulled up in front of the dorm, guard hustled over eagerly, guess I didn't fool him … picked myself up, my hosts, catching on to my motion, very quickly and understandingly got to their feet … no worry, no worry, said one, leadin me down the hall to a window, washroom was pretty wild, showerheads torn outta the wall like there'd been some kinda battle … wash, here, what for? in these kindsa places people gave up on more than just keepin clean, I squeezed through the window and jumped … hunched down in the nettles, bolted out back, cut through some woods toward the car, came out on the road … one of the ones I'd given the paper to was sittin in the ditch, head on his chest, the other two had Smoothy sandwiched … I broke into a run, they scuffled without a word … I let loose: Hola ho! They jumped back, saw it was me, took off, but I blew right by em, hopped in the car, and as soon as I sensed the gasping Smoothy — after all those trips, we knew each other by sound — climb in back, I stepped on it.

We drove in silence. I was just starting to wonder whether Černá had any cash, maybe enough to get to Vienna, Budapest ... anywhere, when Smoothy said: Stop the car. I did, under a bridge, figured maybe he was wounded or somethin ... but then someone knocked at the window, it was that Vietnamese I'd seen in the ditch ... I yelped, clutching the wheel, but Smoothy patted me on the shoulder: Why, that's the gentleman! Things have worked out beautifully today. That's Captain Zueng ... or something like that.

Great, Smoothy, whatever you want, but I'm pullin off for some coffee.

It was truly a beautiful roadside restaurant. The Vietnamese were refused service and I couldn't use the toilet. Since I wouldn't order without them. We drove on, Smoothy chuckling and jabbering away with his new acquisition, and me ... I was ashamed. Even if it ended up the only ... manly act of my life. I pulled a U-turn and started back in the other direction. Mr. Potok, ahem, said Smoothy ... we have a mission, there is no point in getting upset ... mother-fuckers, bloated dumplings, I fumed ... screw the mission, Smoothy ... this is the mission, I'll crush him, I muttered, picturing the waiter in my mind ... worthless bum, half-wit European mishmash, talks like a TV show, dreamless heathen ... a Czech pig, one of millions ... I pushed that machine like a horse outta hell ... Smoothy tried to reason with me: But Mr. Potok, that will not give us satisfaction ... the captain kept quiet, sittin there in his jumpsuit, probably couldna cared less ... who we were after ... I parked the car, flew in there ... not a sign of the waiter ... I ran into the toilet, the kitchen ... Who're you looking for? a short blonde girl asked kindly, reminded me of Elsa ... uhh, he's not here, I went into the dining room ... Smoothy and the captain were at a table drinking beer, heads still foamy ... they do an outstanding svíčková here, I'll take mine with six dumplings, and for the captain here as well, have a seat, Mr. Potok, now now, as the driver perhaps you shouldn't ... I pounded down his beer.

It was an outstanding idea to come back, you show great initiative, the general is very pleased with you ... then Smoothy started in with an analysis of the Czech Foreign Ministry's current policy vis-à-vis the Communist states of Southeast Asia, he knew from experience that had a soporific effect on me ... the captain fed his face ... I started laughing ... the blonde bustled past, back and forth ... Mr. Smoothy, tell me one thing ... Yes, of course, that is what I am here for, my dear friend ... Who'm I workin for?

You are working for a just cause, have no doubts, and by the way you have not heard the story of the captain here yet, he is a pilot, and when he came home from the reeducation camp after fifteen years … you see his mother was head of the Religious Confederation in Hue, and when the captain returned to the house where he was born, in a little village, his mother was out in the field, hanging … you see the Communists had crucified her …

Černá sat there, music playing, candles on the table, waiting for me. She had the white dress on and a different hairdo. Up in a knot. I took the dress off her, didn't go easy on the thing, it wasn't important to me anymore, she just took a quick look but liked it, we fell on the bed and made love … and from that moment on I stopped having those dreams. It's great, I said … And it'll stay that way, she said. Long as you don't have anyone … No, just you … I was thinkin, that dress belongs to somebody. Where is she? … It's just a dress now. And you're on your own? … Yeah … What do you say we go out some time, some night? Yeah. If you're thinkin about that guy you beat up, he's all right now. You don't hafta hide. He's gone. I know. So why're you holed up here, I mean … I'm takin a break, you know. Just tired … Uh-huh.

Then we went to her place, first thing next day. She lived out across from Ohrada. Attic flat. It was a sizable room with a kitchen and … no more plastic bags and no walkway. Just stairs and dens, it was excellent. Table and some shelves. Music stuff. Looked like she coulda wriggled outta there at any moment. Books. Those're … mostly presents, she said.

Yep, assorted Holans* and Senecas, plus Anthologies and Libraries of Wisdom, even Sunshine Meditations, stuff you give in the family on name days … in packages tied with ribbon. I threw a fit in front of the bookshelf once … yep, those're givers, all right! Jeffers and the Lyres of Love, for relatives an smart folks it's a can't-miss … just so long as the girl reads, heh-heh, they say to themselves, tuggin at their caps, that stuff's been boiled to death in the textbook pot, bout as dangerous as milk … won't give the little one crazy ideas, but sometimes … sometimes she outwits em … lyin around and whatnot … nothin goin on … maybe she's got her period, a hangover, the blues, maybe a combination … peace and quiet reign and there's nobody on the phone, no godforsaken visitor to interrupt the moment, and the girl reaches for the book and it happens … the words and sentences come to life, a miracle, how many times has it happened already … aright aright, if the books bother you I'll throw a blanket over em. I just keep em here for the noise, when I rehearse, the neighbors, soundproofing, get it?

I solemnly presented her with the Solingens, she disappeared into the kitchen, and I went through my jacket ... the photos I'd taken from that old guy were gone. Černá ... but I left it alone. She took em, I lost em ... same difference, like when I told her about my search. Bolkon? Never heard of it, maybe it used to be called somethin different ... my folks lived on Lenin, I donno ... Dernet, donno him ... I've met some junkies, who hasn't, but in that part of town? Aright, Černá, it was probly a false trail, I'm glad.

I took a look around the attic, but there was just one other flat up there. In the back. That's Max, said Černá ... quiet type ... that Mr. Dráp guy mighta moved out, haven't seen him for a while.

Sometimes pigeons landed on the windowsill at night, Černá told me she used to give them food. I kept examining her face, her body ... when I wasn't out driving with Smoothy, I would just sit still and, say, pretend like I was reading ... even managed to keep my mouth shut ... and that says a lot, when you don't have to fill the agonizing dying of time with words, that's intimacy ... to call it a happy time wouldn't be right, it was nonstop tenderness, and that's beyond words.

Hey, you haven't turned a page, half an hour now.

I was havin a little dream about you.

I'm right here.

We drank. But the Fiery had a different effect on me now. It was like being rocked in a cradle as we wove our words together, and at times our tongues ... I had a feeling she sensed my need and at first just went along because she didn't have any way out, or just happened to have an urge to be with somebody right that second, but then again ... especially when we were side by side, her touching me ... it was entirely possible she needed it too, that she was hungry for the same thing as me.

She didn't wear any protective stuff, her body was clean, almost ... I don't need silver, she told me, and I believed her. But I didn't take the Madonna off, even though ... Černá wanted me to ... get totally naked ... I can't stand when guys've got circles an hoops. But I never removed that silver of mine.

She told stories, the sound of her raspy voice beside me ... I liked that she'd also acted before, not in Prague, and to my surprise ... you worked at a paper? You, a secretary, I think I'm gonna faint! In TV, no shit? I couldn't picture it.

And then she started to get into singing, into getting somewhere with singing ...
including into people.

Was it fun workin ... at Černá's?

There no. But it was fun singin ... fuckin with those assholes' dicks. An
seein how bad they wanted it, seein em go for it ...

C'mon, they're not all ...

From up there they're just faces. One big face. Sometimes they all merge.

No time to choose?

Sometimes yeah, sometimes you choose ... I chose you. An here you are. I
remember, know what we used to call you guys?

No.

The quiet table. There weren't a lot of em. Always ... someone grabbin my
ass.

I thought you liked that ... an Hadraba told me ... never mind.

I hated that ... there was this kid that used to sit with you, big beak ... kina
skinny, dark ... I liked him too.

Sharky!

Uh ... David, he told me his name was ...

Nope. That's another guy.

Well he said he was David, I donno why. An I been meanin to ask ... why'd
you climb into that receptacle that time ... cut yourself up ...

I got bored, everyone just starin ... quiet table, huh?

I told her the myth about the rib too. How Bog wrenched it outta that first
guy. Said I didn't believe he took just that rib and gave it to her. I was glad she
knew the ancient legend of Hermaphroditus. When she talked about it, it was
like she was telling me about up there and down below.

We were never anywhere else, either.

The days went by. We didn't count them.

Those days ... my dear raising a ruckus on the stairs ... drinking Three
Musketeers beer, sitting in nothing but red bikini briefs with spiderweb lace
around the edges on one of those afternoons ... yanking my hair ... rolling up
her amazing eyelashes with her secret wand, me holding her head ... and wires
quivering in the air overhead, steam rising out of the sewers, walls sagging with
century-old plaster, swaths of savage city skin ... walking past a playground
ringing out with clipped commands, it's muggy, walking along the bridge, slow
and tired, a storm's about to hit ... we feel the first drops and she flags down a

cab, riding uphill, the air opens with a flash, sharp light, light from above. Illuminated street.

It's obvious the guy goes on top, since he gives the seed. The woman's closer to the soil, that's why she gives birth, but the guy flies. So he's more scared of what's up above. The woman holds on an she's underneath, it's obvious, I believe it.

But I mean the ground's also got … dangerous things in it.

So what. The ground you can hold onto.

Well, Černá, if you say so, you oughta know … who's that Moriak on your door, your father? … I don't mean to pry.

That's me. Not my father! Not that guy! I was fuckin sick an tired of draggin around that "ová." That's just a trick forefather Čech invented so he wouldn't hafta remember his wives' names. Now every woman's an "ová."

You're an "á." Ever have kids?

No.

I stayed with her. And one time as I was sittin in the window listenin to some story of Černá's, somethin from the past … I saw an incredible light show, breathtaking colors, a little bitty spider weavin his net at high speed, it wasn't a trap though, couldn't've caught a thing in it, I figured it was a game, or some secret message for somebody about the joy of motion … it was a silky and mysterious web, lifting with the wind, billowing with the gusts, like it was there just for the wind, or the wind just for it, they merged.

Evenings we'd go out occasionally, though for now we stayed away from the usual establishments.

In this one coffeehouse, the only spot free was the chess table. While Černá went off to make a phone call, I didn't ask who to, I set up the board, just for the heck of it … reminiscing about bread knights and bishops … as long as we're using bread for this, an old man there told me, then everything's fine, totally springtime.

Springtime, he said.

You wanna play?

Let's give it a try.

We moved the pieces in various sequences, but with all the talking and drinking we never did finish that first match … the chessboard was like our center of gravity, it's good to have something there on the table … mostly just old ladies went there, we often knocked back a goodly number of shots ourselves

… that made the waiters as happy as us … Černá busted up when the black-and-white … penguin helpin her into her mangy jacket said: Come again, madam … I didn't laugh. And outside she grabbed me and said: This is new to me, let's be together. Černá … don't say that, or I … you'll never leave me. We stepped across a puddle, and for a second it seemed like a pit, a shaft that led to somewhere, and as I squinted, playin around with the flashes of light inside the water, Černá said: You better believe I won't leave you, not ever, it wouldn't work anyway. But … you donno anything! You like me too much. I took a look at her, the look on her face was … nasty, as if she didn't like the idea, as if what awaited us … which I believed was good things together … as if she didn't want it. All you guys piss me off! You too! she said. I turned around and walked off, and when I looked back over my shoulder she was standin there by the puddle, alone … motionless, I could see her eyes, just the gleam, I could feel her, she was inside me … her figure's seared into my body and whatever's outside that outline I sliced off long ago … it lasts to this day, after all that happened … then we walked side by side in silence and the city was friendly. I donno why.

And the next morning Smoothy smiled when I grabbed the envelope, he probly had a hunch I wanted out. We took off for some factory again, we'd been callin around for two days on this one. Got inside no problem. Smoothy was somewhat … shaken up, which was unusual, maybe we knew each other so well by now he didn't consider it necessary to keep the mask on for me … after three months now of livin this life … it went without a hitch, we found the block, the hallway, for once there was no one standin in our way … Smoothy stops and pulls out a smoke … this time, Mr. Potok, he says, this time I am hoping to see my son, so I beg you for extraordinary, yes, extraordinary readiness in the event of an emergency … I swallowed what I had on the tip of my tongue, namely that I'm not some kina gorilla, etc., and asked: Son? I could see he was hesitant … somehow he didn't want to open the door right away … by speaking again, literally by moving his tongue in his mouth, he regained his confidence: As we pushed off in our, so-to-speak, family boat from the shores of our homeland, which had become inhospitable, indeed perilous and harsh, we heard the crack-ling of machine guns … Smoothy dramatically lowered his voice, while I rolled my eyes and clutched my heart … by now I knew he enjoyed it, it was our idiom … we paddled furiously, but one of my sons, the eldest, was hit and fell in the water … we learned later on that he was imprisoned, reeducated, and afterward … like most of the gentlemen we have found and transported to the place of destination … he changed his identity, and his face, Mr. Potok, his face … and I fear I shall not recognize him … Smoothy whispered the end of his speech, and I could tell he was in a bad way … but … clearly full of what he called the mission … he walked up to the door and opened it.

This one didn't look good at all, a bit like a frog or a monkey, eyes bulging out of his gigantic head. He peered at us open-mouthed, obviously not expecting a visit, staring, back leaned up against the fridge, wrapped around, to be safe, with a chain and two locks. But it was definitely him, he stood up and shrieked … Smoothy teetered ever so slightly, Dapper Dan in a suit, and across from him this … hulk. Smoothy spread his hands, started chattering away, loud and fast, I could tell this was the moment, so I slid over to the window, stared out, waiting off to the side.

I was still ashamed. For dorm managers, officials, phone operators, bosses … when they found out we were looking for a slope, they generally behaved impossibly … their inner life manifested itself, absolutely pointlessly, in acts of often unintentional cruelty … callousness … weighing down the sky over all our heads … definitely better to wallow in the muck than to deal with a horrid person.

Maybe there were exceptions, never met em, there wasn't time … after one frustrating inquiry I folded again and got drunk, despite all of Smoothy's reassuring maneuvers I got liquored up in some backwoods dive … the yellows there had a special table and designated glasses, to prevent any accidental mixing, which anyway they never had anything about on TV, so it didn't exist … I shouted out somethin about farmers that came from the area of certain camps where labor had been the great liberator … Smoothy played a Japanese tourist and took pictures of them, or they would've kicked my ass, and they would've been right, I took it too far …

All the old tricks and suits and cons, otherwise known as fast work, didn't give me any pleasure, I was too ashamed for my tribe's people, even around Smoothy, who'd lived here, as he informed me, more than ten years, he'd seen it all before, he just laughed. I didn't even know why it bothered me so much, except that every now and then I'd get seized by this vague feeling that me and Černá were threatened too … brutally and from all sides.

I had no idea what kinda capo Hunter was either, I just took their side by instinct, but when it came to their mission I think … they'd've done whatever was necessary, wouldn't've shied away from any filth, they were warriors and it was a pretty cruel war. Petitions didn't interest them.

Mr. Potok, Smoothy lectured me again one day, it is true we now know that nothing is what it seems, but what is truly meant to be and what purpose it serves, that is the real riddle … this applies of course to the entire universe, including even the most trivial objects, and to be specific, take for example Semtex, you see, you Czechs sent it to our enemies at just the right moment … that was what finished off the Americans back then, but you know, our men … well, you know a lot already, but did you know that our boys from the base in Thailand, who sometimes spend weeks at a time on the trail in order to punish as many Communists as possible, carry little bits of Semtex along for their stomachs? It's the truth, especially, now don't be angry, but especially our men from Eastern Europe have rather damaged stomachs and a bit of Semtex, a truly tiny little bit, can give an exhausted warrior a proper cleaning out, believe me.

Even though it was obvious I already had at least one foot in the trap … see, one day over at Smoothy's place, after we'd found the fifth relative, I spotted a couple familiar-looking suitcases in the foyer, sparkling steel, like you see on TV, couldn't lift even one of em … in the blink of an eye Smoothy was standing in front of me, smiling, a little sadly I thought, I donno. But I shouldn't've touched em. I shouldn't've even seen em. And once I had, I should've acted like it was soap. Maybe it was a test.

It was love for her that got me caught in the ropes, desire makes me manic. Despite everything I'd gotten myself into, despite the agonizing restlessness that kept me on edge, I was happy. I knew that some things you have to pay for … but my time with Černá was the most beautiful time of all … I think few mortals have experienced anything like it, she gave me strength … few men, when it comes time for Starry Bog to run the film, can find a couple frames where they're with their sister … I mean every guy, man or boy, even the poor fucks everyone's written off, is searching for his sister, that's all there is, it's a possibility … for life with the gods here and now, and every move she makes is a war against Evil, and a privilege too, I knew that … and our stay here is limited, and just to find your sister means a lot … and the more time my trips with Smoothy took, and the closer I got to the end of my job, the better prepared I was.

All night long we waited for the arrival of the morning shift. For the sunrise over the brickyard in the valley. Some were just waking up, others, mud-splattered, were just arriving. Ridiculously baggy coveralls, a quilted jacket here and there, earmuffs. How they would recognize each other in that dim morning light, I had no idea. But then Smoothy hoisted himself. Nudged me with his elbow. He'd seen the one he was after, the sixth. We walked to the dormitory, me in the lead, equipped with my ridiculous forged papers in case there was a guard. In case it was a guard from the opposing team, I think Smoothy was equipped with something else. But I didn't ask. One time he told me their country's secret service was called Fighting Fish Under Water. And what about yours? I asked. I take orders from General Vang, he snapped.

And then one day with Černá, my loved one, it happened … the metamorphosis. We were together so much now, knew so much about each other, I was already long familiar with the drawing she had on the skin of her thigh, I knew it by heart, but that didn't prevent … each touch, each kiss, from being ever closer, ever stronger, just like in those trashy romance novels … one morning she screamed, I woke with a start, still inside her, tried to move, but it didn't work, I shifted a little to the side to give her breasts room to breathe, but … we were joined. We couldn't separate. Does it hurt? I asked, still dazed with sleep. No, but I can't get up or anything!

We rolled over and tried to crawl … me on my back, clutching her shoulders and thighs, feeling her shoulderblades move, it was totally exhausting, we stopped for a breather … we were like a naked … spider, a new creature, some weird model, skin and hair and nails, eyes … Sister, I told her, I love you … Well, it's about time it came out, and I love you too … the old words relieved us, that's hard stuff to say … and even though I couldn't move, I could feel her moving inside, very gentle and tender … persistent … waves, circling, and it happened … But I can't have a child with my sister, flashed through my mind as we fell into a tighter tangle, now also joined with our arms and legs and tongues … I wanted to feel her with my tongue because I'd found that when I loved her that way, it was even more beautiful and complex than speech … but the path I traveled inside her, moist and tender, what I learned to achieve with my tongue and its caresses, in her and from her … making her sigh with bliss … was a path beyond voice, which is more than a word and can't be expressed in words … only now … we couldn't separate.

Hey, my dearest, said Černá, if I could get up now … maybe, coffee? Sure, but, I said … you … you've got me clamped … Huh, really? No way, you're the one that got big … get out!

But she had to admit, it was at least a two-sided matter ... I glanced toward the door over her naked shoulder, terrified at the thought of them coming, anyone from out there, and seeing us, surely they'd want to separate us, and that would be dangerous ... we were totally defenseless in this new thing of love's, panic seized me, Černá disappeared underneath me, I pawed my way to the door to at least make sure it was locked ... she threw a tantrum ... banged her head on the sideboard, bit me, her hair flowed down over my face, I couldn't see ... then she stopped holding on and it hurt, so I laid on my back again and she got on top and rested ... I never asked you before, but tell me, where'd you get those scars ... No! I'll tell you that when I feel like it! Are they ... old? She burst out laughing ... This, you mean? Yeah, that's old, way old ... she kept laughing ... Hadraba said you were nasty ... don't seem like it to me. Then I glimpsed movement, her hand fumbling in my pants pocket, she pulled it out ... I heard a click ... Černá, no! Don't! Leaning over, she pricked me from behind with the knife, gently, but I was startled ... she lifted her head and looked at me, knife in hand, wiggled her ass, I was still inside her ... Forgive me ... I read somewhere that shock makes it relax ... Sorry, she kissed me to make me stop laughing ... handed me the knife, guess she realized it was her after all ... I jabbed her gorgeous ass a little, twice, but nothin ... Wait, she said, we gotta wait till I'm not expecting it ... So we chatted ... tried to make coffee, it was pretty funny, I tried cold water, it didn't work, neither did hot ... Černá ... you're just a little too run-down, scraped-up, a she-wolf like you, what's another shock or two ... Let's stay like this, she whispered, because ... the circling motion inside her was starting up again and I fell into her and again we were more together and it could've gone on and on ... we might even've been able to overcome ... death, and stay that way ... like figures in an old engraving, characters embroidered on a rug ... but then the doorbell sounded, jangling, we froze.

And all at once we came loose, tumbling onto the bed, I sat up. And a voice said: Excuse me please ... Černá exhaled deeply ... is Miss Moriak ... ová there? Yeah ... Křepelka here, I'm from the Brno branch of the Philatelists Union, please, could you keep something for Mr. Dráp again, and may I come in, Miss? No! And do you know, did Mr. Dráp happen to leave an envelope with you? No! An I don't have time.

The weirdo left. I was disappointed, never saw a philatelist before. We caressed each other a little with every part of our bodies, but since we didn't get much sleep the night before and I had the day off ... we fell back asleep in a close embrace, but it wasn't as close anymore. I'm bummed, I whispered, hugging her tighter … I know … it was a morning miracle, a metamorphosis … we had no other needs … and if life can be like this, even just for a while … then I'll take it, I thought as I fell asleep, and under my eyelids again I saw faces, colors of chaos and spinning circles and metal towers stabbing into the air … but it was different, all of a sudden I knew why … not that I understood, but it was … joyful, I was part of the chaos, it made sense … even chaos had its own color, I saw it but forgot it again right away, like a smile.

When I woke up and moved to get closer to Černá, the magic was gone, she stood at the window … there's somethin goin on at Dráp's place, she said, somebody went in there … go take a look, please … her scared … that amazed me, livin here so long on her own. Up in the attic.

First thing I noticed was one of the floor tiles … overhead nothin but roofbeams, appallingly dusty … my steps stirred up dust, rising in columns, sunlight poured down through the dormers … the tile glared, a sunbeam glancing off, leaving its light, and the door flew open … a boy stood there, chompin on a piece of gum … Mr. Dráp? I said politely … By Jove, the brat said, get over here, dudes, look what the cat dragged in … the other scamps straggled out, they were a little older … the toughest punker, forelock in his face, says to me: Step off, citizen, lest ya come to harm … scamps combine the old tongue with the new, like me, only they donno beans … Heh, it's the big cheese, screeched one of em, carrottop, medieval breeches, chain around his neck, wrists punched to make it look like he'd slashed himself … another crept out from behind him … there were five of em, that's too many, and the last one had a dog … growling and drooling, it was a fight dog, a bigget, the illegal kind they use for gladiator fights, pimps bored with pseudogames love em … slowly I edged out … saw papers scattered all over the flat, upended chairs, and in back … some kind of crate … guess they're lookin for somethin … one of em, a tall blond with moves like a queer … walked up to me, bobbin flirtatiously, I reached into my pocket as if … the other boys just watched, guess he was the boss … Hey, pussy, the fop says … whose're you? You wouldn't by any chance be comin from … Brno, would ja? It dawned on me. I'm no phitelalist, uh, philatelist, I live here … Where is that pecker then, motherfucker! the blond said. Shit … he raised his hands and a demented leer spread across his face … one of the stooges leaped to his side … easy, Miran, we'll snag im, we promised ya … He went out, I said. Snap to it, pipsqueaks, the black-haired one next to Miran yelped … carrottop and another one in a grungy red cap took off down the stairs … still three left … the boss, probly a speed freak … three's still plenty, specially after my sugar-sweet experience this morning … and that dog! … my legs started shakin, I couldn't help it, I had somethin now, Černá, and … the third brat says: First I'll sic Jolly Joker here on im, chew his balls off, that'll be a blast … member that time with the Derelicts? I mean check this ugly fuck out, dude's from Brno, space case. Who're you, said the boss. I live here in the attic. But … said the blond, and something happened to his eyes, but … there's just one place up here! Yep, I nodded, that seemed to impress him. So you're … that means you must be … Moriak. Morti! Yeah, I live here with my sis. Uh … the blond gulped, the second brat took a step back, and as I … noncommittally and basically sweetly … glanced over at the remaining boy, saw him lean against a beam, study the rafters, he patted the dog on the ass, it sat. But it was eyein me.

Hey, boss, said the blond, sorry, we were just in the middle of a gig … an she knows, we got a contract with her. So you have a contract … with my sister, I raised my voice. Yeah, I swear, the blond one yelped in falsetto. I just came by to check it out, I said … I'm goin now. And I went. Didn't bother with any goodbyes.

My mind raced, what could Černá have … with juvies, maybe from the bar … drugs or whatever, gambling … gladiators, no way. I walked past the odd tile, now the rays clung more weakly to it, the sun had shifted … and I pulled up suddenly, hearing … Černá! … and she was saying: Hurry, go on. He'll be back any second, dammit, scram.

She was … whispering, I broke into a run … the guy went down the stairs, disappeared, Černá caught hold of me, and when I saw her smile I hit her, her eyes bulged in disbelief, she sank to the ground but still held on, hugging my knees, I tried to shake her off, but she held tight … No! No, you can't … not yet! You bitch, but I couldn't slug her again, I'd just lost my head, I picked her up, heard that sound … Černá, I'm sorry, that wasn't me … with all my might I gripped her shoulders, spun her round, but she wasn't sobbin, she was laughin … in my face.

I walked into the flat and started packin … tossin around my things … she planted herself in the doorway and said … Don't do it, it's not worth it. Who was that? Hey … my business. Yeah, I don't even care … but how come you wouldn't let me … It's old stuff, real old stuff. We've got time. Černá, I don't trust you. And I love you.

She knew what that would do to me. Actually I didn't get why she wanted me. Bed ... I wasn't that conceited ... the only possibility was that she wasn't lying, that she ... really likes me, maybe. Or she doesn't know if she does, but she wants to. Or else there's somethin here I don't know about ... okay, I'll wait. I stayed. Gladly. And didn't ask questions.

Again that night we sat over the chessboard examining possibilities, moving pieces. The mirrors were set up on opposite walls, you could look and see from one into the other, and there was another infinity, casual and matter-of-fact, like stringy meat on a cutting board.

Sometimes I'd like hunch myself down over the board and the drinks and succeed in getting the solemn, often passionate face of my love in the picture, sinking and reemerging in the shiny surfaces, farther and farther away, and then here.

Sometimes I had to touch her, sometimes she purred and liked it. Now I gotta hold you, she said, and she did, and now I gotta kiss you, she quick slid under the table and touched it, sometimes she got me so excited, touching her lips to it through the fabric, dancing over it with her tongue, I had to grab her neck ... unbuckle myself ... a couple times we had to go down the hallway to the restrooms, the walls there were strewn with classics ... I'd study the obscenities, or better yet close my eyes, standing up, holding her on top of me, behind the curtain, her hitched around my hips, my arms underneath like bars, like branches ... the penguins suspected but left us alone ... Černá drank more in a night than all the random walk-ins ... see, this coffeehouse didn't have any TV or video shit or pseudogames, it didn't even get the daily papers ... there was nothing there but mirrors ... and a permanently shut Stein piano ... ladies with cakes around us, some we started exchanging nods with ... some of the old ladies used to be actresses and talked about it ... constantly ... their only audience here was the cakes and the eggnog, the mirrors, it was a relatively high-society slice of old Prague ... I was wary ... I didn't want any more contact ... and many no doubt were well aware what Černá was doing under the table, that she wasn't tying her shoelace, we got accustomed to one another ... all guests at the same place, and one time I got up the nerve, we ordered a bottle of cognac for them and JD for us, they twittered, but then we got drunk ... I didn't recognize Černá, she was attentive and polite, I didn't know the girl knew how to talk to old ladies. I know ... when they get together, to chat ... sit a young woman down with them, one like Černá, and it can get sadistic, because sometimes, and especially at night, and in these kinds of cafés, the night opens farther, right through the heart … it goes into the grate, into the shit.

Outside, I babbled, a touch sentimental and blinking back tears, she shoved me away and said: Moron! They're dead! They're already goners! Shoved me again. What's got into you, I said pointlessly. Besides, you're gonna be like that too! Not me, what do you know, you don't understand. She waited for me at her building and gave me a hug: Sorry. I was talkin crap. No, you weren't at all.

We didn't miss it … the Dóm, Galactic, Černá's, friends. Friends of friends. People. Quite often we'd just go out strollin at night. That was enough. It would've been pretty hard for us to deal with anyone else.

Sometimes I'd tell her where I got my cash and what I did. I'd drop hints. She didn't seem interested. Even though we both lived off of it. Maybe it's a certain kinda person, the ones that're used to livin alone … they're more on the lookout, don't like idle talk, too many questions, they guard their freedom and the other's too. Even when maybe they'd just as soon be rid of it.

Sometimes we'd tell each other sagas from our past lives … I sometimes talked about myself in the third person, my former life seemed so unbelievable. But it was complicated to say anything about my last crew. She also had a lot to tell … I listened. And that guy on the stairs … I only got a glance from behind, he was older. Probly an ex.

Chess … I told her where I'd learned to play, patched a few ballads together for her, rambling on …

Occasionally we'd interrupt our game and go for a stroll, look at the people … nothing struck fear into me, we held hands, sometimes. After walking around the block, we'd come back to our coats, tossed over the chairs, to our never-ending match and whatever else we happened to get the urge for.

So what kina contract you got with those little thugs from the attic … what was that boss a theirs goin on about?

If you mean those little darlings, before I started at Černá's I used to be the super … those youngsters had a rehearsal space there.

You're always gettin tangled up in your lies … check!

Those're my truths, and not anymore, your move!

Sometimes though … sometimes Smoothy and his bandits gave me heavy-duty circles. It was too much. We'd just picked up a fella who'd spent a couple years in Cambodia, tank driver, and Smoothy says: Not only is our faith in you unshakable but, as you may have noticed, despite your admirable modesty, duly acknowledged financially, my dear and esteemed friend ... I'd gnash my teeth, by this point I was just about as fed up with his politeness as I was with his horror stories, and he knew it, he would torture me until we ... burst out laughin, usually ... modesty, I say, for I must add that you have returned faith in Czech man to some of our boys, yes, through your flawless work, there it is, Mr. Potok, and that is no small thing ... the tank driver jumped in: Toi da tung song voi puli pozikan tyaap! ... our friend here, said Smoothy, wishes to inform you that he met a compatriot of yours in the United States, some Paulina Porizkova ... Chek gurl, gut gurl! the tank driver smacked his lips. I pulled over and ran off into the woods. My nerves're startin to go, I told Smoothy, both a you shut up or I'm gonna wreck this thing.

He could only hold back for a while. Just imagine, Mr. Potok, take a left here, we will be driving day and night this time and ... Huh? Are you afraid your girlfriend will be worried about you? You can call her of course. You see, our tank driver here is truthfully the next-to-last, we need to bring back one more ... relative and then we can say our goodbyes ... of course it is my hope that we may soon welcome you as a guest of honor in our liberated homeland ... turn! ... General Vang would like to express his gratitude to you in person.

Well, I said to myself soberly, now I'm gonna find out where the place is. How does he know about Černá?

What's that you said about my girl?

Just that you can call her so she needn't be concerned.

How do you know I'm ... with somebody?

I was only assuming.

Yeah right, bullshit, all of a sudden I started to wonder if maybe this character was Vohřecký's contact, he'd make noodles outta Side Pocket, though you never can tell who'll cook who till the banquet's on the table. Till afterwards.

For me Jícha was joined with ... what he'd done to Černá ... and I didn't give him another thought otherwise ...

What are you thinking about, Mr. Potok, my master's voice said from behind me. Perhaps it would be more reasonable to drive straight, it is not wise to elect the left-hand lane. We might be faced with oncoming traffic!

I pictured how much I would earn off this trip ... if it turned out all right, and I was fast ... and how I'd pool the envelopes from Rudolf with the chuckles from Hunter and the two of us'd take off ... at least for a while ... we drove on down the highway ... come night I remembered that guy was a tank driver ...

woke him up and got in back with Smoothy, for once he was quiet … but it was impossible to sleep, I guess drivin a tank in some Cambodian jungle, tryin to make stiffs out of every livin thing in sight, is a little different than haulin down some fucked-up white man's highway … I was pretty rough on Paulina's lover … then Smoothy woke up and started tellin me what Pol Pot and Saloth Sar were like, and what the Khmers Rouges used to do when they ran out of lime for graves … got it firsthand from the tank driver … Smoothy, don't you have a driver's license?

But of course!

Then take over, I can't see anymore.

Excuse me, Mr. Potok, but that's your job.

The jerk at the motel wouldn't take us: said they could've tolerated Smoothy, would've put a cot for him in my room, but the tank driver had a jumpsuit on … even though Smoothy's Czech was better than mine, the guy at the reception desk talked right through him: This is a private establishment, he told me, as if anyone but the Devil cared what kinda pact they'd signed with him.

I kicked at the gravel. Smoothy, amazingly, spoke briefly and to the point. He explained what was at stake. It was all the same to the tank driver … he was used to the factory, being on the road was like paradise for him. Even if he wasn't allowed to drive anymore. The two of us had a beer, Smoothy made do with a cognac, and we spent the night in the car.

Above all, Smoothy told me, you have no idea what it's like for our men when those youngsters attack them … the colonel here could dispatch four of them in eight seconds, just between us, that's the only thing he really knows how to do, but he can't … he has a mission … it's very frustrating for him that he is not able to act correctly in this regard, and the youngsters are very unreasonable and very careless.

He stuck a photo under my nose, cut out of some newspaper … I shouldn't've looked … it was the faces of four girls, Asians, they'd been thrashed, bloodied and battered, noses broken, I figured each of those plucked blossoms for about seventeen … Smoothy talked …

There were times the wheel's motion got me so carried away that I woke Černá up and: Let's roll! Not to give any orders, Sister, but hurry, let's roll!

Where to, what's up?

We gotta get to Paree right now, I gotta measure this classroom there where Pol Pot learned to build a fence, take a string an some chalk, I wanna see it … maybe then I'll understand.

No you won't, an I wanna sleep!

Usually, once we were up strugglin with our night demons anyway, we'd dive all over each other, I used to keep track of who was on top and who was on bottom, now sometimes it got mixed up … who soothed who, who crushed who, depending on our urge, and that was shared. Nothing stood in the way of our desire to hold each other, ourselves. Černá … didn't talk about it like me, but … there was something we had in common. Those little scars. Hers definitely didn't come from a bicycle, or from scoopin out crayfish from under rocks, back in the days of some sweet helpless childhood. She had her own stuff. That's how come the fingers in fists, that's how come sometimes at night … she lay in bed with her eyes open. Sobbin … only when she thought I was asleep. It's pretty disgusting listenin to a girl try to cry so she won't wake the guy next to her. One time I grabbed her hair and yanked her outta bed, I couldn't stand that quiet grief … but she kneed me so hard I saw sparks … afterwards she attended to the spot, which she'd aimed for out of habit, she sobbingly explained, with breath and hair damp with tears … and we began anew.

What did I know. I must've been a pain in the ass sometimes, once the bliss had run its course and our bodies were gathering strength for the next round: Let's roll! Černá, c'mon. Outta here, anywhere!

Number one I don't wanna, number two I don't wanna, number three I don't wanna, an number four it's always what you want an never what I want!

Thanks, I don't wanna anymore.

The night before that last trip we talked a long time. Tell me, Černá, when was the first time you thought you … how come I didn't know you back then … where're you from?

I'm with you, aren't I? The questions you ask in bed … an I'll tell you when I feel like it … but there was one I liked, he had a car.

Hah, I shoulda known … some dumb car …

What do you know, you donno … it was so fast all of a sudden … I'd wait somewhere, by the side of the road, so they couldn't see me … an suddenly we'd be gone, far away, get it? I didn't know anything around there … he showed me churches, graveyards, I never knew before about castles an all that. We also went to a lake together, he wanted some fisherman to take our picture, to remember it by, but I told him: No! It's stupid, you can't take a picture of that, no way. An the castle was huge, I was real young. I never knew knights were that short before, shorter than us, they had shorter doorways, shorter beds ... I was too young.

Knights, I know! They went through doors too, right! What didn't you know about castles though, in school they taught us ...

I didn't listen to that crap a theirs.

Now I get it ... he was older. I'm not jealous!

Yeah you are ... an you oughta be! Cause I gave it to him. Well, it wasn't the first time, not by far ... but I wanted to, he was nice. We had to go someplace without people ... the cemetery. No one bothered us there. People only go on certain dates. We picked up on that. It smelled of flowers. Just on those dates, the rest a the time they put fake ones out, idiots. Doesn't help the dead, I think. So that's where we did it, that was the safest place. But it didn't do much for me. Not like with you, I swear, how come you're not talkin ... what's wrong?

I was sniffin around her ear, checkin it out. It reminded me of a clam, a mussel, it was amazing. I listened, heard something ... but it was just her stomach growling, stuck the tip of my tongue in ... she began to get carried away, but it made me think of ... the sea.

Černá, get up, right now, let's go. To the sea! Why didn't I think of that, I've never seen the sea ... I'll see it with you, that's what we're together for. Definitely! We'll rent a boat, cruise around ... hey, you can ski, I'll steer, my bronze chest glittering with drops of water ... you'll wave to everyone ... afterwards we'll head in for campari an roulette ... we'll be incognito, mysterious foreigners! ... coconuts an palm trees ... we'll scrape up the cash ... you can sing along to the surf, listen, the water's silver foam on your lips along with the words to some song, how's that? Then I'll bury you in the sand so just your breasts an head stick out ... an then you'll bury me!

I sat on the bed and gripped the steering wheel, Černá rode the skis like a queen, vrrrr, vrrrr, I wheeled it around, she caught hold and lay down on top of me.

An there'll be clean air. Beaches, sand. An after you bury me ... ha-hah.

She squealed, I cackled ... only then ... Aw no, Černá, honey, what is it ... she pressed her face to the sheet, didn't want me to see her, I guess to see her eyes ... wet.

Oh no, what'd I do now? What's wrong? What got into her? I didn't get it. The highway. We couldn't sleep. I watched each piece of asphalt go by, remembering every one. So … tomorrow I'll find out where that bungalow a theirs is. An then I guess the spooks'll turn up.

All right, Smoothy, I made up my mind to give it a shot, when we get to the next stop I'll say … So you're working for Vohřecký and them, all I want to know is where's your hideout, and I can guarantee …

Herro, a voice from behind us said, and there stood Hunter.

Ça va? I said with a kind smile. How much Czech does he know by now, I wondered …

Ça va, monsieur Potok.

So as not to waste time, Smoothy traded off with me at the wheel, all of a sudden he'd turned a bit tame. Occasionally he exchanged a word or two with Hunter, but otherwise he was strikingly reserved … Hunter warmly greeted the tank driver … and it was nice … two guys, half a world away from their tribe … greeting each other here on a highway near a motel, right beneath an ad for some idiocy, and in the sky a moon as bright as all the flashbulbs ever fired since that memorable day in the depths of the eons, back at the commencement of all creation … a few words, an ear-to-ear smile, a pat or two on the back, it took a while, then I noticed … Hunter was their boss, their war chief, they obeyed him, but not his words, his every movement, the slightest hint of a gesture.

Next morning I go to get some milk, the gentlemen tucked away in the car, at the edge of the village I stop and stare … donno that. It's in Ukrainian, I ask some fella, he scowls, walks right past me. In the shop they all gawk … damn, shoulda worn different clothes, thought we were goin to a factory and that'd be it, they ladled the milk into pails … one of the women looked like my grandma before she came down with that whatchamacallit … they're talkin … Russian, I guess, Christ, where am I? But the goods were Bohemian, or Czechoslovak, drugstore items, food and stuff, snacks, tidbits … stamps, what stamps? I froze. Fumbled for the wallet Smoothy'd given me … any Moor'd know his way around here better than me, I'm just in it for the mental exercise, for love and death, what an idiot I am, I thought … that guy bumped into me on purpose, better give him some room … I'd like to see the tank driver in here, wonder how many seconds he'd need to take these guys out … couple locals sittin on sacks of potatoes, guzzlin vodka, one of em collars me, plunks me down next to him: I want milk! I say. Aj tuna, guy shoves a triple shot of vodka in my face, yore a man, down it, don't down it, yore a cunt! It was obvious what the guy … might do if I proved to be the latter … I downed the glass, it was awful, but the shop came to life again, the grannies tottered over to get a peek, I sat on the sack, waggin my head, have you got a telephone? Hej! Prague, please … oho, Prague! That set off an uproar, I hid my face behind my hands, but no, it was friendly, one of the grannies tugged at my hair, like I was some kina horse … the fella stuck a wooden platter under my nose, bacon fat on it bristling with fur … Take a bite! They were stuffin their faces. I took a piece, spotted a tomato on the shelf, leaped up, took a bite, wrong, a young hot pepper, another round of great laughter ensued, what would I think of next … I dictated the number to the saleslady, the shop owner … others kept wanderin in, I promised myself to cut my hair behind the next beech tree I saw, there were whole forests of beech out here … a buggy rolled up in front of the shop, a herd of pigs went dashin by … the guy that poured me the vodka started in on an ice cream bar, offered me a bite, someone slapped me on the back: You must be Havel's son, at least that I understood … that's Francek, he's Czech, someone shouted, and up walks this bum … some dog skin or somethin over his shoulders … He starts huggin and kissin me, slobberin all over. Aparatka! I grab the phone … Černá! What, six in the? Sorry, I'm, no, I donno where I am … Francek tears the phone outta my hand: Not to worry, lass, we're all out here in Ubla! All us out here're Ruthenes. Me and yore lad, we were, what … scratches his ear and with a guilty look hands back the receiver … a stream of cuss words pourin out of it, no one but me could understand, I cut right in: I love you madly, no, I'm not at the train station, I'll be back … I noticed the shop had fallen quiet, everyone had their ears pricked up, some a the grannies snuck in closer … No, Černá, I think our side a the border, I think Slovakia, yeah, I'm a little loopy, you too? I slept alone too … with Smoothy, I mean, damn that vodka … What? Somebody was tellin me somethin … Yeah, Černá, listen, I'm somewhere near Uzhgorod or somethin … Ušanica, they're tellin me's the nearest … Ubla … no, there's no way a place could be called that … maybe I'm in Poland … what? For trams? Traps? Yeah, honey, you look out for yourself too … they're starin at me like I'm from Mars … in about two days, maybe there's an airport around, I'll call just as soon as I know where I am. An sorry bout the other night … but anyway, when I'm done here … we'll go to the sea … Bye. Aright, later!

A wave passes through the shop again, someone bursts in: Gypsies! Gypsies! They're not our kind, they're un-Ruthene! The owner drops under the counter, the men duck behind the sacks, and in walk Smoothy and Hunter … jaws plummet, I'm havin a heart attack … Smoothy walks up to the counter and lets loose: Greetings, fine people. Excuse me, but could we have some rolls and milk and coffee? Weal … veal? Voice shakin a little, he muffed it … Someone from behind the bags, Francek, says, they're Czeshes, new Czeshes! Finally we picked out some food, canned sardines or whatever. Hunter remained aloof, even they could sense … he was a somebody. A boss.

We had to stay a while and get acquainted, they weren't gonna let the chance pass by, foreigners like these … but they didn't crowd around Hunter, the conversation was up to me, I just grinned stupidly, couldn't refuse the vodkas, they might've been insulted … Smoothy got in the groove, yammerin on … a cry came from outside, in raced two cops, totally panicked … I bounded out the door and saw the tank driver next to some soggy old wall, wavin a bar around, a little ways off a police car was flipped over, six stick-swingers lyin on the ground … Whose is that? one of the badged men moaned, probly thought the tank driver was some kina animal … Hunter hissed at him … they took us in to the Diet, the whole village was gathered there, everyone from the shop testified to our immaculate behavior … Smoothy and I found the chief of police before they could start the proceedings … We're sorry about the squabble and our mechanic clobbering your young men like that, he's a maniac … I rambled … then Smoothy showed the chief our purchasing power, it worked as usual, and a little while later we were back on the road, the tank driver looked more cheerful.

This time Hunter drove while I sat in back choking, one minute with laughter, the next I guess from the bacon, and then, exhausted, I fell asleep.

One night we were playing chess when out of nowhere she said … she was only slowly coming to see who I was and why I'd latched onto her, but that it had probably been an act of love. Those were her words. Sometimes our language was scrambled because our sped-up idiom didn't always work for talking about what we had together. Much of it was beyond language. The way the body speaks. She told me about people who'd wanted to get inside her and who she'd had to shove out of her way. She'd never had a tribe, but it's rare that women do.

With Černá … for the first time I realized that even the slimmest little vein, every single hair on my body … *was*. At times I didn't understand her sadness … then again at times she had to scald me, or douse me with ice water, or I would've gone through the roof. We hugged hard, in part because we didn't hear any bells. Sometimes she'd jump at me from the side and I'd flip her in the air.

Me underneath, on the broken glass, so she wouldn't get cut, and her up above, pulling down webs, sometimes we'd spin around.

Maybe if the metallic sound of a bell's heart had sliced through the space above the rooftops and come filtering down through the buildings' walls and corners … we could've snatched it up and divined from it right there on the sidewalk. When I said so, she came to life … and told me a story about that … friend of hers with the important car … he took her to a founder, a guy that made bells … one of the last. I considered that an important sign.

I realized my love consisted of many parts, be it her shoulder, her breath, or what she had on, or each little piece of her skin, and always it stunned me that it was her. Maybe she felt the same … maybe that was why we took all those photos. Sometimes we even needed beating. The chill of ice and the warmth of butter. Our enormous hunger refined everything, and therefore everything was allowed. Death was everywhere, but Černá had her arms outstretched, palms up. And I tried too.

I'd found her, dragged her out of the web. Cut the straps. I wasn't afraid to tell her I wanted her. But then she started making me. One time I saw a grave with her name on it, she woke up too.

It was bad, Černá … it was terrible! In my dream I was standin at your grave, or wait, it wasn't yours! There was just a name, I remembered the first time I saw a woman naked … I was sick, often, as a little kid. My father took me to see the doctor. An army doctor … did I ever tell you my dad was a soldier? But the Communists gave him the heave, then he got some job sweepin … He still had friends, though, oh yeah. Those guys taught me Latin, for cryin out loud. The doctor ordered me to strip, they took my temperature. I used to get these high fevers where it felt like my hands an head were so big I couldn't fit into my room anymore. My grandma'd soak my hands in a bowl of cold water. Finally they took me to the doctor … but then there was the waiting room with those retarded posters, remember? And Jesus … this one loony bin had a sign: CHEERFUL THOUGHTS ARE THE OIL OF THE HUMAN MOTOR. Yeah, that got me. I was one big wreck when they brought me in. Shook like a dog when I saw it. That's ages ago. Want the ashtray?

Yeah okay. Put it there. Good.

It was just … my dad didn't tell me till we got there that they were leavin me … said I would like it there. The hospital was clean, my room was nice an big. There were lotsa kids, my mom brought this one boy a huge seashell, I was furious. Actually, Černá, you know … how I was talkin about the sea … that was cause of your ear! It reminded me of that shell. It was mine. My mom explained to me that that sick kid came from a children's home an didn't have anybody. My uncle, though … he brought me a cannon, a model from the Napoleonic wars. I'd longed for one for ages. The hospital was the first time in my life I saw a woman naked. First night, I'm lyin by the window, can't sleep, so I'm lookin out. And there was this little house over there, the lights were on, afterwards the kids in the room told me it was a morgue. I could see in and there were dead bodies laid out on tables. Two people came in with a body in a bag. Then they took the bag off and left. I looked. She had black hair, like you … only longer! And gorgeous breasts. I could tell even then. She was dazzling, I didn't care if she was dead. I just kept lookin till I fell asleep. After that the lights were never on again.

Maybe you just dreamed it.

Whatever. Oh … Černá. Sometimes I'm scared too … I fight. So do you. Where are you, I fumbled for her.

Wait a sec … here I am. She turned on the light. Cut it out! Got a smoke? You chose me as your sister an I said okay. I'd like you just the same if you didn't want me … I mean we know each other. But you'd be deprived without me. I'm … sometimes I'm proud. You're always goin on about how dangerous it is … cut it out! If people weren't such cowardly shits, the world'd be a different place … although … that's bullshit too. But still … that's where hang-ups come from, an hang-ups I think're real dangerous. We're not that scared though, are we, honey? We're givin it a try … I mean we go together, you an me. Be careful, please.

Černá, don't think … I gotta tell you. I'm afraid too, sometimes … even with you. You're right, notice how now the masks're peelin off, it's rotten underneath … people, when they wanna, can be real scums, you said so yourself … I mean even me, I mean you know … they're afraid to say, yeah, to say! … somethin's nice, somethin's good … it's easier to crush it, strangle it … I know all about that … the hardest thing of all is tellin someone what I told you, you know … when I told you I love you.

Sister shrieked, sat up in bed, and gave me a look, foolin around … took her hands and made like a telescope, peerin at me through the cracks … you said it, I'm embarrassed! Hey, she kicked off the blanket, why don't you come over here … an fuck me, hurry, I want it … now.

Her skin touched My Protective Animal, my flying, dancing symbol, and one time she said: I was — you're gonna get jealous again but that's stupid! — this one guy I was with, his … cock was like this. He had an eagle on his skin.

What … I jumped up. What was his name … Bohler?

I donno. Didn't ask. We were only together once. We met once. Whatever … but what you told me an I told you, the important thing … trust me. Always. Sometimes I'm not myself, I mean with us drinkin an all. But I've never loved anyone this much before. So actually no one else's been inside me. And I'd destroy anyone that tried to harm you. Mercilessly. You have no idea …

Pass me that lighter, would ja. I do have an idea, Černá. Maybe I already know who you are … I've got a hunch … an could ja nudge that ashtray over, yeah … good.

In time we expanded our territory. The city was growing, always some new thing … we'd walk out in the street at night, confusing taxi drivers, on the slow trams sometimes we'd get jumpy and wrap ourselves around the bars, especially me. In the subway we'd sit solemnly, staring blankly ahead, pretending, in front of and along with the rest of the passengers, like nothing was going on at all … we'd even go to the theater, now and then. At least there we didn't run into anyone we knew.

We studied the gowns and masks and then used some of it later on. I think the singers pissed Černá off a little. I knew, I noticed … sometimes she'd hum along and harmonize. I guess she really missed it. But it fascinated her how I'd always guess what each piece was about and how it would turn out. She'd look at me, eyes shining, and gasp: You're amazing! I didn't tell her that most of the plays I'd read. Once upon a time. One skit in some out-of-the-way local theater I even wrote. Under my own name though, so she didn't realize.

Occasionally we'd have a couple vodkas in the lobby, Černá rattling the jewelry she'd borrow for nights on the town. Me powdered up. Planting kisses in her décolletage and throwing roses at her. Champagne for Chekhov, whiskey for Shepard, we didn't mix that up. *The Lantern,** Jirásek! Water goblins, myrtle. We saw that one five times. During the performance we'd rustle papers. She'd leave chewing gum on her seat. That's so they'll see … so they'll see it's no joke, Sister would say. The ladies hissed. When that unfaithful Yaga throttled her husband the Moor, Černá broke down sobbing, she shouldn't do that! she cried. They tried to escort her out, I intervened. Idiots, what've you got against negroes, Černá railed at the usher. Then she told me the story. I was jealous. Still.

And after one brilliant play I fine-tuned the plot: Černá! I had a dream. That's not how it was in reality, see, it's true Ulysses slaughtered those suitors when he got home, but that was only cause … they were younger an better-lookin an richer than him, he was gettin to be an old dog … an they were just boys, don't gimme that look! That's all he did in those islands anyway, was kill an plunder, plus charm Circe an take over her pig byznys … so he comes home to his castle an Penelope's there waiting faithfully, like a good wife … but Ulysses bursts in an says: Sorry. You've waited faithfully an long. I was off fightin, I'm a man. That's why you wanted me, right? Sorry, though, you're gettin old now. So I brought back this splendid sixteen-year-old slave girl. Girl! Lift your arms over your head, turn around. See those breasts, Penelope, see that ass? See that mane, see how her hair shines? See those teeth? Does it remind you of anything? That's right, that's how you used to be, Penelope. Ages ago. It doesn't bother you that I'm bein frank, does it? I am a man, you know. Do you know how many enemies I crushed an songs I wrote on my travels? That's why you wanted me. I met this one, Penelope, an now she's here! She's the one I've had under my eyelids all my life, you just wandered into my path. That's the way it is. Sorry, Penelope, it's been nice. Now … get out.

Černá put her shades on. Are you hungry, friend?

Yeah.

Unfortunately all I've got is a little dried-out piece of … mortadella. An coffee. Just black though. How bout it?

Okay.

Maybe you oughta try a little more, you're always bullshittin … what about comin up with a happy ending for once, I know it's hard, are you scared?

Yeah. A little bit, yeah.

There was one thing I couldn't stand. When she put on her shades, I'd lose her eyes. Think it was somebody else under there. I'd known her eyes as green, now more often they were speckled brown. Maybe it depended on the light, on whether we had candles or a lamp, or if it was daytime. I never did find out. But then she started wearin her shades to bed even. I told her I didn't want her to. She just laughed. Trust me … it's good for you too … not to see for a while.

I focused so much on her body and her breathing that sometimes I didn't notice her eyes. We also tried a mask, and sometimes I put a pillow or a pillow-case over her face. I guess there really are times when you wanna be alone. Just you an your grimaces. It's impossible to smile all the time.

But in my heart there was love. I kept it locked inside. That's the way it was. With her I was in reality. I know it.

Sometimes … it got in there. I came home from a foray, Smoothy's crap ringin in my ears still, and she had the radio on. First the announcer spoke about India, then took Pakistan, dipped into Iran, cut across the north back down toward the south and then said a thing or two about Egypt, took it all in one fell swoop, didn't even leave out Libya, he didn't leave out a thing, bet he had to loosen his tie. I opened the window and looked at the street. The hustle and bustle. Some tanker of something drove by. It was yellow.

What's up, said Sister after a while.

Nothin, I don't think I can take it anymore. Nothin's goin on at all … notice all the natural catastrophes lately though?

There's also nice things.

Like what?

The air hardened in my ears like chunks of basalt.

Hey, hey, stop talkin, have yourself a glass a wine, have a smoke, come over here, be with me, hop to it.

I noticed she had a new … I guess T-shirt. Nothin on her shoulders, just these thin little strings … it was white. An besides, she was right.

But then she started throwing up bile. All I could do was hold her head. And that night, before Hunter got in the car … she didn't want to go to the sea with me.

We stood on a path in the woods. I gave it a shot. Fidgeting like I was nervous, I told Smoothy: My work's finished. I'm goin. Let me go. Smoothy threw up his hands. Why, my dear esteemed Mr. Potok, that is out of the question! Think what you like, but Oriental hospitality is an important factor here. Now we are going to walk through the forest, the general first, then our new friend, and after them you. After you will be me, and my dear Mr. Potok … I sorely beg you … try to understand … it would be best if we also arrive in that order, yes?

Yeah right. At that moment I despised … Hunter. That time on the street, him jabbin that bamboo stick around with me at his side … that was different … now he had a mission. But I'm no commissar.

He walked past like he didn't even see me. We followed the path through the woods, crooked trees all around, then we came to a swamp, I watched the worms' bizarre little trails in the puddles … unnamable creatures, it's nonsense what they call em in labs … Hunter stopped as we entered a gully. A tree trunk lay across the path. The tank driver and Smoothy went runnin up and started wrasslin around with it … but didn't take their eyes off me, it was ridiculous! The tree's roots were tangled up, they didn't spot the little snarl of nettles. I freed it all up and rocked the tree off the path. Hunter gave the nod and we moved on. The tank driver tried to take a shortcut and sank into the swamp … just up to his knees, but he got pretty freaked … as we walked on, Smoothy couldn't hold back and started rattlin on again, I would've rather listened to the birds, why put up with human conversation right to the end …

Mr. Potok, a very interesting cultural dissimilarity, did you know that in our country people never go for walks? Most of their time they spend seeking food. Perhaps poets and philosophers once did, but they have all been reeducated now … one does not walk in the forest in our country, the forest there is different, can you believe it? You can only go in with a tiger club … of course I am joking! Can you believe it? My friend here, who so imprudently strayed from the path just now, has traveled dozens of kilometers through the most dangerous jungle on earth. He escaped from the camp and headed for Thailand, truly he is something special … if only he knew how to write, he could publish a comparative study, here is a man who survived a reeducation camp in his homeland, then another one next door in Laos, and then, consider this, the Khmers spent several years making him into a new man … and he survived, even though no one expected it of him. Such a comparative study would be extremely interesting, he emerged from the jungle unscathed and hiked into Thailand, where he survived several refugee camps, and when he was hungry, he admitted, he …

Guess that's what got Paulina, huh?

Your cynicism, Mr. Potok, is entirely out of place. I am showing you a phenomenon here … compare, if you will … the gentleman ahead of you is quite probably the only human on earth to have completed such a journey, and yet he sinks into the mud at the first silly little European forest he comes to, no snakes, no mines … no people, apart from us, naturally. Of course we are all friends.

Oh yeah, it was obvious what kinda friendship he'd show me if I were to start skippin even just a little bit indiscreetly. One minute I wanted to whimper, the next I felt calm. One childish self of mine refused to believe after all we'd been through that they could just … in cold blood … but I know people with a mission are the worst of all. Commissars. They've rid themselves of choice.

We walked through the woods for about an hour, and I've never felt a forest so much. Out of habit, I guess, I examined it, remembering it, putting it inside me. There were moments I felt like it knew. Like it was friendly to me. The men around me, our paths intertwined … but their souls were filled with vines and snakes and orchids… maybe they had the dragon, but in my cells I've got the bear … the pine … those swampy pools of theirs're different, they donno a thing about cuttin through lilac and steerin clear of blackberry bushes. I was on my home turf, that consoled me a little. In spite of everything. When it came to this forest trail, this path, they didn't know a thing. They didn't feel what I did. Then Hunter came to a stop.

We were on a hill, we'd come up out of a gorge and now we were standing on top, hidden by trees, beech trees. Below us shone the white roof of a hideous one-story building made of plywood boards, plastic, and sheet metal. The kinda thing people leave behind in godforsaken places.

Smoothy went ahead of me, teeth shining in a smile … you are our only guest, Mr. Potok, the only one, we hope … notice if you will, he showed me what he had in his hand … a pinecone … this highly remarkable and exotic fruit is worth more to us than all the supergadgets put together … he threw the cone onto the roof below and another one right after … ponk! ponk! … the woods around the building rippled … at first I only spotted movement, then them, hopping out … like this: hop, hop … from the bushes on this late afternoon … the tank driver and I gawked, he was overjoyed … we started off downhill.

The building was just camouflage, they had pits in the bushes, that's where they lived … waiting. Greetings like barking, they didn't waste time … I gave em a nod … the captain slapped me on the back, but I didn't trust him anymore … but the scariest character was Smoothy junior. He was no smoothy, he was … a mankurt.* I don't think he knew he was living. Looked at his dad like he was air, didn't rush over or anything. His eyes hung on Hunter. Aw, shut up, I told myself … What do I know what kina hell they got inside em. Anyway I'm on their side, although … They'd given up trying to convince me that we'd be going to track someone else down still. The day was fading, slowly and surely. I tried hard to absorb. The things of the world whipped me like ivy.

They had a car there. Roomy enough for the seven I'd dragged outta the factories, plus the boss. Plus Smoothy. I don't think they were figurin on a spot for me. They were on a mission. Mine was apparently at its end.

I wanna talk to the general, I told Smoothy. He isn't a general … and he doesn't have time. I went up to Hunter an let loose in French, panting like some kinda Gavroche. The general refuses to speak the language of the colonizers, Smoothy translated for me. I tried Russian. No dice. Then kiss my ass, you nimrod! Smoothy grinned.

Let's go inside, he took me by the elbow, I had no choice. Smoothy … You have betrayed us from the beginning. No, I'm on your side. Don't lie! For once I'm not lyin. You would lead them here. I don't wanna, screw em. You took money from them. They wouldn't've trusted me otherwise, all I wanna do is grab Sister an split … I know, said Smoothy. And do you trust her? I stopped … like he'd bitten me. You know her, Smoothy? I am asking whether you trust her … yeah … but. Precisely, said Smoothy.

Inside it was scorching, they didn't air it out. Everything was bent, banged up, who knew how long that place'd been standin there. Formica looked fresh though. I went and opened a window, turning my back to Smoothy. Wait a moment, he said. It's still too light. Huh? You lied to me constantly, Mr. Potok … all those words of yours … nilly, noo-noo, figling, mickiwick … bimbam, thupdoodle, frickter … I went through every one of my dictionaries, those words don't exist … Hah, they do now, Smoothy! How true, did you know that I am a professor … of comparative literature … does that mean anything to you? Not even close, but what's it matter now, right? An what'd you mean about the light … Not only am I a professor, Mr. Potok, but I have been trained … and Smoothy took a running start, it was tough in that little room, but he's a nimble little guy, rammed his head into the wall, face first … I thought he'd gone nuts, here I am, the only normal one, surrounded by loonies, I mean look at Černá, she's psycho too … he looked a little stunned but took another run-up, this time it made a crunching sound, his knees sagged a little, he wagged his head … seeping blood, his nose, I guess … I am releasing you, Mr. Potok, and I am doing this so they will think that you overpowered me, which, he laughed, will astound them … I am a Christian, Mr. Potok, but my family, what is left of it, are Buddhists … and I am going to tell you something, some words you do not know, he pulled a small figurine from his pocket, some little demon … gold probly … I curbed my comments … this is Sakya Muni, said Smoothy, I had it made in Paris, and he is my family's God of Happiness and Good Fortune, I am releasing you so that in turn perhaps someone will release … one of my people … is night falling yet? Is dusk upon us? Is … twilight drawing near? I guess he was a little giddy from the blows, but he'd been trained … so he sat down an pulled out a gun … with a silencer, I knew it from the movies … an said … if night is falling, then run along, and please, don't let them get you, because I cannot give you a second chance and the general may not give me even a first one, and did you see my son? I smashed my face in, but at least you have kept me amused, perhaps I shall yet reach the end … min-ding, thupdoodle … pan-toong, yes, the borders of poetry are as flexible as the borders of the Chinese provinces … I was already outside, but I leaned in through the window … thupdoodle, but my sis came up with that one … Go! Hurry! And he fired, *thup!* … and again, *thup!* and I didn't make up that exclamation point, and I was halfway up the hill before I looked back and saw that Smoothy wasn't in the chair anymore … I ran … but when I got to the top I checked myself, only fools rush into the woods … and it started … hop, hop … they went flashing past … ahead of me and on either side, and I snuck off, slow and silent, in the other direction … but they were no dodos, that was obvious. My only advantage perhaps was a childhood of make-believe, this was my forest and I was a robber, only now the king's men were menacingly real … I crept slowly … they ran, I think, silent and bowed … and the first beech to offer me its trunk and branches I accepted, and stayed there … toward morning I spotted two of em, goin along, sniffin the wind, and in their hands … all they had were these thin little canes, it scared the hell outta me … next day I stole across the hillside, allowing myself some speed now, swooping in and out of the rocks … and I came around a stone mound and there was Smoothy's son.

He just sat there, holdin a cane, lookin at me, didn't breathe a word. I started shakin, couldn't control it. I think I said: Oh. But he didn't stir, was it a dream? I kicked the stone, the mankurt waved his hand. I walked around him … waiting, waiting. But then … he got tears in his eyes. Shook his head, and a great big one dripped off his chin. Strange creature. I headed back into the woods. He waved after me.

At last I made it to a road. It was falling to pieces, at every bend I was worried the gravel would give out. And after … some time, I donno how long, I heard a familiar drone, it stabbed right through me … it was the weirdest thing, totally unnatural, I didn't hear any technological stuff at all in the area, no robots, buzzsaws, engines, planes, no silver birds in a streak of exhaust … no traffic lights beeping, nothing. Don't get that much anymore.

It was a junker, patchwork job, the guy took a start when I came outta the trees, but he pulled over. Hello, scuse me, could I get a lift? I had a humble expression on and more language tricks in reserve. What ... where ya goin? he asked. Big guy, black sweater, older than me. And around his neck ... silver! I couldn't believe it.

He was a milkman with a pickup full of milk jugs. Came in handy. Did a pretty good business, I gathered. We rode along, he told stories.

He'd left the city. This here all useda be military, strategic area, he said, elbow propped out the window ... vacuated alla the villages. Just opened it up now, after the revolution. Soldiers cleared out, Russians too. Was it a revolution, whadda you think? I gave some answer. Over there, he waved his hand, ya got Poland, over there Ukraine, this here's Slovakia, I think, an over there's nothin, he kidded. We had a good time.

I'll drop ya in Ušanica, at the train. How'd ja wind up here? Aw, just driftin, takin a look around ... I hear ya, he nodded. Locals don't exactly flock here, too superstitious. Couple Ruthenians, in the mountains, come down for vodka an chewin gum, that's about it ... only people we get out here're city folk. There's a family with kids nearby. An the one that herds. The locals ... you wouldn't believe the stories they got. Say there's ghosts round here. Last time they had anything spooky out here was Bandera* an his crew. An sposedly ... there's some factory, from the war still. Buried. They say after the Germans left, the Russkies started it up again. Wives' tales. Was an earthquake here, way back when. But otherwise there's nothin goin on, so they still remember. The time the earth shook.

What're you doin here? I inquired of Mr. Talkative.

Me ... I found somethin! he said excitedly, and pulled over. I flinched, another wacko ... He took me round the back of the truck and unrolled some blankets full of assorted unusual rocks ...

Donno how much biology you had, but those're trilobites! He lovingly lifted one and rotated it to give me a side view ... I discovered caves, hundreds of em! His face was ... happy. Gorgeous, they're beauties ... an there's somethin else in there too, he said, winking. Flowers! Know this one? He pulled a deep orange flower out of his pocket and rubbed it between his fingers. Strong fragrance.

Sure don't.

It's saffron ... there's whole meadows of em, I'm gettin it analyzed, see if it's mutated ... you wanna join the team, we can make a deal!

I felt an almost irresistible urge ... first I gotta go see my girl.

Bring her along, what's stoppin ya?

You're a great guy ... I told him sincerely ... would Černá ... maybe, maybe not ... it's a possibility. But the main thing was, I had material for my dreams.

Word of advice for ya, he said back on the road ... get a haircut, no point in stickin out around here ... they don't like it.

Don't like it anywhere.

City's different ... out here everyone knows bout everyone else, even if they're kilometers apart. They know right away when somebody new comes. Or disappears.

I don't like the sound a that, I said.

That's the way it is, nothin you can do. He kept quiet a while. Then he says ... yeah, I'm satisfied here, the one that herds too ... how long though I donno ... there's times I think I've found my place ... an there's times somethin tells me I should clear out while I can ... there's somethin strange here, that's for sure. Just donno what. Where ya wanna hop out?

At the station. So this is Ušanica?

Yep.

Holy shit!

You'll get used to it.

Keep goin. Step on it!

Standing in front of the station was Hunter.

I dropped to the floor, squeezin up against the metal. My new friend was understanding, he kept goin ... was that a Russian? he inquired.

No. I donno.

Some Kazakh or Kalmyk or somethin ... said the fella, he a deserter? There's some a those round here, don't wanna go back to Mother Russia, they want Germany. Yep, they're real curious bout them over there. Dads hacked the place to pieces an their boys got freedom. Crazy how the wheel spins, huh? Been a long time since I talked normal with anyone. Also useda be Mongols out here worked in the porcelain factory. Mongol in a china shop's what they say out here, good, huh? But it didn't work out ... with the locals. Surprised that one showed his face. You got some racket goin with them? Forget it, all they got's rifles for booze, now the gangs're gettin in on it ... I warn ya, you look like a regular guy ... Where ya headed? I gotta go to the lab ... all the way to ... Mezilavorie, know it?

Nope.

You'll see.

The car wove through the concrete. The only living people were at the pepper market. But it was beautiful. Except for the concrete. Concrete. Formica. Tar.

Here's where they put the folks from the woods, get it? Housin projects! Took their land. Blew up their houses, everything, gone. So there'd be nothin left to orient by. An they gave em TVs for free, get it? Like as compensation … yeah it's obvious! What that musta done to em. Strategic area … ya know there's no maps a this region? An if there are, they're maimed on purpose. It's gonna take years! Drunks lyin all over the place! An maybe this guy wanted me to run inta him, hafta toss him some change then. Never get away in this clunker. Yep, look at that, got his buddies around the corner, that's what they're doin all right, an I thought I was makin it up. He shook his head.

No Gothic here, boy, nothin, my rescuer lectured me. Baroque, hah! Maybe a couple painted chests, about it … herders, man. Nomads. Stone Age to Stalin. Mud huts to housin projects. Tartars'd flip, they came back … There's a few wooden churches, for appearance' sake, synagogues're fucked too, Jews didn't stay, not here, not a one, closest ones now're all the way down in Bratislava … nothin out here cept for bolshevism, an that'll be here forever, construction … hey, a museum, an there's that big Ruthenian artist … I missed the name, since we nearly ran over a cat … plump thing, just lyin there, claws tearin the air … didn't wanna move. It was black, what else. And then it got up and ran across the road.

I dozed off in the train, just on the edge of a dream, enjoying the feeling … now, my sweet, now we'll pack up an move on, wherever … maybe the sea, maybe not, the day rocks along … maybe saffron, maybe some other fragrance … I had the compartment to myself.

Take care, Smoothy, wherever you are, you tall-tale teller and observationist, you dissectionist you, and thanks … tonight I'm taking a holiday, I'm giving it to myself, I want to spend it in solitude.

The conductor stepped in, thoughtful fella, doused the light, it was hurting my eyes, I rubbed my eyelids … we go flying into a tunnel, I hand him my ticket, he's got on a silly hat … buttons with an insignia, a uniform … light whipped out of the tunnel and suddenly Hunter stood before me with a vacant expression, clutching a thin cane, spinning it around his wrist … I know one end of the cane's dull and the other's whittled to a point … I jump up, bang my head on the window, wake up … good gracious, what is it, sonny, someone says …

a granny's sittin there, I'm all sweaty … bad dream, here, take a cough drop, freshens the breath … No thanks, I sat back down … old lady looks like Mrs. Macešková, flower-print scarf, like my grandma had … but I had to go to the bathroom, I leaned over the sink a while, told the mirror: Say hi to Černá, washed up … the granny wasn't there anymore, guess I got the wrong compartment, maybe went the other direction, I donno. I rode the rest of the way without incident, in daylight.

South Station, where Bohler the savior used to do his hunting, it was lively. Too lively. There were even numbered cops here now, characters swarmed in the corners. Loitered off to the sides. I had a cup of coffee and then did something I'd never done in my life. I bought Černá flowers. I didn't know how she'd take it. Roses, yeah, but that's somethin else. They also had wreaths and candles, I just made a face.

I ran up the stairs to the attic. She wasn't there. Nobody was. The flat looked tidied up. Like nobody'd ever lived there. Never knew we had a vacuum. I sat down.

Hours rolled by. They rolled over me, and they were heavy. They were dark. I tried the drawers … spotted some papers, but didn't peek. That's a no-no, they'd beaten that into me, taught me that. She hadn't gone shopping or out for a walk, she'd've left a note, after all we'd talked. The flowers lay on the floor. I left the vases empty. It was still day.

Now, Černá, now that I'm rid of the spooks, now that I've busted outta the trap, the big trap … why now?

16

I TIED HER HAIRS. LET'S GO! THEY TOLD ME.
WHO MY SISTER IS. I SEE IN THE WOODS AND … IN THE MOUNTAINS.
WHAT I HAVE TO DO. THEIR WELL. RAVEN'S WING.

Again outside it slowly darkened, again came the divide … I sat there, something begun without having finished, riding on along its own axis, sucking me in, I felt a hole, an uneasiness, inside me.

Lighting up a cigarette, I hunted for her scent in the armchair she sat in, held the fork and knife she ate with. Bile climbed into my throat and I felt the light pressing down on my eyes. I let it blind me, and groped my way through the hallway, the foyer, where it was dark, without turning on the light.

In the bed I found several of her hairs, and tied my fingers firmly together, in twos. In the bathroom I found more hairs in the drain. Raven hairs. She liked water and cleanliness, but she couldn't get rid of every trace. I tied the hairs under my nails, I could feel them better when they hurt. They smelled nice even though they'd been in water, water that had flowed over her skin.

It was evening, I looked out the window, people were going along the street, artificial people too, mutants, from this high up you can't tell them apart, but some gave themselves away by their gait, their stealthy way of moving. This is my street, my neighborhood, my city, I said to myself, but nothing belongs to anyone, not for long. From the pub next door I heard a fight, drunkards spilled out into the street, beneath a lamp's sparse light. In a puddle next to the lamppost stood a dog. Slurping rainwater. Cracked walls, metal bars on windows. Trashcan, gutter, and a cloud of steam rushing out of it. Obstructing my view of the billboard with the actors and the poster of the politician. The rails gleamed, shining coldly as a tram went clanging past. So this is the way she's supposed to go, I said to myself. This way, by herself? And who else? It can't be good for anyone, it makes no sense, nobody could ever want this. This city, this street, such a lonely walk.

I lit another smoke and wandered around the flat listening to music. I emptied my pockets of all my maps, medications, rolling papers, knives, razors, boxers, cigarette holders, straps, notebooks, games. I attempted to rip a hole in the parquet floor to get at the stash of machine guns and pistols, the metal parts gleamed so bright my eyes ached. I drew back the bowstring and it snapped with a whizzing sound, slicing through the skin on my wrist, interrupting the tattoo. Then I took some nails and, rocking Brother Nail on my knees, cleaned his hide with a rusty knife. It woke the dogs in the building, they joined in the ritual. City degenerates, but that's in their cells. Yeah sure, I know that every second ... someone else is perishing, having the soles of their feet seared, being crushed in a straitjacket, thrown to the pigs.

Maybe ... it's a possibility, my turn'll come too ... now you, someone, lying in a cold eye, in the dark, a day, an hour, a minute before being tortured, and then it comes, sooner or later it comes, you hear your own scream, and in one bright heavy second of blinding pain you absolutely definitely know you exist. No one escapes it, in one of your lives pain will come and you'll know, acutely and positively, that you exist, it will be a single instant and it will hurt, to let you know how reality feels.

That's Bog. So you'll know that pain is real and all the rest is only scenery, delusion and illusion, the first cigarettes, bashful kisses, and idle banter. And why you ... why not me? I already knew the answer.

So take a moment from time to time to give at least a caressing glance to your minesweepers, your grandstand, your guns, slowly I run the burning spear through me, sun blazing down on my helmet, the dried scabs on my leather jacket again ooze blood and pus, alive. Where are you, little sister. It was dark, the only light in the room the pale glare of metal ... glowing ... stole a chunk a uranium off those wiseguys, discreetly purloined it, it worked ... an I knew who I wanted to give it to. Maybe.

I lay on the bed and waited, sat back on my heels and waited, a second before she turned the key in the lock and the door swung open I knew. I scented her nearness, was it a scent? When she moved, in all her living beauty, did she split the air ahead of her, sending forth a wave? I embraced her, squeezing her so hard I didn't hear the answer, she was saying something, troubles, we've got troubles, I'll help you, I'll do whatever you want, I said, by then we were lying next to each other. As the sun came up I saw her face, I wanted to get inside it, I would've liked to see her skull. I wanna tell you somethin ... somethin has to be done ... yes, there is something we have to do, I bit her lip. She rested the soles of her feet on my shins, lying across my thigh bone, I almost couldn't feel her, the weight was pleasant. I could feel her breath on my face. Then she moved over, dissolving into the wall: Be careful, here I come, I heard.

I awoke to the sharp ringing sound of the doorbell.

I lay there, dazed and naked. If I ignore it, it'll go away, I mumbled, or just thought to myself. But the bell kept on ringing.

I got dressed, covered myself in pants and a shirt, my silver I don't remove. It was Vohřecký and Viška, they walked in.

Vohřecký opened the window, Viška stood there grinning. An I remembered … there he was at last, exposed in my memory … rounded shoulders, sturdy build … bald … heh, Viška … I said … Now I know you, Block 12, C-wing, Pankrác … it was him, my mind raced, how did Hadraba classify his crime … oh yeah, little kids, musta felled some little boy, little girl? … it was that cell … just down from me and Bohler and that greengrocer,* they amnestied me, but Bohler did three years, I guess cause he was a priest … that cell where Viška and the murderers were, the bark box they called it, sometimes at night the guard went in there with this German shepherd that barked on command so nobody'd hear em thrashin the prevert … funny how in the slammer even the worst monsters detest the ones that do it to kids, they consider em subhumans … that's why they put the, diaper diddler in there, so the thugs wouldn't beat him to death … hello, I told Viška … smiling at him … got promoted, huh?

Sit down, Vohřecký told me, better sit down.

How did you find me? Where is she, slipped out of me.

Miss Moriaková? said Vohřecký, you're dumber than I thought, little buddy, he sat down too.

There's no way, I don't believe it.

You've sunk so low, boy, said Vohřecký, you're not even defiantly silent when questioned anymore.

Easy Evie? Easy Evie, the knucklehead means, said Viška … Eve the skeeve, he's talkin about.

Go find the Viets, or whatever they are, yourself … an as for Černá, you don't have anything on her anyway.

But we do on you, boy, said Vohřecký, and he meant it seriously … a good couple Fridays now, told ja I combed through all the leads, an not only them … see, we found Závorová … whadda ya say to that?

I held my tongue.

An she's dead.

Don't say that! You donno nothin, spook.

An we think you did it.

Zat right?

So now we know where she was all those years. An know where we found her, what was left of her? Under a heap of coal … in a cellar. Yeah, you know where she was. Barbara Závorová, beautiful girl … strangled to death. Lousy, huh?

You guys donno nothin …

But that's not all, Vohřecký jumped up and grabbed me by the shoulders, tore off my shirt, with one tug ripped open the buttons … Viška watched.

Yep, that's it, said Vohřecký … an ya know we got a lady says she saw the killer … gave us a pretty exact description what he had around his neck, one a those old ladies sells candles in church, she don't live there no more, so don't go gettin any ideas … an she gave us an exact description of this thing here, this saint a yours, you piece a shit. Is it even silver, yeah, guess so. That granny went down for coal, saw the two a you, you an the victim, she was scared a you. But we got it in writing. She saw you rape the girl too.

That's not true! An this is the Madonna!

An then you choked her. They'll tell us that in the lab too.

But they didn't tear her off me. The medallion was still on my skin. It was cool.

You killed Závorová. Let's go, you freak. Get up, we're goin down to the station. They'll give you a nice warm welcome! Wait'll they get a load a the artist …

I sat there.

Or maybe we oughta take a ride … step out a while instead? Whadda ya say?

I couldn't've cared less that Rudolf was in the car, but there … in the seat next to the driver … shades on, she sat stiffly, didn't even move her head … I was still hopin they'd forced her, that they had her to get at me … even now that they'd found what they found, knew what they knew … but as soon as we got on the highway, Viška, who was driving, began clowning around, honked the horn, and then one more time … we honk at the pharmacy, at the signal we come out, and … he turned around and laughed at me … I was broken, crushed … I wasn't gonna talk, but when Viška … grabbed her thigh and said: Easy Evie, she can take it … man, can she ever, slut with an overbite, whadda ya say to those sweet little teeth … sharp as the Reaper's scythe … I slugged Rudolf and then shouted at her.

Viška, looking like he'd expected it, slammed on the brakes, jumped out the door, but Vohřecký stopped him … they held me down … and Rudolf said into my ear, soothingly … softly: It's the only way, sorry, don't be surprised, you blew it, and then jabbed a needle into my forearm … the vein absorbed it gratefully, sucking it in, I didn't care what it was, all I could see was my girl's black leather jacket and her hair … from behind. I was powerless.

When I came to, it was daylight. I was in the backseat and the first thing I saw … Hello there, said Vohřecký. We were stopped in front of some … little wooden church, I could see cobwebs all over the corners, the belfry, Vohřecký touched my shoulder, pretty gently … wake up now, c'mon … the only other one there was her, in front, back to me … take off those shades, baby, look at me, just once … I begged her … Shut the fuck up! Vohřecký commanded, she didn't move … easy Evie, I was glad Viška wasn't there … they're out eatin, the other spook informed me, want somethin? Černá, no way, I don't believe it … she flung herself at the door, opened it, slammed it shut, walked off.

Doesn't work, man, you can't do that sorta thing an then have everything go okay, said Vohřecký … now show us where they are an you're free as a bird … we'll go in a while, you don't want anything?

No.

Little Evie had to go and get mixed up with a hooligan, Viška joked, winkin at me as he drove, just to get to me … out of sheer love, isn't that right, kitten? What's the matter now? Easy Evie loves her old daddy. Don't cha? Isn't that right? He groped her thigh again.

Rudolf sat next to me, not saying a word, I could see him sweating. I'll take you guys there, I told Vohřecký, but make him be quiet … Yeah, Michal, said Vohřecký, that's enough now … Fuck you, I'm drivin here! … I was embarrassed to talk to her in front of them, and then suddenly I realized I wanted to die, the thought came in a flash and stayed … I'll go first, I said to myself, an I'll never come outta those woods again, I don't wanna live, this is the end … I was a little scared of She-Dog too, I had a hunch she was around somewhere … we pulled over at the spot where Smoothy had stopped … it hadn't been that long ago and now my life was shattered … Vohřecký tied my hands with his belt … I sat down on the ground … Viška kicked me, Sister … Černá saw it … they held him back … not like that, said Rudolf, he looked comical, like some good little student, next to these louts, Vohřecký with his gut stickin out, Viška like some kina wrestler …

After a few steps Rudolf untied me, made me lead the way … I only stopped once, where the tank driver'd gotten stuck in the mud, and I realized Černá had stayed in the car, she'd let me go … sacrificed me, who knew what for … I could've explained what happened with She-Dog, but no, I would've kept quiet … so that whole time she … I must've been dopey still from the injection, cause I wasn't eatin dirt, I was walkin on top of it … they won't let me talk to her, I won't ever see her again, if I could slip off through the woods somehow … I stopped, wait a minute, please, wait, I wanna say somethin … they stopped, maybe because I spoke softly … What is it? said Rudolf. There's … eight or nine of em an they're soldiers, you'll never take em.

The gentleman's shit his pants! said Viška, if only the girls were here now, huh? Don't worry, said Rudolf, shoving me ahead.

And then we were standing above the valley, me gripping a stone to throw on the roof, and for the last time I whispered to Vohřecký … don't be stupid, I mean … we're gonna get … I mean they're gonna put up a fight … our only chance is if they're already gone … but then a shadow peeled itself off from the trees and started toward us, Hunter, and Rudolf spread his arms and said: Sakya, sir … Sakya … it's us … and he said the word one more time and then his eyes bugged and his knees folded and he had a cane stickin out his throat … Vohřecký, two steps ahead of me, reached under his arm, but then sputtered, clutching his belly … I was already off and running … and the forest began to move … I felt it more than heard it: that hop, hop of theirs again, somebody crashed through the bushes, I made a circle and then one more, caught a glance of Vohřecký, white windbreaker billowing in the wind … they were on him, probly to finish him off … and then all around me again: hop, hop … a branch lashed me in the face … thanks to Rudolf my hands were free … I came to some mud, the color of moss … somehow I guessed right and jumped across … whatever it was he'd shot into my vein … my side didn't hurt, I was breathin all right … the whole way, actually, while I was knocked out, I'd been resting … an now I'll find out, if Černá's there an by herself, if they got em … I was gonna find out and that gave me wings … I ducked down between the rocks, cautiously weavin in and out … took a breather in a trench or whatever … an joy again flowed through my veins … but hatred too … cause if she'd betrayed me like I thought, I had a hunch what I would do … there's the car … I saw him but couldn't run fast enough … Viška pounced, he'd been waiting, I sidestepped … got to the car, she gripped the wheel, hurry up, go, he rattled the handle, I slammed the door on his fingers, he howled in pain … go, you cow, what're you waitin for … slowly he walked around the car and settled in next to her … go on, girly, give it some gas, now the clutch, just like I taught cha … let's get ridda this dumbfuck, huh?

Aiming at me. Both of us panting. Černá shot off.

Here I am, Černá, I hissed. No answer. Won't be long now, Viška said. Pull over by that haystack, Evie. Yeah, here. An you, out. Into the field, hurry up. Move! Černá climbed out too, I moved toward her, but he was faster.

Into the field, I said. One, two, five steps, an hold it. Turn around. An you hurry up, kill im! You went down on him plenty a times. Now you'll see … how he goes down. Do it, Evie! I order you … kill him!

I turned around and time came to a standstill … I realized … that woman aiming the gun at me, Černá, now I knew who she was … the mist ripped open behind their backs, somebody was standing there … I hoped, but it was only a scarecrow, made of straw, the mist swallowed him up again … I know now my sister is death … I'd searched for her and now she had me … I closed my eyes and heard: bang! and then one more time … this is my sister, it's death, and this is the end.

I stood there, still deaf from the gunshots. A sharp dry wind sliced into my face … I heard a scream, like … an animal, and opened my eyes … he was flat on his back and Černá was kicking him, kicking him in the face, and then she jumped up and came down on her heels … I ran over and knocked her off … screaming, out of her wits … What? What? I bleated, somehow I managed to drag her off … the pistol lay on the ground, its barrel hot, stuck it in my pocket and hauled Černá away … we went and lay down in the woods, out of sight of the car … and of him.

She lay facedown in the moss, shoulders twitching … we gotta get outta here, shoulda taken the car, shoulda stuck him in that haystack, I didn't know what to say, held her … then I heard an engine, somebody drivin down the road, what if it's … yeah, let it be them, the yellow guys, I shoved her forward, stumbling, but we made it deeper into the woods … somehow I had to break through her silence, I gave her a shake and tore off her shades … her eyes looked like they were inside out, sharp and deep, but it was her, I hugged her on the ground, she'd fallen down, and I said: Thanks, you're mine … you're brave … you got tangled up with em, doesn't matter, it's gone.

Idiot, she said, that was my father.

Him? Aha. What month is it? I asked.

What'd you say?

I donno. Just wonderin if it'll be cold tonight.

We both knew we couldn't go anywhere.

Do we stay here? I wanted to talk to her.

Doesn't matter to me.

No, c'mon, before it gets dark.

I don't want it, she screamed.

But you got it.

Know what I was thinkin the whole way?

No.

That I was growin into the car, that I *was* the car, like upholstery or somethin.

Aha.

There's no way to put it.

But now … it's gonna be all right. I thought you were death. Not just mine, just … death … hey, look at that stump, it's like a person.

She screamed.

No … aright, it's not. C'mon.

We spent the night in the forest, in the leaves. I fell asleep, regardless of the fact that my sister lay, eyes open, trembling next to me. But then I was the one who couldn't sleep. Because She-Dog came for me.

I saw her when I got up … it was the forest that had woken me, it wanted me to keep going, somewhere, I knew it. What I didn't know is it would be so close. First she was hanging up in the trees, then she came down. The moon at her back. Standing before me. Little She-Dog. Her head by my shoulders. But I didn't dare touch it. She was smiling. In a white dress with her hair down. She was beautiful.

You see, she said, you found her.

An you, She-Dog … have you forgiven me?

I have. It hurt, you know. But I was too tied to you. I think it was true love. So even after … I wanted to see you.

I wanted to see you too, I still love you.

I know.

Why did it happen? She-Dog … I donno!

Me either.

An She-Dog … did it hurt a lot …

No. I was mostly just startled. You're fast … an I, somehow I forgot about it … it happens … things're different out our way. That was to make you laugh. You know that one, right?

Yeah … that was a dream. She-Dog?

Hm?

Is this a dream too?

Guess away, guesser. You talk too much. Get ready, you've gotta go now.

But I can't … not with her here! … not yet. You know what she did!

Don't worry, you can still go back. For her sake.

Can I ask somethin … before we go?

Make it fast.

Do you like her?

Well … She-Dog scowled, I knew that face so well! That serious look of hers … her lips.

Well … you guys're … a little different now. Something's changed. But go now! An don't worry … I'll protect her when you're not around. Trust me an don't worry about her. As for me, my loved one, you'll never see me again.

I flew. Her last words echoed inside me … hurting, and I felt like a scoundrel and a lost dog, but then all of a sudden … a wave came crashing over it … a wave of joy, an I think it was her who sent it, cause as long as I'm flyin an goin … somewhere, wherever I have to go … an She-Dog's keepin watch or whatever … over poor miserable Černá, then Sister is safe … I could sense that … then I was walking, in snow, but I felt light, walking hard and my breath was sharp, I was going in a straight line, the path of the warrior, I knew it, mountains, maybe she was trying to give me a dream … I walked a long time, growing stronger with the motion, then I was lifted up again so I could see what I had to see … my footprints in a circle … so that's my straight line, I nearly groaned, and then there was grass around me again … I stood on a hill, houses below me. Smoke rising out of them. It was summer, it was warm, and my tattered jacket was just right. I touched Madonna and walked on. I had a hunch where she'd sent me … I didn't know why. But I really, really wanted to see him.

He stood out in the garden, at his side an old woman … and oh my god, slipped out of me old-fashionedly … the woman was steering him toward a chair … he shuffled along.

See him? She-Dog hissed in my ear.

Yes. But what … what do I do?

You'll see, said She-Dog. Go on.

Something gave me a nudge from behind … a wing, a breath …

She-Dog, is … is he better? That lady's steerin him around.

That's what they do with idiots. Go on! An do it.

I took a step, and then didn't hear from She-Dog again.

Dogs came charging out, sheepdogs, I stopped in my tracks. A man walked out the door of the … estate. He peered at me suspiciously, but chased off the dogs.

C'mon in! Here fir that icebox?

No sir … Mr. Losín. I … I'm here to see David.

His eyes popped … he dashed inside, I walked into the yard.

David! Buddy, it's me! … he sat in the chair looking straight ahead, the old woman screamed … the man charged out the door with a rifle.

Step aside, Maw! It's one a thim gangstirs! Ah'll kill yew!

She wrenched the rifle out of his hands. No! Came on his own, yew donno why. C'mon in, son. Let David be.

I … stood next to him and when I touched him he was like ice, didn't notice me at all … his folks were arguing, the old man wanted to shoot me, I remembered how David had told us his dream … exaggerating the dialect to make us vain city hooligans laugh …

I stayed on … and in time I began to lap up their tongue, it was old, but they'd been living out here cut off for so long it had mutated … it was impure, and then I discovered that over the hills and up in the mountains, in all kindsa hovels and tarpaper shacks, the people spoke … Czech … I discovered the tongue was different all over, warped differently, like time here had gone through a grater … I noticed, for one thing, they called the old tree fungus they washed the dishes with detergents, and the plates they called frisbees. That was the underground influence.

After I'd settled in a bit and David's bros were no longer a threat, one day Abram and Kubík, with much important conspiratorial winking, took me out to the Cave, which belonged to the Holecek estate, and the young Holeceks, with more significant winking and putting of fingers to lips, led me inside … to the underground, as they called it … there were some youngsters there from the settlements, even girls, who darted, squealing, off to the sides, and there was a television.

For a couple hours we watched a movie about the construction of some dam, then was some snow show with ads or somethin, music videos … the youngsters gawked. What else … when evenings they'd bring their gramma down and she'd start in with that singsong voice: … come a ridin in on thir wagguns, lookin fir promises, an nothin … all's there is out here's thi Benat firest, thi Benat marshis … an up above thi Benat stirs, an thi olduns set to diggin, diggin an clearin an burnin, an lo an behold: Halob's balk … an thi lovely, most loveliest, Losins' field … an Kropacek's ditch … and their gramma'd go on like that night after night, the young ones knew it all by heart … they didn't have anything written down … just that old Bible … from the good monks of Kralice* … where old Losín wrote down the names of his sons and daughters as they were born or passed away, as his grampa and his grampa's father had done before him … it wasn't till afterwards I realized why they poured my green-onion soup in a plastic bowl with an ad for Coca-Cola on it while they put theirs in earthenware … it was a big rarity, all the boys envied me, the littlest ones couldn't control themselves … as I finished eating, slowly and ceremoniously like the rest, they'd climb all over me, wriggling around to get the best view … first you'd see the writing on the sides and then the bottle of Coke, I didn't want to torture them, so I'd start gulping like a dog till the old man would hiss at me and Abram knit his brow … this all came later on, of course, along with many more things.

But first I stood there out in the yard, amid the chicken droppings, somewhere big dogs barking … all sorts of weird sheds and lean-tos, the house, well, from up close it was pretty squalid … and then I saw his thumbs, bandaged thickly and soaking wet … still bleeding … someone whacked me from behind, the boys … next thing I knew, there were four of them on top of me, and that was fine, since they were mostly just scrapping with each other, but the old woman intervened again, shooing them off … my head churned like a horse pit, Černá … out there in the woods, she'd better have strong protection … and sitting down on a wooden bench I felt a prick … She-Dog's so powerful, what if she harms her, but again I felt the puff of wings and my heart swayed up, relieved … the old woman set down a bowl of soup in front of me … the men and boys, David's bros, sat along the walls, the old man at the head ... praying ... and me, dunce, spoon in hand ... one of them, the lanky one, glared up at me from his prayer with great hatred ... I put down my spoon and quick clasped my hands, totally just like once upon a time ... long as the old woman is gonna protect me, I'll hold out, I thought ... and next to me sat David.

He didn't pray, gulping down the hot stuff ... it wasn't him anymore. Face puffy and white ... a gourd, I thought, sweating guiltily, yeah, guess it was us ... and we didn't tell Helena where he was either, we didn't know, we didn't watch over our brother ... but nobody asked any questions ... they just let me be there. The old woman parried their first hateful lunge ... and then I guess innate kindheartedness triumphed, I thought at the time ... and also curiosity.

What protected me at first maybe ... it was totally stupid ... but when those two busted into Černá's flat an Vohřecký tore open my shirt, right after I gave em the nod I'd slipped on some T-shirts, the ones Černá used to appraise with a screwing up of her left eye ... in other words I was now draped in a remarkable jumble of cotton, reigned over by some reincarnation of I guess it was Travolta, underneath I had a matching set, SUPER DISCO, for one ... all my hamburger-shack loot I'd yanked off the coat rack, plus a jacket of Černá's she probly got from somebody else, I didn't ask ... and the boys followed me around the yard, I was afraid they were gonna do somethin to me ... but they were just checkin me out ... at first they wouldn't let me near David, I tried ... assuming She-Dog'd sent me to help him ... and perhaps, though it might've been blasphemy on my part, to somehow atone for what I'd done ... to her.

Where yew from, mistir? One stepped in my way ... from Prague ... they yelled, grabbed me, and dragged me in to their gramma ... she got up and started talkin ... I caught some ... they thought Prague was going to send out its people to bring them back, all the best people live in Prague, they earnestly declared ... big-hearted ... rich and happy ... an where'm I? I asked Abram, he was obviously the boys' boss ... Banatka, this here's Banatka all arown, an Vladan Dragač, lord a thi barrow ... Barrow? I wasn't any wiser for asking ... then the old man's sharp voice rang through the yard and the boys' siesta was over ... I watched David walk away ... most of the boys were pretty strapping, probly worked their tails off, and even if they didn't know all the flimflams and treacheries I did, I wouldn't've wanted to offend even the ones goin on fifteen ... one of em was a hunchback though, started trailin behind me, yakkin away ... I went out back to look in on the boys, it was pretty wild ... they were tillin the field, but the way they were tillin, two on the plow, the third one urgin em on an steerin … they had a horse, but only one … what I gathered, he was for Abram, him or Kubík'd go for supplies … the little cripple kept scuttlin after me, tuggin at my jacket … I began to understand … he wanted to see my shirts, went totally nuts for this one heinous thing with the Eiffel Tower an Café Bitch, where I got it from I donno … I gave it to him … he didn't trust me … put it on right away, it hung down to his knees, he dragged me off … somewhere, granary I guess, scurryin up the steps like a squirrel, flingin his little body around … then he shows me: Pssst! Drags me over behind the sacks, whips out a crate an scrabbles around, then hands me a book like it's some kina sacrament, an old thing with photos of ancient Egypt, pyramids, camels, I had some acquaintance … then he whips out … a postcard of the Clock, the one in the Pearl, puts em both on the ground, Eiffel shirt in between, slaps the floor, an says: Speak! Not only that, but he said it totally normally … so I settled in on the sacks … Losín, pointing to him, Potok, pointing to myself.

Potok, yeah, he said, what else?

Where are we … you boy you!

Banatka! he started jabberin on, an I didn't get much, but it sounded kina like Romany or Romanesque, an old word here an there …

Me Benjamín, knockin his chest. Then he whips out a book again, a notepad … ships stuck all over it and … *la mare,* he says, *la mare* … taps the paper, lookin at me …

Not me! I said fast, donno that one … or the sea.

No?

That night … the old woman took me in to see David, in the settin room as they called it, had it all to himself, slept on top of the stove, I realized I was sposta climb up there too, that didn't thrill me … I don't handle close quarters too well … but objections were no help, she had practice with her whipper-snappers, so she put out the candle and I lay there in the dark, next to David, my blood brother … who fell asleep right away, I guess, breathin regular, on his back, had to squeeze in right up next to him … what's that old bag want from me, what kina punishment is this, didn't fall asleep till daybreak, then got woken by some squeaking noise … I figured it was David, over by the window … started to say somethin … took a look, he was standin on an overturned foot-stool, the squeaking was comin from underneath, he was squashin some mouse or whatever, poor thing.

That morning the old woman showed me how to change David's bandages, brought us into the kitchen, to a tub of warm water, outside it was just getting light out, but everyone was up already, all ten or twelve brothers, there weren't any girls … everyone quiet as we rewrapped him, they gathered like that every morning to look … at David's wounds, the flesh was clean, I was worried it was infected, but no … it was totally clean and the blood seeped out … from some bottomless inside, and David held on.

Then Benjamín took me by the sleeve and we went. With David. The little hunchback boy took care of the sheep. Didn't have my T-shirt on anymore, but he gave me … what might easily've been a shirt at one point. Back in Napoleon's days. I put it on. It made him happy.

We sat on the hillside among the sheep, Benjamín grillin me, me grillin him, and it wasn't gettin anywhere.

Banatka, damn it! I took a stick and scratched in the dirt … Here's the world. Where're we?

Here, he banged the ground. Took a clump of dirt and set it down on my very imprecise map. Jabbed his finger into it and said: Lord Vladan Dragač.

Lord Barrow? I inquired.

Benjamín nodded happily. That was all I could get out of him.

I tried to spend time with David, but … he'd just squat wherever we put him, runnin his hands through the grass … I told him stories, but only Benjamín got anything out of that … every now an then he'd fire one of my worse words back at me … so I toned it down a little … here I am with the sheep, on one side an idiot, forgive me, David, on the other a cripple, forgive me, Benjamín, an me in the middle, like King Salaman, me I won't forgive.

She-Dog, what do I do. How do I get outta this, there's gotta be some scam, some trick. Helena! I shouted at David. Nothin. But … Benjamín perked up.

Bitch, he says.

Huh, Benjamín, c'mon … David's wife, Helenka!

Yup, nodded Benjamín.

Was she here?

No answer.

She ran off when she saw him, is that it?

Nope.

What is this crap, you donno, you're just makin it up, show-off …

Eyed me askance. But he took the bait. Shilly-shallied … yeah, I had to swear up an down the holy of holies I'd never tell a soul, which of course now I've broken my oath.

Abram said: Bitch. No be here with Davidko.

But she was pregnant!

Ah know. That's haw cum they chaysed hir off.

That was as much as I learned.

David. He still looked the same, all of us'd definitely changed since then. Yep, turned old and hoarse.

Not him. But there was a strange quality to his face, even in spite of the overall, unfortunately, dimwittedness … an enthusiasm, perhaps. There were moments, but only moments, he looked like he knew it all, like he had it all under control … and there was something working inside him. With a design. But then again maybe I just imagined it.

The boys treated him with respect when he walked around the yard … with that awful mechanical stride, either clearing outta the way or gently steering him around. They never called him anything but Davidko or Davidik. Even though … they were constantly ribbin each other, givin each other lickings … the old man harried em, the old woman too, she made em toe the line … but … in all the days I was there I never saw a single one snivelin off in the corner cause his bro'd trampled his matchbox car or some similar mortality … no, most of the time they were … exhilarated, they were untamed … sometimes they fought like horses … but, I noticed, no kicking in the balls, no ganging up or eye-gouging … more like practice for who versus who … soon I came to realize they were savin their brutality for somebody else … an when from time to time a genuine disturbance broke out, Abram an Kubík were there to tame em down … there was also one called Daník, evidently the family pride, he didn't even haul the plow … Daník was a wisenheimer … a bit of a loner, like Benjamín, only Benjamín was the family jester, the cheerer-upper, the crackpot … Daník had a place of his own too, out in the barn … one day, stuffed full of herb soup again, they hauled me out there … the old man an Abram an Daník an me, I took a look … he had these pits in there, an in one of em was this thing covered in rawhide, a stick, but smoothed an shaped, an Daník takes the string, draws it back, an goes *fshhh … tok!* I gaped … they mumbled somethin, all I could get was they were talkin about Benjamín, Abram walked off … they all went back, Benjamín proudly luggin the book about Egypt under his arm … barely draggin, but it was clear he wasn't gonna let Abram get his paws on it, set the book down on the threshing floor, slowly, painstakingly … relishing it … turnin the pages an jabberin away, the old man went stompin off … Benjamín gets right up an points, a painting in some ancient crypt, mummies, yeah yeah … taps his finger, there on the wall, hunters an bowmen … my eyes pop, yeah … bow … it's a bow! I barked out the proper word. They just stared. In Prague that's called a bow, an you invented one, Daník! A bow … there's bows in Prahah? Yeah, lots, it's normal there. Daník's lip sank, probly thought he was the first … c'mon, your gramma told you they've got everything in the world there, right, an her gramma told her … so he calmed down.

One day the old man got me in a corner, wanted to know when they're going to come … after all, they'd written mighty Prague that they wanted to go home … now it's time … their time here was nearly spent … so when're the Czechs comin for em? They can't just leave em here, no way! Well, I rattled somethin off … and that same day I'm standin out there with the sheep again, and all of a sudden Benjamín says: "The river of love floats streaming past, we stroll along its lush green banks, singing like the rain, sugar in my coffee" … and looked to see my reaction. I jumped outta my socks.

See, the ones that gathered every so often around the TV, which the old folks would've stomped to bits, since there was nothing about it in the Bible, occasionally picked up a Czech pop tune or two … that was their underground, that was how they learned the tongue, secretly findin the modern meanings … so I wasn't at all surprised when … Kašpar an me're traipsin through the woods, an all of a sudden he lets loose: "Here they come, tuning their trumpets, arise, sweet breeze, my only love." So I go: "Headlong toward the trains my white steed dashes, wind in my face, whipping my lashes." *Train* he knew a little, *lashes* too, *steed* I had to explain. After that they'd ask me things every now and then. I began to act as a missionary.

One day me and Benjamín were analyzing a song, he couldn't figure out "twilight of the gods, gods creeping out of every bathroom and kitchen," I couldn't either, when all at once the hazelwood parted and two men were standin there. Benjamín let out a shriek an hid his head in the grass, I glanced at David, nothin, he just sat there, hands in the dirt.

These two looked very much like Losíns, everyone around here wore the same tattered hundred-year-old manmade wool, even young boys had hats, here and there a white shirt … and one says: Yew thet fellir from Prahah? Yeah. He sat down next to me. Ah'm Cermak, this muh bruthir, also Cermak. Wi're out yondir, waved a hand over the mountain. C'mon ovir to owr place, Losins, he screwed up his mouth an spat … wi're gud Szechs, onli ones rown heer, Losins eee. Perti thing, that's frum houme … fingering my jacket … all of a sudden he noticed David, leaped up, an him an the other walked over to him, Benjamín vanished into the grass, fled without a sound … but they didn't mean David any harm … just gaped in outright adoration … heer he is, thi one that herds … see his thuhms, so it's thi trooth, thi holy trooth … it's him, he's got thi stingmata … he bleeds … I wanted to take off, there was somethin in the air, but I couldn't leave David … I go up to him an see … so that's why he's always got his hands in the grass … I'd noticed wherever he sat he'd always fiddle around with those hands, an whenever I'd come over he'd scoot forward a little, craftily, it struck me once … and now I saw why … he was tearin up grasshoppers, ants, crushin larvae left an right … teeny-tiny drops of blood, it was a sickening mess … an behind him, where he'd been sittin before … more wings, legs, pinchers, tiny insect bodies torn in two, a fly crawlin around, no, not even crawlin, its wings an legs were gone … an I flashed back to one time Benjamín had tossed him a lizard … an another time he'd brought him a wounded baby swallow … I took the little one aside an asked … Davidko's playin with thi aminals, he said … yeah, he was playin all right … it was horrifying, and if the Cermaks wanted to play with him now, well, I guess I'd let em, my stomach turned … and they gaped at him, just silently movin their lips … suddenly there was a sound like thunder and one of the Cermaks dropped flat on his back, a hole in his head … the other one went tearin off … the Losíns all came runnin toward us, all of the boys, with pitchforks an axes, Daník had a flintlock, they didn't even notice me, runnin after Cermak … then Benjamín came draggin in, all outta breath, threw me a glance, peeked at David, an knelt down by the slain Cermak, ran his hands through his pockets … came up with some rope an a bowie, stuck em under his Eiffel T-shirt … that night I lay on the stove next to David again, in that cramped little room, an I told She-Dog … that motionless body with the gourd face touchin me, there was no way to avoid it … an I told She-Dog, this is too much, I can't take it, I got a hunch what you want now … David, I guess in his sleep, swung his leg over me, I jerked outta the way an looked, he lay there, eyes open, not movin a muscle … like he was waitin … uh-uh, She-Dog, I can't do this …

And next day when Kubík, who'd gone for supplies, didn't come back, the boys went out to look for him. They knew where to go. Him they brought back, the horse was gone. War preparations got under way, I think you could call it that … the only one who came to see me that day was the old woman … kept on sayin: How's Davidko?

I shook my head. She gave me a sideways look, slyly … did she know?

These old women that live their whole life outdoors … Some of em. Definitely know a lot.

Suddenly she told me: You'll be goin now, soon. That shook me up, see, I … sometimes I'd feel sick that I was here, while Černá … was out in the woods, somewhere. Everything would go dark on me. Sometimes it was exhausting, but the environment was so new … I hadda be careful … and sometimes, when I no longer knew which way to turn and my spirit was sinking … sometimes I'd feel a slight pressure, like wings … I trusted She-Dog, no … I believed in her.

The boys were out in the yard, Daník … was showin em what a bow was. He himself had a rifle slung over his shoulder. Everyone was in high spirits, little Benjamín gave me a nudge an said they were goin out that night to crush those disgusting Cermaks once an for all … just then one of the little ones they had standin lookout in the hills comes rushin up an shouts: Vlado, here comes Vlado!

And I heard: budda-boom, budda-boom … like horse hoofs. The Losíns fell silent, all of a sudden everyone looked tired and downcast … dejected … I didn't get what was goin on … we all went out in front … of the estate, and there I saw, heading toward us over the plain, a horseman, crimson cloak flyin … hoofs poundin, but there was something unnatural about the way the sound carried, like maybe some kind of echo … or maybe there was nothing else alive at that moment, motion had come to a standstill … the rider hurtled toward us and Kašpar gave me a nudge and said: Headlawng into thi wind ma white steed dashis, wind in ma face, whippin ma lashis, ah know, ah know thi words to that song tew … that's not how it goes, I told him … but tears ran down his cheeks, and he said: That is too how it goes.

Now I could see the horseman, oh no, I said to myself … it was the proud Prince, yep, the Dark One, knew him right away … eyes flashing wrath, he dug his spurs into his horse's flank, it didn't even bleed … the rider's teeth gleamed, long and sharp … I started trembling … the old woman whispered: He don see yew. This is owr wirld. This is owr lord Vlado.

And he was on us. Abram stepped forward and said with a humble bow:

Yore servant, Abram. Not you, barked the horseman, his armor in the setting sun ... the fiery ball was just going down ... glistened, but the hands in which Dragan held the reins were dark ... probably grave-rot instead of blood.

You, said the horseman. And pointed to Daník. He slowly laid his rifle down and strode forward. No one lamented, they accepted it ... like nature, it struck me. I knew ... I wasn't from this world, the old woman had told me, I had a hunch now who she was ... it was awful, but I think she had a pact with the Prince ... the old man stood there crestfallen, similar to his sons ... Daník walked up to the horse and vanished ... into the folds of the cloak, and the rider slowly turned around and ... rode off.

I snuck into Benjamín's sailor's berth an dug out that postcard a his with the Clock ... some instinct for self-preservation gave me an idea ... Rudolf injected me with some drug an this whole thing is just a dream, I'm ridin in the car with the spooks ... but then I'd still have all that to come, no way, I gotta admit, I broke down sobbin right there in the granary ...

Hey, mistir! It was Benjamín, pale but holdin up ... yew dunno nothin! Lord Vlado, lord a thi barrow, is gunna stick Danik up on a stake, yis he is. But ma bruthirs don go after thi Cermaks an they don git dead, yew know. Just one. Danik, ma bruthir. Lord Vlado is real, real good to us. Lettin us stay here. C'mon, ah'll show yew sumthin!

Our soup was eaten in peace that night. But I'd made up my mind. Even ... the way the boys tilled the field, for instance ... takin turns, the old man and Abram kept an eye on that, so whenever one of the boys took the whip too much to his brother, he got it right back the very next day ... and whatever one didn't finish was left for the next, had it all balanced out like scales ... and they treated each other great all around ... and all those stories their gramma told em ... how every balk and forest path and ditch came to be, they had all that firmly inside em and they knew the land they walked on ... they'd come into contact with others, apart from the Cermaks, and even with all that hardship ... it seemed to me somehow they knew what the universe was, they knew they were alive, and that made em happy ... even with all his hootin and hoppin around on those crooked little legs, Benjamín noticed every honeybee ... and breathed along with them ... what David did with his hands ... Benjamín told me he'd never do that, that Davidko was just lost, that's how he took it, as an exception ... and I saw into that awful visit: They didn't try to please anyone, their life flowed along in orderly fashion ... even if they did long for their old land, which they'd dreamed up entirely, including the Pearl … I guess they were happy here. But whenever I brought up girls, I ran into a wall.

Somehow I'd heard the Losín daughters had left … an they weren't talked about. The bros … every now an then, one of em'd disappear for a time an the others'd go out lookin for him, an when he came back on his own … scowlin … it hit me, the old woman had hinted … they were all related. Chalups, Holeceks, Bendárs, Kecliks … everyone that made up this tribe. An one day Kašpar … who, after Kubík, played first fiddle with Abram … left.

That day the old man didn't show his face outside his settin room. The boys that weren't workin hung around the yard, bored … an some of em already knew, probly, that they were leavin too … that it was comin to an end there. Cause … bringin in a stranger … nobody here'd ever done that yet. Helena they'd chased out.

It's up to you, Abram, bring back a girl, c'mon, you wanna protect your bros from the Prince, then show em this, pick up some … chick, an outsider … she'll be good! … for you … you can teach her your stuff your way, an she'll teach you too, hey … I told him with the voice of experience. I was two or three years older.

I think he didn't understand a word. An before supper, before that last bowl of cabbage soup, little Benjamín showed me. Down in the cellar.

He led me down a hallway full of potatoes an cabbage, then we climbed down a ladder an the little guy … showed me a well, the lid was rotten through, Benjamín giggled an made the sign for woman … pretty disgusting at his age, then grabbed his crotch, drew out his face, pale an twisted with scrofula, says: Here Ondráš, ma bruthir, an here Jula … his concubine … Cermacka!

Plainly reveling in the fact that justice had been duly administered … he raised the lid an threw down a woodchip … there were two skeletons down there … plus hair, hair doesn't rot … in the old well in the chill in the webs, tangled up in each other, plus somethin else, some wire … Ondráš an his Jula, said Benjamín, grinning as he joined the two signs he'd made with his warped little fingers … donno what got into me, I gave him a slap … Benjamín, feelings hurt, sniffled … Maw tol me … said his mom ordered him to show me the family secret, the disgrace of the Losín clan … they'd run away, those two … together, but not far … Benjamín … a plague on both your houses … that's one tune you donno yet.

Nobody cracked too many jokes around the supper table that night, Daník's seat was empty ... I snuck a peek or two at the old woman, but she just kept refillin my bowl, actin like she always did ... everyone kept quiet, but Benjamín was probly right, if they'd gone after the Cermaks, who knows how many more empty chairs there'd be ... the Devil, that's who.

David breathed without a sound, eyes open again ... I lay down next to him so we were touching ... for the last time I tried, David, pal ... you want it ... you really want it ... if you do, then close your eyes, just gimme a sign, please ... but then the candle went out, I couldn't see beans, licking my thumb I extinguished the wick and said to myself, aright then ... leaning over him, I grabbed a pillow and laid it across his face ... had to smother him with my whole body ... holdin his legs so he couldn't kick ... but it was like he was sucking death in ... a minute later it was all over ... I laid on my back, waiting for the wings, persuaded that now that I'd done it, She-Dog would take me away ... but nothing happened ... I just waited.

David was gettin stiff, I reached over to shut his eyes, but then left it ... for his bros an dad ... shudderin in horror at my deed, I climbed off the stove, she left me here! only she knows why ... an then someone knocked on the door.

I had the window open when the old woman walked in. My Davidko, she said softly ... I didn't budge ... she had a candle ... went to him, then turned to me and said: Let's go. The words fractured and broken, her voice quivered like the candle flame ... I went ahead of her ... yeah, it occurred to me to deck her an run for it ... but in front of me were two rooms full of heavily breathing sleepers ... at any moment I expected the scream that would wake them up, an then what would they do to me ... She-Dog, I whispered, I guess I'll hafta suffer a lot, give a lot for the pain I caused you, but afterwards will I be with you? ... I banged into beds, tripped over feet, but the old woman ... kept quiet ... and the sleepers lay as if under a spell ... breathing open-mouthed, in and out, they didn't even stir ... the last one by the door was Benjamín, snoring away too, crutch beneath his bed ... here's Benik, arn't yew gunna tell im gbye? ... she was taking me away! ... clumsily I searched myself, flailin my sleeves around, but I managed to get that T-shirt off, the SUPER DISCO one, left it on his pillow ... and then we went ... the old woman led the way, walkin up the trails ... I'd never been up that far with the sheep ... she walked both ahead of me and beside me, hard to say ... I'd killed this lady's son ... at the top a breeze blew as we walked through the boulders, her thin strong fingers caught me by the elbow, I thought for support, but it was so I wouldn't stumble … draggin me along … and then we were on a plain, I guess up at the top, and in the distance stood a boulder … I shuddered … a barrow, a burial mound … that's where she's takin me, to the stone … lady, no.

Don't worry, silly … I peeked at her incredulously, under her scarf her eyes flashed, the corners of her mouth drawing up in a tiny smile … an old lady, but that voice … are you She-Dog? You're She-Dog … I am who I am, an c'mon … you talk too much, always do … you're goin back to her. Treat her with love.

She led me to the barrow, there was a little fire burning, I shuddered to think I was goin to see the Proud One in his suit of armor … but it was just an old fella sittin there in patched-up rags, looked like one of the shepherds … Grampa! Ah'm bringin the gennilmin, said the Losín woman … he's goin back, done an did it with his hands.

Sint thi youngun off ti heaven, did ji, took yi long inuff, ol witch … set yirsef down!

I didn't understand what they said after that, at any rate it wasn't much, the old fella tossed some leaves on the fire, herbs and … I think a raven's wing, into my eyes an up my nose he drove the stinging smoke … at first I could make out individual feathers, but he kept wavin it at me, an the old woman began to sing, I saw her unbraid her hair … then run a comb through it, singing and combing … no, she was rending herself, tearing her hair out and bleeding … Grampa kept to himself, minding the fire, as the song grew softer and softer, and I sat down and couldn't help myself, swaying to the rhythm … it was a long melody, and then … I was alone in the night and high in the air and flying … flying, without my willing it.

17

ANTHILLS. BONES. SHE KNOWS MANY THINGS.
HONEY … YOU WERE TALKIN CRAP!
THE HUT AND THE FIRE. THE WOLF DREAM.

I opened my eyes, startled to see two blazing spots right up next to my face … she covered them with her eyelids.

Sorry, said Černá, stretching out in the leaves, you were smilin in your sleep just now, an that's interesting … cause all night long you were grindin your teeth an …

Sorry. It was amazing! I was flyin an … I jumped up and threw off my jacket and …

Ants? Sister said with concern.

No, hey … SUPER DISCO, it's here!

She sat up.

Yep, the Eiffel Tower, I've got em.

I'm not too wild about those … disguises a yours … but whatever, she toppled back into the leaves, face to the ground.

It hit me … where we were and why … and what had happened.

Hey, I squeezed in close to her face … it's gonna be fine, it'll pass … I had a dream …

You're always havin dreams, but listen, Černá turned to me, after all that, I had a really odd dream. Wanna know what it was?

Yeah.

It was odd … you were lyin next to me an I couldn't sleep … I was too scared, the trees, in the wind they look like ghosts, an I was thinkin about those days … with him, how he useta abuse me … you know what he called me, it's crazy, you know what he useta call me: Buns! Buns, fetch this … Buns, hold that. It was awful … an also … I'll tell you that after … an suddenly it wasn't you next to me but a woman … a girl, touchin me, holdin me … I said to myself in the dream, I'm a monster, I'll do it, I'll kill … an then I have a dream … with a woman! One time I … well, never mind … but she was holdin me … an feelin me up, my breasts ... an down below too, she was checkin me out ... exploring me, but not like it was a turn-on, an I had this warm feeling ...

I might ... know who it was!

Wait ... so you know she had a white dress on, like a bride ...

You bet I do!

Well ... I guess you do know then, I guess you know it all ... how when I opened my eyes, she was ... a little like me at first, I thought, like lookin in a mirror ... all except for the dress ... an she smelled, you know ... of earth, somethin cool ... an it struck me she smelled of the grave an that she was my death. Or she was me. Dead.

No, don't say that ...

I'll tell you one more thing an that's it ... it's about him! After all that time with him, an me runnin away, I didn't realize till in that dream, ach ... it wasn't ... the way he talked to me: Buns ... I was thinkin about it last night, an now I know ...

Černá put her lips to my ear and whispered.

I know that sometimes ... I even liked it! I even ... Černá breathed into my ear ... wanted it. Sometimes. Isn't that awful ... you can kick me now if you want ...

No, for me you are what you are. It doesn't matter.

Yeah, you mean it? You were off flyin again, aright ... an if I tell you maybe I was on the other side ... in the ground, down below, an that I went to ... certain places? An even had to crawl! An one of the places was real quiet ... an empty. You want?

No. Not yet.

I guess we were both a little crazy. Tramping through the woods, me in the lead, Černá behind me. There weren't any paths, but going between the trees worked. At first we were glad there was ... no one around. No smoke to see, no sounds to hear. An odd, empty landscape. Černá kept going slower and slower. She had on her, shall we say, rocker ... boots ... and occasionally we'd stop. We didn't talk about how hungry we were. When her feet hurt too much, she lined her boots with leaves and for a while it was okay again.

Černá ... a lot of stuff's finished now, an when we get home ... let's take off, somewhere. For a while at least.

You think they're after us?

I think they found him … the yellows. An they'll know what to … they'll take care a the bodies. You're fantastic, any other girl would've caved in, but you …

What're you sayin, I am caved in.

Yeah, me too I guess … for now let's keep goin. An Černá …

Hm?

Did they tell you anything about me … what I … did?

No, Černá said quickly. No, they didn't, but …

What?

Well, they made fun a you.

Uh-huh.

We came to a road. Not tires, I noticed. Wheels … wagon wheels. The road led into a valley. Černá spotted the first buildings. They were ruins though. Where once there were roofs now whole trees punched skyward. The road was overgrown with brambles and weeds. I nearly stepped on a rusty scythe. We made our way through the houses, sticking close together, we wanted … to get through as fast as possible, the village was surrounded by cliffs, there was no way to get around it.

Somebody told me … they evacuated some people from here …

Look!

She pointed … it used to be a church, but it must've been destroyed by an explosion … the roof, the copula, was torn wide open … we saw scattered gravestones, splintered crosses …

Those're anthills, Černá said.

On a lotta the graves … I thought it was dirt, but then I took a closer look … it was alive, ants in motion … the grave looked like it had some kind of living matter coming out of it … we went on … me in the lead, and suddenly there was a creak, I winced … No! Černá shouted … Don't even move! You're on a well … I peeked cautiously down at my feet, the lid was made of rotten wood, teetering … Wait, don't make a move or you'll fall … she didn't have to tell me, but maybe if I hop up … stretch out your arm … she couldn't reach, but that was probably good, at least I wouldn't drag her down … the lid's edge crunched … it's breakin, I'm goin down … grab on, I peeked in her direction … Černá stood, body pressed against a young oak tree, hands in front of her, and in one … I grabbed the end of the belt and pushed off … she held on, my weight pressed her into the tree, she scraped her face … we lay in the grass … you know many things, Černá … Yeah, I knew right away there hadda be a well there, my folks had one just like it, right next to the house. Where? Doesn't matter, maybe I'll tell you someday, but not right now, I can still see him there. Even now? I said. Especially now, she said.

We walked through the valley, going through a few more villages, and everywhere there were churches and graveyards demolished by the explosion, and everywhere ants lived on the graves … red ants with pinchers … we went by a little graveyard with stairs leading up to it carved into the rock, I wanted to take a look at the names, maybe figure out where we were … Don't go up there, Černá said, she stayed on the road. But in the graveyards at least there were no rusty scythes, no abandoned wells, we weren't scared a wall would collapse, and then … twilight caught us out, we went into a graveyard, the ground there was solid … we squeezed together out of fear, one of the anthills had some kinda phosphorescent twigs in it, I'd read somethin once about rotten wood.

No, Brother, those're fireflies, you got em in your hair, she brushed my mane back from my forehead, I lay on top of her … we probly shouldn't've, that poor guy down in the dark grave beneath us, I don't want to know his name, then I'd have to think about him … let's just say it makes him happy, said Sister, moving beneath me, legs propped up against the stone tablet full of cracks and holes leading somewhere else, into the chill … but then she said, stop it! Let's stop, I think … that tree there's watchin us, I got a feeling … I looked over my shoulder, by the dangling graveyard gate stood a lone tall tree, branches trembling in the wind, it was watching.

We got up and walked on through the night.

In the other villages … well, we got used to it. What was weird and distressing was, here and there, even though everything was smashed … in some houses, and we could see in through the crumbling walls, there were all sorts of desks and chairs still … bowls … a cross or two on the walls here and there, and I was glad they hadn't been heathens.

You think, yeah, my companion snorted, like it did em any good …

Oh, you bet it did!

You're so smart, aright, aright, maybe it did …

I sat down on a tree stump, we'd just come out of a village, and I said: Hey, sweetheart, I never hassled you about faith, but know this … once upon a time there was a fella, a priest, Bogomil, an he said, don't make pictures of Bog, it's not for everyone … just for the strong people of cruel Bog, an he an his woman

... whose name can't be uttered, it's always changing! She's eternal ... have got two sons, Logos, word, an Lupus, i.e. wolf, i.e. Warrior, the younger brother an the older brother, an they stick up for each other ...

Cool, got a smoke?

Yeah.

Well, go ahead, she said, taking off her boots, you've sure got some interesting theories ...

Old Orthodox Bogomil, a.k.a. Theophilus, was smart to come up with censorship, just imagine, some people're usin images of Bog now in ads ... subtitlin him in the old tongue, yep ... for example, God smokes Jupkas, so should you ... or God on TV, prime time, when they show those illegal gladiator fights, snacks on Avízo pretzel sticks, so can you ... I saw it, pisses me off ... now God an the whole happy family drink only delectable Dagoberts coffee, know that one?

That one, yeah.

There, you see ... an this priest said the world's an embrace, always in pairs, day an night, man an woman, an so on, nonsense too, an that it's unknowable, like a dream ... an you fight against it all, but you're part of it. An sometimes, just sometimes, you catch a glimpse ... just for the blink of an eye, you glimpse the wheel of the world ... an then you return to make your way through more snares an traps an delusions, makin your way through the deceptions ... an it's all just about bein free, bein yourself, avoiding slavery ... and we who know about the secret, boy do I love you!, we love eagles, cause they see ... they're still around in some places ... an it's about findin your being in the vale of tears, in other words your other half, so you can be whole, at least for a while! an be there for someone, an through passion an strength of feeling, he said, you can overcome even your own pain, drown out the awful solitude ... an you also fight with the other one, just like with yourself, but in love all things're permitted ... on the other hand there're rules, but! ... if they're after you, you can do anything ... an in order to find that being, you gotta get past the snares ... the eagle of course sees into the future, or more like senses it ... you're asleep!

No, look at my boots. A nail came through, it's diggin into me.

An sometimes you can fly even, at least for the blink of an eye ...

Yeah right ... you an your flyin ... but look at my feet. They're all bloody.

I'll give you my shoes.

That's stupid, then you won't be able to walk either.

I gave her my socks and she stuffed them with leaves, put bark in her boots, left em untied ... we walked on in silence ... I had a feeling that what'd happened, what she'd done, the forest and houses we'd gone through too, our motion was wiping all of it out, the horror ... I mean she had to do it, I said to myself.

That pistol ... you got it? She asked.

I do, an it's stayin with me.

What's wrong? She stopped.

I, don't get mad, Černá ... I think you wanted to shoot me too.

You said the morning after that you wanted me anyway ... the way I am. Still mean it?

Yes.

Aright then ... so, when you were standin there lookin at me with that terrified expression ... an that piece a shit told me: Kill im. I squeezed the trigger.

She grabbed me by the elbow as I winced ... hey, let's not sob an grovel here, that's the way it was. I squeezed the trigger but it didn't go off. An you closed your eyes ... like that time by the sink, when I slugged you ... back when we met, remember?

You bet I do.

Well an then I let him have it. Maybe ... maybe he wanted it? Why else would he've given it to me? I mean he musta known ... how I felt. He's, he was, a smart guy, don't think he wasn't. He even ... loved me! His way though. It was the only way he knew. She shuddered.

I don't wanna think about it, Černá, it's all too fast. At least I know that I know how to close my eyes at the right time in the right place. Hey, don't look! Not there!

But she saw it too. In one of the houses with crumbling walls, bright white among the nettles, a skeleton, human ... and next to it in a tangle of furniture ...

That was a dog! said Sister. Big one too.

The human bones were strewn across the filthy, rotting floor, but the dog's bones ... he was lying down, maybe passed away in his sleep, no ... either way he probably starved, since he couldn't let himself out.

Excuse me, but what's with tellin me not to look ... after all that, they're dead, so what.

I guess I didn't want, that skeleton … the long hair, it was a woman.

Aha. I didn't notice. Think there's still some people hidin out here?

I looked around. The forest we'd entered was dark. Not a sound, not even a bird cheeping. All we could hear was the leaves beneath our feet.

Think we'll make it to that Ušanica place? There's a train there, you said.

We'll make it somewhere.

Then we walked through meadows, the sun shining, and … we were hungry, but maybe the walking … made us more cheerful … Sister broke into twitters … even sang.

It's strange, she said, actually I've never sung, never tested my voice like this, totally out in the open, sounds different … it fills space boldly, I concurred.

Her voice made everything better. I recalled the first time it reached my ears, out at the Rock … it must've been hers … I told her.

Maybe I had a window open in the attic.

Yeah, it was summer.

Eventually we came to enjoy wandering … we'd make it somewhere … we were together. Gallivanting in an oak grove, shaking down nuts and snacking on them … pears and wild cabbage smiled on us along our way as we nibbled lanceroot and sampled wild ploughnuts … that worked … scrambling over rocks and marveling at pools, drinking from cool springs … tossing pebbles and twigs at each other. Then Sister went for a swim while I admired her … her body totally white in the water, her tenderness … on the bank she turned blue.

Get down, quick.

I'm cold …

I saw four walking single file on the opposite bank, dressed in green, but I guess the sun blinded them, they didn't see us … maybe … Sister's teeth were chattering, but it wasn't the cold, I don't think … they had uniforms, but rumpled and tattered … rifles too, crossing the slope like an apparition, they vanished into the woods.

Those weren't cops, I said, maybe soldiers.

Better slug me, little brother, I think I'm … but I'm awake, they were like some kina SS or somethin … that first one's cap said CA, or SA.

Aha, so they were deserters … get dressed!

I don't feel so cold now … an it's strange … I got an urge. Wanna?

We harmonized our movements, fast and slow, probly wasn't a wise idea, I thought … what's become of us … they'd given us a fright, maybe that awakened in us … no, we'd just been without each other too long. Without ourselves.

We might hafta be outdoors another night. Were you cold?

Sister was pluckin up flowers an weavin … a wreath.

I yanked it away.

Cut it out, what's gotten into you … aha. Yep. That's dumb, I'll stop.

We walked in silence.

How're the feet?

Bad. Are we there yet?

Where?

Anywhere … you're the one leadin the way, you're lookin where we're goin, tell me a story to pass the time, or no, better yet, I'll tell you … Odysseus was a dirty old man!

Hah, too bad! That's just the way it is. Man in his fifties, sixties! If he's a man, an a good one … there's nothin you can do, but a woman … soothsayers maybe, but that's spiritual, it's cruel, I know!

Well, I told you how I also used to act, not in Prague … but there's somethin you forgot, Odysseus had a buddy … lemme tell you what you forgot … Agamemnon, he boozed it up with Odysseus an the rest, they all fought together, an they had slave girls in their camp, an their women were waitin at home. An you know how it was, you know very well … when Agamemnon finally got the urge for home an his faithful wife, he comes stormin into the castle, flings off his boots, an goes: Clytemnestra, come! Hey … watch the scalps … he'd filthied up the rug … I've composed many manly songs, I'm the rex, he said … look here, an he showed her all his knives an swords an daggers stolen from the weak … the sharp edges startled her, but she was used to it by now, after all that time she'd been with him, with the rex … an look, woman, he showed her a golden mask an various suits of precious armor with scenes of him crushing his enemies or composing songs … oh yeah, an here, woman, here's some coral, but … he drew back his hand, were you faithful to me, need I ask … You bet I was, after all you're the best, did you miss me? He mumbled some answer … miss her, right, with all the work he had … drags his ass home after all those years an starts yakkin away about who all he got … an how they didn't get him cause he's the best … an Clytemnestra goes, yes, you're a hero, how about a little bath before the banquet? … an I should tell you, there'll be … mortadella. But he didn't listen, tippin back the cannikin an bellowin some song

... an you know, my friend, said Černá, how it was in the bath ... the one Clytemnestra loved was in there with her, an they were waitin for him with axes, know that one?

Yeah, but Odysseus ...

Beg your pardon, honey, but you forgot, you were talkin crap! You didn't tell me, an hell if I know why, the way it really was, you forgot a lot ... I'll be glad to tell you, said Černá, and suddenly her feet didn't seem to hurt so much ... Odysseus told Penelope ... get out. He explained everything honestly, after all he was a man. An Penelope turned pale an trembled an drew back her outstretched hand ... an you know what was in that hand, my dear? You know, you know very well: the key to the bath. An one of Penelope's suitors was hidin in there, like you said, a boy ... more handsome an refined than Odysseus, he wasn't covered with knife an axe scars, didn't have rough skin ... never burned himself with butts, or cut himself, or rolled around on the street in puddles, or roared at banquets when it was uncalled for, he was poised ... an his body wasn't all coarse an hard from battle, an forget about booze, this boy was an athlete, ran an threw the discus, an knew his way around women too ... he knew a beautiful robe when he saw one ... back home, you see, times'd changed, dear friend, an Odysseus, out knockin around the islands, didn't know ... an that boy ... was Penelope's boyfriend, that's the way it was ... his hair was thick an silken, fleece! An ... Černá rolled her eyes and gave me a wink, I covered up my SUPER DISCO and maybe turned a little pale ... his body was smooth, but he was very strong, don't think he wasn't, an clever ... an Penelope was fond of him, she was wise an he ... knew it! An Penelope, in spite of everything, still would've handed that key to Odysseus, but he knocked her down an broke her heart ... an went off with his slave girl, laughin an slappin her ass an tippin back the cannikin, till he came to the dung heap ... an then he tossed aside the cannikin an ran off, without even a look back at the slave girl ... an meanwhile Penelope walked off, stooped not with age but from the blow, hair gray not with age but from waiting and grieving, an tears flowed down her proud, beautiful face ... she opened the bath an let in the boy, then led him to the bedchamber an took a sword off the wall, Odysseus had his collection in there ... bayonets of all shapes an sizes ... an pointed her hand out the window ... to Odysseus in the dung, lying there petting a blind old dog ... an they both had tears rollin out their eyes, they recognized each other ... the dog was an old bastard, Devil was his name, that was typical of Odysseus ... the two a them used to hunt together, conversing for hours on end … an that dog was the only living being Odysseus truly loved, the only one he was faithful to, with him he didn't fear for his freedom an didn't need to think up tricks so he could be alone … the dog licked his old scar … Odysseus planted a kiss on his snout, an at that moment the dog died, Odysseus wallowed in the dung … an wailed … an Penelope's lover ran down the stairs an pounced like a tiger, sword in his fist … that's the way it was … nobody was happy there, for a while maybe … Černá sighed … cause all they had inside was fury, not humility … but now I'm talkin crap, what do I know … she walked and walked, and I hid behind a tree, on purpose, to see what she'd do.

I chuckled into my stubble, expecting her to scream and start looking for me. But then … I didn't like it by myself, not one bit. I dashed back out onto the road, not a sign of her … Černá! Come out!

Okay, you got me, you're right, that's the way it was, just like you told it … I dashed outta the woods, lowland, grass, hills … not a sign, she'd vanished … maybe … soared off into the air … I fell on the ground, no, just like She-Dog, no … I can't be like this … I love her, maybe that's why … no, I'm me and I know what I'm doin … maybe that's why … I looked at my hands, killing hands … ran in a circle, calling her name, maybe she'd gone back into the woods and was wandering around there looking for me … I thought of the village behind us, the skeletons, not a good place … and then on the hill I saw a silhouette … she really must've flown, but maybe she's talking to herself … thinking I'm somewhere behind her, or I ran off just for a sec … it has to be her, I scrabbled up the hill … she stood there immobile, guess she was pissed … I ran up to her and froze, it was a scarecrow made of straw, instead of a face it had a gourd with a carved mouth, hole for a nose, holes for eyes … a dummy on a pole cross, straw pokin out of an old jacket fulla holes … my legs buckled … Hey, what're you doin up there? Cripes, wait for me! Černá shouted from the bottom of the hill. I was at her side before she could say goddamn.

Hey, she squinted, a scarecrow! Great, that means there's people around, right? People … train station's what I mean. Is that a field there? Hey, city boy, can you even tell rye from wheat?

She was a little puzzled why I was so ardently and affectionately hugging and kissing her, but then again not that much … occasionally we expressed tenderness and fondness for each other, and if I forgot to mention that most of the way we held hands, I don't know why.

It was corn. We stuffed ourselves.

Look, Černá, they're like scalps! Tearing off the husks, I gathered them into a barbarous clump …

Ever had pickled corn, roasted or stewed or shucked? I'd make some if I had a pot. Back home sometimes the scarecrows had pots on their heads, not this one … my grandma'd say we're in poor country …

Hm.

We skirted the field, the road led upward, back uphill, and there, at the very top, stood a tall, solitary tree … we made a beeline for it, raindrops came down … warm and balmy, and then the first lightning bolt shot through the sky … Wow, look, Černá, it's gorgeous, that scar is smiling! … hurry, run, it's unsafe to be out in the open … yeah, let's take cover … flashes of light painted the sky, thunderclaps shook it … Sister laughed … I tore off my clothes and ran out in the rain … she sat under the tree, in spasms of laughter … I howled too, somehow I guess we were cleansing ourselves … I rolled in the grass, yelling and shrieking … Sister stripped too, pounced on me, we skidded down the slick hillside, squawking … light exploding overhead, thunder pounding mightily. She tried something out with her voice, and her purring and meowling grew into a cloud above our heads … soon her voice was whipping through the air like energy, maybe a little like radiation … I bellowed: Hah, you Bog you, take us both, you Murderer of Young, you Old Fuck … and I shouted: Why're we here, Up yours, Maniac, and then it occurred to me that maybe *maniac* came from *Manitou*, and I kind of liked that idea … I tore up blades of grass, quietly, Sister crawling under my knees, it rained, drops lashing down like endless ropes, I chopped them in flight with the edge of my hand, dancing and skipping, and Sister tried to do a headstand, found an indentation, head in the ground, long white legs swaying, I caught on and held her … and then … a fireball hissed past my elbow, Sister fell, I had to let go, the pulsing orb shot through her legs as they swished to the ground, I was worried the tail had singed her ankles … the lightning ball shot all around us, I stood still, Sister lay there, watching … and then the thing began hopping around the plain, high in the air and back down to the ground, and vanished … Think it'll come back, I asked, actually I shouted, over the rain … No, said Sister, now on her feet … we both had goose bumps, and just to be safe we hugged.

Under the tree, it was still friendly … not so much rain came through its dense leafage, we put on our clothes … the rain began to die off … the cornfield was somewhere below us, damn, should've ripped some up for reserves … but what about the other side, surely there must be a village … I think, though, my dearest, that tonight we'll be outside again. It's not that cold … maybe we can find a haystack or somethin … I don't care, said Sister, I'm startin to like it, an besides … maybe, you know, after what happened … it's not a bad thing if we're not home right away. Think they're after us? It's always better to act like they're after you, I recited to her the words of the teaching. You held my legs up real nice. So you weren't cold last night? C'mon, I told ja … I slept with that girl … how could I be cold. An tonight I'm sleepin with you. Yeah you are. An I'm thinkin even, you always wanna go to the sea, hey … maybe it really would be better to take off. You think … cause of. It's easily possible, though, that if the Viets found him they cleaned him up an everything is cool … or else … Drop it, please. You're right, Černá, it's like a dark cloud. It's a lot better now though, huh. Yeah, oh yeah, I said. Got a smoke? How're you for cash? I combed through my boots and all my pockets … I'd say two tickets to the Pearl an a couple drinks an meals, could be. You're makin me hungry! All I have's a couple thou too, got that smoke? Aright aright, here … she lit up. I watched the glowing ash. Shifted my vision slightly, and there they were … those unforgettable lashes, each and every one a living continuation of her soft eyelids' tenderness, she moved them, gazing out into the landscape, emitting rapid searching looks … targeted flashes … I stretched out to hide any targets on me. I stretched out to touch. We were close. The storm was over.

It was totally dark when we came to the hut. The roof was made of sticks with waterproof fabric stretched over them. Inside, a hole lined with blankets. And there was a firepit.

Potatoes! Cried Sister. An a … whatchamacallit … a rutabaga!

I found a bottle. That was all there was. Remember, Sister … those deserters … but I was already building a fire. We'd better get lost, said Sister, but she was already opening the bottle … aright, we'll stay an see where it lands us … making love in that hole, we had the feeling, which we shared with each other, that it must've been something like this back in the cave days … in all likelihood, I told Sister the anthropology, based on the drawings of the time … kneeling and from behind, cause with your back on the rocks, ick, my sis filled in with a grimace, the potatoes meanwhile burned. We put in a new batch.

We drank ourselves silly. My dear … stop me mercilessly if I start goin off again … but my heart … a couple times I sat down on a stump when you were walking ahead of me an we weren't holding hands … an I took it out an I wanna tell you, my heart in spots is black an stabbed an burdened, maybe that's why I'm always ravin on about the sea an the islands … I donno what that girl who held you last night told you … but my heart is heavy … an I oughta tell you that on my way … see, in the former time my heart …

You, said Černá, moving closer … always rattlin on about your heart … what about my feet … they hurt!

Sister sat by the fire, waiting for her things to dry, I gaped in amazement at her skin, golden and soft in the flickering glow … I examined the bony outline of her ribs, jutting out beneath the skin, holding fast the sweet paradise of her innards, her, the eden of her body, her raven-black hair merging with the dark and the paleness of her face reflecting each time she dodged the blaze's tongue or tossed her head … then, sitting back on her heels and resting her hands on her thighs … she turned around and the flames' reflection flickered on the skin of her back, her slender neck, I'd never seen her through fire before, through a frolicking wall of flames, shimmering with the air's motion … we both turned, toward the sound … the guy was gigantic, one eye agog, across the other a black patch, I was crouched at his feet, hidden in shadow … his lace-up boots, green pants, the deserters, my mind raced … but if he didn't notice me, he saw Černá very well, just let out a groan, for a moment he seemed petrified … it isn't often a guy comes home to find his fantasies come true, a warm fire and a naked woman … when I looked at Černá, I froze too … she'd scooped up her clothes, but … she smiled at the giant invitingly, running her hands over her breasts … I thought she'd lost her mind … that guy could squash me like a bug if he wanted … the second it hit him that a naked woman was really there and smiling at him, he let out a gasp, threw open his arms, and charged at her … moving faster than I could think … I knocked his feet out from under him, as he fell I grabbed a branch from the fire and conked him, as he raised himself on his elbows I bashed him over the head and stabbed the branch into his face, both of us were roaring … Černá snagged me by the elbow and dragged me out of the hut, running and stumbling … we didn't stop till far away, still trembling … why'd you do it, why, said Černá, shaking me … Huh? You're askin me … you're the one that did it, an c'mon, there's probly more of em out here. More who? Sheepherders? What sheepherders, that was a deserter, we saw those guys. Now you're really mixed up, he had long hair an a beard, that was just some oaf, a local! What about the uniform? I saw his boots … He was in rags, that was a sheepherder, army boots're what people wear in the country … We could've made a deal. You slut! Don't gimme that crap, you were strokin your tits, leadin him on! What're you babblin … idiot … I covered my chest cause he was starin at me is all … an why'd you jump him, anyway? I mean you got the gun, shit! I mean we coulda tried nice, an then if somethin went wrong you coulda … threatened him with the pistol. An don't call me slut! Flying into a rage, she hurled herself at me, fingers curled, we tumbled through the grass, her biting, me holding her off with my hands, and I don't know why … I guess the whole thing … I started laughing, she fell still on top of my hands and whispered: Look. Take a look.

I let her down, she rolled off into the grass. I turned around, in the distance was a fire. It stood out strongly in the dark. The flames whipped the night, billowing white steam … the fabric was soaked with rain … but I knew it was that hovel.

So he stayed in there, I said nonsensically.

Sister turned her face to me and it was full of tears, c'mere, she said, burying her head in my armpit and weeping. I couldn't. I looked at the stars. Guess it'll come some other time. An I hope she'll be there for it. Just let me make it through tonight, I said to myself.

She fell asleep. Maybe he'd come because She-Dog didn't want me to tell this love of mine … and the pistol, it dug into me, I took it outta my jacket and tucked it under my belt … I wasn't at all eager for my little sister to know where I carried it. There was only one round left in the gun, and that one … that one I'm savin.

I peered up at and into the stars, chill springs, unmoving eyes on a creature's wings, openings to elsewhere. And then I also fell asleep. We were pretty tired.

An I had my … it was a wolf dream. We ran off, Raksha squealing with joy … me too, we knocked the lock off the cage and it rattled through the zoo the whole last night, one of us knocked it off with a paw, the chain fell away, and then we ran, running over the hard frozen snow, through the woods, over the dirtclods, along the stones, claws clicking, and we didn't worry about our tracks because we were running … away.

Her eyes glowed like coals … sometimes she would nip at me, lick me … there, where I had a scar from my collar, the bald patch on the nape of my neck where the fur hadn't grown back in … she touched her snout to the spot on my ribs where once upon a time the barbwire had cut me, and pieces of wire were left in there, they'd grown into me … I nipped at her too, her scars were inside

… the drill where they'd taught her to beg and hold out her paw and roll her peepers and pout her lips, where they'd dressed her up in ribbons and suits so she'd grow into a good little girl, a well-mannered little woman … always at attention, like a snowman kind of, but sexy … where they showed my little sister how to wiggle her ass to please the bosses … to live with idiots the rest of her life in exchange for cash to get makeup and food and a flat … consuming energy on learning how to go ooh and aah whenever the fucking bosses lay down the gospel … but now we were running … and the only trail we left was the fast frozen breath that fell from our fangs … my loved one was a bee and a butterfly and knew how to cut with her claws and her tongue, and I tried too … we learned from each other what was good for the other, and that made both of us stronger … running, and the earth turned beneath us, running by graves and leaping across them, avoiding the bones and glassy stares and empty eyesockets … of wolf skulls … and steering clear of traps and snares, we had experience … with falling stakes and poisoned meat … we made it without harm through the red pack's territory … and met the last white wolves, they were wracked with disease … and the big black wolves chased us, but we escaped … we, the gray wolves of the Carpathians, had an age-old war with them, they were surprised we fled, their jaws snapping shut on empty air, they had a hunch it was their turn next, the helicopters were on the way … we ran side by side, our bodies touching … running over the earth as it turned, with the wind whistling in our ears like a lament for every dead pack … and the clicking of our claws made the earth's motion accelerate … we ran over the earth, a mass grave, running away … away from there … and then … but then we stood on the final cliff, above the depths, and nothing was left but to jump off and plunge into the surface, that was where it all began … the depths below sparkled like a mirror and Raksha, my sister, shrank back, tongue drooping, a growl, dark and savage, escaping her throat … Akela nudged her flank with his snout, but she snapped at him … we're here … come on, Sister, we can't go back now … come on, let's jump … let's fly, we can be together forever … but Raksha turned and ran back … Akela stood at the edge, hesitating, but just for a moment … he ran after her … Raksha had found a hole in the hillside and wouldn't come out … and Akela didn't get it, he didn't know a thing … he stayed outside alone … the only sound from the hole in the ground her growling … warning him … and then it was quiet … Akela was alone … and there was no point, he could go back to the cliff by himself … and fly … but there was no point … he howled, the moon was all he had and it drove his nerves crazy, Akela had no one to lean on … he ran into the woods and killed the first animal he caught scent of … carried it back to the hole … Raksha dragged the meat inside … days went by, and Akela went mad with grief … the solitude, so close to the precipice, and the betrayal … he didn't know anything … and then he saw Raksha come out of the hole, dragging wearily, creatures all around her … sucking the life from her, taking it for themselves … Akela attacked … but Raksha knew, she'd been expecting it … knocked him off his feet, and he exposed his unprotected belly, offering his neck, the jugular, nothing mattered to him anymore … but she didn't break the rules … she returned to the creatures … leaving Akela alone with the moon, but now he knew … and his howl was different.

What're you screamin, for God's sake, what? You donno how to sleep, said Černá. No, you don't. Either you grind your teeth or but now you were even screamin!

Sorry. If you knew what I dreamed though, hah! You'd be amazed!

Did the gentleman fly?

Yeah, actually no … it was a lot different this time. An it told me. See, you crawled into this hole an …

Yeah sure, listen. I practically didn't sleep. Or else it was a dream. It was really weird. Listen, I got woken up by this awful din, this ruckus. Like machines, you know? I donno, I think I was awake, an it came from underground. I tried to wake you. The earth was shaking. Like there was some airport or factory or somethin underneath us. I walked around a while an then I went … she pointed to where the grassy plain sloped downward, I listened and it sounded familiar … over there, I wasn't even scared, I kept lookin to make sure I could see you … an there's a gorge there, man, I lie down an look, an there's these little carts flyin around, an the people pushin em were totally emaciated, down to the bone, horrible … an in the side of the gorge were these metal doors with guards out in front … an there was this racket from inside, an this light like they were meltin down iron or whatever … the people had on these suits striped like zebras, but you know … that was enough for me, I got outta there, metal doors … there was ivy or somethin all over em, an it was rolled back. I donno if it was a dream.

Well … Černá, if you want, after the obligatory morning grooming … we'll go take a look.

Yeah, let's. Go ahead, there's this little stream over there, past the trees, go wash up. I'll wait, I already went. An … be back soon.

Her dream reminded me a lot of another one, is it logical, is it magical, is it at all? I jabbered to myself … Josef Novák the skeleton, I'll never get rid of my dreams … underground death camp … there was the brook, I knelt down, bathing my fingers … well, Černá said to wash up … my fingers carved a furrow in the water, just for a moment, then the two streams merged, the water coursing over stones and pebbles, along and above the sandy bottom, stubbornly flowing into the unknown, always the same and ever changing … repeating itself and changing, goin somewhere, like speech and like time.

I stood up, took out my knife, and for the last time snapped open the blade, hah, I said to myself, this'll fool em! I just won't defend myself, I won't be part of it … *churi des, churi hudes*, not anymore.

I tossed the knife into the stream and the water closed over it. It's so simple, I thought, after all, I had that dream … about the tribe, we were five and I've got five senses … is it nonsense?

We were five, an if my sister is death, I don't exactly hafta love her, but I can learn to live with her till the end. Death can't suffer after all, death is scar-free … I'm gonna trust her. We'll make it somewhere.

I was in a very humanistic mood when I sat back down on the stump next to Sister, smiling and saying: honey this, honey that … unlike her I had a hunch she hadn't been asleep last night … I sang my good knife a little farewell tune … Černá pulled a package out of her jacket … imbued with benevolence and Saint Francisness, I gazed caressingly on every crawling bug and spider … my knife won't threaten them ever again! *Churi des, churi hudes*, not anymore! … Černá slapped a mosquito … I frowned a little … but I had to get up and adjust my belt, the pistol was digging into me.

Hey, look what I got! I mean we.

What? Food … good woman!

Yeah … where'd I … swipe it, I don't even know, I don't get it … I mean I stuck a piece of … mortadella! … in my pocket for the trip. An now there's a whole dead naked chicken … incredible! Did it ever occur to you that maybe we're under a spell an what happened didn't happen?

Occurs to me all the time, little sister … but try … I pinched myself hard … only pain is real.

An pleasure, said Sister. You want?

Yeah. Like a wolf.

We munched the chicken, it was so defenseless! grinning at each other and tearing the flesh from the bones, nibbling them clean, ripping out the veins with our fingers, just like kings.

So maybe, said Sister. We can go take a look. If that gorge is there?

We don't have to, it's there. I know it. I saw it, this fella, what I mean is, let's just say I was advised it was there.

But shouldn't we report it? To the police, the UN, UNESCO, I donno.

What, that your new dream confirmed my old dream?

They'll come, take a peek …

You know how that goes.

You're right. Let's go, on your feet!

We struck out, refreshed and fortified, pores prosperously opening in the wind and the grass … we didn't talk about what we'd done to those people. All in good time.

Though we remained on the alert, Gretel here and there climbing a tree, ripping a hole in her jeans, and me occasionally dashing off, looping through the woods, somersaulting through the grass, and relishing the open air, the trip proceeded without any further incidents or encounters.

Just once … far off in the valley, we saw some wagons riding single file, wooden wagons roofed with canvas, pulled by horses and mules, circled by men on horseback … those're covered wagons, Sister, maybe there isn't a train around here … no, they must be evacuees, hey look, there's little kids in em too … who's movin, I wonder, an where? … always somebody goin somewhere, big whoop, Sister said wisely … we also saw mountains in the distance … sparkling in the sun, maybe it was the air, maybe there was a storm over there, some of the cliffs glowed phosphorescent green, or swam in the blue of the distant sky … on top the snow glittered, if we'd been closer it would've hurt our eyes … I stopped, suppressing a howl with all my might … some day we'll go there … yeah, an how bout the sea, said Sister, or both?

Both, get this, one time I met this Greek girl from Cyprus, maybe she was Turkish, but she told me that on their island you can ski downhill right onto the beach! Now, though, it's all wired off, she said.

Maybe later, Sister suggested.

I can tell you wanna go, an that's fabulous.

Of course, said Sister, kicking a stone … Odysseus preferred to be off fighting with Agamemnon an Menelaus … maybe you too?

Oh, not me, my dear, I'm exempt from the service, you know that, an besides, war …

And surely, Brother, you also know the first part of the Odyssey … where he made like he was crazy, threw his son in front of the machine … then he ended up likin the army, that was his son, but the two of us … you the brother, me the sister … I just laughed, because she didn't know about my wolf dream … I hadn't told her yet, all in good time, I thought back then.

In the dream we had babies.

18

BY THE OLD WALL. IN THE HALL. GUY WITH A BRICK.
BY TRAIN. AND ONWARD, ELSEWHERE.

Eventually the road broke off and we were standing in mud and dust, broken glass and plastic bags at our feet, with a little town spread out before us.

There was a sign, UŠANICA 3 KM. We didn't much notice the buildings or look for anything at all. Just the train station.

Maybe some little boutique, dear, after recent events, have a drink, splash off the dust, ramrod the blunderbuss … cracking jokes, we stole along the walls, wondering whether they'd found our victims and whether finding them had upset anyone enough to call in the commandos.

The station was different than I remembered from my last, fleeting visit. Ticket window closed, not a soul. Then some hobo surfaced behind the bars. Shove a thousand crowns at him and he says, Here in Mezilavorie* … huh? Ušanica's a good 70 miles due east, he explained. But the sign? Ehh, signs're a dime a dozen! Trains don't run much, but if we're goin to Prága … there's one comes through right at midnight, but he doesn't recommend … it's very, he said some word that might've meant expensive … doesn't bother us … well, just so long as we don't get confused and end up paying too much.

We sauntered around this way and that, tryin to be inconspicuous, which was tough … had some drinks, mixing for speed … I guess our stay in nature improved our health, cause the alcohol didn't work, but then Sister said maybe the opposite, maybe it works so much we can't tell, we only think … sure, only think, only! You, dear, know instinctively what takes me years of work an prayer to arrive at, I admire you tremendously, and so to love is added respect, the big sister of relationships … see, the booze does work, there you go, rattlin on again … we leaned against the corner of a beautiful old wall covered with putrid fungus, it was a synagogue.

Battered, with glazed windows.

You don't know this, little sister, but my great-great-greats came from Odessa, led by old Aladdin, or Apollo, or maybe Ahasver Potok, on that point the records in the family Bible differ. I never told anyone, it's nobody else's business, I keep my back covered! They were the only ones who settled in a village, cause Potok means something in the Bohemians' tongue too an my ancestors wanted to drop out of sight a little, first thing they did was set up a tavern ... the others crawled off into the ghettos, but mine opted for the disguise an the mask, taking their double-meaninged name as a sign from Him ... when they crossed the border into Bohemia, they contentedly smacked their lips at the taste of the garlic balls, an delightedly tugged at their peyos, cause there wasn't a Cossack in sight, nothing but good jovial folks ... only my forefather was suspicious an careful, an that's why I'm alive an here with you ... he had flying dreams too, in Odessa he raised pigeons, an a certain bocher that used to shop there wrote a story about it, he was a journalist, hah, he was stupid an wrote about himself, so in the end the stalingos hunted him down an killed him ... nobody knows that about me but you, I keep a lookout!

An here by this old wall I'll let you in on somethin too, my friend ... I first saw the sky at my grandma's somewhere in Transylvania, I don't even know what country it is now, things there change fast, an I don't wanna know, an when my mom died the wolves tore her to pieces, she was out pickin blueberries ... so she could buy me a primer to learn that foreign language ... Sister broke down, crying uncontrollably ... then that thug, my father, turned up, an the whole village went gaga when he drove up in his Zhigulik, an he stayed with us all summer, an the first time he did it to me I said so, but no one believed me ... a champ like him, handin out chewin gum an pocket mirrors an lighters, an even if he did, it's all in the family, their business ... an all those boys that turned their heads at me ... girls're women there at fourteen, you know? ... but I wasn't even that ... not one of em killed him, like anybody there woulda done to their own brother for a thing like that, no, the scum, on Sundays they went to church an at night they cast spells an everything was hunky-dory ... an then he arranged for the papers an bought me dresses an cremes an candies ... an the virgins an everyone congratulated me cause I was gettin outta there, to the West, to Czechoslovakia, an my grandma? She knew ... an listen, I think she let me go so I'd sink all the way to the bottom ... you know how I told you that time ... about my feelings, the awfulest one?

An then Grandma sent me you, an gave me that pistol an the two of you for me to decide ... an now I'm free an you'll never order me around ... unless I want you to. An I told it in school again, years later, cause sometimes ... I couldn't stand it, down in the cellar so the neighbors ... but I'm not gonna tell it all right now … at school they called me Vampire because of where I'm from, they didn't believe me either, the scumbag was a big shot, so they just made like nothin was goin on … and then Sister fell silent as an icy gust snatched at us from around the corner, and Sister, sobbing, began to tremble like an aspen leaf … I told her … like an aspen leaf, yeah, she said, an a stake, she clutched at her heart, good one, she caught hold of me, and then, continuing the chain of association, I guess, whispered: You're probly gonna get older for what you do to my sweet little body. I didn't have anything to say to that.

Heh … we walked on and the weather changed, it began to drizzle a little, we ducked into the first open door … it was an odd hall.

Dark. We tread cautiously, then I let out a scream. Curling off the wall was a rag, no, a piece of paper with a woman's face on it, I donno why I crossed myself, the face was a sweet one … Černá wrinkled her brow critically, hey, it's some broad, an actress no doubt, some big star … I went closer, yep, almost too sweet, and … blonde … next to her was another one, the walls in there were dripping … blech, that's … Sister, that's an electric chair, an that'd be the murderer … I think we started shaking, what kind of horror show is this, here in this bizarre land of enchantment … And then Sister whispered: An now I'll tell you the last thing, it's good an also real real bad … hold onto me, there … I think that guy wasn't even my father, he just weaseled his way in … I'm really scared my grandma sold me to him an everyone there knew it, there's a lot of poverty there. I've been thinkin about her ever since, but if I wanna know the truth, I might have to go an ask the old crow. Will you come with me?

Černá, I'll go wherever you want, but … if it's true we'd have to … we'd have to do it to her. I'd have to.

Maybe not, said Černá, maybe we'd find out she had to. For some reason. I've been thinkin! Those mountains back there, you'd like to see em, wouldn't you? Things're different there. They've got legends an fables, you're into all that …

Do they have a legend there about a horseman from the barrow, a Prince? How do you know? Did I tell you that?

I donno. Maybe you mighta mentioned … hey! Anyway, you can't sell somebody. That's forbidden as long as I'm with you. Forbidden! No selling. You shouldn't keep in touch with certain people, you make phone calls, I donno who to, I'm gonna protect you … we'll change.

Tsss, Černá hissed. No givin orders, you know that!

We had to yank off a sheet to see the next painting. A guy's face, looked nice enough. Some Joseph somethin or other, charged with murder, I sounded out the words.

Mug shot, they got him, it's obvious. We just looked at each other and grabbed each other's hand.

Next … a hacked-up car … I remembered Viška, that was about how his face looked by the time I got Černá off of him, I kept that one to myself.

Some of the rags were canvas, but waterlogged and damaged by plaster didn't look it anymore. None of the pictures was very uplifting.

Hey, the old butcher Kim Il Sung, slaughtered his own people, I showed off my education in front of the politician in the field uniform.

Mug's tight as a bitch, no doubt he's watchin someone's nuts get roasted, Černá appraised him. Whoever took his picture musta been a psycho too.

It's a painting, I corrected her.

Whatever, she said.

Next act, and that got both of us: cash. The lunatic painted cash, somethin musta been eatin him.

No, actually he took it easy, Černá proposed.

The colors, if there had been sunlight … but here in the gloom, all sopping wet, the cash curled like worms, one minute ludicrous, the next almost triumphant … now we gotcha, you peepin Tom, you're ours. When I explained to my woman how I saw it, she said: I think that chick, that blonde, is dead now, that's why you got startled but you're not afraid … the reason the cash is curlin, though, is cause it's still alive. It lives, changes things. People.

Yeah, an how bout this one? Some cans of somethin, fancy labels, hadn't seen that before, my mom never gave me snacks like that. Weird, I said. Actually, that's how people look, nowadays.

Yeah, but not here. Luckily!

It won't be long though, people're already dressed mostly in stickers … they wanna be the same, shiny like tin … we cheerfully shouted back and forth, and when Sister gave a quick toss of her elbow I nodded back, I'd heard it too, behind the pillar … someone was there … we gabbed on about stupid stuff, casually drifting … around the corner, I let out my belt a little.

Mordy tvoyay keerpicha hochetsia! somebody screamed, we sailed around the corner and a tiny little fellow with glasses peeled himself off from behind a pillar …

Hey vagabonds, wanna buy a brick, he shouted in a forced bass.

I took a look at him and left my belt alone. Sister said so he could hear ... What's he want, is that man nuts? I mean we're only lookin around, we didn't take anything! And to me she whispered ... c'mon, the guy's like a matchstick, he doesn't know who we are ... forget him!

We stepped out from around the corner, slowly and goodnaturedly walking toward him. He stood by the pillar, testing the brick's weight like some manufacturer makin the rounds of the ovens ... but you could tell he didn't mean it seriously.

Hello there, I said.

You're from Prague? You came all the way out here to see it an they went an closed the place! He threw down the brick.

What's with the brick, said Sister.

Oh, we get all sortsa ... sneakin in here an trashin it. Oughta put in a minethrower. They don't even want it! An he was a local native, I put in a lotta work on this thing an they don't even know who he was.

I didn't know either, but I was embarrassed to ask in front of Sister. I think she had the same dilemma. The fellow squatted down on his haunches, looking pretty crushed.

There there, Sister said, patting him on the shoulder, I mean c'mon, they're only pictures.

Jesus an Mary! the guy cried, folding his head into his hands. Animals ... he muttered ... beasts ... it's insane ... it's typical ... civilization! I'm goin back! Let it all collapse, see if I care! I've got my own stuff ... Andy! Ach, Andy, fuck it all.

Slowly me and Sister retreated. Outside, after that gruesome display, I let out a deep breath. Poor kid, said my sis, guess he was off the mark on what the locals' taste was like. Think he painted all that? Obviously, he looks it. But he said somethin about a local. It was probly that Joseph guy, said Černá, the only locals he does portraits of're some killer an a blonde slut, an he wonders why they don't like it, talk about naive. What they want on the walls around here is cash, murderers, soup cans, corpses, car crashes, execution chambers ... Černá counted off on her fingers ... they're dumb, they don't know that's all they got ... practically. Who else'd want this stuff, no big town.

You're a smart one, Černá, that's the way it is!

It was dark outside ... in front of the battered synagogue, now a margarine warehouse, which I noticed but thought better of sharing with Sister ... we told each other our secrets, and hers was a terrible one … I only told her part of mine, didn't dredge up the main thing.

And so for once we were quiet, but then Sister poked me, the clocktower showed nearly midnight, we fled to the station, hopping on the train just as it was pulling out, a fella stood by the door, pale as a candle, I asked: Prague, yeah? Praha, Prága! Nach Prag, sonuvabitch … he just nodded and gave me a faraway look, probly sloshed … we found a free compartment and snuggled up, smiling … and since all's permitted in love and war, as the Old Bulletins of the Elders of Zion say, and in a passionate embrace the two merge, and it's never a bore, and especially not when it's always the same an always new an goin somewhere … we provocatively drew the curtains, audaciously bolted the door, and began feeding on each other in the figurative sense. Then we succumbed to dreams. The door flew open and in walked … that pale guy that'd been by the door, in a uniform though, a conductor's. Hope I hadn't offended him. He stood there smiling, drew back his pale, narrow lips … two to Prága, I said, I was surprised to see him lift the cash up to the light and inspect it with amusement, like it was the first time in his life he'd seen the new, independent Czech moola. Then he handed me two tickets, I stuck them in my pocket.

Hooh, Sister shuddered, guy was weird. He smelled funny.

Yep, shepherd's son in an ill-fitting uniform. I mean everyone out here crosses emselves. But that guy was weird. So're we. By morning, maybe afternoon, we oughta be in Prague.

God willing, said Sister.

An why wouldn't he be? Uh … I hushed up.

After a while I got thirsty … and hungry.

I wouldn't mind somethin either … but don't go anywhere. It's dumb, I know, but do you hear the train?

Aha. I didn't hear any ties, or wheels. I darted to the window, the landscape rushed past, changing, not the darkness, just an occasional flash of light from some town or *gorod* or wherever it was we were.

Oh, know what, it's probly one a those ultramodern Western turbo-charged … shinkansens.

You're all pale! What's wrong!

Nothin, nonsense. I'm goin to scope it out. Come with me if you're afraid to stay.

Me? She bristled. But I just took off my boots, it still hurts, be back soon!

I walked down the aisle, peeking into compartments, not a soul ... the train was empty, butt or two on the ground here an there, stains, bottles, I picked up one that rolled under my feet ... didn't know the brand ... but inside was a spiderweb with a little black ... don't clean too much here, do they ... I walked on, just about ready to give it up, the curtains flapped out the windows of the empty compartments into the night like they were tryin to get away, curtains with a mind a their own, idiot? Hush up, you're only hurting yourself ... but at last I found the dining car, it was empty too ... on the tables tablecloths and fake flowers and salt and pepper shakers, the waiter busying himself in the back by the counter, back to me, I went up and coughed politely, he turned around an I felt my heart start poundin wildly ... that same guy ... smilin ... beer, I rasped ... he bowed an took off, after all why not, I mean the train's empty, he can handle it, bigger take for him, I reassured myself, on the whole unsuccessfully ... he handed me some bottles in a plastic bag, again smiling and shaking his head at the coins ... I made sure to keep my distance, some types I just can't stand, instinctively an right off the bat.

Fear gripped me. The thought of going back through that empty train, curtains flapping to nowhere ... I opened one of the bottles on a window in the dining car, and chugged it, Sister, forgive me! Černá ... my vision went black. She's back there all alone, I rammed into the door and almost fell. A Gypsy family sat in the aisle, splayed out on their bundles. I stared at them, I guess ... like some goof walkin into the bedroom on his old lady an she's, well, I'd wish him all the best ... one of the men stood up. I climbed over them. The whole train was a ruckus, columns of cigarette smoke billowed everywhere. I fought my way through a pack of drunken soldiers, held my nose with two fingers by the toilet, clambered over a teenager wrapped in a jacket with an embroidered skull winkin up at me, belly to the floor. In one compartment a German shepherd sat on the bench, a tramp sprawled on the floor with his guitar, I barked. People in the aisle were guzzlin beer an gobblin crackers, I got a close-up look at their ruddy faces, stomped on one of em's foot, to see if he was alive, he swung round. Ugh, guess so ... train must've stopped while I was in the dining car, yeah, that's it ... me and Černá both're gettin hypersensitive ... Ušanica's by the border, it's obvious, they just got on, why bother with customs ... smokes! She'll get testy, me too. I traded two beers for a pack of ... Bělomorka, well, we'll see. White Plague, didn't like the sound of it, but I was in a hurry. Every now and then a figure peeled itself off from the aisle, full of smoke and the moon's night mist, and slipped past me, I stood still, collecting my breath, Uchryujte, I heard, a greeting, a curse, a secret password? Chrunchru, said a mamluk in a turban apologetically, shoving me out of his way, step aside, said one of ours, ramming into me. From some compartments I heard snoring, from others shouting, boozing, gorging, bottles smashing. Spotted a Soviet Army uniform. He lay snoring away on his back, next to him some bum with an officer's cap on his head, red T-shirt, earrings, blue tattoos all over. They sprawled across each other, the soldier's gold teeth on display, a puddle of drool on his shirt collar. The muffled sounds of a brawl near the toilet. Someone hadn't paid for something, did something, lost something, stole it, better not to know. The whole train unanimously celebrated the successful traversing of another border. True, a couple hucksters were removed from the train, but the rest were unstoppably headed for Prague. It stank like hell.

But Černá wasn't there. Just her boots. I flew out the door, going through every toilet in the area and peeking in on the neighbors, which didn't come off without a few minor tiffs and exchanges of pleasantries, and came back and all that was there was the boots. I fell to my knees and begged him: I know we're on the shinkansen, but please, we've done some really bad things … give me whatever I deserve, her too, I don't care, just as long as we're together, I can take anything …

Černá fell laughing into the compartment, I could tell right away she was liquored up, a tall, strapping guy came charging in behind her … bald head topped with a derby, bottle of Jack D. in hand, looked like a wholesale pig dealer … easy, honey, Sister wrapped her arms around my neck, she can tell very well what's bugging me, even when she's bombed … this gentleman's got news for us, it isn't goin to Prague, Černá spluttered, tipping over on the seat … Truly, young man, I'm pleased to know you're Czechs on the go, this here pociąg, which is to say train, is going to Warsaw, and there's a suburb there called Prága and that's where I live, the name's Josef Švejch and you're Mr. Potok, your little sister tells me, she's gone beddy-bye, isn't that the sweetest thing! Sister sat, legs spread, snorin away … you wouldn't happen to know a Mr. Potok from Poříčí nad Sázavou, would you? Old Vávra's got a drayery there, and he told me once how the year I was captured a fireball wiped out both their churches, and why, do you think? Because the foreigners pulled into town … he leaned toward me and said … soon as it stops, grab the girl and hightail it out of here, and don't look back, believe me, I've been helping out around here quite a while, it's straight down from here on in! We'll just put little sissy here's booties on, tickle the señorita's hoofs, heehee, the man gestured wildly toward the ceiling and then to his ear … the sign that the place was bugged … I was flabbergasted … so I'd been right! The question is whether he's lying, I decided to chance it, I didn't like that train one bit … the guy nodded and the train pulled to a stop. I grabbed Černá and flung her at the door, and again, she woke up: Let's fly, run, I said in a voice reserved for awful moments … dragged her down the aisle, it was … totally empty again … not a soul, just the door at the far end creaking … we staggered along, Černá started to kick back in, didn't ask any questions, smart girl … past three more empty compartments, at any moment expecting someone to reach out of the darkness, I looked over my shoulder, that pale thin guy was runnin after us, and how! … he was leaping, I caught a glimpse of his face, like … a wasp's … mouth and nose merging into a single orifice … bubbling yellow foam … I had to stop and watch, it was like the foam was boiling, and I could see the pinchers … as he ran his … face grew, filling up the aisle … he raised his arms, tried to strangle me, slashed my neck with his nails … then somethin … Černá grabbed my hand, tugged, and I fell out onto the platform, hard … and the train was gone.

Little brother, are you hurt, she knelt down next to me. Move, please, move.

What're you doin, I'm fine. Just a little banged up. I hoisted myself.

Oh, you're … I thought you got hit.

Huh. By who?

That disgusting guy that was after me, c'mon, he shot at me! I was afraid he got you, didn't he? It totally hurt when you fell on me. But thanks for yankin me out, I was out of my mind with fear. The barrel on that thing. It was totally growin, seemed like it filled the aisle. It's a wonder my head didn't burst I was so scared. I'm amazed that train even left.

But you yanked me out! That's how come I fell on you.

What do you mean … you yanked my arm. I was in the aisle with him an he was shootin, it was horrible … she covered her face.

Černá, wait a sec, I think I get it … you with the pistol, me strangled, those were … demons. An we made it through, I think we're past it. I might've even prayed. I donno.

I prayed too, the whole time.

Hey, but that one guy saved us!

No he didn't, I was about to make a move when he started gabbin at you how we oughta get off, an I knew he was gonna start shootin. He pulled a pistol on me an forced me to take him to our seats. I just pretended to be drunk. On that Fernet a his. When he was tellin you how we should get off, I wanted to scream. But I couldn't move. It was real bad.

We went on discussing the train of horror for a while. The cool night air got it out of us. Peace and quiet all around, small platform, not a soul. We were together alone in the night and we'd just wriggled out of a trap, what more could we ask for.

Whatcha got there, Sister wondered.

I hadn't let go of the plastic bag, astonishing!

I reached in my pocket and there were the cigarettes, only Cleos, marvelous Cleos. Warily I lit one up, and a smile spilled across my face.

Yep, Sister, now we're in reality, let's sit down a while.

There's one thing still … we both know why he tried to shoot me, but why would they try to strangle you? Don't cha wanna tell me?

I winced.

Why don't we wait on that, huh?

Whatever you want. I trust you. An I think I know. Don't get mad, but that girl who held me, the night after … you said you know her. Did you love her?

Yeah.

Was it her? Sister gasped.

Leave me alone.

I'll never leave you.

We sat against the shabby waiting-room wall, taming our thirst and puffing away. The beer was real. Černá remarked that she didn't give a damn if it was bewitched, she'd had her fair share of swills anyway. I had a feeling it wouldn't throw me off either. And besides, I'd paid in normal money, there's gotta be some logic still! Sister fervently concurred. Just to be sure we kissed a few times, hungrily and passionately. Then softly and tenderly. Our hands roamed over each other's bodies. That worked too. Wait … have we got any cash? I gotta buy myself some shoes, this isn't workin anymore. She took off her boots. We searched ourselves. Almost nothing, a couple thou, good for about two lunches. In Prague. Here maybe more. I'll swipe you some sneakers somewhere, or we'll hitch, or stow away, or somethin, I consoled her. I reached in the pocket where I'd put the tickets that pale Azazello had sold me. Came out with two dry leaves that crumbled in my fingers. We eyed the empty bottles with a touch of concern. But so what!

All at once Černá twisted up and started squirming, I alertly dropped to the ground, gropin for her … but she was screaming with laughter … Brother … don't even lift your head … I lifted my head and saw a sign hanging there: UŠANICA. I didn't laugh, I swore like crazy.

We lit up another round of Cleos.

Maybe something'll go from here?

Sister started squirming again.

Listen … the only way … I'll get on that train … here … is with a pack of nuns … at least they … won't be curious … about me!

I was curious how long she could keep up that laughter.

Idea, Sister, we nap here, an at daybreak we'll see more.

Yeah … what stumps me is, with all those dreams you have, aren't you afraid to sleep?

Yeah, that's been my problem ever since early childhood, that's why I hafta go crazy in the daytime. Drinking puts me to sleep all right. I confided in this shaman my concern that I drank too much, she heard me out a couple times an then we went for some vodka. She said go ahead an drink, at least it puts a brake on your insanity. But I'm talkin about the old time. With you, love, it's different. I feel much better an I'm calmer!

Maybe … it's the lovemaking?

Definitely. An everything.

Yeah. Since we're together, everything's easier.

All at once she broke up laughing again, guffawing and roaring. This time I didn't get why, and tried to fall asleep.

I woke up … gazing straight into a … the word *iris* occurred to me, or *nonthorn, crimson cloud, treasury of rosebushes* … it was kind and familiar, I blew out a puff of air and my dream's orgiastic landscape trembled imperceptibly … focused my gaze, it was Sister's ear, inserted the tip of my tongue, she jumped up … ick, oh it's you? Then out with it, now … what were you dreamin?

This time I was too lazy to invent anything.

Nothin. Nothin at all! An you?

I'm not tellin. She blushed.

We walked down a lane and then through the streets. Just to have a look around. Not a soul, we loitered on streetcorners. Studied the situation. Explored shredded posters from last year's festivals. Windows. Behind some of them were family things, we often spotted the outlines of furniture. And people. Sometimes nothing. Up above, the same sky; down below, trickles of mud. The movie theater was playing *Chainsaw*. We deciphered that, the pictures were inscrutable. At the end of the sidewalk, we found a little park with a statue in it. Sit down, said Sister when we came to a bench, I'll tell you somethin.

You're probly not gonna like this. I've been havin dreams … about someone. I like him a lot, an I feel safe an pretty blissful with him. I'll just spew it out: The guy's washin me. I'm in the bath an he's splashin water on me an soapin me up an touchin me. He's gentle but strong. An I know that before, I was really … dirty. Are you angry?

Not at all! Surprise, but no! Can you see his face?

No, my eyes're shut an I can't open em. Then somebody walks in, somebody bad, an the guy chases him out. But only with words. This dream keeps comin back. Don't get mad, but maybe when I find out who he is … I'm gonna wanna be with him.

She eyed me from the side. Saw I was smiling.

That doesn't bother you?

No! C'mon, let's keep goin.

Next to some building with a shop selling something, not food, sat a bus. The driver was starting the engine. A small, rather obese guy with glasses. We ran over, not caring where it was headed as long as it was away … from here. It only had seats in front, otherwise it was empty, apart from a few crates. If he'd tried to throw us off, I probly woulda pulled the gun. We'd had it up to here with Ušanica. I let Sister do the negotiating, she's prettier. But the guy … it pissed me off, Černá may be petite, but when she sticks out her chest … gave her an appraising look. It's not like I care if some fella looks her over. My eyes're active too. It's those disgusting market looks that go right for the price. Since that time in Berlun I've been sensitive to that stuff. I couldn't hear what they were talkin about over the roar of the engine. Shoulda been more on guard with my sister.

She came back … furious, guess he musta gotten raunchy with her. Who wouldn't, girl in distress.

What's his deal?

Aw, you know these fuckheads … laid all sortsa bullshit on me, yeah, you know. Plus I think he's drunk. Czech.

Where we goin?

It's cool, said he's going through a place where there's a railway hub to Prague, ends at some market near the border with Hungary, some Kyselice* or somethin.

Hungary, that's weird. An what's the first place?

He said Hungary, maybe there's Hungarians there, I donno. An that hub's in the Czech Lands! We're in luck.

What's it called?

Ahh, said Sister softly … some Bezbožice.*

Hah, not a chance! Are you crazy? It's obvious! Forget it, hey, we're outta here …

Take it easy. Wait a sec.

She grabbed my hand, which helped.

Let's go to that Kyselice or whatever. He's got a stall there, there's a market, there'll be connections.

What's he sell?

Donno. He didn't say.

But the way she said it was weird somehow. After a while we dozed off again. The bus rocked us to sleep. And the landscape around us was empty, I noticed during the short time I was awake. Fields. A road or two. And the occasional scarecrow stuck up on a pole.

Up an at em, kids, nighttime! The fella stood in front of us, circles of sweat under his arms, swaying side to side, the bozo, uninviting guy.

Brother, said Černá astonished, he's gropin me!

The big man slid his paw off her breast, made a playful face, said: Hoho! Enjoy the snooze? I'm Pepek, an you're the only menagerie in my parlor, we'll eat in a while, gang! An shoot the shit a little.

I eyed him incredulously as he fondled Černá's thigh.

Sister … this guy's a suicide case, I blurted.

Ah, so you're siblings! Said to myself right away, an I'll take your word on it, sir … seein as you two're on the lam, you lamsters! You two … what? Addicts, that or you pulled some heist. Sit down! That paw of his was stronger than I expected. Gripping my shoulder, as she lay there feebly like … some body dragged outta the river … he kept it there. As it stands, you owe me a pretty nice wad for the trip, but I don't want any horror shows, the young lady here's quite a piece of work. I mean, compared to what's around. Ride with me an we'll make a deal, shake on it.

What do you want?

Little missy here knows. She's not so much a snoozerist as some people. A fine little brother you are! She's a bright girl all right. One week an you'll have enough for a trip around the world! An a shower'll do the trick. You know that one, right … lady goes to the doctor …

We know it.

Then off we go. Brake an skid, the squeal of speeding wheels … hah-hah!

Our driver settled in at the wheel. Černá didn't say a word.

Tell me, what's up … an I bet if you had your shades, you'd be puttin em on right now. What'd you cook up with him while I was asleep?

Nothin, are you crazy! He's a jerk … wants me to sleep with him or whatever.

Wanting's okay, I'm not surprised, who wouldn't, with you … you're a nice piece of work, although, then again … we're not seventeen anymore, Sister!

I think this is some kina travelin whorehouse or somethin, she said.

Let's take off then, this guy stinks, hey look, a village. Stop! I hollered, getting to my feet.

Wait … Černá tugged at me, let him drop us off first an then we can split.

No, we're goin now. But he wouldn't stop till I kicked the steering wheel. Didn't get pissed, pity.

Don't get off here, you'll be stuck. I didn't mean it!

Outside the windows it was hopping. A market, I guess, people all over, wooden carts, hens, looked lively … but otherwise, maybe we really were near Hungary.

There's gotta be a bus or a train around here.

There's nothin here! Puszta!* What're you, blind? Take my word for it, c'mon, not another word about your girl, promise, I was only jokin. How was I sposta know you're such a priss.

Open the door. Černá, let's go!

Pepek exploded: Go on then, beat it, the hell with you. I had a sick little shit like you at home … ingrate!

We stood on a mucky village green. It must've been what was left of my mystical third eye that saw the hustle and bustle, through a cataract most likely … a few splintered wagons sitting in puddles, but otherwise not a soul, a dog trotted past. The squat cottages' roofs … guess that must be thatching. They had tiny little windows, most of the yards were filled with bizarre odds and ends. All of it made of wood. Sister touched my hand and I saw … some old crone walking through the puddles in a black dress with a huge wig on. Carrying a hen with its head hanging off, throat slit. We looked at each other. Over there's a … tavern, Černá pointed. Looked more like a shed. Three old fogies in black coats standing out in front, it was odd, as we passed them … standing silently, breeze ruffling their beards, some ropes or something dangling from their waists … Sister and I noticed the breeze right away. It was cold. A frosty föhn. She shivered, let's go in an ask, she said. Inside it was all wood. Not a single poster, or TV, still rely on their imaginations out here. A couple tables occupied, the whole place was quiet … no one paid us any attention … I looked for a menu … not a one … on the wall opposite sat an old fella, also in a long black frock, caftan or somethin, nibbling at an egg, dog at his feet, yolk drippin all over his beard … innkeeper leaned on the counter, like a character out of an old movie, a cap on, full beard too … all of the guys had caps on their heads. I looked at Černá … her face had turned all pointy and pale … for once I looked for the sign, little brother, but there is none … no, there wasn't a cross on the wall … but that's normal in dives … I know where we are, said Sister, looking out the window, over there, GOLETICA,* only it's written all funny. Never heard of it, I said, at the next table sat a guy with a red nose, belting back the hard stuff … also without a word, and in his hand he had a whip, a coachman's I guess, but a book sat at his elbow, an old one apparently, all black … the coachman had a jacket on, not a black robe, he stood out a little from the mournful haggard band around him. And I think he reminded me of … someone … his features. Look at him, I told my mate, it's weird, it's like I know him … hah, that's how you're gonna look if you don't watch it with the booze, yep, he's got your nose, my dear. It's incredible, Sister said softly. It gave me the chills. I'm a little superstitious, I admit. Member that hen, Černá, uch, there's somethin in the air here an they're actin like they don't see us. Should I go to the counter, I inquired of my love. Not that I wanted to. Hold on, that girl's tryin to tell you somethin, do you know her? Really, I hadn't noticed her before … a beautiful girl … standing at the counter looking at me … up until that moment, I'd never seen eyes you could fall into, tunnels to somewhere, sparkling with light, grabbing hold and not letting go, like her long dark hair, I wanted to tell Černá, but my throat was choked … that girl, I donno her, but … raising her fingers, she put them to her lips, and then made a V sign … she was speaking in letters, I realized, saying: VOICE, and again VOICE, and again … I rose … Černá grabbed my hand, I'd forgotten she was there. No, don't go, said Černá, let's get outta here, nobody's sayin a word an now they're watchin ... she got up and led me out, I felt pain, physical pain ... like something tearing inside my body, touched my fingertips to my chest ... I knew if I left now I'd never see that girl again, and it made me sorry, her fingers and hands were moving faster and faster as Černá dragged me out, telling me VOICE, HANA, VOICE, HANA, and then again I saw her eyes.

I saw infinity and the chill of it.

Real treat, that little brother a yours, always zonked out, or'd you put a spell on him, c'mere, you little chinny you ... I leaped out of my seat and the guy dropped his hand. We weren't alone on the bus anymore. Some woman was in the other seat. That's Vlasta, Pepek introduced her, you're ridin together now, we'll be on the spot in roughly an hour.

Černá, why'm I always sleepin?

You always told me you didn't sleep enough.

Maybe it's cause with you I feel good. Either that or I'm comin down with somethin.

I hope not, we gotta make it somewhere. Else.

We are somewhere else.

Vlasta came and sat down with us, it was obvious what she was. But she seemed pretty nice.

How'd Pepan find you guys? How old're you, you're a young girl, where ya from?

Černá told her something.

So you gonna work for Vandas?

Then she edified us. Vandas was Greek or Hungarian, kind of like the ruler of the market, the local boss. Probly a real gorilla. Vlasta kept rambling on about him, evidently worshiped the guy. I didn't listen much, drifting off again, knowing Černá'd keep her ears perked up in case of any info ...

19

AT THE MARKET. THE SPINACH BAR, SHE SMILES.
IT HAPPENS. AN I GO. I'VE GOT A SONG. THE EARTH SHAKES.

The market was outside town. But. This was a market of the dregs, next to this Berlun was some place with a Ku'damm. Some place. Here was whirling chaos, protoplasm with a face or two peekin out here an there, most of em pretty scary. This was something unfinished, something that vanishes at the moment it's conceived. An anomaly. What I saw hadn't been in any photos yet. And never will be. Maybe on some scrolls from someplace in China, but the people here were a mix. It no longer exists, except in my mind, and the images in there stack up on top of each other fast. Many of the people I'm sure aren't alive anymore. Definitely not the ones who could've been worse off. And the ones who made a profit and hung on are somewhere else.

Not long ago I was flipping through *Global Magnates Annual.* There was a guy in there that looked very much like Vandas. Donating a check to Charity. Caught in the act with a flash. Posing in paper eternity with the outstanding figures in politics, society, and culture from one of the key nations.

No, this wasn't Berlun, or the Pearl. Pointy leather caps, the whizzing of arrows, that muddled image of the marauder flashed across the screen at the base of my consciousness, I've got it in my cells like the degenerate city mongrels have the wolf howl in theirs.

In the distance, through the near-sheer air, lay a little town I didn't even want to imagine, the vanguard of the housing estates was bad enough, and in the other distance, since wherever I stand is where the universe divides, was flatland, a steppe maybe, puszta. We were definitely near some border. This was the bottom. It was a mixture, the dregs of Eastern Europe, mainly Russian, Polish, and Romanian hucksters. But the kind that had nowhere else to go. Černá and I strolled through the stands, most of the stuff on blankets, in shoeboxes, in vegetable crates, on plastic tarps. From toothbrushes to bayonets. Ugh, Sister, what did Adam an Eve see when they took walks in Eden? Bubbling brooks, willows, friendly monkeys, apples … don't take it as a reproach, Sister, uh-uh!

I'm over it now. Yeah, said Sister. There was tons of Soviet Army surplus, like a smalltime ragpicker's crazy dream, backpacks and uniform parts all over, who'd wear that in this country, I wondered, c'mon, people wanna live. Some of the uniforms were filthy, this was no bridge in Prague, maybe they were for scarecrows. I was intrigued by a set of green scales with a label in Russian: Military Command, Second Army, what had it weighed, off in some kitchen, measuring out into mess tins the daily dose for shit, the daily dose for survival, they had the mess tins too, even spotted a few that were unmistakably prison-issue, the kind that once upon a time dripped tea and gravy onto my hands through holes in the wall, and sometimes a message would appear on the bottom — *Charter 77, I want pussy,* or *Good grub!* — the bottom's always got some extra surprise to keep the Dark One from gettin bored. The bayonets were kept chastely hidden under a blanket, unlike the army alarm clocks and Zenit cameras they'd kept their shine and still looked functional.

Listen to this, Černá, there was a kid in my class at school that useta have a camera like that. They took us for military training, just the boys, down to the basement of a school on Havel Marketplace where they had a shooting range made outta mats an pieces a wood, an we shot at targets, an when the instructor took off we got this horse, you know, like they use for gymnastics? an set up a big bakelite doll, someone stole it from the caretaker's daughter, her they left alone. Then they spread the legs, which were the color of meat, that's the only way I can put it, an wedged em in the grips. It was a lot more fun nailin her than some dumb paper targets. I pegged her twice, once in the belly, once in the eye. We blew her to shreds. Bajza was a good shot, Hála too, I remember. Then Lucky Boy whipped out his Zenit an snapped a picture of us with our target, the artificial corpse. Made a mint, I'm tellin ya, everyone wanted a copy. Little boys do that sorta thing, I don't think it means anything. Or does it?

You have no idea what little girls do.

I can dig up the photo, I've still got it back at Gasworks somewhere. Wanna see how I looked when I was nine?

No, I don't think so.

If you can imagine, I used to be pretty scrawny.

Yeah, it's possible. People change.

When I hit puberty, I started eatin more and goin out with girls.

They musta flipped their lids over you.

We ambled through the sorry emporium … eyeing the Rambo T-shirts and the cocky little mutts getting tangled up in everyone's legs. Reigning over the market was a huge tent … filthy, there's no other word for it. Inside were crates piled high with wares, stacks of cosmetics, sixth-rate doodads, clips, bellybingers, shampoos, mostly women rummaging through them. On the other side was a huge cauldron with a fire underneath … reminded me of an upside-down bell … I stepped up … goulash? blurted a tall fat guy, drenched in sweat, his gut cloaked in an unbelievably disgusting apron … still, when I saw that intriguing slop, heat coming off it in waves, I couldn't resist … he stood looking through me … at Černá … one goulash, *egy gulyás,* man, I alerted him … nem, two, he said, you are two, *kettő* … he tossed two servings into bowls and set them down on a board laid across two kegs, Černá, curious, stepped closer … know how to say my name in Hungarian? my loved one asked as we finished eating … no, an I'd rather not … Fekete, isn't that pretty? Amazing. Hey, those peppers pack a punch, I told her, I could go for a …

You want? the goulash seller asked me, eyes glued to Černá.

No, I answered for Sister too.

In one part of the tent was a guy selling vegetables, all colors, big and little, jumbled together. We traipsed through the market this way and that, taking in the curios and costume jewelry, a closeout sale of the most hideous junk … this is all gonna disappear, Černá. In any other country they'd sic a bulldozer on it … I saw entire orchards of ashtrays, all of em the same, inscribed with the name MITROPA … at one end of the market sat a few cars, some clunky old Pobedas, a Trabant, and a Czech model I call the Coma … we trudged through the sand and the dust, perusing the people and what they were selling, at a stand with red wine I had to lean on my little sister … laugh all you want, Černá, but I'm totally touched, check out those deer figurines, the way they're crumblin to pieces, look at all those Lenins, an hey, Jesus an Mary! Stop yellin or I'll buy you one, she warned … I must've seen a hundred of those beer mugs with Švejk's portrait … I'm all soft an my insides're trembling, take a look, Černá, this is our last chance to see this stuff … c'mon, it's abominable … yeah, but I mean I've seen it all my life an so've you an now it's gonna be gone … hey look … at one of the stands they had maps and charts, I recognized a pterodactyl … probly robbed a school … what for I donno, schools're broke, everyone's in byznys these days … how bout that stuffed weasel, or is it a marten? butterflies! a hedgehog … aright, Sister, I know it's abominable an lotsa these people're nothin but dim-witted snot-nosed burglars, but wait'll they plow it all over with ads … let's get another bottle, I can't stand it, my head's spinnin … then I went to one of the stands and sold my jacket, it was pretty mangled but partly leather, got a warm-up jacket instead and felt better right away, didn't stick out so much … Listen, Brother, looks to me like there's a halfway normal bar over there, let's go in for a while, I gotta wash up a little … I took off the warm-up. It was like surfacing on another map. Clean and empty. But the waiters snapped to attention the second the door creaked open. Černá gave them a gracious nod, and I was grateful for the healthy SUPER DISCO glowing on my chest. I ordered something, wine I guess, and stared out the glass wall at the insectlike swirl of the market, the merchants didn't come in here, this spot, strategically placed by the road, was probably for tourists only, they'd occupied it just in time. Maybe even too soon. The kellners spoke German, I gave it a shot and they melted. Germany? I said to keep the conversation moving, and Ich bin turist … aus Nederland! Austria, the waiter bowed gallantly. Spinat pitsa, I read off the menu, zwei mal, bitte. Ja. I'll surprise my beauty, we can't just drink all the time … I haven't had this kind before, she said, is it … sea spinach? Never come across anything like it before, maybe it's seaweed though … from the Sargasso. From the Dead Sea … steeped in salt, an I'm thirsty, said Sister, flashing her freshly brushed teeth. A ray of light pierced the glass. Over the bar was a photo of a veteran with a mike, plus some ballerinas and a pair of surefire actors. Black Numa in gloves was up there too, snarling at us through his dagger sheath. And I told her. Everything. I told her what happened with She-Dog. I don't know if it was courage or if I was just too big a coward to bear it alone anymore.

We stopped eating. She stared at her paper napkin. After a while the waiter turned up. Schmeck gut? Ja, natürlich. Picking the spinach out of the crust with her fork, Sister said: I'll never forget this spinach. And then she smiled at me.

I don't remember leaving there. I had that smile inside me. Outside it had turned chilly, I put my warm-up back on. Through the glass I spotted the waiter. Černá waved goodbye to him. We'd left all our cash there. That spinach pitsa was expensive.

And then … I babbled incessantly, we'd had a lot to drink … Černá wanted to walk into town, take off … I talked her into staying, to observe life … in a few spots there were fires burning, apparently some of the marketeers spent their nights here too. By one of the fires we saw Pepek and Vlasta, the only people we knew. They had slivovice. We sat down with them. Holding hands.

In the morning we woke with a start all at once. We were on the bus, wrapped in a blanket. But the inside looked different, divided in two by plywood, with a mat on the floor in one part. As we clambered out rather groggily, we saw the bus was adorned with a plywood sign: MASSAGE PARLOR, it said, with a painting of … the Věstonice Venus,* I joked … but I wasn't laughing. The bus steps chilled my feet. There were other coaches too, most of em full of wares. A greasy-lookin guy or two waking up and starting breakfast. Hungover … we straggled through the market as it came to life … I looked to see if there were any tomatoes lyin around at least … it's awful here, Sister, sorry, mea culpa. Huh? Well, if you're done with the tour an you've said your goodbyes, let's clear out … better hitch, that new jacket a yours, you are stylin! Well well, look who's out of bed already, sweetiepie and … honeybun, come and have yourselves a nice cup of coffee, the day's under way, you need nourishment, no fasting! It was Pepek, sitting in the tent and waving. I went in first, yeah, to say our goodbyes … to the pimp. Vlasta was sitting there too. In her face I could see the truly devastating effects of the previous night. She was coverin em over with makeup. How old're you anyway? I hissed to Černá in our language. Twenny-six now, why. You look younger, Sister. An how bout you? The same, I lied. I guess I'm infantile, a bum, an all that. I'm feelin down. Yeah, said Černá, but the coffee's good. Mr. Vandas here would like to ask you, Pepek pointed to the fat guy who'd served us the goulash the day before … so that was the boss makin lecherous eyes at my girl … what language do you speak? Oh we were just foolin around, said Černá, sipping her coffee. Otherwise we speak normal, Czech.

And then it began. Something happened to me. Like I lapsed. All day long I was racin around in the whirl and the hum, draggin Černá behind me. She was patient with me, after all I'm pretty witty. And then, that morning, as we were sitting there drinking our coffee … Pepek half-jokingly offered her a job, Vlasta nodded her head … into the tent walked two cops, I broke out in sweat, they settled in next to Vandas and poured themselves a cup of coffee, gabbing away, Slovaks … Pepek tugged at my sleeve, winking and sticking out his tongue, want an intro, those two're the filthiest officers under the sun, you bet your ass … eagerly he regaled me with incredible anecdotes from Vandas's dizzying career … making no attempt to hide his admiration … an you bet you got me to thank that you're sittin here with him now … yep, an your sister too, heh, skinny, but nice tits on her … shut up, I said, more astonished than anything else … c'mon, that's just guy-talk, Pepek said with a smirk … bullshit … now that's more like it … like I was sayin, those officers're real dogs an they bark when Vandas tells em to, get it? I got it all right, so did Sister.

Vandas, Vandas. He made and sold the goulash himself. Guess he enjoyed it. Slicing meat. He had a few flunkies around, why he put up with Pepek I don't get. Vandas was there to handle taxes and also served as arbiter. Determined who set up shop and where. Who got the nod and who got the boot, who started and who was finished.

Me and my little sister understood his arrangement with the local cops all too well. Maybe that's why she wasn't in a hurry and let me screw around the market. Seriously, it was like a lapse. By afternoon I was drunk again. In my euphoria I traded my pants and belt for a pair of fatigues. Even got some cash, the transaction took more than half an hour, and I think both me and the small Asian man got more satisfaction from the exchange of words than from the deal itself. While I changed, behind some shack, I got so wrapped up in looking forward to scarin Černá that my pistol nearly fell out. Couldn't be easier to buy a holster, I mumbled, a dozen shapes an sizes … but I bought another bottle instead. The pants were big on me.

I made friends at the stands, swaggered … in the dust. Listened. One thing I found out was that in Albanian "death" is *vdakya* and "prison" is *burg*. The first one sounds almost too Slavic to be true, and on hearing the second my brain floods with delicacies from McDonald's, does it mean anything? My verdict was yes. Most of the storytelling took place at the cologne stand. If those flasks weren't stolen, then I'm Pako Rabon. But they didn't swipe em in Cologne. One pharmacy there sprayed their flowers with the stuff. Why all the biggest storytellers and fibbers congregated by the perfumes, I don't know. Maybe it was the Albanian girl. I pointed her out to Černá. That's kina how you useta look ten years ago! Y'know she keeps starin at me? Sittin there starin … An that Gypsy lady tells fortunes. Know what she told me, Sister?! Where'd you dig up those pants, holy shit! So what … I rolled up the cuffs, they're big. You know why they always lie? So one day they can tell the truth. You just keep on lyin an lyin an then nobody knows when you finally come clean. But you get it outta your system. That's the thing about storytellers, little sister! Pity old Homer's dead, but nah, he'd probly be splicin movies, these days …

I know I was still with Černá when they rounded up the horses. For Vandas. Whole herd disappeared. Most of the riders were Gypsies. Then the days started flashing by. One night I got in a fight with some guy by the fire. Rolled around on the ground was all. The fun wore off fast. I got scared he'd lifted it. Luckily I went back to the spot later on and found the gun.

Somethin's wrong with you, said Černá as we snuggled inside the bus. Pepek and Vlasta were snoring away on the mat.

I donno what it is, Černá, I wanna but I can't. Sposedly it's normal. He doesn't wanna!

You're too drunk. Not like you usually are. Not like with me. You're not happy.

Today, Černá, I saw, they got this bigget an they do fights … out by that cabin they got this mud hut built into the ground, an they stick him in there an let rats loose. I won three hundred. It was sick the way he snarfed those things. It was insane. I thought he'd just bite em, I didn't realize. Maybe they're actually mice.

My sweet … snap out of it, we gotta get outta here, c'mon, right now. You're … sorry, you don't exactly smell like flowers.

Yeah, it's the dust. Černá, we're never gonna see this again, it's all gonna disappear.

But c'mon, it's revolting.

But you're gorgeous. A woman's not a woman next to you.

They're wasted, if I lived like them, you'd see! C'mon, let's go.

Wait'll morning, I really feel weird.

But in the morning … in the morning Černá sold her jacket … then I saw her with Vlasta scraping a stack of potatoes for goulash. And Vlasta! A couple times I'd seen the line at the bus, guys making small talk, smoking while they waited … it was the market's top draw, that Massage Parlor. One time I was standing there and it struck me that if Černá … he said in a week we'd have enough for a trip around the world, but that sick shit … and besides, without a shower, just a washtub … better me go in there than her … it was too much.

Černá! Is he still buggin you? She rolled over next to me.

Who?

Pepek. For you to do like Vlasta.

Don't be stupid. Sober up, or don't even bother, let's go.

What's Vlasta like?

Pretty okay. Run-down though. One minute she's buggin me to do it, sayin it's no big deal, the next she's tellin me to beat it while I can. Says rubber makes her teeth numb. An know what else she told me? That some a those guys've never seen a lady naked before! Ones from the sticks, the mountainmen, just in the dark, she says. Yeah, they go nuts over her. An then some of em, get this … some a the old-timers that just saw porn for the first time? They think that's the only right way to do it … has to be if they printed it!

How'd she hook up with Pepek?

Donno, I'd say they're related. She's nice though, just stupid.

Are they married?

Donno.

Cut my hair.

You really want me to? How come?

Donno. I just do.

She borrowed a pair of scissors from Vlasta. Afterwards I was more naked, it felt weird, next morning I found myself a cap. A flat one.

Least you won't get lice. I never saw your head like that before.

You like it?

It's yours.

Černá, c'mon, it's just a disguise, c'mon, we're losin it. Tomorrow … we hit the road.

But with the rags we had on, we didn't stand a chance hitching anyway. I burned the hair.

Černá began working in the kitchen, in the tent. I checked it out right away … Vandas had disappeared somewhere, probably on business. He wanted her, I could tell. Pepek kept an eye on the johns, got drunk, fought with Vlasta, and in his free moments prowled around the Spinach Bar, begging whenever travelers from the better countries passed through. Knew the spiel in umpteen languages bout the entrepreneur who'd missed his train. Putting on a face that said "honest to the bone." Sometimes they'd toss him a few pfennigs. Usually, though, they drove through pretty fast. The Austrians behind the glass must've been pretty sad about their strategic location. Europe just couldn't quite unify somehow. The ecu wasn't happening. Spinach is gonna go on the block, I laid it out for the manager.

Sometimes during the day they'd put a few tables outside, I'd go and drink coffee. The waiters knew by now I was no Dutch boy, but they didn't care. They also knew I wouldn't break anything, and that I'd pay.

After I told Černá though, I never went back inside. I'd sit under an umbrella, drinking one bitter espresso after the next, curing myself of my hangover. I had one constantly. Coffee brought me back. When I had the cash. Every now and then Černá'd slip me a little something, but usually I had luck with the bigget. There was just one trick to it. Most of the bettors were passin through, so even though a lot of em were countryfolk, they didn't notice at first … the more of em he ate, the lazier he got. The farmers usually expected him to bite one rat and then go for the rest. But the rats … would go into a frenzy when they realized they couldn't escape … they'd start biting, and he'd slow down. It was simple. Usually the guys seeing the show for the first time got burned. Cause to start with the dog was ferocious and fast. And the start was what got the inexperienced bettors hot to trot. Štefan, the mutt's owner, and me cut a deal. He noticed me. Then I lured people in for him.

Černá … maybe because I'd told her … I was a little shy around her. I knew we had to take off, it pounded in my brain every day. But as long as Vandas was gone, I wasn't worried about her. And maybe we were both a little scared to head out on the road again.

I bummed around the marketplace, made a few connections, I knew I could sell the gun and there'd be cash. But I was saving that as a last resort. Just like that last round. In one of my clearer moments, I was sitting with Černá by the pump, over near the Spinach Bar, and I looked at my sister … and I was startled … Sister, you've got wrinkles too … around your nose, an here's a silver hair … I know, she said, I've had that ages, didn't you notice, an so what? … nothin, it's nice … but … something about her was strange, and then suddenly I saw what … she had on a dress, an ordinary dress, the kind women wear … in the kitchen … she'd sold her old stuff, or traded it … this's gotta stop, it's like we're in a trap … Černá, I'm sellin the gun an that's that! We're outta here. I patted Madonna under my shirt to make it official. You talk with Pepek? I steer clear a that moron … I met a guy, says his name's Štefan, an he's got a car … Pepek says those officers've been askin around about us, says some guy an a girl held up a gas station nearby … yeah, so? Don't you get it, as long as we're with Vandas, it doesn't matter what we did … but the cops're lookin for them, an if they happen to nab us somewhere … then y'know, you know … Sister, if we go with Štefan, he's got family in Hungary … hey, we got no cash, no ID, we can't even buy food, are you nuts?! I got the pistol. Sell it, but watch out. I mean, you know … that Greek, or whoever he is, you know damn well he wants to get me into bed, an how're we sposta protect ourselves? What're you talkin about, c'mon, you're with me! You're so fulla shit … how many times've you been drunk or off with your buddies while he was hittin on me? An how many people has he got around here?! He can do anything. Is he harassin you? No, cross my heart, an that's what scares me. Maybe he wants more than just to sleep with me, maybe that's why he's so serious. Aha, I said thoughtfully. An you know he's got that Pepek guy, like his jester or whatever … an know what he told me? What? He told me he admires me for scrapin potatoes instead a doin that, an that if I did … he says Pepek goes berserk when Vlasta's on the rag, low turnover, the brute says … if I did do it, he said, he wouldn't like me anymore … Černá, I'm amazed, you blushed just now, damn, it's flattering on you! Listen, little brother, this dress is from him, since you obviously don't give a shit. Huh? You just don't get it, if it wasn't for Vandas I couldn't even walk through this market alone practically … an what'm I, a bar singer … an you … who're you … honey? What're we, what've we got, what the hell've we got … nothin. That's the way it is. What've you got to say? What've you got to say for yourself … you're a wreck. Those rats're makin you stupid. Vandas may be horrible, but at least he's a man. But you're my sister … Yeah, I am. Don't worry, I hugged her, squeezing her tight but … gingerly … Like I said, I'll sell the gun, an we'll round up some clothes an hop a train, an in two days everything'll be back to normal.

I trust you, she said. But I don't have much strength left. We can't stay here anymore. Do something.

I did. I went to find Štefan to tell him about the pistol. But along the way I got caught up in an argument with some asshole. We made up over a bottle and went to place our bets. I took him and then bought another bottle. The vodka with the skull on the label, most expensive stuff they had. I didn't want to see her after that. I slept outside, just peeked in to make sure she was there. She was lying down already. I'll stand guard … I can see the door from here, I said to myself. Reflecting off the metal stairs, the moon chilled my eyes till I fell asleep. Next morning she woke me up. See you at Spinach, she said. You okay for coffee?

Yeah.

After two I felt better. After the third she finally came. Looking pretty fresh, it was the dress … actually it suits you. It really does, Černá … if those fan clubs a yours could see you though …

Yesterday I wanted to hurt you … but you were asleep. Lucky you! Černá said angrily. You have no idea how worried I was where you were. I wanted to take the pistol. I'm gonna sell it myself.

Uh-uh, darlin, I said. I'm outta your league.

I don't wanna be in your league. I want outta here. An fast. Or somethin bad's gonna happen, I can feel it.

She got up and walked to the pump. Two rusty-haired curs lapped at the damp stones. Suspicious, they looked up, the bigger one bristling, showing his teeth. Shoo varmint, I'll tap you one, she said, pumping the handle. The dogs crept warily toward the stream of cold water splattering against the stones, both flashing their canines.

From my vantage point by the watering hole, day in, day out, I could see why the stray dogs, living off whatever they could beg, scavenge, or steal, had plenty of reasons not to trust anything human. Their lifestyle fit the marketeers' to a T, only they didn't drink, do drugs, smoke, or blaspheme at all, I don't think. It occurred to me that afterwards … they'll have a better chance. When they go riding off on that doggy shinkansen. Anyone anyplace on this shared planet of ours who says dogs don't have a soul is an idiot, I don't care how high up he stands in his worldly church. He could have a cap a gold an a cassock to his heels, I'd still think ill of him.

The canine bandits' purchasing power was of course negligible. Unless you call a bone for a kick, a lump of suet for a rock in the head, commerce. They traveled in the market's lowest circle, a whole pack of them.

Pepek teetered over from his post at the Spinach Bar and tried to give Černá a slap on the ass, fuck off, she told him, irritated. The pimp turned his attention to the dogs instead. Pussycat doesn't want any, so I'll give the pooch a pet, he said, but he didn't. The mutts froze, baring their fangs. Pepek went on a while giving us his spiel, which we now knew by heart, and then staggered off toward a carload of German tourists. He was a professional, the instant he caught wind of prey his swaying frame would tighten up, a look of "reluctant and perhaps somewhat humble pride" appearing in his eyes and spread across his boozy face like a map of freshly conquered territory. No doubt he had already zeroed in on the Germans climbing out of their car as he donned the mask of the "well-meaning lush" for us, hand outstretched toward Černá's body. He didn't really want to touch her, he knew by now.

The dogs, who had meanwhile retreated to a safe distance, slowly began creeping back, scanning the area cautiously, and when neither of us made a move they drank. The smaller one, with a speckled muzzle, had a rope around his neck with tiny red sores underneath. Probly considered it pointless to belong to anyone. His big brother had one dead eye. After drinking their fill, they slunk off on their bellies to about a meter away from us, hoisted themselves with dignity, and trotted off. I didn't see them again till a few minutes later. Černá stormed off, splashing water at me. She was mad. Today I make a move with our fate, I promised myself. She's scraped enough potatoes. And as for me … aright then, bye, I bid farewell to that dusty place, to the mountains of junk, I know what's cookin here, I know what it's all about. I can tell. I've got every stand, every one a those ugly mugs inside me, an that's not it. But actually I donno too much else. What'm I gonna do? The Austrians brew their coffee without grounds, I tossed back the whole cup, gargling a little for fun. The waiter, who'd been staring at Černá the whole time, turned away from the glass in disgust. Closin time, I said to myself, letting the water stream over my face, it sloshed into the mud in the drain, pump creaking, like a requiem, I thought.

Just then they came tearing over, accompanied by screams and curses in Hungarian. The puny dog dashed out in front, the big one lagged a little behind, tripped over a huge carrot jutting out of his mouth.

The dogs took cover under a bus, a battered Czech coach. From their insistent, soft, menacing growls it was plain they had no intention of giving up the carrot. The bus belonged to a crew of Gypsies who'd just pulled in. They communicated with Vandas in Russian until the basket seller, a shady character, stepped in to translate. It looked like Vandas wanted to be done with the dogs once and for all. His tent, full of heat and smells, full of food, must've been a big draw for them. The Gypsies were apparently arguing that no one was gonna mess with their bus while the dogs were underneath it. Hard to say if they were hoping for some doggy delight, or if they just didn't want to fall afoul of whoever owned the little thieves, but they most definitely weren't eager to have anyone poking around that bus of theirs with who knew what inside … all those oddballs, lured out of inactivity and away from their byznysses by Vandas's furious uproar, cause there's only so long you can go on peddling T-shirts of Batman, who flies wherever he wants, while your average guy's gotta stick it out in the heat, picking his nose, waiting for a miracle … and the most he's got to look forward to's a bottle of rotgut. Or Vlasta.

You can't argue, haggle, steal, and wheel and deal all day long either, and Vandas's efforts, assuming he could penetrate the dogs' defense, promised to be an exciting spectacle for the growing crowd. Tiring of his debate with the Gypsies, who were gently but emphatically trying, with several willing interpreters' help, to persuade him to forget the dogs, the boss got down on the ground. His paunch brushed the soil, leaving it armored the rest of the day in a sticky plating of dirt, goulash grease, and sweat. From his back pocket he fished out a piece of metal, which with a click like a quiet "yes" turned into a lengthy dagger, and plunged under the bus, poking and stabbing. He wheezed with the effort, it wasn't about the carrot now, for him or the dogs. The people from the market accompanied him with advice and jeers in several languages, while the Gypsies, who'd stiffened a bit on first seeing the dagger, exchanged haughty grins. They looked like they would've preferred to settle things fair and square with the mutts, after all they had sought asylum with them. I wanted to get up and walk away. But I didn't budge. Screaming, Vandas yanked out his now empty hand, gushing blood, from under the bus, raised it skyward and collapsed on his back, it was shredded up to the elbow. Now the dogs had the carrot *and* the dagger. The crowd howled with laughter. One of the dogs barked and charged out into the legs. The crowd rippled to the sound of sparse applause, legs dodging as the dog snapped at them wildly, rising, falling, stirring up clouds of dust, until eventually one well-aimed kick drove the dog back under the bus. Growling, he crawled off into the back where he couldn't be seen, it was the one with the bad eye, the big one, the carrot thief. The little one didn't show himself. Vandas was back on his feet now, holding his hand while some woman tried, unsuccessfully, he wouldn't keep still, to wrap it in a wet rag. He fed bills to the Gypsies. Urged them to run over the dogs, I gathered, they just shrugged their shoulders, telling him, Nyema benzina, nein gazka, neni petrol, sir, looked like they were squeezing enough out of him for a good couple kilometers instead of the short stretch it'd take for a dog's backbone.

Pepek appeared behind Vandas holding a long pole, the kind used in proper households to prop up the clothesline, nails set in one end to hold the line in place.

I was waiting for a swarm of good spirits to appear, a gracious princess, say, for Rambo to suddenly step down off the T-shirts, for I myself to be gifted with the power of a bull that I might scoff at death, O Lord, if I were to save a single canine beast, though he may return the favor by chewing off my finger, surely my karma would bump up a notch at least. But I didn't get up.

Pepek took the pole and began flailing furiously and methodically into the space where the sparse heat-scorched grass gave way to the dusty earth of the road, flailing, where did that alkie find the strength, flailing, and surely the prospect of bolstering his gainful friendship with the merchant boosted his strength, flailing, and the growling changed to wailing, dog moans, an unbroken litany, an animal prayer of agony, the crowd stood quietly around the bus, occasionally someone shook his head, spat with a hiss, shouted out a curse or word of advice, then Pepek scraped out a quivering dog, belly punched open, head bashed in, and finished him off with the pole. It was One Eye. The smaller one I guess got the dagger. Caving in to public opinion, the Gypsies backed the bus up and ran the mutt over, hard to say if he was gone by then or whether he still felt the wheels. The onlookers briefly commented on the two carcasses, next to them lay the gnawed carrot, as long as the little one's trunk, mocking the life-or-death struggle of the animal kingdom. Vandas bent down to pick up the dagger, it vanished into his pocket with a click of relief. The wise guys all of a sudden remembered their stands full of junk, peppers and T-shirts and socks and bottles of vodka, and disappeared. The two carcasses were left on the road, I sat gaping at the blowflies' first reconnaissance flights, the thin ribbon of shiny ant bodies intently setting out on their promising expedition for nourishment, for the morsel that had dropped onto their plate from on high, from the heavens. The first ones went for the eyes.

Behind me the market came back to life, I listened to the sounds of Babylon, and nothing was going on. Not now. Not anymore. Maybe I oughta brighten my life with one a those T-shirts, I thought, or maybe it'd be more sensible to purge my imagination with some liquor from Vandas's tent. The spiffy waiters from the Spinach Bar disposed of the carcasses later, I heard, claimed they were bad for business.

I sat in the tent next to Černá and Vlasta, behind a mountain of potatoes. Vandas ladled out the goulash, full house today. In all about six alleged owners turned up wanting compensation for the dogs. In their greedy eulogies the dogs became the most noble of creatures, masters of the canine race, superdogs as amazing as people. Broccula'd go for at least twenny thou, he was an Irish setter! hollered a lush. What a man, what a gladiator, killed two pure-blood bidgets, they attacked him, I saw it, said someone who liked the goulash. Vandas ignored them. His hand was bandaged. Had a plastic bag slipped over it, I guess to keep from splattering the gauze. He didn't trust anyone else with that goulash.

I saw Černá wrap it for him. He held still, a dense sweat standing out on his forehead. She washed out the wound.

Learned that at St. Francis, huh? I inquired.

I just know it. She tossed a potato in the pot and reached for another.

What's that cha got, Vlasta leaned toward me. Is that silver?

Lay off, don't touch.

Why so brusque, young sir?

Calm down, Černá told me.

Got another scraper?

No.

I'll go grab a knife an help you guys.

How kind of you. But the knives're here in the tent.

Aright, I'll be back in a while.

But I wasn't. I kicked around in the dust somewhere, drinking shots and amusing myself by taking off my cap and scratching around in my crewcut, or whatever it was.

Next morning I couldn't get up. My mouth was parched, my tongue was heavy and ached. Every bone in my body was sore. There was a buzzing in my head, one minute I had the chills, the next hot flashes. I was in the bus alone. Then Pepek showed up, I could tell it was him, he kicked me in the ribs. Get the hell out, less you're interested in Vlasta, heh-heh. I tried to say something but couldn't move my tongue. Then a rush of black water came over me.

Little brother, get up, stand up …

I could hear her voice … talk to me, I said … the voice was like a waterfall, scattering into vapor before it could reach me, Černá's voice, it sounded like. I was being carried, taken somewhere.

Then I opened my eyes, I was lying in Vandas's tent behind some crates. They smelled of wood. I opened my eyes and there was a face, soft, the guy had glasses.

Well, it's about time, this'll put him back on his feet. That's no typhus, miss. Tongue like that … who knows what it's from. But he ought to get to a hospital.

Then I was looking at feet, from under the canvas I saw feet wearing clodhoppers, black shoes, age-old Masaryk half-boots, shoes flapping open like shark jaws, slipshod things with studs poking out, threads trailing off, newspaper flopping out, scuffed and muddy, sand stuck to the mud like talc on a wound, I saw snazzy moccasins and slippers with the head of Pifík the dog, flip-flops, sneakers, lots of sandals, some with rope for straps, and I saw white shoes too, and with all the dust it looked like bare ankles shuffling past on dirty white clumps, I saw bare feet too, those were children, and even waders, despite the heat, and combat boots and shabby yellow slip-ons, and all those feet were going somewhere, crossing paths and kicking up dust, I coughed and coughed, I couldn't move … and I couldn't get through them … and then I heard next to me … hold still, you slut, and pay, say it … say it now or I'll give you an exam that'll make you shit your panties … hold still, you little slut … and move it, my time doesn't come for free, say it … say you're a slut … it was strange, even with my eyes glued shut I still had those feet under my eyelids, the shoes in the dust and those sounds of sex … maybe I'm on the bus … when I opened my eyes again, it was dark, I could smell the wax in the tent canvas … and next to me lay Černá, asleep … from the other side of the crates I heard conversation, people playing cards, they had an oil lamp, I felt better … tried to stand, stumbled, grabbed hold of the crates, but it worked … I walked outside, slowly … relieved myself. Guess I had a fever still. I felt light. It was nice.

Černá … breathing deeply, fists clenched, usually, being a light sleeper like me, she woke as soon as I touched her. I stroked her hair, letting it slip through my fingers, there're the gray ones, no, they're silver. I noticed my nails were long. Černá, I breathed, moving down to her feet, my strength was coming back, I had an urge to stroke her … but no, that wouldn't be right, not when she's sleepin so soundly … she had different shoes on, must've hocked her rockers … some dull little things with fringe … wouldn't occur to her in a million years to wear somethin like that in Prague … I took them off, she didn't stir, her fingers were covered with band-aids and … she, who was always washing herself … but she didn't know I was the guy in her dream! her feet were dirty … I kissed her thumb slowly, then the nail, cracked traces of polish, she twitched her leg and sighed … like some kina little kid.

Vandas let me stay in the tent behind the crates and Černá brought me water and pills. I didn't eat much. A couple times I had half a mind … but the thought of booze now gave me bad forebodings.

I was stunned when she told me I'd been unconscious three days. Then some doctor, she said, gave me a shot, some guy Vandas knew.

Let's not talk about it, said Černá, but if it'd gone on any longer you woulda had to go to the hospital. You're still weak now, but you know we can't stay here.

Černá, there's still a possibility. I know people. You can head back to Prague on your own an find my buddy Micka. He'll give you cash. An there's other people too, maybe a phone call'd do the trick.

Listen, friend … what you don't get is if I leave, whether they let me go or I just split, Vandas wouldn't let you stay an hour. An he might … get mad. You know what I mean.

Aha. Yeah.

We'll wait till you're better. It's all we can do.

Hm.

The doctor came one more time. The guy with the soft face and glasses. He refused to make any calls or take a letter to the post office, said he didn't have time. Gave me a shot of penicillin or whatever. Didn't even want any money. He was pretty nice.

And on my first day as a convalescent I stomped through the sand, delighting in my slow motion … strolling around … then I stood in front of the bus with the plywood sign and Černá went up the Massage Parlor steps with the weary stride of a different woman. She turned around when I said her name, and her face … I'd never seen her like that. It took a while, but then she laughed, the delicate grace returned to her face … and she said: You're on your feet. What's up?

Whatcha doin in there. Cleanin?

But I already knew, she never wore makeup like that. Some of the girls in Berlun looked like that, all done up so you couldn't see much. Some clients liked it, they said. You donno who's who. You just get off.

Černá, uh-uh, get down here.

What … you're tellin me? Whadda you know, don't order me around! An besides, there's people here.

A couple of characters stood there. All guys, ugly fuckers.

Černá! C'mon, you might, I mean you might have a kid an I'll leave!

You! Ramblin on again … an what're you babblin about kids … you? She stomped up a step but then turned back to me.

Get down here! Now!

Don't yell at me!

One of the bystanders said something. Somebody spit and laughed. Someone said: Get in line. I stood in front of him. Waving my hands around, saying something. He stepped around me. The door clapped shut, she was inside. And the guy moved, walked up the stairs, went in.

I heard an odd noise, I was scared it was just in my brain.

But no, Pepek sat at the wheel, leering at me and honking: toot toot. Doing it with his mouth too. He waved to me and then joined his hands in a gesture. Somebody grabbed my shoulder and the faces went blurry. Up above was the sun. It all fused.

I walked through clumps of dirt. A field. Barbwire, with sheep on the other side. I started toward them, but the voices made me stop.

Do we kill him?

You want to? He's unconscious though.

Let's wait till he gets closer then.

It was the Shadows. But this time I saw them. Only very vaguely, one second they were ravens, the next they were bodies in outline, moving through space, two of them … I pretended not to notice … yanking wire off the fence and coiling it as if I'd been hired to … they came from the left, silently … I knew who the Shadows were … and I knew I couldn't look, holding the wire in my hand, I tread cautiously, and a new song played inside my head … one no one had ever heard yet … about old things that I knew.

All right. Here we are. Are you going to say anything?

There's no point. Ready to pounce?

Yes.

At that I made my move, horror gave me strength, and I grabbed them without looking, eyes shut tight, they thrashed around but their hearts were small, each of them fit in the palm of my hand. They died, hissing like snakes, now at a loss for words. I strung the beaks and claws on the wire. I wanted to give thanks for the victory, but was afraid what it would bring. I took the wire with the remains and wrapped it around my neck, it hurt, so I tore some bark off a tree. I wore a scarf of bark, rough and fragrant. I went through a forest of crooked trees, I was going home. I don't know how long. I steered clear of a village and slept in a haystack. I wanted to walk at night too, but the moon didn't shine. I fell and stumbled. Then I stayed on the ground, and in my mind I saw pictures of me with Sister. The two of us, tangled and naked, and not moving. Not a breath, not a hair moved, nothing. Sometimes my eyes got tired and the picture would crack. But then I figured out that if I moved my eyelids a few times fast, the color was restored and our skin was whole again. When the moon appeared, I walked all night and again I heard that song ... the one I had inside me when I tore the stuff off the Shadows and put it on the wire:

> I heard a voice
> I saw machines
> there were ravens there.
> Two black birds with whore-licked feathers
> hissing whore spit
> dripping on the hard earth I tore off the wire
> and killed them claws and beaks and wire
> became a necklace.
> The sun shone
> but it was a winter of war. I had my own religion.
> People were fodder for death, I held it in my hands
> and stroked it. And I was afraid.
> Monsters were born in blood.
> Blotches grew in the soil.
> Water washed over the dirt and the bones.
> I came to a city and found the place
> my love was there
> with a white dress on
> laughing
> and she was dead.

I sang it and I said it. It was a lot of words. Sometimes I changed them. At daybreak I was stopped by a dog. A little white puppy sat on the slope as if trying to block the way down. My head stopped buzzing with words and I tried to speak to him kindly. He backed away. Then I saw a fire, someone was sitting there. As I made my way downhill, the puppy romped around me but didn't bark even once. The person at the bottom stood. Behind me I heard a rumbling, the earth began to shake. It was like she was drawing near.

Silver

Back at the outset of it all, he bent down over me as I slept and, parting my ribs, took one, then removed my heart from the cage of my body and gave it to her; at least part of it. She left me in the room with the mirror, every path was in there too. And when I looked, bending over the shiny surface, I saw her face. Now I'm counting the shards.

20

COWS. THAT TIME IN BERLUN.

I got used to it there. And soon I knew when to run up to keep the herd from droppin off. I was alone. There on the hillside my lonely path began. It was beautiful on the hillside. Suka and Shorty herded the cows.

When you came walkin up an collapsed, I didn't know, said The One Who Herds. From the pistol I figured you for a deserter, or some gangster. Where'd you get that Chezetta? Me, I always liked the Parabella an the Beretta, specially the names. Magnum, now that's intense! That sucker can blow!

Tomáš is the first thing I remember about my new home. The look of him. Had me stumped, the herdsman. Lying there in his shack, I'd see him through the cracks in the wall, walking back and forth, poking around the fire. He looked familiar. And also: The first day I felt better, he brought milk; crouched down at the doormat, I did too; set the mug on the ground, I mimicked him, empty-handed; sat down, me too.

What're you doing? he said, confused. I repeated his words back at him. Then I told him I must have a fever still, I'd thought he was me. Or maybe it was just that aping him helped me clamber back into life.

You look familiar, he said.

So do you.

You're lucky you came this way, next valley over's old Varhola, good luck tryin to understand him. Yeh, feels good to talk normal again. Now where do I know you from, way you talk I'd say the Pearl … Galactic maybe, I useta sweep up there … or Černá's, useta play there sometimes.

Oh, now I know, I said. You had that crazy act with the wires, you're that singer … the Blue Negroes.

Yeh. Yes sir. That's ages ago. Then there was that what's-her-name.
Yeah.

I had to get away. Least for a while. All I got here's the radio. An that day you came … I had kind of a hunch. Russkies pulled a raid over the hills there in Kysucní. Lookin for deserters. Shot some girl but that was it. Tea?

No thanks.

I still had an image of her inside me, but something had happened. Sometimes I told myself I'd just … get healthy … and then head back to the market and find her. But. I couldn't bring myself to picture it, I didn't want to. The massage parlor. What she was doing. How long she'd been doing it. It was too much. It was shattered. Sometimes I had a terrible longing for Černá, sometimes my thoughts of her were like glass. But if what Tomáš had heard on the radio … then it didn't matter anyway. And maybe, it occurred to me … maybe I'd wanted it to happen to her.

Stay the rest a the season an you can make yourself some cash … my new pal said … I been out here eight months now … need a break. Out here … everyone's leavin for the city. Nobody wants to do this. It's over, puttin em out to pasture now. That or they slaughter em.

During the day there was mist in the valleys below. But at night sometimes I saw lights, just these indistinct sort of flashes, I asked Tomáš about it.

Nothin down there. Past that's Bukovina. Galicia, ever heard of it? Hasn't been anything down here for ages. Yeh, he waved to the north, you mighta run into the Milkman up there, useta be villages. Then the bolsheviks said they were buildin a dam an evacuated everyone. Never even built the thing, probly wanted to get rid a those people is all, bastards. May they an those engineers a theirs rot in hell. Understand, the Ruthenians'd been livin up there with their own customs forever. Bolsheviks came along an slapped their National Committees on top of em, but the Ruthies just kept on goin same as ever. Didn't even learn the language. Eight villages. An they were self-sufficient. Well, you get the drift … when their power got cut off, they lit candles. Didn't have fridges anyway. Didn't give a damn. Only thing they ever came down for was vodka. Rather cook their own stuff. All that's ancient history. Yep, they were Christians, you saw the crosses on the graves … but hey, in the woods around here! You watch your ass. An they all had shotguns, poachers. All the fronts rolled through here. Benderites* too. An there were partisans from the Uprising* here right up to the fifties. Started lockin em up after the war. It was all mixed out here. An that over there, the Cow Boss waved, that's Łupków Pass … mighta heard of it … not in the textbooks. Germans marched through once on their way into Ukraine, an once on their way out. What was left of em. Then the Russkies an then our guys. Sposedly an entire army clean disappeared. People saw em comin, they hid … oh yeah, they hid from all of em. With their cattle too. Just ask old Varhola! what it was like in the caves … an when they crawled out, not a soul. They say a whole army corps sank into the swamps, that's a crock. You wouldn't believe the stories the locals tell, things goin on underground. Not too many left though. Cops were still scared out here in the sixties. Only reason anyone comes out here now's to escape. Yep an then … a dam, hah! Yeah, doesn't surprise me the Milkman told you, that guy was obsessed. Churches all got blown up. Varhola says it was one a them, a Ruthenian, ran the whole thing. Then the Zmijak came an took him. Those're the kina fairy tales they got out here. Say this Zmijak lives underground. My first few days out here I didn't feel too good an I was drinkin a lot. An with all that talk a theirs, I saw him too. Know what helps? I mean if you're not useta solitude an trees … an stuff. I picked that bush over there an got used to it. It was spooky at night sometimes, like a head. Like somethin. But then I got used to it an it was fine. An when it was a head, I'd say to myself, yeah, so? An it was fine. You don't mind me talkin all the time? It's a novelty havin someone around.

No.

You might think this is old stuff, but time out here is … preserved. You don't mind me talkin about it?

No.

It suited Tomáš that I liked running up the hill. He knew what it was like already. The cows did their grazing on the slopes above the hill, and when the dogs drove them into the corral the herder had to stand there and pay attention. Because some of those clunkers were so dense they would've just kept going. Once they'd bothered to start. I nearly fled the first time the herd came thundering down, all horns and hoofs … the cows' bodies, the sun in my eyes, I was scared they would sweep me away, and Suka chasing after them, and Shorty … he was still learning, from time to time he'd catch a hoof and tumble head over heels, catch one in the skull … but he was a tenacious mutt.

Old Varhola gave me him … said he'd hafta put him under otherwise … know how I started out here? I come walkin up to the old man with my backpack on, lookin forward to the natural life, an the guy doesn't even talk practically, just cocksucker this an cocksucker that ... an, man, on a stump there's a TV set. Runnin on batteries, nonstop. So I ask ... what's this yellow flower here, sir? ... an he's ... cocksuckin yeller flower ... an goes an kicks Shorty here in the head ... I'm standin there like, aw no, this is what I ran away from ... an then I find out, two days back the pooch stole his meat. So I go, that dog doesn't even remember that now. An Varhola's like: Whudda yew know, yew heap a dung! So I shut up. Shorty really is a thief, though. I don't beat him, but the second I leave ... he's a goner.

I stood on the hill, stick in hand, for appearance' sake ... and the cows streamed past me, the first ones still at a dignified pace, then the middle of the herd, moving faster, and finally the last ones ... Suka had fun rounding up the stragglers ... and Shorty, what a clown ... barking and snapping, rolling around in the grass ... and the cows lumbered past me, snorting and snuffling ... Git along, big girl, git along, little girl, ho there, Whitey, get a move on, Bessie, an you too, Sonya, ho there! ho! ... and they rumbled past me, spotted and brown, handsome Mona and cunning Mordvina, little Bekta, and Beka too, lolling an eye my way and chewing ... and chewing ... cows, nice cows, git along there now ... yep, cows don't ask why, all they do's chew, get wet when they're expectin their bull, nothin against em though ... beautiful cows ... hola ho, go cows go, git, Mahulena, move your bones, Stáza, keep it rollin, Polka, Žveka ... ho, hop to it, ladies, ur-Slav mothers ... slide along now, Goddess, you too, Huna, ho Donna, let's go! hey there, Okta, c'mere, Muna, I slapped the cow's behind, she whipped her tail ... into my eye, it was symbiotic, I was recuperating ... leave her be, Shorty, or I'll take a stone to you. I put myself in tune with the hillside to keep the cows from falling off. Shorty would've chased them over the side ... and sometimes I had to close my eyes as the pain inside me melted ... where is she? Traitor. And who betrayed who, I said to myself, and it was unbearable.

Where's my gun?

On the shelf. Behind the books.

I gotta go.

You're crazy! Potok ... what've you got to look forward to? Elevators? Video games? Don't be a jerk, there's plenty of time. Got any cash?

No.

Then wait. I'm goin down for a week. You can take over for me, I was watchin yesterday. Suka let you pet her. So it's cool.

What good's a week?

I wanna have a drink. Go to the movies. An there's a whorehouse in Ušanica. That's right, eight months now. Last winter I was up at this one chalet. An sposedly there's girls out in Kysunica too, or whatever it's called. Know anything about it?

No. Drop it.

When he left, I didn't need to get used to any bush. I slept out by the corral, with the cows, it did me good.

I was totally empty, alone. And at night ... after the beauty of the roundup I'd have dreams. They came to me from the valley. Every night, before I fell asleep, I saw the lights down there.

When Old Varhola went for supplies, Tomáš gave me some cash and an old jumpsuit. A clean one.

I'll buy the pistol offa you ... sometimes wolves come out this way. From Poland. How bout it?

I want it. Only one left in it anyway.

I could come up with more. Well, have it your way. Later!

Thanks. Later.

And I left another way station behind. Now I knew where I wanted to go: to the place with the sign and into the cellar. I knew that the pile of coal wouldn't be there anymore. But the old time might be. I'd lost Černá. I'm always losing myself, with each move of my heart. But the pistol's cool butt kept my belly warm and I hadn't forgotten anything.

Maybe if we had met each other sooner ... back then in Berlun ... when I first saw the end ... stood next to death.

Černá, she'd been there too around that time, like lots of people I knew, hung around the same places as me. I asked her once what she'd done there. She laughed. What else ... I sang, an stuff. Where at? Around. Maybe we saw each other. Yeah, maybe. I'd say I saw you there.

But the time we'd had together was so jam-packed that to ask all those questions ... I just didn't care.

I sat on the train, riding ... toward the place. The old place with the sign.

And maybe I'd see her there again ... one last time? Hear her voice? Or aren't you guiding me anymore? She-Dog?

Because it happened to me in Berlun. I'll be brief. The Kanak Empire had fallen. One made it to America, two coupled on paper and took off for Australia, another got lost in the subway and was never seen again ... someone bet on the Foreign Legion, someone else burgled flats till they nabbed him, Rosie signed up for classes at the university, and another buddy sank so low on drugs and booze he was practically an animal ... then the borders cracked beyond repair and lots of them went back ... home. One became an entrepreneur and another one wrote a novel, there's even new kids bein born.

Me and Kopic were standing around ... down to our last two marks, the roulette had gone bust ... oof, how're you gonna explain this at home? I worried ... some of it I'll tell, some of it I won't, let's go, he said ... we bought two peel-off tickets for the Bundeslotterie ... legs and fingers shaking ... I can't believe it, Kopic whispered ... I won a Yamaha! Congratulations, wait ein moment, bitte ... carefully I peeled back the corner of my ticket like silver folio ... Kopic! I got a Kawasaki!

We rode through town, solemn and somber on our new machines, our time here was finished, it was obvious, we parted with Kreuzberg, other crosses and crossroads awaited, this place was changing ... then I remembered the photos Chiharu and Shimako had of their native realm, including the temples ... and noticed the faces on our machines were slanted like Shinto demon faces, the same aesthetic ... better sell em, Kopic agreed ... and we were back to being loaded again.

Kopic got hold of some brand-new documents, and he and his family set out ... for the border ... I heard there's a sign, Kopic said: Welcome to Free Czechoslovakia! Wouldn't wanna miss that ... it's new ... you gonna stick around still? Look for the Queen? Yeah, she got me, but don't ever talk about her in public, there's no point. Aright, aright ... and I stayed by myself in another flat that belonged to somebody else. And one day ... to shorten the chain of events ... I got thrown out, so I'm bummin around the train station, keepin a lookout ... and I spot a familiar set of crooked legs, that bouncing stride ... Ça va? Chiharu! Ça va! ... it was a reunion, we even hugged, and there was no end to the questions and clarifications ... the one thing she sadly declined to mention was her pal, and then something grew in her eyes, an idea, apparently ... she asked what I was doing ... Rien! I gasped happily. Notwithstanding the fact that the cash from the bike was scattering left and right. Getting rid of chuckles I love, it's comin up with em I don't like. I prefer my money to appear miraculously.

The next day she offered me a gig, I consented, a little camerawork, no problem! But ... it began to smell fishy the moment I arrived ... first a little cup of tea, get nice and relaxed ... said Chiharu in a kimono ... so that's what you meant by cinematography, aha. And after the tea, as I expected ... relaxation gave way to madness, I didn't care about the guys runnin around with lights and cameras. And that tea of theirs was so strong and exotic, it's quite possible I didn't know exactly what I was taking part in. In a tight tangle of bodies, once your pupils are exposed and subjected to the air and the action, you mostly only look in one direction anyway, what's going on around you is like behind a wall. But you can hear it, of course.

Yeah, sick stuff. I believe that if I'd been harboring any feelings for a girl at that point I would've felt alienated, to say the least. But apparently I'd entered a weary period. The kind of depression where you search in the gloom for the fleetingest glimmer of any sort of excitement at all to give you the feeling that you're still alive.

Besides ... insofar as I vaguely recall, it's entirely possible that by then I didn't like anyone at all. Least of all myself. I was searching for my Queen ... and I already mentioned the kind of woman ... the lady in black ... I'd met at the whorehouse ... mistakenly I assumed that after what I'd seen there, I wouldn't be sensitive to horrors like that anymore.

I didn't know yet that the levels of the body's hell are infinite. That the torture never stops, as one classic says. I was a mere youth, after all.

After one particularly impressive round of gymnastics, Chiharu brought in a delightful little creature and the whole thing started up again.

The one thing I don't get, I told my celluloid initiator ... is I'm not exactly a discobolus ... my bod's nothin to be proud of ... doesn't matter, she assured me, this one's special, just wait'll the end ... we still spoke Kanak, only now that it was just us it didn't sound the same anymore ... the sense of discovery was gone, the phrases and expressions were all established ... what end ... there's more than one part, an don't worry, you're just right, it's good that you're not handsome ... excuse me?! ... on film I mean, you're just the kina klutz we need.

Chiharu!

After all, you always wanted me.

I did, Chiharu, but this is like eating when you're not hungry.

You don't even know how to do it, sorry, but you're like a child, she said.

Huh?

But that's just what we need for this film, all you guys're like that.

Who?

You know, you ... it's not your fault.

We shot once, sometimes twice a week, and since I was constantly in a drug haze I could handle it ... even when they began to fiddle with the sets ... historical costumes and stuff ... and besides that pretty girl Chiharu had brought, some guy joined in, squatting on a throne with a dragon mask on, not even moving, luckily ... in my state of intoxication I enjoyed the colors ... they'll cut out a lot, Chiharu informed me ... it's gotta be perfect, it's only for a select few ... I didn't find their film that amazing compared to blockbusters like *Moscow Triumphs* ... but in my clearer moments I admired the props, genuine carved wood, but too many pillows, cushions, and lace curtains for my taste ... are those diamonds real too?

Yes, exactly, Chiharu laughed, it's the real thing, you nailed it!

The walls of the room with the throne in it were covered in swords and daggers ... that's funny, they don't have any hilt, an that's what knights had for a cross, an I believe, Chiharu, that Richard the Lion-Hearted could strew a whole arena with those samurais a yours ... Now that'll be the day, the samurais didn't need any cowardly hand protectors, they twirled theirs ... like this! Taking down a weapon, she began gyrating her wrist at such furious speed the blade was like a strip of light, the glittering diamonds slashing through the air like thunderbolts ... I backed off.

Eventually ... I guess she couldn't resist, Chiharu began to teach me, and the basis of her secret, what she really loved the most, was one ... great ... big ... slow. She did it all, but slowly. And the end was like a dam bursting, or a city burning down. To the ground ... and then it would start all over again, slowly, from the foundations up. Thoroughly.

As slowly, I guess, as when you prune that crooked little tree, with care and devotion ... and it becomes a mini tree, complete in every way and like a gem. For whom it pleases.

At times I was concerned that when it was over I would forget my moves ... don't worry, she said, it stays in you, like swimming, here, drink this! I took the tea ... then they slipped a suit of armor on me, I guess Chiharu liked that it somewhat crushed her breasts, at least she acted like she did ... though pushing away and holding back were often part of going slow ... they gave me a helmet with horns ... I look like a devil, this doesn't feel right ... just wait, you'll do fine, you must have intuition ... cause this time you play the white devil ... wow, you've got a name for everything, Chiharu. Why don't we go out sometime, take the girl along ... and she's the yellow dwarf, get it? See, I'm the Sun Woman, and you attack from in front, and she comes from behind, like China ... that's a pretty perverted parable, who's it for? Perverts. Aha. But she's not goin anywhere with us. Why not? Because. An what's her name? She doesn't have one, she doesn't matter. She's nobody.

As time went on, I took an interest in the little one ... it started gettin a little drastic ... Chiharu flipping her this way and that, dragging her by the hair, stabbing her with needles ... I was doped up on the tea and whatever it was they put in it, but I started to think that little girl wasn't just acting her pain. And then they killed her. I was right there. When the guy stood up from the throne and ran her through, I thought it was all staged, including the blood ... then Chiharu stabbed her too, it was awful what they did to her. And I couldn't move. They slit her open and ripped out her guts. I stood there naked, my brain awash with the drug, intensifying the colors, jiggling the images ... hearing the whir of the cameras as the guys ran around ... maybe a little faster than usual ... then Chiharu, after all that, slit the girl's throat and the guy with the camera leaned over her, straddled her ... while she twitched. I started hopping.

You couldn't hear a thing in that cellar. No windows. I was scared.

I didn't bother asking why she got me out of there. Maybe it was because we had known each other so long. I found her revolting ... indescribably so. That got to her a little. You don't understand ... she said, there's hundreds of thousands of girls like her, maybe millions ... they dug her up in some camp, at least she got to live like a human being a while ... do you know how many there are, in Thailand, in Hong Kong, just waitin for someone to help ... they'd do anything to get out ... they used to shoot these films over there ... you know how much they cost? An believe me, the people who watch these things ... who need em ... for every girl they ... shoot, they pay the way for a hundred more, she's a sacrifice. That's how they appease the evil powers. Not just anyone can shoot this stuff. Only us. Leave it alone. How do you know what's right? Even you're not good enough to be with me.

That's for sure. But thanks anyway. I thought it was my turn next.

She broke out laughing again. Just imagine, she said, the camera jammed. That never happens. Otherwise the Dragon would never've let you go. That's the only reason, I don't take chances. You're lucky, no one believes it was an accident it jammed. That's why you could go. Trust that you're intended to meet a different end. But don't ever mention this. It would be very dangerous. For you.

So, Chiharu, where's your girlfriend, where's Shimako?

She didn't answer. And I laughed. I laughed at her because I was overcome with … heavy-duty hopelessness. No, Chiharu, I donno what's right. An you don't either. Where's your girl? Tell me …

I guess because I was laughing, she turned around, walked slowly toward the door … very slowly, as if we still had something to say to each other … but then slammed it behind her. With a strength no one would expect from such a fragile being. And the door remains shut to this day, because we never met again. And I hope we never do.

After that I got outta Berlun. And I carried that little girl's face around inside me a long time. I still remember the bitter taste of that stuff they gave me too. That stuff that changed the colors so much it made me a worthless witness. I still have the taste on my tongue, I've forgotten the taste of the skin. I haven't said a word about it all this time. It's so sick I don't think anyone would believe me anyway. And my description of what they did to her was exceptionally restrained.

21

TO THE PLACE WITH THE SIGN, BUT … THE STRING.
KING KRONGOLD'S CRUSADE. THE MISSION.
WHAT I'M CAPABLE OF. AN I SCREAM.

At the train station … it was the same as before, maybe a few more colors and glass surfaces, I knew I could be at the place with the sign on foot in half an hour. I was on my home turf. And I had the pistol from Černá, and down there in the cellar was where my journey had begun. I'd come full circle. Only …

Only then I had a shot. And another. And another. I stayed.

The people I fell in with were from all over. The only thing they had in common was the face cover. The mask. A dull mask of indifference, maybe it was already a mask from the other side. I'd escaped an aviary only to end up in an aquarium. Piranhas included. Sometimes the faces would open up, ignited by a memory, or more often a bottle, or rage. Even the weepiest ones had so much hatred inside. I steered clear of … people, but even then you only end up backing into more. Carbon copies. Gangs I avoided too. Usually they were transitory, just met, hung out … and moved on. The station was a dangerous place for anyone who had anything. Soon I knew the corridors too. Knew all you had to do was tell Gramps: Fuck off! The stronger ones he left alone, the weaker ones had to pay to sleep downstairs by the crappers.

Help yourself, said Howdoyoudo good-naturedly, nudging a bowl my way. The gentleman who'd gone and got the soup slid over without a word. Thanks, I mumbled. Only Howdoyoudo could get away with stunts like that. Even the staff of the cafeterias and stands got a kick out of her. Their crews changed constantly too. Almost as fast as the bums'. I spent most of my time in the halflight in the corners. Didn't want to take the chance of meeting someone I knew. Not that I was ashamed, I didn't give a damn anymore. But I was thinking things over and didn't want to be interrupted. Sometimes I could think two hours, sometimes a half, it was torture. That's what I wanted. Recollecting people and fragments of sentences, pondering my mistake. Otherwise, I clouded my brain. Watched the steam from the ventilators, sometimes it was misty outside, sometimes it was dark. A couple times I tried to go out, but the heat would always stop me. That and the bugs. In the concourse, which was built into a hill, and that means underground, it was nice and cool. As long as I sat down somewhere and kept my mouth shut, people left me alone. I didn't take part in the contests for scraps of meat, various revolting leftovers, I found stuff here and there. The only thing that mattered to me was keeping the darkness in my head in balance with the light that flickered on … furtively … every now and then. My head hurt. A couple times before, I'd had a wincing toothache. Now it was a vein in my head. A tensing and relaxing, like a short cord or a length of wire. It pulsed, it twitched. In my head. It hurt.

Then Howdoyoudo started giving me food. She also gave me wine. I followed her around like a puppy dog, they told me. Howdoyoudo Lolly was an older woman, probly had a few drops of black blood in her. Kinky hair, thick lips. Picked up her nickname hunting customers. She'd always say How do you do and then trot out her offer.

Once I was feeling better, I'd sit out on the hillside, by the ventilators. The air there was cool. I often slept. It was still warm outside. One time … I ran my hand under my shirt … the pistol was there. Quite possibly, quite possibly I'd tried to get rid of it in the course of my wanderings. But there it was.

What's with you? someone said. Shut the fuck up! Well look who's up, everyone, it's Ducky … what'd you call me … you been waddlin roun like a duck … they almost took you away, but Howdoyoudo wouldn't let em … kch hch hch. We sat out between the railroad cars drinking. Want Drool? Hey you, wanna drool? a scabby face bent over me. I shoved him away and went out to the ties … I'd found a pile of railroad ties out back, tossed a few together one day, built myself a fortress … no one else knew about it. That was where I spent most of my time. Time. It didn't move. Inside the ties, it was like being sealed in a can. No one knew about me. It occurred to me I could do it in there. I'd sit and lie around and hang my head … because sometimes it hurt a lot. The string.

One day I was walking past the ticket windows and some old nun gave me money, didn't even have to babble much … not much. But it was enough for a bottle. Next day the nun was back again. I rushed right over to her. Spilling out thanks like a waterfall. I liked her old face. That one knew! About many things, no doubt … I sensed I could tell her a lot. After a long spell, I got talking again. Gargantua. I murmured to her, jumping around and hissing my words. She didn't say a thing. And as I walked away, she stood there, short, stooped, in one of the few uniforms that women can wear. Stood there, crowd pouring past her … it was unsettling: that look of hers. I clutched the cash in my fist.

Sometimes I managed to pour so much alcohol through my mouth into my head that the string would get inundated and couldn't move. In my hangovers, though, it returned, like a pendulum. I guess the trick is to snap the string, I thought to myself.

I never forgot what I'd done with the knife. So I kept out of the way. You never know with bums. One minute some old ass-kisser is givin you a hug, the next he's goin for your eyes. And I didn't want to be part of it anymore. Their speech was skeletal, pared to the bone. But I didn't like it … when my head was clear for a while, free of haze and pain, and their words would get in there: Unh. My old lady's a cunt cause she's a twat. Unh. Usually all they talked about was where they'd eaten what, who got tanked how, what they'd scrounged up where … totally the same as the people outside. Here it was just a little bit faster.

Around the end of the summer … I felt better. Plus I saw where in fact I was living. I picked my way through the hurrying people, going somewhere with suitcases, backpacks, heading somewhere in ties and skirts. I joined the procession, marching … with them. Down by the ticket windows, the crowd broke into clusters, making for the exits, I did too, occasionally someone would stop and buy a paper, smokes, something to eat … under the hall's fluorescent lights, there were posters there to look at … and then they ran for the trams, surging out into the park, there were buses there, I noticed … on the other side they made for the cabs, leaving me alone by the exit. Pondering, or whatever. Then I went back to the platform and waited for the next train.

I sat by the ventilators, dozing, maybe my strength was coming back, my head didn't hurt anymore, I stretched. It's time to make a move, time to go … even the station people disappeared from time to time. To other stations. Some had a place to live but came here anyway. Here it always looked like there was something going on.

Ondra was there too, claimed he was sixteen, but he was a shrimp. Followed me around. Stole all sorts of reading material and then told me stories about it. Liked to hear himself. I guess so he could relive it. He'd walk up to me at the ventilators, sit down, and let loose. I didn't listen … at first. But he really lived for those comic books. So then, get this, he tells me, King Krongold spurred his horse an went ridin off with his army a crusaders to the Holy Land, but how'd it turn out with Queen Eleanor? Will she be with King Krongold, or did that scumbag Merlin capture her? The next one doesn't come out'll next week … don't worry, Ondra, they published all that stuff in the sixties … Queen Eleanor stays in the tower, Merlin's cast a spell on her, an she gets these visions of things an places she's seen with King Krongold, but it's just a bunch a shit, lemme sleep. Wait, tell it … how does it go? Ondra was on the edge of his seat. Steal it next week, leeme alone. But what if it doesn't come out, an plus they know me everywhere now, it's not that easy anymore. Aright, I'll tell you, but how about a bottle.

Ondra, you see, was a thief's treasure. All kindsa parasites tried to bamboozle him, all kindsa assholes tried to wrangle him onto their teams … especially Howdoyoudo Lolly, I steered clear of her after I found out about Drool … but Ondra didn't give a damn … he'd spent all his life in institutions and knew his way around … stole, but just for himself. Just food, occasionally cash, so he could make a move somewhere, get outta town. And when he begged, people gave. Patted him on the head. I saw it. He was bent on going abroad. Got the idea from those comix of his, all those deserts and jungles. The Dead City of Macchu Picchu. The Holy Grail. The Monkey People. Lugged around a tattered atlas. His dream was to join the Foreign Legion. Dude, just wait'll I'm strong! But don't you hafta go to school? Aready been. I nodded, after all he knew how to read. I'll tell you somethin, he said one day … by the ventilators … but you gotta promise not to tell anyone! Swear it! Yeah, yeah. No, dude, raise your hand an swear for real! I did. I'm not sixteen, dude, I'm thirteen. Yeah, so? If they find out, they'll put me away. Uh-huh, I closed my eyes and tried to sleep.

He came right back with a bottle. Yanked the cork out with my teeth. So … Queen Eleanor dreamed of King Krongold, but she was far away and under a spell. And the king meanwhile … clashed with the Tatars, and it was a terrible battle, his horsemen fell under the infidels' spears, but then the infantry penetrated their defense and raided their camp and engaged the enemy in man-to-man combat … this wine's great, Riesling! where'd you get it? … What happens next, what about the Tatars, they had bows, right?! Yeah, and that was the thing, they pelted the King's army with salvos of arrows, inflicting huge losses, but at close quarters the king's knights were stronger, and had better armor ... the battle raged for two days, and when it was over King Krongold had only a handful of loyal men left ... hey Ondra, got any smokes? Thanks! So, they snuck into the galley and sailed into port and ... damn, what next ... oh yeah, disguised as merchants they went to the capital and sold silk and fruits and vegetables ... that's dumb, said Ondra angrily ... just wait a sec ... but the other merchants plotted against them, and one night, disguised in black masks, they attacked, King Krongold and his loyal men fled through the darkness ... their horses' hoofs clattered across the planks of the bridge, and the moon was veiled in mist, and they came to a plain afflicted by plague ... and several of the king's loyal men were struck down by the abominable disease ... an what was Eleanor doin meantime, Ondra inquired ... Merlin had her spellbound, she was forced to do his bidding, and he'd order her around, do this, do that, move it, Queen, heh heh, Merlin cackled ... that fuckin scumbag, Ondra yelled, cheeks burning ... but she was proud, and inside her was a smile for King Krongold, because she knew he was searching for her ... and at night she would sit alone in her chamber ... and get totally shitfaced, and in some parts of the tower were trap-doors, and the only thing that kept her from stepping on the wrong stone and plunging into the cellars full of gruesome spiders was her love for King Krongold, it held her up ... did the cellars have rats an skeletons in em? Ondra wondered ... course they did, don't interrupt! ... and King Krongold came to a jungle where he was attacked by wild men called the Utnapishtims ... hee-hee, snickered Ondra ... but with the help of his trusty laser he swung out on the creeper vines, but of all his loyal men now the only one left was Sir Dolphus, and their swords were all they had ... to be continued. No fair! No fair ... you got the wine! It's all gone. C'mon, anyway I'm just talkin crap. No, that's the way it was, said Ondra, wait here ... the string was quiet and my head was totally clear, I had an urge to go and ... maybe pick up some threads at some charity, mine stank like shit ... hey, good boy, Ondra, Riesling again ... that'll pick me up ... I got burgers too, paid for em an everything, try one. The first mouthful was awful, but after that it went all right. Okay, this is gonna be short now, though! You know what's weird? Ondra said. When I hear it, it's like I see pictures. Like a movie almost.

Right, so Sir Dolphus tells Krongold ... my lord, I cannot go on, there is an arrow in my side ... I am dying, O virtuous lord, in truth and on my honor! My friend, says Krongold ... you did not lose honor, sir knight, you fell in battle ... only those who live may lose honor ... I must tell you something,

King Krongold … the reason I am with you is that I too love Queen Eleanor, the Shining Star, 'tis a sin … No, Dolphus, we all love her, 'tis no sin at all … and Dolphus, contented, breathed his last … Ondra fidgeted … so now he's just got the swords? Exactly, now the king had two, and when the Bedouins attacked him he let out a roar and charged, the camels bolted, kicking up sand, and the Bedouins began fighting each other … that one Krongold knew from the Legion … and Dolphus's confession filled him with power so he fought like an army that day … and also he was intelligent, slipping a burnoose off one of the Bedouins he cloaked himself in it … and then he came to a Zulu village, and they surrounded him with spears and clubs, fearing that he was a Bedouin chief who had come to take them prisoner, it was a dangerous moment. The Zulus were painted with mud for war and the shaman was rattling his rattle … but Krongold revealed his identity … and they rejoiced, because they feared Merlin, and they showed the king the way, and he walked through the desert … but isn't he gonna get another army? Ondra huffed … wait a sec … till he came to the cave where the Old Man of the Computers lived, and he had a thorn in his paw, he was a lion … a lion with a festering wound … and spying him, King Krongold planted his sword in the sand, nobly reached out his right hand, and plucked the thorn from his paw … an the old guy made him an army on his computer! Ondra yelped … exactly! and they rode off through the dunes with Chief Joseph's braves at their flanks, eerily painted in yellow and black, their veins pulsing with speedy strength, between their teeth they clenched stone knives and their quivers beat against their thighs … the notches on their six-shooters gleamed … and in front strode the giant Ninjas, followed by the waving standards and banners of the Nestorians, and Spartacus and his rebels were there, gladiators and former slaves, it was one great big mix … and they chanted in rhythm to the march: Whip, sword, blood, cross … six thousand of them, just like in Capua later on … the sisters of mercy went with them too, they were very powerful, nobody knows why they went along … then the metallic ranks fell in, halberdiers, flailers, and slingers, and the Skipetars, with their bambitti, and the murderous Richard the Humpback headed up the cavalcade, riding under the sign of the cross … the shields of the Lithuanians sparkled in the crimson sun, the Egyptians carried baskets … and had elephants and bazookas … the Old Man assembled a massive army in Krongold's honor … and Eleanor … Eleanor had to obey the disgusting Merlin's orders, had to grovel and make coffee for him … listen to his bullshit!

… he laid his charms and lures out before her, be a free woman, forget Krongold, you can be whatever you want … and I can change myself too, just tell me what to be, the abominable Merlin fawned over her … I can be twenty years old and play guitar … or I can be a racecar driver … I can even change myself into a fifty-year-old writer in a sweater with a pipe … just tell me what you want, Eleanor … forget King Krongold, forget … Merlin yelled, and that word, *forget,* echoed down the halls and corridors, startling the bats … that disgusting pig! Ondra cried, how'd he get that hocus pocus? I donno. But King Krongold was drawing near, and he pitched his camp at the foot of the tower, and the fair Eleanor stretched her arms out the window … the king withdrew to his tent with Richard and his valets and the rest of the knights to dream up a plan … and meanwhile the Nubians rigged up the catapults and flung fire-balls and dirty tricks into the city, and Merlin got hit in the eye with an arrow … Ondra applauded … but it didn't do a thing to him, he whipped his robots onto the ramparts … Krongold went for a ride on his steed, and ho! what did he see, an eagle soaring down from the sky! Yep, an eagle! Fuckin A! … yeah, an then? … then, Ondra … then, oh yeah … then it got bad, man … see, Krongold had a goblet of wine before the attack, but the computerized army vanished in a blink under the blows of Merlin's axe, and King Krongold was alone … alone … and couldn't get to the Queen, screaming up in the tower, so he had another goblet, betrayed her, the scoundrel, oh well … now leeme alone, Ondra … that's the end … You're lyin! You lie! That's not the way it was! Ondra yanked at my shirt, I swung round … he pulled my hair, I think he was crying … you're a retard … just like everybody else.

Afterwards I was sorry … I'd pissed off the only person around I could talk to … gimme a break, Ondra, I screwed up, you're right, that's not the way it was … he walked off in a huff, pretending not to see me.

But I felt better. Charity gave me pants and a shirt. My SUPER DISCO was worn thin. I traded it in for Mickey M. Picked up a quilted jacket too, I needed the padding … because where everyone else had nothing, I had a pistol … and the Madonna. My silver Madonna. And her I had to protect. She was the only living thing I had left. And if anyone had spotted it, I would've had to fight. Assuming I'd even have a chance. I also had my keys. But I couldn't go there yet.

That's just horrible, I'm callin the mayor's office, Gramps complained, I still got friends! Lookit um, the shameless hussies … two Romanian Gypsy women sat on the ground, newborns feeding at their breasts … I knew Gramps liked to spy on them … but now he was outraged … they're bad for business, I'm Vltava baptized, not enough all the hicks we got crawlin aroun, now on top of it the furriners're movin in, trash oughta be swept out … but he didn't dare lift a finger, they weren't alone, and their menfolk would've made fast work of him … it's funny, I said, I mean who's makin slaves outta who, those pimps … lousy bitches, go to hell! Gramps shook his fist from a safe distance … or those women an their kids … this is goin in the papers, honest Czechs're bein robbed … or maybe they truly can't provide for the kids so they feel like they got no choice, it's all they know how to do … shoot em all! … you an yer who's makin slaves outta who … nice rack on that one though, Gramps licked his lips. Yeah right.

I may be aggressive, but the Book is aggressive too … the preacher said for probably the sixth time already. We were packed in there at the Mission … Gramps'd dragged me in … in the stench of our grubby rags, but there was soup on the table, and sandwiches and rolls, ugh, I said to myself, shutting my eyes … yes, this book is a book of war … now watch him whip out the Scout Handbook, dipshit, said someone behind me … you have wronged and been wronged … yeah, that especially! shouted another voice behind my back, and a guy built like a mountain stepped forward from the door … the preacher, short and stooped, raised his hand to stop him, they had their act down pat, those two … the doorman had a T-shirt on that said Jesus Loves You, the rest of his upper body was plastered with tattoos … on our way in I'd told him: And you too, on purpose, to see what he'd do, but he just lowered his eyes and said, Enter, sinners, I didn't tempt him further … yes, my book is a warlike book, and it's the Bible! the preacher shouted, climbing onto a chair … grasp at last the meaning of history … start with yourself, cuntlips, a voice behind me muttered, my belly growled, the others looked on, intrigued … the preacher teetered a moment, then decided to climb back down … close the door, brother Arthur, it's full, and the draft … you are going to fry in hell! the preacher roared. The life you lead now is a stroll! Gramps picked at his scabs, while some woman in front turned on the waterworks. Yes, a stroll through the rose garden, Satan is going to skewer you on his pitchfork down there! What the hell's he scarin people for … a voice behind me grumbled … what people, asshole? I don't see none, another voice replied. Silence! the preacher thundered, there is but one hope! Let Jesus into your hearts, he knocks softly, but the dragon fights his way in with the whip … the preacher paused dramatically to illustrate … but Jesus! He was no sniveler, no, he was no coward like you. Like you! He pointed at a woman, she let out a shriek. Like you! And you! The preacher ran around pointing his finger, pissed me off. No, you are mistaken, he exclaimed, like anyone'd even opened their mouth … remember Babylon, remember centuries of man humiliated and beaten, remember the pyramids, the lowly, who suffered under the whip, and the lofty, who suffered in their souls, the flames devoured each and every one, and they had to make war, to burn their savagery in blood, their enemies' and their own … I'm ready to chow! said a guy behind me … puke is more like it, another said quietly … like rabid beasts the people lived, for they did not know … in every land on earth they murdered, nothing but tears and gnashing teeth and conflagrations … but then he came along, the warrior, he alone had the courage to say: Enough! The preacher jumped back on the chair: And the name of that most fearless warrior is Jesus … and he said: Love one another, there is a way … for otherwise your torture shall be prolonged unto eternity! And some heeded his words and found life eternal. You riffraff, you will never be known as anything else, you in your humiliation and pain are closer to Jesus than those who dwell in the sumptuous towers, say Yes! A few Yesses sounded out, guess they wanted to get it over with … Many stuck by Jesus and left behind the world of cruelty, only the fools and the defiant remain, and sectarians! they will burn, oh, how they will burn … And Jesus was brave enough to accept the human body and be martyred on the cross, to prove … that it could be done! Out of love for his fellow man! He left the message of his pain here for you, because pain is all you believe in, pain alone is real for you, the wretched … don't shit cher pants, bozo, the guy behind me said … this time I got pissed off, cause in the midst of the stench and nothingness, at least the preacher had a story, yep, they killed him back then an it's been goin on ever since, an they say nothin's happenin … an I realized, those words from kids' nursery rhymes, like *honor* an *faith* an all the rest, the only place they're left anymore's in the old stories the preachers tell, it's similar … but Bog was in me, an I knew this guy here was leavin out plenty … and Luke the Evangelist was the only one, you poor souls, continued the preacher, who set down for the record that in the garden, that ancient, desolate garden, Jesus was alone, sweating in agony … someone fell off his chair, a little commotion ensued as the others picked him up … because he had accepted the human body and its pain, and he didn't have to, but he was brave, unlike us, and Luke the Evangelist, you motley crew, was a doctor and he knew what he'd seen, that agony was human, Jesus feared torture no less than the most wretched of men, and that was his war … and he was victorious, and he showed that it was possible … to love.

The preacher wiped the sweat from his brow, eyelids fluttering, then went on talking about the body on the cross, and the next time the guy behind me made a wisecrack, I flew out of my seat and told him: Shut the fuck up! Softly and menacingly … then quick sat back down as the doorman moved from his post … instead of nabbin the cracker behind me though, he latched onto me an dragged me outta the row, it wasn't me! … I said, but next thing I knew I was on my knees, a twist of the arm was all it took … and the preacher said: My son, you have seen the light, hallelujah, you have seen the light and risen to the defense … he went on jigging around me a while with the doorman holding onto me, and then it was time for soup and tea.

Before I had a chance to get any though, the preacher dragged me into the back an gave me some pamphlet an a stack a holy pictures, still talkin away, but the power was gone … socks, I said … what, my son … socks, if you have any … oh, yes … he knelt down on one knee and took off his shoes, rolled off his socks … handed em to me … I can't, Father, thanks … but really I can't … somehow I staggered outta there … in the hall it was still pretty rank … and all the food was eaten. I lifted up the soup lid … cue violins. A couple crumbs left, I swept em up.

Luckily Gramps was waiting outside with the guy I'd gone off on, he let loose: Nice show, boy, that's what it takes, otherwise he'd never finish, heh heh … improv! They had a few rolls stashed away for me, plus Gramps had a chunk of salami. And a bottle of rum. We headed out to the railyard.

The Blue Army … I was scared of them at first, a uniform's a uniform, but the railroad guys didn't give a damn about us. Gramps'd even become a station mascot of sorts. I didn't make any trouble, even when I was loaded, so sometimes they'd let me sit on the platform. I'd just sit and act like I was waiting for a train. Look around … occasionally I'd doze off. I think I looked normal enough.

On our way out back, ah, Gramps called out full blast, how do you do, lick your lolly? Howdoyoudo was hustling through the concourse … leading Drool by the hand. It took me a while to get it. Besides, I didn't keep track much, content to let it all merge as long as everyone left me in peace.

Drool was a mongoloid. No one knew for sure whether she was Howdo-youdo's daughter. No one cared either. They were heading out back toward the out-of-service trains.

You wouldn't believe, Gramps told me once, the cars that stop out there an the fellas drivin em ... saw this set a wheels the other day ... even remember the license plate, but not a peep to anyone. I don't want any trouble. They keep an eye on it! We know the top dogs at City Hall, heh, we still got friends! ... Maybe what he was saying was just part of the station mythology, everyone here had a story to tell. Everybody was Monte Christo, every thief an ex-millionaire, every junkie blathered on about the golden hit and how they were gonna do it ... tomorrow ... the junkies were just passing through, they didn't live here ... every lousy washed-up alkie claimed to've been some famous actress or singer. Lies and inventions and sob stories ... everybody here lived a life of pure fantasy, the day-to-day worries of finding food and warmth and a place to sleep didn't leave time for anything else, and sometimes it was brutal. Of course ... the main thing was to cloud your mind. I wasn't the only one lost in a fog. Some of those derelicts' lives were real drudgery ... they went on babbling their tall tales and lies because that was all they had. Nobody cared if people believed them ... apart from those moments of hungover weeping ... and besides it was fun. It made time move.

Drool really did drool. I saw Howdoyoudo Lolly feed her once. Dunking her bread in a cup of milk.

We sat and drank, slowly, so it would last ... it was summer, but the air was ... different already somehow. I was about to throw away the stuff the preacher had given me ... but Gramps yanked the pictures outta my hand, scrawny old scarecrow bawled me out. I let him have em. I sat on a barrel, the others flopped out on ties around the fire: Gramps, the fella from the Mission, some Polish guy. Ondra shuffled up, sat down next to em, acting like he didn't see me. The conversation flagged. Hey Gramps, I winked at the old man ... didn't you want me to finish tellin that fable about King Krongold? Gramps squirmed ... oh yeah, that's right, you promised ... I winked at Ondra, he still had his back to me, but it looked like he'd perked up his ears ... Mission Guy grumbled testily, but Gramps gave him a kick ... I mixed it up last time, got totally off track ... Merlin did mow down that computer army, only, get this, Gramps ... there was still one slinger left, the Old Lion's page, an he was with Krongold too ... but what you gotta understand, Gramps, is this kid was sharp

… looked sixteen, but he was actually younger … didn't matter though, because, an this is historically documented … trink! the Polish guy yapped, I passed him the bottle, sposedly he'd chipped in … the kid'd spent his childhood in the orphanages of Genoa, learned all kindsa stuff there … so it didn't matter that he was small … an not from a computer, he was flesh an blood, so he didn't feel Merlin's axe, not even when the troops were fallin left an right … that's the way it was, an this page, the slinger, was extremely valiant, so as soon as he sees King Krongold's unconscious … this slinger, who's called Ondráš, sneaks into the tower an sees … Merlin creeping toward the chamber where the fair Eleanor lies weeping … an he's got a dagger an his shadow falls across the floor an … errr … errr … the floorboards creak, an Ondráš winds up his sling an bang … pegs Merlin in the eye! Heh! said Gramps. Wait, but that arrow didn't bother him, said Ondra … that arrow didn't bother him cause it was computerized, an what Old Man Lion didn't know … nobody knew! … was that Merlin was a program too! … so programmed arrows couldn't hurt him, hah … but Ondráš used a real-life stone from the desert … an Merlin was reeling … that was all the slinger needed, quiet as a mouse he raced past Merlin into the chamber an fell into Queen Eleanor's arms … no, wait! … they, uh, what was it … jou ar all paranoyt, the Pole declared, wrapping himself in a blanket … right, they take the blanket an sheets an start wavin out the window to Krongold, he spies the movement … an comes to his senses! … an he leaps on his noble Arabian charger an gallops forth … meanwhile Merlin … now you *know* he's furious … shaken but furious, an he starts tearin the door to shreds with his nails … Ondráš stood, sling at the ready … an Eleanor sank to her knees, extending her snow-white arms: Make haste, my dear, make haste, Krongold … an throwing off his breastplate the king dashed up the stairs … just then, the bedroom door flew open an in came Merlin, pouncing at them with his ghastly claws … but Ondráš was sharp, he'd been expecting it … so he quick let fly, an boom! In the other eye! Merlin lurched into the wall … a second later he was right back at em again … but that second was all it took! Krongold bursts in, sees Merlin, an stabs him! Eleanor faints in his arms. Who is this lad? King Krongold frowned, gesturing to Ondráš … that, my king, is a virtuous soldier, twas he who twice felled the powerful and evil wizard Merlin! the fair Eleanor said, and she presented Ondráš with a braid of her golden tresses. So it is then … I declare you a knight, the king exclaimed in a thunderous voice … accept this gift, O valiant hero … and he handed Ondráš a huge sword covered in diamonds … the sword of the fallen Sir Dolphus … only heroes may carry the swords of heroes, the king said, his voice shaking the chamber walls … so Ondráš became a knight … Aha! so that's why Krongold had two swords, I get it … and finding countless treasures in Merlin's castle, they rigged out a splendid argosy and set sail for Genoa … an Krongold an Eleanor were wed … an Ondráš … uh, right! … Ondráš stayed with em! They adopted him … an they all lived together in a huge castle up in the mountains … high in the air, an kept an eye on the roads … an then comes the next part, where Ondráš takes out his Arabian steed, throws a shabrack on him, an rides off toward his next adventure … heh? … here I am goin hoarse an they're all sleepin … the Pole'd finished off the bottle … yeah, great … everyone was snoring away, Mission Guy drooling … Ondra curled up at Gramps' feet, also in rags, fast asleep. I walked out past the ties.

That string in my head, I only felt it rarely now … I'd set up a regular time for sitting on the platform, that was my time to think about Černá, I'd given up believing she'd ever step off the train … given up being scared of it too … and when I'd jump out of my skin, it was always a different girl … and somehow I'd make it through the rest of the day, walking, wandering, sleeping … it occurred to me to try leavin the station, goin by my place on Gasworks, pick up my clothes and some money, there'd be something there, wash up so I wouldn't stick out so much, and then go where I had to go, and do it. I gave my pistol a pat.

She talked to me first. Nothin much, but young, strawberry blonde, face kina runny. Took my hand. One word led to the next, our shoulders touched. I groped her under the table so it'd be obvious. She held on. Egh, I neighed on the inside … checked my getup, the lighting was dim, puffed out my chest … after a few shots we were all over each other … and I was turned on, so I'm absolutely positively getting better, I thought to myself. I kept drinking till nightfall so she wouldn't notice how keyed up I was. I was looking forward to Gasworks. This way it would be … healthier. Up until now I couldn't've imagined standing next to that sink again. Like I had that time with her. There might even be some of her things there still, trifles.

Ginger was a sociable one. Nurse on vacation in the little mother. Bullshit, no doubt, but it sounded nice. So if I trip an bust my face, you'd bandage me up, right? I'll bandage you so good … you haven't lived till you've been bandaged by me, she poured it on. We made a deal, I'd get the drinks, she'd get the cab. Either we'd stay at my place, or grab the cash an go somewhere. I'll hit the cellar first thing in the morning, it'll be a classy farewell … I told myself. With a manly smile. She got a little wild in the cab.

Yep … this is Gasworks, the driver said. Same name still.

I recognized the store on the corner, but except for that … my street, which used to be one of the worst … lots of buildings had new facades, wait a sec, leggo, I pushed her off, a fashion boutique, a toyfil store, a crystal shop, here? … a bank, this is unbelievable …

You gettin out, or do you want me to keep goin?

Wait here, I told him and the redhead, moving as if in a dream. At number 23, where my place should've been, was a hotel. Glass doors, dish jockeys, cactuses … Hotel Evropa, yeah, that's original … Chinese tombs on the walls, all the frills … unobtrusive music, red carpet …

Where do you think you're going? A fellow in a uniform stopped me, reception clerk. He surveyed my attire under the glowing chandeliers.

I live here.

Uh-huh … we'll see about that. Which étagère?

Which what?

Which room.

Number nine, on the courtyard.

Oh, that's gone now, sir. This is a hotel now, as you see for yourself.

Where's my stuff, dammit!

Make an appointment at City Hall, sec. 77. All previous tenants who failed to submit claims were relocated to the City Dump. You must have neglected to submit your claim by 9/7!

What claim? That's my stuff!

We've had cases like yours before. But if you haven't submitted your claim yet, I'm afraid it's too late.

What the … ?

You won't get any space from us.

Where're all the resta the people that used to live here?

Where do you think? They went somewhere else.

I staggered back to the cab. This is unreal … my nautical maps, my photos … a couple blazers …

Where to?

Back!

It took Ginger a while to get it. So you don't have anything? Nope. The driver pulled over to let her out. We didn't even say goodbye. I took off through the bushes and stiffed the cabbie. It was sad, but I had to.

I managed to get drunk just like old times. How far can it go? I asked myself. What am I capable of? The lid was blown off for good. And from all those black corners … all those train station faces, an evil power made its way into me, I don't excuse myself, it was me who let it in. First I went out behind the ties. To my chamber. Found a bottle there, good boy! Ondra knew that was where I hung out, and left me in peace. Kid's got this station cased better than anyone, he knows his stuff. And what awaits him, too. If he survives, he'll turn out a bum. Maybe king of the bums, if he's strong. Heh, knight on horseback, he'll get over that soon enough. I got mean … accused Gramps of owing me money … he was by himself and scared, coughed up some change. I drank. What am I capable of? What'll I do next? That was my refrain. Outta my way, asshole … I shoved someone aside … someone who maybe the day before I'd drank with, hugged, searched for the same words, maybe even bedded down next to in the same lousy rags … his story, I bared my teeth at the loser, he kept his mouth shut, slunk off. His luck, motherfucker. Coulda had it all behind him, miserable piece a shit. I don't remember anymore who it was. I went to the men's room, where sometimes I retreated when the string got too loud … sat there shakin my head, wishin it would stop … and I had to hear all the sounds and the bullshit … it hurt so much! I ripped the mirror off the wall, trashed the place a little. Some upper cruster slipped out. I'm human, what am I capable of. This, I stomped up the bakelite, an this, I punched out the lightbulb, the red stuff came trickling out, that only enraged me more … I went downstairs, at this time of day the hookers were usually by the ladies' room … you, come with me … no, not you, she was too young for what I wanted, you, picked out an old biddy, some raspy old hosebag, barely draggin … how much ya got? As much as you want … but c'mon, move it … out by the bushes … We walked outside and went up toward the ventilators, into the scanty light's shadows, I noticed drops on the bushes, dew I guess, can that be? What'd you say … what dew? How do you wannit? She ran her hands over my crotch. I saw that it was Howdoyoudo Lolly. But what would she be doin downstairs, she works a different post … groping me, painted face like a mask … you ain't even hard … how much ya got? I got this … she knelt on the ground, mouth open, I put the barrel to her forehead, quick, so she wouldn't see, wouldn't be scared … squeezed the trigger, she had a hole in her head, and then the sound kicked open the night, blood spurting, mouth still open wide, she tipped backward, legs shooting out, the blast deafened me. No, it couldn't've even hurt, I wasn't holding the gun anymore … you see, I told myself, that's what you're capable of … and if you'd wanted, she could've suffered, the possibilities, it's horrible. So I can do … even this. I stood waiting … somebody must've heard it go off, waiting … for someone to come, the cops … anyone at all … but nothing happened, she lay there under the bushes, drops on them. Glistening. Leaves hanging there in the cold light, everything as before. I leaned over her … is it Howdoyoudo or not … and agh … I screamed, or gasped … it was an old lady's face, white hair, swollen body … the body of my She-Dog, this was the old lady I'd held in my arms there, where she'd given herself to me, in the cellar.

I fled through the park, hands pressed to my face, I could hear my breath and my teeth knocking, couldn't control my jaws … my face was twitching.

I lay down under a bush, it was almost daylight. My head ached. But the string lay peaceful in the dark. It was a dream, my mind raced … I wouldn't do something like that … but I didn't have the pistol … I got up … found the spot. The grass was flattened, yes … this is where she'd been, but there was nothing there now, stains on the leaves … not blood, I tore one off, brown, crusty, barely alive in the wind and the dust … went back inside, dragged myself through the concourse … in the men's room I ran water over my head … place was all smashed up, but when isn't it, I can't tell … they could've changed the light-bulb. I went looking for Gramps. By some miracle … I had a little money, bought him a cup of coffee. I know I owe you, Gramps, but about yesterday … yeah, you got sloshed an went off to snooze in the park. Yesterday, Gramps … I heard some lady got killed … hey, what do I know, people talk all kindsa shit here, what's wit you? Hangover. Yeah yeah … hookers come an hookers go. I guess it was a dream then … I took a sip. Maybe not, said Gramps. Ah! … scalded my tongue. C'mon, Gramps, you know a thing or two. I donno nuttin, what do I know what kina dreams you got … Christ … he shuffled off … you're goin nuts here, he shouted back at me, better hurry … while you're still young … get out!

I believe that I prayed genuinely for the first time in a long while … thought about my folks too, the old family … I'd told them to go screw themselves, back then, in the ancient past, which was hollow … but they used to take me. To church, when I was little. I had to. Now I said: I am not worthy for you to come under my roof, but speak to me just one single word … and my soul will be healed. I said it with affection. But there was silence. And I screamed because … I patted myself down to make sure I hadn't lost the Madonna too … then I really donno, then I'm lost. She was there. Around my neck.

I walked out of the concourse and off through the park, not because of what Gramps'd said, not because of the day before … and even if it didn't happen, it was still an important dream, it meant something. I walked away … the sun was coming up, it's usually a little misty and a little cold then, and suddenly I heard behind me: Wait! Where ya goin?

Away.

Hey … I'm goin with you!

No way, not where I'm goin …

Aw, lemme go with you.

No.

I knew the kid … was still there. Heard him start running and spun around.

Ondra! He stopped.

I'm tellin you … no way!

Way!

Look … I picked up a stone. Cut it out. You can't come.

Take me with you …

And he started running, so I threw the stone.

I didn't want to hit him. But I knew he was used to it. He wouldn't've understood otherwise. The last time I turned, he was still standing there. His puny build. Pissed me off. I walked out of the park.

22

IN A FIELD OF EVER-CHANGING COLORS.
WHO I'M SCARED OF. ONWARD, TO THE LAB. THE STONE.
SHE'S GOT A VEIL, SHE'S KIND. SHE SAYS: YOU HAVE TO.

I didn't go to the place with the sign. But once I found myself downtown, where all it'd take was a little jog to get to her attic flat … to the place where we'd shared our things … I couldn't go there either.

I had the key. Tucked safely in my jacket's inside pocket. Everything on me hurt. The string didn't make itself heard, that I kept a watch on. But the pressure on my chest. There, where I had the silver, I could feel every bit of skin, it was like it had scales. Like Madonna's wise and kindly face was tugging me toward the ground. The ground. I mostly walked with my eyes lowered. I didn't want to see the others. The thought of disappearing into the trams' iron bellies struck me with horror. People inside hung on the bars, looking out. I went very cautiously and slowly, following the path. There was only one left.

I hadn't remembered the Dump like that. Sure … I'd heard a thing or two. It had expanded. The town fathers found it profitable to lease out unused plots of land to big foreign firms, which not only tossed out lots of stuff still usable by the locals, but even paid to do it.

Now the Dump extended from the last housing estates as far as the eye could see. A yellow haze hung over it, lashed by an occasional wind. Smoke climbed skyward in many spots. The clouds, steeped in water, barely moved. I had to walk carefully, paying attention to what I stepped on. The soft stuff often reeked. But soon I came across a trail. The Dump only seemed to be dead. Tires baked on either side, the wind swept heat into my face. A pool of something gurgled beneath the papers. There were artificial mountains. They'd been trucked in. I skirted the mountains and hiked through the canyons. Covered my mouth with my hand in some spots to keep out the ashes tossed by the wind. Between the heaps of garbage it was occasionally calm, sometimes out in the open I had to run from the heat's scorching tongue. There were patches of hard ground here and there. That didn't sag. I walked through a field of tin. Pocked with holes. That was where the scrapyard began. Met my first person there, I tried to avoid it but would've had to leave the trail. It was a girl, fifteen, sixteen at most, raggedy-looking and scrawny. Her nails were chewed to the quick, I noticed that because she kept waving them in my face. Spit flying, she fired right at me: Seen Bašnák? Where is that guy? I gotta talk to him! I took a step back: I donno. Oh pardon me, she said … got any change? I stepped around her. Now I was deep in the Dump. Other trails crossed the one I was on, intersecting it. I saw piles of crates, all the same, some giant force had stacked them up. Some had burst open. All of em were the same, only some lay on their side, others end on end, I must've seen every combination. Broken sides, lids, bottoms. Bound in wire. It struck me this might be infinity. If I was a graphic artist, I'd make postcards from space like this, once we conquer it. Then I found a receptacle full of rotten lemons. Their greenish skins were coated with shiny insects and black flies. But some of em were whole, I stuffed them in my pockets.

I don't know where they came from. Maybe they crawled out of some hole. There were three, and one said: Hit the road. Hit the fuckin road! I did as I was told. I'd heard about the Dump People. And after all, I was on one of their trails. There were stakes plunged into the greasy slop. I kept them to my left. I came to a pool buzzing with insects, walked past with my eyes and mouth shut. The sound alone was enough to make me itch all over. Maybe they were being born, maybe some of them were just leaving the ground for the first time. I wanted to get somewhere that didn't belong to anyone. Assuming there was such a place here still. The Dump was filling up fast. I spotted the rusted-out skeleton of a bus with a sheet-metal chimney. Smoke coming out of it. A kid sitting on the steps. Laundry drying on clotheslines. I picked my way around them. Farther along were the machines. Some looked like monster bones, snarled and shattered. Doors, levers, wheels. I crawled under something that used to be a conveyor belt. Changed trails. Saw two old-timers squatting around a fire. A rusty pump bundled in rags looked to be all that was left of the old setup. Water was boiling in a big tin can. One of the old gents had a dog on a leash. It barked at me. I took a trail at random. I was afraid of sinking in, into something I'd never heard of. They could've had fake trails too, for people that had no business here. If I lived here, I would. Even the Dump can't be bottomless, it's not for everyone. A heap shifted under me, I tumbled into a burst of colors. Plastic bags and packages. Of juice. Multivitamin Nectar. There must've been millions of them.

I came to a spot where there was nobody else. Couldn't see the ground. Just paper and plastic, but it didn't stink. There weren't even flies here. In most parts of the Dump it reeked, some spots it was pungent, others it was sour. I came to a metal fence. On the other side, the Dump stretched into the distance. The fence was hidden between the heaps, I'd found it by accident. Alongside it were barrels, a whole row. Painted yellow but peeling now. A corrugated metal roof was set up in one spot, the kind they use for bus stops. I crawled underneath. The barrels were lying on top of sacks, I yanked them out. It was getting dark. I ate the lemons. Then wrapped myself up in the sacks and watched. It started to drizzle, I crept back under the roof. Heard laughter and conversation. At first I thought it was just in my head, but then I made out the flicker of flames. It was far away, the wind carried the sounds to me.

The next day I found some boards in the scrapyard. Sniffed, they smelled like tar, I made a wall out of them. Near the barrels there were also some sacks of hardened cement. When I did construction I used to flip those things onto my back no problem. Now it took me hours to stack them up. Then I took a long break. That evening they were back by the fire. I had to go. I was hungry and thirsty.

You wanna stay, I don't see why not, don't make no difference to nobody else, said Vulture, tugging his beard. We even winter here. Jus find yerself a stove. Foxy tossed some planks on the fire. They started it with gasoline. An Jasuda's comin tomorrow, boy're you gonna feast. Vulture handed me a piece of bread. Stuff yerself.

The first thing that struck me about the bums ... a few were obviously boozed-out derelicts, but all of them were dressed pretty normal. Vulture clued me in that they'd found it all at the Dump. Yup, wasn't worth diddly till Jasuda come along. Even promised to build a shower! For the ladies. Ain't too many a them though. Stick clambered down from the tractor and said: Forget the shower, wait'll we get a proper rain, Dump'll change. You'll see! They even had wine, in cartons. Said there was hectoliters of it. Fermented red. But my body said: Enough. I took one sip and threw up. You sick? said Foxy. Everyone perked up their ears ... cause if you're real sick, like for real, then uh-uh, ya can't be here ... Vulture said earnestly, Mr. Jasuda looks out for that ... otherwise we'd all end up sick ... no, I'm not sick, just tired ... Vulture threw a poncho over me ... here, take it, he said ... rains a lot out here, drizzles ... you're gonna need it. Cushy livin though, best home I ever had, best grub ...

an they're always truckin stuff in. We got it easy here. An the Dump'll be aroun long as all the rest of it is.

They told me where to come the next day. And to bring a sack.

That night I couldn't sleep. It rained, drumming down on the metal, and to its rhythm I remembered … thinking and dreaming. That day I'd found a magazine. Inside it was an ad for some … movie or something … there was tension in the picture, I don't know why I tore it out, and then an ad for spinach, You've never tasted better … it reminded me of Černá, what I'd told her. But maybe what I'd told her wasn't true anymore … no, these things don't go away, it'll be there long as I live. I tore out that one too. There were tons of newspapers and magazines, floating around all over the place.

Jasuda. The trucks rolled up one by one. Dumped food into the pit. Turned around and drove off. Made room for the next. The pit was left over from something. Looked like an explosion. There were a few others like it down at that end of the Dump.

They clued me in around the fire, the stuff came from supermarkets, all expired, but lots of it wasn't spoiled … and I saw … fish, lots of stiff fish with metallic eyes … chickens … and then packages, bright-colored packages with stuff inside … salamis … melons, then some fruits I didn't recognize … doesn't it rot down at the bottom? I said to someone's back, but they didn't even turn around … pheasant, fuck, I could go for a pheasant, said somebody else, and others began walking up, I spotted the girl I'd met the first day, she had to be crazy, laughing, didn't belong to any crew, just laughing, wriggling in the mud that was left behind from the rains … I saw an old woman with a wheelbarrow … they started tossing meat into the pit out of the back of one of the trucks that didn't have a tilt-up bed, and it was disgusting, the people around the pit fell silent … I saw half a pig, sheep's heads, they were tossing sheep's heads into the pit, one after the next … the meat covered over what was in the pit from before and flies began to swarm … I shuffled impatiently, even licked my lips, I noticed … my stomach was growling, but then the next truck came and the meat, the chunks of flesh, got buried under an avalanche of packages, yogurts, more salami … that's Mr. Jasuda, Vulture nudged me with his elbow, on his head a Tyrolean cap with a feather … Jasuda strode around the pit, a tall guy in a suit, but with slippers on his feet and an umbrella in his hand, waving it around and rattling on, I couldn't hear what about … we came too late, said Vulture mournfully, giving me another swipe of the elbow … when he points our way, move it! Jasuda waved his umbrella to a cluster of people who raced into the pit and began rummaging around, cramming food into sacks and bags, they didn't have to fight over it, there was plenty for everyone … and then, I couldn't believe my eyes or ears, Jasuda pulled out a silver whistle and gave a shrill blast, the people in the pit froze … slowly picked themselves up and walked off with their spoils, Jasuda gave the nod to another crew … hey, Vulture nudged me, old lady aksed me ta give ya this, we got no use for it … he handed me a jacket, dazzling … green, but a new shade, the kind of thing only skiers used to wear till it caught on, it was warm though, zipper and everything … I was taken with it … thanks, thanks a lot, it's beautiful … Jasuda brought duds in once, liquidation … wasn't sellin or whatever, no need for thanks … a lot of the people here had coats like mine, ski caps too … a commotion broke out by the pit, the girl was still in there scrounging around despite Jasuda's emphatic whistle … Vulture grabs my elbow and says: That cow's gonna ruin everything, oughta get rid a elements like her … if she gets Jasuda pissed, he could jus call the whole thing off, an with winter comin … damn, what's that guy's problem, blowin his whistle at me, I say … can it, pal, says Vulture, where do you think we'd be without Jasuda, he's the one maintains aroun here, he's the one keeps order, don't ever say that again! … finally it was our turn, I crawled down into the pit with two other guys, the choice stuff was already gone, we stood on top of the slippery meat, passing up the stuff in packages, I stuck with Vulture's crew, the people from the fire … the girl drifted in again, had to shove her out of my way … it was like one great big bowl of goulash … in there with the sheep's heads, they made me sick to my stomach, hunks of flesh hanging off their throats, eyes shut … I snagged a head of lettuce, tossed up a bunch of rotten bananas … Stick suddenly staggered and slipped, reached out … I gave him a hand, and when I peeked up … Jasuda was looking right at me … a second ago I'd stuffed a piece of cheese in my pocket, packaged, hope he didn't see me, maybe it's not allowed … he didn't say a word though, just smiled at the crazy girl … I flung up canned goods, Vulture collected them in a sack … I didn't know how often the trucks came and I was afraid I'd hear the whistle … and I did … holding a chicken wrapped in foil, and as I raised my hand to toss it up I saw Jasuda again, tensely following me with his eyes, I put the chicken down … he smiled. Stick helped me up and together we dragged out the third, Míra they called him … c'mon up, I stretched my hand out to the girl, she sat on her haunches nibbling a stick of salami, covered with blood from the slaughtered animals, but so were all of us who'd been in the pit … Stick gave me a nudge, we gathered up the sacks and tied them shut. Just one truck left now, waiting I guess for Jasuda … le's go, c'mon, gimme a hand, said Vulture, wrestling a sack onto his back. We were almost the last ones left on the trail, we had a pretty long walk ahead of us … my sack was heavy … wait, Vulture … he didn't mind me calling him that … what about the girl? Who, that cow? … she'll stay. What? That's right, an he'll be there too … he'll wait! What's he gonna do to her? Hey, c'mon … ya can pick up a water bottle over at our place, got no water there where you are. Wait, Vulture … who is that guy, who is he? That's Mr. Jasuda. Nobody knows where he's from. An stop askin questions aready, we got a lot to be thankful for.

Besides the frequent rain, it drizzled constantly, and the nights were different too. It was light. Maybe because of the moon reflecting off the tinfoil, there were shiny surfaces everywhere, glass, sheet metal … at night you could see. It was bright. Silhouettes of trash heaps undulated through the Dump, so this was the sea I'd finally reached, not much murmuring, no waves crashing, one over the other, going forward, going nowhere … but underneath, the Dump was alive, sometimes it erupted, once I saw a fire break out, breach a trail, but since everything was soggy with moisture from the rain, the fires never spread, they only smoldered out … here and there a cloud of smoke would pass over the Dump, it occurred to me there might be some new creatures being born … out of the chemicals … some new thing … some kina dragon.

I found out what Stick'd been getting at about the Dump changing after a rain … after a real downpour the surface changed, at least where I was … paper mountains flattened under its weight, in other spots the surface swelled … where there used to be pieces of orange stuff now there was slimy muck, even the trails changed, but I didn't go out much. At least the rain drove off the bugs.

But there tended to be a lotta mud on those trails.

Occasionally I stopped by Vulture's, sat around the fire. Listened. Same stories here as at the station, even met a guy who'd hung out with Gramps for a time … but these people weren't as frenzied … there wasn't so much move-ment, there were even families here. From what I could get, the mysterious Mr. Jasuda had something like a police force … people with kids weren't scared anymore … Vulture told me he'd been one of the first to come to the Dump, back when people used to get jumped.

But there were still plenty of wild people here, a guy could never be sure. And I didn't have anything to take in hand, I'd thrown it away. Lost it. Not anymore, I'd told myself.

Oughta lay down a rope at least … so ya can always find yer spot, Vulture suggested. But I kina hang out all over, I said. Sometimes on my way back from the fire I'd take a detour on purpose, there was no need for anyone to know where I was. If there was a string they could find me. Mr. Jasuda. Or someone. No, thank you very much. Not anymore.

I kept playing around with magazines. Tearing out pictures of stuff and people, along with their names. In the head of lettuce I'd pulled from the pit were slugs, repulsive little things. I wondered if I threw them into one of those gurgling orange pools whether they'd grow into mutants. That's the kind of crazy stuff I thought about. But I kept quiet.

Food. I hadn't eaten so much since the days of the Organization. I fed myself even when I didn't have an appetite. I used to be a dancer, knew how to leap high. But now I dragged. The green of my jacket merged with the colors of the Dump. Here the mountain patrol in all likelihood would've been at a total loss. It was a colorful world. In that, it resembled the world in the magazines. I lounged around the barrels stuffing myself. No longer tortured myself with thoughts of Černá. Sometimes I'd see us making love. Sometimes I'd call up the silkiness of her skin. It didn't matter that two of my toenails had fallen off and the skin on my palms was peeling. I lay there sated, and on those increasingly rare truly warm days I'd strip naked and lie in the sun. It fed me too.

Sometimes I went for walks. Even when I didn't have to go anywhere, I did it for the movement. My head had stopped hurting. I only drank by the fire sometimes. It was the only way I could stand the lamentations and braggadocio. Some people have the unique ability to curse and beg for help all at once. Here almost everyone spoke that way.

Lying behind the barrels, I saw: the wind wafting pieces of paper, a trickle of water sparkling between the old train tracks, pulp oozing out of a burst plastic bag, two pigeons pecking a hunk of salami, then a dense black cloud spread over the scene, and when it floated off again the birds were gone and the paper had settled to the ground. All of it at once. I sensed a miracle. I was awestruck, filled with awe. This is happening? This exists? And I'm here to witness it? On the inside I was all curled up, but my body was taut. I didn't take anything for granted. It's here. It is what it is. And I'm part of it. It's … sometimes it's even beautiful and I enjoy it. That's enough.

Maybe it was the food, or maybe it was not talking so much, but I grew stronger and more peaceful. I'd put it aside. The idea that I'd kill myself if somebody else didn't kill me first was still in me. I'd betrayed a lot. I'd lost my tribe, my people, there was nothing tying me down.

Around the fire the tramps and drunkards spoke into the flames, conversations intertwining and crisscrossing like the trails of the Dump. It was the speech of the train station, a barebones tongue. Not trash. Always someone yammering: So I slug im, right, he's shittin his pants, right, an so's the other one, right, relating the wreckage of his odyssey in leftover language, a warrior without a war … yeah an I'm on her an she farts so I says, hey cow, are you shittin or fuckin, bitch … I says to him, I go, an I walk out, I tell ya …

And sometimes they fought. I surprised myself. The night Hippo kept goading me on. Why ya by yerself … you a homo? Yeah. Yer a disgustin moron! Hippo told me, obviously proud of his putdown, beaming around at the others. Cut it out, Vulture said, you know Mr. Jasuda doesn't like scuffles … he ain't here, said Hippo, slamming a branch into the fire. Then he yanked it out. Reminded me of the sheepherder. I whimpered, I'd almost forgot. Listen to him, whinin like a dog … are you a dog, you stinky-ass hobo? … Hippo gave me a shove. I fell into the fire on my knees, but then, getting up, the words tumbled out of me … shut your fuckin face or I'll kill you, I'll chop alla you into little bits, an as for you, you piece a shit, I'll skin you alive an carve you like a goose … I kicked him, he wasn't expecting it … Vulture stood up … suddenly I saw it all, the fire and the shadows, said: People, forgive me, I was asleep, he woke me up … yeah, he provoked cha, I saw it, said Vulture … shake hands, you're buddies now … we shook.

To Vulture, Jasuda was a god … and one day when I made a few disrespectful remarks, Stick … he was a little younger than me and one of his legs was shorter from some botched operation, so he walked with a cane, ergo the nickname … turned to me and said: Better watch what cha say, the old man works for Jasuda. Never know what might happen to ya! An … he took me aside, the old man's got a flintstick under a board out in the shack, Jasuda gave the okay, so watch it. I took what he said seriously, I'd met a pretty wide variety of bosses and their methods of enforcing obedience were all the same, the only difference was context, the most dangerous fucks're the ones who get off on their power … only the next day Vulture said the same thing about Stick … I decided to believe them both and kept my trap shut. After all, they'd probably saved my life, and did it like it was nothing, didn't feel the need to talk about it. If they hadn't taken me in, as a matter of course, without any bullshit or questions, I most likely would've gone down the first few days I was there. And not the way I wanted to, either.

Stick showed me where not to step. Stay away from the brown stuff, sticks to your soles, an don't ever step in those pools. Saw this one old bag fall in … Stick shuddered … glad it wasn't my granny … there were a lot of old people there at the Dump.

Among the machines, among their skeletons, I found a heavy iron lever, dragged it back to the barrels … lifted it every day. As the sun warmed up, I established a sort of daily routine. The only thing I wouldn't interrupt was my dreams, when images, words, and sentences emerged. I didn't move much then. Other times, though, the rhythm of the images forced me to walk around. I even went without water one day.

The Spinach Bar was still in my brain, that was where I'd spoken to her, that was where my love was, let her be a whore, let her be a single slit in the body of a whore, but let her *be*, let her be mine, I realized if I picked up and left it would only be to find her, because there was still hope … the images were also of all the trips I'd made by train, wherever, luggage swaying in the nets overhead, someone else's … and I supplemented my dreams. The magazines took up a lot of my time. I took my world from their pages too. Sometimes I had to peel all kinds of sticky stuff off of them.

One had photos I guess from some movie. Showed a kid standing there with a T-shirt on that said "Give me freedom or give me death." He was facing down a tank. Two meters away. Surrounded by pagodas with dragons all over em, some square, probly Asia. From the blur of the tank, the motion, it was obvious the crew'd made up their minds, the kid was gettin the latter. It got to me for a minute. Ah, it's just a movie, I waved it off.

The ads and photos got me going … I even recalled that first appointment with Micka, at the Tchibo coffee shop, I know a lot of ordinary stuff happened to people close to me that day. Like always. I added one more exercise to my routine, preserving words and sentences, writing them under each other. Sometimes they were connected. But the point was that it gave me material for my dreams, I didn't have to fumble around in my memory anymore ... in that cellar of mine, I had it down on paper.

I filled in empty spaces on magazine pages, the ones where there weren't photos. Got a ballpoint pen from Stick for my Mickey M. T-shirt, the one from the Mission. There were plenty of threads around. Plus Stick had a thing for Mickey. On the side of the pen was some ballerina or dancer, when you turned it upside down her skirt came off ... Stick told me he used to masturbate to it, then it got old and he found some porn.

While I wrote I thought a lot about Sister and the attic. This is my Firewater, I'd think to myself as I braked time with my writing, making it mine alone ... it was like a drug.

I tried to give a name to what mattered to me. It would exist more then, I felt. Even if just in my memory. What I'd lost. That was all I lived for anyway. It didn't seem right to avoid cruelty and hunger.

Hey, Bog, it's mine ... I've got it in my coat pocket. You need yellow wind, people as they are, pigeons that peck meat, you've got Jasuda an pits, cold rain an barbwire, I guess that's what makes the world go round, fine, I've got my time grenades, the worst they can do is blow my head off. These were the tales I put in my pocket:

Old Words

Today he sleeps under his dream can't bear it anymore. He's afraid
of truck wheels mounds of gravel animals the knife sickness.
But he's in her he's with her
they're together they'll protect each other.
Strong feelings. And he's battling in the arena
for his grandpas in the crematorium too.
It was B. that dragged em out on the ramp.
How did it happen? Were they too weak?
Let me be a Hun be a Devil-killer
he says to himself.
Sometime later Sister lifts herself up on her elbows
and says: Hey it's light out!
And it is. It's day, night is done. That's the thing
anyone can see.
A day with people like any other

and if it's summer
something's growing. It's January
and still the same old dirty
street of whores. Trade. That's all there is here now.
And maybe the whole city'll change in the night
like a brain written off by a dose.
Just to be safe he's relearning
quickly the old words of love.

Firewater

My sister is Firewater
I tell her: honey
she tells me: tenderness
and we tell each other: I love you.
And we drink Firewater.
Today the moon protects me from danger
at the head of my sister.
I'll swim in the water
in the power of fire till morning I get up
and clear out
through the dark hallway by memory down from the top floor.
My sister is Firewater
she's got messy hair and in the morning she says: go to work
I think: I take what I want and give what I can
and we tell each other: I love you.
The moon blazes and the two of us're here in the Firewater night
skin on skin. And everything
is important. Sister. Now, at night.
You're next to me in my dream
and after. Sound of breathing and touch of a fingernail
to the rhythm of blood in my brain. You.
Be with me. Closer still. My Firewater.

"Now go in peace"

the man in the cassock told the crowd
of Christmas people below.
Now I can see you every night.
I saw the words: Freedom or death.
I made them up. They're Sister's.

As the Ghost strode up the stairs toward me
I got a cramp in the elevator down
in my guts.
I'm thoroughly awed
brother
life.
Hey — I say
An my life's like ABC. I don't do a thing
I organize verbal matter
just what my cells tell me.
Singed brain.
My mafia.
I said: freedom or death.
I wanted and searched. And now I know they're Sister's.
I sleep with em. In the same flat. In this smallish sorta
room.

He's There

I slash my back
so I'll know that it's me.
If it hurts he's not an actor
stride altered by band-aids.
On the riverbank were trees
dampness settling into their tops
now there's just a hole.
Is this still the same city the walls
and streets my turf? Would I tell
him myself the child Hi Take care Good night
pass him by standing there
key around his neck in a raggedy sweater
with a puppy? Would I bring him home? Or
is that brat still there?
An are pedestrians passin him by? Nasty faces? Yes.
He's still standin there and he's alone. He's lost. His feet burning
over and over through that same that one that fiendish block of asphalt.

Into the City

On a sleepless night
sometimes faces swim in the dark
here and there one pops out
someone you used to know.
Then they all disappear with the morning trams.
Every madman knows how that is.
So tonight again in this home
full of Czechs in their in our
very own genuine state.
I guess it's better than bombing
definitely.
Sleep you don't gotta die you do you say to yourself it says softly
into your brain. But even that isn't for sure.
Shadows shift slowly along the walls and the moon's been there
for hours now. It's like past lives.
If you went into the city
you would feel it with all its shards.
That can be managed.
Here and there in the wind
a trash can creaks like a living thing.

Another Story

I felt
the friction of the future
and in your face my own one, love.
Fate, its weight. Waves of life
true happiness etc.
B-o-g willing
before the year is out I'll be an averagely agile businessman
dealing in used cars
that're fast as an eagle
as a pig
as someone else.
A guy's gotta live off something
if he wants to.
I'm also someone else.
I put my head on your arm
a little big but it was her.

Then I met my double he finished
my sentences the city was warming B.'s dead for you Brother
went away and at 7 a.m. the day caught my woman
at a fire drill tuning up
a hellish band
played to please all and the important appointment was
at 2 p.m. in the Tchibo coffee shop
but that's another story.

Me, for Me and B. and Defense

For me he's changed into B.
I call him Bog and hey Bog and think of hearts and of skin.
Someone was casually kissing caressing thinking of nothing
and someone was walking alone into a tunnel of corpses
B.'s all I've got now
and some words aren't at all pretty.
Dreams can be horrible someone screams and he's there
in a bayonet dream and some live their lives and they're totally theirs.
Some things you watch with your eyes find out
from others some things
are already written down. It's obvious.
You've gotta believe a little in all of it.
So you don't get lost
so the big dogs
don't catch you defenseless
the wheel doesn't run you down
the black widow bastard doesn't get you at home
at the end of the world in the dark.

Morning, Still

My hero that fella
I killed a rat killed a man yeah right another time
another place lying in the sand of a desert island beach
with a naked woman.
The fella laughs
and then someone forgives him
maybe
we've lost more than that and is B. here at all?
Anymore? He wondered that morning thinking of the court.

The one that sits nonstop from the very first second
from the very first cell from the dawn of the Earth
guess so he told himself looking in the mirror
as he shaved himself with his old razor
forever fucked up with
crud and rust.

Along the Way

Two little birds perched on branches
like in prehistoric times.
Even the blood looks the same
maybe thicker. Luggage jiggled in a threaded cage
by the lightbulb over our heads.
Up under the spider's web.
It was in my brain.
In the concourse they offered newspapers fliers flowers
kitchenware rags a whore and among the other passengers
I recognized the devil a man who wants to kill and a man
who's going he doesn't know where and there was no way to hide
among the trash cans or even in the elderberry bushes.
I was slowly beginning to love the spider now I knew:
he's got something going.
That time in the bar over spinach pizza I told
the most beautiful woman in the world my innards my everything
and the vein in my brain that link to the universe
nearly burst.
She smiled because she knew about life
and what it does: that's the way it is.
On the walls were faces of singers actors and boxers
some we knew.
We smiled a little the shine threw light on our faces
while the others walked around outside.
Had I turned my palms up they'd have been full of light
but there was no need.
I touched her hips and was gentle.
We groped each other. I said the worst I had in me
and grinned out the window. To where we'd been standing.
It was all behind glass. And it was secret.

Any Time At All

With any one of his next movements
Bog could cancel theater and actors.
Or else let them be in their colors
writhing crawling pacing
let them speak. At home. With the others.
In a room with walls. Where there's air.
Where there's love like a plant.

I mixed new and old words. Some of it I meant seriously, so I hid it away in more words. Spread it around. It was all about the same thing. Some of the pages I ended up losing.

And that night, as I wrote the word *plant,* I heard a cry. It came from the fire. Then there was howling and screaming … it wouldn't stop. A wail of pain. The wind kept rolling in my direction. I figured a brawl had broken out, so I didn't go over to look. Spent the day behind the barrels, crossing out and scrawling my stuff. And the next night it came again. A cry. And then howling. It was a person. Not calling for help. Howling. Then suddenly it stopped. And I heard … a soft rustling of paper, a little ways from my lair … something was walking around out there, I heard soft … little footsteps. I knew that it was out there and that it was looking. In my direction. I didn't even blink. Then it went away.

Next morning I went to see Vulture. He was there, along with his woman and somebody else … but they were … torn to shreds … blood all over. I had to throw up, crawled off, doubled over. But then I went back, averting my eyes from the dead … and the flies … I had a hunch where he kept it.

I tore up the boards in their shanty. There it was. A good old AK-3, un-wieldy perhaps, but compared to the horror around me … elegant. So, I said to myself … you're back in the wheel.

It was terrifying what happened to them. I saw part of Foxy's torso with tiny holes punched all over it. Whoever killed them had tortured them first. That explained the screaming. What kind of monsters were they … how am I supposed to include them in my awe when they could do me so much harm … Bog, I know your ways and traps … I know what it's all about. I'll survive as long as I can. I no longer wanted to kill myself, I'd stopped having dreams about it. Not now, now someone was after me. Someone other than me for a change.

As it grew dark I was afraid. They marched past. Just a pack of scamps. Scamps may be little, but when they get together ... Vulture'd told me stories about them setting tramps on fire. Douse em with gas an toss a match, that's how they got their kicks. He said that in the days before Jasuda,the stalingos used to come to the Dump and do it to people too. Keepin the city clean, they'd said ... he'd had to hide from em a few times himself. I hoped that when the scamps went ridin off on the shinkansen, He'd count it to their credit that they did it so they could see, so they'd know ... to get a whiff of death, they needed to know there really was such a thing. But not the stalingos, those guys had a fuckin ideology, a mission. Well, either way, to the victims it was all the same.

I poked the muzzle out through the barrels and got the crew in my sights. The one leading the way had his hair shaved on one side. On the other it was dyed blue and down to his shoulder. He leaned on a metal bar as he walked. Two scamps ran up onto the heaps and took a look around. Jumped pretty nimbly, they knew what they were doing. The others walked single file. All of them had something in their hands. Their getup was the usual. Something on top, something below, the main thing was fast shoes. They didn't come my way. Maybe they were just tryin to find a trail that'd been wiped out by the last rain. The wind tossed me a sentence from the two at the end of the line: I'm glad we're outta here. They disappeared over the heaps.

That night I heard the screams again. Far away. Next morning I went for water. Every step of the way I was afraid I'd run into a body. Some oldster was at the pump. He was glad to have someone to talk to. All he talked about was the Creature. More people showed up. Everyone was talking about it. We're packin it in, declared a guy scarred with smallpox. It's those motherfuckin stalingos, they're tryin to drive us out. Nuh-uh, said a woman in a blue men's robe, this is some new ting, sumpin from here, I was talkin wit da reporters, they tolt me. An those guys know! They got a inside track ... I'm gonna be in the papers. TV's comin too! Some decided to leave, it'd been a long time since Jasuda's trucks last showed up. On my way back I ran into Hippo. Hi! I said to my buddy, jutting out my chin ... but he had no hatred in him. Said I should join his crew, it was all over here ... c'mon, Hippo, some killer creepin around, we'll spring a trap on him ... Naw, this's somethin weird, you saw

Vulture. Yeah, I'm sorry bout that. He helped me out a lot. How bout Stick? He's comin wid us, you oughda too ... Where you goin? Train station. No thanks, aready been.

I don't know why I stayed. When it got dark I took out the AK and stood watch ... and then I heard soft steps coming toward me, broke out in sweat ... they went off to the side, my heart lilted with relief ... but then they came toward me again and I realized I didn't have ammo. I clutched the rifle like a club and waited.

Hello, said a voice. Soft and sweet. I peeked out. It was a child. A little boy stood there smiling. And his eyes ... they glowed ... I knew him.

Remember me, Potok? Uncle? The boy kicked a barrel with the toe of his sneaker.

Can I come in, can I come visit? In your little house.

Blood pounded in my temples. I had no doubt this was the Creature, it was him, the demon ...

Are you gonna kill me? I stammered.

I'll think about it, Potok. Why don't we have a nice talk, huh?

Even his voice was childlike. He came in. The glow from his eyes lit up my burrow, the barrels shining ... silver.

You're ... I squeezed out, you're from the well, Kučera's boy.

Yeah, he said, hanging his head. A little kid with a crewcut, in shorts, a T-shirt, and sneakers. White socks, standing there, hands in his pockets.

An you know what I saw down there? You know what all of us saw?

Uh-uh.

Torture, you know? They showed us torture. An they let us touch it, they let us get inside it a little. Just a little teeny bit. But each of us was all alone an we were sweating blood. Blood. Get it? Me an those big girls an the granny. Why us, I don't know. Do you? An we were afraid someone was gonna do it to us too. What they were doin to those other people. We didn't know how bad it could be till we saw. Anyone can do it. Anything's possible. An we were all by ourselves, an then we weren't even human anymore. We changed down there. An you know what we changed into, Uncle Potok, do you? the boy whimpered.

What do you want from me?

I want you to help me.

I crossed myself. The boy smiled. His glowing eyes smiled too. I touched the Madonna on my chest, the boy nodded his head.

That's why I'm here. I hadda do some real bad things, you know.

He stuck out his tongue, licked his lips, gave me a wink, then rocked up on his toes like he was stretching ... and took a step toward me. I was afraid he was going to touch me.

I'm just a little boy, you know? he said. An I can't take it much longer. It's too much. Little boys like me, when they don't have a daddy ... he winked at me again ... or mommy, they get tired real quick. You know?

I just gulped.

I want you to do something ... to me, he took another step closer ... I'm just a lost little boy, said the Devil, an it took me a while to find you. I had to ask around, he laughed, rocking up on his toes again, but now here I am an I've got you. He blinked, and in the glow that came from his eyes his lashes were totally white ... he stood looking at me ... and I realized to my amazement that I was standing upright inside my cave, like all at once the walls had grown, I saw stone and wood, smelled the rot ... yeah, that one you called Vulture was scared of rats, so I did a rat for him ... another one was scared of cops, so I showed him a cop, well, they're in hell now, how bout you? What're you most afraid of? Do you know? ... we were standing in a tomb and lying on the catafalque was a little white coffin, not for me, flashed through my mind ... nope, said the boy, it's for me, I want peace ... you gotta do it, said the Devil, my little boy body's all tired out, it was horrible doin those things.

How? I stuttered, my voice sounded like it was coming from out of the sacks on the ground.

Shoot me, the boy said. With what you've got in your hand. An whatever you've got that's valuable. Once you do it, you'll be able to protect yourself. Forever. I'll be back tomorrow. An if you aren't ready, I'll hafta stay on earth like this ... an it'll hurt you a lot. Bye now, Uncle Potok. The boy walked out of my barrel shack. Without a sound.

I couldn't sleep. That was no dream, uh-uh. What'm I supposed to do it with ... whatever I've got that's valuable, and from then on I'll be able to protect myself ... he'll come for sure, that glow, everyone who came out of the well had that glow in their eyes. Then I realized what he meant.

The next day I spotted some people again. They'd said they weren't leavin, that they were gonna stay till the end, but the night before they'd found another shredded body ... one insisted they oughta call the cops ... yea an den dey chase us outta hea ... naw, man, the guy laughed, we call em in, an it eats dem ... heh heh, the bottles went around the circle.

Found a mold among the wrecked cars, I think some thing for ball bearings. I didn't say goodbye to Madonna, just gave her a pat like a thousand times before ... my grandpas, she'd protected every one of them, but now I guess the world's different an I gotta fight ... I melted her down, the bullet came out pretty well ... I think I know who was helpin me, the fire got the black coating off, then I scraped and smoothed the surface ... turned the silver bullet in my hand ... pretty handsome ... I stood up ... for the first time in ages I did a little dance, just with my elbows an heels ... then I roared, true ... and good thing I'd been in the army, I took apart the AK-3 and put it back together ... then waited, had a few cigarettes.

It was a full moon. One minute I was shuddering, the next I just grimaced. An when I do this, will I go back to bein human? With a kind face and a sneer underneath, or the other way round, or both at once? An maybe ... you know, Černá, wherever you are. I hope you're doin all right.

He stood before me.

Look, big man, I cut up my knee, he sniffled, we were playin monkey in the middle ...

I didn't move.

Are you ready? said the Devil.

Yes.

Yesterday ... it's funny ... the guy was scared of trucks so I changed myself into a car, you should've seen his face ... I shredded him to bits. It hurt him. Are you scared?

Yes.

Then watch this, the Devil said.

And the little boy began making faces, leering, laughing, his face peeled off from inside ... like it was being swallowed by fire, dissolving in some solution, his eyes were glowing though, you could almost touch the silver glow, and then ... he had on a warm-up suit, it was still a tyke, but another one, in a striped T-shirt ... sulking, soccer cleats on his feet, and around his neck ...

No, I said.

He was blond, skinny, elbows scraped, the way little boys' are, around his neck was the thin imprint of a string, and on the string ...

I can't, I said, dropping the rifle on the ground.

Because that key ... I knew it, I'd opened the door with it a thousand times, and there was the vestibule, my father kept his sack of birdfeed in there, I was scared of that sack ... scared the Blind Man from the pirate movie was hiding inside and would jump out and grab me, I'd raced past it into the kitchen a thousand times ...

I wanna go home, the boy whimpered.

His eyes were blue, a little bit cock-eyed, I recognize him, myself, I remember ... I remember every mirror from back then ...

Where am I? Lemme go home. I don't wanna be here, said the boy.

I picked up the rifle.

I picked up the rifle and placed the barrel to his temple, clenched my teeth, and squeezed the trigger ... bang! ... he tumbled onto his back, head spurting blood, the bullet had torn his face wide open ... the body curled up, eyes twinkling a moment, then he shut them and he was gone.

You did it, I heard a hiss. You're free.

I know, I screamed, squatting on my heels, rifle in my lap, the barrel was warm ... I had to sway, just with my head ... back and forth ... back and forth ... the hissing voice I guess came from me. I don't know if it said anything I was supposed to remember. Anything of value.

I knew where to go. As fast as possible. When I woke the next morning, there was frost everywhere. Don't they even get fall here, the one season I was fond of, even if autumn stuff did occasionally throw me off pretty good ... I needed to warm up, slipped into my duds. Took the rifle and tossed it in one of those gurgling holes. Then headed out. Made it through the Dump in a couple hours. By now I knew the way.

On the street people turned and stared, bundled up in that quilted jacket, plus the skier's thing on top ... I made quite an impression. And then I realized, I must stink pretty bad. Compared to how I'd dragged at the Dump, I was moving fast now. I had a reason, too. And maybe I was too late.

The sign was still there, though rusted now. And the balcony was covered with wire mesh. I rang the buzzer and almost instantly a head appeared behind the netting. I recognized him, guess he couldn't say the same for me.

Open up. It's cold as hell.

You the messenger?

Huh? I'm Potok.

Huh? The head disappeared.

A moment later the door opened, photoelectric cell I guess. I slammed it shut behind me. The old entranceway was gone. In front of me was a TV screen with me on it. Then the next door opened and I stepped into … a cage. Ugh, you gotta be kiddin … they came walkin up, two. I didn't know em, either that or they'd grown a lot … where's Montague? I asked. One of em pinched his nose with his fingers and offered me his hand, they walked behind me … what kina act're you guys puttin on here, Montague … but then I clammed up. He'd turned out pretty hefty. Oh yeah … you're … ex-boss Uncle Potok. Didn't recognize you at first. What up, Uncle? … barely got the word through his lips, he was big now … Stein an the boxes? … an the resta my uncles? … they're all somewhere, Montague, but look, it's urgent, I gotta talk to your dad … your sisters turn up? … yeah, he said, and from the way he said it I could tell something had happened … where are they? … in with Dad, been a week now, said Montague, eyes glued to me … Father's in there with em an that's what's got us worried, yeah, said one of the young men behind me … Dad's like, sick, said we're not allowed to come near him … I think I know what it is, Montague, I gotta get in there … my name's Gyros, said one of the two, you don't remember me, I was little, what happened to you, Mr. Potok … I realized it was the first time any person apart from waiters and cab drivers had actually called me mister … it stunned me … apparently I'd gotten rather old and cracked … can I wash up? But first lemme see your father … Maybe, just maybe, said Montague thoughtfully, you might wanna take a bath first. No time, your dad can take it … Montague gave in and led me … downstairs, metal doors all the way, and as he unlocked them, one by one, he told me the story: Some a my bros left, but there's still plenty, thought you were one a the Vondráčeks, they're how come we're barricaded in here like this … they insist they also got a restitutional claim … to the lab, Vondráčeks at first, nother old Prague famiglia … we got a feud … he stopped at one of the doors. Dad doesn't wanna see me, he said weirdly … any of us, but give it a shot … wait'll I leave, gotta lock you in, Dad's orders … then slam it hard … wait, Montague, are the girls in there? Took em in soon as they turned up … kay I'm goin, he walked slowly, peeking back at me over his shoulder.

I waited till he shut the door, then pounded. Now I couldn't turn back. I stood in a dark hallway between two metal doors. Just a chilly little light blinking over the last one. Looks like a bunker … I shuddered and pounded again.

Doctor! It's me, Potok! He came to see me … little Kučera … from the well. If it's just you in there, girls, open up, I don't care anymore … Doctor …

The door opened, I don't know how, he was sitting in an armchair in the corner. Vats, scalpels, flasks everywhere, water bubbling …

I see you. He said.

Now I knew why Montague had left so quickly. This wasn't the voice of old Doctor Hradil, the clever Mohawk beast … this was the Beast itself talking … he stood up, I gazed into the flat gloss of his silvery eyes.

I reached for my throat.

He tore the cord with the scalpel off his neck and tossed it on the desk in front of me.

I know everything, the voice croaked. It's a good thing you came. An don't be afraid. I'm not like them yet … but I will be. It's getting closer.

What about your girls?

He pointed to one of the vats.

Of course I could tell right away, I'm their father … I finished them off. They would've killed my other children.

That grating voice … broke. Or seemed to. He sat down.

I donno what force brings you here, old Potok, by the way you look ghastly, like some scarecrow or somethin, but you're just in time. I tried … I know that one of my sons has to do it. I tried, but I can't bring myself to tell them. I had em lock me in here so I couldn't, you know … but I can already tell, another door or two, he waved his hand. Take this upstairs, he patted the silver scalpel … an one of em has to come, tonight. Tell him what he has to do. I know about Kučera, they're … they were linked. The boys'll get over it, you can explain. An you donno how sweet those daughters of mine were. Nobody knows. Now they never will. Marie and Anna were their names. They were … lovely, they were sweet girls. I donno why it happened.

I took the scalpel and carefully stuck it in my pocket.

Wait, said the Doctor. Look at this.

On the table sat a vat. Inside it a transparent liquid. The surface quivering. I could see through the smooth glass sides. The smell drifted over to me. It smelled good and I felt a great hunger. I wanted to touch the vat, clutch it tight.

I knew this was what I wanted. I stood at the table. Doctor Hradil's hand flashed through the air and the glass shattered against the wall.

Yep. That's it, he said. I finally did it. You're probly the only person who's ever seen the Elixir. In today's era.

Elixir? But …

This is the genuine stuff. But it's made of … that. They're in it. You wanted it bad, huh?

It was strong.

Again I inhaled the aroma. As it faded into the walls' dampness.

Now go tell them.

Aright, M.D., I understand. I'll tell em how to do it. An I've got a great sorrow inside me. For everything. Bye. I'm goin.

Tell them … to sort it out with the Vondráčeks somehow, put an end to it. It's what I want.

If that's what you tell em, they'll do it.

Maybe. An one more thing … which one's it gonna be?

Montague.

Montague! My favorite … why does it have to be him …

He's the only one I know. An Doctor, surely you know the old Jewish joke. Why me?

Why not. Said the Doctor. But you've got it mixed up, that's from the old Doctor's Heap of Anecdotes … it's the patient that asks … hah, well, same difference.

I guess so. Later then.

Yeah. Later.

I wasn't in any hurry. First I told Montague okay, a bath. Climbed into the tub and instantly fell asleep. He shook my shoulder, the water was cold. What time is it? There was still time … Montague brought me some of his older brothers' clothes … we torched that getup a yours … I felt a little jolt inside me … yeah, no big deal, I said … there were some papers too, my sisses read em … And? I was all ears … Well, Montague blushed, some of em said good an all … an some, he turned away … What? What'd they say?! Well, they were laughin. He handed me the pages, but I was in the tub, the poems got soggy, tossed em on the floor … Montague passed me the clothes … Here ya go, jeans, black … zip or buttons? Rivets, said Montague … Some dress shirt, green silk … World War II parachute, Montague alerted me … I nodded …

the only T-shirt he had was one with Batman on it, whatever ... tall leather boots ... those're my oldest bro's, David's ... huh, who ... David, you know, the one that stayed with the Mohawks ... aha ... want a cap, it's yellow ... not a chance! ... here's a dark green one ... give it here! Next an excellent coat and a belt around my waist. All dressed up. And after what I'd been through at the Dump, deep down in my soul I began to consider myself a new man. You look a little like the old Potok, said Montague.

Then I gave him the scalpel. Told him. What he had to do. Left him alone.

It occurred to me in the kitchen that it wouldn't be bad to stay a spell ... if only for the sake of my tongue, on my last two stops I'd lost the habit of speaking normally ... and some of my expressions weren't at all appropriate around the girls ... I felt for Montague, but maybe because of what I'd just been through ... I was at peace inside, like fatalism or somethin ... the daughters leaned over the fire, roasting a lamb ... I felt a stab in my heart, Černá, where are you, I couldn't stand the way one of the girls moved as she arched her back, carrying a pot, I got up ... Montague escorted me out through the corridors, it'd floored him when he first heard, but now he was calm ... he'd been through more than enough for his age, and knew the things of the box, he'd been able to answer the ancient question on his own ... he locked the door behind me.

Again I was leaving somewhere ... but not clearing out hastily, fleeing madly, slinking off in a fever ... walking, with the city in front of me. Even fingered ... my clothing a little, I was walking without Madonna, and I hissed through my teeth, I'm goin to see Černá, I'm comin to see you, my sweet ... because if you're dead, then I'll make it through my time here without you somehow ... dreaming of a woman ... and we'll meet afterwards, in eternity. It's the only way. Walking, neither avoiding people, nor feeling the need to crash into them, walking ... and then I saw the stone.

It spoke to me. Not that I heard anything, no talking stone. None a that mysticism. It just captivated me. A cornerstone, the kind they used to give buildings so the carriage wheels wouldn't bang up the plaster. That stone was somewhere in my memory, something was going on ... and then I glanced up, I was on that street. The street above the German Embassy, I was back at the beginning, from here it stretched uphill ... it was after a rain, the air was cool ... I saw roofs and house signs, there was the lion, I'd aimed here without even knowing it ... I felt my hands and throat and breath again ... and raised those hands … to clasp them … and then something hit me on the back, like wing-stirred air, I fell, and flew a while, and for an instant felt my skull, the bones, the walls of the depths, the bony walls of my world, and I fell on the stone headfirst. It hurt, and then it went dark.

I was coming to … I heard ringing … maybe the bells again, crowding into my mind … and then I opened my eyes and saw a woman's face. It was beautiful, I wanted to speak but couldn't move my tongue, I couldn't move … honey, I dredged out … and then focused, no, it wasn't Černá. It was a gentle face, viewing me from up close with concern, a girl with some kind of veil or hood over her head … the room was dim, I could feel her touching my hand, and it was bliss … she was close, I noticed that she didn't have even a smidgen of makeup on …

Thank God you're recovering, she said. And walked out.

It was a nun.

I was in a small room, whitewashed, over my head hung a crucifix. The sheet was stretched tight, and the blanket, no, a down comforter, it had been years … smelled good, I caught a whiff of old lavender, none of that new stuff made outta monkey guts … I couldn't move though.

I didn't wake again till the middle of the night, and there on the wall … where before there'd been nothing, I spotted another face … a woman's, also in a hood, a veil, her eyes were smiling … on her face she had a scar though, some saint, I thought, and felt … guilty, maybe I'm in some convent, it occurred to me as I looked at her … because, I admit, that face was sexy … turned me on, but in a friendly way, not like one of those wrestling matches with stuff sprayin right an left … I studied the face, she was an ambitious woman, I think, there was something burning inside her, she was strong. And then I closed my eyes, and suddenly I hear … little brother, hey … get up outta that fuckin … deathbed … it was her, that raspy voice … I hear you unmistakably, Černá, that means you're alive, no Saint ever talked like that, do you think about me, Černá … at least sometimes … and I waited, tense and ready, but I couldn't move … and nothing else happened and I fell asleep.

Yeah, Bog knows I'm recovering, I thought … Sister Maria Coseta came to see me every day. At first I was a nervous wreck, I knew whose bride she was … but she knew how to talk to me. She was younger than me. Yes, definitely there's a lot more people younger than me around. Than at the beginning of my story. I'm aware of that. That's the way it goes in ordinary time.

As time passed ... it struck me that she enjoyed coming to see me, and I said so. She told me the story of her order ... the Silent Sisters of the Divine Child. Its members swore an oath of silence.

That's why I like visiting you so much, said Sister Maria. To chat. And you've been so many places. How's the head?

Doesn't hurt at all now. I've only traveled around Bohemia, but maybe that's not what you mean. Anyway, you never told me how I wound up here. This is total salvation for me.

You mustn't speak of salvation that way. They found you on the street, not far from here.

But I mean you can't go puttin up every stiff ... pardon me, Sister, every needy person ... you find.

You know why we took you in? Perhaps I shouldn't, but ... she took a step toward me ... undo your pajama top, yes, there ... she touched me with her finger, and all I wanted was for that hand to stay there, she must've been able to tell ... she quick drew back her finger ... we eyed each other ... how long've you been in the order?

Over a year now.

Sometimes I could sense in her ... not exactly the street or the bar ... but we had something in common. I didn't like that idea at all. My ... friend was alive, she knew how to move. I think she knew how to be pretty fast. That chamber of mine was full of her. And the life she gave off, it was like even her skin was breathing ... it was probably the best medicine I could've had. I told her she was rescuing me with every move she made. She laughed. But one day she said: That's why we're here. That's why we're all here.

Since I couldn't read yet, she would read to me. Her voice was bright and clear. Sometimes when she was speaking, formally and properly, an ending would drop off. Sometimes she would swallow conjunctions. Every now and then she would laugh from her throat, a laugh that didn't seem to go with the silent corridors around me. Sometimes it was like she was telling me old things beneath the words. Her eyes gave off flashes and mist.

If a nun, God forbid, put on makeup, she'd look the same as a waitress, I theorized pointlessly. And the other way around. Sister Maria was the only one I saw, maybe that's why I was so preoccupied with her. I tried to lower my chin

to my chest so I could see the spot where she'd touched me, gently, like silk …
and then I saw it and threw up on my pillow. I looked again and again, until
my neck was sore. There was the Madonna. My Black Madonna, tiny as the
medallion, in all her beauty, in the pain of her scar. She who weeps eternal. It
didn't look like a tattoo … you'd think a tattoo would embarrass a nun, but
Sister Maria told me she liked the dragon very much … the Madonna looked
like it was seared into my skin, or maybe like an engraving … right above the
dragon! … I was very happy to have her there.

So they took me in because of that?

We had both gotten into the habit of referring to the order as *they,* Maria
was a novice.

I suppose so. I don't know too much about it though.

Are there a lot of sick people here?

No. Just a few.

Why did you take down that picture?

Huh?

I told her about the woman's face, the picture I'd seen my first night. That
upset her. She was holding a book she'd brought me, nearly dropped it on the
floor.

So you saw her … no kiddin, yeah?

She ran out of the room. About an hour later returned … I tried to sit up
straight or whatever … this was the first time I was seeing the other nuns, they
had different habits … there were three, just one young one … and she looked
strict … the two older ones had an air of kindness … they were ladies … I
mean you can tell, whores or ladies, even when they merge, that was the sinful
abomination that flashed through my bandaged head, I admit … Maria stood
beside me, unpainted eyes not even blinking, apparently it was a serious moment.

They wanna know if you saw her besides the first night.

Yeah. Yes. Can you hear them?

Yes. They already taught me that. They want to know how you feel and
whether your head hurts.

Tell them I've tried walking already and I feel fine. Just weak is all.

They can hear you. Wait a sec, she turned to them.

They'd like to see what you have on your skin.

You mean the dragon?

She blushed. I undid my pajama top, personally I've never owned any. Then I thought of something and froze.

So can they hear what I'm thinkin too? I asked Sister Maria.

One of the older nuns looked at me, smiled, and ... shook her head.

Just in case, I said.

They leaned over me and inspected the Madonna. But didn't touch me.

It seems weird me not seein a doctor, I declared.

They say you don't need one. Not anymore.

Then they left us alone. Maria had already told me a lot about the order. But apparently she didn't know that much herself. She said they came from Spain and that a lot of the sisters were South American. The first thing I asked about was the bells.

You see, said Sister Maria Coseta, you're Catholic, I suppose ... weelll, I said, I didn't even mention that stuff about Bog, not me, I was glad to be there ... the sisters feel themselves bound by their mission, so it's just ... the chapel where they assemble, the bell's in there ... uh-huh, I said, attempting to catch a pesky fly ... they care for the Divine Child, the Baby Jesus, all through Latin America ... the Indians worship it ... you've no doubt heard of the Carmelites, my little sister lectured me, she'd brought in a chair, not like at the beginning when she'd sat on the edge of my bed ... this order split off from them in the seventeenth century, but wasn't recognized ... seventeenth, that's baroque, right? I inquired craftily, Sister Maria had brought me a book of poems called *Rose of Wounds** with some old and beautiful words in it ... even read the flaps, out of boredom.

It was only when I asked her how she came to the order that she wouldn't give me an answer ... but one day, as I pried insistently while hunting flies, and by then we were pretty much buddies, she said: Just like you.

Huh?

I'll tell you, why not. They found me. I recovered here. I stayed.

What'd you do before?

What's it to you?

You're right.

The first few days I felt sick, my head hurt, the string began to make itself heard again in the distance ... I was scared of it, scared to sleep even, because of the dreams, Maria brought me some tea, though, that made me sleep like a rock ... sometimes I told her I couldn't stand it there ... and after a very long time and much begging and pleading Maria brought me a cigarette, I smoked it in the bathroom, fighting off a couple faints, she laughed. Steered me back into bed. I guess that cigarette messed me up, I touched her. She sprang back.

Cut it out! Do that one more time and you'll never see me again. I'm Maria Anna Fatima Coseta now ... an I belong to the order of the Silent Sisters. Don't forget it! Don't ever forget.

Sorry. Forgive me, Sister.

Ever since the three nuns' visit, Maria had been casting mysterious glances at me, puffing up my puffed-up pillow, walking around the room, telling stories ... what's goin on? I asked. What's it mean, that visit a theirs?

Oh, she said, that was a big honor for you, a great honor, the mother superior spoke about you at the staff meeting, I mean, you know, they don't talk, but ... Why not? I'd asked that one several times now, she always gave an evasive answer. So as not to defile ... their tongue! I guessed ... the paths to the Lord, they say ... and anyway they don't need to, I mean, you know, since they can ... tell me, Sister Maria, what secret're they protectin, some of em have their tongues cut out, I read something somewhere ... she put her hands in front of her mouth, I donno, she gasped, maybe some ... but listen, they really did talk about you, and that's a big honor ... what'd they say? She got flustered again ... listen, you know how much this treatment would cost you anywhere else, and you have a room to yourself ... and you ... yes, and I'm free to come here and talk with you whenever I want, it's unbelievable, you know you're the first person I've spoken with normally for any length of time since I came ... why, Maria, whadda they want from me?

You know ... Mr. Potok, she flashed a smile, it may sound fantastic to you, but nothing surprises me anymore, that woman who appeared to you was Sister Samaritas, some say Samargas, and this order reveres her and is searching for her, truly searching! That's their mission.

How ... I don't get it.

I found out, Maria said softly, she's alive, that is, just an incarnation of her, of course, but she's out there somewhere!

Well, why not, I wriggled on the bed.

And she, Maria swallowed, she was from the tribe of the Samaritans and knew Jesus, she knew him well! They met by the well that time, and this order believes that Jesus ... the Samaritans were shoved aside like dogs, you know, it's in the Bible ...

Way things were then, I said, why not ... I mean, Mary too, but sayin that kina stuff scares me, Sister, I can't ... so this is the order of the Baby Jesus, the Child?

Exactly, said Maria, it's connected ... that's the connection! and they might want you to go somewhere, carry out an assignment for them.

Gladly, Maria, gladly.

It might be another country, they might send you somewhere, you have the sign, they said so yesterday at the staff meeting, and listen, you're getting bored here, huh.

Not at all, I sleep a lot, catchin up from all those crazy nights, an I dream an get beautiful books an talk with you.

The sisters say you've tried a lot of things, that you've done harm even.

Uh-huh, lots ... Maria! So they know ... and out it came.

Maria ... I really love this one woman, but she, she became a whore, see, I couldn't stand it ... and my first night here she spoke to me, she's out there somewhere ... I abandoned her, betrayed her, and now, if I could have her, I'd chop off my hand, or do whatever, I really long for her an I donno where she is. A harlot, sold herself, get it?

Lie down ... she pushed me back into the covers and grabbed my hand ... you can't talk that way about her, you don't have the right ... maybe she had to ... what do you know about women, what do you know about her, lemme tell you somethin. You wanna know if their tongues're cut out ... tongues, pfeh, what about me! An what was I sposta do? An what can I say? I'm standin outside, back then, I'd left, and I say to myself: Where do I go? Where am I supposed to go now? And then I fell, bad, you're not the only one. To the bottom. That's all there are here. Just people who come back. To life. You have to hang on, you have to. You have to hang on to life.

Now I was the one shaken ... she'd told me a lot, a strand of hair had slipped out from under her veil, she was twisting it.

And the next day I was feeling much better, pacing around the bed and calling my room a cell, purely in jest ... the next day she brought in a little man in spectacles carrying another chair ... this is Father Antonio, also known as Lobo, Father Lobo, Sister Maria said, flashing that smile of hers ... and he's going to teach you Spanish ... I hope you won't refuse ... of course not, great idea, I love the sound of that language ... *galeón*, I barked at the little man ... *caravela*, I said, he sat down ... *caballero*, I gave it a try ... *misericordia*, he volleyed back, and I shut up, having exhausted my vocabulary. He began cleaning his glasses. I saw that movement afterwards many times, every day. It astonished me how similar Spanish grammar was to the Bohemian tongue's, and I liked the upside-down question marks, chopping back at the sentences, spearing them like hooks.

Out? Maria, out is the last thing I want, I don't want to see anyone … I'm dying to go to her place, but I don't dare yet, no, I have to wait … can't imagine myself on the street yet, but I gotta start runnin or somethin … I missed movement. We had an agreement, a pact, that I wouldn't wander around the convent.

Maria said there weren't any men there at all, Father Antonio walked over each day from Břevnov,* and I rejoiced when he told me what Lobo meant, el Lobo … the only man there was the gardener, he was deaf and mute … Maria got an idea and made a few inquiries … yes, you can help him out, but …

They let me walk around the garden, I had to tie a little bell around my knee … some of the sisters are strict and don't want to see any men, this way they'll know when you're coming … so I got my own clothes back, winter was closing in, I'd been there a long time, I was feeling strong, a couple times it occurred to me, jump up an swing over the wall an I'm gone, who knows what they got planned for me … in the garden was a ladder for the apple trees, I watched them a lot … but I think I stayed for Maria's sake, slacking off with the gardener and carting around manure, jingling at the sisters, occasionally they'd go for walks dressed in their flowing vestments, like something from another world … sometimes it was misty.

The gardener was a smoker, the first few I could barely stomach, but I was coming back … coming back to life.

I might, said Maria, I might have to go away.

What? No!

Yes, we have missions, in the Andes and elsewhere … and now I can tell you, you may go one day too.

With you?

No, that's out of the question, she laughed, I told you, the order may ask something of you.

They've found other people with signs …

Yes, said Maria.

And the order sent them somewhere?

Yes.

And hey, sweet Maria, did they come back?

Yes, on my honor, they did come back. But they belong to the order.

Didn't find anyone, huh?

That's right, said Maria. No one.

Tell me what it's all about, Sister.

Come on, you know.

I got a hunch, but I donno nothin. And let me tell you, sweet Maria, thank you for everything. Now, since there might not be an opportunity.

You're going to run away? Leave?

Not just yet.

Now you're lying.

You can understand, Maria, my girl's all I care about. Černá's her name. I can't just wake up one day, learn Spanish, an set out into the jungle, or the mountains, or I donno where, to go look for some Saint.

You of all people can, Maria laughed. I could tell you that I'll be punished, severely punished, if you leave. But it wouldn't be true. If you do run away though, I warn you. You owe a debt to the order. And one day, sooner or later, you'll have to pay it back.

What, you mean they'll come after me?

They'll know where you are.

For another week or so, I would learn Spanish in the morning — *Yo no tengo dinero*, for instance — and then, between lunch and supper, I'd learn sign language from the gardener. Mostly all the old fogy taught me was phrases like: get the rake, bring the watering pot, weed this, water that, more manure, want a smoke? We jingled.

And one night … I couldn't sleep, all riled up thinking of Černá … craving her with all my might … the door to my room flapped open like a black wing, noiselessly, a chill gusted in from the hall, and in walked Maria, leaned her back against the doorframe, some simple coat on over her habit, gasping for breath … this is it, she said, I have to go … I got up, then quick snatched the covers back … she just shook her head, that movement that says, yeah yeah … so, she said … watch yourself out there, Sister, an I owe you a lot, really … forget it, and you watch yourself too, then at last I walked over to her, caught hold of her shoulders, but she gently pushed me away … placed a finger on my lips, said: God be with you … and was gone.

I didn't go after her, I never went after her, we had a sort of pact. I couldn't sleep a wink afterwards. And during my morning lesson I was rather unfocused.

I expected a scar when they took off my bandages, but I'd only lost a little hair … on the side that wasn't wounded, it had even grown out a little. I'll get my do fixed somewhere else, I told myself. Since Maria had left, the only people I'd seen were Father Antonio and the gardener. I'm betraying you, dear sisters, but for her sake … I'm more bound to her, don't be angry … and to the spot where I'd seen the image of the Saint, I said rudely: I don't know who you are, but thank you for showing me your beautiful face … and don't you get mad either, you know what I saw in your face … I think you definitely get what I'm sayin, and wish me luck on my journey … after all, what do I know, you're the Great One … just that time is still running and the order knows about me. Samaritas, protect your Maria Anna Fatima Coseta, I mean it! … and me too, if possible … Christ, protect us all if you've got the power, everybody needs it … or if you choose, your business … I nearly crossed myself, but with the order still unrecognized … I worked it out somehow.

In the morning I left my pajamas there.

It woulda been pretty shitty to steal em.

And then … despite the fact that he was making the sign for the watering pot, I snatched the ladder and propped it against the wall, the old geez leaned on his rake and watched … afraid he'd try to stop me, I crept up the ladder … keeping on the alert, he made another sign … all right, I said to myself, I'll risk it, on purpose, see what it does … I jumped down and went over … he handed me one and lit it, I kept watching in case he made a sudden move, wouldn't've advised it, but no, he just nodded his head and blinked his eyes, rapped his forehead and pointed to me and then pointed … I quick undid the bell, the gardener grinned and laughed, forcing the laughter out like some kind of substance. I'd gotten used to my sleigh bell, the gardener was right.

I was glad to be able to tell him goodbye. We stood there, the faint sun of early spring glaring in the mist above us, like a medallion I guess. When I'd finished my smoke, he slapped me on the back and made a sign like he couldn't see, struggling with the rake … At the top of the ladder I got a slight case of vertigo, but I swung myself up and was over the hump and holding on and dangling down, let go, and rolled up to the feet of some pedestrian, a baldy in a tie with a briefcase … back again, I told him, he moved his legs out of the way … I got up and felt fine.

I rubbed my eyes, shut off my view, then stared back … the door had a knocker, yep … and that symbol, the sign on the door, I was there the whole time … another place that'd changed masters, now it belonged to the sisters, oh She-Dog, I was right on top of the spot the whole time … and surely, my She-Dog, it's thanks to your forgiveness, because you forgave me, that I came back … and I'm alive, I won't go there, not down those steps and into that cellar, I just climbed down a high wall, now I'm on the other side … and I'm going to live and I'm not going back in there, not anymore.

23

BUT I WASN'T SURPRISED. ODD JOBS.
I WAIT. I SEE … THE CURVE OF HER NECK.

Černá wasn't there. At the entrance my heart was pounding and I had to lean on the banister, the rest of the floors I sprinted up, and burst in the door … and she wasn't there, she couldn't be. Everything was as she'd left it. As if nothing had happened since. I remembered our last night together. Never did forget it.

There were candle stumps and dust all over. Her clothes and mine. I went through the flat. A bottle still chilling in the bathtub, refrigerator full. I threw out the spoiled stuff, wiped off the dust and swept away the cobwebs. Calmly and quite methodically tidied up. Fine, I'll start over. With everything. I'll wait and ask questions. And if she doesn't turn up, I'll hit the road. Just as soon as it gets warmer. I was lured to her desk, maybe she had some papers in there. But I didn't dare yet. That was her territory. I could turn to the authorities. I mean there's no way a girl could just vanish, is there? In a small country like this? Oh yeah, there's a way, you know there is. I sat on the bed. I was scared to lie down. I might start howling and tear up the pillows.

And that little piece of metal was gone. The one I swiped that proved to me the whole story was true. It wasn't there. But I wasn't surprised.

Černá's didn't exist anymore. Galactic had different owners. I realized I knew a lot of people only by their nicknames. I hunted around for Micka. Couldn't find him in the phone book. At the Dóm they told me he showed up from time to time. With his partners. But where he was or what he was up to, they couldn't say. Or didn't want to. They didn't know me. I'd sit around the Dóm, nursing my drink, hadn't found much money back at the attic. Everything here was going fast, and the loot I'd saved up in the Organization era wasn't valid anymore. I took it as a sign.

You been gone long … said some of my friends … yeah, an far, I laughed. And I admit I spent a night or two with Cepková … out of loneliness I guess. Hers and mine. But. I couldn't make love. I was sick a long time, I told her … an you probly still are, that's okay … I think we were both secretly studying our wrinkles and guessing at the deep scars in each other, yeah, more that than sex … didn't see each other much after that, and when we did just said hello … slowly I sank back into the old acquaintances and habits and talk … nobody'd heard about Černá, Spider an Hadraba're in Germany, got some clubs goin there … the bartender grinned, but bartenders never know nothin … I began asking around for work and eating out of cans, it was a shock after the fare at the convent, but I was used to extremes from the train station … I didn't really believe Černá was living with someone else out there, and if so, that's fine too, as you like, my dear, you're free … but I've gotta see you an it's gonna happen, you've got to come to the little mother, you she-wolf … where're you traipsing around, girl, which way does your path lead … I sent out signals to her, and she was in my dreams.

And one day … one of those smiley city days when the autumn sun so casually bestows its gilding as generously on any rat snout as on the faraway deep forests' ancient trails … having bottomed out on cash, I strode into some new establishment to make an inquiry … there were more and more tavernas every day … I walked the city, put myself on the job market … I got up early, when it seems like the air is still fresh, and the people are too, everything just getting under way, like how many times before … striding through the underpasses and taking it to the sidewalks and crossing on green, I eyed Prague the Pearl like a hawk, and I studied the rotten vegetables, how their leaves'd gracefully float to the ground while the salesman impatiently stuffed em into some held-out plastic bag … and I saw clouds of dust, mysterious maps changing in the air, and windows full of things I don't need, but someone might … and I noticed the wires running out of the walls, and I liked the movement of the wires woven into the bicycle that just rode by, and the traffic lights with their three-stanza composition, the pedestrians as the refrain … I shook my healed head in wonder, striking out with the footsoldiers, like when the king sends out his army into the labyrinth of the streets, but watch out which king, and watch out, your labyrinth's mirrored … I gawked at colorful jackets in bookstore windows, and some of the books sent out a signal, I went after them … I'd begun to read again … since my honey wasn't around … and besides, amid the city noise, the slalom, the rattling trams, and the chattering waterfall of the crowd when you go fast and the voices merge … books at least seemed polite … saying: Here we are, take us or leave us, guess you'll be leavin us, huh? Yep, books're polite, don't bark an pounce like those fucked-up

Martian machine melodies, alla those computerized hits churned out with impunity by the brutal robot narcomafia to fool you along the way ... a book you've got to fold open and weigh for yourself if you want it, that's your business.

Supposedly there were times when people had to cut each page open as they read. Not only did they read with a knife in hand, which is always a great advantage, you never know who's out there creepin around disguised as a mail carrier ... but they had to at least dance with their wrist bones, move a little at least, and surely when it was gripping, their breathing speeded up, an impatient curse or two sounded out, and so their words merged with the book's ... by the kiosks I spotted a fella, the one I'd come to see, at Galactic they'd told me he worked here and might have a job for me.

Hey-hey, Kája! What're you doin here ... in the dust, like a nut ... ciao ...

Potok, lookit you, you look like a ghost, I work here, head honcho! Where you been all this time ... what do you want?

I'm lookin for work. Lucky coincidence meetin you. Got anything?

Heh, Potok ... can you lift that crate?

It lay in back of the vegetable kiosks, thing would've been a hard job for four guys.

What're you pullin on me, Honcho, this is like out of a book ... forgot the author though ...

What's an educated guy like you want peasant work for?

Rather have somethin physical, but somethin away from people.

I took it thinkin it was short-term too, but, man, I stayed with it! It's different nowadays. You're a hired hand, you're a hired hand. Boiler rooms're different too. Don't you know anyone?

I donno. I know you. To tell the truth I'm broke. I was gone a long time an got behind on rent ... I was amazed at how practical and to the point I was ... growin up, yep, happens to most.

An Karel ... know this one ... I don't need work, I need cash?

Yeah, I know it ... that's me ... I'll take you to the warehouse. You've done stock before, but this is different. You're gonna be unloadin fruit. Give this piece a paper to Burda. An don't let that scumbag forget about the gloves! Remind him, gloves.

Thanks, I owe you.

Yeah, but you can bet I won't be lookin for work with you.

I wouldn't take you anyway.

So I got a job. Socialized myself. It numbed me.

But then ... I saw the Romanian Gypsy ladies with their kids again ... the beggars, and it hit me, aha, He sends em here, I get it now ... hey Honcho, I said one day on our noontime break, I figured out the theory of relativity, here's how it works, listen: He sends em here, an there's times it seems to em like they're in Paradise, what with the packages an the leftovers, yeah, this is the Vest, an they can get by on a couple crowns, but the real reason they're here is for the sake of the native inhabitants, that's the theory ... What? said Honcho, but it began to dawn on him too ... notice, Honcho, nowadays it's fashionable to say: I don't have time, it makes people feel tremendously important that they don't have time, that they're workin, makes em feel almost American, sittin in those meetings a theirs tryin to solve the unsolvable an not lookin around anymore ... they wanna look like the people from the TV series, pissed-off professionals, success, dude, satellites, fast cars, five blondes, etc., get it? Yeah, whenever I'm in a pub I ask: D'you read *War and Peace* an *Gilgamesh* yet, or how bout *The Man Without Qualities,* or *Welzl the Eskimo,** you can get through it in a night ... yeah, you oughta see the look they get on their faces, like: That's thick! I don't have time for that ... these days! Isn't there a movie of it? Like the Bible? Yep, when someone tells me, all dignified and lofty, or with a drained look: I don't have time, I hear the rattle of the spit an shudder for the fate of humanity ... they wanna be like machines, like slaves hitched to the clock, an the only result is an increase in the number of zombie varieties ... an what they see on the evening news, those lousy wretches gettin mangled under the wheel of the world, Monday the Kurds, Tuesday the Somanians, Wednesday the Cambodians, Thursday the Halases, Friday the Rennets, Saturday the Ethiopians, Sunday the Bosnians, an the other days're full of it too, an sometimes it's all at once, so the dear viewers end up not believing it anymore ... that there's people without plastic, without grub, without teeth, it's not real anymore ... an so crafty Bog sent these raggedy Gypsy women with their deadened urchins out into the world, into the metropolises, so people could see ... poverty an how it dulls you, get it? It's a new tribe, a secret an very important community, they're everywhere, you know ... I saw on TV, the Brits're tremendously surprised to find they're even in London, how did those barefoot brownies make it across La Manche without any pounds or ID ... not like Venclovský,* that's for sure ... they marveled in Parliament ... the witches flew there, straight from His palm, to provoke. An every disgusted glance at them is also the question, why me? Why not you? An every time they give their breast to one of their frozen children, it's like they're tellin that pedestrian dashing past with his tie aflutter: Just wait, maybe tomorrow you'll be the one to fall, you never know, fella, heh … you know?

I know, said Honcho, but how bout you … sure you don't want a little vacation?

No, work is a pleasure for me.

And it was true … except for Burda and the other packer … then I got why it pissed them off that I was there … I unloaded fruit from the trucks and put it in trays, they shipped it in sacks, grade-F stuff pretty much, my job was to pick out the whole ones and put them in boxes … and they were labeled SUPER SPECIAL KLASA NUMBER ONE BORN IN BOHEMIA, so right away I was in the picture. My shed, or as we modernly said back in those days, my hangar, had bluish plastic walls, together with the fruit it was a constant dance of colors. You could track the sun by it. Burda supplied a jumpsuit but told me the gloves'd just run out. On the other side of the tropical-smelling packing house was a kiosk that sold smoked meats and a shack with a REFRESHMENTS sign. We were outside town, by a woodland park, a free range. Large parties of daytrippers made their way here, souring my life with their noisiness, bustling with byznys. Occasionally they'd bum some fruit. Yep, then I began to do a little selling on the side.

The refreshment stand regulars were mostly forestry workers from the nearby Obora,* grazed cattle there. I'd done some exploring … these guys had time galore, but they all looked to be about two or three steps from the train station, by now I could tell. They favored rubber boots and swung their fists as they walked. I spent my time with lemons, switchberries, peaches, the trucks brought kiwis, bananas, parsley … old Burda believed that kiwis spread AIDS, he was always hassling me … one morning, counting over my trays, I realized ten were missing. Burda and Křepek sat at the refreshment stand, the thieves … just grinning at me, and Burda says not to stuff myself so much with raspberries, they're expensive, said he's seen me an he's gonna tell the Boss, couldn't get anywhere with him. The next day it was the same … give me back my lemons … made a fool of myself … Křepek wore a cross, the dolt, I had half a mind to dance him one, they didn't know … they thieved like baby magpies, but not a uniform in sight, I began putting in even rotten pieces, just

to give me more, and slightly smudged the invoices, it was the only way ...
you're in the wheel, heel, so let it ride an wait for her, I said to myself ...
nothin else I could do. But I enjoyed the work ... it gave my nose a workout,
now and then I had to use a shovel for the older pieces, Burda cracked up
when I asked for gloves, Křepek had new ones I saw, eat shit an die, you
proletarians ... the lemons smelled good. Lemons don't waste time with talk,
I envied them.

And up in the attic ... sometimes I got claustrophobic, there was too much
of her smell, too many of her things ...

I made some minor repairs around the place. A thing or two to the
windows. Rearranged objects. And the bookshelf ... I painted red. But I didn't
bring home any flowers. That seemed premature.

And I swore and I begged and they merged.

But I lost my job. It was in the bananas. I thought it was a twig, quite
possibly a sprig even ... grabbed it, a message from a distant shore, but suddenly it moved, slippery in my palm, I jumped back, a little green snake, a whole
nest of them, and they ... came shooting out, whizzing past my ears with a
sound like a pod cracking open, I raced off, Burda laughing, grabbed the
Minimax off the wall an sprayed em, crushed em with my boots, then I had to
sit down. I walked up to Burda and he quit laughing. Křepek looked on with
interest. But I went back. That day was jinxed. Glimpsing movement out of
the corner of my eye, I watched, cautious, and then my eyes really opened
wide. It was hairy, big as a soccer ball, and moved at terrifying speed, scamperin
up the sack, legs flickin one over the other ... I mean I'm an animal lover, but
this thing ... I snuck past it ... away, patting the spot out of habit, raced out
of the hangar, and slammed into Burda ... he gave me the fish eye ... you're
lookin pale, c'mon into the warehouse, they came ... the gloves ... Go over
there, Mr. Burda, we've got ourselves a visitor ... no, I grabbed him by the
sleeve, no ... we finished the monstrosity off with a rake ... Burda swept him
up, what mush was left, to this day I still get goose bumps whenever I
remember. An bananas I can do without.

No, Honcho, not even in asbestos armor. I got somethin I wanna wait for
... that was too much.

Heh, most people quit when they come across em, but they're not
dangerous, sposedly ... old Burda's not afraid of em, that other guy either,
they're the only ones that can stand it, weird people, huh?

You can say that again. Why didn't ya tell me?

You wouldna believed. Plus you'da wanted to see.

That's true. You could show that shit at carnivals.

You know, old Burda already thought a that.

But he mowed it down ...

He enjoys that too. Forget it. Hey, there's a spot open at the stand. Why doncha take it? That kid Kasel's there on his own, kinuva twit.

While the first job was a fragrant plant with dangerous flesh moving in its midst ... this flesh reeked and was dead. Still, it seemed safer. Now I sold human beings scrag ends, veal, and lardlings. They wanted it.

Occasionally it was a wild ride, the surface was always greasy. I was glad I'd kept my hair short since that time Černá had cut it. My current employment was just as tough to fathom as the rest. But if the world were knowable, you'd run up against its borders. This way at least you get somewhere.

Daily I saw hundreds of people, that part I liked. The idea of Sister ... on her way ... coming here to buy this, was exciting. Mothers would visit the stand with fairly little kids ... for market reasons I couldn't refuse them. Doctors, soccer players, miners, vagabonds, metalheads, civil servants, all stepped up to the counter ... I didn't recognize myself in the mirror anymore. It pissed me off they bought the stuff, I overcharged like crazy.

Kasel tossed dead meat on the grill, sizzling it beyond recognition in fat, my new partner was a surly young man, eternally lost in thought. Whenever there was a moment free he'd hunch in the corner, casting suspicious glances, and sometimes scribbling to himself. I was afraid he was taking down my mistakes ... knew that from my other jobs ... waiting tables for instance ... addition mistakes: So, Mr. Supreme Commander in Chief, sir, that gives us 6 lardlings, 8 Melinda sodas, 4 brews, brewskies, ho-ho, 16 veals, those boys a yours sure can pack it in, yes siree, Boss Coal Baron, an two double portions of scrag ends for the lovely young lady, which makes: eight thousand two hundred an twenny, on the nose! ... but if the old fart added it up himself and said pompously: Hah, it's six thousand seven hundred an ten ... I'd break out the trench tactics, my words flying like turds into a cesspool: Oh my goodness gracious, why I added this here from the next table, pardon me, I'm on my own today, an that's three thou straight up, cross my heart an hope to die! He gave me four, it cost two, and it wasn't worth a thing. Everyone did it. I wouldn't've lasted there a week otherwise. That's the way it went in kiosk paradise. They explained that to me fast.

One day Kasel dropped a sheet of paper … leave it, he twisted his hands into claws … but I got a glimpse, man, you're writin verse! … he blushed … but I didn't tease him. At least he wasn't ratting. I breathed a sigh of relief. Felt like an asshole.

After work … couldn't stand it in the flat, it occurred to me … to go out to the Rock, see Bohler, pay the old buddy a visit … but I still felt a little guilty about what'd happened … back in the slammer … and without a rowdy bunch around, I don't know … I sat around Galactic checking out the people, Micka might turn up, there were lotsa familiar faces there, new and old alike, I knew that if Černá showed up in town her steps would surely lead to these places … and besides, you can be alone in a crowd if you're smart about where you sit … there were always videos and tapes going, back in the bush, I stuck my head in the sand, and once again speech was starting to grab me, I met people … now it was mainly Prague 3 … after being raised their whole lives as atheists, they began to pull new words from the vocab of the sects that were suddenly teeming all over … heavy, serious words, like *lot, penance, punishment* … some young people mixed biblical expressions with the language of grunge guitar groups … sorry dude, plug that in, an've you, like, ever done penance? … I heard once … and international drug lingo got a dash or two of protectorate argot, and poking out of it all like straw was a Marxist pictur-esqueness … got a copacetic metajoint here'll knock your bulletin board off … I picked up idioms and images … and English, the Latin of today's com-munities … *broukn ingliš* … and *broukn ček* … a broken tongue, and a new feeling grew from the unsoundness, maybe, or the other way round, I don't know … in any case it was accelerated.

I sat of course with my back to the screen, and one day … froze, hearing a voice, hers, it was unmistakable, I got up, gripping the table, but it wasn't just in my head anymore, I turned to the screen, a split second … merer than mere, the woman put on a mask, a Cat Head, walked off screen, the News came on … What was that? I guess I shouted … heads turned my way, Tusk says, what's the big deal, some ad … for sumthin … I fought my way through to the office upstairs, the guy the clips belonged to was there, looked familiar, but I didn't take the time to flip through the index in my head … it'd started to ache … I tape it off TV, all over, I donno … I stuck to him like a leech, he played it for me that night … it was her, Černá.

Maybe … yes. Her face was there for literally just the blink of an eye … she seemed skinnier and more carefree, but maybe I was only imagining it. And I could see in my loved one's face that she'd paid … my little sister had dearly paid.

But I couldn't find out who'd shot it or where. The agency didn't exist anymore. The stuff the ad was for wasn't sold anymore. There weren't any credits, just pseudonames. No one even puts a date on videos. It didn't exist. From time to time she'd flash by, at random, in front of a few stoned, drunk, or apathetic faces. In a pub. But she was alive.

I had it made into a photo. A pretty big one. And then … I spotted her again. Bumming around the street, I stepped up to a bookstore window, eying the silent covers, and suddenly … there she was, in negative, but it was her. The book was some kina … nonsense … nothin to do with the cover. I held it in my hand. And the chase was on. Kasel had a little more work at the stand. Only … history repeated itself … the publisher was some small-time bootlegger, now extinct … I bought em out, small print run, movin slow, the salesclerk said … so maybe there's not too many people droolin over my little sister, the author hadn't written anything else, some poet guy, used a pen name … the photographer's name was in the colophon though … I took off running and didn't stop till I got to the hospital building, I was already dressed the part, human, and with that stench of burnt fat on me … they let me in, but … he didn't live there anymore, I rang the neighbors', pretty insistently, an older lady opened: You don't know? Mr. Meždek passed away. Car accident. Why, it was all over the papers, and the car … Only I didn't read the papers. And that was another mistake. Could've saved myself a lot of trouble.

I also went to Bolkon Street, went … and my heart knotted up at the sight of that lady, it choked me up … different guy sittin around in the kitchen, same type though … somebody'd sent them money a couple times, the old man figured it was her … I sat very dejectedly, he slugged me on the back, you'll get over it, there's plenty of fish … yeah, but without my little minnow, the sea'll be black and stormy:

the dark star of love
took me by the hand
and led me into old age

and left me there

and we won't make love anymore

ever again

came to me. They were talking at me, both. Then I went down the stairs, slowly, holding onto the banister. Like someone that was pretty crushed.

And then I bounced back from the bottom again and lightened up.

A few days later, at Galactic ... the ad for Muorex came on again, and I studied the face a second, Tusk elbowed me ... got a thing for cat food, dude, or're you checkin out Černá ... looks like her, huh?

Ee! He shrieked as I grabbed his elbow.

You know her ... talk!

Chill out, haven't seen her ... a while, you mean that singer, right.

Uh-huh.

Yeah, I knew her when she was hangin with Morti, buddy a mine, the Martian, you knew him, what're you lookin at ... Potok, careful, it's one thing drinkin all day when you're twenny, but doin it now with the same body ... an brain, hah, yeah, well, ain't what it useta be ... I knew her back in Berlun. After the Wall came down. Or was it before?

What was she doin there!

Let go a me, whadda ya think you're doin ... anyway, then Morti freaked, military an shit, she blew him off, an good thing too, he really freaked ... then I guess he took off, it's been ages now since I ...

What did she do in Berlun?

What else, nothin ... I donno, waited tables in some dive I heard, I donno ... same as everyone, I never had nothin with her.

That I believe, Tusk, hey ...

What'd you call me ... somethin wrong with my teeth? ... you should talk, look like an ad for Paradentall, only prior to use, heh heh, that's a good one ...

Know anything about her?

An you smell kina funky, Potok, sorry to say ...

Know anything about her, or anyone who knows her?

No. But why don't you go look her up at Moony's?

What's that? Where is it?

You know, Moony Bank, that new one over on Liberation Ave., she's right there, next to the entrance ... wait a sec ... wait!

I didn't wait, I ran … but I should've waited and let Tusk finish. Saved myself the trouble.

They threw me out. I got all the way to the director. Took me about two hours. A minute wasn't enough for me to state my case. He wasn't interested. Some sheriff types chased me down the stairs. She wasn't employed there, nothing. Not a clue. I stood outside fuming, high noon … and then, then I raised my eyes … and saw her.

A guy, slick type, dazzling teeth and splashed with cologne, climbing out of a car and smiling, cheerfully striding up the bank steps, turning around and waving, and waving back from the car an elegant lady, with a veil across the temperamental glint in her eyes, dressed in the delicate tulle of high society, there you were, Černá, lightly and gracefully waving your arm, clad in a white glove up to the elbow … the movie ran in a loop proclaiming that Moony bills made everyone happy … and the guy got out and hustled inside, waving to the lady … and over … and over … and over … after ten loops the name of the bank's founding father came up, glowing in neon, and then it ran again …

Oh my Černá, there you were, done up as a gorgeous lady, a lady who knows, and they didn't even hafta bother with the makeup, very gorgeous …

And then I figured it out, it was in her eyes … she's just tryin it out, foolin around, takin a little break from it all, like me at the stand, and maybe … maybe she's tryin to give me a sign.

The bank was a dead end. But I found the studios where they'd made the ad. Wouldn't let me see their records, and the billing office naturally threw me out. Anyway, who knew what name she'd used. If any. The studios … were endless unfortunately.

I thought back to the mirrors in the old coffeehouse we used to go to together, here it was doors and Makeup Toucher-Uppers … I talked my way in as a journalist … prowled around, she could be anywhere, down any hallway, behind any door, in some disguise, behind any mirror … could.

I flashed through prop rooms, crept down hallways, sidestepped gaffers, emerged from trapdoors without warning, and passed many girls, one I chased down … burst in on a crowd scene, they were shooting the Battle of Lipany,* and one of the wounded, I wiped the ketchup off her face … nope, wasn't her, I had to bolt, the director … and his crew chased me around the flaming barns … I absorbed their language, walking around with a carpenter's satchel, that's the way us Czechs sneak into Parliament, St. Matthew's Fair, and Freemason

Lodges, it's like a broom … I ran through the middle of dramas, speech … Beda, flip the synch there to number two, an lights on the balance beam, great, bring in that jib an here we go … the place was like a spaceship, maybe you're wandering around here, little sister, among the aliens … in one office I spotted a familiar-looking folder, a catalog … young rising stars and breakout starlets, slashes and crosses and numbers marked next to them by pudgy, sweaty, clumsy fingers … 1's with stars and swooning exclamation points, I ran through the rankings with a pounding heart, photo after photo, she wasn't there … though one face, in profile, no, uh-uh … I moved on … that actress there's got some of her movements … she was all bleached white, though, with scales on her body, couldn't see her face … but the voice, raspy, different … maybe some hardships behind it though, found a suit in the men's room and put it on, lady made me do an interview with her, wouldn't let go a me … I grabbed my satchel and slipped through the opening … next door they were shooting a gothic horror, I changed into a priest's costume in a nearby prop room, begging forgiveness, it wasn't blasphemy, I just … I gotta test it out … and the voice that came from the Iron Maiden, and the corner of the snow-white veil, I interrupted the scene, ruined the movie, dragged the captive into the light … but it wasn't Černá, just some regular old pasty-face … I left the studios in a gloomy mood. The light lurched along the cliffs.

The stand began to annoy me. Once I knew the tricks, I wanted to move on. Anywhere. Though me and Kasel were getting close. Now I was waiting for Černá with every movement of my heart, she'll definitely come to the attic too … and I'd left a note for her there … maybe she's abroad, I thought. And fixated on that. Of course, maybe she went to the islands, the sea, we talked about it all the time, her especially …

Now I was out of Honcho's jurisdiction. We saw each other from time to time. But then they locked him up. And Burda became boss of the grounds. He called me over one day.

Hey … you … c'mere!

Right with you, maestro, I promptly obeyed.

Hey, you always got that look … an you ain't no fledgling, boy, no sir! You ain't no boy no more … musta had some schoolin. Isn't in your papers though, why's that? You got strange papers, real strange! Who are you … flappin around, gawkin? The fellas say … hey … answer me! Seems to me you're … some kina lumpenproleterrier!

No I'm not, but you're dumb as a guinea pig, Mr. Burda.

Huh?

Just what I said … shit … I tore off my apron … yeah right, grinding my teeth, it's always somethin, fuckhead, questions, I'm goin … goin!

Now look, you don't hafta … what's buggin you, son?

Nothin, an I apologize. But I'm goin.

So you don't want the job?

Can't you see? I'm a bigger dummy than you, I know. It's just that it doesn't matter.

I knocked over a pan and the lardlings started to burn, Kasel was off in the woods somewhere … probly writing, the twit.

Don't be so unhappy all the time!

Yeah yeah. Aright then, I'm … goin.

Go ahead, for today. But come back tomorrow. If you want.

It annoyed me. I annoyed myself. Casting sinister glances into shop windows, ugh. Hm! Lumpen, yeah maybe. If you insist. I still reeked of grease, cut my hair … left the smell on for mystical protection … against debauchery, I'll give myself a good washing-up later, when the time comes. When the Conductor at long last raises his baton and hews into the forest of intermingling symphonies. I stink. But it's good to wash up before you kill yourself. It's the decent thing to do, right? Didn't your mom ever tell you? I tried to be mean to myself, talking tough and brassy to my reflection … whenever it flickered past, in a shop window, a puddle … but my face just mocked me, leering at my soul …

Next day I was back at the stand again. With Kasel. He was more cheerful now, not so closemouthed. Started luggin in all sortsa tabloids, magazines, ploppin em down in the lardlings and goose necks next to the bubbling pots … and then one day on break he couldn't hold back and whipped it out, a photo of him, hair slicked back and parted … one magazine had him loungin in the grass … man, you're all over the place, I marveled … yeah, that's excellent … he went off about some youth anthology, comin out next week, he's in it! Got it all lined up an squared away an ridin high from here on in!

He spoke feverishly of receptions and readings, full-page interviews, literary polls! We started talking about it … I'm the best, said Kasel, flushed, everyone's finally startin to get it, I'm the best, an I'm a couple lengths out in fronna the rest, he said, stirring the lardlings … but, I told him sagely, recalling Sister

Maria Coseta and her *Rose of Wounds* … I mean it's not like art's a steeplechase, I mean the dead are outta your league anyway … but I'm alive! Kasel screamed, hacking open a roast lamb's neck with the cleaver … good point … but I thought back to Jícha and the Kulchur section, maybe it was best to leave the imparted paths of my murdered friends inside me a little longer … don't take it too fast, I told Kasel … after all, anyone that knows how to read can write somethin good … screw you! Kasel said to my smart remark, it's not about writin one good poem, it's what comes next, what's in between, it's survivin from one to the next, an after … that's what's interesting! Aha, I said … but I didn't bring in those scribblings of mine I had at Černá's flat, it would've wounded him, and I didn't want a mortal enemy.

He'd show me pictures of authors in magazines … they're out there somewhere, here in the Pearl, an they don't know it yet, Kasel said, but I'm here too an they're outta luck … he spoke like that sometimes … so what're you doin here, with all that ambition … an talent! … in a dumbass job like this, I inquired … he made a mysterious face, but I soon figured it out.

An odd crew had begun turning up among the daytrippers … hysterics or somethin, I presumed … together constantly, arguing, but I noticed … as soon as one stepped off, the others would get these weird smiles and start jabberin away, pickin him apart, it was obvious … various types, guys and gals, dressed funny … together constantly … boozin at the picnic tables, stuffin emselves with provisions … every day they'd come and walk the trails, fencin excitedly with their arms, terrifyin the squirrels with abrupt, unexpected motions … I was stumped … must be some sanatorium for neurotics around here, I concluded, and went to tell Kasel, but he … stood like a pillar of salt, bug-eyed, and I heard bum … bum, the irregular thump of his blood-red muscle … move it, Kasim, your veal's burnin, hop to it … he stood there, magazines in his hands … I kept him in the corner of my eye … next day he brought napkins. You're a strange one, partner, I said … he didn't react … then the scarecrows showed up again, picked out a table, and ousted a couple families, Kasel got out the paper plates, piled on lardlings and all the rest, covered it up with napkins … are you nuts, since when do we deliver? Since now, said the poet, and off he flew … I picked up the slack and pondered … napkins … and then I got it, yes … he'd stuck those poems of his in with the napkins, and then again … bum … bum, the sound of his heart, I splattered him with beer, I'd knocked back a few, there was no talkin to him that day … the patients out there raisin a ruckus, one screamed so loud the whole park could hear: It is dead, it is no longer possible! and another one said: On the contrary, now it is possible because it no longer matters! and they said: disproportion, discrepancy, identity has taken a blow, reality ... I shook my head, reining Kasel in, as they tossed his writing in the trash, it fell to the ground as they finished their meals, evidently Kasel had piled it on, they mopped up their plates with the fruits of his imagination, wiped their hands and chins with it, the pages soggy and translucent with grease, tossed the sheets in the dirt, I saw a high heel pierce a piece of paper, left it there in the mud, with the remains ... among the bones ... but that's perfect, I consoled him in vain, that's the way it lives in real life, that's exactly the way it is, an ... who are those people anyway? That is ... he stammered ... the elite ... they built a Creators Chalet here outside the city, they're ... lyricists and authors and critics, he gasped.

They came all the time, and I got to thinking ... actually, what if I ... it could be a message for Sister, she'd be able to tell from the words who wrote it, some of them were hers ... Kasel got mad though ... my idea! All right ... I get the veal, you get the lardlings, half and half on the scrag ends, I stood my ground ... we grudgingly sized each other up, but he had to give in, of course I wouldn't allow him to read my verse, or whatever it was, anyway he wasn't interested ... he was dreaming of a new way, the possibilities ... a crimson robe and the prince of poetry's lyre ... it started to mess with me too, and then ... up to the stand walks a man of about fifty, solid build, graying temples, pipe clenched in strong teeth, pure silk sweater on, parts his red lips ... Kasel's gaspin for breath, an the guy says: Beer! We nearly got in a fight, two cups stood before him in the blink of an eye, a dark and a light ... ach, this is almost surrealism, he said, studying the cups ... duality, Manichaeanism, he took a sip, smacked his lips, if not ... schizophrenia, alcoholism ... he staggered, clasped his head, and walked over to his car ... the Maestro doesn't have it easy, said Kasel, but I barely heard him, there, by the car, a flash of white, she was shaking a pebble, some sand, from her shoe ... her back was to me, but the curve of her neck ... and her calves, as she leaned a heel into the dirt ... I dashed out ... the writer started the engine ... NO! I screamed ... the woman climbed in, and they drove off ... I leaned against a tree, panting ... saw the stand, it brought me back ... Kasel went insane, ran out there hollerin, pourin stuff all over em, throwin clumps of lard, the crew, shrieking, beat a retreat, I leaned my forehead against the tree, shut my eyes, and stayed that way.

24

WHO I MEET. AND WHO I'M WITH. KARLOVICE.
CRYSTAL S.R.O. AND WHAT IT'S FOR.
OLD WORDS, THAT SOUND. I LIFTED MY HANDS.

And one day, one smiley city day when the sun again showed its experienced face through the dust, I saw in the distance, by one of the kiosks ... a distinctive gait, her hair, she was walking ... leading a small child by the hand, my eyes popped and I ... ran over ... spotted her again in the crowd of daytrippers, elbowing through, I did too ... shoving them out of my way, faster, again the crowd closed around her, but it was her, my friend ... and at the end of the road there was nothing again but a whirl of dust from a bus.

I hastened back to the kiosk where I'd spotted her ... Viets or whoever ... shirt, pant, digital, casset, one let loose with a wide smile ... no, quick, that girl that was here, he reshuffled a stack of jeans ... she's a friend of mine ... she was here with a child ... where do they live? His face shut down, looking like an Aztec from a stone frieze in a temple in the festering jungle, the silent face of the full moon itself ... aright, I picked up a pair of jeans, he snatched them back ... I no know nobody, turned away ... wouldn't get anything outta him, that was obvious ... made the rounds of a few spots in town where she might've been, in vain.

There were lots of Asians at the markets, but among the Vietnamese I didn't have any friends. It had all been too fast with Smoothy. I waited, even set up a rearview mirror over the flock of sizzling lardlings so I could see, Kasel was puzzled. And absent. Getting more vexed and restless every day ... uh-huh, it's everywhere now, he mumbled to himself ... they print it all over, there's even a book, an nothin ... nothin's goin on ... so maybe, just maybe, yeah, it isn't just for its own sake, I knew it, there's no destination, there's only the way, the path ... you're burnin the scrags, I alerted him ... he was lost in reverie.

And then ... Hi there! I said, she looked at me, the little one in tow, sizing me up like a rapscallion ... but there was a twinkle in her eyes ... we were reunited. Tempestuously. I admit, I was taken when she spoke.

I's you ... tha's goo'. This is Son!

He hid behind her ... yelped when we hugged. The poet was on his own with the meat that day. It was too much. What she told me. It was horrible. From then on, she came to see me often.

We'd sit on a bench in the park. The boy eyeing the squirrels with interest ... well, he wasn't exactly a looker ... Bohleresque features ... but maybe later, his mom's beauty, all that cat and gazelle, then again in a boy I donno, I donno ... she told me stories ... dea', she said of my buddy ... and then, when we were living together, in the one building where we could, I began to visit the Press Center and piece it together from old newspapers, because there were times I didn't understand, and also, she didn't like going back much ... but some of it she told me the very first day, through tears.

I didn't want to go back to the buildings at all, but with her and Son it was different. Besides, the attic ... when I thought of Černá I still ... I still trembled.

And that was the first thing I had to share with Lady Laos. After all the things she'd told me as I held her in my arms ... taking the weight off her ... maybe it was cruel ... but I considered it essential to say: Don't get mad, honey, but there's a woman, she's traveling ... an when she gets back I'm gonna be with her. Or we're gonna be together somehow. That's the way it is. How about it?

We all gonna be together? inquired Lady Laos.

We lived together, side by side, helping each other. Protecting each other.

The little boy enjoyed prowling around the old farm equipment just in back of the sheds, seemed the technical type, into levers and chrome stuff ... took apart the watch I'd bought, seeing as I had a job now ... but ... the boy couldn't speak much, his Czech was like his mom's, Bohler hadn't had much time, I took him on as my student ... but he sti' need schoo', Lao decided, I didn't take that away from her. She herself called him Son, sounded to her like a proper name. He also had a Laotian one, that one I couldn't pronounce, plus the one Bohler had baptized him with ... at times the youngster had trouble in the sandbox with the locals. Because of how he looked. How he spoke. He soon stopped being afraid of me. Asked questions himself. Bohler had wanted his name to be Vojtěch.*

Lao had landed back in the buildings a while ago. They didn't have any bad vibes for her, just the opposite ... though she was surprised to find the cellar filled in with concrete. With a diligence unique to her, she had set up a tailor and dressmaker workshop. She and her compatriots sewed for sale, I was awed

... on flywheel Singers. Their husbands and brothers and cousins dropped them off in the morning and the ladies would sit there going all day, there was always lots of chatting involved and now and then a song or two. At first I was very cautious around the guys. But the copper, blue, and dark one patted me on my scar one day and said: You crasy ... you safe he'e, no way fo' Hun'er ... you jus' imagine!

I had my doubts. But me and the men would exchange greetings, solemnly, ceremoniously, sincerely, and with many smiles, slipping through the hallways.

The capitalists advanced. What they sewed went to the kiosks, where the other tribe members took over ... they even set up a nursery and something like a school, I noticed Vojtěch was in charge there, and I glowed pretty bright ... no no no, he stomped the sand, not baroon! he told a slant-eyed boy, balloon, but have i' you' way ... the lessons bore fruit, we'd go for walks on the lawn, once we'd cleaned it up ... the rest of the street was nearly deserted, a fire or two in the ruins at night, but Lao had taught me ... safety first ... I noticed two or three husbands or cousins were in the sewing room at all times, and they may've looked condescending and lordly ... but they were looking out.

I lugged some books over from Černá's place and settled into a flat on the second floor ... me and Lao were together only occasionally, but more and more often. And if anyone honorable feverishly opposed it ... I could only gently point out how extremely fortunate it is when all the cruelty that's been, is, an always will be isn't so visible cause you're with someone you hold, an your palm's just right to cover their heart, worn paper-thin with anxieties ... to shield it from the barb of solitude that drives you mad, pounding, an you hold that someone so tight that you also cover yourself. Lao. Peeking across the bed at each other in our unwritten agreement. We got close.

And then one day the little boy said: I'm tired! I'm ... so tired! He was startled to see my eyes bug, I interrupted our ball game, it reminded me ... he watched me run off ... I flew through the buildings in horror ... but Granny Macešková wasn't there. Not a trace. Not a trace of anything ... that might remain of her. Even walked across the concrete in the cellar, examined the surface ... maybe here. Maybe she's here somewhere.

I combed through the buildings, checked around the flats, the remains, there weren't any tenants left and Lao had hinted one of her friends would like to move in with her family ... it was strange, sometimes she treated me as though it were still the old times and I was one of the owners, I guess it suited her, she was settling into our contract on her own terms.

And mornings, every morning on the days commonly considered working, I flew out the door to the tram to see Kasel, who'd tell me how he'd sent out grant applications, better look aroun for someone, I'll be packin it in soon … he'd say confidently … headin out to an Art Colony, hey … an when I get there I'm gonna write about how we worked our balls off here, you'll see … yeah, definitely, it'll be a bestseller, I can't wait, Kasim … and we'd flip the lardlings and chop up the rest, and the third possibility we'd fling into the sizzling fat, by now we were a pretty fine-tuned duo.

And now and then … I'd poke around the studios, since that was where the trail left off. And also go to the Press Center, putting together that short Bohler story …

Out at the Rock, you see … in the surrounding woods and villages, back in our times, there still lived Gobs.

Bohler had always maintained friendly contact with the creatures, and he didn't have to twist our arms either … some of the Gobs were a lot of fun … it doesn't make one bit a difference if folks out here say Gobs aren't people, it's no one's business anyway … they're here! Bohler thundered.

He would go on religious and reconnaissance missions among the Gobs, they let him instruct their young ones, after a brief moment of hesitation and self-searching he even baptized them, to be on the safe side, as he put it … it's the one thing that can't be neglected, he claimed … and the Gobs, when Bohler preached to them, may've wagged their furry heads, but they admitted: Yeah, could be somethin to it, leave the seedling in our hearts a while, we'll play around with it, see what it does, we got the Black Daliah, you know …

Shy creatures, those Gobs … right at the onset of the Sewer period, the Communists smashed their wagons, adopting Gestapo-style edicts against "vagrant lifestyles" and "the Gob public nuisance," by the end of the Third Reich there weren't a lotta Gobs left either, whole tribes had disappeared, it was just like with the Gypsies … what was left of them the authorities ordered into the factories … well, the Gobs didn't sweat it out there long, that sort of movement was foreign to them, they lived in a different time than mere machines … so to keep the Gobs from pickpocketing, the state instead gave them cash, stolen from somewhere else, and that's what did them in, they spent most of it on the Fiery … and then, when time exploded, the Gobs no longer knew the old way of doing things and didn't get the new one at all … some lived pretty miserably, stealing … picking pockets … the losses weren't that heavy, but for the Karlovice town councillors it was enough … infertility, retardation, forty years of the Sewer, black comets, escaped convicts, floods, every scar the township ever suffered they threw at the Gobs, trashed a few of their hideouts … Bohler spoke out against it … and in the *Karlovice Courier* I found: "This decadent, un-Czech figure canvases his neighbors dressed in a faded cassock. Point your finger at him! He is a heretic, a Pragocentrist, and is urging Gobs to commit attacks. Again yesterday, two people were assaulted by individuals of Gob origin …" etc.

The citizens of Karlovice formed the Society of the White Hood for the Defense of the Purity of the Noble Czech Nation, and it began … some Gobs fought back, but it was the old ethnographic imbalance … the townspeople went out on raiding sprees, strong men with sticks and knives … and the stupid Gobs sat in their hovels scared out of their wits, old folks, children, all together … and then some Gobs said, not anymore, and also took things into their hands … at this point the accounts in the *Karlovice Courier* get pretty confused … Bohler and several others had begun digging tunnels so the Gobs could flee the township, but demonstrations against them began outside it too … and the Gobs had no country of their own they could flee to, they'd been born here after all … Lao couldn't understand … the people encircled the Rock just as Bohler and the Gobs and the rest were crawling into the barn, and when the people sicced the dogs on the Gobs, they fought back, as did the others, the theologian skewered an attacker on a pitchfork … I remembered his perverted old smile and that *olovrant* of his … Evil must be countered with violence, immediate an brutal, remember, colleagues … the priest of the tribe had preached to us … they drowned the Gobs outside of town, cause Gobs donno how to swim, and Bohler went down with em …

Lao?

Mm-hm.

So … someone'll hafta go out there, I said, jotting notes in my notebook … it's too late, she told me, and she was right.

Meanwhile … we'd been torn apart … David, now Bohler … Sharky's off fighting a war, and Micka's around here somewhere, I felt a pang of nostalgia and said so … and Lao got up and brought me a byznys card, said she'd found it a while back but didn't know how to read and forgot … I leapt up: Mr.

Micka Co. Crystal s.r.o., of course it was a riddle, there hadda be some catch, but at least it gave an address: Golden Cross, Skyscraper 33 … Lao tossed me my clothes and I dressed on the fly, it was late, but knowin him he'd be grindin away … you wan' snack, she asked with concern … all those memories and she was worried about this old schemer …

Many remarkable buildings had sprung up at Golden Cross, actually not that many, but their shiny glass walls gave the pedestrian, squeezed suddenly beneath a lower horizon, an impression of abundance that greatly amplified any feelings of inferiority … just to be safe, all over the place were submachine gunners and doormen decked out as rear admirals … and I ran aground. It was unbelievable, I mean I was practiced in hallways, walls, holes, trapdoors, me and Micka had learned together, jump, scramble, crawl, fly, smash, go! But here it was a no-go. Not a single garage or barred window or service entrance, and the skyscraper's walls were smooth … then again it was only logical. This eminent figure had the same schooling as me, he knew how to build a barricade … I didn't even get to the secretaries.

I made a sport out of it, going over every day in a different getup, mustaches, beards. Lao and Vojtěch kept their fingers crossed, sometimes I took them along … me and the rear admirals and submachine gunners were soon on a first-name basis, swapping remarks about our mothers, amatory abilities, appearance, attire, etc., it was quite entertaining.

I spent plenty of time with Kasim though … he was brooding and distraught, the Art Shacks were all he talked about … old Burda started roaming around again, wearing an odd smile … the literati didn't come anymore, now they knew about Kasim, and they'd socked it to him in the press pretty good, he'd turned rather bitter, mumbling: Get outta here, dude, here everyone knows ya right away, place is a fishpond, I filled out the application, enclosed translations, bibliography, photo, c'mon, let's go to a pub, but some-place we won't run into any writing fucks … that'll be pretty tough, I replied … he got furious.

I'd disappear straight from the stand to the studios and run around there and … I had a plan now, I'd found a few people I knew that still remembered me from the old times, when I used to recite other people's monologues, till I got the bug and started in with this thing … remembered me as an actor … earnestly I sought a role, I wanted to leave a trail for Černá, not in a field or the sand anymore, and not on a lake either, uh-uh, not some bent blade of grass, or a notch, or stones, no ... now I knew where I had to leave a trail so she'd know that I still was. In this world.

About sixty of us stood there, naked, in a damp cellar, nothin to eat or drink for hours, till the director had time ... then he walked in with his entourage, we all fell silent, he pointed his switch ... Beda, you know what I need an what for, move it, Jesus, look at those figures ... move it, Beda, take him into synch, profiles an straights, let's get this outta the way an we can all go get laid ... Beda pointed to me, I was thrilled. All around me I could sense the daggered looks.

Yes, only I could play Fly Man, it was an ad for Bohemia Halucia Milk of Milks ... disguised in fly garb and a fly mask, I flapped my wings around in a huge cup of bad old milk while next to it a gorgeous young lady sipped the one and only proper milk, the totally new Bohemia Halucia Milk of Milks ... it gave off these vapors that killed flies in flight, and they plummeted to all sides of the glass at a safe distance from human lips ... a prominent Czech composer wrote the music, it was a zinger ... I flapped around in there, and in an unguarded moment I made a typical move, a rap of the knuckles, you know it well, my dear ... raised a shoulder, you've leaned on it, little sister, surely that you'll recognize too ... I hit the jackpot. After that they wanted me everywhere. I also played a fuzzball in the Dust Sucker ad, but you couldn't really see me.

And then I went back to Crystal and tried to get inside again.

But carpenters didn't work on this place, there wasn't a single opening ... it was an enormous structure, reaching toward the clouds ... maybe touching them ... astronauts musta built this tower, Gaudí'd be floored ... I thought up some new tricks. Wait'll the rear admirals see me on TV, that'll make em button their lips. Cut em down to size.

And then one day old Burda walked up to the stand: Say, boys, you eat that stuff you sell? We laughed wholeheartedly. Good, cause as of next week City Hall's declarin that shit illegal ... Finally! said Kasel ... I'm glad, boys, that you're takin it like that, see I'm gonna build ... Křepek an me been savin up to buy us a little Mack Donald's, already signed an everything ... an I got some great outfits for ya, fit cha like a glove ... laughing our heads off, me and Kasim began dousing each other with beer, we stank like hell anyway and at least the beer attracted wasps so you had to be alert, didn't get too sluggish ... Burda stared ... this is no joke, they'll give ya an allowance for clothes an shaves, plus a uniform, red on top, green below, copacetic slippers to boot, an you can work your way up … so ya really don't want it, huh? spoiled brats … in the end Burda got drunk with us, we closed up shop, leaving the dead meat to its natural course … let's torch the place, Kasim suggested, but Burda wouldn't allow it … his good mood didn't last long, old fogies, sometimes when they get a drink in em: Go ahead an leave, boys, see if I care, pissed me off anyways … but me an this park, we remember the Kaiser, an there's always been squirrels here, an what'll happen to them now … this is all gonna be an amusement park … ah, they'll survive somehow, an if they don't, no big deal, I wrote a poem about em, Kasim consoled him, we turned gloomy anyway though …

Then we told Burda goodbye, he'd seemed somewhat suspect to me anyway since that incident with the spider, we stole what cash there was and staggered off … we hit every place we could think of, and then, at Galactic … I was entertaining Kasim with stories from my shoots … and suddenly on TV … a perfect ad, kick-ass … Soapy Happysoap, hey, that's me too … in the washing machine, donno if Sister'll be able to tell … listen, said Kasim seriously, this is unadulterated commercialism, what'll the city underground say … it doesn't matter, Kasim … you gotta spread yourself around if you ever want her to find you … and the Grainy glows even in the circular corrals of the Ojibways, in icy igloos, even if Sister's plodding through the desert it'll catch up to her at the first oasis, she'll know it's me, even if she's hiding her beautiful face beneath a black veil among Muslims, the Grainy'll chase her down even in an old log cabin in Sázava, get it, even among the bronzed, happy youth on Mykonos, Ios, Sumatra, I'll come on screen, and my sister, out there in the islands, will see that I'm waiting faithfully for her … an not washin much, to discourage the others … just then a girl with braids the color of fire pulled up a seat at our table … we'd been eyeing each other a while now, that was one of the reasons I'd been braggin about my film work … Titiana swept her hair back from her forehead and laid her hand on my shoulder in an unmistakable way … why're you shoutin, what's all the shoutin for, c'mon, the News is on, an you there watch, watch closely, she told me … Kasim was asleep … and Titiana added: So, my place, or yours, or nothin?

I was about to choose from the options when I heard vzhhhh Headline News vzhhhh, and on the Grainy I saw: a fella with a mike … standin in the Dump, on a purple heap, couple people behind him, dazzling jackets, but Dump faces, drifters … and the guy said into the camera … garbage monster

... killing ... bloodshed ... tellin how they'd finally made it in and how a couple TV crews had gone down fake trails and were never heard from again ... briefly they showed what was left of Vulture's pack ... Titiana dug her nails into my shoulder ... the man on TV said the police were in pursuit of the deviant killer, they showed the food pits veiled with flies, even found a skeleton in there ... I should hope so, I said ... a woman's skeleton, the reporter announced, pointing to it ... he said Bohemian supermarkets were in the process of building an oven system to burn expired food products and leftovers, and that technology subsidies were needed, on that the newsman agreed with the chairman of the Food Product Trust ... once this food ceases to exist, so will these people, the chairman said, and they flashed a picture of a kid that looked like Stick ... the doozy and reassuring thing was that the police were hot on the killer's trail ... that made me burst out laughing ... you're jolly, said Titiana, but still, you're all pale ... an didn't you used to wear your hair long, she inquired mournfully ... yeah ... well, next to them, darlin, you'd look pale as an angel ... know that one?

That gave me a little chill, yeah, I know it, I said ... an who're you?

Guesser guesser guess away, said Titiana, parting her ruby-red lips to reveal her dainty teeth ... so which option will it be? she asked ... here you are, fella, sittin here with everyone else like it's nothin, like nothin's goin on at all ... scuse me, I said, and I entered the restroom, opened the window, yanked out the screen, and crawled out, hauling myself up on the wall ... she stood in the street looking me in the eye ... I locked myself in a stall ... chattering my teeth. I saw white.

And then ... I think I didn't have a body, I was inside a barracks, wood, fences and stakes, bunks, and on them people. Some in rags. Through the windows, which were bare, I saw the sky, medieval clouds, driven by the wind, apart from that no other movement.

Halflight. Opposite me a figure cloaked in black. I saw a field, I was looking through barbwire. Aright, I mumbled to myself with the tongue that remained to me, aright, me too. I was starting to see ... I saw faces around me, if I'd had a body I would've frozen, opposite me was Viška ... my enemy, I thought, and I heard: She wanted it, it's obvious ... that look, hey, I don't make mistakes, I'm a man ... I heard coming from Viška, sitting there, gaze fixed ... somewhere else, maybe inward, I'm hearin his thoughts, it hit me ... the little slut, I mean the way she looked at me, there's no way ... yeah, yeah, she was grateful to me for gettin her outta there, maybe I should've held off … but that time in the cellar, she offered herself, I could tell … she seduced me, I can't be wrong … and I loved her, I did … pulled her panties down herself, wouldn't've done that if she was afraid … but maybe I shoulda been firm … and then, then I couldn't hold back anymore. But I shouldn't've beat her. She told on me. And later … she was all grown up, but she still belonged to me … she couldna been serious about that chump, that hooligan … I gave her a choice, I loved her. And what I turned into, she did that. It was like I was obsessed. But I don't regret a thing.

This came out of Viška at me, a constantly altering stream … but I don't believe a word, the goon … he's deceived himself, the truth's gotta be different … hers.

And then I heard: Back then, when we crossed the water. Yeah, Morales told me how it goes. That time by the fire … and I saw Vohřecký, and it came from him too, a stream of speech … I felt good there, standin guard by the fire at night, how many times did I wish it could last forever … everyone else asleep an me keepin watch with my weapon, the only one awake … that's life, that means somethin … came out of Vohřecký … that was where I realized what I wanted to do an who I wanted to be, an one day Morales came, an that was an honor … he was somebody, an he says to me: Hey, amigo, you know how it goes on the Congo? Took a cigarette from me and lit it off a twig, cupped it in his hand, we kept to the side, off in the shadows, cause a the freedom fighters … but he was there with me, an he says: Scorpion's sittin on the bank of the Congo, river's flooded, bridges're all swept away, an he says to the hippopotamus, hey, pal, I gotta get to the other side, there's this chick I got over there … how bout a lift? But the hippopotamus knew him … not you, lovebug … you're poisonous, you'll sting me, you're wicked … c'mon, that's nuts, the scorpion says, if I sting you I drown too, right? It's only logical … so the hippo thinks it over a minute, gives the nod, the scorpion climbs on his back, an the hippo goes swimmin off into the muddy waters … he's swimmin along, the scorpion starts laughin … an when they get to the middle … the scorpion stings him with all his might, fucks him fulla poison … are you insane, says the hippo, I mean you promised … sorry, pal, the scorpion says … but that's how it goes on the Congo.

An Morales was right … that's how it goes, that's the way it is, it's cruel, I know … came to me out of Vohřecký … an I got it, an that's how I was from then on, even after they killed him … I don't regret a thing that happened. Just those people over there … some of em suffered a lot, we had to do it … an as long as I'm here, God … here … then it's true … even this is true …

Hi, Potok. Said the figure in black, couldn't see the face, but the voice I recognized an felt joy.

I knew I'd run into you, we never did get a chance to talk …

Not about that, said Bohler.

I was ashamed the whole time.

An I hated you, he said.

I really like her, the little one too.

You of all people. Maybe it's good. But you better not hurt her.

We've got a contract.

Baloney, with a girl, what contract? Either you're with her or you're not.

I kept my mouth shut. Just like that time. When they pulled that trick with the soap on him. Some dumb young con in the showers, soap in his eyes, bends over to wash himself, two guys grab him, an the third rams it in. An when they broke somebody that way, they'd usually toss him around a pretty long time. As long as they felt like it.

Didn't happen to me. I had practice in speech from all sortsa environments … an soon me an the German shepherds were conversin, me an the dylinas, somehow it worked, soon I had it all scoped out, even the corners, an then the mop an bucket was child's play, I knew my way around, all those boiler rooms an warehouses an factories from before, in my youth, that did the trick, it's always the same … but Bohler, straight outta seminary, with his vocabulary an those ministrant moves of his … they ate that shit up … an what was I sposta do? Get myself beat up, killed? Those guys were psychopaths … we were just psychopaths of freedom … foolish kids among cannibals … I stood by the wall, shower running, and they brutalized him. Maybe I should've scalded them with the water or whatever … but then it woulda been my turn … wet wedding, they called it, initiation, cable installation, kaolin mine, the old prisoners had lotsa names for it … it wasn't a question of just one fight, the thing was you hadda hang on there … I didn't know … maybe years, an I wanted to survive. One joker called it the shower of happiness … monsters. For them it was normal.

Bohler lost his mind. Didn't speak for weeks. It was too much. We were in a cell together, us an some greengrocers, an one night I say to him ... who gives a shit, right ... he wasn't asleep, and declared in his new tongue ... I do, he laughed, sperm up the ass, stuff'll shit right out ... but what gets me is the others, the rest of em ... what, those guys that did it to you? Nah, the other ones. And he changed.

You pissed me off pretty bad, Potok, later on too, in the buildings.

I didn't know. Where are we?

Guess. An watch.

Outside the windows, the field, soggy and swampy on the other side of the wires, drew closer all of a sudden ... there were women, a procession, they were marching ... walking through the muck, moving their feet, but in place ... I saw them, in rags, scarves, it was raining on them ... on their naked arms I saw goose bumps ... I looked into their faces, horrified that maybe ... they were barefoot, I saw their battered, bloodied feet ... some didn't have nails anymore ... I had no body in that place, but I shuddered, my mind a blank as my eyes drifted over the women's faces, terrified I'd see her ... I had a clue now where we were ... those're Chatterers, with too-sharp teeth, a voice said ... an Sadies that tortured, that's how they made their lives ... an Shells that suffocated inside, an whores ... an poisoners, an Lacties that killed their own kids ... an they all hafta do it over an over, do it till they get it, an this is just a stroll in the park, a rest stop ... Bohler, my guide to purgatory, told me, the men're here in the barracks, they can't move an they can't get at each other, not here ... here they're separate ... and then one of em, her scarf slipped off her raven-black hair ... why're you here, dear, feet still hurt? if it's you, then I'll lie down in the muck an you can walk over me, go ahead ...

Yep, said Bohler. Exactly. I heard you. Be glad. You're lucky. Some it takes a while. An I've got nothin against you anymore.

I never had anything against you. I was just ashamed. Bohler?

What?

An if you're here ... I mean you fought!

Yeah.

An if you're here, you saw his face ... tell me.

What?

Why?

Why what?

Why everything. Why is it?

It's by design, Potok. Well … at least I think.

An … that's sposta reassure me?

You gotta trust a little.

But I wanna go back, I want her.

Potok … how do you know … you won't do to her, you know what you did.

I can't, Bohler … not anymore. It won't happen. I trust … myself.

There, you see. It's the same.

And Bohler got up, tore off his burlap. We were still inside the barracks, but I couldn't see the others that he'd shown me anymore. His face was all puffy, my drowned buddy. And I saw his wild animal too, the one he'd had tattooed on. They hadn't taken that away. A clear-sighted eagle, spreading its wings. But that's not what he wanted to show me. He watched me through unmoving eyes. Like they were made of glass. All at once I had a body, and leaned toward him.

His eyes didn't move.

Bohler!

Yep. I'm blind. Blinded. An you'll meet her, don't worry.

I was woken by someone kicking on the door, it was Kasim. He helped me get up. We'd run out of steam. Didn't talk much.

After that I walked around, daydreaming and pondering. Quite likely the Vatican's seasoned lawyers would've mocked me, or even worse. After all … I'd confessed to a murderer, an a dead one to boot. Yep, I can only nod my head an say: That's the way it is. I don't say it in my defense. I don't want to defend myself anymore.

I didn't tell Lao about the encounter. With all my activities, there wasn't much time for it either. I was busy playing Popeye the Sailor in an ad.

I was all spiffed up for it too, I left the costume on, thinking, this'll flood the rear admirals … but then … in front of the studios. In a gray Daimler. Just ran my eye over it, took a couple steps and went back, following my heart … she was starting the engine … hat on her head, veil across her face, tulle … gripping the wheel with both hands, in muslin up to her shoulders … you're leaving, I said to myself, more like the words fell into me from nowhere … I guess you know why you're leaving me, the woman drove the car away … on the seat next to her … maybe it was a pistol. Maybe she wanted me to see. I don't know. Maybe it wasn't her but just some wacked-out actress, there were throngs of em paradin around, I reassured myself. Pointlessly.

At Skyscraper 33, finally a metamorphosis took place … Popeye … swaggered in there in my frayed striped T-shirt, flashin my earring an puffin my pipe, the submachine gunners reined in the dogs an the doormen opened the doors, bidding me on with a bow … into the chambers and rooms, at the elevator a young lady took charge of me … Mister Octopedes the shipbuilder, traveled mouth to mouth down the hall, I nodded, belching smoke so they couldn't see my grin … we rode all the way up. Another young lady opened a set of armored doors … in an expansive study behind a desk under a fan sat Micka.

Bowing, he came forward, then sped up and slowed down and stood still, opened his mouth and shut it again … me swayin an puffin … he turned to the window and said: Took you long enough.

I just said, sheesh, or somethin like that … then we sat there in leather club chairs, legs crossed nonchalantly, sipping drinks and getting into the groove, we yammered … our throats, I admit, at first somewhat constricted, opened wide to spew again … and after a good while talking and relating our travels, Micka laughed and said: You musta been snow-blind back in those woods, cause Vohřecký … that's unreal, but I had it taped an I got the cassette! … he's head of the Unshod now, gives sermons in a tent up on Letná Plain … I tipped over, along with the chair, but we let it go and went on talking, primarily about Bohler, I asked about Sharky … an from the way Micka tugged at his brilliant trousers, wriggled inside his impeccable jacket, an examined his tiger-stripe tie with the masterful knot, it hit me … yeah, said Micka, he's on the missing list, Palestinians got him, they say, a rock, some scamps. But I got contacts, I hope that's obvious … an it's not all that clear! Hey … think about it … he was on guard with another guy, an you know what Sharky's like, maybe the army pissed him off … keep a pretty short leash on those Israeli troops, I hear, what with the Arabs pitchin bricks an molotovs all the time, on account a world public opinion … or the other way round … rubber bullets only, yep, anyway, they were on patrol, Gaza Strip, two rookies, an you remember Sharky … you bet it pissed him off, lettin himself get suckered in! … havin to salute … or maybe the other guy nudged him wrong, provoked him somehow, had better smokes … an Sharky, you knew him, the way he is … stabbed him, switched uniforms, traded IDs, maybe mashed up the other guy's face a little with a rock or his rifle butt … an hopped the wires … an split … yep, joined up with the Arabs an …

Whoa, Micka, hold your horses.

My pseudodroog winked at me … that's how I woulda done it, I mean … before … you know that one, over the fence an gone! But you know what I'm sayin … there's various possibilities, various paths, I just don't believe he's done for! More likely he's off somewhere organizin some gorilla resistance, or …

Well, hey, more likely he's done for.

Probly, yeah, but there's …

I know.

I know you know. I'm not settin a trap for you here, not pullin any riddles, old brother, but Sharky …

The two of us remained in silent meditation.

The same followed after my report on David.

Only then Micka tossed some … photos on the desk. A guy in a white frock down to his knees, with a long shepherd's pipe and a hat on, his face, from the sun I guess, blurred … but in the background, that rock … it stuck in my head.

Well, fill er up, fill er up, Micka said.

When's this from, I asked.

Hm … Micka scratched his forehead … I donno actually.

Uh-huh.

Forget it, let's get to the crux of the matter, said Micka, puffing the diamonds on his fingers. What're you doin?

I didn't mention Sister. Just the studios.

Puhleeze … what for?

That I didn't tell him.

By the way, Potok, that was a good gag with that Octopedes thing … if you're interested …

Heh?

Well, said the byznysman, you went to school with a certain Špelner, if I recall the old list.

Yeah, kinuva pussyfoot.

Well that quiet little boy is now chair of the National Assembly. An Fiala, back in our times he was head of the Chamber of Commerce, but nowadays he covers the full spectrum of petroleum products, hey ... an he's the son-in-law of that MP Vašegis, a player, so if ...

Micka.

Hm?

I'd rather not.

I thought so. Follow me.

He led me down a hallway ... to the men's room. Went to the sink, nodded, we bent our heads down, he turned on the water an the fan an the drier ... I can't hear a word! I hollered. He ran from stall to stall, flushin every one, hollerin at me ... Helenka! ... an whisperin frantically into my ear ... that thing a yours with David, even if it wasn't a dream, it doesn't matter ... Helenka! He hollered again, and ... child ... where? I hollered back ... in a safe place, I understood ... it's taken care of, an the kid, the racket subsided ... the kid, man, could be ... there's definite signs ... for real? I forced out, and had to lean on the tiles ... then that'd mean that everything, that all this, maybe after all it wasn't ... in vain ... YES! said Micka, turning off the water and the machines, we strolled down the hallway ... that's fantastic, I shouted, hallelujah, so there's hope that the child, that it might be the M. himself? An you're keepin an eye on him? Rest assured, said Micka, matter of fact this building, this whole firm, an all the deals we got goin're cause a him, but shhh! he pointed around the room in an obvious gesture.

But, Micka, I asked again, what does the possible and anticipated coming of the M. hafta do ... with byznys?

What do you know what it might do ... to oil prices for instance? An so on?

Aha.

And outside ... the gray car again. Driving away. I shuddered, some kid asked me for an autograph, then burst out sobbing ... not Potok, Mr. Popeye ... I'd like to be sitting with her in that old coffeehouse with the mirrors, taking joy in our moment together ... but the car had driven off.

And sometimes, sometimes you would come between us. I'd be kneeling in front of my girlfriend, clasped between her thighs, the two of us moving together, me stroking her breasts, circling my spread palms over her nipples, just the way she likes it, and we'd be rocking back and forth, and you would come between us. Suddenly you would be facing me, and not just your eyes, all of you, jealously lifting my hands off Lao and pressing them to your chest, you would be on top of her, her holding your waist, clinging to you with her lips and stroking you with her tongue, and we moved like a three-headed body, relaying tenderness to one another ... me inside Lao, as far as I could be, and holding onto your hips, you would smile, Černá, as I kissed you, I could tell from your lips, feel you holding back a smile as we rocked back and forth, and we could hear each other, and it was beyond words, it was finally beyond words ... and you know I don't like to blaspheme unnecessarily ... but there was grace in it. And it would always end with your eyes half shut, and you gasping out ... only then, underneath you, Lao ... would start to suffocate, gagging ... with laughter ... and you weren't there. And something else happened.

That time ... the rain drummed down on the roof of the shed, we stood there in that stuffy attic, Lao leaning her belly on me, sticking out already, me peering round at the shadows ... her son playing around with ancient reject gadgets, twisting wire off or whatever, I was about to give him a moderate scolding, when Lao said: Bell ... I thought maybe she'd bought a new phone, but then I heard it too ... the wind was carrying the sound out of town in irregular gusts, it even caught Vojtěch's attention, he came over to us, asked: What's that ... hey! he screamed at me as I stood, lapping up the sound. The bells! I told him ... they're ringin again ... had to make him a drawing ... and find it in a book ... sometimes, when we've both got time and are in the mood, I teach him some of the old words, the ones I haven't forgotten yet.

Now I knew you would come. In the attic, on your desk, I found a flower. It was a rose, the kind you like so much. Lying by the notes I'd left. I had one old box of soap, left over from my travels, ready on the edge of the tub, filled it up right away ... it had been a while since I worked at the stand, but ... and I heard quick steps and you opened the door and walked into the room. Černá. We were next to each other. All at once. You had your head next to mine and I hugged you.

Let's not leave each other anymore.

Not anymore, you said.

And just then the doorbell rang. You jerked, I didn't even ask ... I could see in your eyes you didn't know. The ringing wouldn't let up. Whoever it was was holding his finger on the button. A little ... just a little, I pushed you away an lifted my hands ... but you took them, lightly, took my palms in yours, and laid them on your shoulders.

Let's not open it, you said. Not anymore.

No. Not now.

Notes to *City*

19. German for "Hands up, Faster, swine, Look out, mines, Work will set you free [the slogan posted over the entrance to Auschwitz], Come fuck, my love."

21. The Church of Our Lady Victorious, the first Baroque building in Prague; it houses the pražké Jezulátko, or Bambino di Praga, a wax effigy revered throughout the Catholic world and especially in South America.

22. Státní bezpečnost (State Security), Communist Czechoslovakia's secret police.

23. German for "The Unknown," as in "the unknown soldier."

24. 1938 book by Bonn, who died in Terezín (see note for p. 63)

27. German for "I am a foreigner."

34. With the disintegration of the Roman Empire, in the fifth century A.D. eastern tribes launched a series of raids into Central Europe. First came the Huns, followed by the **Avars**, who were then pushed out by Slavic tribes from east of the Carpathians.

36. A combination of Josef Stalin's full name with the name of the main character of Jaroslav Hašek's extremely popular humorous novel *The Good Soldier Švejk* (1923).

46. A play on *My Sweet Little Village* (1985), a film comedy about a village idiot, directed by Jiří Menzel and nominated for an Oscar. Libuše Šafránková was the female lead.

48. A statement released in January 1977 calling on the Communist government of Czechoslovakia to abide by the human rights provisions of the Helsinki Accords.

52. The **Lučans**, People of the Bow, were an ancient Slavic tribe that once inhabited the Czech Lands. Defeated in battle by the people we now know as Czechs.
    Čech: The mythical original Czech. His name means "Czech" in Czech.

56. Karel Hynek **Mácha** (1810-1836), famed for his lyrical-epic work *Máj* (May, 1836), which scandalized his contemporaries but is now regarded as having been the starting point of a new direction in Czech poetry.

58. A reference to the story "Footprints" by Czech author Karel **Čapek** (1890-1938), from his *Tales from Two Pockets* (1929).

64. **Terezín**: Concentration camp in northern Bohemia set up by Nazis to fool outsiders into believing that conditions in the camps were basically good. Prisoners were transported on to other camps.

  Batas: Named for Tomáš **Bat'a**, who founded the company in the Moravian town of Zlín in 1894.

65. **toyfil**: From the German *Teufel*, "devil."

  toluene: a liquid solvent sniffed like airplane glue.

67. **Ribanna** was an Apache heroine from the writings of Karl May (1842-1912), a German author best known for his series of popular novels set in the American West, although he also wrote about Arabia and Turkey. Though his works have sold nearly 100 million copies in Europe, he remains virtually unknown in the U.S.

76. Warriors of the Southern Cheyennes. Also the name of a popular band led by the author's younger brother, Filip Topol. In the group's early days, the author wrote their lyrics.

78. Lady Midday, the Midday Witch. Seen at the hottest time of a summer day. Also the personification of sunstroke.

82. **Maryša**: the title of a play by Alois (1861-1925) and Vilém (1863-1912) Mrštík about a village girl who is forced to wed a rich man she despises. She murders him by pouring poison in his coffee.

  Josef **Lada**, illustrator of *The Good Soldier Švejk* (see note for p. 35), also known for his folksy calendar illustrations.

93. According to folk custom, lit during storms or at the bedside of a dying person.

97. Characters from *Hunters of the Woolly Mammoth,* a children's book by Czech writer Eduard Štorch.

101. **Josef Novák**: Czech equivalent of John Doe.

  Žižkov: A working-class neighborhood in Prague.

102. The **Protectorate** of Bohemia and Moravia, an occupation government established by the Nazis on March 15, 1939.

  Adinka: Adina Mandlová, Czech film actress, possibly a lover of Goebbels'. Her memoir was called *I Laugh About It Now* (Dnes už se tomu směju).

103. German for "Heil Hitler, my officers and doctors and scholars. I'm a little Czech swine, born from Žižkov." Note: this is not proper German.

105. Karel **Poláček**: popular Czech Jewish novelist, journalist, humorist (1892-1944).

109. A phrase coined between the two world wars to boost the morale of craftspeople and designers at a time of increasingly machine-driven production.

111. Czech for "Falcon," the name of a Czech patriotic and gymnastic society founded in 1862.

120. Emil **Hácha** was the Czech president under the Protectorate (see note for p. 101).

122. Andrei **Chikatilo**, a.k.a. the Soviet Hannibal Lecter. Estimated to have killed 52 people, mostly young boys, between 1980 and 1992.

124. *We Were Five* (1946, posthumous) is the title of a popular novel by Czech writer Karel Poláček (see note for p. 104) about a group of five boys growing up in a small town.

130. **gotwaalds**: A play on Klement Gottwald (1896-1953), the first Communist president of Czechoslovakia.

Jaroslav **Foglar** (1907-1999), author of a popular illustrated adventure series called *Speedy Arrows*. His advocacy of the scouting movement led the Communists to prevent him from publishing for many years.

Kcharal ben May: A play on Karl May (see note for p. 66).

132. **Myslivec:** "Huntsman," a cheap Czech brandy.

In Czech *Potok* means " brook."

Notes to *Sister*

141. Towns in northern Bohemia.

142. At the end of World War II, Czechoslovakia's three million Germans, most of whom lived along its northern and western borders (known as the Sudetenland), were forcibly expelled. This process was preapproved by the Allied powers at the Potsdam Conference and officially referred to as a "transfer." The Czechoslovak government, in a move supported by every political party and the overwhelming majority of the population, seized the Germans' property and redistributed large portions of it to Czechs and Slovaks. To this day the expulsion remains a highly charged and emotional issue in Czech-German relations.

143. In Czech **Černá** is the feminine form of the adjective "black." It is also the female form of the common surname Černý.

144. Semion **Budenny** (1883-1973), a Soviet field marshal.

145. Normally *dylina*, a Romany word meaning "idiot," "jerk," "asshole."

149. **Moravian**: Reference to Sigmund Freud, who was born in the north Moravian town of Příbor, known as Freiberg to German speakers.
    Romul: A play on Jan Ruml, minister of the interior for Czechoslovakia and then the Czech Republic, 1992-1997.

161. A play on Topol's first collection of poems, *I Love You Madly* (1991). The original samizdat edition of 1988 won the Tom Stoppard Prize for Unofficial Literature.

164. **Battle of Britain**: in which Czech pilots flew with the Royal Air Force against the Luftwaffe (1940).
    Milan, King Vladislav: In 1158 Vladislav II, of the Přemyslid dynasty, was granted royal title as King of Bohemia by the Holy Roman Empire.
    Reinhard **Heydrich** was the SS officer in charge of the Protectorate (see note for p. 101). In June 1942 he was assassinated by a Czech and a Slovak who were parachuted in from England. This led to the Heydrichiad, a wave of recriminations against the Czech population, including deportations to camps and the razing of two Czech villages. The assassins themselves were hunted down and killed by the Nazis after taking refuge in a church in Prague.

170. **Gingerbread**: *Perník*, a homemade amphetamine named for its color, popular in the Czech Republic.

Brno: A city two hours' drive southeast of Prague, the capital of Moravia and the Czech Republic's second-largest city. Reference to a well-known literary talk show that was taped there.

172. Rafał **Wojaczek** (1945-1971), poet described by some as Poland's postwar Baudelaire.

177. **Di do prdele**: "Shove it, "up yours," in Czech.
   Chłop zasrany: "Shithead," "piece of shit peasant," in Polish.

178. "Give the knife, get the knife." A Romany saying.

179. The **Stag Moat** is located at Prague Castle.
   small works: a philosophy advocated by Tomáš Garrigue Masaryk, cofounder and first president of Czechoslovakia, in which large-scale change is brought about through the accumulation of small, individual efforts.

201. An untranslatable pun: *samo* means "by itself," i.e., the boy is answering that it happened "by itself," but his questioners believe that he is telling them his name. **Sámo**, however, was a Frankish merchant who united and ruled the western Slavs in the seventh century. According to German sources, he was actually a Jew by the name of Samuel, but as far as the Slavs were concerned, he was a Frank who betrayed the Franks. Sámo was also responsible for teaching the Slavs modern warfare.

202. The **Boii** (in Czech, *Bojové*) were the Celtic people who gave their name to the region of Bohemia.

212. The people of Ingushetia, a small mountainous territory in the Caucasus next to Chechnya. The **Ingush** are Muslims, and after Stalin deported them for siding with the Germans in World War II, they were not allowed to return home until 1957. Now a republic in the Russian Federation.

230. German for "Foreigners out!"

235. The horses of Winnetou, an Apache, and Old Shatterhand, a white man, from the Western stories of Karl May (see note for p. 66).

241. From *The Bagpiper of Strakonice* (1846) by Josef Kajetán Tyl. A drama in which a bagpiper leaves the Czech Lands to make his fame and fortune abroad, but is morally tainted by foreigners. He is saved when he returns home and takes a Czech wife.

250. *Land of Dreamers*: The title of the Czech translation of the German book *Die andere Seite* (The Other Side, 1909), written and illustrated by Alfred Kubin; not actually filmed.

Winnetou: an East-German film based on Karl May's Western stories (see note for p. 66).

Mrazík: "Grandfather Frost," a Soviet fairy tale designed to replace St. Nicholas (Santa Claus), shown every year on Czech TV.

254. Jiří **Korn**, Czech pop singer famous in the 70s and 80s.

256. Play on **Edward Kelley,** one of two English alchemists (along with John Dee) invited to serve in the Prague court of Emperor Rudolf II in the 1580s.

258. English for Neználek, protagonist of a Soviet series of children's books with titles like *Neználek on the Moon, Neználek in the City on the Sun,* and *The Adventures of Neználek.*

260. In Ukrainian, Chernobyl means "wormwood."

269. Divadelní Akademie Múzických Umění, the theater school at the Academy of Performing Arts in Prague.

285. The word *luna* for "moon" was introduced into Czech poetry by Karel Hynek **Mácha** (see note for p. 55).

293. Vladimír **Holan** (1905-1980), major Czech lyric poet.

315. *Lucerna* (1905), an allegorical fable by Alois Jirásek (1851-1930), popular Czech historian and ethnographer.

319. Described in a book of Kazakh legends, *The Day Lasts More Than a Hundred Years* (1980) by Chingis Aitmotov. Young men captured in battle are shaved bald and fresh-stripped patches of camel skin are placed on their heads. As the skin dries in the sun, it shrinks around the victim's skull, squeezing it like a vice. Most either die or lose their memory forever, becoming a **mankurt.**

322. Stepan **Bandera** (1909-1959), Ukrainian nationalist who fought with Hitler against the Communists in World War II. At the end of the war, he turned his forces against the Germans.

328. Reference to Václav Havel's famous essay "The Power of the Powerless" (1978), in which Havel used a **greengrocer** to illustrate how even minor deviations from accepted behavior represent a threat to the Communist power structure.

336. Site of the monastery in Moravia whose monks produced the first complete translation of the Bible into Czech (1579-1593), known as the **Kralice** Bible. The language of this work served as a norm for some 250 years.

367. A play on Medzilaborce, the eastern Slovak town where Andy Warhol's family comes from, and where, due largely to the efforts of Czech artist Michal Cihlář, a Warhol museum was set up in 1990. *Cihlář* means "brickmaker," thus "the guy with the brick."

379. **Kyselice:** "Acidville" in Czech.
   Bezbožice: "Godlessville" in Czech.

380. Hungarian word for treeless plains or steppe.

381. Reference to the title *Golet v údolí* (Exile in the Valley, 1937) by Ivan Olbracht (Kamil Zeman, 1882-1952), stories based on the life of Jews in the Carpathian region. The subtitle of the book is *The Sad Eyes of Hana Karadžičová.*

387. A Great Mother-type figurine discovered at a 25,000-year-old site in Dolní Věstonice (southern Moravia), the earliest evidence of clay firing.

Notes to Silver

406. **Benderites**: See note for p. 322.

Slovak National **Uprising**, August-October 1944, in which some 80,000 insurgents, both non-Communist and Communist, battled German forces in the mountains of central Slovakia. Though nominally independent, Slovakia was a puppet state of the Nazis during World War II.

460. English for a Czech collection of seventeenth-century baroque German poetry, translated into Czech in 1959.

463. Neighborhood in Prague 6, home to the Benedictine Archabbey, oldest monastery in the Czech Lands, founded by St. Adalbert c. 993 (see note for p. 488).

470. Jan **Welzl** (1868-1948), a Czech who spent some thirty years above the Arctic Circle as a trader, hunter, and Inuit chief. Upon returning to Czechoslovakia in the 1930s, he wrote several books about his adventures.

František **Venclovský** was the first Czech to swim the English Channel.

471. **Obora**: Park in Prague 6-Liboc, site of the battle in which the Protestant troops of the Bohemian Estates fell to the united armies of Austrian Emperor Ferdinand II and the Catholic League on November 8, 1620, the famous Battle of White Mountain.

477. Battle in which the mainstream branch of the Hussites, known as the Utraquists, allied with Catholics to defeat various more radical branches (1434). As a result, the Hussite Church was accepted by the Papists.

483. The saint known in English as Adalbert (955-997). Named bishop of Prague in 983, he encouraged the evangelization of Poles and Hungarians, as well as Czechs. Died a martyr's death at the hands of Prussian heathens in Pomerania (see note for p. 467).

If you liked this book, you might be interested in other Czech literature from Catbird Press. Here is some information about these books. For more information, including excerpts, visit our website at www.catbirdpress.com. If you would like to order any of the books or receive notice of future Catbird books (i.e., our bi-annual catalogs), please call us at 800-360-2391, e-mail us at catbird@pipeline.com, fax us at 203-230-8029, or write us at 16 Windsor Road, North Haven, CT 06473-3015. Shipping and handling is $3.00 total, no matter how many books you order (at least as of 2000).

Other Contemporary Czech Writers

DANIELA FISCHEROVÁ, *Fingers Pointing Somewhere Else,* translated by Neil Bermel. The first work of fiction by a Czech baby-boomer to appear in English. Meticulously well-crafted stories about various stages in a woman's life, plus two other tales that take place in Asia. "Fischerová creates a mulitlayered meditation on truths and fictions, innocence, curiosity, politics and expressions of love both physical and imaginative." —*Prague Post.* $19.95 hardcover, 192 pages, ISBN 0-945774-44-3.

The Poetry of JAROSLAV SEIFERT, translated by Ewald Osers, edited by George Gibian. The largest collection in English from the Czech Nobel Prize-winning poet's entire career. $14.95 paperback, 255 pages, ISBN 0-945774-39-7.

VLADIMÍR PÁRAL: *Catapult,* translated by William Harkins. This twist on the Don Juan story looks at the attractions and difficulties of freedom. "Páral masterfully switches from farce to drama and back again, so that in the end we feel Jost's dilemma even as we're laughing at him." —*N.Y. Times Book Review.* $10.95 paperback, 240 pages, ISBN 0-945774-17-6.

_____: *The Four Sonyas,* translated by William Harkins. In this darkly comic world, people will do almost anything to attain their dreams, and Sonya is their principal target. "The ways in which *The Four Sonyas* … conceals its larger meaning just beneath the surface of the narration is wonderful to behold." —*Newsday.* $22.95 hardcover, 391 pages, ISBN 0-945774-15-X.

DAYLIGHT IN NIGHTCLUB INFERNO: Czech Fiction from the Post-Kundera Generation, selected by Elena Lappin, various translators. Stories and novel excerpts from the generations that came of age after the Prague Spring of the 1960s. "This important anthology … places some marvelous talent on display." —*Booklist.* $15.95 paperback, 320 pages, ISBN 0-945774-33-8.

Pre-War Czech Writers

Karel Čapek

TOWARD THE RADICAL CENTER: A Karel Čapek Reader, edited by Peter Kussi, foreword by Arthur Miller, various translators. Čapek's best plays, stories, and columns take us from the social contributions of clumsy people to dramatic meditations on mortality and commitment. This volume includes the first complete English translation of *R.U.R. (Rossum's Universal Robots)*, the play that introduced the literary robot. $14.95 paperback, $23.95 hardcover, 416 pages, illus., ISBN 0-945774-07-9, 06-0.

WAR WITH THE NEWTS, translated by Ewald Osers. This new translation revitalizes one of the great anti-utopian satires of the twentieth century. Čapek satirizes science, runaway capitalism, fascism, journalism, militarism, even Hollywood. "A bracing parody of totalitarianism and technological overkill, one of the most amusing and provocative books in its genre." —*Philadelphia Inquirer.* $11.95 paperback, 240 pages, ISBN 0-945774-10-9.

TALES FROM TWO POCKETS, translated by Norma Comrada. Čapek's unique approaches to the mysteries of justice and truth are full of twists and turns, the ordinary and the extraordinary, humor and humanism. Selected by *Publishers Weekly* as One of the Best Books of the Year. $14.95 paperback, 365 pages, illus., ISBN 0-945774-25-7.

THREE NOVELS: Hordubal, Meteor, An Ordinary Life, translated by M. & R. Weatherall. This trilogy of novels approaches the problem of mutual understanding through various kinds of storytelling. "Čapek's masterpiece." —*Chicago Tribune.* $15.95 paperback, 480 pages, ISBN 0-945774-08-7.

TALKS WITH T. G. MASARYK, translated by Michael Henry Heim. Never have two such important world figures collaborated in a biography. Tomáš Garrigue Masaryk (1850-1937) was the original Philosopher-President who founded Czechoslovakia in 1918, an important inspiration for Václav Havel. $13.95 paperback, 256 pages, ISBN 0-945774-26-5.

Karel Poláček

WHAT OWNERSHIP'S ALL ABOUT, translated by Peter Kussi. The first novel translated into English by the most prominent Czech Jewish writer between the wars. "Poláček studies the effect of power on the values and dreams of ordinary people, revealing their weaknesses and skewering their pomposity with a deftness and dark wit reminiscent of Chekhov." —*Library Journal.* $21.95 hardcover, 238 pages, ISBN 0-945774-19-2.